A SEARING SAG [text obscured]
AMBITION, LUS [text obscured]
NEVADA WHER [text obscured] **WERE BIG AND**
REWARDS EVEN BIGGER

Jim Delavane, parlaying luck and ruthless skill into a vast silver-mining empire . . . Ruby Surrett, the flame-haired beauty who ignited the passions of three men . . . Buck O'Crotty, battling all odds for the cause he believed in and the woman he loved . . . Francie Delavane, stunningly sensual, and damned by her own forbidden desire . . . and Tony, heir to a legacy of brutal ambition and secret shame, moving up the ladder of power in the glittering gambling palaces of Las Vegas run by the most feared emperors of the underworld . . .

A scorching novel of family betrayals, forbidden love, desperate men, and high-rolling gamblers—men and women whose passions lit an era when fabulous fortunes hung on a swing of a pick, a turn of a card, or a pull of a trigger. . . .

"Intense, deeply haunting and enlivened by charismatic fictitious and real life characters . . . suspense . . . turbulent emotions and confrontations . . . a spellbinding tale by a superlative storyteller."

—*Publishers Weekly*

CLARK HOWARD

QUICKSILVER

A SIGNET BOOK

NEW AMERICAN LIBRARY

PUBLISHER'S NOTE

This book is a work of fiction. Names, characters, places, and incidents either are the product of the author's imagination or are used fictitiously, and any resemblance to actual persons, living or dead, events, or locales is entirely coincidental.

Quick Silver previously appeared in a hardcover edition published by E. P. Dutton, a division of New American Library, 2 Park Avenue, New York, New York 10016.

SIGNET TRADEMARK REG. U.S. PAT. OFF. AND FOREIGN COUNTRIES
REGISTERED TRADEMARK—MARCA REGISTRADA
HECHO EN DRESDEN, TN

SIGNET, SIGNET CLASSIC, MENTOR, ONYX, PLUME, MERIDIAN and NAL BOOKS are published by NAL PENGUIN INC., 1633 Broadway, New York, New York 10019

First Signet Printing, March, 1989

1 2 3 4 5 6 7 8 9

PRINTED IN THE UNITED STATES OF AMERICA

To
William Targ
for all those fine talks

Part One

Tony

1950

ONE

Buck O'Crotty unlocked the front door of the union business office and switched on the lights. It was a storefront office, at the extreme edge of the town's commercial district. At nine o'clock on Sunday morning the district was silent and deserted, with rarely any automobile traffic, even more rarely any pedestrians. In Virginia City, Nevada, most people reserved Sunday as a day of rest. Buck usually did too, but this Sunday was an exception. He had risen at five A.M. and gone to six o'clock Mass to get his religious duty out of the way so that he could attend to something else.

Closing and locking the front door behind him, Buck went to the back door and opened it to let in some air. In his own small inner office—PRESIDENT on the door—he sat down behind his desk and thoughtfully drummed the tips of his callused fingers on the desktop. What he was about to do was right—he was convinced of it. But there was still a nagging question that he had not been able to put to rest: Was it right for the others it would affect? Or was it only right for him alone, right for Buck O'Crotty?

There had been a time, Buck reflected, when he was absolutely sure about nearly everything. But that, he knew, had been youth, not wisdom. At twenty and thirty, even forty, life had many areas of white, many of black. Only, it seemed, when you got to be fifty and sixty did so many views of that same life turn gray. He had not made many mistakes in life, compared to some he knew. But the ones he had made—God help him, they had been, in retrospect anyway, momentous.

Like the one he made with Ruby.

Unlocking a bottom drawer of the desk, Buck took out a Cavalier Supreme cigar box that was at least a quarter-century old. Fingering through an assortment of mementos in it, he found her photograph. Ruby Surrett Donovan. A pretty, vivacious figure dressed in a World War I nursing cap and cape. It was the only picture Buck had of her. Actually, it was a copy of a picture; Buck had given the original to Ruby's son a decade earlier.

Sighing quietly, Buck looked at the photo and thought, Ruby, Ruby, my dearest Ruby. Will you be able to forgive me for breaking my promise to you? For failing you when you needed me most? For hurting you so badly?

Staring at her likeness, it would have been very easy at that moment for Buck to renege on the promise he had made to himself; the promise to do what he planned to do this morning. Very easy to forget the whole thing and let life simply go on as it had for all the time past. In another ten years, fifteen if he was lucky, he would pass on to the grave and it would all die with him. The problem was, could he live with it another ten or fifteen years?

Buck had already made up his mind that he could not. More than that, he *should* not.

I'm sorry, Ruby, my dear, he thought, and put the photograph back into the cigar box, the box back into the drawer, locking it away.

Reaching for the telephone, Buck dialed the operator. When she came onto the line, he said, "I want to place a person-to-person call, please. To Tony Donovan at the Flamingo Hotel in Las Vegas. I don't have the number and I don't have his extension, but everybody knows him; he runs the place."

Drumming his fingers again as he waited, Buck glanced at the desk calendar. It was June 11, 1950. In a few weeks he would be sixty.

Presently, the operator came back onto the line. "Sir, Mr. Donovan is not in at the present. They expect him around ten o'clock."

"I'll call back," Buck said. "Thank you."

Hanging up, he frowned. Was this an omen, a sign—his not being able to get Tony on the first attempt? Then he grunted softly. You fool, he thought, you really *are* getting old.

At that moment, there was a sound at his office door and Buck looked up from the desk. His eyes barely glimpsed the figure in the door, then the first bullet slammed into his chest.

Then the second.
Then the third.
Then nothing mattered to Buck O'Crotty anymore.

Two hours later, Tony Donovan was at his own much larger desk in his own much larger office, looking over plans for a new wing on the Flamingo, when Arnie Shad burst into the room without knocking.

"What the hell do you want?" Tony asked. His tone was not friendly.

"You haven't heard the news?"

"What news?"

"Buck O'Crotty's dead. He was found murdered an hour ago in his union headquarters office."

Tony stared at Arnie. He could not believe it, could not imagine it, could not conceive of it. Invincible men did not get murdered. Indestructible men couldn't be killed. Buck was a hardrock. Only God could break a hardrock.

"Are you sure?" he asked, stunned.

"I'm sure," Arnie said. He was a pugnacious, curly haired, wiry man of thirty, the same age as Tony Donovan. There seemed constantly to be an unlit cigarette between his lips. A newspaper reporter for the *Las Vegas Star*, he and Tony had once worked together for Ben Siegel when he was building the Flamingo, the first luxury resort hotel-casino in Las Vegas. They had been close friends back then. But no more.

As Shad watched, Tony's expression slowly changed from disbelief to sadness. Quickly from sadness to anger.

"The bastards," Tony said through clenched teeth. "The dirty bastards."

"Who are you talking about?" Arnie asked.

"The mine owners. They did this. They had him killed."

For a moment there was silence in the office. Then Arnie replied quietly, "That's nonsense, Tony. You know as well as I do who was responsible. The only question is whether you'll admit it or not."

Tony stared at Arnie for a moment. "If you're talking about Meyer Lansky, you're crazy. Don't start that 'organized-crime' bullshit with me again."

Turning his back on Arnie, Tony looked through a large picture window at the desert behind the hotel. A frown settled on his face, underscoring a dark, brooding countenance. His was not an easy face to know; even in repose he often appeared disturbed, angry. His blue eyes were deep and concealed their warmth. Dark hair and eyebrows, along with his name and the dark eyes, labeled him Black Irish, and a straight, scalpel-thin scar lying horizontally on his left cheek added a slighty sinister touch. He was considered handsome by most women; some of the showgirls, particularly the younger ones, referred to him as "dreamy." An infrequent smiler, when he did so it was always spontaneous and genuine, and could brighten the mood of everyone around him. On this summer Sunday, he was deeply tanned and dressed in expensive slacks and polo shirt under a new lapel-less Cugat sport coat named after the popular band leader.

Tony Donovan was the most successful gambling executive on the four-year-old ribbon of resort hotel-casinos on Las Vegas Boulevard South, popularly known as "The Strip." His rise to the top had been a swift rush, his position marked by respect and envy. Rumor had it that he worked directly for Meyer Lansky, reputed treasurer of a national crime syndicate, which FBI director J. Edgar Hoover claimed was nonexistent. That and other stories, such as how he had been orphaned as a boy, grown up in the silver mines, fought heroically with the Marines, all underscored the Donovan myth. Highly visible, well-known, Tony was glanced at, scrutinized, studied, and generally admired wherever he went.

Standing at the window now, he thought of Buck lying dead. He was gradually, inevitably filling up with terrible grief. And tremendous guilt. The last time he had seen Buck, they'd both been violently angry; they had nearly come to blows. As usual, it had been over Tony's life, one of the many such scenes between them.

Except, Tony thought, his throat going dry, always before there had been the possibility of reconciliation. It had never occurred to Tony that there was a chance of that disappearing; a chance that the harsh, bitter words would be their last.

Sighing, he turned from the picture window to his desk, picked up his telephone, dialed the hotel operator. "This is Mr. Donovan. See if someone can locate Mr. Ebro for me."

As he hung up, Arnie came over to the desk. "You always have to call Denny in, don't you? Always have to have your loyal sidekick for support."

Tony's jaw clenched. "Why shouldn't I call him? Buck raised Denny just like he raised me."

Arnie leaned forward several inches. "Listen to me, Tony," he said urgently. "You're getting in too deep. This is murder and it's very close to you. You need to get away from Denny, away from this hotel, away from everything you're involved in here—"

"You mean like you did, Arnie?" Tony asked cuttingly. "Quit like you did? That's really what's always bothered you, isn't it? I stayed and today I'm at the top. You quit and ended up a two-bit reporter. No thanks."

Stiffening slightly, Arnie fixed Tony in a penetrating gaze. "You sound just like Meyer Lansky. He owns you now, doesn't he, Tony? He owns your soul."

"Go away, Arnie," Tony said wearily. "Leave me alone." Sitting down at the desk, he buried his face in both hands. Buck, Buck, Buck, he thought. Why in hell did it have to end like this for us?

Arnie's shoulders slumped. "Okay, Tony. Okay. I should know by now that there's no reasoning with you." He put a cigarette between his lips but, as usual, did not light it. "The paper's sending me up north to cover the funeral," he said. "I'll see you there."

"No," Tony said. He raised his head to look at Arnie with eyes as deep and dark as two bullet holes. "No, you won't see me there. I'm not going to his funeral."

Arnie stared incredulously. Then his expression changed to disgust. "Forget what I said a minute ago about Meyer Lansky owning your soul. You don't have a soul, Tony."

Arnie walked out, leaving Tony at his desk, face ashen, stomach churning up a miserable nausea—not because of Arnie's comment, Tony was not concerned about his soul; but because he suddenly realized that he had never told Buck he loved him.

With a trembling hand, Tony opened a desk drawer and took out a fading brown photograph of Ruby Surrett Donovan, his mother. It was a photograph that Buck had given him long ago. For a moment he studied the pretty, vivacious looking figure in her World War I nursing cap and cape.

"Buck's gone, Ma," he spoke in a strained voice to the photograph. "He's been murdered. And I can't even go to his funeral."

Tony started to cry, the tears falling on Ruby's picture.

Part
Two

Ruby

1919

TWO

The three young Marines, still wearing their discharge uniforms, saw Ruby Surrett for the first time when she boarded their Central Pacific train in Chicago. They were on the platform of the big underground depot having a cigarette and stretching their legs, when she came by in her army nurse's uniform and boarded one of the coach cars in front of their Pullman sleeper.

"There's a looker," said Buck O'Crotty, a knobby, bow-legged sergeant with kinky hair showing under a pushed back barracks cap. "Wonder where she's going?"

"Maybe to Silver City, like us. Didn't you say there was a miners' hospital there?" This from Mike Donovan, a corporal, big and brawny, solid as an oak, but the softest spoken and gentlest of the trio.

"San Francisco," said Lieutenant Jim Delavane, the cleanly handsome one, "it's written all over her."

"Probably on her way back to the farm," said Buck. He winked. "But she won't stay long. Like the song says, you can't keep 'em down on the farm after they've seen Paree."

They did not learn which of them was right about Ruby until several hours later when she came into the dining car where they were eating lunch, and Mike Donovan, napkin tucked in his collar, rose and said, "Join us, miss? We'd be pleased to buy your lunch. My buddies and me, we all owe some thanks to the nurses' corps."

Ruby's direct green eyes, shiny like emeralds, gave the three of them a quick study and decided they were just being friendly, not on the make, so she said, "All right, thanks," and sat down with them.

"Looks like you're just out," said Buck, bobbing his chin at the discharge pin on the front of her uniform.

17

"Right," she said, noting his own discharge pin and those of Mike and Jim, "like you three." She also took in the campaign ribbons they wore. "You've seen some action, looks like. Blanc Mont, Meuse-Argonne, Belleau Wood."

"Fifth Marines," said Buck, as if that explained it all. He nodded toward Donovan. "This here's the one and only Iron Mike Donovan. That's the Navy Cross, that blue-and-white ribbon."

Ruby's eyebrows went up. "You're the one that advanced on the Huns carrying a machine gun under one arm and a mortar under the other? That's you?"

Mike grinned and blushed and finally admitted it was him. "But my buddies have decorations too," he quickly pointed out. "They've both got Purple Hearts, see—"

"Those are awarded for carelessness under fire," Buck said wryly. Jim Delavane, who had not spoken, chuckled, and Ruby looked at him with interest.

"And you're an officer, I see. A first lieutenant."

"Jimmy got a battlefield commission at Belleau Wood," Mike praised.

A waiter came and gave Ruby a menu and a pad and pencil. Buck winked and said, "You have to write out what you want. Railroads are cautious. Don't like mistakes."

"Order whatever you like, miss," said Mike. "We've got our mustering-out pay."

Ruby ordered a sandwich and coffee. When she finished writing, she noticed Jim looking at her. "You don't talk much for an officer," she said.

Jim shrugged easily, "I let these two do all the talking. When people get tired of listening to them, I say something intelligent."

"Like what?"

"Like you haven't told us your name yet."

"Ruby," she said. "Ruby Surrett."

Jim held a hand across the table. "Pleased to meet you, Ruby. I'm Jim Delavane."

Ruby put her hand in his. Jim shook her hand and held onto it longer than necessary.

"Jimmys engaged to be married," Buck said. "A school-teacher in Eureka. That's in Nevada. By the way, my name's Buck O'Crotty." He held out his own hand, forcing Ruby and Jim to uncouple.

"Nevada's where I'm going too," Ruby said, with delight. "A place called Silver City."

"So are we," Mike said, smiling because he had been correct about her destination. "We're going to work in the silver mines there."

"So you're silver miners? All three of you?" She glanced at Jim again, hoping it wasn't too obvious that it was him she was really asking about. He was the dandy of the three, by far the handsomest. It was difficult for her to picture him as an underground miner, all dirty and sweaty. His hands, which had black hair on their knuckles, looked to her as if they belonged other places than around a pick handle.

"We're not silver miners yet, but we will be," Buck answered for them. "Jimmy and me, we're copper miners. This big lug"—he gripped Mike's neck fondly—"was a coal miner in Pennsylvania. We talked him into coming back to Nevada with us to mine silver. We're going to go partners and try to put together a grubstake for some digs of our own."

Ruby kept glancing at him, so Jim finally felt that he had to speak again. "There are still some fortunes to be made in silver in Nevada," he said, shifting slightly in his chair and resting a hand on the table between Ruby and himself. "Plenty of high lodes, mother lodes that haven't been tapped, and probably quite a few quick silver veins too—"

"Quicksilver?" said Ruby. "You mean mercury, like in a medical thermometer?"

"No. Two words, not one. It has nothing to do with mercury. They're just called quick silver veins because the silver is in ore close to the surface. It's quick to find, quick to make money on."

"Not that we're going for that," Buck said at once. "There's only a certain type that goes for the quick silver. That's surface mining, y'see, it strips the land bare, ruins it for anything else. Real miners don't do that. Real miners go deep down for their ore. They leave the top land as it was. Nevada's raw and rugged, but she's got a lot of beauty to her. Real miners leave that beauty—and the quick silver —alone."

"You understand now?" Jim asked Ruby. They were still looking at each other.

"Sure," she said. "I learn fast."

Buck did not like the way their eyes held. "Speaking of

beauty," he said, "Jimmys fiancée's name is Edith. Her father's principal of the school in Eureka. Mr. Solomon Bloom. Her and Jimmy and me, we went to school together for a bit. Mr. Bloom, he sent Edith off to college somewheres when she was old enough, and she came back a teacher herself. A fine woman. What she sees in this hardrocker, I'll never know."

"Sometimes," Ruby said, "a woman can see things in a man that the man can't even see in himself."

The waiter brought her lunch and Ruby joined the three men in eating.

Later that afternoon, in the sitting area of the sleeping car, Iron Mike was slumped down in a chair dozing, and Jim Delavane was reading a newspaper that had been put on the train in Clinton, Iowa. Buck rose from his own chair, stretching and yawning, and said as casually as he could, "I'm going to walk up and down a bit. Stretch my legs."

"Sure," Jim said with a knowing look, which he tried to conceal behind the paper.

Buck made his way forward through the other sleeping cars, through the empty dining car, to the line of day coaches that made up the front section of the train. He found Ruby in the third car, sitting alone, reading a magazine. She had removed her starched nurse's cap and the afternoon sun on her side of the car picked up highlights of a deeper red in her mostly auburn hair.

"Join you?" Buck asked.

Just a hint of a smile. "Sure."

Buck sat. Working a pack of Chesterfields from his shirt pocket, he asked, "Smoke?"

"This isn't a smoking car. It's the next one up."

"Oh." He put the cigarettes away.

"Where are your friends?"

"Both napping," Buck lied, in case she thought of suggesting they join them. He looked around the coach. A man in bib overalls and a Central Pacific cap, with his Chinese wife and three halfbreed kids, sat just across the aisle. In the next seat was a sleazy looking slicker in a checked suit and celluloid collar, toothpick in one corner of his mouth. Two elderly women in musty dresses that smelled of age were across from him. Their odors combined with everyone else's to thicken the air and make it heavy, like the air in a closed barn. "Day cars," Buck commented, "the only time they're worse is when night comes."

Ruby smiled tentatively. Buck leaned forward and lowered his voice to a confidential tone.

"Listen, I was thinking. If you'd like to take my lower berth for the night, why, I wouldn't mind switching tickets with you. I can't sleep on trains anyhow, might's well be sitting up as lying down." He saw that Ruby was looking at him with the same kind of knowing look that Jim had tried to hide behind his newspaper, and that Buck had seen and ignored. But he could not ignore this one. "What's the matter?"

"Why are you being so generous?" Ruby asked.

Buck shrugged. "I just thought it might make your trip a little easier—"

"I don't suppose you had any ideas about what I could do to thank you for your generosity?"

"Thank me? I hadn't—"

"Like maybe we could spend the first hour in the berth together? Something like that?"

Buck leaned back, ramrod straight. "I never thought anything of the kind."

"No, of course not. You're just a gallant gentleman taking pity on a poor helpless woman traveling alone." Now it was Ruby who leaned forward, almost in his face. "Well, I've got a surprise for you, Sergeant. I'm not poor and I'm certainly not helpless. I could have purchased a sleeper if I'd wanted to; I chose not to because I am a thrifty person. As for being helpless, I assure you that I can more than take care of myself; if you try anything funny, you'll find that out quickly enough. Do I make myself clear?"

Buck was aghast. For a moment he was speechless. When he finally got hold of himself enough to speak, it was with cold indignation. "Of all the colossal gall," he said. "You must fancy yourself quite the one. I'll bet somebody once told you that you were fetching. My God. The nerve! Gloria Swanson and Constance Talmadge, look to your laurels—there's a great new beauty arrived on the scene, Miss Ruby Every-Man-Desires-Me Surrett." Buck rose and made an elaborate bow. "Please forgive me for disturbing you, Irresistible One. And just so's you'll know, it is no longer any concern to me whether you have an easy trip or not—nor where you rest your oh so lovely head. Good day."

Buck stalked away. When he got back to his own car, Jim looked up from his paper and asked, "Any luck?"

Buck looked at him incredulously. "You too, for Christ's sake? Jesus! If I tried to do a really good turn for someone, I'd probably get charged with murder!" Finding a chair alone at the back of the car, he slumped down to sulk.

Twenty minutes later, Ruby came into the car. Stopping just inside the door, she tried to get Buck's attention by gesturing. When that failed she made several audible "Pssst" sounds in his direction. Several others in the car looked up and Ruby smiled self-consciously. Finally Jim noticed her and went over to Buck.

"I think you have a visitor, Bucky."

Buck glared at Ruby for a moment. He might have tried to stay mad, but it wasn't in his nature; the best he could do was pout. When he went over to her, his expression was as sullen as he could make it. "Yes, what is it?" he asked impatiently.

Ruby put a hand on his arm. "Listen, I'm really sorry about what I said. I shouldn't have doubted your sincerity. It's just that I've been over there, you know, in France, for so long and it seemed like every soldier and Marine and medical corps doctor and ambulance driver, not to mention the frog officers, all had their little systems for getting a girl out of her bloomers, and your offer, well"—she shrugged— "frankly it sounded pretty much the same. I only realized after you got so upset that I had probably misjudged you. I'm really sorry and I hope you'll forgive me."

Buck shrugged and put his hands in his pockets. "You made me feel like a fool for trying to be nice to you."

"I *know*," she said, emphasizing it with a really sad face and by wringing her hands. "Please say you'll forgive me."

"Do you want to use my berth?"

"Sure. If you still want me to."

"I want you to. And I forgive you. Will you have supper with me in the diner?"

"Okay." She looked past Buck at Jim. His eyes were on her.

"I'll come up to your car and get you when they announce the first call for dinner."

"Okay." She touched his arm again. "Thanks, Bucky."

Turning to leave, she took one last, quick glance at Jim. He was still looking at her.

* * *

At midnight, Ruby worked herself into a chenille robe over her cotton nightgown, slipped bare feet into her white nurse's oxfords, and left Buck's lower berth. Quietly making her way down half a car length, she let herself out onto the train's rear observation platform. They were crossing Nebraska; the evening summer air of the plains was comfortably warm. From her robe pocket she took a pack of Sweet Caporals and lighted one. Leaning back against the car, she exhaled into the night.

The cigarette was only half smoked when the door opened and Jim Delavane came out. He had a Marine Corps officer's raincoat on over his pajamas. Putting a cigarette of his own between his lips, he took Ruby's hand and raised her glowing cigarette to light his.

"I wasn't sure you knew I was out here," she said.

"I've known where you were every minute since you got on this train," Jim replied. He leaned back, as she was doing; their shoulders pressed together.

"I'm afraid I got your friend Buck really sore at me this afternoon. I couldn't help it. I was half daydreaming about you and those great eyes of yours, and half reading a supposedly true story about a bigamist married to two women in the same city, and all of a sudden this Marine sergeant is offering me his lower berth, and I thought, whoa, what's going on here? I rebuffed him rather severely."

"I think he got over it. You two looked pretty cozy in the dining car this evening. Iron Mike was really miffed that he and I weren't invited."

"What about you, Jim? Were you miffed too?"

"Maybe."

Ruby turned her head to look at him. "When I first sat down at your table at lunch today, did you feel the same thing I did?" She wanted to know. It required no further elaboration.

Jim turned his head. Their faces were very close. "You know I did," he answered. "Why the hell do you think I took so long to say anything? I couldn't trust my voice."

"That's what I thought." Ruby threw her cigarette into the night. "You smoke too much," she said, doing the same with his cigarette. "Do you want to go to your berth or mine?"

"Who the hell needs a berth?" he asked.

Stepping around to face her, Jim opened her robe and pulled her gown up around her hips. With one hand under each of her thighs, he sat her up on the recessed ledge of the observation window. Sliding his hands down to her ankles, he lifted and planted her feet firmly on each side of him against the guardrail that went around the platform.

"What if somebody else comes out?"

"Pretend you don't notice them. They'll go away." He sat down on one of his heels, using the other foot for balance, and started licking her.

"Sweet Jesus—" Thoughts crowded her mind: the black night of Nebraska going past; somebody seeing them; stories she'd heard of what Parisian women were teaching American servicemen to do. Jesus God but his tongue felt wonderful—"Did you learn to do this in Paris?" she had to ask.

"No. A farm girl near Rouen showed me how," he replied between long, languishing licks. "Do you like it?"

"God, yes—" The first consuming tremor rippled through her body.

He kept it up until her juices, mixed with his saliva, were running freely down her buttocks and down his chin. Then he stood, removed his raincoat and pajamas and stuffed them behind a handrail; naked, he moved his erection slowly into the soft darkness that he had made so wet. Holding her face between both hands, he bent his head to press his lips against hers, letting her taste what he had tasted, at the same time beginning a slow, precise roll of his hips that settled into a long series of deep thrusts.

When their kiss ended, Ruby turned her head slightly; off in the blackness of the night, she saw a single faraway light and wondered if some farmer and his wife were doing the same thing on their feather mattress that she and Jim Delavane were doing on the back end of the speeding train. Probably not, she decided; somewhere she had heard that Midwestern farmers never even did it with the light on. Obviously, she thought with a grin, that did not apply to silver miners; apparently they did it anywhere. This silver miner anyway. She thought about his name: Jim Delavane. God, she had fallen hard for him. Hard and quick. Like the quick silver veins of which he had spoken earlier, maybe this was quick silver passion: close to the surface, ripe, ready to be taken. Was it less valuable because it was so easy to get? Ruby wondered if she had any chance at all of winning this man. As he continued to drive himself into her, she bent her head forward and rested against his shoulder.

"What's your fiancée's name again? Ellen?"

"Edith."

"Edith, yes." She had known it. The name had seared into her mind. "When will you be gettng married?"

"I don't know. Soon."

"Have you done this with her yet?"

"No." He took one hand off her hip, lifted her head up, and with his palm covered her mouth. "Don't talk." As if afraid she would anyway, he kept his hand there. Presently he felt her working her tongue between his fingers, moving it in and out in tempo with the movement of his erection. It excited him and he increased his impetus, almost impelling his testlcles into her. As he felt his ejaculate begin to roil and spread, when he knew it had passed that minuscule point of time and movement when it became irreversible, he pressed his lips to her ear and whispered, "Here it comes, something to fill your little pud—aaaaah—"

Ruby knew she should have shared the instant of ecstasy with him, but for some reason all she could think about was Buck O'Crotty in the day coach, sitting all alone. As the product of Jim Delavane's body shot up into her, a product of her own body, a single tear, left her and rolled off her cheek into the racing night.

THREE

The three young ex-Marines applied at four mines in Silver City—the Eclipse, Hale and Norcross, the Confidence, and Potosi—before being hired on at the Empire. The works superintendent for Empire said, "I can put youse two"—Buck and Jim—"on as muckers. The big guy"—

Mike—"looks like he's got enough muscle to make a good hoister."

They went right to work, on that very shift, in their mustering-out uniforms, with no time even to buy underground duds. "Jesus H. Christ," a hauler said when they got aboard the cage to be lowered to the bottom of the shaft, "hide the women and girls, the Marines have landed."

"This is risky business, boys," said another. "You'd be better off reenlisting."

"Never look up, big man," one of them said to Mike, who was peering up at the crank and cable that noisily lowered them away from daylight. "You'll get dust in your eyes and gravel in your mouth."

"Ain't dust and gravel he's got to worry about," interjected an older miner. "It's them goddamned toplanders that work up above. Careless, that's them. One of 'em dropped a hand wrench down the shaft last month. Fell a thousand feet and went so far into Billy Kiley's skull it was plumb out of sight. Lad never made a move after it hit him. Buried him with it still in his brain."

Mike moved to a corner of the cage.

"Give him a break, men," Buck requested. "Me and Jimmy here's from the copper digs in Eureka, but our friend's from the coal fields, a strip miner, and he ain't used to this kind of work yet. By the way, so's you'll know—his name is Mike Donovan. Iron Mike Donovan. You might've read in your newspaper what he done in France. He was a hero, like Alvin York."

"Quit it, Bucky," the big man said. "I can hold my own."

"Sure, buddy."

At the bottom, Mike asked, "How far down are we?"

"Thirteen hundred feet," Jim replied. "From here on down the works are stoped. Each drift is about six feet lower than the one behind it. From here to four thousand feet is called 'great' depth."

"What do they call it after that?" Mike asked.

"Insanity," Buck cut in. "Steps to hell."

The stope foreman pointed to Mike. "This is your bucket, Donovan," he said, indicating a tin container roughly the size and shape of a washtub. Four winch hooks in its sides were held together by a rope running up the shaft. "At the top of this here portal is a windlass that the rope is attached to. It'll guide the bucket. When the bucket's full of ore, you pull it up. A toplander will empty it. You two"—he gestured to Jim and Buck—"grab a shovel each and start filling the tub with diggings. That's all there is to it, boys. Get to work. Your twelve hours will go by before you know it."

That last was wishful thinking. The shift could be interminable. The noise alone was enough to drive a new man crazy. Each mine had a pulse of its own, a combination of vibrations from the hand-held sinker drills in the lowest stope and the Cornish pumps that sucked water from the violated earth, mixed with the thuds of picks, hammers, and wedges, the creak of the windlass and its winches, and the grating screech of the iron-and-steel incline car that brought the broken rock up to bottom of shaft where the three new men worked.

"What in the name of God is that?" Mike Donovan asked the first time he heard the awful screech. Buck and Jim paused and waited for the incline car to labor up from the depths, its noise like the agonizing cry of a great wounded beast.

"It's called the 'giraffe,' that incline car," said Buck, "because the iron track it runs on is long like a giraffe's neck."

"And it makes that noise," added Jim, "because it's carrying two tons of rock."

As the three men watched, the giraffe car rumbled to a stop at the end of track near them, and a self-acting gate opened to spill a new mound of rock for them. Exchanging resigned glances, Buck and Jim bent and threw their shovels back to work. Iron Mike resumed pulling the bucket rope, his arm, shoulder, and back muscles swelling to the job.

Periodically throughout the shift, a line of miners would file up out of the lower works and wait patiently at bottom of shaft while a crew of blasters, known as powder monkeys, went below to generate new rock to be dug. The muckers and hoisters had to follow them down to form a plating crew.

"What's a plating crew?" an apprehensive Iron Mike asked. "What do we have to do?"

"Wait, you'll see" Buck told him. "For now, watch these powder monkeys and you'll see true artists at work."

The powder monkeys, each with a jackhammer, drilled a hole straight back into the breast, or face, of the stope. Into that hole they slipped paper cartridges taken from a wooden box stenciled with the red figure of a muscular male torso and labeled "Hercules."

"Those are a mixture of potassium nitrate, sulphur, and charcoal," Jim told Mike. "They call it black powder."

Mike watched in fascination as the powder monkeys carefully inserted one after another of the cartridges into the drilled holes and with a wooden stick gently tamped them into place.

"They always use a wooden stick," Buck explained, "never metal or rock; one little spark would blow them—and us—to kingdom come."

When the holes were filled, each blaster snaked a stiff fuse all the way in to the farthest cartridge. Leaving a length of fuse extended, they then packed the opening of the hole with mud.

"That's called crimping," said Buck. "It directs the force of the explosion inward. A loose crimp can result in a misfire, with all the force coming out into the stope. That happens, it can blow us all to kingdom come." Iron Mike gave him an annoyed glance.

When the blast holes were ready, the powder monkey foreman yelled, "All right, plate it!"

"That's us," said Jim. With Buck, Mike, and the other laborers from bottom of shaft, Jim moved to a side wall of the tunnel where a huge, flat sheet of iron was leaning. With the strength of fifty arms, fifty hands gripped the great plate of metal and shifted it around until it lay up against the face that was to be blasted.

"That's what plating the blast is," Jim said. "When the powder goes off, all the blasted rock will form up into a smooth working surface for the muckers down here."

"That's if the plate's been put into position properly," Buck hedged. "If it hasn't, we could all be blowed—"

"I know!" Iron Mike cut in. "To kingdom come. Do you have to keep saying that?"

The plating crew filed back up the drift, stope by stope, until they were a safe distance away. There they stuffed rags in their ears, wrapped their heads in shirts, coats, sweaters, or whatever they had, and crouched at the sides of the tunnel as close to the wooden roof props as they could get. All was silent for a moment or two, then the powder monkeys came running up from the front stope yelling, "Fire in the hole!" That was the warning that fuses had been lit.

Instinctively the crouching men tightened up: jaws, fists, sphincters. Sometimes it would seem to them like an eternity of heavy, terrible, threatening silence before the rumbling explosion was heard, before the ground beneath them—the ground they had already violated and were violating further—trembled as if in sexual climax, shuddered, then seemed to balk and draw into itself, checking, steadying itself, as its newly wounded wall settled in tens of thousands of pieces behind the iron sheet. A rolling cloud of dust brought silence again. Then it was all over for a while. The drift advanced another two feet and provided three to four tons of muck. The men moved back to their places. Tools were picked up. Work resumed.

In the middle of the shift they were allowed time to eat. The regulars had lunch buckets with them, but the three new men had to buy box lunches sent down by the shift foreman, who charged the outrageous price of a quarter each. The boxes were brought down by "nippers," youngsters sometimes no more than twelve years old, who earned half pay by turning chipped and dull drills up to topland for the mine blacksmith to heat, hammer, and reform their edges. When a nipper had put in his time, built his muscles, learned to see in the dark, tolerate the incessant noise, acclimate to the constant steam and heat, conquered or at least concealed his fear of the depths, of cave-ins, of spurting water, of insidiously seeping gases, of fire, of pneumonia contracted by going from ninety degrees at five thousand feet to wintertime's ten degrees or zero or ten below at topland, and when he had decided that life had nothing better to offer, then he could ask for a pick or shovel or sledgehammer and finally, at full pay, become a man. So he believed.

"Jesus, I've got a beauty of a headache," Iron Mike complained as they ate their box lunches the first day. "Must be the noise."

"That's a powder headache," Buck advised. "Black powder does something to the air. I'm not sure what exactly. You'll get used to it, but it'll take a while."

"The coal mines back home are looking better all the time," Mike declared. "How did I get talked into a lash-up like this anyway?"

"Stop complaining," Buck said. "If you've still got the headache at end of shift, it'll give us an excuse to stop by the hospital and see lovely Ruby for some pills."

"Us? Why us? It's my headache."

"Right, and I'm sure you'll be half blind from it by then, so I'll be glad to lead you over to the dispensary."

"You're all heart, Bucky," Jim threw in.

The short break to eat was ended as it had begun, just as all things in the mine began and ended, by the shrill, clear blast of the mine whistle. Heavy eyes opened, heavy legs moved, heavy torsos were reactivated, sluggish forms unfolded and stood upright: a tribe of underground Neanderthals imprisoned in the bosom of earth another six hours before being allowed to resume human form.

Well into the second half of their shift, the three new men heard an urgent cry from the stopes: "Water hit! Water hit!"

"Jesus, what's that?" Mike hurried over to ask. "Are we flooding?"

"Water hit! Water hit!" The men in the upper stopes took up, and passed along the cry. Jim Delavane trotted over to the main shaft, and yelled up, "Water hit! Cage down!" He repeated it several times until an acknowledgment came from above. "Cage coming down!" a toplander called.

Already sounds of scurrying feet and urgent voices could be heard coming up, stope by stope, to bottom of shaft. Iron Mike stepped around nervously, beside himself.

"What in the name of God happened?"

"Somebody down there stuck a pick into an underground water reserve," Jim told him. "When that happens, it's like busting a water pipe, only a hundred times worse. The water shoots out with pressure you have to see to believe. It's like being hit by a train."

"Usually," Buck added, "the pressure's so great that it enlarges the pick-hole to the size of a baseball as soon as it feels release. Sometimes the shooting water gets half a dozen men before they can cave-in the hole and seal it."

The cage hit bottom and several toplanders hurried over. Sounds from below of rushing feet were now louder, accompanied by grunts, curses, admonitions to hurry, be careful, go easy there, and mutterings of reassurance: "You'll be okay, lad. I've seen this before. Come on, take it like a man now. That's the lad."

When finally they came into sight at bottom of shaft, Iron Mike Donovan was appalled at what he saw. Three men, drenched top to bottom, being led by other miners because they could not see: their faces were swollen grotesquely from the enormous pressure of the jet of water that had hit them so suddenly and unexpectedly. Besides their eyes looking like skin-covered golf balls, their noses were spread flat and bleeding down over lips that stretched wide in a macabre smile of agony. Cheeks were puffed as if with mumps, distended ears looked waxy and Halloweenish, necks and throats appeared goitrous.

"Mother of God," Mike whispered. Jim put a calming hand on his shoulder.

"Sometimes it looks worse than it is, buddy. Sometmes the swelling goes down in a few days."

"Other times," Buck amended, "it takes weeks. Now and then, if a man's taken a blast right in the eyes, he goes blind."

"Come on, Bucky, you know that's a rare thing," countered Jim.

"Didn't say it wasn't rare." Buck stood his ground. "Just said it's been known to happen. You're not disputing that, are you?"

The two friends locked eyes in a moment of rare animosity, while Iron Mike watched in awed revulsion as the three mutant-looking miners were led to the cage and hoisted topland. His expression was ill, color pale. Nothing like this—even *remotely* like this—ever happened in the coal fields. Filthy, grimy days, yes; cave-ins, yes, sometimes; but *this*—Jesus! Explosions, steam, sweltering heat, unremitting noise, bursts of high pressure water, falling hand wrenches—Christ, what else faced him?

"Back to it, lads!" the stope foreman ordered, blowing his pocket whistle. "Let's get our backs into it! There's lost time to be made up!" He blew the whistle again. The sound of it drilled into Iron Mike's head like a hammered spike.

"Jesus, my head! This pain is driving me crazy!" In frustration, the big Irishman who had carried a machine gun under one arm, a mortar under the other, pounded his fist against his forehead to try and beat away the hurt.

As all things do, it ended. The big mine whistle, underscored by the stope foreman's pocket whistle, told them to lay down tools, straighten crooked backs, wipe away some of the sweat, put on shirts, coats, something—it was always cooler topland, even in August heat—pick up lunch buckets, and trudge wearily, stope by stope, to bottom of shaft, the cage, and the ride back up to the world where men worked upright in a thing called sunlight.

"Christ, this headache has me blind," Iron Mike said, actually appearing groggy from it.

"I said I'd lead you to the dispensary," Buck reminded him. "The lovely Ruby Surrett will minister to you and you'll feel like a new man. Coming along, Jimmy?"

"No," Jim replied, looking away. "I've got some things to do."

"We'll tell Ruby you said hello. See you later at the boarding house?"

"Sure." Jim wanted to say *don't* tell Ruby I said hello. Don't mention me. For Christ's sake, I'm getting married on Sunday. But he knew such a statement would have demanded explanation.

Jim had last seen Ruby Surrett when they all got off the Virginia-and-Truckee train, which they had boarded after leaving the Central Pacific in Reno. Ruby had gone to a small house near the hospital, which she had rented by mail, and the three men had found lodgings in a boarding house at the edge of town. Their paths had not crossed since, and Jim thought it best to keep it that way. Ruby had been something on the back of that train, but Jim was committed to Edith Bloom. He loved Edith, had proposed to her; she had waited for him to return from the war, and in his mind it would have been unthinkable not to honor the plans they had made. Jim Delavane was a man of his word; in that there was no compromise.

Ruby was able to conceal her surprise when Buck and Mike showed up at the hospital and Jim was not with them. It was obvious from the condition of their mustering-out uniforms that they had found jobs, so it gave her a natural excuse to inquire about Delavane. "Did Jim get on too? Same shift?" she asked.

"Sure. He's mucking alongside me at the bottom of shaft," Buck said.

"I'm a hoister," Mike told her proudly. "Because I'm so strong."

"Good for you, Mike."

"But, Ruby, I've got this devil of a headache—"

"Powder headache," Buck said. "You heard of 'em?"

Ruby shook her head. "No."

"You will, around mines. Ask a doc."

Ruby inquired of one of the doctors on duty. He knew at once what Buck meant. "The black powder they use for blasting," he explained, "releases sulphur and potassium into the oxygen down there. When the men breathe it, it relaxes the capillaries. That causes increased flow of blood to the brain. The result is a severe headache. Give him half a morphine tab. He'll probably be back for one every day for a week; after that his system should acclimate."

As Ruby was halving a morphine tablet, Buck asked, "How is it here?"

"Fine," replied Ruby. "Seems like a good hospital. I'm learning new things all the time, like powder headaches."

"What days do you work?"

"Every day but Sunday."

"Want to go with us to Jimmy's wedding over in Eureka then? It's next Sunday."

"I wasn't invited, Bucky."

"I'm the best man and I'm inviting you."

"Sure, Ruby, come with us," Mike seconded. "I don't want to be the only one there who don't know everybody."

"No, I couldn't; not being invited." She gave Mike the half tablet with a drink of water, then stepped behind him and started massaging his temples.

"All right," Buck said. "I'll have to tell you the truth then. Jim asked me to ask you. He meant to himself, but what with looking for a job, looking for a house for him and Edith, well, it just slipped his mind. He didn't want me to tell you because he was embarrassed."

"Is that the truth, Buck?" she challenged skeptically.

"I swear it by the Church of England."

"Ha. You're Catholic. Mike, is it true?"

"He wasn't there when Jim asked me," Buck said quickly.

"That's right, Ruby. I wasn't there."

"We'll all take the bus over early Sunday morning. What d'you say, Ruby?"

"All?"

"Sure. You, me, Mike, and Jimmy." He smiled broadly. " 'Course, Jimmy won't be coming back with us in the evening. He'll be busy doing things."

"Come on, come with us, Ruby," Mike renewed the plea. "What if I get one of these headaches and need help?"

"This rubbing isn't part of your treatment; that's my idea.

Anyway, they aren't getting married in a mine shaft, are they?"

"They're getting married in Mr. Bloom's house," Buck said. "Edith's father. Then he's going to visit friends in Elko so they can have the house for a honeymoon."

"And Jim will be taking the bus over on Sunday morning?" Ruby asked. "With us?"

"Exacty."

She nodded her head once, pertly. "All right, I'll go."

The bus would not have an observation platform, she thought, but at least it would give her the chance to be around Jim Delavane for several hours to see if this consuming feeling she had for him was real or merely imagined; was it love or just the wake of an hour of extraordinary passion?

Ruby hoped to God it was the latter.

Jim was not surprised to see her at the bus depot early Sunday morning; Buck and Mike had already told him they had invited her. He had not been pleased at the news, but had the composure not to display any consternation that would have puzzled either of his friends. He merely said, "That's nice. Glad you remembered her." And to Ruby at the bus depot, in front of them, he said, "Hello, Ruby. Glad you could come." Only when the bus made its first rest stop, at Fallon, did they accidentally have a moment alone, and then Jim asked bluntly, "Didn't you realize this would be awkward? What the hell made you accept Buck's invitation anyway?"

At that moment Ruby realized she had been lied to. *Buck's* invitation. Jim had not wanted her there, after all. She got so angry that she had to become very quiet to control it.

"I guess I didn't think," she said. Inside she began to seethe—at being lied to by Buck, not wanted by Jim.

"I suppose we'll just have to make the best of it."

"I suppose." Outrage boiled in her breast. She looked away from Jim to keep from exploding in anger.

They reverted to cordiality when Buck and Mike returned and they got back on board the old Willys Overlander bus and settled onto its innerspring seats. One of the few other passengers was a farm boy who had a mouth organ in the bib pocket of his overalls. Buck and Mike encouraged him to play and began to harmonize on "Somebody Stole My

Gal." Ruby and Jim were asked to join in but demurred and threw irritated glances at them instead. After brutalizing their first song for ten minutes, the men switched to "After You're Gone." Neither of them could understand why Ruby wouldn't sing with them. Between songs, Buck said, "I can see Jimmy sitting out; he's a nervous bridegroom. But you don't have no excuse to be unhappy, Ruby. Come on, give us a few choruses."

Ruby could not be swayed; she sat by a window and stolidly watched the lower Dixie Valley go by as she silently fumed about men who lied and didn't care. At Eastgate, the bus made another rest stop. Ruby deliberately cornered Jim this time.

"Didn't what happened between us on the train mean anything at all to you?" she challenged without preliminaries.

"Sure," he answered, "it meant you and I wanted each other very badly. It meant we were attracted to each other right off. It meant we did what we wanted to do and we both enjoyed the hell out of it. Was it supposed to mean anything else?"

"It might have—if you'd given it a chance. Why haven't you come to see me in Virginia City?"

Jim shook his head impatiently. "Jesus, Ruby. You knew I was engaged. Buck told you I had a fiancée waiting for me."

"Engaged isn't married," Ruby asserted. "I fell for you hard, Jim. The least you could have done was ask me how I felt."

"Look, Ruby, you've got Bucky and Iron Mike both crazy about you—"

"Don't say it," she warned, holding up both palms. "Don't tell me to pick one of your friends as second choice."

"Ruby believe me, I—"

He never got to finish his sentence because Buck and Mike came out of the men's room of the Humboldt Oil filling station and it was time to reboard the bus.

"Come on, Ruby," Mike begged when they were on the highway again, "come on and sing with us."

"Sure," Ruby finally said resignedly. "Why not?"

She sat between them on one of the side benches and they went into a rendition of "Hail, Hail, The Gang's All Here!" While she was singing, Ruby's hurt feelings conjured up some spite. Personally selecting the next tune and whispering it in the farm boy's ear, she stood up in the aisle of the rickety bus and proceeded to do a vigorous shimmy as the harmonica jazzed out "They Go Wild, Simply Wild Over Me." Buck and Mike gave her enthusiastic hand-clapping and foot-stomping support, while Jim could only force a tight, humorless smile. At the end of the number, the other passengers on the bus applauded and the driver even gave Ruby a "Shave-and-a-Haircut, Two-Bits" toot of the bus horn.

"More, Ruby!" Iron Mike urged.

"Encore, encore!" shouted Buck.

But Ruby decided that was enough. Being vindictive helped with her pain, but it also made her feel guilty. "No more now," she said, "I'm tired." She moved to the rear of tie bus and sat down by herself.

The remainder of the trip was quiet, almost melancholy, everyone sitting alone, dozing or meditating, lulled into various degrees of repose by the asthmatic but haunting strains of the harmonica. The sun rose high in front of them as the bus proceeded due east and wound down the seven-thousand-foot Austin Summit. Early in the afternoon it rattled into the Central Nevada hill town of Eureka.

The wedding of Jim Delavane and Edith Bloom was small, quiet, and dignified. Jim and his best man, Buck, as well as Iron Mike, wore newly purchased black suits and neckties. The bride was dressed in a handmade lace-and-silk dress in which her late mother and maternal grandmother before her had been married. Edith Bloom was a proper, pretty girl, pink-cheeked, almost boyishly figured, with dark hair worn fashionably short. There was a friendly directness in her eyes exactly matching that of her father, Solomon Bloom, a tall, stately man with the precise bearing of the educated. He was a third-generation teacher, his daughter and only child a fourth.

After Edith Bloom had become Edith Delavane, she was introduced by her new husband to Ruby Surrett. Taking Ruby's hand, she said warmly, "It's so nice to meet a friend of Bucky's. I hope we'll see a lot of each other in Silver City."

Ruby had turned red, knowing that Jim had told his bride ahead of time that she, Ruby, was Buck's friend, not his. "Yes, I hope so too," she had replied, although seeing Edith Delavane in Silver City was the very last thing she wanted to do. Nothing against Edith; she seemed very nice, very sweet. But Ruby knew that the mere sight of her would stimulate images of her in bed with Jim, of her being fondled and kissed and licked the way that farm girl in Rouen had taught him—

After meeting Ruby, Edith had whispered to Jim, "It must be serious between Bucky and her. Just the mention of his name made her blush. Wouldn't it be nice if they got married and we could all be friends in Silver City? Of course, we'd all have to try and find a girl for Mike. He seems like such a dear—and so strong! Did you see him lift that barrel of cider for father?"

"I don't know how much time we're going to have for socializing," Jim had evaded. "You remember I told you that Bucky, Mike, and I were going to be involved in some speculation to try and raise a grubstake for some land to do our own digging on. I'm afraid that's going to take up a lot of my time, especially early on. I hope it won't be too hard on you."

Edith had taken it in stride, squeezing his arm and putting her head on his shoulder. "I know how much you want to get ahead, Jimmy. You do whatever you have to do. I'll find some way to keep busy. Maybe Ruby and I can spend some time together."

While Jim fretted over that possibility, Solomon Bloom and two other middle-aged widowers were entertaining Ruby and making friendly threats of stealing her away from the young bachelors who had brought her. Meanwhile those young bachelors, Buck and Mike, were having their first serious discussion about Ruby. Buck initiated the conversation, deciding that if he and Mike were to remain friends, which he hoped they would, there had to be an understanding on the matter. He waited until they were alone, standing off to the side of the Bloom front yard, drinking cider into which Buck had poured a taste of rye.

"You seem to like Ruby a lot," he said casually to Mike. "Quite a lot, I mean."

"I do," Mike admitted. "I like her more all the time."

Buck sighed quietly, looking off at the mountains, "So do I," he admitted.

"You mean you like her like I do?" Mike asked. "Like, you know, *that*?"

"Afraid so, buddy. Like that."

"Jesus" said Mike. It was more a prayer than an oath. They stood by the fence in silence for a while then Mike asked, "Bucky?"

"What?"

"Do you think a guy like me could ever have a real chance with a girl like Ruby?"

Buck squinted at him. "What do you mean, a guy like you?"

"You know. A hardrock miner. A lot of muscle but not too bright. Probably never really get nowheres in life. Don't have all that much to offer a girl."

"Hell, you got as much to offer her as I have," Buck scoffed. "More, you're better looking. Got as much to offer Ruby as Jim has to offer Edith. Besides, if we get our grubstake going like we plan, who knows how far it'll carry us?" Buck reached up and put an arm around his friend's shoulders. "Main thing is you and I can't let our feelings for Ruby come between us. We'll both court her, fair and square, everything above board, and whichever one of us she chooses, why, that'll be that. The other one can be best man at the wedding and we'll still be friends. Deal?"

"You bet," Mike said, smiling. "Thanks, Bucky. You're a real pal. You and Jimmy both. I'm real lucky I met you."

"No luckier than we are, buddy. Come on now, let's take our girl away from those old men."

For everyone but Ruby the wedding afternoon was as pleasant a time as could be remembered. As evening approached and the air began to cool, shawls and coats were put on and the guests began to drift off homewards. Solomon Bloom put on his duster, set his grip satchel firmly in the rumble seat of his Marmon, kissed his daughter goodbye, and set off on the one-hundred-mile trip north to Elko to visit friends for a week. The Willys Overlander bus, which had continued east to Ely, near the Utah border, then turned around for the trip back, drove up and parked to wait for its return passengers; the new Mrs. Delavane invited the six strangers already aboard to get off and eat, which they did. Ruby went in to use the Bloom bathroom to freshen up for the return trip, and while inside examined with morbid curiosity the sleepwear Edith had laid out for herself and Jim, sleepwear she had made by hand: matching cotton nightgown and nightshirt, white with blue piping, a rose embroidered on the breast of hers, a good luck horse-shoe on his.

Out in the yard, Jim took Buck and Mike aside to make plans. "I'll be back in Silver City Wednesday afternoon," he told them. "Between now and then, it's up to the two of you to find us an honest game somewheres. The sooner we get started, the better."

"Leave it to us," Buck said. "We'll have something all staked out by the time you get back."

"You going to be able to start right in?" Mike asked with concern. "Just being married and all, I mean."

"Sure. Why wouldn't I?"

Mike shrugged. "I thought you might not want to leave Edith alone so soon."

"Let me worry about Edith," Jim advised him, in a tone that caused Buck's forehead to pinch. "I want to get moving on this. We've been putting half our wages in the kitty for three weeks, so we've got nearly a hundred greenbacks to play with. Let's test these jokers, find out if we learned anything about cards in the Corps. What d'you say?"

"We'll be ready when you are," Buck assured him. "But if you do need a few days to help Edith get settled, why—"

"Edith will be fine. Don't worry about her. She's already got several things lined up to keep her busy. Matter of fact, she was too embarrassed to say anything, but she's going to be so busy for a while she won't be able to invite you two and Ruby over for supper. Not right away anyhow. I told her I was sure you'd understand. You're all at the top of our list, though."

Later, after everyone had gone, when he and Edith were alone in the house, Jim had covered that lie with another one.

"I'm glad you liked Ruby Surrett so much," he said. "She'll probably end up married to Bucky. I invited them to supper after we get settled in Silver City but they had to beg off; Ruby works long shifts at the hospital, and Buck is going to be busy in our new partnership. They have such little free time, I guess they want to spend it together. Anyway, I told them you'd understand. We'll all get together when things settle down a little."

"Yes, of course," Edith said.

There was disappointment in her voice; Jim felt bad about it, but was sure this way was best for all concerned. With them all closely associating, there was too much chance that something would be said, some hint dropped, a deliberate remark made in anger. One thing he had learned as a Marine officer: Keep the ranks separated. Privates from sergeants, sergeants from lieutenants. The less one grade knew about the other, the better. Jim needed everyone at this point—Edith, Bucky, Mike—everyone except Ruby, of course. He did not want to risk affecting his grubstake plan by alienating anyone.

Everything was going to work out fine, he was certain of it. As he went around the house pulling down the shades, only one thing bothered him. He should have been thinking about Edith, who was at that moment taking a warm bath to prepare herself for him. Instead, he was thinking an entirely different thought.

He was thinking about the rear platform of a speeding train.

FOUR

When Jim came over to the boarding house on Wednesday after supper, Buck was waiting for him on the front porch.

"Where's Iron Mike?" Jim asked, glancing around.

Buck put an arm around his shoulders and led him away from the porch, where other boarders were also sitting for their after-supper smoke. Once out of earshot, Buck said, "Mike's pulled out of it, Jim."

Jim's lips parted in surprise. "Pulled out? What the hell do you mean?"

"Now don't go getting upset. He and I talked it over. He asked if he could pull out and I let him."

"You had no right to do that, Buck!" Jim put a finger on Buck's chest. "We had this figured as a three-way partnership. We needed Mike's share of the kitty to help bankroll us!"

"We don't have to have it three ways, Jimmy; we can have it just you and me."

Jim shook his head vigorously. "That won't give us enough of a bankroll."

"All right then, I'll put in part of my mustering-out pay—"

"No good, Buck. The deal was equal shares. Equal shares means an equal vote. If you put in more than me, we won't be equal partners."

"Then I'll *lend* money to the partnership and it can be paid back off the top. We can work it out, Jimmy; it ain't that big a problem—"

"It *is* a problem! Goddamn it, the minute I turn around, something goes wrong."

"Come on over here," Buck said, taking his arm. He led Jim across the street from the boarding house and they sat on a spur track of the Virginia-and-Truckee railroad line.

"What the hell did he pull out for, anyway?" Jim demanded.

"For Ruby."

"Ruby? What's she got to do with it?"

"Mike and I," Buck said with a grin, "have agreed to court Ruby for the purpose of matrimony—"

"Does she know that?"

"I'm sure she knows of Mike's interest by now; he's over seeing her tonight, with a box of chocolates. I haven't made my own intentions clear to her yet." Buck looked curiously at him. "Why do you ask?"

Shrugging, Jim looked down at the cinders on the right of way. "Just wondering, is all."

"Oh. All right. Well, we've come to an agreement, Mike and me, to court Ruby like gentlemen, on the up-and-up, with no back-stabbing and the like. When she makes her choice between us, the other will back off. Iron Mike feels that a girl like Ruby will be more impressed by a thrifty saver and a little nest egg than she will by involvement in a poker scheme to get a grubstake to dig for silver where there might not be any. And put that way, I wouldn't blame her. Anyhow, Mike asked if he could pull out and I said he could. It was the only fair thing to do, Jim. He asked how you'd feel about it; I told him you'd understand."

"Big of you," Jim sulked. "How much bankroll does that leave us?"

"We had ninety-nine bucks; now we've got sixty-six."

"We can't even buy into a six-bit game with that." A six-bit game required a seventy-five dollar buy-in.

"There ain't any decent six-bit games around anyways," Buck told him. "But I found us a beauty of a four-bit game. It's in the back of a saloon. Goes from eight until when. Run by a dealer name of Roone McKee. Everybody says he's the straightest player in Virginia City."

"*Virginia* City?"

"It's a short enough drive. I thought it best to keep our gambling separate from where we live and work. Especially for you. Edith might want to start teaching here—"

"It seems to me, Buck, that you're taking an unusual interest in the welfare of my wife," Jim said pointedly. "You wouldn't be insinuating that I'm not capable of properly looking after her, would you?"

Buck looked at him in surprise. "Come off it, Jimmy," he chided. "I'm thinking of you as much as her. Look, suppose you want to buy Edith a little house and need to borrow money from the bank. Don't you think it would look a lot better if you was just a mucker for Empire Mines, instead of a mucker by day and a card player by night. It's common sense, Jimmy."

After he was placated, Jim asked, "How in hell are we supposed to get back and forth to Virginia City?"

"That's a surprise, Jimmy my lad," Buck replied with a wide smile. "Come see what I've got." Behind the boarding house he showed Jim a fenderless 1914 Mercer with a canvas top. "I bought it from the butcher uptown; he's got a new Hupmobile. In addition to getting us to and from Virginia City, I figure it'll keep me even with Mike as far as courting Ruby is concerned. He'll be able to see her every night during the week, since we'll be busy either playing or dealing practice hands, but in Silver City there's not much they can do—listen to the radio or walk uptown to the picture show. But on Sundays I can take Ruby for rides in the mountains, picnics, even to Reno. What d'you think?"

"Where are the fenders?"

"Rusted off. It don't need fenders anyways. Looks pretty good otherwise, eh?"

"Pretty good," Jim agreed absently. He thought of Ruby

riding around in the car with Buck. It did not please him. "All right," he said getting back to business, "we'll share the cost of the gasoline to and from Virginia City. Everything's got to be equal shares, just like we originally planned. Where's the sixty-six bucks?"

"Right here," Buck said, producing a roll of bills with a rubber band around it. Jim took the money and pocketed it. They got in the Mercer.

"What's the name of the place in Virginia City where the game's at?"

"Callahan's," said Buck.

Roone McKee wore a soft, unstarched, snow white shirt with the sleeve cuffs turned up twice so that all players at his table could see that he was not wearing a brace or any other contrivance used to conceal or manipulate cards. He wore no tie but had a blue silk scarf tied around his neck. There were no pockets on his shirt. He kept both hands above the table, in sight, at all times. The only time his hands touched anything other than cards, chips, or money was when he occasionally reached up absently to feel the patch of skin where his thin, sandy hair was receding.

"Did Mr. Callahan explain the buy-in?" he asked Jim and Buck after Callahan had brought them into the back room.

"Yeah," Jim replied. "Fifty, right?"

"That is correct, yes."

Jim counted out the fifty, trying to conceal how little was left. As McKee pushed a precounted rack of chips across the table, his eyes flicked to Buck.

"May I ask what this gentleman's status is?"

"What?"

"His status. Why is he here? You've only bought one chair."

"Oh. We're partners."

"I see. Would you mind sitting back awaw, from the table, sir?" McKee said to Buck. "And please refrain from kibitzing during play."

"Your game, mister," said Buck, moving back to a chair against the wall.

Roone McKee shuffled a deck of cards precisely three times and placed the deck in front of one of the four players to be cut. "The game is five-card stud poker, gentlemen," he said with quiet authority. "Nothing is wild. The ante is two dollars each hand." As he spoke, he picked the deck up and began to deal.

The game started at eight o'clock. By nine-thirty, Jim Delavane had lost his fifty dollars worth of buy-in chips, as well as seven dollars cash bet on his last hand. As McKee raked in the pot, he said, "Additional chips are twenty-five dollars a tray. Are you staying in the game?"

Jim shook his head, pushing his chair back. "Not tonight."

"Thank you for playing," Roone McKee said smoothly. "Come again."

As Jim and Buck walked through the saloon in front, Callahan, the owner, said to Buck, "Jesus, that was quick."

"A little too quick," Jim replied for them, pausing at the bar.

"What d'you mean by that?" Callahan asked coolly. He was a slight, wiry man from Knock, a bit pugnacious.

"I mean we're strangers here, mister. How do we know your game's straight?"

Callahan smiled a tight, controlled smile. "Come here, lad," he said, leading them down to the middle of the bar. He pointed to a glass-covered picture frame mounted above the cash register. In it was a one-thousand-dollar banknote bearing a portrait of President Grover Cleveland. Below it was neatly hand lettered: *This bill will be given to any customer who can prove that Callahan's games are rigged or Callahan's whiskey is watered.* "Any time you can do more than insinuate, boys, be sure and let me know. In the meantime, if you can't afford to lose, don't gamble." Jim flushed red and walked out. Callahan's eyes flicked to Buck. "I thought you said he was all right."

"He is," Buck defended his friend. "It was just a bad night for him."

"Better find him another game," Callahan said. "He's too hotheaded for my taste."

"Come on now," Buck chided. "He didn't make no scene or nothing, did he? You've got to give us a chance to get our dough back."

"All right" Callahan said grudgingly. "Just see that he don't cause no trouble."

"You have my word on that. We'll be back," he promised as he hurried out.

Jim was sitting in the car, muttering dark curses. "I never lost that much that fast in my life," he said indictingly when

Buck got in. "He must have stacked the deck on me or something."

"I think he beat us fair and square, Jimmy. The cards just fell wrong. It happens."

"You were watching the game, do you think I played badly?"

Buck shook his head. "Not really. Couple of times I thought you should have dropped out instead of staying in, but—"

"Do you think you could have played better?" Jim challenged.

"Not better. Different, maybe. But it would have amounted to the same thing, Jimmy. The cards weren't right. We'll make it up next time."

"Maybe you should do the playing," Jim said sullenly.

"We decided you'd be the one to play, Jim. When it was you, me, and Mike, we decided you were the best player. That hasn't changed."

"You're a good player too, Buck. Maybe we should take turns, at least."

"Let's stick with our plan," Buck insisted. "We've got nine dollars left in the kitty. With each of us putting in eleven bucks a week, we'll be able to buy another chair in two weeks. In the meantime, we deal practice hands every night and keep memorizing that book of poker odds we bought in New York. We'll get him next time, Jimmy."

Buck started the old Mercer and headed back for Silver City. Inside he felt sick because the money had gone so fast. But he did not want to add to Jim's guilt by admitting it, so he pretended it did not matter. They both knew it did.

Two weeks later, Roone McKee beat Jimmy for every dollar of their fifty-three-dollar stake and sent them home flat broke. He did it in just under two hours of play.

"The son of a bitch has got to be doing something," Jimmy insisted. "Were you watching him or me tonight?" he asked Buck.

"You mostly, but him sometimes."

"I want you to watch just him next time. If we catch that pasty-faced bastard doing anything with those cards, I'm going to personally tear that thousand dollar bill off Callahan's wall!"

Three weeks later, they were back with sixty-six dollars. McKee won it all in two and a half hours.

"Did you watch him?" Jim asked angrily when they left.

"Like a hawk."

"And?"

"I think he's beating you fair and square, Jim. If I thought otherwise, I'd find us another game. But we're better off staying with this one. The odds are with us here; we can't keep losing indefinitely."

They did. Every three weeks they went back with a sixty-six-dollar stake, and every three weeks the soft-spoken gambler in the snow white shirt won most of it away from them. It went on for three months: the rest of summer and most of fall.

The more he lost, the greater became Jim Delavane's irascibility. His distemper was constantly at the boiling point. When he walked gloweringly out of Callahan's now, drinkers stepped aside; everyone knew of his losing streak, and everyone recognized the fury in his eyes; no one was about to antagonize him, even by accident. Buck stayed as close to him as possible for several days after each loss, a buffer against the chance careless remark, the casual brush of a shoulder, that might set him off. Buck wondered what life must be like for Edith, but dared not ask. He did not even discuss the matter with Iron Mike, for fear the big man might try to help and do more harm than good. When Mike asked occasionally how the play was going, Buck would simply say, "Pretty steady," or "We're holding our own, pretty much." Suspecting that he had made a wise move withdrawing from the plan, Mike did not press for details.

The only person Buck did tell about it was Ruby. Because she was being induced by sheer boyish charm to spend several evenings a week with Iron Mike, while Buck was dealing practice hands to Jim and coaching him on odds at the boarding house, Ruby felt obliged to let Buck take up her Sundays. She knew the two were competing for her, but because with neither of them had it reached the serious stage, she was letting it continue for the time being. She had already made up her mind to leave Silver City in the near future, although she was not certain yet where she would go. In the meantime, she spent Sunday afternoons with Buck.

Over the weeks, Buck kept her advised about the losses, having first sworn her to secrecy. As time went on, she saw Buck become more and more apprehensive about the effect their incredibly bad luck might ultimately have on Jim.

"I've never seen him like this," he finally told her. "On our way back from the games, he's like a crazy, man. His eyes practically pop out of their sockets and his jaw clenches so hard I think the blood vessels in his temple will burst. He's starting to make some very serious threats. I can't convince him any longer that he isn't being cheated and made a fool of. Sometimes it's hard to even convince myself."

"Have you thought about talking to his wife about it?" Ruby had asked cynically, and immediately regretted it. Buck did not catch the derision in her tone.

"I couldn't do that," he replied simply. "Edith doesn't even know about the game. She thinks we're trading stocks and speculating in land, that sort of thing. She's no idea it's a poker game. I'm afraid it would be quite a shock to her."

"Poor dear," Ruby muttered and at once mentally scolded: *Stop it!* "I hope Jim doesn't do anything rash," she said quickly, and sincerely, to cover her sarcasm.

Somehow, as the weeks went by and Buck's reports on their scheme became bleaker and more foreboding, as she heard of Jim Delavane sinking deeper and more completely into the despair of defeat, the premonition grew in Ruby that Jim would come to her. From premonition it evolved to possibility, to probability, and finally to foregone conclusion. Whether he came for sympathy or sex, he *would* come.

Late on a cool night in early October, he knocked on the door of her little rented house. When she let him in, Ruby saw that he was pale, drained, wasted. Gone from his marvelous eyes was the lively challenge she had first seen there, the spirit, the confidence.

"I'm sick, Ruby," he said. "I think I'm losing my mind."

She sat him by her little fireplace, put an afghan over his legs, and had him drink a coffee and whiskey.

"You're not sick and you're not losing your mind," she told him resolutely. "You are simply under a great deal of pressure and have no outlet for it. There are positive forces and negative forces in life, Jim. You've let the negative forces get control. Your losing streak has got you down."

His expression flashed anger. "That goddamned O'Crotty. He told you."

"Yes, he told me, and I'm glad he did. People have nervous breakdowns over this sort of thing, Jim. You've got to turn it around."

The anger in his face was replaced by desperation. "How?" he almost begged.

"Work at it. Fight it. Talk about it."

"Talk about it? With who?"

"You've got a wife, Jim." His immediate, barely audible grunt told her many things. She sat on her heels in front of him. "What's the matter with your marriage?"

"Nothing. Edith's a perfect wife. She doesn't complain about anything. No matter how many nights I'm gone, how late I'm out, she doesn't say a word. I never take her anywhere; all we do together is eat and sleep; yet she never complains. I only give her half my wages to run the house, and she manages to get by. She goes to church without me and never nags me about it. She's left alone most of the time and doesn't seem to resent it." Jim held both palms out in resignation. "She's perfect, Ruby."

"Why can't you talk to her about your losing streak then?" Ruby had to challenge. "Why can't you share with her what you're doing?"

"I don't know," Jim said, shaking his head. "She's had such a proper upbringing and she's so well educated, it just doesn't seem like the kind of thing that she'd approve of."

Wonderful, Ruby thought. Miss Goody Brighteyes. We mustn't show her anything but sunshine. Her husband was heading for a high-blood-pressure stroke and she wasn't doing a goddamned thing to relieve his tension. "What about sex?" Ruby asked bluntly.

"What do you mean?" he said, averting his eyes.

"You know what I mean, Jim. Please don't play games with me; I'm trying to help you. Do you and Edith have a decent sex life—no, let me ask it a different way—do you have a *good* sex life?"

"We have sex—" he said tentatively, shrugging. The shrug was Ruby's answer.

"You have the kind of sex that would be satisfactory if you'd never been to France, is that what you mean? You on top, her on the bottom, do it as quickly as you can, and try not to look at each other. Have you tried the other ways with her, Jim? Have you asked her to—well, experiment?"

"I can't," he replied in utter frustration. "I've thought about it, but I just can't bring myself to talk to her about things like—that."

Ruby took his hands in hers. "Jimmy, Jimmy. She's your

wife. You've got to give her a chance." What the hell are you *doing?* her mind screamed. This is the man you want for yourself. Why are you promoting *her*?

Jim buried his face in his hands. "I can't, Ruby. I try, but I can't. I'm afraid she might—" He shook his head in abject misery. "I just can't." Taking a deep breath, he got control of himself and sat up straight. "Listen, I'm sorry I intruded on you like this. It's my problem, not yours. I'll work it out. I just needed someone to—be with for a few minutes. But it's late and—"

"Just a minute," Ruby said, patting his hands. "Stay here for just a minute."

She left the room. Jim drank the last of his laced coffee and rested his head against the back of the chair. God, it felt good just to sit here, away from Edith, away from Buck, away from that son of a bitch Roone McKee, away from the steam, sweat, and sludge of the mine. There was still a knot in his esophagus, aches at the top and bottom of his spine, and a throb in his temples, but somehow sitting there, with no one on the face of the earth knowing he was there but Ruby, was like some kind of physical and mental limbo in which he sensed that his misery was stalemated, that it would not, at least for the moment, become worse.

Ruby, he thought. Ruby was a woman a man could talk to. A woman who would understand a man's problems. Was it, he wondered, because she had been off to war as he had, instead of being restricted to an elementary school in a little Nevada hill town, as Edith had? Or because she was sexually knowledgeable and Edith was barely beyond virginity? Or was it the way each of them saw things, the way each of them viewed the many windows of life? Background, experience, attitude—any or all of those reasons? Just wondering about it was refreshing to Jim Delavane; it was the first time in weeks his mind had not steadfastly and morbidly dwelled on his losing streak.

"Jim—" Ruby's voice called.

Turning his head he saw her standing naked in the lighted door of her bedroom: auburn hair down over her shoulders, hands on hips, feet apart, the vision of every virgin-whore a man dreams about.

"You don't have to ask me, Jim," she said evenly. "Just come and do anything you want to with me. Kiss and lick and suck anything you like. Put it in me anywhere you want to. Do it for as long as you want to, as many times as you want to, any way you want to." She held a hand out to him, causing one broad, freckled breast to rise. "Come on, Jim."

Without hesitation, Jim Delavane went to her.

FIVE

J im started winning.

In his very next game, he played steadily for four hours and ran their sixty-six-dollar bankroll up to one hundred fifteen dollars.

"Congratulations," said Roone McKee when the game ended. "Looks like your luck finally changed."

"Yours too, maybe," Buck said over Jim's shoulder. He quickly assumed mock contriteness. "Sorry, didn't mean to kibitz."

McKee's smile was humorless. "You've got enough to buy two chairs tomorrow night," he suggested. "Why don't you sit in too, O'Crotty?"

"Jim's the player in our partnership," Buck replied. "We'll stick with one chair."

Outside, they were jubilant. "Forty-nine dollars!" Jim said gleefully. "I beat the son of a bitch for forty-nine dollars!"

"We're going to beat him again tomorrow night too," Buck said grimly. "And every night afterward." He slapped Jim smartly on the back. "I told you we couldn't keep losing indefinitely."

When they got back to Silver City, Buck as usual dropped Jim off at the corner of the block in which Jim and Edith rented a small house. Ironically, it had been Buck's idea to do that. "The noise this old clunker makes," he had said, "might wake Edith if we drive right up to the house."

"That's thoughtful of you, Buck. The corner'll be fine."

After he had started seeing Ruby, Jim would walk away from the car as if heading home, then double back when Buck had driven away, and hurry along several blocks of darkened streets and into an alley to Ruby's back door.

The night he broke his losing streak and won for the first time, Jim arrived buoyant and exhilarated at Ruby's. "I beat him, Ruby!" he declared, hugging her heartily, swinging her around. "I beat Roone McKee! I took him for fifty dollars!" he exaggerated, determining that fifty sounded better than forty-nine. "You did it, Ruby!" he praised. "You straightened me out! I love you, Ruby Surrett!"

"I love you too, Jim Delavane, but please keep your voice down unless you want it all over town tomorrow that you love me. I have neighbors, you know."

"I don't care who knows it," he avowed, but Ruby noticed that he at once lowered his voice. He still had her pulled up tightly against him. "I couldn't have done it without your help, you know that, don't you?"

"Maybe." She felt him erecting between them. His lips began to nibble at her neck as his hands unbelted her robe.

"Everytime I see you in your robe and nightgown, I think about the train," he whispered.

"I know . . ."

The kitchen table was mere steps behind her. Backing her up to it, opening her robe, raising her gown from the bottom and lowering it and the robe from her shoulders, he was able, by arching backward, to enter her and draw a swelling nipple into his mouth at the same time. The synchronous movements, one thrusting, one drawing, never failed to enrapture Ruby; she leaned back, gripping the table with both hands, as a massive orgasm consumed her.

"Ruby, Ruby," her exuberant lover whispered, "I'll beat— the son of a bitch—again tomorrow night—"

He did win again the next night, increasing the hundred fifteen to a hundred seventy-six.

"Sixty-one dollars tonight!" he exclaimed with elation on the way home after the second winning night. "We've got him running, Bucko!"

"I think you're right, Jimmy," Buck agreed. "But let's not lose sight of the fact that he's playing with our money still. We were down four hundred thirty-four dollars before we started winning. We need another two fifty-eight to break even and start taking his dough."

"We'll get it, Bucky," Jim asserted confidently."Listen, how about buying two chairs tomorrow night, like McKee suggested? We'll both take him."

Buck shook his head. "Let's stick with the original plan. We rode out the losing streak; now we're winning. Let's don't do nothing that wasn't part of the original plan."

I already have, Bucko, Jim thought slyly. Ruby wasn't part of the original plan. But she's sure as hell part of it now. Every night, on the way back to Silver City, in the darkness of the front seat, Jim kept a hand cupped over his growing desire for Ruby Surrett.

He continued to win. For ten consecutive nights he won, adding more than six hundred dollars to their bankroll, increasing it to nearly eight hundred. On the eleventh night, Roone McKee said, "How about a heads-up game, Delavane? Just you and me."

Jim looked back at Buck, who shrugged and said, "Why not? We own this man."

McKee's pasty complexion turned red and a little knot appeared in each cheek as his jaw clenched. The game was five-card stud poker, nothing wild, man-to-man, ten-dollar ante, twenty-dollar bet, fifty-dollar raise, McKee doing all the dealing. They played for four hours. Jim won six thousand and eighty dollars.

"I'd like to play you one more time, Delavane," the gambler said at the end of the night. "I've got a couple of thousand in cash at the bank, and I hold title to several unmined parcels just east of town. You and your partner wanted a grubstake to buy some land to work; if you'll let me bet the value of the deeds I hold, I'll give you a chance to win the stake and the land."

Jim and Buck went into a corner and discussed it. "How do you feel about it?" Buck asked.

"Good. I feel good," Jim said.

"Can you beat him again?"

"I can, yes. I can beat him again."

Buck looked into Jim Delavane's light blue eyes and saw, without knowing that Ruby had put it back, the confidence and alertness and eagerness to face challenge that had been there before the losing streak began. It left Buck without a doubt that Jim could beat Roone McKee again.

"Take the game," he said.

*   *   *

In Ruby's kitchen that night, Jim paced back and forth, wringing his hands, like some hyperkinetic mourner. He wet his lips constantly, swallowed rapidly, and blinked as if fending off blindness. Outside, a sudden electrical storm had started; the crack of lightning punctuated his staccato speech.

"I've won nearly seven thousand dollars. I can hardly believe it. We're going to play a heads-up game tomorrow night for all the money that McKee's got left, and for some land deeds he's won from other players. Callahan says it'll be the biggest game ever played in Virginia City; he's going to charge admission for spectators in the card room. Look at me, I can't stop my hands from shaking—"

"It's nervous anxiety," Ruby said. She patted his face with a towel. "You're sweating profusely. Give me your arm." She checked his pulse. "Racing. You've got to calm down, Jim."

"I can't stop thinking about it—"

"Are you worried that you might lose?"

"Yes."

"Then don't play."

"I've got to. Buck and I have agreed to the game."

"Let Buck play. You said he was as good as you."

"I said *almost* as good as me. Which might not be good enough to beat McKee. Pour me a drink, will you?"

As Ruby went to her liquor cabinet, there was another loud crack of lightning and it began to rain. She gave Jim two ounces of brandy. "Just sip it," she tried to tell him, but he was too quick for her and bolted it down. "Come lie down," she said. "Let me massage your neck and shoulders; you're probably tight as a drum."

On the bed, coat and shoes off, he began to relax a little as her strong, practiced fingers kneaded the top of his shoulders and sides of his neck. As she rubbed, he rambled, his words and thoughts disconnected, until finally she put a finger on his lips and shushed him. "Be quiet, Jim," she said softly. "Try to relax. Close your eyes."

"I can't," he told her, "I'm too keyed up. My mind feels like it's going a hundred miles an hour."

"Here," she said, "I'll help you."

He felt her fingers at his trousers, inside, handling him as he became firm. Then she was stroking his shaft and ministering to him with her mouth on the underside where it felt so incredibly good. Outside the storm raged violently as if to protest what she was doing. Her full lips pursed and kissed, then nibbled at him; her tongue ran up, down, around; she bared her teeth and dragged them over the wet flesh that her tongue had just covered; then she took him in her mouth and held him there as her hand finished its work on the length of him.

As he ejaculated, there was yet another shattering split of lightning outside, and in the flash of its light Ruby saw a figure at the bedroom window.

"Jim, there's someone outside looking in!"

Jim was off the bed and moving out of the room, buttoning his trousers, crossing the kitchen, Ruby right behind him, when the back door was thrown open with a sudden slamming of wood. Buck O'Crotty stood in the doorway, drenched from the rain, staring at them in revulsion.

"You lowlife son of a bitch," he said, pointing a finger at Jim as if there was some reason to distinguish him. "And you," he said to Ruby, shaking his head incredulously. "You went to his wedding, for Christ's sake. My God, what kind of woman are you? What kind of dirty, contemptible—"

"Just a minute, Buck—"

As Jim stepped forward, Buck dropped into a crouch and hit him in the face with a solid, anger-driven fist. Caught completely off guard, Jim dropped to his knees, dazed. Ruby rushed to him.

"Stop it, Buck!" she snapped, kneeling to grab Jim and keep him from pitching forward. She glared up at Buck. "What the hell were you doing looking through my window anyway?" she demanded. "How long have you been doing that?"

"I haven't!" he snarled. "But maybe I should have! At least I'd have known what kind of—" He shook his head in disgust and suddenly turned away, looking ill. Standing in the open doorway, he used one hand to wipe the rain from his face. "When I got back to the boarding house after dropping him off," he said, spitting out the word "him" as if it were now an obscenity, "I started getting ready for bed, and then I had a sudden urge to come share with you how well we did in the game tonight. I was going to—to tell you that I'd have something special to ask you on Sunday."

Ruby's expression softened momentarily, but as Jim's limp weight shifted in her arms, her face at once resumed its severity. "That doesn't explain why you were prowling around out there peeking in my window."

"Oh, stop trying to crucify me about the goddamned window, will you?" Buck lashed back, turning to face her. "I knocked on your goddamned door, three times! Maybe you didn't hear me because of the storm. I thought maybe you'd fallen asleep with the lights on; I came around to tap on your window. That's when I saw that you couldn't answer my knock"—his tone became venomous—"because I'd caught you with your mouth full."

"Get out, Buck," she said coldly. "Get out of my house, right now!"

"Sure," he said, "sure, I will. Just as soon as I take care of a little business matter."

Buck reached down for Jim and Ruby sought to fight him off. "Leave him alone, Buck, goddamm you!" Taking her firmly by the wrists, Buck snatched her to her feet and flung her across the room.

"I'm not going to hurt him," he assured her. "I'm just going to dissolve our partnership." Dragging Jim onto a kitchen chair, Buck roughly tore open the front of his shirt to expose a suede money belt. Unsnapping its two pockets he emptied them of the currency and tossed it onto Ruby's table.

"What . . . are you doing?" Jim asked thickly, fighting the disabling dizziness brought on by Buck's brutal, unexpected punch.

"Splitting the money," Buck replied coldly. "You and me, we ain't partners anymore."

"What . . . about the game?" Jim's mind groped for its first priority. Across the room, Ruby realized that he had all but forgotten her. She started to tell herself it was the blow to his face, that he wasn't cognizant, but she knew down deep that it was a lie; he was cognizant about the game. "We made a deal," she heard him say, "to give McKee a chance to get his money back. *All* of his money. You can't back out on that, Buck—"

"Don't you tell me what I can and can't do," Buck retorted harshly. "And don't lecture me about making deals. Seems to me *you* made a deal not long ago too—with Edith."

Shaking her head, beginning to cry, Ruby left the kitchen, retreating to the bedroom, slamming the door to close off the sight and sound of them. Grunting scornfully, muttering, "Hope her poor feelings ain't hurt," Buck continued to divide the money. When he finished, he pushed half of the currency across the table to Jim and began to stuff his share into his pockets. "Thirty-four hundred and thirty-four dollars apiece," he said flatly. "You and me are quits now."

As Buck got up to leave, Jim unsteadily followed him. "If we don't put everything we've won on that table tomorrow night," he warned, "your word and mine won't be worth cold piss in Nevada, Buck."

On the roofless porch, in the rain once again, Buck stopped and faced him. "I know that, you bastard. You don't think I take my word as lightly as you take yours, do you? I'll keep my word to a highbinder like Roone McKee more than you do to your own wife. All the money will be on the table tomorrow night. But McKee will have to play both of us to get it."

Buck walked off into the stormy night.

Roone McKee had no objection to a three-hand game. In fact, the quiet gambler was delighted to at last have a chance to beat Buck, toward whom he had developed a growing animosity. "As long as it's understood," he said, for everyone to hear, "that it's each man for himself, and you two aren't throwing in against me."

"We aren't," Buck assured. "Our partnership has ended."

"Can't say I'm surprised," McKee commented. He glanced at the ugly purple swelling under Jim's left eye. "Two things that will break up a friendship faster than anything else are cards and women. Which was it with you two?"

"That's none of your business, McKee," Jim said levelly. He knew the pale gambler carried a gun in his hip pocket, but he did not care.

"We're here to play poker, not talk," said Buck. "Let's get on with it."

"Of course." McKee smiled softly. His words had irked both of them, as he had hoped; discomposed players were careless players.

The game began: twenty dollars ante, fifty dollars high bet, one hundred dollars high raise. At those levels, all three men would be playing very cautiously; rarely would a player take his hand past the third card unless he had a compelling combination of cards forming—or unless he had decided to bluff a hand and see if he could steal an occasional pot. The back room at Callahan's was filled to capacity, sixty men each standing on a chalked x on the floor, the front row having sold for five dollars a spot, the second for three, the back row for two, making Callahan the evening's first winner with two hundred dollars profit before the cards were even dealt. He also was to receive ten percent of Roone McKee's winnings for providing the room, table, food and drink when required, and a guarantee of honesty. That ten percent, his normal cut, had become nonexistent since Jim Delavane's winning streak had begun.

The game began slowly, no large pots building up early, no fall of the cards creating straights or flushes or anything else exciting, each man winning ante and small bet pots of one hundred to one hundred fifty dollars on high cards showing or the threat of small pairs hidden. The first break in the slow tempo came forty-five minutes into the evening, when McKee's hand started a possible spade flush and Jim's hand threatened with a mixed straight. Buck folded his hand after three cards and let the other two butt heads. They bet back and forth, raised back and forth, and built a pot of slightly more than one thousand dollars. McKee did not get his flush and Jim did not get his straight; Jim won the pot on a pair of sevens.

During the second hour of the game, there were three pots of more than a thousand dollars, six of more than five hundred. Of those nine healthy pots, Jim won four, Buck won three, and McKee took two. By the beginning of the third hour, an unmistakable trend had materialized: Jim and Buck were winning, Roone McKee was losing. McKee had started the evening with four thousand cash and three land deeds worth one, two, and four thousand dollars respectively. With a bankroll of eleven thousand, which was roughly sixty-five percent more than the combined bankrolls of the two men he was playing, he felt that he had serious odds in his favor—which on paper he did. But the game did not follow the path of straight predictability; there was the momentum of Jim Delavane's winning streak to contend with. Just as Jim's losing streak had in the beginning upset the odds and weighted them more heavily in McKee's favor, so now was his winning streak cutting McKee's odds off at the knees. Winning streaks and losing streaks: they were what made gambling a gamble—and they were what broke Roone McKee that night.

McKee held out for six hours, twice seeming as if he

might make sudden and surprising comebacks, only to slide back to loser's status as the momentun of Jim's winning streak and the grim, careful playing of Buck slowly chipped away at his bankroll and his nerves, letting spectators see him sweat for the first time, until finally his cash was gone, Jim had the larger land deed, Buck had the two smaller ones, and for McKee it was all over. He left the table, the room, and the saloon slighty ruffled, greatly frustrated, but with the quiet aloofness of the professional he was.

"Been a pleasure, gentlemen," were his last words. "Let's do it again sometime."

At that point, Jim Delavane had slightly more than six thousand dollars in cash and four thousand in land, and Buck O'Crotty had nearly five in cash and three in land.

"Will you give me a minute in private, Buck?" Jim asked across the table.

Buck had nothing to say to Jim, and did not really care to listen to anything Jim had to say to him, but prior to the previous night they had been friends for a very long time, as young boys, as young men in the mines, as young Marines in war, and Buck O'Crotty was too much a man to humiliate Jim Delavane by rebuffing him in public. Rising, Buck led the way to a corner of Callahan's kitchen where they could talk unheard.

"I want you to know that it's over between Ruby and me," Jim said. "The things you said last night, to her and to me, made us both take a long look at ourselves, at what we were doing. I love Edith, Buck, and I want you to know that; I probably love her too much—sometimes she's so perfect she doesn't seem real. Ruby and me, well," he shrugged almost helplessly, "we just fell into something and got carried away with it. But we had a long talk after you left last night, and we decided to end it. We won't be seeing each other anymore. So if you and Iron Mike want to—"

"That's enough," Buck interrupted. "I don't propose to make Mike a part of this conversation, nor do I intend to discuss my own feelings for Ruby Surrett. You said you're through with her, fine, so am I. What Mike does is his business, but I don't see as there's anything else for you and me to discuss."

"What about the game?" Jim asked, nodding his head toward the card room.

"What about it?"

"We don't have to go on, Buck. We've each got enough cash and land to go our separate ways. Or we can bury the hatchet, pool our winnings, and be partners again, big time." Jim looked away. "We don't have to go on."

Buck's eyes narrowed a fraction. He thought he smelled fear. "You don't want to play me, do you?" He tilted his head, studying the other man. "You want to quit, don't you? But you can't unless I do. So you want me to let you off the hook."

"I'm trying to look at it the smart way, Buck, for both of us."

"Sure, sure." Buck smiled coldly. "Tell me another."

Jim's chin came up slightly, his shoulders squared a bit. "If you think I'm scared of you, Buck, you're wrong," he said evenly.

Buck's smile became wider and colder. "Prove it."

Jim's jaw clenched. "Let's go."

They walked back to the table and sat down.

"One hand of showdown," Jim said. "Callahan deals. Everything I've got against everything you've got."

"You're cheating yourself," Buck pointed out. "You're up two thousand over me."

"Everything I've got," Jim repeated, "against everything you've got. It all came from the partnership we had; it should all go to one or the other."

Buck pushed his money and the two deeds to the middle of the table. Turning to Callahan, he said, "Deal the cards."

Jim pushed his winnings and the larger land deed into the pot and sat back. "Deal," he seconded.

The room fell absolutely silent as the cards were shuffled, cut by Buck, shuffled again, cut by Jim, and dealt.

To Buck, first card: six of clubs.

To Jim, first card: six of diamonds.

Buck, second card: three of clubs.

Jim, second card: six of hearts. A pair of sixes.

Buck, third card: ten of spades.

Jim, third card: Queen of hearts.

Buck, fourth card: ten of hearts. A pair of tens.

Jim, fourth card: ace of diamonds.

Buck, last card: three of diamonds. Two pair, tens and threes.

Jim, last card: six of spades. Three sixes.

"Pot to Mr. Delavane," said Callahan. It was the first time he had ever called Jim Delavane "mister."

Buck stared unblinkingly at the six of spades; a slight frown of disbelief settled on his face. *What had he done?*

Jim Delavane did not hesitate for a second. As soon as Callahan spoke the official words—"Pot to Mr. Delavane" —he rose, collected the stacks of money and the three deeds, stuffed it all into his pockets and inside his shirt, and left the table.

From that moment on, Jim Delavane never looked back.

SIX

For the next two months, Buck O'Crotty mostly did two things: worked and drank. Little else. He ate, of course, a usually huge breakfast, and at midday whatever the boarding-house cook had put in his dinner pail; this only because he knew he had to have nourishment to maintain his job as a mucker for Empire Mines; and he slept as a last resort, usually drunkenly after skipping supper and drinking for several hours at Callahan's. He did very little talking, to anyone about anything; noncommittal greetings and farewells at beginning and end of shift were all his peers came to expect from him. At noon break he sat alone and ate, encouraging no company. Everyone knew about the showdown game, but no one dared mention it to him. Or would have known how. What does one say to a man who had bet the equivalent of a decade's underground wages on a single hand of cards? The vast majority of the other men would never accumulate that much money in their lifetime, would never have deeds to two parcels of land, would only daydream about such things; how could they form questions, much less comments, about it?

So Buck became a loner, keeping to himself, brooding,

for the most part communicating at length only with Callahan. It was Callahan who kept him current on what was going on in Virginia City. Though Buck professed disinterest in most of the subjects on which Callahan spoke, the saloon owner was aware that Buck could have done his drinking in Silver City without making the nightly drive; he could have taken his whiskey to a table instead of bracing up the bar. The fact that Buck did neither was more than enough excuse for Callahan to keep talking.

Some things Buck had firsthand knowledge of, such as Jim hiring Iron Mike. Buck had been lined up with the day crew, waiting for the cage on the morning after the big game, when to his surprise Jim strode up and said to Mike, "I'm fixing to start my own digs up in Virginia City. You want to go to work for me?"

"Your own digs?" Mike replied, impressed. "Say, that's keen, Jim. Have you got backing?" He glanced at Buck. "Or did you and Buck strike it at poker?"

"Leave me out of the conversation," Buck advised.

"I don't need backing," Jim told Mike, and everyone else within earshot, "I've got this—" He drew a thick sheaf of currency from his pocket and flashed it around, pleased with the impressed response it drew. "That's just part of it," he boasted to Mike. "I need a general foreman for Delavane Mines. I know you're still new to silver mining, but what you haven't learned already I'll teach you. And I'll double what you're getting as a hoister here."

Mike smiled widely. "What about Bucky? Where does he fit in?"

"I told you to leave me out of it," Buck said.

"This is between you and me, Mike," said Jim. "Do you want the job or don't you?"

Iron Mike looked uncertainly at Buck, then back at Jim. "I don't understand this—"

"Take the job," Buck told him. "What have you got to lose? You can always find work as a hoister," Buck flicked his gaze onto Jim, "if things go sour for your new employer."

Jim smiled tightly. "Things aren't going to go sour for me," he said confidently for all to hear. "I'm going to be one of the biggest mine owners in Nevada. And I'm starting today." He fixed his eyes on Mike. "Last chance. In or out?"

Mike did not have to answer. The Empire Mine whistle

sounded loudly and the crew began filing into the cage. Buck pushed Iron Mike out of line and he remained behind.

That night at the boarding house, Mike asked Buck what had happened between him and Jim. Buck's response was as honest as he could make it without hurting anyone. "Jim and me, we've had a falling out," he said. "It's a personal matter that doesn't concern you in any way, and I ain't going to discuss it with you. No hard feelings about you going to work for him; I'd have done the same thing myself. No reason why you can't remain his friend as well as mine, if you want to. I'd appreciate it if we could consider the subject closed now."

Mike did not question him again on the matter, not even when it became apparent to him that Buck was no longer competing with him for the attention and affection of Ruby Surrett. Better to leave well enough alone, he decided, and take whatever good fortune came his way: the new job with double pay, as well as an unchallenged course to Ruby's love.

After Mike moved out of the boarding house to live in Virginia City, Buck saw very little of him. Buck was kept aware of Mike's as well as Jim Delavane's fortunes through Callahan. "Iron Mike got hisself an automobile," was the first report Buck heard, "so's he can drive to Silver City of an evening and on Sundays to court Ruby Surrett. A nice car, I seen it meself. One of them Hudson Super-Six models with mechanical wipers to clean the windshield. Oh, and it's got fenders all around."

The saloon owner kept Buck apprised of Jim's activities as well. "He's putting in a blind shaft on each of the three parcels he owns." A blind shaft was one which was put into the ground without benefit of geological testing or advice, a large hole dug with no assurance of good ore being found. "Everybody says he's crazy," Callahan commented. "He'll be risking everything he's got. Unless he strikes a good vein, he'll be right back where he started."

Some nights the news was about others. "I heard tell that Roone McKee is opening his own place down in Carson City. The rumor is that he got backing from a banker here in Virginia City, but nobody knows which one. It's probably that Harmon Coltrane who bought the old bank building at C and Carson. The man's got a seventeen-year-old pregnant wife, I hear, and him old enough to be her father. Personally, I don't think bankers and gamblers should be in cahoots. It don't look good."

One night Callahan said quietly, "Bad news for Jim Delavane's wife. Her father had a stroke over in Eureka. Died at his principal's desk in the schoolhouse. Shame." Buck drank a little more than usual that night. But a few nights later, after the Delavanes had returned from the funeral, he did not drink at all; instead he bought a bouquet of fall flowers from a widow who grew them for income, and stood in the shadows down the street from where the Delavanes now lived in Virginia City. When he saw Jim leave the house for something, he hurried to the door and knocked.

"Why, Bucky!" Edith, dressed in mourning, exclaimed when she opened the door. "How nice. Come in."

"I'm sorry, I can't, Edith, I'm on my way back to Silver City to work the night shift for a man who's ill," he lied. Holding the flowers out to her, he said, "I just wanted to offer my condolences about your father. Mr. Bloom was one of the finest gentlemen it's been my privilege to meet." Seeing tears welling in her eyes, he hurried to finish what he had rehearsed. "He himself may be gone, but you can rest assured that the things he taught will live on in the many pupils he guided over the years."

"Oh, Buck, that's beautiful," Edith said, crying. "Buck, please come in. Jim will be back shortly and I know he—"

"I would, Edith, but I promised to work for this fellow who hurt himself—"

"You said he was ill."

"I mean ill. Anyway I've got to hurry. You have my sympathy, Edith," he said, and kissed her on the cheek. Then he was gone before she could protest further.

It was only a short time later that Callahan had news of the Delavane digs. "Your ex-partner struck it today, Bucky. On that smallest parcel, the thousand dollar one, that you won from McKee and Delavane won from you. Rumor is that he hit what looks to be high-grade ore at just thirty feet. No assay report yet, but rumor is that it's fine looking diggings."

The next day, Callahan confirmed the rumor. "Delavane's ore was assayed today. It's sweet stuff. Fifty percent lead with an estimated two hundred ounces of silver per ton. Mr.

Jim Delavane just became a big man in Nevada mining circles." Callahan poured Buck a double shot. "On the house," he said.

When Jim Delavane had set out to sink a blind shaft on each of the three parcels of land he had won, he had hired off-shift men from the nearby Fair and O'Brien works and from the Overman Mines, both good income-producing digs. While maintaining their regular full-time jobs, the men put in as many hours as they could safely do for Jim. After his strike, he closed the two blind shafts that had as yet produced nothing valuable and summoned all the men to the shaft at which they had hit the silver vein.

"Men," he announced, "this is going to be the first major dig of Delavane Mines. I need three full-time crews. My offer is a nickel an hour above what you're earning now. I expect to be able to offer long-term employment to anyone who's interested. Delavane Mines is here to stay. Iron Mike Donovan will be the works super. He'll be the one picking shift foremen. Sign up with him."

Callahan duly reported the results to Buck. "All but two men switched over to Delavane Mines. Looks like the new digs is off to a fast start." Callahan polished the oak with a bar towel. "Now all's that's got to happen is for Iron Mike to wed that pretty little nurse of his and everybody can live happily ever after, just like in the bedtime stories. Ain't that right, Bucky?"

"Sure, sure. Whatever you say, Callahan." Buck pushed his whiskey glass over. "Hit it again."

"You're all right, Buck O'Crotty," said the saloon owner. "I knew you was too good a man to let this thing get you down."

"Sure, sure," Buck said again.

Inside, his guts felt torn apart.

Ruby was waiting one night where he parked behind the boarding house. His headlights picked her up, huddled in the cold in her blue greatcoat from the nurses' corps, its service patches and pins now removed. Buck sat behind the wheel, staring at her without extinguishing the headlights. Finally Ruby came around to his door and opened it.

"I'd like to talk to you, Buck. May I"

"Sure, go ahead." He did not turn to face her or show any desire to get out of the car. Ruby shivered in the thin night air.

"It's cold out here, can we go inside?"

"Sure."

He led her into the boarding house and down the deserted hall to his first-floor room. He had previously shared the room with Iron Mike but now had it to himself; the extra bed had become a catch-all and was littered with laundry to be done, laundry that had been done, a few old newspapers, some empty whiskey bottles waiting to be thrown out. Buck had the uncomfortable feeling that he should apologize to Ruby for the condition of the room; he shook his head at the incongruousness of the thought.

Still clutching her coat around her, Ruby sat on the room's one straight wooden chair while Buck knelt before a small kerosene heater and dug his thumbnail into a stick match to light it. His hands trembled slightly, not from the cold but from having Ruby so near again. For weeks he had been trying with Callahan's whiskey to wash her out of his mind, to erase all pictures, images, memories of her; now he had a new one with which to contend: shivering, pale and fearful, with the big blue coat around her, looking much like a lost, helpless little girl. Another incongruity for him to deal with.

"Buck," she began tentatively, "I know how you probably feel about me—"

"Do you now?" It was a rhetorical question, meaning: No, you don't. You couldn't.

"Certainly I do," Ruby said, as if reading his mind. "I have feelings for you, Buck; you know I do. I am very aware of how I've hurt you, and I'm very, very sorry for it. I'd do anything in the world to be able to undo it—"

"What do you want, Ruby?" he asked wearily, removing his coat, tossing it on the littered bed, sitting on the end of the other, the bed in which he slept, sometmes drunk and fully clothed. With his elbows on his knees, he held his head in both hands. "Why are you here?" he wanted to know.

"I'm pregnant," she said simply. Buck's heart jerked in its chest cavity as if it had been kicked.

"I'll not inquire who the father is," he said dryly.

"It's Jim's baby, of course," she told him, overlooking his malice.

"You haven't been servicing poor Mike?" he asked with mock but spiteful innocence.

"Buck, don't . . ." Ruby began to cry.

"Jesus, Ruby, why are you here?" he asked again, desperately now.

"I need help, Buck."

"Getting rid of unborn babies ain't in my line," he replied coldly.

"I'm a nurse," she reminded him. "If I wanted to abort, I could do it by myself. I want someone to help me *keep* my baby. Someone to be a father to it."

Buck raised his face and stared at her incredulously. "You're looking for a husband?" He could only shake his head at the brazenness, the audacity of her. "You let Jim Delavane fuck you, you let him put his brat in your belly, and you come to me proposing *marriage*. You slut—"

Without moving from the bed, Buck reached out and slapped her smartly across the face. Ruby's head snapped sideways and stayed there as her cheek turned fire red. She did not move or touch the place he had hit, and he saw that her tears, instead of increasing from the pain, dried up and stopped. Buck stared at her, looked in revulsion at his offending hand, and shook his head in weary defeat. This was too much. He could not deal with this any longer. He felt as if his very soul was shrinking within him.

"I'm sorry, Ruby," he said abjectly. "I'd no right to hit you." His own eyes filled. "But why are you doing this? If you need a husband, just take Mike. It's obvious he wants you. He doesn't know about you and *him*." He could not bring himself to speak Jim's name in her presence.

Ruby finally turned her face back to look at him. "Buck, I came to you because I want to get away from here, away from Jim Delavane. And I think you do too. We've both been hurt by him, but we don't have to stay around and relive it every time we see his face or hear his name. Sure, I could go to Mike; he'd take me in a minute. But Mike is so caught up in Jim's new ventures, his successes, the money that Jim's paying him, the position he's been given, that it wouldn't be fair to ask him to leave. Where else would a man like Mike ever do so well? But you're different, Buck— you're smarter and tougher. You and I could leave here and make a whole new start. The baby could be *our* child. And I'd be a good wife to you, Buck, I'd do for you—"

Ruby suddenly blushed, knowing what he must be thinking, seeing in her mind as she had a hundred times how she must have looked to him through that window, Jim's erection in her hand, his semen on her chin; the memory returned to her now and caused her to shudder. Buck was still sitting on the bed, staring at her. Suddenly she felt like dirt.

"I'm sorry, Buck. I shouldn't have come here. How in the name of God can I ask you to forget what I can't forget myself?"

Gathering her greatcoat even more tightly around her, Ruby rose and hurried from the room. Watching her go, Buck wanted desperately to stop her but he did not. When she was out of the room, he rushed to the door and watched her hurrying down the hall; he wanted to run after her but did not. When she left the boarding house, Buck ran to his window, raised it, and looked out at her running off into the night; he wanted desperately to call out and stop her but did not.

Then she was gone. For several minutes he felt sick and wasted, dead inside. Kneeling, he folded his arms on the sill of the open window and put his head down. He remained there for an hour, letting the high, cold air make his face pinch, not moving until he felt as if there were a thousand tiny needles in his cheeks and eyelids and forehead. Then he wearily dragged himself up and closed the window.

Pulling his old kit bag from under the bed, he began to pack.

SEVEN

Ruby Margaret Surrett and Michael Anthony Donovan were married at Saints Peter and Paul Church in Virginia City on Saturday, November 8, 1919. The bride's maid of honor was Edith Delavane, and the groom's best man was Jim Delavane.

There had been absolutely no way Ruby could have avoided having the Delavanes in the wedding party. Without her prior knowledge or consent, on the day after she had accepted his proposal Mike had gone to the Delavane house and asked them. Edith, though she had not seen Ruby since her own wedding, had been delighted with the invitation, and Jim had subsequently seen no unsuspicious way out of it. Everything that goes around comes around, he had thought, recalling Ruby's awkward attendance at his own nuptials.

When Mike had told Ruby what he had arranged, she could not conceal her displeasure. "I wish you'd asked me first, Mike," she said. "Especially about the maid of honor. I was thinking about having one of the other nurses. I hardly know Edith Delavane."

"I thought you'd be pleased," he said. "It seemed like the right thing to do, what with Jim giving me the superintendent job and all. He's really the one's made the wedding possible, you know."

He's the one who's made it *necessary* Ruby thought sourly. Then she thought: no, that isn't fair. It was her fault as much as Jim's, maybe even more. Yes, definitely even more. She could have stopped him anytime she wanted to. Jim Delavane didn't do anything to her that she hadn't wanted him to do. Except get her pregnant, of course.

"I suppose there's nothing to do about it," she finally conceded on the wedding party. "You can't very well renege on the invitation." Why in hell she wondered, hadn't Jim found some excuse to turn Mike down? Jesus! What an impossible situation.

Instead of being upset about it, Ruby told herself that she should be damned glad there was going to *be* a wedding, never mind who her maid of honor was. After her disastrous meeting with Buck, when she realized that there was not going to be an easy way out for her, she had decided to abandon the marriage idea, leave Silver City, and go back east to a home for unwed mothers. The only thing that made her finally discard that idea was the uncertainty of keeping the child after it was born—and Ruby was determined to keep her baby: that was a constant with her. Trying to do it on her own, she realized, would involve expending all of her savings during her term, paying all the doctor and hospital expenses herself, finding someone to care for the baby after it was born, and obtaining a new job and getting back to work as quickly as possible. There were too many elements of risk involved, she decided, too much chance of having to give the baby up for adoption—or having it taken away from her because she could not support it. Finding a husband was the most sensible solution.

It had been a natural thing, after Buck, for her to revert to Mike Donovan. He was, even in Buck's mind, the logical choice. Whether or not her life was a lie, Mike Donovan would, Ruby knew, be a good husband and a good provider; most important, he would be a good father. That he was crazy about her there was no doubt. He had been pressing his courtship for several months: chocolates, bouquets, even an awkward love poem or two. Now with the new job that Jim had given him, he had bought an automobile in order, he made clear, to court her more properly: uptown shopping on Saturday afternoons, church on Sundays, trips on holidays. The problem was that, although courting, he had yet to actually propose. Ruby had to find some way of expediting Mike's ardor. And quickly, she was already six weeks along.

The next evening when he came to call, Ruby had told him a lie she had concocted. "I had a long distance telephone call today," she said excitedly. "My first one ever! All the way from San Francisco. It was clear as could be, just like talking to someone right here in Silver City."

"Who from?" Mike wanted to know.

"A girlfriend of mine from the nurses' corps. She works at San Francisco General."

"What did she want?"

"She called to say they were expanding the nursing staff and asked if I'd be interested in a job there. San Francisco! Doesn't that sound keen?"

"I guess. What did you tell her?"

"I said I'd think about it."

Mike became sulky. Ruby let him pout for a few minutes, then asked innocently, "What's the matter?"

"Nothing."

The very tone of the word screamed *something*.

"You're not upset about that telephone call, are you?"

"Shouldn't I be?" Mike asked, in order not to have to admit outright that he was.

"I don't see why," Ruby said defensively. "After all,

Mike, a career girl has to consider her future. I don't want to be a nurse at a miners hospital forever. Silver City, is fine for you; you're getting somewhere in life. You've gone from a hoister to a foreman to a superintendent in less than a year. But I'm still exactly where I started."

Ruby crossed the living room and cranked up her Victrola. The cylinder she put on was as preplanned as her lie about the call. As she sat back down, a soft rendition of "Somebody Stole My Gal" wafted into the room. Iron Mike began to fidget.

"It's your future you're worried about then?" he asked finally, after clearing his throat several times.

Ruby shrugged now. "Sure. If I don't, who will?"

"Would you consider letting me look after you?" He almost blurted it out.

"How do you mean that, Mike?"

"Marry me," he said. "I'm asking you to marry me."

Before the song ended, Ruby had been on his lap, running her fingers through his hair, promising to make him the best wife he could ever imagine, and Mike, a hand on her thigh for the first time, was eagerly telling her about a house for rent on E Street in Virginia City, a nice little place with a porch and a swing, that he intended to see about first thing tomorrow. Then he became self-conscious about his hand on her thigh, and moved it, muttering something about not taking liberties, and that was when Ruby put her lips on his ear and whispered, "We don't have to wait, Mike, if you don't want to."

He could not believe his ears. How many times had he dreamed about this? How many times in the middle of the night had he had to put his arms outside the covers and sleep with them cold to keep his hands off a throbbing erection brought on by erotic thoughts of Ruby Surrett? Ruby naked: walking, turning, sitting, bending, standing, while his imagination concentrated on first one, then another part of her fleshy, freckled body. Now after all the frustrating nights, some of them resulting in wonderful but bountiful, therefore stickily disgusting wet dreams, the object of his lustful desires was whispering warm words into his ear that all but invited him to make his dreams come true.

"Really?" he asked. "You mean it, Ruby?"

"I mean it, Mike." The sooner the better, as far as Ruby

was concerned. As Mike lifted her into his arms and carried her into the bedroom, she tried not to think of Jim Delavane. Forcing herself to concentrate on her new fiancé, she wondered if Mike knew all the ways Jim did. She guessed he probably did; they had been to France together. But once in the bedroom she found that she had guessed wrong. Naked, Iron Mike Donovan was a magnificent specimen of manhood, with an absolutely spectacular erect penis, vein-corded and purplish-headed, but sadly, other than a basic knowledge he had no skill whatever in lovemaking, no expertise in the tributaries of sex, the feeding of one sensation into another until the massive effect was achieved. Mike had his great muscular form on top of her, his splendid appendage inside her—and here she expressed sincere pain because of his thickness and length—but after a period of grunting and sweating, he was finished and it was over.

"How was I?" he asked after his labored breathing slowed.

"You were wonderful, Mike."

"Did I hurt you much?"

"I'm not going to lie to you, hon. Yes, you did."

"I'm so sorry, Ruby. I'll try to be easier next time. I just love you so much."

"I understand. It's all right."

It had been the very next day that he had invited the Delavanes to stand up for them at their wedding.

When the day finally arrived, Ruby was surprised to see what a radical change had taken place in Jim Delavane's appearance. She knew, as did everyone in Virginia City, that he had become very prosperous very quickly, but not having seen individual changes in him as they occurred, she was not prepared for the cumulative effect. He was dressed in an obviously expensive suit of fine gabardine, a white polished broadcloth shirt, silk cravat, soft leather ankle boots, and a gray beaver hat. In his tie was a silver stickpin made from the first assayed ore of his strike. He was handsomer than Ruby had ever seen him, handsomer than *any* man she had ever seen.

It was not until after the ceremony that they had a chance to speak for the first time. "You make a beautiful bride, Ruby," he told her quietly. "I wish you the best of luck."

"Thank you, Jim."

"Lovely wedding."

"Edith was a great help to me."

He lowered his voice. "I'm sorry about our involvement, Edith's and mine. There was no way out of it."

"It's all right. Everything has worked out fine."

After a moment he asked, "Have you heard from Buck?"

"Buck? No. What makes you think I'd hear from Buck?"

Jim shrugged. "Some of the things you said that last night—about how you had hurt him and how you'd have to find a way to make it up to him. I kind of assumed you had taken up with him."

"You assumed wrong," Ruby said, her tone cooling.

"Sorry. I'm just being honest with you. I was very surprised when you and Mike became engaged. I thought all along you had been seeing Buck. I thought you probably started seeing him right after you and I quit."

"By 'seeing him,' I presume you mean sleeping with him?"

"Well," Jim shrugged, "yes."

"I see. Without even letting the bedsheets cool off, I'll bet. You must have a very low opinion of me, Jim."

"That's not so, Ruby." He seemed genuinely hurt by the remark. "I'll always consider you very special. I hope you believe that."

"I have a favor to ask of you, Jim," she said abruptly.

"Ask it. I'll do anything I can for you."

"I want the Donovans and the Delavanes to see as little of each other as possible in the future. I think all our lives will be much less complicated. It shouldn't be too difficult to accomplish; at the rate you're going, you and Edith will soon be well above our social level anyway. Mike tells me you have someone designing a house for you to be built high on a hill so that it looks down on everything and everybody."

Jim stiffened slightly. "I'm having a home designed, yes."

"Well, I think if you will handle Edith on your end, I can handle Mike on mine, and between the two of us we should be able to squelch any future social engagements that come up. Do you agree?"

"If that's what you want," he replied, a hint of resentment edging into his tone.

"That's exacty what I want," she asserted.

Jim Delavane nodded curtly. "Good luck, Ruby," he said, and walked away.

Before the wedding reception ended, Edith Delavane confided to Ruby that she was pregnant. "I haven't told Jim yet," she whispered. "I'll tell him tonight; it'll be the perfect ending to a happy day. Are you and Mike planning a family right away?"

"Yes, right away," Ruby replied without hesitation. The two women discussed pregnancy. Ruby was glad for the opportunity to lay some preliminary groundwork for her own as yet unannounced condition. It was part of her overall plan. She had already selected the doctor she would use, one of the older general practitioners in Virginia City, a man she was sure would take her word about how many cycles had been interrupted and how far along she was. She planned also to prepare Mike for her impending "early" delivery by giving him periodic false reports of the baby moving toward its position in the birth canal faster than normal. She also would tell Mike that premature babies were common with women in her family, but that he should not worry because they were usually as large as full-term babies and always healthy. With a little effort here, a little preparation there, Ruby was certain that she would be able to effectively disguise the fact that she was pregnant before she slept with Mike Donovan again.

Ruby had been somewhat surprised to learn that Edith was also pregnant—although when she thought about it in retrospect she did not know *why* she was surprised. Ruby gathered that Edith was about as far along in her term as Ruby herself was—which meant, of course, that Jim had been having intercourse with both of them during the same period. There was no reason for that conclusion to have been unexpected; Jim had never intimated in any way that he and Edith had discontinued their sex life. But somehow Ruby had felt, or *wanted* to feel, that they had. No woman, she supposed, wanted to believe that what a man was putting into her, he was also putting into another woman—perhaps even on the same night.

Ruby found that she was not in the least upset by Edith's pregnancy. She would have been if it had happened two or three months earlier, when she still cared so deeply for Jim. But her affection for Jim had diminished radically, and so had her vulnerability regarding him. Ruby knew the exact moment at which she began to stop loving Jim Delavane. It had been the night Buck caught them together—but it had not been *because* Buck caught them. Being exposed that way would not have bothered her if it had been *them*—her and Jim—joined against Buck, Edith, society, the world. But in the space of mere minutes the situation had been reduced to *her* being exposed, *her* person and reputation being reviled, while all Jim had been concerned about was that goddamned poker game and the reputations of Buck and himself. Jim had apologized later, after Buck had gone, but the damage in Ruby's mind was irreversible: he had claimed to love her, yet when she had been practically labeled a whore in his presence, he could think of nothing except whether the man doing the labeling was going to play cards the next night. True love it obviously was not.

The one thing Ruy was certain she could count on Jim Delavane for was that he would keep his agreement about the two couples not socializing. Whatever lip service he gave to considering her a special person, it was obvious to Ruby that he felt even more uncomfortable around her than she did around him. He proved good to his word as winter came, Thanksgiving and Christmas came, the new year of 1920 began, and the Donovans and the Delavanes drifted further apart socially. Edith was not even aware that Ruby was pregnant until the two happened to meet on the street one day. Both were a little embarrassed, Edith because she was afraid Ruby would think she and Jim, now living up on what was becoming known as "the Hill," had become snooty and too good for Ruby and Mike; and Ruby, embarrassed because she was certain that Edith remembered the exact date of the Donovans' marriage and would have been sure Ruby was further along than she claimed, therefore would assume she had been sleeping with Mike Donovan before they wed. Both women suggested during their chance encounter that they *had* to get together very soon, but neither of them thought for a minute that it would come about. And it did not. A strange but persistent social uncomfortableness was settling permanently between them.

It was one day in late spring when Mike came home from the mine with an expensive cigar in his shirt pocket and the news that Edith Delavane had delivered a baby girl that morning. "Frances Grace, they've named her," he said, "after their own mothers."

"They're both well?" Ruby had asked.

"I'm afraid not," Mike said. "Edith apparently had a very difficult time of it. They had to take the baby, you know?"

"Cesarean, you mean?"

"That's it. She bled a lot. And I think she had some other problems, I'm not sure what. Jim was white as a sheet when he told me about it. God, I hope you don't have to go through anything like that."

She did not. A week later Ruby went into labor exclaiming, "My God, I'm still a month away from being due," a phrase she had been practicing for a month. At the hospital, she asked, for Mike's benefit, "Doctor, aren't I a month or five weeks early?" She got exactly the response from her aging physician that she anticipated.

"Early, late, it makes no difference as long as the child's healthy."

Ruby's child was a boy. "I want to give him your middle name, Mike," she told her husband. "Anthony. So we can call him Tony. Is that all right?"

"Anything you want is all right," Iron Mike replied. He held the baby in his big arms and said, "You've made me very happy giving me this fine son, Ruby. I love you even more for it." Iron Mike Donovan could not have cared less what the date was, or whether little Tony was early or late. His son was perfect; nothing else mattered.

It was while Ruby was in the hospital after giving birth that she got the letter from Buck. "Looks like it's come from halfway around the world," said the nurse who brought it in. "Look at them heathen stamps, will you?"

Ruby was astounded. Even more so when she read it.

Dear Ruby,

I hope this letter finds you well, and I hope you will be kind and forgiving enough to read it.

I have given a lot of thought to what happened between us before I left. I feel I was wrong in the way I treated you and I ask you to try and find it in your heart to forgive me.

I hope all has been resolved for you. You will probably be a mother by the time you receive this letter. I hope you have found a way to keep your baby.

I am back in the Marines and serving over here in China. If you want to write me I will be glad to hear from you. Please look after yourself.

Your friend,
Buck O'Crotty

Reading the pencil-scrawled letter caused Ruby to cry. Bucky, oh Bucky, she thought, why couldn't you have felt that way the night I came to you? How much simpler and more honest things would have been. Then she chastised herself. No looking back, she scolded. Things didn't turn out for the best, but they didn't turn out for the worst either. Her baby was healthy, it had a name and a father. She must now concentrate her entire being on making a good life for the Donovan family. Ruby wanted everyone, including the Delavanes—yes, even Jim—to be happy. Buck too. Especially Buck, because he had been hurt so badly. As she was thinking about it, little Tony was brought in to be nursed. Ruby put the letter away. With her infant suckling, she began composing an answer to Buck that would convey to him that which he seemed to be seeking so desperately: her forgiveness. Presently she glanced over and was surprised to see Jim Delavane standing in the door. He looked haggard.

"Hello, Ruby."

"Hello, Jim."

"I've just been to see Edith. She's still in a bad way."

"I'm sorry, Jim."

"Congratulations on your son. May I see him?"

Apprehension seized her. *Stay calm!* she silently screamed at herself "I—yes, I suppose."

Jim approached the bed and looked down at the black-haired infant with Ruby's swollen nipple in its mouth. He stared at the baby for what seemed to Ruby like an unusually long time. Then he said, "Edith won't be able to have any more children. She won't be able to give me a son to carry on the Delavane name." With one finger, he touched her baby's cheek. "He's a handsome boy, Ruby. Do you think he looks like his father?"

Ruby stared at him, too surprised by the question to answer it. Jim smiled wanly at her, then turned and left. Ruby continued to stare after him; finally she shook her head emphatically. *He can't know.*

Only two people knew: herself and Buck. She had to make certain that no one else would ever find out. Holding her suckling infant a little tighter, Ruby began to recompose her letter to Buck. She would convey to him the forgiveness he sought, but in exchange she would extract from him a promise never—*never*—to tell Jim Delavane that Tony was his son. The secret of Tony's real father must be kept forever.

Buck O'Crotty must promise to take it to his grave with him.

Part
Three

Tony

1950

EIGHT

At the desk in his office, after Arnie Shad had told him about Buck's murder, Tony Donovan had looked at the old photograph for a long time; finally, blotting as best as he could the splash of wet drops with a handkerchief, he put the photo away. He wiped his eyes and crossed the office to a built-in bar to mix a gin and tonic.

As Tony was fixing his drink, there was a soft knock at the door and Madge Bellamy entered. She was an attractive, no-nonsense woman of forty-five, whose expression, Tony noticed at once, was decidedly sad. It did not surprise him. Nearly everyone in Las Vegas knew that Buck O'Crotty had raised Tony Donovan from a young orphan; word of his death had obviously already spread among them.

Taking the drink back to the desk, Tony skipped the preliminaries with Madge and simply asked, "Anything on the radio about it?"

"Not much, Tony," she told him quietly. "Just that Mr. O'Crotty's wife and daughter—stepdaughter, I mean—dropped him off at the union hall on their way to Mass. When they came back an hour or so later, they found him shot to death."

"Has anyone been able to locate Denny for me?" Tony asked.

"They're still trying, Tony." Madge paused a beat. "Are you all right?"

"Sure. Thanks for asking."

Madge bit her bottom lip, distressed because there did not seem to be anything she could do to comfort him. Tony Donovan had made her the first female head cashier in Las Vegas. In doing so, he had provided Madge with the income necessary to properly raise, support, and educate three daughters. A week didn't pass without Madge mentioning one or another of them to Tony: showing him their pictures, boasting about their grades, praising their many virtues. She would have killed to get Tony interested in one of them. That aside, she knew the criticism he had taken when he put her in the traditionally male job she held, and was fiercely loyal.

"If there's anything I can do, Tony—"

"I know, Madge. Thanks." Then quickly, "I'll be getting some calls, I imagine. Tell the switchboard to put them through."

"Sure."

When Madge left, Tony took a long swallow of his drink. He thought about Arnie Shad, how close the reporter and he had once been. Arnie could be right up where Tony was today if he'd stuck with Ben Siegel, as Tony had when Ben needed him, if Arnie hadn't quit. Tony was sure Arnie regretted leaving. It was probably the reason behind Arnie's irresponsible insistence that Meyer Lansky, for whom Tony now worked, was some kind of national mob boss. It was a position that even Arnie's own employer, the *Las Vegas Star*, did not support; it refused to print any of Arnie's stories about the so-called national crime syndicate.

The telephone rang and Tony quickly picked it up. "Tony Donovan speaking."

"Tony . . . this is . . . Kerry . . ."

Her usually clear, young woman's voice was strained with choking, word-seizing sobs. It was strange to hear her in grief. Kerry was another one that Buck had raised, but in all the years she had been Tony's foster sister, he had rarely known her to cry. Half Paiute, the Indian part of her was usually in control. But not now. "Buck's been—killed—" she sobbed.

"I know, honey. I just found out." Tony felt his own eyes well. "Where are you? Where's Rosetta?" he asked. Rosetta was Buck's wife, Kerry's mother. She was the full-blooded Paiute woman who had helped raise not only Kerry and Tony, but also Denny Ebro, the third person who had grown up in Buck O'Crotty's home.

"We're at the house," Kerry told him. "They took— Buck to the—morgue. Mamma didn't want them to—but they did anyway. Oh, Tony, he looked so awful when we found him—"

"Who's with Rosetta?" he asked, in an attempt to direct the conversation away from the dead man himself.

"Some of the neighbors," Kerry said, "and some men from the union. And some policemen"—she drew in her breath to control a wracking sob—"and Father Juan."

Tony leaned forward and put his free hand across his forehead, as if shielding his eyes from a bright light. He tried to think of something comforting to say, something that might ease the terrible hurt that he knew Kerry felt engulfing her. But what was there *to* say? That Buck was an old man, that he'd lived a full life, that he'd done a lot of good for a lot of people, that underground miners in Nevada had rights today because of Buck's efforts, that he would be remembered forever, and that now all his earthly tribulations, including Tony himself, were over and he was at peace? All of that was true, but Tony could not bring himself to verbalize any of it. Those words were better left to the priest who would eulogize the dead man. The only words Tony could muster were those that could be spoken by rote.

"You're going to have to be strong, Ker. For Rosetta's sake. To help Rosetta. Your mother is going to need you to lean on—"

"How soon will you be up here, Tony?" she suddenly asked, putting the sentence together without a sob. As if his trite words had actually bolstered her control. "Will you be coming today?"

"I don't think so—"

"Tomorrow then? Early, Tony, please—"

He forced himself to say it. "Kerry, I don't think I'll be coming at all."

"What?"

"You know how things were between Buck and me. You know how he felt about me, about what I do for a living." Swallowing, he stared down at the desktop.

"I can't believe you're saying this," Kerry said incredulously, her voice now under icy control. "Buck's been *murdered* and you're telling me you're not even coming up here? My mother's husband has—the man who raised both of us—gave us *homes!*"

"Kerry, listen to me. Buck wouldn't *want* me there."

"You son of a bitch! You dirty, low-life son of a bitch!"

Tony heard Kerry slam her receiver down, breaking the

connection. Sighing a heavy, weary sigh, Tony hung up also. Just as he did, the intercom line buzzed.

"Yes?"

It was the chief operator. "We finally got an answer at Mr. Ebro's. His houseboy said he was out in the desert running his dogs. He's expected back any time. We've left word for him. And you have a call from a Mr. Henny, sir."

"Put him on." Terence Henny was Buck's second-in-command in the miners' union. He and Tony had once worked together in the mines. As soon as Tony heard the connection made, he said, "Hello, Terry."

"Tony, lad. It's a sad day."

"Yes."

"I'm at Buck's house now, Tony. Everyone's trying to calm down Kerry; she's half hysterical about you not coming to the funeral. I just called to say I think you done right, lad. It'd be best if you weren't here."

"Did the mine owners do it?" Tony asked without preliminaries. "Did they have him killed because of that silica dust thing?"

"How did you know about that?" Henny asked, surprised.

"Buck told me about it when I came home from the war, when he first became suspicious of it." Buck O'Crotty had been trying to prove for several years that some of the new high-speed drills the mine owners had developed were producing a new type of dust that human lungs could not filter. The owners had refused to cooperate with him. Buck had been planning to go public with the information as soon as he had indisputable medical proof. "Well," Tony asked again, "do you think that may have been the reason they killed him or don't you?"

"No," Terence Henny replied now, "that wasn't the reason, Tony. Listen, lad, I have to hang up; the F.B.I. just got here. You stick to your decision and stay away from the funeral."

Tony heard the connection break and hung up his own phone. Terence Henny, he thought, had answered the question about silica dust very firmly, perhaps too firmly.

The intercom buzzed and it was the chief operator again. "Mr. Donovan, there was a call from Mr. Ebro's houseboy. Mr. Ebro is on his way to your office. And there's a call holding for you from Mrs. O'Crotty."

"Thanks. Put the call through." Tony sat up straight and

took a deep breath, as if fortifying himself for an onslaught. He closed his eyes before Rosetta's voice came onto the line.

"Tony? Hello?" Her smooth Paiute voice was uneven.

"Hello, Rosetta—"

"Tony, oh Tony—"

"Rosetta, I'm so sorry. I don't know what to say . . ."

"Yes, Tony, I know. It's a terrible, terrible thing that someone has done to a fine man."

"He loved you, Rosetta, he really did—"

"Why, I know that, Tony," Rosetta said, sounding mildly surprised. "I know that better than anyone. Did you think I didn't?"

"No," Tony said a little too quickly, opening his eyes. "I mean, I didn't know—I wasn't sure"—immediate chagrin colored his tone—"Rosetta, I'm just very sorry," he told her again.

"Kerry is upset by what she thought you told her a few minutes ago," Rosetta said, changing the conversation's direction. "I said that either she misunderstood or that you did not mean what you said."

"Rosetta, you know all that happened between Buck and me. You know how he felt. You weren't there the last time we fought, but Kerry was. It was very bad; I almost hit him. He told me never to come back."

"He spoke in anger," the Paiute woman said. "Just as you sometimes spoke in anger. That was one bad moment out of two lifetimes, his and yours. Now his is done. Do not make another bad moment in yours."

Tony turned his chair toward the window as tears once more streaked his cheeks. He felt dreadful, like a little boy again, an orphaned little boy. In his duodenum, an ulcer began to seethe; a tension headache engulfed the back of his head.

"You must come home," Rosetta said. "You must sit with Kerry and me beside the coffin of the man who loved us all and saved us all. You must."

"All right, Rosetta. If you're sure—"

"I am sure."

"All right." Tony tried to conceal his crying from the grieving woman but she detected his hurt, as she had always been able to do.

"Our tears are with you and your tears are with us," she said. "Come soon."

A barely audible click told him that she had hung up. Reaching back, he cradled his own phone without turning around. The office became eerily silent. Tony remained where he was, turned toward the window, looking out at the desert without really seeing it. He stopped crying almost at once, and as soon as he did he realized that his headache and stomachache were both relieved also. Removing a handkerchief from his inside coat pocket, he blotted his cheeks and wiped his lips. He thought of fathers and children and the ties that bound them: blood or law or name or just plain acceptance. He had now lost two fathers, both violently, and the pain this second time was as searing as it had been the first time. Boy or grown man, it hurt to the core of him. Blood father or foster father, the loss tore something from his being.

And both, he thought, his face setting in anger, had been taken from him by the same killer. The mine owners.

Tony suddenly became aware of someone standing next to his desk, barely in his peripheral view. Jerking his head around, he saw that it was Denny Ebro. Slightly taller than Tony, slightly heavier and more muscular, two years older, Denny was a Basque who had left the high sheep pastures for the low silver mines, later gone off with Tony to the South Pacific war, and come home to reject the life of a miner and follow Tony into big-time legalized gambling. Denny had an open innocent face, almost childlike: a grown choir boy. Only a bushy black moustache disrupted the illusion; a moustache grown for a specific purpose, a purpose not achieved: the complete concealment of a gross harelip. It was a deformity that would only have been permanently hidden by silence anyway, for it harshly affected Denny Ebro's speech and made nearly all of his words sound as if they were being forced through his nose.

Standing next to Tony's desk now, Denny asked nasally, "Is it true, Tony? Is Buck dead?"

"It's true, Den."

Denny Ebro began to cry unashamedly. He, too, had lived in Buck O'Crotty's household for a time, and had been exposed to the good and bad, the strong and the weak, the kind and the harsh in the union leader's personality. Unlike Tony, Denny now apparently recalled only the good, the strong, the kind, because the verification of Buck's death shook him deeply.

Trembling, sobbing, Denny Ebro, who had killed enemy soldiers with a bayonet, dropped to his knees and buried his face on folded arms on Tony's desk. Tony sat forward in his chair, put an arm around Denny, and laid his own head on the grieving man's hard, muscular upper arm. "Don't cry, Den," he said softly. He repeated it several times.

"Who done it, Tony?" Denny asked despondently.

"The mine owners," Tony replied. "Who else?"

"We gotta make the bastards pay," Denny asserted.

"We will," Tony promised. "We will make them pay."

NINE

On the windswept cemetery in Virginia City, Father Juan Gomesa made the sign of the cross as he blessed the ground that would receive the body of Buck O'Crotty.

Buck lay in a simple wooden casket, the planks of which were covered with inexpensive purple felt. Buck himself had selected and paid for the coffin years earlier, disdaining anything elaborate, even forbidding Rosetta to buy him one of the "burying" suits the funeral parlor sold, decreeing that he be buried in whatever suit he owned at the time of his death, with a plain blue work shirt under it, set off by any of the not more than three old neckties he ever owned at one time. And that was exactly how Rosetta had done it. Buck O'Crotty, Tony had thought when he got to the mortuary, looked in death exactly as he had in life.

Tony stood at the graveside with one arm around Rosetta, the other around Kerry. His eyes scanned the hostile faces of the mourners gathered there. It was obvious that with the exception of Rosetta and Kerry, everyone—priest, pallbearers, mourners—felt he should not be there. They apparently had reached the same conclusion Tony had reached: that Buck himself would not have wanted Tony there. Looking around, Tony could understand why; an overwhelming majority of the mourners crowded deeply around the gravesite were working people—not just hardrock miners, though there were more of them than any other, but also mill workers, truck drivers, highway laborers, store clerks, even the boy who delivered Buck's daily newspaper— all people whose lives Buck had touched in some way with a pat on the back, a wink, a bit of advice, the loan of a few dollars, a job recommendation, a hospital visit, a bag of groceries during a layoff, his presence at the baptism of a new baby; none of them big things but all of them good things; and all of them memorable; all of them taking on larger proportions, greater significance, in death. The sad somber faces around Tony Donovan belonged, for the most part, to what Buck had so frequently referred to as the "salt of the earth common man," which to Buck had been the most desirable and least disreputable status to which a man should aspire. It was a rank which he himself embodied in all that he was, including his longtime reign as president of the Amalgamated Mine Workers of Nevada. To Buck O'Crotty, that title and position did not put him above his fellows, but only squarely in the middle of them; even after he had risen to become general superintendent of Delavane Mines, he had never worn a white shirt to his office. Always a blue work shirt. Somehow Buck felt that mattered.

As Tony Donovan studied the screen of faces he was aware that in his grief he was doing something else beside remembering Buck. He was looking for Francie. He did not really expect her to be at Buck's funeral, but he had to look anyway. He had to search for her because she was the only person in the world who could relieve his grief; she had always been the only one who could help him when he was hurting, from the time they were kids. At this moment, with Buck only minutes from going underground for the last time, forever, Tony desperately needed Francie.

Tony had learned of Francie's return to Virginia City almost as soon as he and Denny arrived. As the Calvada DC-6 was making its slow taxi up to the passenger terminal in Reno, Denny nudged Tony and said quietly "Welcoming committee."

Leaning forward to look out the window Tony saw, waiting at the entrance to the terminal, two state investigators and an assistant Nevada attorney general, Jack Coltrane, whom Tony and Denny had known since elementary school. The son of Virginia City banker Harmon Coltrane, Jack was now the state attorney general's rising young criminal prosecutor. He and Tony Donovan had been enemies since boyhood.

"Wonder how he knew we was on this flight?" Denny asked nasally. "You didn't tell Shad which plane we were taking, did you?"

"They have an office in Las Vegas," Tony reminded him. "They don't need Arnie Shad to keep track of people."

It had not been the pleasantest of flights. Denny loathed Arnie Shad and, after learning that Shad had come to see Tony, spent the entire trip lambasting the reporter. To Denny, Arnie was a meddling, trouble-making traitor, doubly reprehensible because he, too, had once been employed by the same people for whom Tony and Denny worked.

"The son of a bitch is nothing but a double-crossing bastard," Denny Ebro said on the plane, his deformed upper lip curling contemptuously. "Worked for Ben Siegel all during the time the Flamingo was being built, then turned around and became some kind of fucking do-good reporter who wants to expose everybody. You ask me, he's damn lucky he hasn't been left out in the desert somewheres. Serve him right. Turning against his friends."

"I don't like that kind of talk about leaving people in the desert, Den," Tony replied sternly. "It's that kind of talk that convinces Arnie and people like him that we're gangsters." He paused a beat, then added, "And we aren't—despite what Lansky was during Prohibition. *We* are legitimate."

When the aircraft came to a stop and cut its big propellers, a set of mobile passenger stairs was rolled up and locked in place; then the bulkhead exit door was opened. Tony and Denny were the first to deplane. As they crossed the tarmac and approached the terminal, Jack Coltrane stepped out to meet them and said, "Donovan, I want to question you about the murder of Buck O'Crotty."

"Go fuck yourself, Coltrane," Tony said, brushing past him into the terminal. Coltrane nodded to the two investigators, who immediately took Tony by each arm. Tony stopped, stood very still, and stared flatly at Jack Coltrane. Then he said evenly to Denny, "Call Leo Sandler and tell him I'm being detained by the attorney general's office and to get up here right away." Leo Sandler was a well-known Las Vegas lawyer who represented the Flamingo and three other Strip hotels controlled by Meyer Lansky corporations.

"You're not being charged with anything," Coltrane disclaimed. "We only want to question you."

Tony ignored him. "Tell Sandler to charter a plane if he has to," he said to Denny. "I want him here in two hours." Turning to Coltrane, he said, "You're not getting away with this, you bastard."

"It's preliminary questioning," Coltrane emphasized. "Nobody said anything about holding you."

"You *are* holding me," Tony said, bobbing his chin at the two investigators gripping his arms.

Coltrane glared his obvious dislike at Tony. Yet he said, "This is nothing personal; you can believe that or not. You're on a list of persons known to have had differences with Buck O'Crotty. No matter who was in charge of this case, they'd have to question you. We can do it the easy way or the hard way." His voice moderated a little. "I know you're here for the funeral. If you'll voluntarily give me a few minutes, we can get it over with."

Tony, glaring back at the state lawyer, thought about it and finally bobbed his chin at a deserted corner of the waiting room. "All right. Just you and me, Coltrane. Over there."

They walked away, side by side, leaving the others, and went to the farthest corner near an idle baggage conveyor. Tony put his back against the wall and folded his arms. Jack faced him, hands on hips.

"What do you know about Buck's killing?" Jack asked.

"Not a goddamned thing."

"How and when did you learn of his death?"

"Arnie Shad told me this morning. He said it came over the newspaper's wire service. A little while later, Buck's family called me."

"You and O'Crotty weren't on good terms, were you?"

"No."

"You hadn't spoken for a couple of years?"

"That's right."

"If the hoodlums you work for planned to execute O'Crotty you probably wouldn't have objected then?"

"I don't work for 'hoodlums'," Tony replied evenly. "I work for a legal corporation that is on file and approved by the Nevada Casino Commission—"

"You work for a group of New York hoodlums," Jack declared. "You know it and I know it."

"Legitimate stockholders of record own the hotels I'm employed by—"

"Employed as what?" Jack challenged.

"As a general consultant."

"Fancy title for a rackets front man," Jack scoffed. He pointed a stiff finger at Tony. "You work for a bunch of vicious criminals who can order a man killed simply by picking up the telephone. And our office thinks that's exactly what they did to Buck O'Crotty."

"Get your finger out of my face," Tony said. "You're wrong about the people I work for. They had nothing to do with Buck's death. If you're really interested in finding out who killed him, why don't you investigate the people who own the mines: they had a *reason* to want him dead. The people I work for never gave him a second thought." Tony's eyes turned dangerous. "I'm warning you, get that god-damned finger out of my face."

Jack drew his hand away. "I don't believe you. I think you and the rest of the Las Vegas hoodlums want to own Nevada. I think you'd like Nevada to be your crime head-quarters, your control center to spread your slimy business all over the country—"

"You're crazy, Coltrane. People like you shouldn't be in positions of authority."

"—but I'm not going to let that happen," Coltrane went on imperturbably. "I may not be able to get the real big shots, but I'm going to get you, Donovan. No matter what I have to do, I'm going to nail you to a cross. I'm going to make such a horrible example of you that the other hood-lums in Nevada will run like the rats they are."

Tony smiled a tight, knowing smile. "Why me, Jack?" he asked in mock innocence. "Plenty others around you could probably nail a lot easier—*real* crooks, as a matter of fact. Why go to all the trouble trying to pin something on me?" He paused a beat. "Wouldn't be because of Francie, would it?"

Jack Coltrane's face reddened, not with embarrassment but with anger. "Francie has nothing to do with it."

"Of course not," Tony said blandly. "How could I have even thought that? Just because I took her away from you—"

"You son of a bitch," Coltrane said with a murderous look, "you didn't 'take' her away from me; you caused her to *run* away from everything that was good in her life. It was because of you that she got involved with drugs—"

"That's a fucking lie!"

"—you, that she became a whore for your syndicate!"

Tony pushed away from the wall and drove his fist into Jack Coltrane's mouth, knocking him back several feet but not down. Jack's lower lip split in the middle and spurted a stream of blood. The two investigators ran across the terminal, Denny Ebro ahead of them by three feet. As they approached, Jack held up a hand to stop them. "Leave him alone!" he ordered. Taking out a handkerchief, he pressed it to his injured lip. Denny moved past them to stand by Tony, while the investigators stood on each side of Coltrane.

"I've been waiting a long time to do that," Tony said with relish.

One of the investigators drew out a pair of handcuffs. "Put those away," Jack said. His eyes fixed on Tony. "I could see that you got six months in jail for what you just did. But I'm not going to. I don't want there to be any misinterpretation about why I'm out to get you. I don't want some smart syndicate lawyer or some newspaper hack on your gangster payroll saying it has anything to do with Francie, or because you took a swing at me, or anything else except the real reason. I'm going to get you because you're scum, Donovan. You don't deserve to walk the streets with decent people because you're a predator. Even Buck O'Crotty, who loved you like a son, thought so. You're a criminal. That's why I'm going to put you away." Jack motioned to his investigators, started to leave, then paused. "In case you're interested in what became of Francie after you and your friends were through with her, she's back where she started—living in the Delavane mansion up on the Hill. They say she's become a recluse, just like her father did. They say she's lost her mind. Nice work, Donovan."

Coltrane and his men stalked away, leaving Tony and Denny staring after them.

Standing at the grave now, Tony thought of what Jack Coltrane had said—not about Francie but about Buck—that even Buck, who had loved him like a son, had thought he was a criminal. Coltrane, he realized, had said much the same thing about Tony's employers as Arnie Shad. Both men seemed to be convinced that Tony was an integral part of something corrupt and immoral. They were now going so far as to accuse his employer, Meyer Lansky, of having Buck killed. To Tony, their accusations as well as their arguments were untenable.

Tony remained loyal to Meyer Lansky. After Arnie had left Tony's office the day of Buck's death, and after Tony had pacified the weeping Denny Ebro and sent him home to pack, Tony had unlocked his bottom desk drawer and taken out a special telephone that was used to call only one person: Meyer Lansky. Installed as an off-premise, long-distance extension of the switchboard of a small private investment firm in Miami, it reached that switchboard directly with the dialing of a three-digit number. The terminals at both the Flamingo and that Miami office were equipped with intercept pulse devices which detected any additional electrical wattage being used at either end, so that if a wiretap was affixed it would instantly be revealed by a flashing red light either on Tony's telephone or on the switchboard in Miami. The reason for such security, Meyer Lansky had explained, was to keep business discussions confidential. And, Lansky was not hesitant to admit, there were still officials who would be happy to frame him for something unlawful, having failed to catch him when he *had* been involved in bootlegging and illegal gambling in the old days.

The switchboard Tony called was manned around the clock, literally manned: Tony had never heard a female voice answer. Dialing the three digits, Tony waited until a man's voice answered simply, "Miami."

"Mr. Donovan calling for Mr. Lansky, please."

"Hold on."

From Miami the call was relayed either to Meyer Lansky's penthouse apartment at 40 Central Park West in New York City, or to his home in the exclusive Miramar suburb of Havana, Cuba. Tony never knew to which location he was connected. It usually took only about three minutes before he heard the genial, dispassionate voice of Meyer Lansky. It was a voice that somehow never failed to provide reassurance for Tony Donovan.

"Hello, Tony."

"Hello, Mr. Lansky. How are you, sir?"

"I'm well, thank you. Yourself, Tony?"

"Fine, sir. Mr. Lansky, something happened up in northern Nevada this morning that I thought you ought to know about. Buck O'Crotty, the labor leader in the mining industry, was shot to death in his union office."

"O'Crotty? The man who was your foster father, Tony?"

"Yes, sir." Tony frowned, uncertain as to whether he could detect any surprise in Lansky's voice or not. It was such a calm, imperturbable voice, a natural characteristic of a man Tony had rarely known to be surprised by anything.

"I'm very sorry, Tony," the voice said now, in a tone not perceptibly different. "I am aware that the two of you have been estranged for some time, but please accept my condolences nevertheless. Was there some particular reason you wanted me to know at once?"

Wetting his lips, Tony had to swallow quickly before he could say, "It's been suggested that you or some of your associates might have been responsible for it."

"No," Meyer Lansky said without a trace of indignation or rancor. "No, I can assure you, Tony, that it comes as a complete surprise to me. No one of my acquaintance has any reason to harm a small-time labor leader like O'Crotty. It was probably the result of some union dispute that we know nothing about. Or a personal matter of some kind. At any rate, please rest assured that it is not connected with me in any way." Lansky chuckled quietly. "I won't ask you, of course, but I imagine it was Arnie Shad who laid it at my doorstep. I had high hopes for that young man at one time. I used to work alongside his father in a tool-and-die shop when I was a boy, back when I used my hands instead of my brain to earn a living." Lansky sighed. "It distresses me that Arnie has turned against his friends the way he has, but I suppose I have Ben to blame for that."

An image of a handsome, smiling Ben Siegel flashed in Tony's mind. Ben had been dead for three years now, but the repercussions of his life could still be felt. Like Buck O'Crotty, Ben Siegel had touched many lives, in many ways, indelibly.

"Ben had such an unfortunate penchant for alienating people," Lansky continued. "It's to your credit, Tony, that you remained his friend until the very end, despite his temper and other difficulties. I wish you and Arnie were still friends. Perhaps through you he would see the error of his ways and realize who *his* real friends are." Lansky paused, then asked, "Was there anything else you wanted to discuss?"

"No, sir, I just thought—"

"Very well, Tony. Thank you for calling. Good-bye."

"Good-bye, Mr. Lansky."

The conversation had made Tony feel better. It was a mystic thing talking to Meyer Lansky, much like going to confession as a boy; Tony came away somehow purged of sin, of doubt, his comfortable beliefs reinforced, his position once again, if not on the side of the angels, at least on the line between them and the devil.

The short talk with Lansky also reinforced Tony's opinion that Arnie Shad's accusations were inaccurate and irresponsible. As were Jack Coltrane's. And this business of a so-called national crime syndicate—F.B.I. director J. Edgar Hoover himself was on record as saying that such a thing did not exist. Tony was aware that Meyer Lansky had once been what newspapers delighted in calling a "gangster," in partnership with Ben Siegel and Charlie Luciano, but that had been in a different time, before the war, during Prohibition, the Depression, *years* earlier. Lansky and Siegel had subsequently become legitimate; they *had* to have been legitimate when Lansky sent Siegel to Las Vegas in 1945 to build the Flamingo; if not, how had Siegel been licensed to build, open, and run the new hotel-casino?

Based on cold, hard facts, there simply was no substantiaton for the indictments made by Arnie Shad. Arnie had tried writing newspaper stories and magazine articles about organized crime, even naming Lansky and Luciano in them, hoping to generate some kind of investigation, but for the most part he had been ignored. Among some journalists he was even looked at wryly, as a crank. A long magazine piece he had taken six months to research and write had been rejected by *Esquire* and *Argosy* and had never been published. Sometimes it seemed to Tony that Arnie had turned into some kind of fanatic who was beyond reasoning with.

Tony closed his eyes tightly for a moment and forced the troubling thoughts of Arnie from his mind. He had enough to worry about at the moment, with Rosetta clinging to his left arm, her rawboned, strong face stolid and tearless under a black veil; and Kerry, her own veil pushed up, weeping against his right shoulder. All around him were men in Sears Roebuck suits with ineptly knotted neckties, standing with wives in their church dresses, daughters with pigtails and dicky collars, sons with hair pasted down with Brylcreem, the lot of them looking as sober and proper as Buck himself had looked at Finnerty's Mortuary. And there Tony stood in a four-hundred-dollar Italian silk suit from the Baer Brothers and Prodie tailor who visited him twice a year from Chicago with swatches. Only a few of the men had spoken to Tony at the mortuary or the church, and none of them with sincerity. These were men, some of them, with whom he had labored in the mines from the time he was sixteen until the war began five years later. They were men he had drunk with, arm wrestled with, laughed and sung with, argued and bet on sports events with, he'd gone to their bachelor parties and weddings, some he had even helped escape a cave-in in 1941. Yet because they knew that Buck had ostracized him, that Buck considered him a "gangster," they either greeted him hypocritically or not at all.

Directy opposite Tony, on the other side of the grave, Denny Ebro stood in the company of these men. Wearing the same kind of suit, silk shirt, and silk tie that Tony wore, known to work for the same people in the same business, Denny had nevertheless been warmly received by the miners. The difference, Tony supposed, was that Denny had always been the follower, Tony the leader, and somehow that made the one innocent, the other guilty. Even Buck had never condemned Denny for going with Tony: only Tony for taking him. Tony was the gangster, Denny merely a simple kid with misplaced loyalty. Denny's harelip helped, of course, as well as his good-natured shrugs and replies of, "Whatever Tony tells me to do," when asked what his job was at the Flamingo. Despite himself, Tony could not help feeling irritated at Denny's acceptance and his own rejection.

Studying him now, Tony realized that it was Denny—at least indirectly—who had caused him to so quickly blame the mine owners for Buck's killing. Although Tony had been estranged from Buck for a long time, Denny had not been; Denny maintained close contacts not only with Buck but Rosetta and Kerry as well. It had been Denny who kept Tony apprised of Buck's progress in attempting to prove that silica dust was hazardous to miners, Denny who brought Tony news of the growing animosity between Buck and the mine owners over it, Denny who therefore had sown in Tony's mind the first seed of suspicion about the owners. Not that it wasn't easy for Tony to accept; he had hated mine owners since he was ten, since his father, mother, and two younger sisters had been killed.

Denny, Tony observed, was standing with Terence Henny. Tony could not help wondering how much Terence Henny knew about Buck's death, and how much he had told Denny. Both of them were linked with Buck to the union's early days, as Tony himself was. They, like him, had been close to Buck, privy to his private thoughts, aware of Buck's acceptance of the violence so often inherent in labor-management relations. Buck had always known he was vulnerable. Had something finally come out of the union's past to prove that vulnerability—something that both Terence Henny and Denny Ebro knew about, but Tony Donovan did not? Tony promised himself that he would find out.

It seemed like hours before the final Latin incantations had been spoken and the mourners began filing between the flower-heaped mound of dirt and the casket suspended over the open grave. Some of the men cried despite themselves, all of the women cried, most of the little girls, and none of the little boys except the newspaper delivery boy to whom Buck had always given two crisp new dollar bills in a red and green envelope every Christmas. There were so many mourners that it took twenty minutes for everyone to shuffle past; the top of the casket was littered with single flowers when the last one came by, an old man with a black patch over one eye from a faulty dynamite cap. Then only three people remained at the grave.

Rosetta approached the casket and placed both black-gloved hands palms down on the lid under which Buck's face lay. Closing her eyes under the veil, she whispered a Paiute death prayer. Next to her, sobbing uncontrollably, Kerry, taller than her mother by five inches, clutched her by the shoulders, and managed to blurt, " 'Bye, Bucko," then urged her mother away from the casket. Rosetta allowed herself to be led away, still praying in her own ancient language.

When Tony was alone there, the last one left, he looked at Finnerty, the mortician, and said, "Open the casket." Finnerty hesitated, glancing after the departing Rosetta. "Open it," Tony said again. Finnerty felt for the latches and raised the lid.

From his pocket, Tony took the faded brown photograph of Ruby Surrett Donovan, his mother; the same photograph on which his tears had fallen when he cried on learning of Buck's death. Buck had given him the photograph years earlier, after Tony's family had been killed. "Your mother gave it to me when your dad and I were both courting her," Buck had told him. "She was a nurse at the miners' hospital in Virginia City, and your dad and me, we used to take turns dating her. Gave us each a photo, she did. I loved your mother and I wouldn't give this picture to anyone else in the world. But I want you to have it now, so's you'll remember her."

Fondly, briefly, Tony touched the likeness of his mother with his fingertips, then quickly slipped the photograph into Buck's folded hands. He tried with every nerve in his body not to cry for this man who had helped him and hurt him with equal dedication. But he could no more control his tear ducts than he could his thoughts at that moment, so he allowed himself to weep without further resistance. Nodding to Finnerty, he waited until the casket was closed again, then he put his hand on it and said, "I'll find out who did this to you, Buck. I promise."

It was as close as Tony could come to telling the dead man that he loved him. He hoped that the photograph of Ruby would somehow speak for him.

TEN

Late in the afternoon, following the funeral reception at the O'Crotty home, Tony and Denny were having coffee in the living room with Kerry. Arnie Shad was sitting with Rosetta in the kitchen. All the other newspaper and radio reporters who had covered the funeral were gone. Denny was irritated that Shad was still there.

"What the hell's he talking to her about anyway?" Denny asked indignantly. "Why don't he leave her alone at a time like this?"

"He wants to do a series of articles about Buck," Kerry explained. "About how he came back to Virginia City and started the new union. There had been a miners' union once before, you know, before the turn of the century, when the Comstock lode was discovered. But over the years the mine owners broke it. Mr. Shad thinks that the story of how Buck reorganized it and reestablished the rights of miners will make a good human interest story."

Denny grunted contemptuously. "I hope Rosetta don't tell him no secrets. *Mister* Shad has a very big mouth."

"He's talking to Mamma about how he'd write the series. He said he wouldn't do it without her approval. I thought that was nice of him."

Denny grunted again but made no further comment. He and Tony had just come back into the house after having a talk with Terence Henny on the front porch. Tony understood now why Henny had not wanted him to come back for the funeral; he did not want any problems as he moved into the union presidency vacated by Buck's murder.

"I hope you'll be smart enough, Tony," he said, "to let the proper authorities handle the investigation of this matter. Denny here has told me that you think the mine owners might have been responsible. I think you're mistaken, but I can see why you'd believe that." Henny paused to light a cigar. He was a heavyset, red-faced Irishman, a decade older than Tony, with the beginning of a beer belly. His suit coat was too tight in the sleeves where his biceps were oversized from years of pick-and-shovel work. "What you might not realize," he continued, "is that things ain't like they was in the old days. When you say 'mine owners' today you're not talking about men; you're talking about corporations. It's not Big Jim Delavane's mine anymore; it belongs to a combination now—a group. Everything's all legal and tidy. There's no more goons and strikebreakers. Nobody buys cripplings and killings anymore."

"Who does the Delavane mine belong to?" Tony asked.

"Consolidated Minerals and Manufacturing," Henny told him.

"Who are the people who own that?"

"That's just the point: people don't own it; a corporation owns it. Nevada Land and Mining, Incorporated."

"Who runs the corporaton?"

"Something called a management group," Henny said. "Western Efficiency Counselors is its name."

"Jesus," Tony muttered in frustration, "who does the union negotiate with, then? Who did Buck deal with, Terry?"

"Locally there's Martin Pitt, the attorney, and Clinton Randall, a C.P.A., and Harley Kent, the general manager—"

"Those are the same men who worked for Big Jim Delavane when *he* owned the mine," Tony asserted.

"But now they work for Consolidated," Henny explained patiently, "which works for NL&M, Inc., which is run by Western Efficiency. Don't you see, Tony? It's all *groups*." Henny shook his head sagely. "These people don't order murders, lad."

Tony was not convinced. When he got back inside, he called his secretary in Las Vegas and asked her to have someone at the state capital get him all the information available on the three companies Terence Henny had named. Denny did not support his skepticism; he seemed convinced now that the mine owners were not involved.

"It makes sense," he said when Tony finished talking to his secretary. "Maybe these guys *wouldn't* buy a killing."

"We'll see." Tony reserved judgment. "Remember what Buck used to say—a pig in silk is still a pig. Just because Delavane's old bunch works for corporations now, doesn't mean they've changed their ways—or their thinking. To them, a union man has always been a troublemaker—and Buck was the biggest and worst offender of all. They hated him because he stood up to them. Maybe you're convinced by Terence Henny's argument, but I'm not. I don't think any one of that old bunch would hesitate a minute ordering Buck's killing if they thought they could get away with it." Tony shook his head emphatically. "I still want some answers."

In the living room where they had joined Kerry for coffee, Denny sat in a club chair opposite the couch which Tony and Kerry shared. The furniture was new, and so was the frame two-bedroom house on G Street for which Buck had paid ten thousand dollars, via a mortgage, just six months earlier. Small, comfortable, homey, it was very much like Rosetta had made the company house in which they had all lived during their younger years. It was, Tony had thought when Rosetta and Kerry showed Denny and him around earlier, exactly the kind of home in which anyone who knew Buck O'Crotty would have expected him to live: totally unpretentious, completely respectable. A stranger could have looked in any closet, any drawer, without experiencing even mild surprise.

As Kerry and Denny talked about Arnie Shad, Tony sat slighty sideways and studied this young woman whom he had known since her infancy. Twenty now, she was an unusual mixture: the planes of her face had Rosetta's angularity and she had Paiute hair, crow black and straight, worn unfashionably long, nearly to her waist. From Dewey Morrell, her natural father, she had inherited exquisite aquamarine eyes and a lighter complexion than Rosetta's hawk-brown color, as well as the lanky Welshman's height. Kerry was five-nine, much taller than the average young woman typified in movies, offices, and on college campuses by girls next door like Diana Lynn, June Allyson, and Wanda Hendrix. A lot of Kerry's height was in her unusually long, slender legs, which, having removed her shoes and nylons when the last mourner left, were curled up under her, skirt hiked up, knees exposed.

As Tony studied Kerry, he had a sudden memory of Buck. It was a Buck he had just met: the man who had come and adopted him when he was ten years old and taken him to a shabby little company house where he first met Rosetta and her infant. "This is little Kerry," Buck said, holding her up for him to see. "She'll be your little sister from now on."

"My little sisters are dead," Tony replied in a surly tone. "Their names were Megan and Maureen. They were twins with yellow hair. Big Jim Delavane killed them along with my ma and pa." He looked at brown little Kerry with her black hair. "She's not my sister." Little could he have realized that day just how much of a sister to him the little half-Paiute child would become.

Tony had not seen Kerry since his last violent dispute with Buck, an incident that she unfortunately had witnessed; a fight over Tony's relationship with Francie. At that time, Kerry had been a somewhat gawky junior in high school; now she was a sophomore at the University of Nevada studying pre-law, because Buck had ambitions for her to become the first female labor lawyer in the tough, traditionally male United Mine Workers union. Knowing Buck's penchant for enforcing his own morality and values on other people's lives, Tony wondered in passing whether such a career was what Kerry wanted. Sitting with her now, he briefly considered asking her; then he decided that the day of Buck's funeral was hardly the appropriate time to question Kerry about Buck's influence on her.

Denny left them and went down the hall toward the bathroom. Tony, having noticed a book on the end table next to Kerry, reached across her to pick it up. It was titled *1984* and had a bookmark a third of the way through it.

"Yours?" he asked.

Kerry nodded. "Yes."

"What's it about?"

"It's kind of creepy. About a totalitarian state where the people in charge control everyone's mind. Buck gave it to me for my birthday. It was just published last year and its author, George Orwell, died a few months ago. Tuberculosis. He was only forty-six."

Tony thumbed idly through the pages and put it back. "You read a lot, I guess."

Kerry made a wry face. "Too much. I'll probably need glasses in a few years."

"That won't be so bad."

"You know what they say—'Boys don't make passes at girls who wear glasses.' "

"I'll bet you get your share of passes," he ventured.

"I do all right" she replied. She made an attempt to be impish about it but the attempt failed and her words came out strained and awkward. They gave Tony pause to wonder.

Presently Rosetta led Arnie Shad in from the kitchen and Tony could tell by the pleased expression on Arnie's face that he and Rosetta had reached an agreement about the writing of Buck's story. Arnie confirmed as much just as Denny returned. "Now all I have to do," the reporter said, "is sell the idea to the paper. I'm going back to the hotel right now and call my editor."

"Why don't you walk back with him, Denny," Tony said. They were all staying at the Ormsby House. "I have something to talk to Rosetta and Kerry about. I'll see you back at the hotel later."

Arnie and Denny glanced distastefully at each other, but Arnie was in a hurry and Denny was too accustomed to following Tony's orders to object. The two men said good night to Rosetta and Kerry, and went out the door together.

"It's only a four-block walk," Tony called after them. "Try not to kill each other on the way."

When the three people who had been Buck O'Crotty's family were alone for the very first time since Tony's arrival, Rosetta poured fresh coffee and tried to get Tony to move from the couch to the only piece of furniture in the room that was not new, an old Morris chair that Tony recognized as having been Buck's for many years.

"Sit here in the big chair, Tony," the widow said. "You will be more comfortable."

Tony shook his head. "I'm fine right here, Rosetta."

Without arguing, Rosetta sat in the chair Denny had vacated. Like Kerry, she was still wearing her black mourning dress, but had replaced her black oxfords with felt house slippers. "It is so good to have you with us again, Tony," she said, smiling a sad, affectionate smile. "Isn't it good to have him here, Kerry?"

"Yes, Mamma." Kerry gave Tony the same kind of smile. "Like old times." She reached over and squeezed his hand briefly. "You know I didn't mean those things I said on the phone, don't you? The names I called you. I was just—"

"Sure," Tony interrupted quickly. "That was my fault. I upset you. I'm sorry, I was a little confused." He paused thoughtfully for a moment, then added, "I'm still a little confused, except now it's about something else."

"What is it?" Rosetta asked, delicately sipping her coffee. She had more natural grace than any woman Tony had ever known. Every movement was soft.

Tony glanced from mother to daughter. "I've heard that Francie is back in Virginia City. Living up in the Delavane mansion. Do either of you know anything about it?"

Kerry and her mother exchanged quick, significant glances. Tony at once felt a tinge of distrust. Had these two become that much like Buck?

"There has been talk that Francie is back," Rosetta admitted quietly.

"You knew I'd want to know," Tony said. "Why didn't you tell me?"

Looking down at her cup, Rosetta replied, "People say Francie's not . . . the same as you remember her, Tony."

Kerry rose and stood by her mother's chair. She put a hand on Rosetta's shoulder. "Who told you she was here?"

"Jack Coltrane was at the airport to question me about Buck's murder."

"My God," Rosetta said. "Surely he doesn't think *you . . . ?*"

"He thinks some of the people who have interests in Las Vegas might have wanted Buck dead. And he knows I'm associated with some of those people. He's wrong about them and I told him so. Then we had words about Francie. He told me she was back." Tony's gaze was flat now, without warmth, still moving from one to the other. "You wouldn't have told me, would you? Either of you?"

"No," Rosetta replied quietly, "we wouldn't have."

"Why not?" Tony's tone became accusing. "The same reason Buck used to use? Because it was 'for my own good'?"

"There's no need to get nasty about Buck," Kerry said sharply. Rosetta quickly touched her hand to silence her.

"We would not have told you because we felt that knowing might somehow hurt you, Tony," the Paiute woman explained. "I suppose you are right about it being the same reason Buck used. If our not telling you has made you angry, we are sorry."

Tony rested his head back against the couch for a moment, sighing quietly. "I'm not angry, Rosetta. I just don't want you and Kerry taking Buck's place trying to be my conscience. As unlikely as it seemed to Buck, sometimes *I* know what's best for me." Sitting back up to face them again, he asked, "What do people say is wrong with Francie?"

By a glance, Rosetta deferred the question to her daughter. "No one is sure, Tony," the younger woman said, returning to the couch. "No one really *knows* that she's really there; it's more a rumor than anything. No one has actually seen her. If she is there, she's totally reclusive."

"Could she be ill?" Tony wanted to know.

"Physically, you mean? I don't think so," Kerry said. "She's never sent for a doctor, so it doesn't seem likely. Again, Tony, it's only talk. She might not be there at all. The only people ever seen around the mansion are Cavendish—you remember him, Big Jim's butler, he's been there for years; and Chalky, the albino man who came to town with the strikebreakers back in 1940; he was with Francie when she came back to Virginia City in 1944. She left him here with Cavendish when she went away again. It's possible that people only *think* Francie is there with them.

Some people say she comes and goes, here for a month or so, then gone again. No one is even sure how the talk started that she *was* back."

Tony rose from the couch. "I'm going up there to find out."

Expressions of dread came over the faces of both mother and daughter."Tony," Rosetta and plaintively, "that is not a wise thing to do."

"They won't let you in," Kerry warned him. "They don't let *anybody* in, even delivery people."

"If Francie's there, I'll get in," Tony assured them.

"What you are doing is a mistake," Rosetta said as Tony kissed her on the cheek and walked toward the door. Her tone now became grave. She started to speak again, to elaborate her objection, but Kerry rose and moved to her side again, touching the Paiute woman's shoulder significantly, the daughter soliciting silence from the mother this time.

"Would you like to take Buck's car?" Kerry asked, walking to the door with him. "The keys are in it."

Tony hesitated a fraction of a second, then decided against it and said, "No, thanks, Ker. I'll walk. I need some exercise." Somehow, using Buck's car to go looking for Francie did not seem right. Buck, Tony knew, would have thought him foolish. Buck probably would have said, "It's just a car, lad. A lot of metal with an engine in it. It's got no memory, no loyalty." But now, just as then, Tony Donovan had his own values, his own ethics.

At the door, Kerry squeezed his hand and kissed him lightly, half on the cheek, half on the lips. "Please be careful up there," she said.

"Sure. Denny and I will see you both in the morning before we leave."

Rosetta joined Kerry at the door. Both women watched as Tony walked briskly down G Street toward Sierra, which led up to the mansion.

As he trudged up Sierra Street, Tony's mind flooded with thoughts of years past, thoughts of Francie and years past. Sierra Street had been an important part of their young lives, the link that connected them both physically and spiritually. They once had a pact about Sierra Street: whenever Tony walked past it below, in the poor section where he lived, he would think of Francie; whenever she passed it above, in the wealthy section known as the Hill, she would think of him. They considered it "their" street.

Sierra was for a long time the only paved artery extending between the town itself and its richest residential community. Because Virginia City was built on a succession of natural tiers, all of its north-south streets, like Sierra, resembled a series of steps that angled up at thirty degrees or so, leveled off to intersect with east-west thoroughfares, then angled up again. The difference between Sierra and streets like Silver Street, Maple Avenue, Miners Walk, or the other parallel, or "ladder" streets, was that Sierra had been longer and gone higher, all the way to the top of the Hill. Eventually, as residences on the Hill increased in number, several other streets were extended to the top, and Sierra Street was no longer unique.

By the time Tony got to K Street, having climbed four blocks, he was winded and beginning to regret not having taken Buck's car after all. If he could have been sure no one would have seen him, he would have turned around and walked backwards up the inclines, as he and every other boy in town had learned to do from the Chinese. Walking uphill backwards was far easier than doing it frontwards; one could stand upright and breathe much better walking backwards, instead of leaning forward, trudging, with one's lungs compressed. But Tony felt it would look silly, a grown man in a suit and tie walking backwards, so he labored along in the conventional and more difficult manner.

When he reached M Street, Tony could see the Delavane mansion. It sat alone, at the very end of Sierra Street, its wide, circular drive crowning the terminus of that avenue like the top of a scepter. Other large homes now dotted the Hill, many more than the half dozen that had been there when Tony was a boy, but the Delavane place was still discernibly elevated, still perceptibly separate, still a distinct, discrete structure the sight of which generated a single thought: It was here first. It was *the* house on the Hill. Three-storied and marble-pillared, shuttered and verandahed, stained-glassed and corniced, at its completion the *Virginia City Chronicle* had editorialized that their "fine little mountain oasis could now boast of having a mansion as stately and palatial as that of a Rockefeller, Carnegie, Vanderbilt, or any other Eastern millionaire." Everyone in Virginia City believed it, of course, because no one had ever seen the mansions of the wealthy Easterners, and even a glimpse of the Delavane mansion was enough to reinforce any claim about it to the uninitiated. More than a quarter of a century old, it still looked stately and splendid from M Street where it first loomed into sight. Even Tony Donovan, having now been exposed to the wealth of Las Vegas, New York, Havana, and Beverly Hills, was still taken by the sight of it after so long.

Francie's there. He was certain of it. The thought seared his whole being, warming and exciting him—and also frightening him as he recalled Jack Coltrane's statement: *The rumor is she's lost her mind.* And Rosetta's: *People say Francie's not the same as you remember her, Tony.* And Kerry's: *If she is there, she's totally reclusive.*

As Tony trod closer to the Delavane mansion, passing tributary drives leading back into stands of tall pines to other, lesser mansions, he concentrated on purging those remarks from his troubled mind. Tony could not convince himself Francie was crazy, anymore than he himself was crazy. What others saw as madness was probably only their view of torment, of anguish. Reclusive? Why wouldn't she be? When the world wiped its feet on you, you tried to close it out. Tony saw himself as no less reclusive emotionally than Francie was; of necessity, he was simply more on public display.

We are one, Francie, he thought with grim optimism. *We always have been.*

Reaching the end of Sierra Street where it divided into the wide circular drive that surrounded the mansion, and now even branched off on both sides to other, newer streets leading down the Hill, Tony stepped off the pavement and crossed a broad expanse of lawn that had once been manicured and flowerbed-lined but now was unkempt, weed-ridden, unfit for the great house it fronted. Or was it? Tony thought, frowning. As he got closer, he saw that the mansion, too, was ill-kept: mold was advancing around its foundation, paint peeling in places from its exterior, outlaw ivy encroaching on the great marble pillars that had come all the way by freighter from Italy. It surprised Tony to find on closer scrutiny that the property was not stately and splendid after all; it looked decrepit, pitiful.

How Edith Delavane would have hated this, Tony thought, because it was evidence of slovenliness, which she abhorred;

and how embarrassed Big Jim would have been by it, because it would have marred the image of perfection he was consumed about projecting. But it was Francie's house now, and clearly it meant less to her than it had to them. No matter, Tony thought. If he had his way, today Francie would leave the place forever.

Twilight had come and only a single, thin reed of sunlight crossed the front portico and slanted up the massive oak door with its ornate brass knocker—which, in keeping with the rest of the estate's appearance, was tarnished. Heart pounding in his chest as it had not done since Guadalcanal, Tony lifted the knocker and struck its plate four times. Like a man going to the electric chair, he waited, nerve ends feeling as if they were under one thin layer of epidermis, exposed, adrenaline rushing. He clasped his fingers together because both hands were trembling. Perspiration surfaced along his hairline and upper lip. When there was no answer after an eternity, he knocked again.

Still there was no response. Tony tried knocking with his knuckles. No answer. He felt desperation building. Be here, Francie, he silently pleaded. Be here, *please*. He knocked several more times, calling out as well, but got nothing in return but silence. Slowly he began to feel as if he had been emptied out. A sense of helplessness settled in. Was Francie this near, somewhere inside this fortress of a mansion, and he could not get to her? Anger flashed momentarily and he tried to bring up his fists to pound on the door in outrage, but his hands were suddenly too heavy to raise, his arms too limp. He could only stand there, impotent. So certain had he been that Francie *was* there, that he was going to see her again after such a long time, that to be denied it momentarily traumatized him.

Presently a hand touched his sleeve, an arm went around his shoulders. He looked and saw that it was Kerry. She guided him away from the door. Parked in the drive, to his surprise, was Buck's car; he had not even heard it drive up.

"Come with me, Tony. I've got something to tell you," Kerry said.

Tony allowed Kerry to direct him into the passenger seat. He stared straight ahead, mutely, as she got behind the wheel and started the engine.

She slowly drove him away from the decaying mansion.

*   *   *

Instead of going back down the grade to town, Kerry drove to the newly paved Route 341 that went over the Hill to connect with the Reno highway. It was one of the new "scenic drives" that the state tourism board was promoting; at various points along the route, it had places designated by markers as "scenic views" where automobile travelers could pull off the road to take pictures or picnic or merely marvel at the mountainous landscape. At one such spot, the view looked down on Virginia City, much the same as it did from the Delavane mansion except higher, wider, more panoramic. It was there that Kerry Morrell pulled Buck's car over and parked.

She reached past Tony and rolled the window on his side halfway down. "The fresh air will be good for you, Tony," she said. "It's cool and clear; it'll help cleanse your mind."

"You sound like Rosetta," a depressed Tony replied listlessly. " 'Paiute talk,' Buck used to call it."

"I am like my mother in many ways," the young woman replied matter-of-factly. "Sometimes the Paiute half of me is very useful in dealing with white situations."

Tony rested his head against the seat. A breath of the thin air, more than a mile high, brushed the right side of his face, the scarless side, like a feather. By turning his head slightly, he could see the lights of Virginia City: a handful of sparkles in a vast bowl of darkness.

"I remember Buck used to call them 'heathen nonsense,' some of the things your mother used to say," Tony reminisced. "Back when we first started living together. You were just a baby, weren't even walking. It was after you got older, when Rosetta would rock you and tell you stories about the Paiute tribe, that Buck came to appreciate them as people and not savages. He used to secretly listen to your bedtime stories, did you know that?"

"I knew," Kerry told him. "So did Mamma. She told the stories as much to teach Buck as to teach me."

Tony grunted softly. "Sometimes I think Rosetta is smarter than all of us put together." He was quiet for a while, then sighed an almost inaudible sigh. "When did the rumor start that Francie was back?" he asked. It was inevitable that they would talk about her.

"I'm not sure, Tony. I'm up in Reno at school most of the winter; in summer I'm busy working at the union office. I haven't really kept track of Francie. I think it was about a year ago that I first heard it.'' There was a three-quarter moon rising above the mountains; in the faint light it provided, she saw Tony shake his head in frustration. Turning sideways behind the wheel, she touched his cheek. "There's something I've got to tell you, Tony. Buck was getting ready to contact you. I don't know if he realized his life was in danger or what. But I overheard him tell Mamma that he was going to talk to you. His exact words were, 'I need the lad, and he needs me—whether he knows it or not.' We've got to resolve our differences before it's too late.' Later I asked Mamma what he meant, but all she would say was that he was talking about things that only he knew, that only he could explain.'' Kerry fumbled in her purse for a moment, then dabbed at her eyes with a handkerchief. "I think it's important for you to know that Buck didn't intend to let the breach between you two go on any longer. Mamma would have told you tonight if you hadn't run off up to the mansion. Buck was going to come to you, Tony; he was going to give in for the first time in his life. But before he—before he could—well—'' Her voice broke.

Tony stared incredulously at nothing. Kerry's words were hard to accept. Buck O'Crotty *never* gave in—to anyone. He was hardrock stubborn, to the core. But even as Tony was resisting the notion, he was thinking: suppose it was true? Suppose Buck *had* known that his life was in danger? Christ, Tony wondered, swallowing dryly, could Buck have been coming to him for *help?* Coming to *ask* Tony for something—for the first time ever?

At once Tony was consumed anew with grief and guilt. Would Buck still be alive, Tony asked himself, if he had stuck with him after the war? If he had come home and gone back into the union, stood at Buck's side like a proper son, helped him with the big things that came up, like the silica dust business? What if he'd been there to back him up like Buck had raised him to do: would that have made the difference for Buck between life and death? Was it possible that the one time Buck intended to come to Tony for something, sudden, violent death had stopped him? The terrible irony made Tony feel ill.

Beside him, Kerry reached to the floorboard of the car, made shadowy motions, then Tony saw her turn and toss something onto the backseat. Her shoes, he realized, as she drew her feet up and sat back to face him.

"Listen," she said nervously, "can we stop talking about Francie and Buck and Mamma and everybody else in the world, and talk about you? And me? Us? In the three days you've been here, we've hardly had a moment alone together." She found one of his hands and clasped it in both of hers. "Buck wasn't the only one who planned to get in touch with you, Tony. I was too. I was going to come see you. I'd already made up a lie to cover the trip: I was going to tell Mamma and Buck that I was going to San Francisco for the weekend with some girlfriends from school. But I was actually coming down to Las Vegas and spend the weekend with you."

Tony smiled fondly at her. "That's sweet of you, honey. That would have been fun. But always let me know ahead of time," he cautioned, "so I can make plans."

"You mean so I won't catch you by surprise with one of those voluptuous showgirls I see in all the Las Vegas travel ads?"

"I don't mean that at all," he said. "I mean so I can line up some good-looking young guy to show you the town. I've got this college kid named Stan who parks cars at the Flamingo—"

"Tony, stop!" she said suddenly, her voice losing its conspiratorial tone and turning snappish. "Don't tease me."

"I'm not—"

"This isn't kidding around. I said I was coming down to spend the weekend with *you*." Letting go of his hand, she shimmied her skirt well up her hips and maneuvered herself over to straddle his legs, facing him. She took his face in both hands. "I was coming down to sleep with you, Tony."

He stared at her pretty, angular, open face in the murky light, totally surprised. After watching her grow from infant to toddler to little girl to teenager to the lanky, quick, very warm female now so very close to him, Tony realized that he did not know Kerry at all. She was very much a stranger to him at that moment. Her words reverberated in his mind. To *sleep* with him? *Kerry*?

Her constantly moving hands dropped from his face in disappointment. "You don't know what I'm talking about, do you?" she asked accusingly.

"I know what you said," Tony assured her. "I just wasn't prepared for it."

"Here's something else you're probably not prepared for

then: I love you, Tony. I've loved you ever since I was a little kid."

"I've loved you that long too—"

"I don't mean that kind of love," she said, patting him on the head, "or this kind," tweaking his cheek; she took his face in both hands again. "I mean *this* kind—"

Bending down and forward, she put her mouth on his and massaged their lips together in as passionate a kiss as her twenty inexperienced years could conjure up. It was every kiss she had dreamed of at night; every kiss she had practiced in high school and at college; it was Jennifer Jones and Joseph Cotten in *Portrait of Jenny*; it was a magical, orgastic kiss that wracked her lithe body in a sudden shudder.

"Did you feel that, Tony?" she asked, removing her lips from his mouth barely enough to speak. Her words were spurts of warmth to his mouth and nose, her breath coffeeish, almost balsamic. "Did you feel what just happened to my body? It's the first time I've ever felt it *with* anyone; I've always been by myself—"

"Kerry listen to me—"

She would not allow him to finish, closing her mouth over his again, working her lips, probing with her tongue, sucking at his mouth until the tremor of pleasure took her body again.

"Kerry, goddamn it, stop this!" Tony took her by both shoulders and shook her fiercely. "Stop it!" he shouted. "Stop it right now!"

Kerry froze, stock-still, eyes widening like she had been suddenly awakened from a nightmare and remembered it. Momentarily she stared at Tony. As cognizance returned, her lower lip began to tremble.

"You don't understand, Tony. I love you. That's why I want to—"

"For Christ's sake, Kerry, we've just put Buck in his grave—"

"This has nothing to do with Buck," she said.

"It does," he insisted. "It has a lot to do with Buck. He didn't raise us to do this. It's hard enough remembering all the things I did that he disapproved of while he was alive; now you want to do *this* on the day we bury him?"

Awkwardly, Kerry uncoupled from him: she half stood, bent, managed to get her leg over him, and turned forward again in the driver's seat. Tony looked away from her. The window next to him was still partway down, letting once-familiar high night sounds come into the car: the far-off cry of a coyote; the whistle of a zephyr, that whirling wind that came spinning down like a top from the mountain peaks; the rustle of cone-laden pine needles: all sounds from Tony's boyhood, when life had been so much simpler and had only *seemed* so terribly complex. Where had they gone, those days when all he had to worry about was learning arithmetic, being in the house by eight-thirty, and fantasizing some way to murder Big Jim Delavane? When—at what point— had innocence begun to fade? When had boyhood started turning into manhood?

With love, Tony decided. Everything, no matter what, seemed to begin and end with love. It was the great tester and the great torturer. Buck had deprived him of Francie out of love, he said, for him. Tony had hated Buck out of love, he thought, for Francie. Kerry wanted to share her body with him now because, she thought, of love; he had rejected her and hurt her because of love, he realized, for Buck. It was never ending, this love thing. With you all your life.

Kerry eventually broke the silence by asking, "Do you have a cigarette?"

"No. I gave up cigarettes. When did you start smoking?"

"I haven't," she admitted. "Now just seemed like a good time. Why did you give them up?"

"I have a stomach ulcer. Smoking irritates it."

"I thought only old men got ulcers."

"So did I."

"Maybe you should get out of the gambling business if it's giving you ulcers."

Tony smiled knowingly in the dark. That was Buck talking. "I didn't get it from the casino business, Kerry. It was the war. Denny's got one too."

"Oh. Buck never told Mamma and me that."

"Denny and I never told Buck. A lot of guys brought ulcers back."

"The things we have to live with." Kerry turned her face toward him, as if to study him in the increasing darkness as clouds covered the moon. "Isn't it odd," she said, "all the things inside that hurt us? Physical things, like your ulcer. Emotional things, like love. And nobody ever knows it unless you tell them. I'm hurt emotionally right now, so are you. Francie hurt you, you hurt me."

"Francie's got nothing to do with this," Tony said. It was, he realized, the same thing she had said about Buck.

"Of course she has. You ran up to the mansion tonight because you thought she was there. You thought you were going to find your precious love again after all this time. When you didn't, it hurt you. Then when I offered you *my* love, you hurt me. Now we're both wounded. What do we do—live with it, like you do your ulcer?"

"If I hurt you, Kerry, it wasn't because I was thinking of Francie; I was thinking of Buck. How Buck would feel about it."

"It seems to me there should be an extreme measure we can take," she said, ignoring his explanation. "Like for your ulcer. Surgery, for instance." Her tone was suddenly becoming spiteful. The hurt of the moment had gone deep into her; now it was coming out again with aggression.

"What are you getting at?" Tony asked.

"Getting at? Nothing. Nothing at all. I'm simply talking about extreme measures. If you wanted to get the ulcer out of your system, you could have it taken out. If I want to get you out of my system, I suppose I can employ extreme measures also."

"Kerry, don't make this thing worse than it already is," Tony quietly implored.

"If I can't sleep with the one man I do love, maybe I should sleep with all the men I don't love—"

"You're upset. You don't mean that."

"Maybe in order to get you to love me, I should get on drugs—"

"Be careful what you say, Kerry," he warned.

"Or become a whore—"

"Kerry, shut up—"

"—and spread my legs for all the gangsters and their crooked politician friends like Francie did—"

Tony slapped her smartly across the cheek, snapping her head back. "Shut up, I said! Shut up about Francie!" Throwing open the door, Tony got out and stalked around to her side of the car. He jerked open her door as if trying to tear it off.

"Hit me all you want, Tony!" she blurted, sobbing. "But it's true! You know it's true."

"Move over," he ordered coldly. "Get out from behind the wheel." She hesitated and he gripped her upper arm, pushing. "Move over!"

When she was in the passenger seat, Tony got in and started the car. I'm driving Buck's car after all, he thought incongruously, wondering: what the fuck does that have to do with anything? It's only a goddamned bunch of metal bolted together. Revving the engine a little, he made a not too careful U-turn on the dark highway and directed the car back down the mountain.

Revulsion gripped him. One of the things Buck had been proudest of in life was that he had never lifted his hand to Kerry, had never even *spanked* her while she was growing up, preferring instead to reason with her when she had transgressed. Now Tony, in one violent moment of weakness, anger, outrage, had violated still another of Buck's principles by slapping Kerry. Buck, he knew, would have labeled him for it the way Buck labeled everyone and everything that he judged reprehensible. "You're detestable, lad," Buck O'Crotty would have said. *Was* saying, from the grave, in Tony Donovan's mind.

Halfway down the mountain, in front of them the sparkling lights of Virginia City now twice as large, twice as bright as from above, Tony managed to say in a strained voice, "I'm sorry, Kerry. I'm sorry I hit you."

Kerry had stopped crying and was very quiet, face turned away from the lights, watching the void of the forest. In the light of the dashboard, Tony could see that one hand was in her lap, the other holding a crushed handkerchief to her mouth. When she did not respond, Tony apologized again.

"Did you hear me? I said I'm sorry I slapped you."

"I heard you. It's all right."

"It's not all right. It was a rotten thing to do. I feel rotten about doing it. Buck never—"

"Oh, Tony, forget about Buck. Stop equating everything you do with Buck."

"I don't," he protested.

"You *do*. You either try to live up to his standards and be like him, or you turn away and defy something that he stood for. It amounts to the same thing. You've got to try and put Buck out of your mind now."

"You apparently already have," Tony said offhandedly. The remark surprised Kerry.

"What makes you say that?"

"What happened a few minutes ago. Do you think Buck would have approved of us making love?"

"Making love isn't all that I had in mind, Tony," she replied softly. "I told you, I'm *in* love with you. I was aiming for the whole package—engagement, marriage, kids. Yes, Buck would have approved of that."

"You're not serious," Tony said incredulously. "You and me? You think Buck would have wanted that?"

"Buck only loved three people in the world, Tony. Mamma, you, and me. For us to have married and given him a new generation to love would have been the best thing that could have happened to him. I'm surprised you don't know that."

Tony was astonished. Such a desire on Buck's part had never occurred to him. Thinking about it compounded Tony's already tumultuous confusion about the man. Could that have even remotely been Buck's motive for interfering with Francie and him? To save him for Kerry, ten years younger? It seemed incredible. There had never been any indication from Buck, any hint or suggestion however vague, that he harbored such a wish. Yet Kerry voiced it and seemed to accept it as if it had been a foregone conclusion for many years.

"We really knew two different Bucks, didn't we?" he said as they entered the city limits.

Kerry was looking away from him again. "I guess we did. And we really don't know each other at all. We even have completely different ideas about what represents love."

"You're exaggerating the situation, Kerry."

"I don't think so," she quickly replied, looking at him with fresh bitterness. "As far as love is concerned, the only person that's ever been important to you is Francie Delavane. You don't care what she's been—drug addict, whore—or what she is now, a deranged recluse living in that evil place up on the Hill. No matter what, you run back to her." Kerry shook her head in disgust. "You're as sick as she is."

Tony clenched his jaw and accelerated. The car screeched around a corner into C Street and he sped three blocks to the Ormsby House, the tires squealing again as he brought them to a halt at the front entrance. Tony got out and slammed the door. Looking in at her, his expression was as dark as the high mountain night had been.

"Tell Rosetta that Denny and I will stop in and say good-bye in the morning."

Tony stalked into the hotel. At the desk he was given a message to call his secretary. Walking over to a house phone, he placed the call to her home number. "What's up?" he asked when she answered.

"I have the informaton on those three companies, Mr. Donovan. Do you want it couriered up to you?"

"No, I'll be back tomorrow. Do you recognize any of the names on the corporation papers?" Somewhere far back in his mind lay the fear that he would find Meyer Lansky connected with the companies.

"No, sir," his secretary said. "None that I'm familiar with. The companies are all owned by different groups of men. There's only one name that's on all three."

"Who's that?"

"Someone named Harmon Coltrane."

After he hung up, Tony stood with his hand still on the receiver for a long moment, staring across the lobby. Harmon Coltrane. The man who had been Big Jim Delavane's banker and close friend for many years. Father of Jack Coltrane, who was investigating Buck's murder for the state. And trying to blame Tony's employers for it.

Harmon Coltrane.

A man, Tony recalled Buck once saying, who would go to any lengths for money and power.

Even murder.

ELEVEN

Denny Ebro shook his head emphatically.

"I don't think that's a good idea, Tony. You go to see Harmon Coltrane and you're asking for trouble."

"I'm not asking for anything," Tony replied, "except who killed Buck."

It was eight o'clock, the morning after Buck's funeral. They were packing in the twin-bedded room they had shared at the Ormsby House. Tony had awakened a little while earlier full of fire and eager to hurl gauntlets about Buck's murder. Denny was oddly reserved about it.

"I think you'd be better off listening to Terry Henny's advice," Denny told him. "Let the officials handle the investigation."

"The 'officials'?" Tony scoffed. "You mean Jack Coltrane? Whose goddamned father is involved in every company that has anything to do with Delavane Mines? You think *that* son of a bitch is going to conduct a fair investigation? He's so busy chasing so-called 'organized crime' members that he's completely overlooking the fact that his own father might be involved." Tony paused in his packing. "Or maybe he isn't overlooking it; maybe he's covering it up."

"Whatever he's doing," Denny reasoned, "somebody'll get wise to it. Henny, the F.B.I., somebody. It won't do no good for you to get involved."

Tony stared at him over his suitcase. "What the hell's got into you, Den? Four days ago you were crying and getting me to promise that we'd make somebody pay for killing Buck. Now you're talking like you want us to back away from it entirely." Tony cocked his head. "Has Henny told you something that I don't know?"

"Nobody's told me nothing," Dennny disclaimed. "I'm just trying to keep you out of trouble like I always do." His tone became slightly injured. "I only give you advice for your own good, you know."

Tony was carefully folding some shirts into his suitcase, Marine Corps neat. "Jesus Christ, you sound just like Buck!" he said irascibly. Throwing his hands up in defeat, he stuffed the rest of his clothes into the bag without regard to neatness. Denny came over and took them out again.

"That ain't the way you was taught," he said reproachfully. He proceeded to fold Tony's things in a regulation manner. "If Sergeant Hillis saw you pack like that, he'd climb out of his grave and kick your ass." Sergeant Hillis, their Marine drill instructor at San Diego boot camp, had died on Guadalcanal. "Why don't you call down and see if this dump's got room service," Denny suggested. "Get us some breakfast sent up. I'll do the packing."

"Yeah, sure," Tony said listlessly. He went into the bathroom first and splashed cold water on his face. Got to get hold of myself, he stressed. Got to be steady and in control when I confront Harmon Coltrane.

Suddenly he thought of Kerry. Staring at himself in the bathroom mirror, he remembered the inexcusable slapping incident. He would give anything if it had not happened. But the scene in the car had begun so quickly, when he was still reeling from the disappointment of not finding Francie, when his alertness had been off, his defenses low. Before he knew it, she had been all over him, his foster baby *sister*—on him like one of the barracuda divorcées who prowled Las Vegas. And he had slapped her. Christ, he thought miserably, and wondered how Kerry was feeling this morning. Probably twice as bad as he felt, poor kid. Thanks to him.

Goddamn, he thought, shaking his head. So much was careening in on him at once: Buck's murder, the grief he was feeling over it, the guilt of not being there the one time Buck needed him, anger about the murder itself, disturbing new thoughts of Francie, the incident with Kerry in the car. Tony ran the cold water again.

Back in the room, Tony called the desk and found out that the Ormsby House did not offer room service before 5:00 P.M., but there was a coffee shop open down the street if someone wanted to get an order to take out. "Go get us something," Denny suggested. "The walk will relax you."

Tony put on his coat against the chill air he knew he would encounter that early in the morning, and left the room. Fifteen minutes later he was back with coffee and breakfast rolls. They ate at a small table next to the window, from which they could look out on part of C Street.

"Place sure looks smaller," Denny observed through a mouthful of jelly doughnut. "Used to look like the biggest, widest street in the world." He took a swallow of coffee. "What are you going to do about Coltrane anyway?"

"What do you mean?"

"You know, those things he said at the airport . . ."

Tony shook his head indifferently. "I'm not going to do anything. Why should I? He can try from now until hell freezes over and he won't get anything on me. How the hell can he, Den? I haven't *done* anything."

"Lots of people in jail haven't done anything. You planning to tell Lansky about Coltrane?"

"I'll keep Lansky informed whenever I'm seriously questioned by the law about Buck's killing or anything else," Tony replied precisely. "But I'm not going to go calling him every time Jack Coltrane shoots off his mouth. Lansky can't be bothered with petty things like that."

"I think you should tell him," Denny argued.

"Just leave that to me, okay?" Tony said sharply. What the hell was going on here? he wondered. He said he was going to see Harmon Coltrane, and Denny said he shouldn't; he said he wasn't going to tell Meyer Lansky about Jack Coltrane, and Denny said he should. Denny, his rock, the one person on whom he had always been able to count, was suddenly his first line of opposition. "Have you got some kind of problem I don't know about?" Tony asked. "You're arguing with every decision I make."

"You don't have to listen to me," Denny said. Pushing out his lower lip, he turned to the window in a pout. "I'm only your best friend. Feel free to ignore me."

"Look," Tony said, chagrined, "I just want to find out who killed Buck. That's what you want too, isn't it?"

"You know it is."

"Then trust me, Den. Trust my instinct and my judgment. Harmon Coltrane is involved—I can *feel* it. I'm not going to accuse him or threaten him or do anything else to cause trouble. I just want to ask him what he knows—and I want to see his face when he answers. That's all."

Denny raised his hands in capitulation. "Okay. If you've got to do it, let's get it over with."

"Good," Tony said, smiling. He slapped Denny smartly on the arm. "Let's go."

They carried their own bags down to the lobby. While Tony checked out, Denny went to get the 1950 Chrysler sedan they had rented at the Reno airport for the drive to Virginia City. Because everything at town level was within walking distance, it had been sitting in the hotel parking lot since their arrival.

When he finished at the front desk, Tony saw Denny waiting just outside the hotel entrance. He seemed to be talking to someone. Tony crossed the lobby and pushed through one of the big double doors to the sidewalk. At the curb, behind their rented Chrysler, a police car with a large gold shield and "Storey County Sheriff" lettered on the door was parked. Leaning against the front fender was long-time sheriff Sam Patch.

"Howdy, Tony," he drawled easily. "Didn't get a chance to speak to you at the funeral yesterday. My condolences about Buck. He was a damn good man."

"I appreciate the sentiment, Sheriff. Thank you."

"They can dust off the hot seat down in Carson for whoever done it. Ain't a judge in the state won't give him the death sentence."

"I hope you're right." Tony paused a beat, then added, "Nice to see you again, Sheriff," and started toward the Chrysler.

"On your way out of town?" Patch asked.

"Yes, we are."

"Heading right out or stopping somewheres first?"

Tony turned back. "Why do you ask?"

"Had a phone call to the effect that it might be a good idea if I kept an eye on you. Just in case you took a notion to start any trouble over Buck's death. You got anything like that in mind?"

Tony felt his stomach churn. "Who called you?" he asked, exerting immediate, tight control over himself.

"I'd rather not say," replied Patch. He glanced over his shoulder as a second sheriff's car pulled up and parked. Two husky young uniformed deputies got out and stood alertly by their vehicle. "Don't like to name folks in case they've made a mistake." Turning his head, Patch spat tobacco juice into the gutter. "But I would like to know whether you're headin' straight out of town."

Tony walked over and stood face to face with the lawman. "Suppose I say no. Are you going to tell me to leave?"

"Not gonna tell you that at all," Patch disclaimed. "Don't have no legal authority to tell you that. But me and the boys here, we'll tag along wherever you do go. In the interest of public safety."

"In the interest of public safety," Tony said evenly, "why the hell aren't you out trying to find whoever killed Buck?"

"That's being done, don't you worry about it. The attorney general's office and the state police are handling the investigation, and the F.B.I. has officially entered the case too. My office is cooperating with each agency. Meantime, I still have to keep the peace in my county."

"Which means harassing me?"

"If you want to call it that. I call it surveillance."

Tony nodded tensely. He wondered who had called. Terence Henny, maybe. Or someone up in the Delavane mansion, in case he planned to return there. Perhaps even Harmon Coltrane, who might have guessed that Tony would eventually single him out. Not that it mattered; whoever called had effectively curtailed his movements. Someone knew him well—and knew he would do nothing under the scrutiny of Sam Patch.

"I presume you have no objection if Denny and I go say goodbye to Rosetta?"

"Not a lick," Patch assured him.

"Nice of you," Tony said. The enmity he felt for Patch at that moment did not surface in his tone. He and Denny got in the Chrysler, Denny driving, and pulled away from the curb. Sam Patch and his deputies followed along behind them in their respective police cars. "The son of a bitch," Tony said.

"Think he's planning to escort us all the way out of town?" Denny asked.

"Bet on it."

At the O'Crotty house on G Street, Denny parked in the drive behind Buck's car. As they walked to the porch, an image flashed involuntarily in Tony's mind of Kerry straddling him in that same car the previous night. And another image of him slapping her across the face. Stepping onto the porch, as the two police cars parked in front, Tony hoped he could reach some kind of truce with Kerry before he left. He cared for her too much to think of losing her affection completely.

Rosetta greeted them in the living room. Even that early, on the day after the funeral of her husband, she was up and dressed for the day, wearing a clean, starched housedress, her black-and-silver hair tied at the back of her neck with one of Buck's faded old bandannas, legs bare, feet in soft deerskin moccasins she had cut and sewn herself; ready to continue life, with no mourning past the day of burial; ready to go on as usual, even if Buck would not be there with her; ready on this new morning to resume her normal homemaking chores.

"Hello, boys," she said pleasantly, stretching up to kiss each on the cheek, as she had once bent down to do when sending them off to school in the morning. "I have hot biscuits and gravy in the kitchen."

Tony shook his head. "Thanks, Rosetta, we just—"

"I'll have some," Denny interrupted.

"We just ate," Tony reminded him irritably.

"I don't care. I'm eatin' again," Denny asserted. "Can't get decent biscuits and gravy in Vegas. I'm not passing up the opportunity."

"Good for you, Denny," Rosetta said, patting him on the cheek. She had a special fondness for the harelipped young man. "Come in the kitchen," Rosetta said, taking his arm. "Would you like some eggs too?" Denny threw Tony a haughty look as he left the room with her.

Stepping over to the window, Tony parted the curtains an inch and looked out front. Sam Patch was sitting in his car reading a newspaper; the deputies were in theirs, talking. As Tony swore quietly under his breath, he heard the floor creak behind him and turned to see Kerry entering from the hallway. Her long hair was tangled around her shoulders; she was barefoot, wearing wrinkled cotton pajamas with the middle button undone.

"What's going on?" she asked. "I saw the police cars from my bedroom. What are they doing here?" At the window, she pulled the curtain back all the way and stood looking out. Over her shoulder, Tony saw the two deputies look at her and exchange grins. He took the curtain out of her hand and let it close.

"Someone—Patch won't say who—called the sheriff's office this morning and advised him to keep an eye on me in case I meant to cause any trouble."

"Somebodys got a lot of nerve," Kerry said testily. "I can't believe Sheriff Patch is going along with anything like that. I've got a good mind to—"

"Forget it," Tony told her. "We're leaving in a little while anyway." He studied her. "Are you all right this morning?"

Kerry shrugged. "I guess. You?"

"Sure." He glanced away self-consciously. "Did you tell Rosetta I slapped you?"

"No, of course not," she answered matter-of-factly. Tony had not really thought she would, but he was relieved to have it confirmed as fact. "Did you tell Denny anything?" Kerry asked.

"No."

"Our secret then." Kerry smiled. "Come on, let's have a cup of coffee." She pulled at his arm, and as she did so the unbuttoned front of her pajama top parted and one of her pliant young breasts was revealed: a lovely slope of smoothness rising to an almost black, Indian areola and nipple. "Oops," she said, aware that she was exposed, but she continued to tug at him playfully, making no effort to cover herself. The sight of her like that, apparently not caring, immediately annoyed Tony. He pulled his arm away. "Put on some clothes, Kerry," he said reproachfully, locking his eyes on her face, forcing himself not to look at her breast. "We're not kids anymore, for Christ's sake."

Tony walked away, leaving Kerry there, her face crimson. He went in and sat down at the kitchen table where Rosetta watched approvingly as Denny wolfed down eggs, sausage patties, biscuits, and gravy. From a side dish, he occasionally ate a slice of cold tomato to keep his palate keen. Rosetta got up at once and poured a cup of coffee for Tony. Presently Kerry came in, now wearing a seersucker robe over her pajamas. Getting her own coffee, she avoided Tony's eyes but paused to muss Denny's hair before sitting down. Denny grinned up at her. "Get you for that, brat," he said with his mouth full. Kerry stuck her tongue out at him.

"Look at them," Rosetta said to Tony. "It could be 1939 instead of 1950."

"I wish it was," Kerry said cynically. "I liked 1939 better."

"Not me," Denny said, finally swallowing and pausing between bites. "I 'member 1939 better'n you do, kid—"

"Please don't call me 'kid,' " she interjected sharply. "Not *this* morning."

"—and I 'member that was the year the strike began," Denny continued, as if she had not spoken. "I was hungry most of the time."

"You weren't *that* hungry," Kerry argued.

"What do you know?" Denny said. "You got a free hot lunch at school every day."

"Okay, maybe you're right," Kerry admitted, her face suddenly glowing with a new thought. "I guess it was a pretty bad year, at that." She tried to look coy. "I know it was bad for Tony. That was the year his secret girlfriend Francie Delavane ran off with that low-life hoodlum—"

"Kerry!" Rosetta snapped. "Don't bring up things like that! You know how Tony feels."

"It's all right," Tony said impassively. "It's not true anyway."

"It is so!" Kerry contended. "Everybody in town knew who she ran away with!"

"That's not what I meant wasn't true," Tony said calmly.

"Well, what then?" Kerry pressed. "You aren't going to deny she was your secret girlfriend, are you?"

"No." This was Tony as he wanted to be, *tried* to be, at all times: controlled, emotionless, unintimidated. The way Meyer Lansky was.

"Then what the hell isn't true?" Kerry demanded.

"Watch your language, young lady," Rosetta warned.

"It wasn't 1939; by then it was 1940," Tony said with complete composure.

As Kerry rolled her eyes toward the ceiling in utter disgust, Rosetta tapped a stiff forefinger on the table. "I mean it, Kerry Morrell. You are not to say 'hell' in this house. This is still Buck's house and you know how he felt about women using unseemly language."

"Tell your mamma you're sorry," Denny said, absolutely serious.

"What?" she asked indignantly.

"Go on," Denny insisted. "Say you're sorry."

Kerry looked at the deep-set, steady eyes of Denny Ebro, the mismatched lips parted tentatively, the forkful of food poised halfway from his plate. She had the oddest sensation that Denny was not asking her to apologize, he was ordering her to do it. She glanced at Tony for guidance, protection, something—but Tony only met her eyes implacably, without sympathy. What in the name of God had made her think, even fleetingly, that Tony would take her side, *anyone's* side, against Denny? Especially when it was a matter involving Rosetta. And, more especially, when Kerry knew she was wrong. That part of her that was still a little girl began to rise to the surface.

"Go on," Denny said again.

"I'm sorry, Mamma," she said, voice trembling, eyes misting. Rosetta reached over and squeezed her hand.

"That's a good girl." Buck's house was inviolable again.

"Excuse me," Kerry managed to say. She fled the table.

"Kids," Denny said in exasperation, as if he had raised scores of them. He resumed eating.

"She'll be all right in a few minutes," Rosetta assured

them. "I know my child well. She has what Buck always said I had. Paiute resilience, he called it." She found that Tony was studying her thoughtfully. Smiling deferentially, she touched his hand and asked, "What is it, Tony?"

"Buck was planning to contact me," said Tony. "Why? What about?"

"I do not know, Tony."

"Kerry said he talked to you about it."

"About calling you, yes. But not why he had decided to. He just said there were things to be straightened out with you; that you and he had to resolve your differences before it was too late."

"You don't know what he meant by that?"

The Paiute woman hesitated a beat. Then said, "No, Tony, I don't."

Their dark, penetrating eyes were fixed on each other: she who could stare down a hungry wolf, he whose brooding nature had taken him to fathomless depths of despair. She was the only mother he had known for twenty years; he was the son she never had—by either of the men she had loved. To him she sometimes seemed shrouded, esoteric; to her, he was more like an Indian than any white person she had ever encountered. They were kindred because they wanted to be. Yet for some undefinable reason, for the first time in his life Tony was finding it difficult to believe her.

"If you did know something that I would want to know, Rosetta, would you tell me?" he asked.

"If I was certain that what I knew was right," she replied without hesitation, "and if I knew all of it. Some things cannot be told in part. There can be much heartbreak in half a story. I would not cause you more sorrow than you have already suffered."

Tony nodded slowly. Resiliency and propriety were not by any means the strongest traits of this Paiute woman; she also had a resoluteness as granitelike as the rock Tony had seen men dynamite to get at precious ore. Rosetta resolved in her heart what she believed was just; once that was done in the heart, her mind could not be changed.

"I hope," Rosetta said quietly, "that nothing I ever do will make you hate me like you thought you hated Buck."

Tony covered her hand with his. "You've been my mother for twenty years, Rosetta. I'll never feel hatred for you. Not after all the love you've given me." Tony rose, bent and kissed her on the temple. "I'll go in and see Kerry for a few minutes, then we have to leave."

As Tony left the kitchen, he heard Denny say, "No wonder you like me the best, Rosetta. Those two are nothing but trouble. Are there any biscuits left?" Shaking his head, confounded, Tony went down the hall to Kerry's room. Her door had been left partway open; she expected him, but if he had not come she would have been able to hear Denny and him getting ready to leave, and would have come to him. He looked in and saw her sitting against the brass headboard of her bed, knees up, hugging a pillow, pouting.

"Okay to come in?" Tony asked.

"No, I want to be alone."

"I won't stay long then." Entering, he sat on the side of the bed next to her. "Mad at me?"

"Yes. I hate you. I hate Denny too."

"I'll tell him that. Soon as he finishes eating everything in the house."

Tears welled in her eyes again. "Why does life have to be so screwed up anyway?"

"Wish I knew, Ker. Lots of things I'd like to have straightened out too."

"I know," she said sympathetically. Instinctively she put a hand on his cheek. "I'm sorry for anything I've said or done to hurt you, Tony. Really, I am."

"I feel the same way about you. Let's just try to stop right now and not keep it up."

"If only I didn't love you so much—"

"Are you sure you really do, Ker? Are you sure it's not just a schoolgirl crush from when you were younger?"

"I'm very sure," she asserted. "I'm twenty years old, for God's sake."

"I know how old you are. I've been your foster brother nearly all your life, remember?"

"Please don't start with the 'foster brother-foster sister' argument," she implored. "You have never thought of me as your sister and you know it. Your little sisters were blond-haired twins named Megan and Maureen, and they're buried over in Miners Union Cemetery with your parents. You've told Buck and Mama and me that a hundred times over the years—"

"So I wouldn't forget them," Tony explained. "So I'd never forget them . . . or what happened to them."

"I know that. We all know it."

"But I always considered you my foster sister."

"Foster sisters and brothers aren't blood sisters and brothers," Kerry insisted. "I never loved you like I would have if we'd had the same blood. Since as far-back as I can remember, I've loved you in a different way—a *wanting* way. I've desired you, Tony." She fixed her aquamarine eyes on him. "I desire you right now."

"You know me, Ker," Tony rationalized. "I'm familiar, comfortable to think about—"

"Fantasize about," she told him. "You'd be surprised."

"Okay. That's normal; you're healthy. What I think you're overlooking is that the whole thing might just be a fantasy. You're old enough to love, you're ready, you *want* it, you just haven't met the right young man for yourself yet—"

"You say 'young' like you're an old man, Tony. You're only ten years older than me. Not fifteen or twenty or thirty. Ten!"

"In actual years, sure," Tony allowed. "But as far as maturity is concerned, I'm much, much further ahead of you, Kerry. Remember I worked in the mines for five years; I went to war for four; I've been up and down the emotional ladder with Francie so many times—"

"I *don't* want to talk about her," Kerry stated emphatically.

"All right, we don't have to talk about her. You see the point, I'm sure. For half my life, since I was fifteen I've been doing a lot of living, a lot of hard growing up. *All* your life you've been sheltered and protected by Rosetta and Buck, and for a while by Denny and me. You've never been anywhere, never done anything; you go to college less than twenty miles from here, for God's sake." Kerry tried to turn away, but Tony put a knuckle under her chin and made her keep looking at him. "I'm not saying that this feeling you have for me isn't love, honey; I'm only saying that I don't think it's exactly the kind of love you've convinced yourself it is."

As Tony talked, trying to pacify her feelings, mitigate her behavior, it surprised Kerry that he was so outwardly calm. She knew the turmoil that must exist in him: truths he did not know, fears he could not understand, loves and hates that had plagued him interchangeably since he was a boy. His façade to outsiders had always been impervious: he was tight, cold, hard, obdurate. But Kerry knew better. Kerry knew that despite the years, the maturity, the experiences of which he had just spoken, there was still inside the man a hurt and lonely boy. It was both the man of now and the boy of the past that she had tried to reach last night in her clumsy, totally inadequate attempt to show her love. She had failed. So badly, in fact, that he did not even believe she felt the way she did; so badly that he was now trying to convince her that the love was not what she thought it was.

"What kind of love *do* you think I have for you?" she challenged when he finished speaking.

"I can't answer that," Tony admitted. "I think it's probably a little bit of a lot of kinds. A little bit puppy love, a little bit hero worship, a little bit of good, healthy lust—"

"A lot of that," she interjected.

"Okay, fine. But as far as being honest-to-God true love, the kind that leads to marriage and kids—"

"All right, all right, all right!" she protested; she held her hands up, palms out, in mock surrender. "We could probably argue about it from now until doomsday and never agree with each other. Maybe you're right; maybe I *haven't* grown up enough. Maybe I do need to go up and down that emotional ladder you mentioned; maybe I need to know a few other men before I make up my mind."

"You're not going to start that sleeping around talk again, I hope."

"I might, Tony," she replied with an edge of defiance. "If I'm not going to be part of your life, I'll have to make one of my own, won't I? I'm certainly not going to become a nun. I know it sounds trite, but I saved myself for you, Tony Donovan; that's how sure I was that you'd want me. Since you don't, I'll have to find another candidate." She tilted her head as if considering her problem. "Maybe I'll look up Jack Coltrane," she pretended to muse. "Might be poetic justice or whatever they call it. I mean, he's your age, and you deprived him of Francie Delavane at one time. Maybe this family owes him one."

Tony stared at her for a long, pensive moment. Useless, he thought. I'm wasting my time. The more I talk, the more involved it becomes; the more hurt she becomes. If I don't back off, we're going to end up despising each other. Finally he leaned forward and kissed her lightly on the lips. Then he rose. "Got to go, Ker. You saying good-bye to Denny?"

"Why not! Might as well kiss both of you good-bye once and for all."

They went into the living room where Denny and Rosetta were looking out the window at Sheriff Patch and his escort. "I tol' Rosetta about the phone call," Denny said. "She wants to go out and tell Patch a thing or two."

"No need," Tony said. "We're going now, Rosetta." He walked over and put his arms around her. Denny took Kerry by the hand and pulled her to him. He slipped his arms around her waist.

"You behave yourself, brat," he admonished. "And you let me know if anybody bothers you or Rosetta, okay? I can be here in a couple of hours if you need me." He grinned his crooked grin under the thick moustache and put a finger on the tip of her nose. "Don't step in no puddles at school, you hear me?" Kerry had to grin; it was something he had said to her a hundred times as she grew up.

They all went onto the front porch, exchanged good-byes and hugs and kisses again, and Tony and Denny proceeded to their car. Sam Patch got out of his cruiser and walked over to them.

"My deputies will escort you down-mountain a piece, Tony," he drawled. "Nothing personal, you understand. It's just that I don't really know you anymore. Heard a lot of rumors 'bout who you're in business with, what you've turned out to be, that kind of stuff. Hell, I don't know how much of it's true no more'n anybody else does. I just know this here's my county as far as keeping the peace is concerned; folks have voted me into the job five times, and they kind of depend on me. So I don't take no chances. Prob'ly be best if you don't plan on spending too much time in Storey County. You make people a little nervous."

The two men had locked eyes as Patch was speaking, and throughout neither of them even blinked: a traditional stare-down like the kind one sees in schoolyards and boxing rings. Tony instantly felt back in control: poised, steady, his whole self collected. He had waited to see if Sam Patch would make the mistake of not saying anything that required Tony to respond—and Patch did. There were no questions to answer, nothing to which Tony had to agree or acknowledge, nothing to reciprocate verbally in any way. Patch had delivered a lecture: get out and stay out. Tony had listened. When Patch finished, Tony turned away from him without a word and got into the car. Denny did likewise, and a moment later they were driving away. In the rearview mirror, Denny saw the car carrying the two deputies fall in behind them.

"Fuckers will prob'ly follow us halfway to Reno" he said testily.

Let them, Tony thought, looking out the window as they drove through town. Sam Patch and his hick sheriff's department was not going to change Tony's mind or his plans. He still intended to prove that the mine owners—Big Jim Delavane's old bunch—were behind Buck's murder. Sam Patch might be able to interfere with Tony's personal movements in Virginia City, but there were other ways of doing what he had to do. Delavane's old bunch might have Harmon Coltrane and his corporations to hide behind, but Tony had someone also.

He had Meyer Lansky.

As soon as he got back to Las Vegas, Tony would call him. Lansky, he had no doubt, would help in any way he could. Wouldn't it be ironic, Tony thought, if the very person whom Jack Coltrane and Arnie Shad believed to be behind Buck's death, turned out to be the one who helped prove that someone else did it? Particularly if that someone else turned out to be Jack Coltrane's own father.

I'll get to the bottom of it, Buck, he thought, renewing his promise.

They were passing Miners Union Cemetery. Both Tony and Denny could see Buck's fresh grave with its mound of flowers. Once again Tony was engulfed with a great surge of regret about his and Buck's last meeting. They had parted disliking each other again, as they had so many times in the past. But in that respect, Tony realized, the last time had been much like the *first* time they ever saw each other. In 1930. Man and boy, they had disliked each other on sight.

Looking out the car window at the grave, Tony touched the thin scar on his cheek and remembered.

Remembered seeing Buck O'Crotty for the first time through the bars of a jail cell.

Part
Four

Buck

1930–1940

TWELVE

Ten-year-old Tony Donovan, the left side of his face swathed in a large, professionally taped bandage, lay on one of the two iron bunks in the jail cell and listened quietly, indifferently, to what he could hear being said in the sheriff's office beyond a nearby open door. Two men were talking. One voice was familiar, one was not.

"Officially, he's a ward of the court," said the familiar voice. That was Sam Patch, the sheriff of Storey County, Nevada. The jail was at the end of Silver Street in Virginia City. "The court left him with me while it decides what to do with him. The boy's lived all his life right here in town; don't seem quite right to send him to the orphanage in Reno, but that's prob'ly what'll end up happening to him." There was a pause and Tony heard Sheriff Patch spit tobacco juice into his cuspidor. Then he continued, "Way things is around here, prob'ly won't nobody apply to adopt him. Times is too hard to take on a extry mouth to feed. Only families that could afford to take him in are rich folks up on the Hill, and they're not really interested in what happens to a miner's kid. Big Jim Delavane's wife Edith— you remember her, don't you?—she's the only one who'd be likely to help, but she's had a breakdown—"

"I didn't know that," said the other voice, the one Tony did not recognize. It sounded surprised.

"Sure," said Patch. "She's in a sanitarium over in Reno. One of them nervous collapses. Big Jim came to the hospital here to see how the boy was doing, but the kid was still unconscious. Maybe Delavane would've offered to help if one of the doctors hadn't told him what Iron Mike's last words was."

"What was that?" the other voice asked.

135

"I ain't exactly sure," Patch admitted. "But it had something to do with Delavane being responsible for what happened to the Donovan family." Tony heard the sheriff spit again, making the cuspidor ring. "Anyhow, ain't nobody else offered any help. The county ain't got no budget to pay for somebody to take him in. Only thing left to do is turn him over to the state."

"Where's the boy at?" asked the voice that Tony did not recognize. He could have gone over and peeked through the open door—his cell was not locked, but he had neither the curiosity nor the interest to find out who it was. Almost lethargic, he was still in a pit of despair over what had happened to his father, mother, and younger sisters. He went into deep fits of depression over it, had nightmares about it, sometimes sat and stared at nothing for hours to keep his mind blank so he would not think about it. A doctor had come up from the asylum in Lovelock and spent a few minutes talking to him, then told Sheriff Patch that Tony was suffering from "moroseness" and "melancholia." He would, the doctor prognosed, "grow out of it as he got older." As far as Tony was concerned, he did not even *care* whether he got older; he felt his life was over.

"He's been using one of the empty cells," Sam Patch said in reply to the unfamiliar voice's question. "I let him take his meals with me and my old woman in that shack out back the county provides us. You want to see him?"

"Yeah, if I could. For a minute or two."

Tony heard footsteps on the rock floor. They stopped just outside his cell. He remained on the cot, facing away from the door, hoping this intruder, whoever he was, would go away. But the footsteps did not resume; the man with the unfamiliar voice waited a moment, then said, "Boy? You awake?"

Tony turned his head around and raised up a little. He saw a short, bulky man looking at him: a man dressed in a cheap gray suit and blue work shirt buttoned at the collar, heavy work shoes with scuffed toes, a snap-brim hat with a dark sweat stain above the band; with a face that looked like a cousin to a cauliflower; with black, kinky, hair turning prematurely gray; with big hands and thick wrists showing below the frayed cuffs of his coat. He was the kind of man who if he didn't have a pint in his pocket, you'd be surprised.

"My name's Buck O'Crotty, boy," he said. "I used to live

over in Silver City. I was a friend of your mother's. And your dad's, of course." His voice had a hint of Sligo in it, but a lot more too, from a lot more places.

Tony said nothing, merely looked at him, giving him the token attention he was required to give an adult, any adult.

"I'm sorry about your folks," Buck said. He cleared his throat and pursed his lips for a moment, weighing words. "I was thinking, maybe I can do something to get you out of here. You know, keep 'em from sending you to that orphanage. What would you say to that?"

"I don't care what they do with me," Tony told him in a sullen voice. His eyes flicked up and down Buck. "You don't look like you'd be much help no how."

Buck's expression darkened. Smart mouth, eh? "Your mother would care what they did with you," he said, "and it's her I'm thinking of. Your dad too." Suddenly he smiled. "Him and me, we was in the Marines together. Sure. Belleau Wood. Blanc Mont. Meuse-Argonne. We was in all the big battles."

Tony just stared silently at him, his left eye squinting from the large dressing on his cheek. He wanted to lie back down; his face hurt less when he was lying down. But he was determined to remain propped up as long as the man named O'Crotty stood there. That turned out not to be long; Buck had very little patience with ungrateful whelps.

"All right, boy. It ain't necessary for us to like one another," he said pragmatically. "I'll go see what I can do for you. Or for your mother and dad, however you want to take it."

After Buck's heavy footsteps passed back into the sheriff's office, Tony laid his head down again. He hoped the man never came back.

Buck went to see the county judge, with negative results. "I appreciate the charity of what you're trying to do, O'Crotty," the judge said. "But the law's the law. The statutes regarding placement of a juvenile ward in Nevada specify that such ward shall be placed in a home with *two* parents." The judge, a wizened old man with purple lips and numerous liver spots, saw the frustration in Buck's face. "I don't make the law," he disclaimed, "I just follow it. Two parents is what it says, two parents is what it'll have to be. Either that or the state orphan asylum."

Leaving the courtroom, disconsolate and irritated, Buck lumbered down C Street to Miners Walk, an unpaved lane leading to Virginia Ciy's subcommunity of shanty frame houses where the miners and their families lived. At the beginning of the Walk, as it was commonly known, stood Callahan's, the same saloon at which Buck had lost to Big Jim Delavane in their legendary poker game. It was now an illegal but wide-open speakeasy. At that time of day, the place was empty and Callahan, still slight and wiry, was polishing pint mugs. As Buck slid onto a shiny, well-worn wooden barstool, Callahan filled one of the mugs from a tap and put it in front of him. "First customer of the day gets one on the house for luck," he said. He had spoken the same phrase every day of his adult life except Sundays for thirty years. Buck pulled a pint bottle from his hip pocket and poured a little whiskey into the beer. Callahan was not offended: Buck had bought the pint from him the previous night, walking in unannounced after ten years, causing Callahan to exclaim, "Jesus, Mary, and Joseph, will you look who's back? The best miner and worst card player the town's ever known." Callahan then did an unprecedented thing: removed his apron, turned the bar over to his wife, and joined Buck at a private table where they drank and Buck told him why he was back.

"So what did his Honor say?" the saloonkeeper now asked.

"Two parents. He said the boy could only be put in a home with two parents."

"Makes sense," Callahan allowed.

"To you, maybe, you've got a wife." A sudden thought occurred to Buck. "Listen, Callahan, you don't suppose—"

"Not on your life," Callahan said, anticipating the question. "My old woman raised five—and barely got through the youngest. I brought a stray pup home one night last year and she wouldn't let *either* of us in." As if to emphasize that the matter was not open to further discussion, he walked down the bar to an Archer table model radio next to the cash register and turned the dial from a sports news broadcast to a recorded music station. Ruth Etting singing "Georgia on My Mind" wafted through the quiet saloon as Callahan walked back complaining about the sports broadcast. "I can't get over that Kraut Schmeling winning the heavy-weight title on a foul. Prizefighting's going to hell in a

handbasket." Back in front of O'Crotty, he paused, grimaced self-consciously, and said, "Look, Bucko, I'd help the
lad if I could. But me and the old woman are barely scraping by as it is. Three of our five are out of work, an' two of
them and their families has moved in with us. Times is hard,
Buck."

"I know, I know," Buck allowed. "It's just that I can't
help thinking about Ruby: how she'd feel knowing her only
son was going to be raised in an orphanage."

"How his father would feel too," Callahan pointed out.
"Iron Mike was a proud man. Up until that last year anyway."

"I've got to do *something*," Buck said, almost as an oath.
His knobby face was set grimly, like a man trying to stop a
car from a collision.

"Bucky, did you ever know a miner named Dewey
Morrell?" Callahan asked casually. Immediately he answered
his own question: "No, you couldn't have. He only came
along about three years ago and you've been gone ten. But
maybe you knew him before. He used to work the digs
down by Minden. Welshman. Married a Paiute woman.
Converted, she was. Anyways, he was killed in a scald
about a year ago, in one of Big Jim Delavane's silver mines.
They hit a pocket of boiling water that caught four men."

Buck nodded absently. "Risky, digging around hot springs."

"Morrell's widow, the Paiute woman, was carrying a kid
at the time. Kid was born after the accident. Little girl.
They live in one of the company shacks down the Walk. The
woman does laundry, and Big Jim, he don't charge no rent
for the shack—"

"Generous," Buck interjected acidly.

"—so they manage, after a fashion. She's skin and bone,
though, not an ounce to spare, and nursing that baby too.
My old woman says it's a miracle her milk ain't dried up,
hard as she works and no more'n she eats."

Buck studied the saloonkeeper. "Are you suggesting
what I think you're suggesting?" he asked Callahan.

The wiry little man shrugged. "It's a solution, Buck."

"What makes you think she'd go for it—even if I would?"

"For the little girl. To get by. Times is hard."

Buck took a long drink from the mug and drummed his
thick, callused fingers audibly on the oak bar. "A marriage
of convenience, they used to call it," he said, as much to
himself as to Callahan.

"Still do. People do what they have to in order to get by. Paper yesterday said nearly a thousand banks have closed this year already. Said more than four million people are out of work. But there's nothing to worry about, we're told; President Hoover, he's taking the bull right by the horns: he's appointed a *committee* to look into unemployment. Meantime, lots of folks are starving. Jesus, did you know that people are going *back* to Ireland? Times is—"

"—is hard," Buck chorused along with him. "If I run into anybody who don't know that yet, I'll send 'em straight here, Callahan. So's you can advise them." He drank the rest of his laced beer in a single long swallow and wiped his mouth with the back of one beefy hand. "How far down the Walk does the Morrell woman live?"

The widow Morrell, Buck found, was lighter than most Paiutes he had seen: she was hawk-brown in color. Pigmentation aside, she was Indian all the way: cheekbones so high and arched they might have had miniature lodge poles under them; fierce eyes that could have stared down a hungry wolf; hair black as a mine tunnel when a lantern failed; angled lips so wide they would have fit a face twice as large. She was not pretty by white standards, nor probably even among Paiutes; at best she was plain; and if her nose had been flat and spread as was common in her tribe, she would have qualified as ugly. She was saved from that by an aquiline nose, which although hooked, somehow served to associate and soften the other elements of her face. She was, as Callahan had warned, painfully thin. Uninhibited in front of Buck, she opened the front of a cruelly threadbare dress and nursed her infant with a pathetic, sagging black-nippled breast that looked like a worn, empty leather glove with but one grotesque finger.

"I know the boy you speak of," she said to Buck, who was sitting across from her at a rickety table on which she had placed a cup of water, all she had to offer. "He must be hurt in his heart."

"Yes," Buck said, thinking briefly of the brooding, unresponsive boy in the jail cell. "The thing of it with me," he continued, "is that I feel I owe his folks this. His father and I were in the war together. And I was very fond of his mother. We wrote letters to one another all the time I was gone. Except this last year . . ." His voice trailed off and for a moment he stared at an unlit kerosene lamp on the table, remembering only he knew what. When he came out of his reverie, the woman was staring hard at him; he had the feeling she was waiting to speak again. "Yes?' he said.

"If you have just returned here, how will you earn money?" she asked. "There are no jobs."

"I'll go to work at the Delavane mine."

"They are not hiring at the Delavane mine. Or any other mine."

"I'll go to work at the Delavane mine," he repeated. "Believe me, I will." He drummed his fingers on her frail table as he had on Callahan's sturdy bar. "I'm sorry, I don't know your name."

"Rosetta," she said. "That is the name given me by the sisters at the reservation school. My own, given me by my father when I was born, is *Pav-ot-zo*. It means 'a woman who dances with a ghost.' My father gave me the name in the hope that I would grow up to be a holy woman of our tribe."

"I see." Buck pursed his lips. Heathen drivel. "And the child, what is her name?"

"She was named 'Kerry' by her father. He chose it before he was killed; it was his mother's name before marriage." The space at the top of Rosetta's nose pinched into a wrinkle. "If we marry, will the child's name have to change?"

"Not if you don't want it to."

"I think it would be good if she kept her blood father's name. He was a good man."

"Most miners are. Some say it's because we're too tired *not* to be good." Buck grinned a tentative grin that was quickly gone. He was suddenly aware, acutely so, of his own shortcomings: unhandsome, awkward except with pick and shovel, uneducated, common as tap water. Certainly no catch, even for a Paiute squaw. "Rosetta," he said, thinking to get things straight right off, "I want you to understand that it ain't my intent to take your late husband's place. That is, I don't expect you to, ah—" Son of a bitch, he thought irritably. Why did these things have to be spoken? "What I mean to say is, I'll not, ah, force myself on you even though I'll have legal right to do so. I'm a decent man, if I do say so myself, and I'll treat you like a decent woman. The thing is, I want to provide a good home for the Donovan boy, and if you'll help me to do that, well, I'll ask nothing else of you." He leaned forward a few inches over the table, as if to be sure he would hear her next words. "Is it a bargain?" he asked.

"Yes," Rosetta Morrell replied quietly, and somehow with dignity despite her emaciation, poverty, and pitiful, exposed breast, "it is a bargain."

"Good." Sitting back, Buck nodded curtly. His eyes sparkled as his mind danced with plans. "I'll bring a justice of the peace around tomorrow to do it up legal. Meanwhile, I'll find us a decent place to live—no offense, you understand—by decent I mean a little better. I'll get that job too. Oh, here," he said, rising and fishing in his trousers pocket. He put a few greenbacks on the table. "I'll be wanting plenty of milk in the house. Between the little one and me and the boy, we'll likely need a gallon a day. Ah, you might want to pick up a dress for yourself, you know, for tomorrow. I'll have my suit cleaned and pressed in the morning, and I think I've got a necktie somewhere in my grip satchel. Well, I'm off. Good day to you, Rosetta."

"Good day to you, Mr. O'Crotty." She lowered her glance to the table, to the money. "And thank you."

Buck mumbled an embarrassed "You're welcome," as he hurried out the door.

Big Jim Delavane looked like a man whose likeness should be on stock certificates, or outside a movie house. Hair slicked straight back as if painted on, chiseled chin devoid of beard shadow due to two hot-lather shaves a day, teeth naturally white as a mother-of-pearl seashell, as white as the starched collar around his neck, as white as the pellicle of his manicured fingernails; he was immaculate. But when he looked up from his desk at Buck O'Crotty in the doorway of his office, that handsome face was drawn and gray. He was clearly a man laced with worry.

"Hello, Buck," he said quietly, rising. "Been a long time."

"That it has, Jim," said Buck. He remained just inside the doorway.

The two men studied each other. The last time they'd been together, really together, had been across the poker table at Callahan's when Jim won everything and Buck lost everything. Over that time had fallen the shadow of Buck catching Jim with Ruby. They'd seen each other now and

again, of course, in the two months before Buck had finally
left; Buck had been there the morning Jim hired Mike
Donovan out of the Empire Mine day crew; aside from that,
there had been no occasion when they were close enough to
speak, or even not speak, which was just as well. They
would have come to blows, the matter of Ruby was so
tender. Not so now. Ten years was a long time. Priorities
changed.

"I heard about Edith's breakdown," Buck said. "I'm sorry.
Is she going to be all right?"

"The doctors think so, yes," Jim replied. "She'll need a
long rest, of course. She was involved in so many social and
charitable causes, she wore herself out; then when she heard
what happened to the Donovan family, why, it was more
than she could stand."

Buck nodded. "You have a little girl now, I hear," he
said.

"Francie, yes," said Delavane, and his expression bright-
ened a touch. "She's not exactly little anymore, half grown
is more like it. A perfect young lady, just like her mother.
Here, look at this." Big Jim turned to the credenza for a
silver-framed photograph of a girl Tony Donovan's age. He
held it across the desk and Buck walked forward to take it.
The gesture saved them both from having to shake hands.

"She's a beauty," Buck said. "Favors her mother, all
right. God is merciful, after all."

"*You* haven't changed," Big Jim said in mock reproach,
taking back the photograph. He crossed the office to an
elaborate mirrored bar built into one wall. "Drink?" he
asked, opening a decanter, pulling forth two lead crystal
glasses.

"You go ahead," Buck said. "I've my own." He pulled
the pint bottle from his hip pocket. Big Jim smiled inwardly,
knowingly, and pushed one of the glasses away.

"I heard you were back, Buck," the mine owner said,
returning to his big leather-covered chair behind the desk,
gesturing for O'Crotty to sit. "Been to see the judge about
the Donovan boy, somebody said."

"Yes, that's right."

"Damn shame about Mike and Ruby and those little girls.
Tragic." Big Jim drummed his fingers on the desk. "Have
you been to see the boy yet?"

"Yes. Once."

"Did he say anything?"

Buck raised his eyebrows innocently. "How do you mean?"

"About what happened. What he remembers."

"No," Buck said honestly, shaking his head. "He's not mentioned what happened." Sheriff Sam Patch had, Buck thought. But nothing would be gained by bringing that up. Buck would learn soon enough whether Big Jim Delavane was in any way responsible for the Donovan family tragedy. In the meantime, he did not want to compromise the purpose of his visit.

Without offering Buck one, Delavane took a cigar from his desktop humidor. "I'd like to do something for the boy," he said. "Perhaps start a fund of some kind—"

"It's my intent to take care of the boy," Buck declared. "He won't need any fund. I'll raise him, give him a good home. But I'll have to have a job to do it. I came to get one from you."

Big Jim grimaced. "Be easier if you asked me for blood, Buck. I'm down to skeleton crews, working just enough men to keep the stope from molding on me. We're barely pulling enough ore out to justify processing; what silver we are purifying, why hellfire, we practically have to give it away. The economy's wrecked, Buck." Delavane took a swallow of scotch. "Like I said, I could give you my blood easier than I can give you a job."

"I don't need your blood, Jim," the visitor said quietly. "I had enough of that all over me at Soissons. Remember Soissons, Jim?"

Delavane's eyes narrowed slightly, knowingly. He had wondered if that was going to be brought up.

"It was at Soissons that they finally sent us some tanks to fight the war with," Buck reminded him. "We could've used them at Belleau Wood, to get through that goddamned barbed wire, but we didn't have them then. We didn't have them until Soissons." Buck smiled. "God, we were green when it came to tank-infantry tactics. Nobody realized that the tanker Marines couldn't *see* into the trenches, and the footslogger Marines couldn't *hear* the tanks behind the trenches because of the bombardment noise. I'll never forget you climbing up out of that trench, blowing your whistle to charge, taking a Hun bullet in the leg just as that tank was bearing down on you from behind." Buck paused enough for dramatic effect, then added, "I only got you pulled out of its way by inches."

Big Jim's expression had become patiently resigned during the story. He had known it might be related, used, drawn on like an old bank account; both he and Buck knew he had no recourse but to listen to it. On Buck's part, he had promised himself a decade earlier that he would *never* use the story; he wanted Big Jim Delavane to owe him until the day one of them died. But promises made to oneself are the easiest to break, even in the strongest of men, and Buck felt he had to break his now. There were higher debts to be paid than to oneself "Calling in your marker, Buck?" Big Jim asked softly.

Buck nodded curtly. "Exactly."

The mine owner took another sip of his scotch. "What job do you want, Bucky? Shift foreman? Mine super?" He smiled a humorless smile. "Maybe you'd like my job?"

"Just an ordinary job, thanks. Mucker. Hauler. Hoister. Nothing fancy. Honest labor."

"What have you been doing?"

"Powder monkey in the coal fields back in West Virginia."

Big Jim's eyes hardened just a touch. "Lot of union organizing going on back there, I hear."

"Quite a bit, yes."

"Never had a union in my mines," Delavane said, and his words hung as if incompleted. Or as if he expected Buck to comment. Buck remained silent. "Unions can cause a lot of trouble," Big Jim added at last.

"They can indeed," O'Crotty said. Particularly if they're run properly, he thought slyly. But Big Jim Delavane would learn that soon enough, firsthand.

"All right, Buck. You'll be backup powder monkey in the new digs. Report to Dutch Coy at the black powder shed on Monday—"

"You're still using black powder?" Buck asked in surprise. "With all its toxic fumes? They use gelatin dynamite back east."

"This isn't 'back east,' " Big Jim said flatly.

They locked eyes in an instant of understanding. Not agreement, merely understanding: of the new rules that had been established now that they were square. Ask nothing for free, give nothing for free. Buck nodded curtly.

"Right."

Buck rose, returned the bottle to his pocket, put on his hat, and touched the brim with his forefinger—the laborer's age-old salute to his boss.

As they had not upon meeting, they did not shake hands on parting.

When Buck went to get Tony at the jail, Sheriff Sam Patch took a cardboard box from behind his desk. "These here are clothes for the boy that some of the ladies on the Hill collected. He ain't got much of his own."

As Buck reached to accept the box, Tony, standing beside him, said, "I don't want it. I don't want nothing from the Hill."

"They're just clothes, lad," Buck said quietly. "Pieces of cloth. They've no memory, no loyalties—"

"I don't want them," Tony insisted. "I won't wear them. I won't wear nothing that came from the Hill."

Buck stood awkwardly holding the box for a moment, studying Tony Donovan, thinking, weighing, considering. He thought it important to establish his authority over the boy, to assert at the outset who was to be the boss, the head of the house, the parent—or at least the replacement for the parent. He sensed in Tony a hardheadedness that he instinctively laid to the influence of Iron Mike Donovan, but upon second thought decided had probably come from Ruby. She more than Iron Mike would have been the strong one of the match. With Mike it was façade and muscle: the image of a mighty young bull of a Marine running across No Man's Land with a mortar under one arm, a machine gun under the other . . . that day in Belleau Wood when he had been called "Iron Mike" for the first time. But those who knew him were aware that underneath his surface of strength and sinew, there was gentleness and graciousness.

No, the deep toughness, the deep stubbornness, that Buck saw in young Tony would have had to come from Ruby. How could he not have realized that at once? Buck wondered. Didn't he remember the obvious about Ruby Surrett: her confidence, her directness, her simple awareness of self that stood her out from other women? Ruby the sassy, Ruby the smart, Ruby the sure: how could he have forgotten even for a moment? s-0In afternoon bonnet, evening shawl, or nurse's cap, she was the same Ruby, the same woman, the same *person*. It was Ruby's pride that Buck saw now in her son, tinged though it might be with obstinacy and defiance.

Buck O'Crotty was not a man to step on such pride. Carefully he set the box of charity clothes on Sam Patch's desk. "No offense, Sheriff, but the lad doesn't want them." He started to put an arm around Tony's shoulders, thought better of it, and said simply, "Let's go, then."

As they turned to leave, the jail door opened and Big Jim Delavane walked in. Behind him came the liver-spotted old judge who had required Buck to find a wife. The sheriff, Buck, and Tony all froze, as if petrified by the sudden appearance of the two men. Delavane, immaculate in a fine suit and white broadcloth shirt, did not, Buck noticed, look as drawn and worried as he had in his office. Now he looked like the old Jim Delavane: quick, crafty—even dangerous.

"Tell them, Judge," the mine owner said.

"There's been another offer to adopt the boy," the old judge said. "From Mr. Delavane and his wife—"

"But I've already been given custody," Buck protested.

"Final papers haven't been processed yet," the judge said. "Until they have, it's the court's responsibility to consider any alternative that might be in the minor's best interest."

"What is this, Jim?" Buck demanded. "What are you trying to pull?"

"I'm not trying to 'pull' anything," Delavane replied evenly. "I'm merely trying to do the same thing you are, Buck—give the boy a decent home. Ruby and Iron Mike were my friends too, remember."

Staring at him, Buck wondered: *Jesus, does he know*? Buck glanced at Tony; the boy's eyes were downcast, shunning them all. Tony didn't know, Buck was certain of that. But Jim . . .? Buck recalled Ruby's letter of long ago: *Promise you'll never tell Jim that the baby is his.* Letting Jim Delavane have Tony now, Buck decided, would be the same as breaking that promise to Ruby. He turned to the judge.

"You say an offer to adopt has come from Mr. Delavane and his wife. I'm under the impression that Mr. Delavane's wife is presenty in a sanitarium."

"Only temporarily," Big Jim said. His jaw clenched slightly.

"Is there a doctor's statement to that effect, Judge?" Buck asked.

"The court will take Mr. Delavane's word for it."

"I won't," Buck stated. "The law requires a home with

two parents. You told me that yourself, Judge. If you ignore that now, I'll go to the state court in Reno and challenge it."

Glancing at Big Jim, the judge wet his purple lips. "We, ah, are only interested in what's best for the boy—"

"Why not let the boy decide then?" Sheriff Sam Patch asked. Everyone looked at him. Patch shrugged. "Makes sense to me. Boy this age, if he ain't happy where you put him, he's liable to run away. Go off on his own, take to stealing and such. Seems to me if you let him decide who he wants to live with, might save a bunch of trouble down the road."

"Would you agree to let the boy decide, Mr. Delavane?" the judge asked.

Delavane's eyes flicked over the shabbily dressed, injured boy. "All right," he said. Stepping over to Tony, he asked, "How'd you like to come live up on the Hill with me, young fellow? Have your own room, new clothes, maybe even a pony to ride?"

Tony did not answer or look up.

"You agree, O'Crotty?" the judge asked. "Leave it up to the boy?"

"Sure," Buck replied. He was taking a chance. The lad didn't like him much. But he liked the Hill even less. "With me," he said to Tony, "it's a cot in the kitchen on Miners Walk. And no pony."

The judge put a hand on Tony's shoulder. "Well, son, it's up to you."

Tony twisted his shoulder from under the judge's hand. Looking up, he glared coldly at Big Jim Delavane.

And stepped over next to Buck O'Crotty.

Tony kept step beside Buck down an early-evening-deserted C Street, neither of them saying anything until they turned into rutted, uneven Miners Walk. Then Buck broke the silence.

"The house I've rented ain't too far down the Walk."

"Is it a company house?" Tony asked.

Buck did not lie to him. "As a matter of fact, yes. It's on a row of houses owned by the mine."

"A Delavane house," the boy said. He spoke the name "Delavane" as if it were an obscenity.

"In a manner of speaking. But my house as long as I pay the rent."

Tony was quiet for several minutes, trudging along with chin against chest, eyes downcast, young lips compressed as Buck sensed that the anger and hurt inside him were just as compressed. Presently, without preliminaries, Tony said, "I hate Big Jim Delavane. Someday I'm gonna kill him."

"That's a serious statement," Buck said. "Why d'you hate him so?"

"It's his fault what happened to my folks. He's to blame for it. I'm gonna kill him for it someday."

Without breaking stride, Buck and the boy looked at each other for a quick, hard moment. Buck said quietly, "You'll have to tell me why you feel that way, lad. If I agree with what you say, by God, I'll help you do it."

Tony nodded curtly, making a pact from deep within himself. It was the first time he had trusted another human being since the terrible night of his loss. But for some reason, he trusted Buck O'Crotty.

Man and boy continued down the dreary street toward their new lives.

THIRTEEN

A year after Buck O'Crotty returned to Virginia City, he rode the hoist up from the mine one evening at shift's end and was stopped by the timekeeper as he got off. "O'Crotty," the timekeeper said, "Mr. Delavane wants to see you in his office."

"Me?" said O'Crotty, surprised. Except for the meeting at which Delavane gave him the job and the haggling over Tony's custody, Buck had not seen or spoken to the mine owner since coming back.

The timekeeper, a wisp of a man who wore a celluloid collar, and garters on his shirt sleeves, had an obnoxious smirk on his face. "Maybe your union organizing has caught up with you," he said, affecting a confidential tone. He tapped a page on his clipboard that listed all the men who had worked the shift just ended. "Maybe I won't have to type your name on my list after today. Can't say I'd mind. Never liked names with apostrophes in them, a needless extra shift of the typewriter keys." The smirk deepened. "You probably don't know what I'm talking about, do you, O'Crotty?"

"Not me," said Buck. "I'm just a common hardrock miner; don't know nothing about typewriting or—what was it you called it, an 'apostrophe'? Is that the little mark between the O and the C in my name? I'll be damned. Interesting word. Probably taken from the Greek word *apostrophos*, to be used in the possessive case in Irish names, meaning I've descended from the original Crotty clan." Buck smiled at the dumbstruck look that spread over the timekeeper's face. "As for typing, you and me we ought to have a speed and accuracy contest sometime. It's me that types all the union material that gets handed out, after it's mimeographed, you know? You're familiar with the mimeograph, aren't you? It's a duplicating machine that works on the principle of passing ink through a stencil. Do you know what a stencil is? A stencil—"

The timekeeper, his face becoming angry red, turned and stalked away from Buck O'Crotty. Feeling thoroughly mischievous, Buck fell back in with the line of men walking away from the mine. He was delighted with himself; the timekeeper was a sour, hairsplitting man who never gave a miner the benefit of the doubt over a minute of working time or a nickel in wages. It was men like him, to Buck's mind, that made labor unions absolutely essential.

The line of men reached a point where it began, erratically, to break off into two: the one, family men, moving toward the road that led to Miners Walk and home; the other, bachelors, heading for the wash trough to rid themselves of some of their underground dirt before going on to Callahan's speakeasy for a pint or a shot to start the evening. There were always a few from each group that intermingled with the other, but for the most part the division was markedly matrimonial. Buck usually walked with the family men, but tonight he fell out with the others. At the trough, a long, shallow tin tub with a dozen water hydrants spaced at intervals behind it, he took some good-natured ribbing.

"Has Rosetta thrown you out, Buck?" one asked solemnly.

"He's just celebratin'," another chimed in. "He learned the difference between the powder and the fuse today. The man's very quick."

"Leave him be, for God's sake," came a mock plea from someone else. "Can't you see he's pining away for those fine coal mines he left back in West Virginia."

Buck washed his face and hands, taking what they handed out without retort, until they were finished, and then he said, "For your information, gentlemen, I've been summoned to the office of his lordship, Big Jim Delavane. I'm certain it's for the purpose of making me a partner in the mine, in which case I'll be discharging the lot of you first thing tomorrow."

An immediate somberness came over the group at the news that Buck had been called to Big Jim's office. "Is it the union business, Buck?" one of the men asked.

"I don't know," Buck replied. "Good chance, I guess." Pulling a blue bandanna from his hip pocket, he dried himself.

"What'll you do if he fires you, Buck?" another asked.

"Get along somehow. I was looking for a job when I came here, you know."

"Maybe he's after warning you, Buck. Maybe he just wants you to stop organizing."

Buck smiled. "The union can't be stopped, men. The union is a necessary thing. An important thing. Getting rid of one man can't stop it." He threw them a wink. "Remember that. One man don't make a union; it takes all of us."

As Buck walked away, someone yelled after him, "Stop by Callahan's, Buck, and let us know."

"Sure," he said, and waved without looking back. He smiled. They were concerned now, and that was as it should be. He was their leader and one by one they had begun first to accept it, then to acknowledge it openly. Soon, enough of them would be on his side—a two-thirds majority, he wanted, sixty-seven percent—to write back east to the national headquarters of the United Mine Workers and request an official charter for a state union. He had already picked out a name for it: the Amalgamated Mine Workers of Nevada. Buck O'Crotty, president. After the requisite election, of course.

Feeling good, feeling chipper, a little more bounce than usual in his naturally quick step, he crossed a big open yard to a dirty white two-story frame building with letters painted in black above its entrance: DELAVANE MINES. As always when he saw that sign, Buck experienced an involuntary but irrepressible thought: There but for the turn of a card—

It was a thought he dismissed from his mind immediately. The part is the past, he told himself by rote. Over and done with. Today's what matters. And tomorrow.

As Buck was shown into Big Jim Delavane's office, the mine owner looked up from some papers on his desk and said, a little irritably, "You took your sweet time getting here, Buck. Shift ended twenty minutes ago."

"I thought maybe you was inviting me in for tea, so I went and washed up," Buck replied blandly.

"Sit down," Delavane said.

Buck glanced down at the underground garb he still wore. "You're sure?"

"The chairs are leather; they'll wipe clean."

"You're the boss." Buck noticed Big Jim glance suspiciously at him, looking for the sarcasm, the double meaning, but Buck's tone had been flawlessly neutral. It was a tone he had learned at the side of a bushy-browed Welsh coal miner's son named John L. Lewis.

Finding nothing obvious in the words for which to rebuff O'Crotty, Delavane leaned forward and clasped his hands together like a schoolteacher. "Buck, how'd you like to be my mine super?"

"I'd like it fine," Buck replied frankly. "Be a fool not to."

"I've made up my mind to get rid of Pete Hasselmann," Big Jim said. "He's a good man in his own way, but he can't seem to handle that bunch of shanty Irishmen that make up the bulk of the crew. He throws orders around like some kraut field marshal and those micks down in the stope start slowing down their work. Not so's you'd notice, mind you, but enough to show up on the month-end production report. Hasselmann's got to go, that's all there is to it."

"I understand." Buck's mind was racing. Mine superintendent. The job would double his income and halve the time he had to spend underground. But what price would Big Jim expect to extract in return? A cessation of union activities? Surely Jim was not fool enough to think he could ask that and get it.

Was it possible, Buck wondered, that the mine owner simply *needed* him? Buck knew that in the last two years there had been four superintendents at Delavane Mines, none of them lasting more than eight months. There was an ongoing joke down in the stope about who was going to be superintendent tomorrow; every time a man dug or hauled or hoisted a little extra ore, someone invariably remarked sagely, "There's our next mine superintendent." But Buck knew it would not be humorous to Big Jim. The quality of a mine superintendent could make or break the digs he oversaw, because it depended on him and his relationship with the men whether they simply put in a ten-hour shift or whether they *worked* a ten-hour shift.

There was a very good chance, Buck decided, that Jim Delavane was trying to achieve two goals at once: get the best man to run the labor force for him—and there was no doubt in either of their minds that Buck was the best—and curb Buck's union activities by sheer infusion of responsibility. Perhaps he also hoped to dampen Buck's enthusiasm by the arousal of old loyalties: their youthful years together in the mines, their training together in the Marines, their fighting together in the trenches. Buck wanted the job, but he had to be extremely careful about the terms on which he took it.

"The job's yours if you want it," Big Jim said, sitting back and taking a cheroot from a leather case in his vest pocket. He turned it around between his lips several times before lighting it. "I'll pay you thirty-five a week plus a five percent bonus on everything that exceeds the diggings for the same month the previous year."

"What conditions go with the job?" Buck asked.

Delavane smiled his handsome smile. "No conditions, Buck. I'm not trying to handle you. I just need a good mine super." Unclasping his hands, Delavane leaned back in his big chair. "Look, Bucky, the past is the past. I figure you and I are even-up all the way around. The thing with Ruby, with the game at Callahan's, with young Tony: it's all gone by. Maybe we can be friends again, maybe not, but we don't have to be enemies. Like I said, I need a good mine super." He was being sincere, to a point. He did need Buck. At the same time, if he could diffuse some of Buck's union activities, well—

"If I took the job," Buck asked, avoiding the issues of the past, "would I be permitted to pick my own foremen?"

"Sure."

Buck pursed his lips. "That timekeeper you've got, Jim; he's a nasty sort. None of the men like him much."

Delavane shrugged. "I'll fire him along with Hasselmann. Timekeepers are easy to find."

Buck drummed silent fingers on his coverall leg. This was too easy. "Are you aware, Jim, how close we are to qualifying for a union charter?"

"I know you've been working at it. I assumed you were having some degree of success."

"We're practically on the brink."

"There's still the matter of a formal vote," Delavane said with quiet confidence. "What a man says in public and how he votes in private are sometimes as different as mud and rock. Right now the men in my mines have just one top boss—me. If they vote to start a union, they know they'll have *two* top bosses—me and the man they elect president of their local. That's too much for a lot of them to deal with. I frankly don't think you'll get the numbers you need. At any rate, I didn't call you here to debate a union. Do I fire Hasselmann or don't I?" Delavane smiled around the cheroot. "He's got a nice comfortable office just down the hall. I can have the name on the door changed in an hour."

Sudden inspiration struck Buck O'Crotty. "That timekeeper," he said as casually as possible, "has a nice office too, I noticed. Across the hall. Gets the morning sun, I'll bet."

Delavane's handsome features radiated confidence. "Take that one then, I don't care."

"It doesn't matter to you?"

"Where you have your office is up to you, Buck. I just want to be able to announce in the morning that you're my new mine super. Do we have a deal?"

"We do indeed," Buck said. "I'll take the job."

This time Big Jim did offer to shake, and as Buck rose to take the extended hand, he could not help feeling surprised at how easily he had outsmarted the mine owner.

You won't be smiling tomorrow, Jim, he thought.

* * *

When Buck got home that night, he said to Rosetta, "I'll be mine superintendent starting tomorrow, Mrs. O'Crotty. That'll mean an increase in your household allowance. New shoes for everybody in the house too, I think. And you might price one of them washing machines with the automatic wringer."

Tony, who had just brought in an armload of firewood, dropped it loudly into the wood box and glared at Buck. Rosetta had not had time to respond to Buck's good news before the noise made them both turn toward Tony. "What is it, Tony?" Rosetta asked. "Did you get a splinter?"

"I didn't get a splinter," he replied. Returning to the back door, he left the kitchen saying, "I don't want no new shoes either!" and slammed the door behind him.

"Tony—" Rosetta started to hurry after him, but Buck stopped her.

"Leave him be. He hates Jim Delavane too much to be reasoned with for now. He thinks I've changed sides. He'll find out he's wrong."

Buck let Tony seethe overnight and all the next day, meanwhile putting in his first day as new mine super, and attending to his office as Delavane had agreed he could. After supper that evening, Buck said, "Come on lad, I need help tonight with some circulars." Walking uptown together, Buck had asked, "Sore at me, are you?" Tony, sullen, head down, hands jammed into the pockets of his corduroy knickers, shrugged tightly. Buck smiled. "Well, you shouldn't be. Let me tell you what I've done."

Buck recited the details of his conversation with Big Jim Delavane and how he came to accept the mine superintendent job. Then he explained to Tony what he had done that morning about the location of the mine superintendent's office.

"Never judge too quickly," Buck stressed when he finished his story, "and never judge at all unless you're sure you have all the facts."

At a rented storefront on C Street, they found Edith Delavane supervising the painting of a huge banner stretched around three walls that carried the name and slogan of a popular anti-gambling movement: DON'T LEGALIZE CRIME. Edith was paler than she should have been, and slightly too thin; she had been back from the sanitarium seven months, and the D.L.C. movement was the first cause in which she had become active since recovering from her nervous break-down. Buck and others in the group tried to keep her from doing too much, but it was difficult; Edith Delavane was dedicated.

When Edith saw Buck and Tony enter, she made her way through a cluster of tables at which volunteers were doing a variety of work to come over to them. After a brief smile and cursory pat on the head for Tony, she took Buck's arm and led him a few steps away.

"My God, Buck, Jim was livid when he came home tonight," she said, not quietly enough to prevent Tony from hearing. "I thought he was going to have a stroke." Tony noticed that Edith's hand was still on Buck's arm. "What you did about the location of your mine superintendent's office was a complete surprise."

Buck patted her hand fondly. "I thought it would be." Glancing around, he saw Francie sitting on a bench by the wall, cutting paper dolls out of a book. "Tony, sit with Francie for a bit. I'll holler when I want you." Tony looked annoyed but did as he was told. He sat on the end of the bench, as far as possible from the Delavane girl.

Frances Grace Delavane was the same age as Tony; they had been in the same class at Comstock Elementary School since first grade, but until recently they had never spoken. Edith Delavane brought her daughter to the D.L.C. office, as she had once taken her on other charitable and civic missions, because she did not believe in leaving the girl in the care of servants. Tony knew that Big Jim Delavane objected; he had overheard Buck and Edith speak quietly of it; so in one respect he was always glad to see Francie there because he knew Big Jim would not like it, but Tony himself was not keen about having to associate with the girl. He never initiated conversation with her. She never failed to initiate conversation with him. On this night, she asked, outrageously, "Want to cut out paper dolls with me?"

Tony looked at her with the utter repugnance that only an eleven-year-old boy can muster. "Boys don't play with paper dolls," he replied with cold disdain.

"Some boys do."

Tony looked away. "Not any I know."

Francie remained quiet for a few minutes, seeming to concentrate on using her rounded scissors to carefully cut out a paper dress with little white tabs on its edges which, when folded, would hold the dress on a cardboard figure. As she worked, she glanced from time to time at Tony Donovan, studying his moody young face, scary black eyes, tousled, almost shaggy hair, and the somehow not unattractive scar that lined his cheek. She knew little about him. Despite accompanying her mother at times, she was insulated up on the Hill with her music lessons, French lessons, etiquette lessons; limited in her social exposure to the other children who lived on the Hill, and exposed to town children only at school because her mother, a former teacher, insisted that a public school education, at least through elementary grades, was preferable to boarding school.

Francie knew that Tony was in her grade; he was one of the boys with whom young girls from the Hill were not encouraged to associate. Francie's mother, however, had told her to "be nice to the boy, dear, because he's had quite a bad time of it." Francie had heard about the deaths of the Donovan family, and knew that Tony had been in the hospital for a while, but that was the extent of her knowledge about him. She and Tony had been casually thrown together several times since Edith Delavane had become active in the movement to prevent gambling from becoming legalized in Nevada.

Buck O'Crotty had belonged to the movement from the start; he was the first to support establishment of a Virginia City branch of the organization, which had begun in Carson City and spread rapidly throughout the state. Edith Delavane's reason for joining the D.L.C. was moral; she felt that general community standards could never be raised if gambling legally became widespread. Buck's motivation was more practical; to him, gambling would just be another way of picking the working man's pocket. Never strictly illegal in Nevada, like the production and sale of liquor was nationally, gambling was tacitly permitted in most communities because there was no specific statute against it. In neighboring, Mormon-controlled Utah, of which Nevada had once been a part, gambling was officially a "crime," and so it was considered by the many Nevadans who opposed it. Thus the movement's slogan: Don't Legalize Crime.

"My daddy is very angry at your father," Francie said after a while, looking up from her paper dolls.

"At who?" Tony asked.

"Him" she said pointing at Buck. "Your father."

"He's not my father" Tony said. "When are you gonna get that through your head?"

Francie shrugged. "Whoever he is, my daddy is very angry at him."

"Too bad about your daddy," Tony said. "There's nothing he can do about it. Buck turned the tables on Mr. Big Jim Delavane, the bigshot mine owner."

"How did he do that?" Francie asked guilelessly.

Tony turned and straddled the bench, facing her. "I'll tell you how he done it. By getting the better of him, that's how." Buck's earlier explanation was still fresh in Tony's mind. "Your old man knows Buck is trying to start a miners' union, see. So he decided to give Buck a promotion to mine superintendent, so's it'd look to the miners like Buck was on his side instead of theirs. He was gonna have Buck move into a fancy office over there where he's got his own fancy office. But Buck fast-talked him and got him to say that Buck could' have his office anywhere he wanted. So this morning, Buck cleans out a corner of the tool shed next to the main mine shaft and has the old mine superintendent's desk moved over there. Now Buck's got the mine superintendent's job but the men know he ain't joined up with your old man." Tony jabbed a stiff forefinger at the girl. "That's why your old man's so fried. Big Jim Delavane got outsmarted for once!"

Looking down again, Francie resumed manipulating her paper dolls, dressing and undressing them from what was now an extensive wardrobe of carefully cut, white-tabbed costumes. The vindictive finger punctuating Tony's last words, along with his tone, told her that he too, like the man named Buck O'Crotty, for some reason disliked her father. When she was certain Tony had finished what he wanted to say, Francie sighed quietly and said, "I wonder why everyone calls my daddy 'Big Jim.' He's not fat at all, like the janitor at school is. He's not bigger than the fathers of any of my girlfriends. He's not really any bigger than Mr. O'Crotty, except maybe a little taller. Why does everyone call him big?"

Tony stared at her incredulously. How, he wondered, could any one person be so stupid and dumb. This girl belonged in the loony bin down in Lovelock.

"Well?" she asked, raising her face to look directly at

him. He did not notice that her soft gray eyes had hardened a touch.

"Well what?"

"Well, can you tell me or can't you? Why does everyone call my daddy 'Big Jim'?"

"Because he owns the mine, that's why."

"Mr. Ed McLaughlin owns a mine," she pointed out. "So does Mr. Pete Ambrose. But people don't call them 'Big Ed' or 'Big Pete.' "

"So?" Tony said in exasperation. This girl was a *fruitcake*.

"So what makes my daddy different?" she asked, refusing to let go, riveting her eyes to his face without a blink. "You don't know, do you?" she challenged. Tony finally had to turn away from her penetrating glare. "You're not very bright," she said after a moment, her voice somehow different, not as little-girlish as before. "My daddy is called 'Big Jim' because he's the most *powerful* man in Virginia City. He's got more influence than anybody else. It isn't very smart to get someone who is powerful and influential angry at you. You might try and remember that, boy."

Red-faced from mortification, Tony Donovan got up and walked away.

For nearly a year afterward, Tony carried almost as intense a hatred for Francie Delavane as he did for her father. She was, to Tony, as much the epitome of the snobbish, bratty Hill kids as Big Jim was of the uncaring, money-mongering mine owners. Both were despicable to Tony. In school he purposely took a desk as far away from Francie as possible, and for months went to great lengths never to pass her in the hall, never to enter or leave school at the same time she did, never to allow himself to be anyplace where he would have to meet her eyes or for any reason speak to her. When fifth grade was over in the spring, one of the immense reliefs of Tony Donvan's young life was that he would not have to see Francie Delavane's face for an entire summer. It was an irony of fate that seeing Francie every day would be replaced by seeing her father.

When Tony went looking for a job that summer, he was hired as a bus boy in the dining room of the Ormsby House, where it was Big Jim Delavane's custom to have lunch almost daily. Frequently joining him at his private table was Harmon Coltrane, the leading Virginia City banker and a

staunch advocate of legalized gambling in Nevada. Tony
was clearing dishes from an adjoining table on the day the
state legislature was scheduled to vote on the bill.

"Shouldn't be long now," Tony heard Coltrane say. He
looked at an ornate gold pocket watch as the men waited for
dessert.

"Can't be too soon for me," Big Jim said."Christ, the
way these D.L.C. people have been trying to block it, you'd
think we were trying to legalize sodomy. Fanatics, the lot of
them," he forced a tight smile, "my wife included sometimes."

"Nonsense" Coltrane said at once."Edith's only doing
what she feels is right, what on the surface *looks* right.
Trouble with the D.L.C. people is that they don't understand economics. These are people who either save their
pennies in milk bottles or, like Edith, have someone such as
you to provide for them and therefore don't have to worry
about pecuniary matters. Unfortunately, when it comes to
money, very few people understand that it's the *movement*
of it that counts, not the accumulation. Legalized gambling
will move dollars around this state like they've got wheels
on them."

While he was listening to Coltrane, Big Jim glanced over
at Tony. Their eyes met in a moment of recognition. Tony
continued doing his work, although now with the feeling
that the mine owner was watching him curiously. Bastard,
he thought. Trying to make up with a goddamned pony for
what you did. I'll get you, someday, you son of a bitch.
Glancing up, he saw that Delavane had turned back to
Harmon Coltrane.

"Do you think the entire legislative package will pass?"
Big Jim asked Coltrane, ignoring Tony. "Including the new
residency law?"

"Definitely," the banker assured him. "Those fellows
down in Carson City know that if the state doesn't establish
some kind of decent tax base, we might as well become part
of Utah again. We can't do it with real estate because the
federal government still owns ninety percent of the land
inside our borders. No, we've got to bring revenue in from
outside the state. That six-week residency requirement will
do it. Reno will be the marriage-and-divorce capital of the
country in no time at all. And with people having the
opportunity to gamble while they're here—well, Christ, can
you think of a better combination? I can't. Unless you

QUICK SILVER   161

throw in some good-looking young whores for the men."
Coltrane laughed heartily at his own humor, while Delavane
merely smiled.

When Tony had the adjoining table cleared and the dirty
dishes stacked on his tray, he carried it back to the kitchen
and set it on the dishwashing counter. Taking a fresh, crisp
white tablecloth from the linen pantry, he returned to the
cleared table and began removing the soiled cloth. He took
his time, ears cocked.

"Speaking of whores," Delavane said, "what do you
think will happen to that prostitution amendment?"

"God only knows," Coltrane replied with a wave of
dismissal. "I don't think the legislators will go so far as to
legalize whores. Damn sure wish they would, but I don't
think they've got the gonads. Rernember, they have to go
home to their wives after they vote. Tell you the truth, I
don't know what the hell they'll do with that one." He
looked at his watch again. "We should have all the answers
by the time we finish dessert; I've got my secretary over at
Western Union waiting for a wire from our man at the state
house." A waiter brought each of the men a slice of lemon
meringue pie. "Has Edith indicated what the D.L.C.-ers
plan to do once gambling comes out into the open?"

Delavane shook his head. "Only that they'll oppose any
casinos on C Street. They want to restrict them to D Street
and beyond, with the brothels. Segregate the illicit, Edith
calls it."

Coltrane shook his head vigorously. "Can't be done," he
said around a mouthful of pie. "Legal is legal. Casinos will
have just as much right on C Street as hardware stores or
beauty parlors." Through the restaurant window Tony saw a
marching band followed by a parade of cheering people
moving down C Street.

"Looks like the news is in," Harmon Coltrane said. As
he spoke, his secretary, a young woman in a fashionable
flapper dress that barely reached her knees, came hurrying
in to hand him a telegram. "Thank you, Elsie," he said,
winking at Big Jim as he gave her a playful pinch on her
fleshy upper arm. "Let's see now"—his eyes scanned the
wire—"looks like a clean sweep, Jim. Six-week residency
for divorce, passed; no waiting for marriage licenses, passed;
open gambling—they refer to it as 'gaming'—passed; prostitution bill *didn't* pass as drafted, but was amended to allow

each county to decide for itself whether it wants brothels. That's interesting as hell. Say, look at that—"

Out the window they saw one of the madams from D Street, a well-proportioned woman named Dolly Slidell, wearing a green satin dress, walking with a local gambler named Monte Remsen, the two of them leading a pair of workmen carrying a large wooden sign lettered: DOLLY'S SALOON & CASINO. Beneath the names was an address: 121 C ST.

"One twenty-one, that's the vacant property where the French restaurant used to be," Big Jim said. "Dolly's not wasting any time."

"Neither is someone else," Coltrane cocked his head significantly.

Delavane looked out to see his wife Edith at the head of a group of women blocking the way to number 121. They had a large banner sign of their own: NO GAMBLING OR WHORES ON C ST. "Oh, Christ," Big Jim muttered in disgust.

"Maybe you'd better go out there and stop her, Jim," the banker suggested. "That looks like a rough crowd with Dolly."

"I *can't* stop her, Harmon. If I could, I'd have done it a long time ago." He sighed quietly, wearily. "Edith's a headstrong woman; when she gets involved with a cause, she's in all the way to the bitter end."

"Is that Francie with her?"

"Of course," Delavane replied caustically. "Edith drags the child along everywhere. Says she's teaching her social responsibility." The mine owner threw his napkin on the table. "You'll have to excuse me, Harmon. I don't want to watch this."

Tony saw Big Jim cross to the Ormsby House lobby and leave by a side door. Removing his apron, he darted into the kitchen. "Back in a minute, Lee," he said to the Chinese dishwasher for whom he worked. Dashing out the back door to the alley between C and D streets, he ran down to Maple, the intersecting avenue, and cut up to C, arriving just as Dolly Slidell and Edith Delavane confronted each other. The band fell silent and everyone pressed forward in anticipation to watch.

"If you'll excuse us, Mrs. Delavane," Dolly said with elaborate politeness, smirking, "you happen to be blocking the door to our new business premises."

"Go back to D Street where you belong, Miss Slidell," Edith replied. "The decent women of this community don't want your kind of establishment on our main street."

"I don't really care what the decent women want," Dolly said loudly, raucously. "It's the decent men I get my business from!"

As the crowd responded with a laugh, Dolly Slidell tried to push past, but Edith Delavane stood her ground. Tony had snaked forward in the crowd and saw Francie, her eyes wide with anxiety, holding on to her mother's skirt.

"Look, Mrs. Delavane," the gambler, Monte Remsen, said, waving a document in the air, "we got a legal lease on these here premises, signed and sealed. You got no right to interfere with us taking possession."

"I have a moral right," Edith stated. The women in her group voiced their support in unison, and the crowd behind Dolly booed. Tony saw Francie cringing. But not her mother. "You'll not put gamblers and harlots on C Street unless you walk over me first!" Edith Delavane declared.

"Have it your own way, sister," Dolly said. The madam drew back her fist and drove it solidly into Edith's face. Edith, who had never suffered so much as a slap on the cheek in her life, dropped where she stood. Her supporters drew back in fear and Dolly and the gambler stalked past the fallen woman. The crowd behind them surged forward. Francie was pushed to the side; seeing her frightened and alone, Tony dashed over and seized her by the arm, jerking her out of the path of the rushing crowd.

As he did so, he caught a fleeting glance of Edith Delavane being trampled by a sea of feet.

Three days later, Tony stood with Buck and Rosetta, both dressed in black, and watched solemnly as the heavy bronze coffin of Edith Delavane was lowered into the ground. On the other side of the open grave, a weeping Francie stood clutching the hand of her father. Big Jim Delavane looked thoroughly wasted; his usually handsome face was drawn to a skull-like tightness, bloodshot eyes sunk deeply in black-ringed cavities, lips colorless, jaw slack with the ultimate helplessness. He did not hold his grieving daughter's hand, he had not the strength to do so; rather she held one of his with both of hers. For all his presence of mind, she might not even have been there.

Watching Francie as she wept, Tony became aware that he was seeing in her a new trait: vulnerability. The Francie Delavane he had encountered at D.L.C. headquarters and in school had been ever self-assured, clever, confident of her identity, aware of her *name:* She was a Delavane, daughter of Big Jim. For an eleven-year-old, she had an extraordinary persona among other children. Her posture, poise, carriage, stride, were all perfectly honed; her direct gray eyes until now had always seemed like the eyes of a much older person.

But today she was a child, a little girl who had lost her mother in a moment of human insanity, and the intense, abject heartbreak she felt was etched as tellingly on her young face as it was on her father's. As she sobbed and wrung Jim Delavane's big hand in her own two small ones, her gray eyes moved nervously from one mourner to another, as if searching for a face that would allay her wretchedness. The eyes scanned above Tony, scoping the adult faces, pausing, finding nothing, moving on. When there were no grownups left to peruse, Francie's wet gaze dropped to her own level and fell on Tony. At once a strange thing happened: she began sniffing, swallowing, using the back of one gloved hand to wipe her cheeks dry as she brought her anguish under control. It was as if Francie had suddenly remembered she had not been alone at that terrible instant of loss; Tony Donovan had been there with her. Just for an instant. She had felt his strong young hands on her arms, felt the solidness of his chest as she leaned against him, somehow felt a fleeting instant of safety; then she was pulled from him by one of her mother's friends and hurried away. No one even knew that Tony had been the one to save her from the onrushing mob. But Francie knew. And at the funeral, she suddenly realized that although she carried the awful, awesome personal loss of her mother, Tony shared with her the *moment* of that loss. The weight of the tragedy seemed somehow reduced.

For the remainder of the brief graveside service, Francie kept her eyes locked on Tony's face, as he did with her. Tony had no way of knowing what Francie felt that day, other than her obvious grief, but his own feelings were terribly at odds and mixed. Here was the daughter of a man he hated, yet he wished in a confused, uncertain way that he could comfort her. He had come to this funeral secretly relishing the prospect of seeing Big Jim Delavane suffering; now he gave not one thought to the man but only to the trembling girl at his side. Tony remembered trembling like that when he awoke in the hospital and was told his family was dead. He had always thought Francie Delavane was so different from himself; now he saw that she was not.

There over her mother's grave, Tony Donovan began having strange new thoughts about Francie Delavane.

FOURTEEN

On the day Tony Donovan saw Denny Ebro for the first time, the young Basque boy was standing alone inside the Comstock Elementary schoolyard fence, looking up and down A Street almost frantically. It was morning recess. Denny had been brought to school earlier that day by his father, Piro Ebro, and met there by a woman who worked for the state department of education. Piro Ebro was under court order to produce his youngest son at Comstock Elementary that morning or go to jail.

When he arrived at the Virginia City school, Denny Ebro could already read and write, after a fashion, having been taught by his mother before she died of diphtheria; he had also learned basic arithmetic by having to account for sheep that were his responsibility beginning at age ten. But he had never received any structured education or been inside a classroom, nor had he been exposed to anyone outside his family, who lived in the upper reaches of the Washoe Mountains. Because of the boy's severe harelip, he had never been taken along on Piro Ebro's infrequent trips into town for supplies; it was feared that people would stare at the disfigured boy. Denny had always been an excitable child. Unable to form words properly, he substituted grunting, snorting sounds, which his family was certain would attract curiosity in town. The Basque family was already alien enough.

Five older Ebro sons had, without incident, grown past the legal age requiring schoolroom attendance; Denny had somehow been found out by the state department of education. When Piro Ebro disregarded several letters from that department, left for him at the mountain hamlet store where he traded, a complaint was filed with the juvenile court, a hearing convened—notice of which Piro also ignored—and a ruling handed down ordering the elder Ebro to have his son attend school. Sheriff Sam Patch managed to get up the precipitous mountain road in his police car, served the court order, and patiently explained to Piro not only what it was but what would happen if he did not obey it. So Piro Ebro had brought his youngest, handicapped son down the long mountain grade and delivered him to the faculty of Comstock Elementary School.

According to his age, Denny should have been in the eighth grade. But after interviewing him, helped in the translation of his grunts and snorts by Piro, it was decided to put him in the sixth. That was Tony Donovan's class, as well as Francie Delavane's and Jack Coltrane's. Denny, because of his size as well as his prominent harelip, was the recipient of the usual juvenile snickering when he arrived in class; later some cruel mocking when he tried to answer a question aloud; still later, at recess, concerted ridicule and physical challenges. Tony, shooting marbles in a circle on the ground with some other boys, watched as Jack Coltrane and his friends from the Hill, along with some miners', and merchants' sons, and even a few of the more rambunctious little girls, gathered around Denny at the schoolyard fence and tried to harass him into talking, singing, fighting, or anything else that might entertain their insensitive young minds. Denny reacted to their taunts, shoves, tweaks, trippings, and other abuses in a confused, plaintive manner, all the while continuing to search past the fence for Piro, who had promised him he would return.

When the bell rang ending the fifteen-minute recess, there was a mad rush to line up, boys on one side, girls on the other, to file back into the classroom. Tony, who made a point of never hurrying during school hours, gathered his marbles in his own good time, including one steely and two aggies he had just won, and put them in a rawhide pouch that he tied to his belt: an old belt of Buck's, actually, cut shorter with Buck's pocketknife and new holes put in with Rosetta's icepick. Tony saw that the big, new boy still remained at the fence, unresponsive to the summoning of the bell. His bag of "mibs," as the boys called marbles, bouncing on one hip, Tony walked over to Denny Ebro.

"Din't you hear the bell?" he asked.

"Whunh?" said Denny.

"The bell. The bell that just rang. You have to get in line." Tony had to exert rigid control to keep his eyes from moving to look at the grotesque lip.

"Oy oh woe," Denny said.

To Tony, it sounded like he might have said, "I don't know."

The second bell rang, a signal for the two lines to begin going in. "Come on," Tony said, jerking his head toward the door. "Just follow me. Come On."

"Awwite," Denny said, hurrying after him.

At lunchtime the molesting resumed. Tony watched it from where he sat with the other marble-shooting boys in a shady corner they claimed for their own next to the school steps. They ate from brown paper sacks: a sandwich on Silvercup bread, made from the previous night's leftover supper meat; an apple (invariably); two cookies, home-made, often traded—but only for other cookies, never for anything else; a penny bottle of milk, given to each student as they filed out of the building, a nickel having been collected from each on Monday morning in payment for the week.

The persecution of Denny Ebro was worse at lunchtime because the aggressors now had something to seize and destroy: his lunch. He managed one bite of his sandwich, slices of lamb loin, before it was snatched from him and loudly jeered as it passed from hand to hand, was sniffed, and generated various degrees of repugnance before finally being thrown to the ground in disgust.

"It's goat!" Jack Coltrane announced. "He's eating goat!"

"Aeh ean ouht!" Denny protested. It was as close as he could come to "I am not!"

His lunch sack was emptied, two biscuits ground under someone's heel, and his milk poured onto the toes of his hightop brogans. As he stared dumbly at the streaks of milk on his shoes, the boys roared and the little girls squealed in delight.

"Why ain't he fightin' back?" one of the boys in Tony's group asked disdainfully.

"Maybe he's a sissy," another offered.

"He don't know how to talk," Tony said, "so maybe he don't know how to fight."

"I was him, I'd learn," the first boy said wryly.

Tony glanced around for the lunch monitor. One teacher was assigned daily as recess and lunch monitor, to keep an eye on and maintain peace in the schoolyard when the savages were loose. For the most part, the monitor merely stepped outside and looked around now and again as a deterrent to serious mischief. Right then, as Tony's sweeping glance told him, the lunch monitor was nowhere in sight.

By afternoon recess, Denny Ebro had become like a zombie: apparently having resigned himself to indefinite punishment, he simply stood by the fence, periodically looking futilely up A Street, while allowing his tormentors, who were increasing in number, to mistreat him at will. More than half the class had joined the fun by now; nearly everyone who had been a spectator early on had now become a participant.

As teachers so often are, Miss Minty, who taught 6-A, appeared blithely unaware of the untoward conduct of her old students toward her new one. She had a schedule preordained by the state board of education: so many pages of the arithmetic book had to be done, so many of the reader, the spelling book, the general science book, the history book; each segment of each hour was allotted for something, and Miss Minty's attention was usually on punctilious adherence to that timetable. Only blood or tears disrupted her routine, and from Denny Ebro that first day had come neither so far. Miss Minty remained insensibly oblivious to Denny Ebro's nightmare.

When the three o'clock dismissal bell rang, the color vanished from Denny's face; by then he recognized that the shrill sound of the bell signaled either the beginning of or relief from this strange punishment that was being heaped upon him. Tony watched him fall in at the back of the line, his eyes wide with apprehension, mouth open, notched lip looking like a sneer even in terror. The lines started moving; unleashed kids burst from the outside door like buckshot. Tony lagged behind, as he always did, in order to get a last look of the day at Francie.

No one paid any attention to Tony for lagging behind. In his closed little group of marble-shooting cronies, everyone went his own way and no questions were asked. They were all unusual kids in various ways: one was the illegitimate son of a brothel madam; another's father was the town drunk; one had a brother in prison; one was unequivocally, hands down, the dumbest kid in class, *every* class, every semester, and was promoted each term not out of charity but rather due to the numbing frustration on the part of the teacher who had endured his maddening stupidity for a full semester; still another was a tobacco chewer, and had been since age ten; and of course, Tony, an orphan being raised by other people—a dark-mooded, scowling boy best left alone. When he exited the school and sat on the banister of the steps instead of racing down A Street to freedom, no one presumed to ask why.

Tony watched Francie every day; he was always aware, his eyes constantly alert, with long stares or mere glances, of her presence. Since her mother's funeral, when he had seen her broken-hearted and vulnerable for the first time, his feelings for her had been distractingly mixed. On the one hand he knew she was still Big Jim Delavane's spoiled-brat daughter, one of the Hill kids that he and his pals scorned; on the other he had come to realize that she was really no different from himself when it came to grieving lost family and feeling desolately alone in the world. When he saw her laughing and playing with other Hill kids, he hated her; when she gazed sadly out a classroom window and he knew instinctively that she was thinking of her dead mother, fighting back tears and hurting in her loneliness, he felt drawn to her, felt an odd warm rush, an urge to speak to her, to tell her that he understood. He never did speak to her, not like that; he was afraid to. She was from the Hill, he from Miners Walk; they could never be friends. He could only watch her, surreptitiously, his emotions tortured.

As Tony sat there waiting for Francie to come out—she and the other Hill girls were the *slowest* creatures on earth—he was also aware of what was going to happen to Denny Ebro. Like children torturing a bug, the kids who had successfully plagued Denny through two recesses and a lunch period, gleefully awaited the end of classes so they could pursue their victimization uninterrupted. When Denny proceeded to his place at the fence to look again for his father, a gang led by Jack Coltrane was at once on his heels. Jack Coltrane, fathered by Harmon Coltrane late in life with a woman considerably younger, might have belonged to Tony's group had he not lived on the Hill, which meant peremptory exclusion. Jack's banker father spent little time with him, his mother claimed she was unable to handle him, and he had evolved into a spoiled, cunning, manipulative, bullying boy. He had his followers because he was tough and could fight, but no one really liked him and he seemed to realize it. Shallow and completely without noticeable conscience, he delighted in causing discomfort, unrest, humiliation, and pain to others. Which is what he proceeded to do to Denny Ebro after school.

Singleminded harassment now became torture. Jack wanted in the worst way for Denny Ebro to fight him; Denny was so much bigger that Jack thought it would be a personal coup to physically disgrace him. He taunted Denny, dared him, put a chip on Denny's shoulder and formally knocked it off, stepped on Denny's toes with his heel, systematically yanked the buttons from his shirt, and finally slapped his face. All the while Denny Ebro only pawed impotently and ineffectively with his open hands to ward off the aggression. Finally, laced with misery, the bigger boy started to cry.

The crying was what got to Tony Donovan. Off the banister he came, untying the bag of marbles from his belt as he stalked across the schoolyard. Through the gathered students he pushed, shoving his way up to Jack Coltrane. In his mind, the schoolboy from the Hill was Big Jim Delavane. All of the Hill kids around him were Big Jim Delavane, at least symbolically. Anything associated with the Hill—residents, servants, automobiles; anything except Francie—ultimately was reduced to the despised figure of the mine owner whom Tony continued, despite his feelings for Francie, to hate. When he looped the thongs of the marble bag around his wrist, curled his fingers around the top of the bag, and used it as an effective blackjack to smash against the side of Jack Coltrane's face, he was hitting Big Jim Delavane. When the Hill boy went sprawling, blood spurting from his nose, it was Delavane bleeding.

"Hey, no fair, Donovan!" one of Jack's gang yelled. "You hit him when he wasn't looking!"

"Yeah, and you didn't use your fist!" shouted another. "No fair!"

Tony turned on the nearest one of them and smashed him in the face also. The boy pitched back to the ground as Jack had. Immediately, three other boys moved together to confront Tony, all decrying his tactics.

"Hey, he's using a bag of marbles!"

"You can't hit with a bag of marbles, Donovan! It ain't fair!"

"Yeah, fight fair, Donovan!"

Cocking his right arm, Tony held the makeshift weapon threateningly. "Go to hell!" he yelled back. "I'll fight any way I wanna fight!"

Denny Ebro, meanwhile, was backing along the fence away from the group. Suddenly he saw, far down the block, the familiar figure of his father coming toward the school. Making a desperate grunting noise, Denny dashed to the now open schoolyard gate and broke into a run down A Street.

Jack Coltrane, his lower face red from a bloody nose, got to his feet and joined the boys, now five of them, accosting Tony. "Only a yellow coward hits somebody when he's not looking, Donovan!" he accused hotly.

"Yeah," Tony retorted, "like a yellow coward who hits somebody who won't fight back!"

The line of boys edged forward menacingly. "Put the marbles down and I'll fight you fair," Jack challenged.

"Go to hell!" Tony told him. Without warning he jumped forward and again smashed the bag of marbles into the face of the boy nearest him, and for the third time a boy was pitched to the ground. The rest of them became even more incensed.

"Come on, get him!" Jack yelled.

They all rushed Tony at once. Tony managed to get in a final, glancing blow against someone's head before he was engulfed by flailing bodies. He felt himself stumbling backwards, finally falling, as they all came down on him at once. The bag of marbles was wrenched from his hand, the thongs torn from his wrist, and seconds later a handful of marbles was hurled into his face from close range. What seemed like a multitude of fists were pounding and punching at every part of his body. Something solid—a thumb or a knuckle—hit his right eye solidly, causing a sudden flash of blue and shooting his face with intense pain. A solid blow of some kind—foot, elbow—shook his teeth and made him bite his tongue agonizingly. Clouts and bashes rained down on him, and all he could do was try and cover himself and curl up in the smallest target possible.

It seemed like the attack lasted a very long time before
Tony finally heard a man's voice yell, "Stop that, you boys!
Stop it, you hear!"

There were a few last punches, then the urgent scuffling
of feet as everyone, attackers and spectators alike, bolted
away from the arriving adult authority, whoever it was.
Between the sounds of many feet running away, and two
pair of feet hurrying up to him, Tony had an odd, surreal
moment of silence in which there was nothing on the face of
the earth except pain. He got to his hands and knees, face
down, blood dripping from his nose and lips, right eye
swelling and rapidly closing, and began to look around on
the ground for his marbles. His shooter, he had to find his
shooter . . .

Tony had found four marbles when a pair of strong hands
pulled him to his feet and he was looking into the bearded
face of someone he did not know. It was Piro Ebro. The
man took a blue bandanna from around his neck and began
wiping Tony's face with it.

"Lea' me alone," Tony said, trying to pull away.

"Wait. There is dirt in these cuts—"

"I gotta find my mibs—" he said, holding out his hand
with the four marbles in it.

"Aih ein umm," Denny Ebro said. I'll find them. He
started scurrying around on the ground. "Ear un," he said
when he found one.

Tony momentarily submitted to the temporary first-aid
being done to his face by the man he now assumed was the
new boy's father. Then from the corner of the eye that was
not swelling closed, he saw a lone figure standing near the
corner of the school building. His puffing lips parted in
surprise. It was Francie, prim in her dark blue school dress,
white anklets, patent leather shoes, holding in one hand the
briefcaselike red satchel in which she carried her school
books. She was looking right at him; she had witnessed his
humiliating beating! Mortified, Tony pushed the elder Ebro's
hands away.

"Jus' lea' me alone, okay!" Turning to Denny, he demanded, "Hand over my mibs, kid." Denny obliged. Tony
looked around for his rawhide pouch, but it was nowhere in
sight. In frustration, eyes beginning to tear, he finally shoved
what marbles he had, about half of them, his shooter not
among them, into one pocket of his dirty torn knickers,

and without another glance at Francie, fled the schoolyard.

Down A Street Tony ran, not to Miners Walk where he lived, but to Gold Street which, a block higher, ended at the woods of the foothills that rose to the mountains. He hurried up Gold, crying aloud now, glad there were only a few houses nearby, glad there was no one out to witness the disgrace of his condition—beaten and bleeding, disheveled and dirty—and the crushing ignominy he was certain showed clearly in his face at that moment. At the top end of Gold Street, Tony plunged into the cool, sunless shelter of the forest and kept going until he was far enough not to see the street.

Sitting on the ground next to a fir tree, Tony drew his knees up, circled them with his arms, and buried his face in the nest he had made. He began to sob in wrenching, jerking spasms as the physical pain and mental anguish melded into a single hurt. Hill kids, he thought wrathfully, they had all been Hill kids. Someday, he thought savagely, I'll get every one of the sons of bitches—

He did not know how long he sat sobbing like that, his mind racing with thoughts of fierce, ruthless reprisal, but he sensed no one approaching, heard no footsteps on the crunchy pine needle and pine cone–covered ground, was not even aware that he was no longer alone until he felt a gentle touch on his tangled hair.

Tony's head jerked up and he found Francie kneeling next to him. Startled, he asked curtly, "What the hell do you want?" Her soft, adolescent face was concerned and sad; she was not offended.

"I followed you," Francie said quietly. "I wanted to see if you were hurt."

Tony looked away. "I'm not hurt. They couldn't hurt me."

From under the belt of her dress, Francie took a small white handkerchief and, as Piro Ebro had done, began to carefully wipe some of the dirt and drying blood from his face. At once Tony pulled his head away.

"I'm okay."

Francie pulled his head back. "You hold still," she said. Her voice was not as quiet as before. She sounded, as usual, as if she had a sore throat. Tony liked her scratchy voice; whenever Francie had to stand and recite in class, he absorbed the sound of it in his mind like a recording and replayed it in his memory over and over again. When he happened to catch a few of her words in passing, in the hall or on the schoolyard, his ears locked onto them and secreted them away until he recalled them at night in his room, in the dark, as sleep neared. Now, when she spoke, he obeyed; he held still. "If you leave dirt in a cut, you can get an infection," she said, as if instructing a child.

She was very close to him as she worked, and Tony caught the scent of her; not so much a scent as an aroma: an odd, pleasant mixture of toilet water like Rosetta used, and talcum powder like Rosetta put on little Kerry, and the smell of the classroom, and a distinct fragrance that he somehow knew came from her smooth, shiny, silky auburn hair, and still something else, a trace, a hint, reminding him of the yellow flowers of a musk plant, this coming from somewhere beneath her clothing, perhaps from under the skirt pulled tautly apart just above her knees as she sat back on her heels doctoring him. He had to keep his own knees up because the nearness of her had given him an erection.

"You were very brave to fight Jack and all those other boys like that," she said.

"I wasn't brave," he replied with a cynicism they were too young to understand. "I was dumb."

"You were not. You were brave. It was about time somebody did something to help that poor harelipped new boy."

"Is that what they call it, the way his mouth is?"

Francie nodded. "Yes. A harelip. Not like this kind of hair"—she pushed a black, curly lock back off his forehead—"but hare like rabbit."

"Oh. Oh, yeah," Tony said, his expression brightening with the image in his mind of a rabbit's indented mouth.

"Your hair is very thick," Francie said, running the fingers of one hand through it. "But it's so tangled. Don't you ever comb it?"

"Sure, on Sundays," he said. "To go to Mass."

After wiping off his forehead, she folded the handkerchief into a square and said, "I'm afraid to touch your eye. It's swollen so badly, and it's turning purple."

"I'll put a piece of beefsteak on it when I get home," he said, in what he hoped sounded like a manly tone.

"Everything has stopped bleeding except a little cut in the middle of your bottom lip." She blotted the lip. "Every time I wipe it off, another drop comes out. There it is again."

"It'll be okay," Tony said, trying for aplomb. "Split

lips take a while to stop bleeding. I've had plenty of them."

"I'm not so sure about this one," Francie said, dabbing at it again. "I might just have to kiss it to make it well."

Tony stared into her eyes, unable to conjure up any reply at all. He was not even certain he had heard her right. But, in the next moment, leaning forward, Francie put her lips softly against his, pressed, held for a brief, thrilling beat of time, and removed them. When she did, a drop of his blood was on her lips. She put the tip of her tongue to it.

"I've never tasted blood before," she said.

"Not even your own?" Words, finally. Francie shook her head.

"Not even my own."

"I've tasted mine plenty of times," Tony said. "When I cut my finger on tin or something, I always suck the poisoned blood out of the cut."

"There comes another drop," Francie said. She smiled ever so slightly. "Guess the first kiss didn't work."

Leaning to him again, she put a hand in the shaggy hair at the back of his neck and held the second kiss much longer. Tony took her by the shoulders and kissed her back. Their mouths opened a bit, but closed almost at once, both of them too apprehensive to engage in "French kissing," of which they had heard but never tried. Tony, in fact, had never kissed a girl at all; Francie had kissed Jack Coltrane and some of the other boys on the Hill at birthday parties where they played "Spin the Bottle," but she had never French kissed. And neither of them had ever felt the strange, surging sensation that kissing each other was now giving them.

"I've wanted to kiss you for a long time," Francie said. His blood was smeared on both their mouths. Tony stared at her incredulously.

"You have?"

"Yes."

Tony looked away. "I watch you all the time in class—"

"I know. Sometimes I see you."

He kissed her again and she kissed him back, and they held this kiss longest of all.

"I like kissing you, Tony."

"I like kissing you too, Francie."

Francie shifted and sat on the ground, her right shoulder to Tony's left shoulder, and they put their arms around each other and continued to kiss. It was electrifying and beguiling at the same time; their young lips were soft cushions, incredibly smooth when the blood had been kissed away and the bleeding stopped. With their upper bodies close upon the other, arms entwined, fingertips kneading softness-hardness, they became enraptured.

"I love you, Tony," Francie said at last.

"I love you too, Francie." Only at the precise moment did he realize that he *did*. Only when he spoke the words, encouraged by the fact that she had spoken them, did he understand that all of his thoughts of her, beginning at her mother's funeral and continuing during the long year that followed, had actually been the first notions, the prophecy, of love.

"I love you," they said, and kissed again. They kept repeating the simple phrase, as if it was a release from all that was wrong and misunderstood in their very young lives. "I love you," they said as they walked holding hands back to the edge of the forest where it met Gold Street. "I love you," they said as they parted and Francie slipped out first and hurried down to the corner. I love you, they said silently as they waved good-bye. When she stepped around the corner out of sight, Tony felt as if he had taken a hard blow to the chest; he had to sit down under a tree and concentrate on bringing his breathing under control. Love: the power of it, the jolt, overwhelmed him.

When Tony finally got home that day, Rosetta rushed anxiously to meet him from the front door where she had been watching for him. She had heard about the fight from Piro Ebro, who with Denny was in their modest living room talking to Buck, who was just off shift and still in his work clothes. Denny's father had found out from the little girl with the red school satchel what Tony's name was, just before she hurried to follow the angry, bloody boy. With the name, he had asked a merchant and learned where Tony lived.

Rosetta led Tony in for Buck to check him for serious wounds. Before Buck could do so, Denny rushed from the couch where he had been sitting at his father's side and, grinning widely, said "Eah," and handed Tony six more marbles, including his precious shooter.

"Thanks," Tony mumbled. What the hell were these people doing here anyway?

"Looks like you took a few, all right," Buck said, when he gave Tony's bruises and abrasions a clinical inspection. "Who was it you fought?" Tony named Jack Coltrane and the other boys. "All from the Hill, were they?" Tony nodded. "Wasn't very smart, fighting that many at once," Buck growled, but his eyes showed a gleam of pride, and he kept one arm around Tony's shoulders. "Did you fight like a miner? Like a hardrock?"

"Yessir." Tony grinned painfully.

"Good lad." Buck nodded to Rosetta. "Soap and water. Iodine for the cuts. Then bring me a two-inch square of raw beefsteak and the ball of twine."

After Tony had been cleaned up and streaked dark orange with tincture of iodine, Buck applied the raw meat directly to his swollen, closed eye and tied it in place with two lengths of string that crisscrossed the beefsteak and held it in place. Then Buck left the room to confer with Rosetta in the kitchen. Alone with the two Ebros, Tony felt distinctly uncomfortable. Denny sat grinning at him like an idiot. Presently Kerry came in and climbed up on Tony's lap to examine the funny streaks on his face.

"You are a brave boy to fight for my son," the elder Ebro said.

Tony shrugged self-consciously. Secretly he was proud of how he had fought, proud that he was a miner's kid instead of a Hill kid. He felt as he had when Iron Mike had been alive, when he'd run out to meet the big mine superintendent at end of shift every day, and Mike had swung him up onto one shoulder and carried him laughing into the house. There had been a time, after his family was killed, when Tony's hatred for Big Jim Delavane had made him hate the mines also. But life with Buck had changed that back again. Tony lived for the day when he would be old enough to follow Buck into the mines.

"My son has never learned to fight because he has never had to fight," Piro Ebro said. "He does not even know how to make a fist. Or what to do with it. That is not required in high country where we live. But down here, where the law says he must study in school to become smart, I think he will have to know how to fight, yes?"

"If he's going to Comstock, he will," Tony stated unequivocally. "There's kids in Comstock'll pick a fight with you just for *looking* at them."

"You can teach my Denny how to fight, yes?"

"I'm no good at teaching nothing," Tony said reluctantly. "Don't do that, Ker," he told the little girl, who was touching the beefsteak. Just then Buck and Rosetta returned.

"I've talked to my missus and she's agreed, Mr. Ebro," Buck said. "We'll board your boy during the school term for the price we discussed a little while ago. He can sleep in Tony's room and they can go to and from school together. Tony'll look after the lad until such time as he can look after himself."

Rosetta took Kerry into her arms and went into the kitchen to finish supper, and Buck invited Piro Ebro to join him in a sip of whiskey. Denny was still grinning happily at Tony. Finally Tony got up and said, "Come on outside with me."

"What are you going to do?" Buck asked.

"Teach him how to make a fist," Tony said over his shoulder.

FIFTEEN

Tony Donovan's hands were sweating on the steering wheel of Buck O'Crotty's old Nash. "You want me to drive right up to the front door?" he asked. Buck, sitting next to him, gave his nineteen-year-old foster son a curious glance.

"Certainly. Where else would you drive to?"

"Just asking," Tony muttered.

It felt very odd to Tony to be approaching the front of Big Jim Delavane's mansion on the Hill. He had sneaked up the back way many times, on foot, moving clandestinely in night shadows so as not to be observed by anyone on the way, or seen by servants coming and going once he got there. Behind the mansion, at the very rear of the excavated shelf on which it stood, the terrain rose gradually in a thirty-degree slope of pine trees, piñon, and mesquite: wild and unspoiled, a natural forest foothill, beyond which the rugged Sierra range jutted up abruptly, a rock fist that had punched up through the ground. At the back edge of the Delavane property was a thick stand of pines, and it was usually through those that Tony furtively made his way when he was alone.

"You think the bastard's gonna listen to reason, Buck?" Denny Ebro asked in his grunting, uneven voice. A strapping, muscular twenty-one, Denny was sitting in the middle of the back seat, leaning forward so that his face was nearly between those of the two men in front.

"I hope so," Buck replied wearily. Then his tone sharpened. "And it isn't necessary to refer to him as a 'bastard.' Jim Delavane was a damn good man when he had to work for a living like the rest of us. And he's not all that bad now, not compared to some I've seen. There's plenty worse, believe me. Those coal mine owners back in the Appalachians, the copper mine owners up in Michigan; those are *real* bastards. Pull over right there, Tony, and park it." Tony guided the car to the edge of the Delavane drive and turned off the engine. "I don't know how long I'll be," Buck said. "Wish me luck, boys."

"Luck, Buck," said Tony.

"Give him hell, Buck," said Denny.

Buck crossed the drive and stood in front of the big white mansion door, tugging once at the bell pull. Chimes sounded inside and the door was opened almost immediately by a butler: a proper English butler named Cavendish, whom Big Jim had imported along with a housekeeper and a governess to care for Francie following Edith's untimely death. Within a month after that tragedy, Big Jim had discharged every servant in the mansion, and since then had refused to have any local domestics at all in his employ. The rumored reason for it was that he was revulsed by the thought of having anyone in the house who might have been a part of—or even been *related* to someone who had been a part of—the crowd that had trampled Edith. He had always had a latent opposition to local servants anyway, because invariably they came from one of the Miners Walk families and, Delavane felt, had divided loyalties at best. While Edith was alive, the locals were loyal to *her*, sure enough, but never to him and he was always aware of it.

Big Jim did not particularly like the Britishers who ran his household, but at least he was not uncomfortable around them, and Francie got on famously with all of them. The main thing was that when Big Jim closed his front door at night there was no question in his mind but that he had, by God, shut out the whole of Virginia City—including the scum who killed Edith.

"Good evening, Mr. O'Crotty," the butler said, taking Buck's weathered felt hat. "Mr. Delavane is waiting for you in the study, sir. This way, please."

"Thank you, Mr. Cavendish," Buck replied. It was Buck's policy to address all men as "Mister," whatever their social status. He did it with his miners, with the Chinese in town, even with the Paiutes now that Rosetta, indirectly by her bedtime stories to Kerry, had taught him that they were human and not heathen. Cavendish thought it odd, but could not help feeling a fondness for this man O'Crotty because of it.

Buck had telephoned ahead as a courtesy, although he knew Big Jim would have seen him unannounced. A miners' strike was imminent, and Delavane wanted to avoid it as much as the Amalgamated Mine Workers of Nevada did. The A.M.W.N. membership was set to take a strike vote at midnight when the second shift ended. That was less than four hours away. A dozen very long bargaining sessions in the offices of Martin Pitt, Delavane's lawyer, had failed to bring about agreement on a single issue. Negotiating for the management side were Pitt, Harley Kent, the mine general manager, and Clinton Randall, the head accountant. On the labor side were union president Buck O'Crotty and his two lieutenants, Lloyd Arlen and Terence Henny, both vice presidents of the Virginia City local. Time was running out for all of them. Buck hoped that a face-to-face talk with Big Jim might save them all from the decidedly unpleasant experience of a strike.

As Cavendish led Buck down a long, main hall toward the study, both men were acutely aware of the striking difference in their appearance. Cavendish, taller than Buck, straighter, with more bearing, was dressed properly in his informal evening attire: navy blue double-breasted suit over a snow-white shirt with a tiny polka dot design necktie.

Buck wore a wrinkled gray suit, checkered cotton shirt, and a poorly knotted, ill-matched tie. He looked more like a panhandler than an elected union official. Appearances aside, each man was also aware, just as keenly, that the one appropriately garbed was a man who served others; the one in the unseemly clothing was a leader.

"Hello, Mr. O'Crotty," a throaty, feminine voice said as the two men passed an open library door. Buck looked and saw Francie Delavane, holding a book and a cigarette.

"Why, hello, Frances Grace," he said. "How are you this evening?"

"I'm fine, thank you. I'll take care of Mr. O'Crotty, Cavendish," she said in casual but not impolite dismissal. Cavendish bowed slightly and walked away. Francie raised one eyebrow disarmingly at Buck. " 'Frances Grace'?" she gently reproached. "That's almost as bad as calling me 'Miss Delavane' every day at the mine. You used to call me 'Francie,' Mr. O'Crotty."

Buck smiled. "You used to wear knee socks and have pigtails and a lollipop. Now it's silk hose, a permanent wave, and a cigarette." She was dressed, he noted, in a turtleneck sweater and a skirt, not markedly different from the blouse and skirt combinations he saw her in every day at the mine offices.

Nineteen now, Francie was plainer than both her parents. She had not gotten prettier as she got older, perhaps, Buck thought, because she seemed to have lost some of her softness; the demureness of the little girl who cut out paper dolls in the D.L.C. office was gone, replaced by a healthy female with penetrating gray eyes and a straightforward manner. Her auburn hair, even after a permanent, never looked like it had that final touch. Although she tended toward fleshiness by three or four pounds, her figure was good, and she moved well, with confidence. Ironically, she had matured in appearance to fit exactly the throaty voice that broke in the high registers. Only when she smiled did she remind Buck of Edith.

A year earlier, Francie had gone back east to some exclusive college which she was unable to endure; after less than one semester she had returned home and insisted that she be allowed to work at the mine and learn the business. Big Jim, outwardly aggravated but privately very pleased, had put her to work for Clinton Randall in the accounting department. It delighted Buck to be able to see her every workday, because she made him think of Edith, his old comrade.

"Anyway," Buck told her now, "your mother never really cared for your being called Francie. She said it sounded tacky."

The eyebrow came down. "I know. You thought a lot of my mother, didn't you, Mr. O'Crotty?"

"That I did, Frances Grace, that I did. Your mother was one of the finest ladies it was ever my pleasure to meet."

"Are you one of those people," Francie asked in a mixture of curiosity and suspicion, "who thought she was too good for my father?"

"Not at all," Buck assured her. "Everything considered, your father's one of the best men I've ever known. I thought him and your mother matched very well together, despite their differences regarding certain social matters."

"Mother certainly thought highly of you," Francie recalled. "She was forever saying what a fine man you were."

"Was she," Buck replied very quietly, not as a question but almost as an expression of gratitude. "That was kind of her." He suddenly felt he had to direct the conversation away from Edith, so stirred was he by this girl, her words, this house. "What's that you're reading?" he asked.

Francie held up the book. "*The Grapes of Wrath*. Have you read it?"

Buck's eyes twinkled. "More than read it. I've *studied* it. Have you come across *How Green Was My Valley* yet?" When she shook her head, he winked and said, "Read that one if you can. You'll like it. It's all about Welsh coal miners. My friend John L. Lewis recommended it to me in a recent letter."

"You really do know John L. Lewis, then?" She was clearly impressed.

"If I didn't, my dear," Buck replied sagely, "I wouldn't be here in this house tonight."

Francie put the book down and took Buck's arm, guiding him once again toward her father's study. "Do you think you and Daddy can avoid a strike?" she asked with a graveness that made her voice even hoarser.

"I honestly don't know, dear. I hope we can."

"So do I." She seemed to become preoccupied for a moment, as if suddenly thinking of someone or something.

Then she smiled the smile that had once been Edith's and took him to the study door. She knocked softly, opened it for Buck and said "Good night, Mr. O'Crotty."

"Good night, Frances Grace."

Entering, Buck found Big Jim Delavane not behind his massive mahogany with inlaid ivory desk, but settled instead in one of two deep, plush Morris chairs before a fireplace alive with dancing mesquite flames. On a coffee table in front of him was a decanter of scotch and two heavy crystal whiskey glasses; in his hand was a sheaf of papers he was studying. "Hello, Buck," he said as O'Crotty entered.

"Good evening, Jim," Buck replied. There was too much of the past between them for Buck to ever call Delavane "Mister."

Big Jim put the papers aside and pointed to the other chair. Picking up the decanter, he asked with a canny smile, "Shall I pour you one, Buck, or do you have your own?"

Returning the smile, saying, "I'll have one of yours, thanks," Buck thought immediately: Mind yourself now, O'Crotty, this man is up on both toes tonight.

Delavane handed him a glass of whiskey, raised his own, and said, "How."

"How," Buck echoed. The two men took their first sip. "I spent a minute with Francie in the hall," Buck said then. "She's got a smile that brings back memories."

"Isn't that the God's truth, Buck? Sometimes when she smiles, I think my heart's going to melt."

They sat for a quiet moment studying the fire, remembering, as the whiskey warmed them inside. They were very close in age, but Delavane, graying hair neatly trimmed, fresh from his second bath and shave of the day, wearing a royal blue velvet smoking jacket with maroon piping, looked a decade younger. Out of the mines for many years, his hands were clean, nails manicured, while O'Crotty's were rough as corrugated tin and ingrained with rock dust that had become a permanent part of the epidermis. Ever unspoken, when they were together, was the invariably shared, albeit fleeting thought: There but for the turn of a card . . .

"How is it out tonight?" Big Jim asked.

"Chilly."

"Probably have an early frost this year." The mine owner's words were considered, measured.

"Could be, you never can tell." Agreeable but cautious, that was the union president.

"I predict a long, cold winter, Buck."

"Let's hope," Buck said, "you and I can keep from making it any longer or any colder."

From his inside coat pocket, O'Crotty removed and unfolded a single sheet of paper on which were the final demands of the union membership.

Out front, Tony Donovan peered through the car window to make sure no one was observing them from the mansion. "If Buck comes back while I'm gone," he said to Denny, "tell him I went to take a leak. Then you come get me. Just go over to the corner of the house there and whistle. Got it?"

"Yeah, I guess," Denny said reluctantly. "I just hope you get back first. I ain't so sure I can lie to Buck without him catching on."

"You can," Tony said confidently. "Just think about making a fist."

'Making a fist' was their secret phrase, their personal code; it meant holding their ground, being tough, standing up to anything and anybody. It originated that first day when Denny Ebro was left at the O'Crotty house. Tony had known from Buck's words to Piro Ebro that until Denny learned to fight, Tony would have to fight for him. Tony had enough battles of his own to deal with; he was determined to make Denny capable of self-defense as quickly as possible.

It was not easy. Despite his size, Denny was a gentle kid, happy, playful, devoid of meanness. At first he resisted Tony's instruction; he liked Tony—the first friend he'd ever had—and treated Tony's roughhouse training as horseplay, friendly wrestling, like his brothers engaged in. Even when Tony hurt him, Denny managed to laugh.

"Come on, make a fist," Tony urged. "Stop slapping with your hands. Make a fist and punch."

But Denny would only grin, say something incoherent, and paw at Tony with open hands. Finally Tony was compelled to teach him the hard way.

Initially, Tony had been Denny's protector on the schoolyard. Denny stayed in Tony's shadow wherever he went. The Hill kids left him alone; they'd had enough of Tony

Donovan's marble bag, and he now sported a new one Buck had made for him. Tony knew that Denny Ebro would never learn to take care of himself as long as he had Tony to do it for him. So Tony played hooky one day. At the morning bell, he ducked out on Denny as the line was filing in. Dashing down the hall, he leaped off the outside steps, crept aroumd to the back of the school, vaulted the fence, and was gone. He spent the day riding a V&T boxcar partway downgrade and walking back. When he got home late that afternoon, Rosetta was doctoring Denny's cut and bruised face in the kitchen. Buck was livid.

"I ought to take the strap to you!"

"Go on!" Tony challenged. "Then *you* learn him how to fight!"

"Mind your mouth" Buck warned drawing back a hand.

"Fair's fair, Buck" Tony insisted. "If I'm gonna learn him, I'll do it my own way."

Buck stared at the boy for a long moment; then, grudgingly accepting his logic, stalked out of the room. Tony took Denny outside. "You learn to fight and I'll fight with you," he said. "But if you're gonna take lickings, you'll take 'em alone. What's it gonna be?"

Denny wiped tears from his cheeks. "Ah bite," he said.

"You'll fight?" Tony asked.

"Ehoh, Yeah."

"All right," Tony said. Roughly, he shoved Denny with both hands. "Make a fist, goddamn it!"

Within a month, Denny Ebro had become the most feared boy in the sixth grade. Now grown, he was considered one of the toughest miners in the A.M.W.N. He was afraid of no one, took nothing from no one, and was totally devoted to Tony Donovan for making him that way. There was nothing he would not do for Tony, although a few things gave him pause to worry. Including telling lies to Buck O'Crotty.

"Buck won't have no way of knowing I'm not just taking a leak," Tony assured Denny now as he prepared to leave him in the car in front of the Delavane mansion. "Anyway, I'll probably get back first."

"I hope so," Denny fretted. "If Buck finds out about this . . ."

Tony did not wait for his friend to finish voicing his

apprehension; opening the door, he took something from under the seat and put it inside his coat, then quickly slipped out of the car. Crouching, he leaned against the door and closed it as quietly as possible. Maintaining the crouch, he hurried along the outer edge of the drive to the corner of the mansion. There he paused and straightened, pressing his back against the side of the house. He waited, listening. The night around him was absolutely, eerily silent.

Making his way along the side of the house, Tony reached the opposite corner at the back and did the same thing again: remained there for a moment and scrutinized the darkness for sounds. He was in familiar territory; any time he crept up to the Delavane mansion on foot, it was always to this particular rear corner he came, dashing over from the stand of pine trees where the top of the steep footpath that led up from the end of Gold Street was.

As Tony stood there, he realized that the thin October air had a bite to it. He turned his shirt collar up around his neck. The silence made him feel safe and confident, so he eased around the corner to the back of the mansion and moved stealthily to the cellar stairs. The stairs were protected by two wooden doors built at an angle against the house, hinged on wooden sides that formed a shelter against the heavy snowfalls of high winter. They had no catches or locks, merely lying in place when closed. Tony slowly raised one of them just enough to descend the steps under it, then lowered it over his head. Where the night had been merely dark, the inside of the cellar steps enclosure was as black as a mine without lanterns. But Tony had been there before, many times; he felt his way to the upright cellar entry door, ran his hand down to its latch, lifted it, and sidled against it with his shoulder. It opened with a dull creak and Tony stepped inside.

At the rear of the cellar on one side was a huge coal furnace; an equally large coal bin faced it on the other side. Toward the front were two sets of storage closets and a flight of inside stairs leading up to the kitchen hallway. Tony could see none of this, but he knew it was there; he knew also that if he proceeded in a straight line, arms extended on both sides, he would, if his hands touched nothing, reach the inside stairs in twenty-two paces. If either of his hands touched anything—furnace vents, coal bin frame, closet walls—it meant he was veering off a dead-on course and needed to make an adjustment. Usually that did not happen; after working in the Delavane Mines for three years, he moved about in the dark with the sureness of a cat.

Tony was taking his fifteenth step when the door opened at the top of the stairs and the cellar light was turned on. For a startling stroke of time, the burst of light blinded him, but he reacted nevertheless. Stepping quickly to his left, he found the shadow of a closet wall and concealed himself in it. Above him, the upstairs door closed and footsteps descended the stairs. He heard Francie half singing, half humming softly to herself.

She reached the bottom step, her hair and breasts bouncing as she walked. She headed from the storage closet directly across from Tony, but he grabbed her before she got there and pulled her into his shadowy place. He put one hand over her mouth to stifle the startled scream he knew might involuntarily emit, and with his other hand held her tightly around the waist. At the same time he put his lips on her ear, kissed lightly, and whispered, "It's me."

When he knew the danger of her screaming had passed, he took his hand off her mouth and kissed her there. She kissed him back, running her fingers into the layers of thick hair on the back of his head. They kissed long and moistly, but when their lips parted she scolded him at once.

"You're not supposed to come in until I turn the light on. That's your signal, remember? How many times do I have to tell you? Cavendish is liable to shoot you as a prowler some night."

"Would you miss me if he did?" Tony asked.

"I might. Until I found someone else to meet at the movies."

"Who do you think you'd replace me with?" he wanted to know. "Jack Coltrane maybe?"

"Maybe," she allowed. "I could do worse."

"Whoever it was, I'd come back and haunt you," he promised.

"You already haunt me," she said huskily.

They pulled each other close and kissed again, longer and wetter than before. Tony's hands slipped under the back of her sweater to unhook her brassiere—but she was not wearing one.

"Surprise," she said against his lips. Then she felt a bulge under his coat. "What's that?"

"Guess."

"I don't want to guess. What is it?"

"You have to guess."

"Come *on*," she insisted. Francie loved to tease but hated to be teased. "*Tell* me."

Tony pulled a paper bag from under his coat and drew out a Shirley Temple rag doll. "Oh, you," she said, taking it from his hands. She hugged the doll to her face. It was something she had seen in a toy store window a few days earlier and mentioned to him how cute it was. "Nobody's given me a doll in years," she said. "I love it—and I love you."

They began to kiss again and Francie put the doll on a nearby box. The cellar was cool but they were both very warm and Francie allowed him to pull her sweater up above her breasts. He fondled them and felt their tightening, firming nipples as they continued to kiss. It always delighted and amazed him how active her nipples were, and how much she enjoyed having them touched. They reacted to touching just as his penis did, and Tony thought that was marvelous. "I never knew girls got hard-ons too," he had told her when they first began touching.

"There are probably lots of things you don't know about girls," she had replied.

"Oh, yeah? Are there lots of things you don't know about boys?"

"I doubt it. I had a very experienced governess. She even taught me how to masturbate. Who taught you how?"

Tony had turned beet red at the matter-of-fact question and was thankful that they were in the dark: on a blanket in the stand of pines behind the mansion, where she had sneaked out to meet him after everyone in the house was asleep.

"You do masturbate, don't you?" she had pressed.

"Yeah, sure, once in a while." Tony had reluctantly admitted. "When I don't have nothing else to do."

"I masturbate every night" Francie said candidly. "Margaret, my governess—I had to call her 'Miss Simms' in front of people but not in private—anyway she told me that in Europe girls suck on boys with their mouths. It's called blowing a boy."

Tony had nervously wondered what he would do if she offered to suck on him right then, but thankfully she did not. They were fifteen at the time, Miss Simms had been gone for nearly a year, and Francie had only recently begun letting Tony do more than just kiss her.

"I usually masturbate as soon as I get back in the house after seeing you," she admitted to him once. "Right when I get into bed."

Tony had been grateful that she did not ask him when he did it. He rarely got out of the stand of pines without relieving himself.

In the cellar, after they had petted themselves into a state of arousal that was barely under control, Francie put both hands on his chest and applied pressure. "Okay, Donovan, that's enough for both of us. Stop now. Tony—stop—"

It was becoming ever more difficult for them to uncouple. They wanted to have intercourse so badly it hurt. Sometimes Tony felt like he had golf balls between his legs, and the crotch of Francie's step-ins became wet with her secretions. But despite everything—the lust, the temptation, the opportunity—they always managed to stop short of committing the ultimate act which both of them thought was wrong. Psychologically they were indoctrinated, disciplined, and prepared for a sequence in life that required marriage before intercourse. In the restrictive society in which they lived in 1939, any exception, no matter how compelling, was considered scandalous and shameless.

After Francie had adjusted her sweater in the cellar and Tony's erection had reluctantly slackened, she took a package of Pall Malls from her skirt pocket and they went into one of the storage closets and sat side by side on a large trunk. "Look at these," she said, showing him one of the cigarettes. "See how long they are; they call them 'king size.' Want one?"

"Sure." Tony smoked with Denny, who was a heavy smoker, when they were drinking or shooting pool, and with Francie because he knew she liked him to share a cigarette with her after they petted, but he rarely bought a pack and seldom smoked alone.

"I saw Buck upstairs," she said as she exhaled. "He didn't seem to have a lot of confidence in avoiding a strike."

"How could he?" Tony asked rhetorically. "Your old man's negotiators haven't given in on one single issue yet."

"They're willing to," Francie defended. "They're willing to offer a wage increase any time the union agrees not to ask for anything else."

"The men will never go for that," Tony asserted. "Too many other things need changing down in those mines."

"Changes are costly," Francie said. "I helped Clinton Randall prepare all the figures for Daddy; I know how much money is involved in the changes the union wants. A mine can't operate unless it makes a profit."

They caught each other's eyes and smiled sheepishly, realizing how much they sounded like the negotiators. "Listen to us," Francie said. "*We* can't even agree on it."

"I'll bet we could if we really tried," Tony said, nuzzling her neck and ear. "What do you think?"

"Well, maybe." She turned to catch his lips with her own. "Especially if I didn't wear a brassiere."

Tony grinned. "*Definitely* if you didn't wear a brassiere."

Francie rested her head on his shoulder and they finished the new Pall Mall kings in silence, after which Francie retrieved an Ovaltine can from behind the trunk in which to extinguish the butts. "I heard on the radio tonight that Thanksgiving is being changed to the fourth Thursday in November," she said. "President Roosevelt thinks that allowing more time for shopping between Thanksgiving and Christmas will help the economy."

"Won't be much Christmas shopping in this town if the miners are on strike," Tony speculated.

"You don't think it would last *that* long, do you?" Francie asked, surprised. Tony shrugged.

"The Republic Steel strike in Chicago did. Even after the cops killed four strikers and put a hundred of them in the hospital."

"But that was Chicago," Francie reasoned. "Those are city people. In Chicago, a person doesn't even know their own neighbors. We're different out here in Virginia City."

"A strike's a strike," Tony said, drawing on Buck's philosophy. "Could last the rest of the year."

"God, I hope not," Francie said with a touch of desperation in her voice. "During the holidays is when I wanted to talk to Daddy about moving you out of the mine."

Tony glanced away. "I told you how I felt about that, Francie. I'm not taking anything from your old man."

"You're taking me," she reminded him.

"I'll do that without any help from him," Tony asserted. "Anyway, your old man wants you to marry Jack Coltrane. He wouldn't do anything for me, even if I let him."

"You might be very surprised," Francie said.

Yeah, I might be, Tony thought, but not by Big Jim Delavane. Francie knew Big Jim only as a father; Tony knew him as a man and a mine owner. And as the person he felt responsible for the deaths of his parents and sisters. Tony had never told Francie of his hatred for her father. Nor of her father's offer to take him and raise him after his family's tragedy. Tony still seethed at the memory of that: a pony, a goddamned pony he tried to buy him with!

Tony's hatred of Big Jim Delavane had never waned through the years; only his consuming desire to murder Delavane had tempered, as Tony matured, into less drastic forms of revenge: measures that would hurt Delavane as much, perhaps more than death, but would not put Tony in jeopardy of prison or the electric chair. Usually those measures involved the two things that Tony had come to realize were most precious to Big Jim: his daughter and his mine.

For a time, Tony entertained notions of somehow seizing control of Delavane Mines: striking it rich on his own, making a fortune, and buying up enough Delavane stock to take over. The older he became, and the more he was exposed to the raw economics of life, the more he realized that such a plan was too farfetched to be much more than a young man's fantasy. Then too, as his desire grew to have Francie for his own, his thoughts involved Delavane less and less and his daughter more and more.

Tony had examined his conscience: did his feelings for Francie have anything to do with his hatred for her father? He was pretty sure they did not. His love for Francie was deep and pure, untainted by anything mean; it became clouded at times by black memories of what had happened to his family, but that was coincidental; Francie had nothing to do with that—only her father did. While still an adolescent Tony made up his mind never to broach the subject with her, never to tell her that he thought her father was a murderer, that he had sworn vengeance on him, that he hoped to someday ruin him. Or that Big Jim, to salve his own guilt, had tried to take Tony into his home to raise. Tony had to wonder sometimes how things would have turned out if he had gone with Delavane instead of Buck, grown up on the Hill instead of the Walk, had Francie for a foster sister instead of little Kerry. Life would certainly have been different . . .

After all the thought he gave it, Tony was convinced that no part of his love for Francie was founded on taking her away from her father. He admitted that sneaking into the Delavane cellar and fondling Francie under the very floor that Big Jim walked *did* give him a secret feeling of satisfaction, but that wasn't his motive—he was crazy about Francie and there was no other private, warm place to meet in the wintertime.

In love or out, Tony and Francie had always been poignantly aware of the class differences between them. The problem became acute when they reached their mid-teens and began trying to figure out how they could be together when they were old enough. For Tony, it was one of the reasons he decided to go from the tenth grade to a mine shift; as far as he was concerned, the only sure path to that goal was for him to put together enough money for them to run away from Virginia City and get a new start somewhere else. To that end he began doing a man's labor when he was still a boy.

For Francie, the problem became genuinely serious when she tried to attend college in the East and discovered that the protracted absence of Tony Donovan from her life was unendurable. Tony was, Francie realized one night at school, the real thing: she loved and was *in* love with the smouldering, shaggy-haired silver miner. This wasn't kid stuff anymore; this was *it*. Frequently as a child she had heard her father tell stories of men who searched for the high lode, the fountainhead of a silver vein. In Tony Donovan, she told herself romantically but in all seriousness, she had found her high lode of love.

How to attain that love completely and openly for herself was another matter, and it was a problem that Francie did not address with Tony's logical if naïve planning. Scraping together a little money and running away to a hard knocks life someplace else was not, to Francie's mind, a solution, it was merely a different problem. Here in Virginia City she had status, money, comfort, and a future promising more of the same. Instead of running away to some new, undefined, uncharted, unpredictable life, better to remain where she was, where it was familiar, secure, foreseeable. What she must do to achieve that, she reasoned, was arrange for her father to make Tony a manager instead of a miner. Let Tony learn how to run a business instead of a drill, how to produce profits instead of perspiration. She thought he would consider the idea brilliant. She was mistaken.

While Tony continued to save for and plan an elopement, Francie had not given up on the idea that there was an easier way for them. She was certain that her father would want to help them once he was convinced by her that the relationship with Tony was *real*. Francie's problem was how to convince him. She had been back from college for ten months, and her relationship with Tony was still a secret. She always seemed to have an excuse for *not* telling her father about it, or a future time at which she definitely would tell him. First she wanted to learn her job in the mine office and become an asset to the company, so her father would recognize that she was a mature woman; then Big Jim had to leave on a business trip before she could tell him; then it was too close to the anniversary of her mother's death, when he always became morose; then it was this or that or something else. Now it was the impending strike.

For Tony's part, it did not matter if Francie ever got around to telling her father. As far as he was concerned, he hoped she did not. Let Big Jim Delavane find out about it the hard way—*after* if happened, after Tony and Francie had eloped and were safely married. Let him hear the news and realize that Francie—his family—had been taken from him, just as Tony had been told when he woke up in the hospital that *his* family had been taken from him. Let the news hit Big Jim right between the eyes like a miner's hammer.

It would be easier on himself too, Tony realized, the longer Francie put off telling her father. Because as soon as it became public he would have to submit to Buck's scrutiny and evaluation—and Buck was not going to take Tony's deceit lightly. As for Francie being the girl he loved, Buck might or might not approve; it was hard for Tony to predict.

Buck seemed to like Francie well enough; he had seemed genuinely pleased when she went to work at the mine, and of course Buck had greatly admired—perhaps even loved, Tony had always suspected—Francie's mother. But Buck was first and foremost a hardrock miner, a workingman, a union man. While not outright contemptuous of the upper class, he was somewhat disdainful of it most of the time. To Buck O'Crotty, the labor class was the only class to which a man ought aspire. If he thought Tony was bringing Francie down off the Hill, Tony guessed, he would probably approve; if he thought Tony had aspirations of joining her up there, it would produce objection, disparagement, and denunciation. One reaction was as likely as another with Buck. Meanwhile, Tony had decided that his best bet was simply to continue saving as much money as he could for the day when they could elope.

"I'd better get back upstairs," Francie said now, sitting on the trunk with him in her cellar, "before Cavendish or one of the others begins to wonder where I've gone." As she stood up, she tentatively bit her lower lip and felt a surge of dread. "I might as well tell you now as later. I can't meet you at the movies Saturday night—"

"Why the hell not?"

"—because the Coltranes are having a dinner party and Daddy insists that I go with him."

Tony became instantly remote. "Have a good time," he said, his tone turning cold.

"I didn't know how to get out of it, Tony," she pleaded.

I suppose Jack's going to be there," Tony said irritably, more a statement than a question.

"He's home from college for the weekend," she admitted.

"Keen," Tony said. "Our night—and you'll be spending it with him. You know he's crazy about you. This is just one more move in a lousy plan by your old man and the Coltranes to get you two together."

"Tony, it is not. Now listen," Francie attempted to placate, "don't be angry. It just turned out that way. Let's make it Sunday night for us instead. The picture changes on Sunday anyway. *Stanley and Livingstone* will be on, with Spencer Tracy."

"I don't like Spencer Tracy," he sulked.

"You do so!" she exclaimed indignantly; she punched him stiffly on the muscle. "Liar. Spencer Tracy's your favorite actor. You made me sit through *Captains Courageous* twice!" Francie put her arms around his neck and pressed herself lovingly against his chest. "You aren't going to be angry with me, are you, precious?"

"No, I'm not," Tony said, but there was a weariness in his tone. "I'll just be glad when all this sneaking around is over, when it can just be you and me, and not worrying about anybody else."

"Soon," Francie promised. "That'll be soon."

*   *   *

Upstairs in the study, Buck O'Crotty was talking about working conditions in the Delavane mines.

"The membership feels we've come down to the absolute minimum on this issue, Jim. We've eliminated all but three demands. We want better lighting, better draining, and better ventilating. If we were in a straight and level tunnel, we wouldn't be asking for all three at once like this, but being in a stope, each section of the tunnel a few feet lower than the one before it, why, sometimes it seems like we're digging the steps to hell. If you'd come down there, Jim, and see what it's like—"

"I know what it's like, Buck," Big Jim interrupted, a little irritably. "I've worked the mines. With you, remember? It isn't necessary to invite me to visit a stope like I was some Eastern investor or something."

"I wasn't inviting you to visit *a* stope," Buck pointed out calmly. "I was inviting you to visit *this* stope, *your* stope. The bottom tunnel's down past three thousand feet now. It's so dark down there with just lanterns that the drillers can't see half the cracks in the breast; they have to feel for them. The air's so thick after the powder monkeys set off a blast that the men have to wave their shirts and caps around for five minutes before they can breathe right again. And the muckers, why, they're ankle deep to knee deep in water all the while they're loading the rock—"

"All right, all right," Big Jim waved a hand to halt the litany. "We both know it's not like clerking in a dry goods store, Buck. Jesus! Silver mines have always been dark and dirty and wet. If a man wants sunshine, clean air, and dry feet, let him be a goddamned dairy farmer!" Delavane picked up the sheaf of papers he had put aside earlier. "These are Clint Randall's estimates of how much it will cost to run power lines throughout the main and tributary tunnels, and upgrade the present ventilation and drainage systems." He waved the papers at the union president. "Tens of *thousands*, Buck."

O'Crotty pursed his lips, considering what to say next. He had to be very careful here, *extremely* careful, because his practiced ear had just told him that he had already won the concessions they wanted in the area of working conditions. Big Jim had said how much the improvements "will" cost, not "would" cost; that meant, Buck felt, that the mine owner had already decided to concede on that issue. Buck's strategy now had to be to skirt the point entirely and concentrate on another: one on which Big Jim would not demand a concession from the union to offset the concession he had decided to make but was not aware he had just revealed. Wages and hours were clearly out. That left only the matter of safety.

"Off that subject for a moment, Jim," the wily union man said, "you heard, of course, of the problems old man Benteen's having with his latest digs up in Silver Springs?"

"I heard. It's all that soft ground up there. The damn fool's going under old shafts from years ago when the Grady mine hit that mineral hot springs and flooded everything underground for miles around." Delavane's eyes narrowed a fraction. Was this casual conversation, or was he being handled? "You're not comparing our dirt to Benteen's, I hope, Buck. Christ! We're digging in good, solid rock."

"The breast is rock, Jim, but on the last few stopes we cut, we found that our ceilings were softening. I reported it to Harley Kent; maybe he didn't tell you. The wooden roof supports are buckling and letting too much ground fall in—"

"Pillars!" Delavane roared. "You're going to ask for pillars again!"

"They'd be safer, Jim—"

"Jesus, Mary, and Joseph! The mineralogists have already told us that if we use pillars, we're going to leave seventeen percent of the ore untouched. *Seventeen Percent*! Is the A.M.W.N. trying to bankrupt me?"

O'Crotty sighed heavily and pursed his lips again. Pillars were exactly what their name implied: natural supports left in place by digging around them; they held up the ceiling of the tunnel much better than shoring it up with wooden beams. But using them did mean, as Big Jim raged, that the ore in those natural supports had to be left alone.

"Some of that ore, of course, would be spoil rock," Buck rationalized. That was waste: barren, unprofitable rock.

"Damn little at that depth," Delavane argued.

"And some of it would be lean." Low-grade ore.

"Damn little of that too. Dance around it all you want, Buck, it's still money left behind."

"All right, all right," O'Crotty said, repeating Delavane's own words of impatience a few minutes earlier. "What about the black powder? If we back off on the pillars, will you give us gelatin dynamite instead of black powder?"

Big Jim shook his head. Gelatin dynamite, fabricated into cartridges or sticks, cost half again as much as kegs of black powder. "You're letting those powder monkeys do a routine on you, Buck," the mine owner said, pointing an accusing finger at O'Crotty. The powder monkeys were the men who did the underground blasting. "The only reason they want gelatin dynamite is because they won't have to work so hard. It's easier to use."

"That's not the point at all," Buck denied, shaking his head vigorously. "There's no toxic fumes from gelatin sticks like there is with black powder."

"I see. It's toxic fumes you're worried about?"

"Yes, it is."

"Clean air?"

"Exactly."

"Safe breathing?"

"Exactly."

"Well then, if I concede on the first issue and upgrade the ventilation system, it won't matter what you blast with, will it? Any toxic fumes created by the use of black powder will be eliminated by the new system. So that's taken care of"

Both men sat back in their chairs and reached for their whiskey glasses. I've got him there, Delavane thought. He's got me there, O'Crotty thought. Buck quickly tallied the score. So far he could go back to the men with a tunnel that had cleaner air, drier ground, more light, and with a ceiling that at least was no more unsafe than it had previously been. If he could get the working hours reduced and the pay increased, the men would probably go for it.

"As far as hours are concerned, Jim, we're willing to forget all the demands for elevator pay, crawl pay, the fifteen-minute washup time, and the rest. All we'd like to do is cut back the shift like the United Mine Workers back in Virginia—"

"*Coal* miners," Big Jim said derisively.

"—based on studies of health and alertness fatigue—"

"Crybabies."

"—cut it back to forty hours a week."

"J. C. Penney clerks work longer hours than that."

"Under the new Fair Labor Standards Act that's been passed, you'll have to do it next year anyway. Why not show the men that you're fair and humane by doing it now, instead of waiting a year when the government forces you to do it. The men want to spend some of their lives above the ground, Jim. Between October and March, they never see daylight except on Sundays."

"Neither did we," the mine owner reminded O'Crotty, "in the old days."

"Because we worked for bastards," O'Crotty reminded him. The union man's meaning was clear.

Sighing wearily, Big Jim fingered through the sheaf of papers until he found a certain one. For several moments he studied it; then he uncapped a fountain pen and began to cross out figures and write in new ones. His lips moved silently as he made calculations. After a bit he sighed again, more resignedly this time, and looked over at Buck O'Crotty.

"All right. Forty hours."

Buck nodded warmly at his old comrade in arms and raised his glass in salute. "You're a good man, Jim Delavane." After a quick sip of whiskey, he said, "Now, if we can agree on a wage increase—"

"The forty-hour week was my last concession, Buck."

"What's that?"

"There'll be no wage increase."

"But, Jim, that's the most important issue of all—"

"Maybe you should have brought it up first then." Delavane leaned forward, eyes narrowing, steady as two bullet holes. "You just got through using that goddamned Fair Labor Standards Act as the basis for one of your arguments. Now it's my turn. Your friend John L. Lewis with his new C.I.O." —Delavane pronounced it like an obscenity, "*See-Eye-Oh*," each letter distinct—"thinks he's in a position now to run the entire country, but he's gone a little bit too far to suit a lot of us. There are some American businessmen left who would rather close down entirely than let that little bushy-browed Napoleon tell us how to operate. The steel makers gave him a good battle, and so did the automobile makers. Sure, the unions win in the long run, but their members *lose* a hell of a lot first. The Fair Labor Standards Act requires me to pay a minimum wage of thirty cents an hour. I'm already doing that; there's not a man in my mines who earns less. Under the new law, I don't have to give anyone a wage increase, Bucko. And, in light of everything else I've given you tonight, I don't intend to."

Buck was aghast. "That minimum wage is meant as a

starting base for apprentices, Jim. Not for seasoned journeymen. You've got men who've been with you for fifteen years or better—"

"They should have *stayed* with me," Big Jim muttered, "instead of throwing in with you and the A.M.W.N. They'd have more today if they had."

"What they'd have would be at your whim; the union gives them rights. Now you've got to be reasonable, Jim. Everyone can't be lumped together in the same wage bracket. You've got longtime workers, hazardous workers, night shift workers, grade workers, a dozen other classifications; I'm responsible to all of them, and their families—"

"Just as I am responsible to my investors, Buck."

"Investors! For Christ's sake, man, don't talk to me about filling some investor's pocket when I'm trying to fill a workingman's belly!"

"Then you be reasonable! Delavane Mines isn't a sole ownership, you know! Without investors do you suppose I could even *consider* mining power lines down all the shafts and into all the tunnels, and upgrading the ventilating and drainage works? That kind of thing doesn't come out of petty cash, you know; I have to borrow to do that, and I can't borrow without approval of the people who represent the investors. On top of which you're making me go to those same people and say, oh by the way, because the men have cut their work week back to forty hours, our ore production will be reduced ten or twelve percent."

"A ten or twelve percent reduction is better than a one hundred percent reduction," Buck said pointedlly. "Which is what they'll get if we strike. Maybe you should point that out to them."

Big Jim grunted, loudly and scornfully. "They'd laugh in my face, for Christ's sake. For most of them, Delavane Mines represents maybe three or four percent of their investments. If we shut down, they won't even notice it until their next quarterly brokerage statements come in. Besides which, these are hardnosed businessmen, Buck—they'd rather see the mine closed than watch it lose money."

"I've *got* to have more money for my men," O'Crotty said obstinately.

"And I won't give it to you," Delavane said, just as stubbornly. "I can't give it to you—not with everything else you want."

O'Crotty fixed the mine owner with a steady gaze. "I thought we could work this out, you and me." His words carried a subtle accusation.

Delavane met the union president's stare. "Apparently you were wrong." His reply rejected any guilt on his part.

Buck O'Crotty stood up, leaving the rest of his whiskey. "Like you said then, it's going to be a long, cold winter."

The union leader walked out of the room.

SIXTEEN

As things turned out, it did not matter what anyone had planned for that Saturday night. When the strike began, all plans were canceled.

No one in Virginia City knew what kind of temper a strike would produce, so everyone became wary and cautious. Merchants along C Street closed an hour earlier in order to lock up and proceed to their homes while it was still daylight: the sight of so many miners moving about town, when they were normally deep underground, was unnerving to many. Sheriff Sam Patch found that the city council, usually tightfisted to the extreme, quickly and with little discussion voted him the necessary emergency funds to hire four special deputies, just in case. Six A.M. Mass at St. Martha's was standing room only every morning as the wives of the miners, viewing the strike as a tragedy of great magnitude, attempted collectively to pray it away. The Coltranes, at Big Jim's suggestion, canceled their dinner party to allow their invited guests the security of remaining in their own homes. Francie was confined to the Hill, at least temporarily, until her father could evaluate the mood of the dissident workers; at the same time, he gave leaves of absence to all female employees, with half pay, so they would not have to cross the picket lines. He required his executives and male employees to continue to report to work, as he himself did, as a show of management integrity.

Buck O'Crotty, in an effort to be meticulously fair, assigned the order of picket shifts according to names drawn from a coffee tin—except in the case of members of his own household. He assigned himself, Tony, and Denny to the coldest and darkest or most inconvenient and undesirable shifts scheduled: early mornings from two to six, Saturday night from six to ten, Sunday afternoon from noon until six.

"Jesus, Buck," Tony complained, "why do you and Den and I have to do *more* shifts *and* the worst ones?"

"As an example, lad. I'm sorry it's fallen on you two in addition to me, but I have to be absolutely certain no one has cause to criticize me for not doing my share, or for favoritism to anyone close to me. Terry Henny, Lloyd Arlen, and the other officers of the local are pulling extra picket time also. Tempers get a bit on edge during a strike; I don't want any petty complaints cropping up. Incidentally, I want no complaining on the picket line from the two of you either."

To Tony in private, Buck had said, "I want you to be my model out there, lad. I want your conduct and attitude to be exemplary." When Tony frowned, Buck explained, "That means outstanding, the best. Remember, one day you yourself might be leading a strike; this experience could be invaluable to you."

Before Buck included Denny Ebro in any strike activities, he took him aside. "Look, lad, I know you're working in the mines because Tony's working in the mines, because you and him are best friends. But I think this is the time for you to give some consideration to going back to your own family. Get out of the tunnels and go back up there in those beautiful mountains where the air's clear and clean, where you can live in the daylight. What d'you say?"

"I can't go home, Buck, you know that," Denny said.

"You mean because of what happened when you were sixteen?" Buck scoffed. "That's ancient history, lad."

"No, Buck, it ain't," Denny shook his head emphatically. "You don't know my father; you don't know the *Basques.* Whether something happened five years ago or yesterday, it don't make no difference. It happened—and they don't forget."

* * *

On Denny's sixteenth birthday, Piro Ebro had come down from his high mountain sheep pasture to get him. In the O'Crotty living room he said happily, "You come home now. Sheriff tell me law cannot make you go to school after you sixteen."

Denny's face fell. "I don't want to go home, Papa," he said, in speech so much clearer that Piro Ebro was shocked.

"You talk well now," He said proudly. "That is good. But is time to come home now. Live with father, brothers."

"Papa, I like it here," Denny quietly pleaded. "I have a friend here," he gestured toward Tony, "and a mother," he indicated Rosetta, sitting quietly, mending one of Kerry's dolls while the little girl waited patiently.

"Ah, so," said Piro. He bobbed his bearded chin at Buck. "New father too, eh?" His eyes flashed angrily at Buck. "You steal my son, make him yours, Irisher?"

"No, Mr. Ebro, I haven't," Buck replied civilly. "I've made it clear to the lad that I think his place is properly with his own kin. But I've also let him know that he's cared for in this household, and always has a place to come to."

"Never should I have left him with you!" Piro roared.

"Kindly keep your voice down in my home, Mr. Ebro. As for leaving him here, I don't recall as you had a lot of choice. You had to make some arrangements or be sent to jail."

"Papa, please understand," Denny appealed. "It ain't nothing against you, nothing like that; it's just that it's so lonely up where the pastures are, nothing to do but tend sheep, nobody to talk to but my brothers . . ."

"Once you want me not bring you this place," Piro reminded his son. "You cry, beg—"

"That was before, Papa."

"Before? Before what?"

"Before I belonged here."

"So! You belong here, eh? Here with strangers and not with blood, eh?" Piro put a finger to his temple. "I think maybe you brain, she twisted like you mouth. Cripple like you mouth."

Rosetta rose from her chair, her expression coldly furious. Taking Kerry by the hand, she left the room rather than embarrass her husband by cursing Piro Ebro in Paiute for his viciousness.

"You shouldn't say that to me, Papa," Denny said, ashamed. "Not in front of people."

"I your father, I say what I wish!"

In order to alleviate some of the boy's mortification, Buck also rose, nodded to Tony to follow him, and left the room. Joining Rosetta and Kerry in the kitchen, they were still able to hear the exchange, growing angrier, between the father and son.

"I say you come home where you belong," Piro insisted.

"If you make me go back, I'll run away," Denny threatened.

"Then I come after you," Piro said, "with razor strap for your back! And," he warned, "I bring law on this Irisher who take you in!"

"I won't come back here! I'll hop a freight and go somewheres else! You can't make me stay up there, Papa!"

"By Christ you not talk to father like that! You need good kick in ass!"

There was the sound of a heavy kick then another, and a third. Buck hurried back into the living room, in time to see Denny crouching back from his father's booted foot. The elder Ebro continued kicking out, aiming for Denny's buttocks but invariably striking his thigh or knees. Denny tried to dodge the kicks, but each one managed to reach him. Tony, peering over Buck's shoulder, was reminded of Denny's first day at Comstock Elementary, when Jack Coltrane had driven Denny back the same way with slaps to the face. But this was a different Denny Ebro, this one knew how to make a fist.

Denny let his father kick him seven times; then he stepped into the eighth kick, grabbed Piro's foot with his left hand, and drove a hard fist into his father's face. The older man, who had not taken such a blow in three decades, dropped to the floor. Sitting, stunned, he reached up to feel blood trickling out of his nose. He stared at his son in shock.

"You struck father," Piro said in astonishment.

"You can't kick me like that, Papa," Denny said firmly. "I ain't one of your sheep."

"You struck father," Piro said again, indignation rising as he struggled awkwardly to his feet.

"I ain't gonna be treated like that—"

"*You—struck—father!*" Piro was now consumed by outrage. Wiping off the blood with the back of one hand, he pointed an impugning finger at Denny. "You are devil, not son!" From a table by the front door, he snatched up his beret. "You want stay here, stay!" Jerking open the front door, he paused to say only one more thing before stalking off "I deny you. You hear me? You understand me? *I—deny—you!*"

Then Piro Ebro was gone and an ocean of great quiet was left in his wake. After the roar of his deep Basque voice, when Buck O'Crotty spoke it seemed like a whisper.

"What did that mean, that denying business?" Buck asked, although fairly certain he already knew.

"Means he disowns me," Denny said. "Means I ain't his son no more, and he ain't my father."

"Ah, well." Buck put an arm around Denny's shoulders. "These things have a way of healing themselves," he assured. "This'll all blow over. Give it a couple of months. You'll see.

Buck had been wrong. Piro Ebro never returned, and despite encouragement from Buck to do so, Denny never went to see him, never tried to reconcile. Accepting the situation as Piro Ebro had ordained it, Denny remained in the O'Crotty household, quit school when Tony did and went into the mines. He had not seen his father in five years.

"You're a grown man," Buck said now, "and it's not for me to tell you what to do. But this strike is going to be a tough one. And I believe the thing between you and your father could be resolved if you were to go on home and offer your hand. Your father's a good man; he'll let bygones be, I'm convinced. What I want you to know is that if you want to pull out now nobody'll think the less of you for it. This is a hardrock miners' problem here; you don't have to make it yours. There's bad times coming; I can feel it."

Denny's cherubic young features, his harelip now covered by a moustache, immediately registered dejection. "Are you telling me I have to leave, Buck?" he asked woefully.

"Not at all, lad," Buck assured him, an affectionate hand at once on the young man's shoulder.

"Well," Denny asked with a hint of injured resentment, "are you afraid I might not do my part for you and the union, that I might let you down?"

"Absolutely not, Denny," Buck stated emphatically. "I know I can count on you just as much as I can on Tony."

Denny grunted inwardly. Prob'ly more, he thought. At

least I ain't sneaking out nights to see no Hill girl. "I want to stay, Buck," Denny told him. It was not a statement, it was a plea—and Buck O'Crotty recognized it as such. He smiled and offered his hand.

"I was hoping you would. You're a good lad."

While Buck went into the kitchen to say good-bye to Rosetta and Kerry, Denny joined Tony, who was waiting on the front porch. "What'd he want with you?" Tony asked curiously.

"Him and me was just talking strike business," Denny replied loftily. "It's confidential."

"What are you giving me?" Tony scoffed, hooking an arm around Denny's neck and wrestling him around.

"Honest to God, I can't tell you, Tony. See, you could get carried away some night when you're feeling up Francie and tell her the union's plans, an' she might tell Big Jim—"

"You phony prick," Tony said, tightening his arm hold. "Tell me the truth or I'll break your neck."

"Only if I let you, creampuff," Denny said, grinning. Tony was big and strong, but Denny was bigger and stronger—when he had enough horseplay, he gripped Tony's wrist and easily pulled his friend's arm out of its headlock position. "Quit now or I'll give you a bear hug," he warned. Denny could get Tony from behind and lift him up and down off his feet like Tony was a rag doll; when he did it, Tony was helpless to extricate himself. Kerry, who was now nine, thought it great entertainment. Tony hated it.

"Okay, okay," he said quickly, backing off. "You win. No bear hugs."

They relaxed into seriousness then and Denny told him what Buck had really said. Tony, too, was glad Denny had chosen to stay. "Wouldn't be the same around here without you, Den."

"You'd manage," Denny said, sitting on the front steps and lighting a cigarette. "Soon's old Delavane makes you his general manager, you prob'ly won't even talk to me no more."

"Bullshit," said Tony, who kept no secrets from Denny regarding his relationship with Francie. "That's just Francie's daydream. I'll be exactly what I am now, a bottom-stope driller, until I get enough money ahead for Francie and me to cut out. Anyway, you and me'll always be friends, Den, no matter what."

Sure, Denny worried to himself, until you and your rich

girlfriend run off and leave me behind. So much of Tony Donovan was in what Denny had become: tough, self-confident, no longer uncomfortable with his harelip; it had even been Tony who suggested Denny grow his moustache. The two of them had been so close for so long: sharing a bedroom, walking to and from school together, in the same classroom with desks side by side, experiencing boyhood adventures on the railroad tracks, in the Truckee River, snooping around Chinatown at night, making slingshots, sneaking into the movies, playing hooky, shooting marbles, lagging pennies, learning to smoke, fighting Jack Coltrane and the other Hill boys, and a multitude of other activities. The only thing that kept them from spending all of their time together was Tony's involvement with Francie. Except for her, life would have been perfect for Denny Ebro. Because of her, he endured his great secret dread that someday he would lose his best—really his only—friend.

Tony sat on the steps beside him and Denny shook a cigarette out of his Camel pack for him. Tony lighted it with the tip of Denny's cigarette. "How long you think the strike'll last?" Denny asked.

"I don't kow," Tony replied somberly. "Buck seems to think it might go into next year. He says Delavane might hold out to see if the men will soften up when Christmas gets close. Says men with families start feeling guilty if they can't provide a merry Christmas for their kids." Tony glanced at him. "If it does last that long, maybe you should take Buck's advice and at least go home and spend the holidays with your family."

Denny looked him in the eye. "My home's right here, same as you."

"Sure, I know," Tony quickly amended. "I just thought you might like to see your father and brothers again. Christmas would be a good time—"

"I ain't interested in seeing them at Christmas or no other time," Denny said unequivocally. "If my mamma was living, I'd go back to see her. She really loved me. But not my old man. If he loved me, he would've understood and not disowned me like he did. Anyway, I ain't part of that family no more. Like I tol' Buck, once a Basque disowns a member of his family, that person stays disowned. I'll stick around here," he concluded, taking a long drag on his cigarette.

Turning sideways on the step and leaning against the banister, Tony studied his friend. Denny was leaning forward on his forearms, intently looking straight ahead, mouth open so that he could breathe better, deformed upper lip looking as if it were curled in a scornful sneer. We're not boys anymore, Tony suddenly thought. Neither of us. Since the day they had gone into the mines, they had been becoming men. The strike, Tony realized, would be the last rites of their passage. When it was over, nobody would be able to look upon them as boys ever again. This was the final step to manhood.

For Tony that meant being closer to getting Francie. For Denny, he realized, it meant greater uncertainty.

Francie paced her bedroom like a lioness waiting to feed when the males finished.

She had not seen Tony since the strike began, and the anxiety of it was making her a nervous wreck. He could no longer sneak into the cellar because her father had padlocked it in case the strikers stooped to vandalism; he wanted his home as secure as possible. She and Tony had talked on the telephone several times, but only briefly, clandestinely, both afraid that someone would overhear, or that one of the nosy operators at the phone company might be listening in. For the most part, the hurried conversations had consisted of declarations of love and expressions of agony at being apart.

"This is absolute *misery*," Francie had whispered at one point. "I feel like I'm serving a term in prison."

"Isn't there any way you can get into town?" Tony asked dejectedly. "Just for a little while?"

"I wish I could. But Daddy won't even let Cavendish or any of the household staff go to town; everything we need is being delivered." She thought of Tony's strong, hard hands. "Almost everything, that is . . ."

"It's stupid to make you stay at home," Tony said irritably. "The strike's been peaceful all the way." He paused a beat. "Almost."

"Daddy says there have been some fights."

"Not really fights. Just some shoving. A lot of name-calling."

"Daddy says it's an 'incendiary' situation."

"That's laying it on kind of thick."

"He also thinks it's going to be a long strike."

"Yeah, so does Buck."

"Damn."

"Yeah."

"God, I miss you. I miss having you touch me—"

"I miss touching you—"

"We'd better be careful—"

"Yeah—"

"—of what we say. Nosy people, you know."

"Yeah."

In her bedroom, Francie stopped pacing and lit a cigarette. Standing in the middle of the room, inhaling and exhaling in short, impatient puffs, she suddenly decided she hated her wallpaper. She had selected it herself not six months earlier and had it sent from St. Louis, a soft rose color with just a hint of gold filigree pattern. At the time, she had thought it very delicate and romantic, like her moments with Tony. Now, she thought, because of this goddamned strike, she had no moments with Tony.

Crushing out her still fresh cigarette in a brass ashtray, Francie abruptly left her bedroom and went downstairs. Crossing the foyer toward the front door, she was cautioned by Cavendish who came to the library door.

"You mustn't leave the Hill now, Miss Frances."

"I *know*, Cavendish," she replied in exasperation. She purposely did not tell him where she was going, knowing he would have to interrupt his work in the library and go to a window to watch. As she crossed the mansion's wintering yellow lawn, she regretted her attitude; Cavendish, after all, was simply behaving responsibly in his duties, as instructed by her father. And the English butler was a sweet and loyal person, dedicated to the Delavane household. She would buy him a little gift, she decided. If she ever got to town again.

Walking down the low sloping lawn, disturbing several red squirrels at play, Francie headed toward a mansion just slightly less opulent than their own: the Coltranes', the Delavanes' nearest neighbors. She was going to visit Libby Coltrane, wife of banker Harmon Coltrane. At thirty-six, Libby was twenty-three years younger than her husband— and only seventeen years older than their son Jack, who, like Francie, was an only child. Jack, once the most intensely disliked boy in Virginia City, upon graduation from Comstock Elementary School had been sent to high school at Culver Academy in California. It had taken that prestigious military institution nearly three semesters to accoumplish the task, but on the Christmas vacation of his sophomore year Jack had returned to his parents a model young cadet. It had been an amazing transition, of which some people in Virginia City were still highly suspicious. But the change seemed genuine; Jack had graduated with honors from Culver and gone on to the University of California at Berkeley where he was a pre-law student. He had been home two weekends earlier—the reason for the Coltranes' dinner party— when the strike started, but had returned to school.

Libby Coltrane was on the east patio of their mansion working on an oil painting of Mt. Davidson when Francie came across the lawn toward her.

"Hello, dear," she greeted Francie pleasantly.

"Hello, Libby." Francie and Libby had an understanding. Libby was "Mrs. Coltrane" only when other people were around. As she herself had said, she was only in her mid-thirties and felt more like Jack's older sister than his mother. Francie liked the secret informality; it was somehow like she imagined her relationship with Edith would have been. "I'll go crazy if I have to stay up on the Hill another day," Francie said now.

"You need something interesting to do in your spare time," Libby said.

I have something, Francie thought, I just can't get to him.

"A hobby of some kind," Libby continued. "Have you ever thought about painting?"

"I wouldn't have the patience," Francie demurred. "Have you talked to Jack this week?"

"Yes, last night. He called to inquire about the strike. He asked his father and me to keep an eye on you. I think he's worried about you, dear."

"That's sweet," Francie said absently.

"I'm very serious," Libby asserted. "I think Jack would like to have you for a steady girlfriend. He just doesn't know how to go about establishing the relationship. Poor baby, he still has so much to live down—what an atrocious child he was! A lot of people still think of him as he used to be, I'm afraid. Some of the Chinese laundrymen in town still cross the street if they see him coming, he terrorized them so." Libby glanced curiously at Francie. "You don't feel that way about him, do you, Francie?"

"No, of course not." She didn't feel *any* way about Jack Coltrane.

"Not that I'm eager to see you two start making any serious plans," Libby disclaimed. "God knows, I do not need to become a grandmother before I'm forty." A pretty pampered woman, Libby had come from a once wealthy family that had had the American franchise to manufacture and distribute Bayer aspirin for its German owners. When the United States entered Wotld War I, the American assets of the firm were seized as spoils of war and later sold by the government to the Sterling Drug Company. Libby's family went bankrupt. One of the bankers involved in taking over the assets for the U.S. was thirty-nine-year-old Harmon Coltrane. He made enough profit on the seizure to start his own bank in Virginia City—and took the sixteen-year-old Libby as a bonus. After the birth of their son Jack the following year, Coltrane quietly resumed the womanizing that had kept him a bachelor for so long. He and Libby had not slept together for nearly two decades.

"I know that Harmon and your father have discussed a match between you and Jack," Libby continued the subject.

"They'd better not let me catch them discussing it," Francie said firmly, her gray eyes flinting. "This isn't eighteenth-century Europe. I'll pick my own husband."

"Well, tell me, dear, does Jack have any competition?" the older woman asked in an oddly neutral tone, as if she already knew what the answer would be. "Serious competition, I mean. Does our Francie have a secret beau that none of us knows about?"

"You never can tell," Francie replied, deliberately vague.

Libby stopped painting momentarily, although she did not put her brush down as her expression became quizzical—whether genuinely or not, Francie could not tell; Libby was a very good actress at times. "If you do have, I wonder who it could be. Of course, it would have to be a young man from the Hill; you're much too sensible to become involved with anyone lacking social standing. Let's see now. Phil Pitt is a possibility, I suppose. Nice looking young man, good family, his father is your father's lawyer. Craig Randall is another. Marvelous sense of humor, and his father has been the Delavane Mines head accountant almost since your father made his first strike. Or perhaps Billy Kent—if you're attracted to muscles. Now *his* father, as general manager of

Delavane Mines, is probably closer to your father than anyone—"

"What is this his father-my father business?" Francie asked with mild indignation. "Is there some kind of rule that says I have to marry someone whose father is associated with my father?"

"Of course there's no *rule*, dear, but common sense should prevail in these matters—"

"Common sense is the last thing that prevails," Francie commented wryly, and instantly realized she had fallen into Libby Coltrane's clever trap.

"So," Libby said with cool, contained delight, "there is someone." Now she did put her brush aside and fixed Francie in an unsparing gaze. "Who is the lucky young man, dear?"

Tell her, Francie's rebellious nature urged. Throw it right in her face and let her spread it all over the goddamned Hill. Let your father find out about it that way. Tell her! Shock the living hell out of her and everybody else. Just part your lips and say simply: Tony Donovan. He's a driller in Daddy's mine. Tell her. Tell them all!

Francie parted her lips to speak—but another voice sounded first.

"There you are, Libby," said Harmon Coltrane, coming onto the patio, home from his day at the bank. "Hello, Francie. Just ran into your father; we pulled our cars alongside and chatted for a minute. He's got a big surprise for those strikers tonight, hasn't he?"

"Harmon," said Libby, "you pick the most inopportune times to appear." She smiled artificially at Francie. "You were about to say, dear . . .?"

But Francie's total attention was now on Harmon Coltrane. "What do you mean, Mr. Coltrane? What surprise?"

"Why, those six railroad cars of copper miners he's bringing in on the seven-thirty from Reno. Their mine over in Utah closed down when the vein ran out—say, you did know about this, didn't you?" Coltrane turned slightly red. "I didn't let the cat out of the bag here, did I?"

"Of course I knew," Francie lied with complete poise. "I'd just forgotten that it was tonight." Now it was she who put on a spurious smile. "Well, if Daddy's home already, I'd better get back. Nice visiting with you, Mrs. Coltrane." Francie picked up the brush and handed it to Libby. "Love your technique."

Saying good-bye to Harmon Coltrane, Francie hurried back up the slope toward the Delavane mansion. She was seething. *Outsiders!* How could he? Whatever the economic dispute between her father and the miners, whatever the social differences between the Hill and Miners Walk, whatever discord or disharmony from or in any quarter, it was all still *Virginia City*. It was among acquaintances, neighbors, friends—yes, even lovers. It should be resolved in the community. This was not Chicago, for God's sake, where people didn't even know the family next door. Outsiders? To Francie, it was unthinkable.

Storming through the house, Francie burst into her father's study. "Is it true?" she demanded. "Are you bringing in miners from Utah?"

Looking up from his desk, his mail, his whiskey, a scowl came over Big Jim Delavane's handsome face. "Are you speaking to me?" he asked, surprised and mildly indignant. "Or to some lackey?"

"I want to know, Daddy."

"So you *do* remember who I am—"

"Daddy . . .!"

"Yes!" he snapped glancing away, snatching up his whiskey glass. He took a swallow and looked back at her. "Yes, I am," he answered again, more calmly. For a fleeting instant there was unutterable pain in his eyes. Jesus God almighty, why—*why*—did she have to look so much like Edith? Blinking rapidly, shedding himself of the abrupt grief, he rose and went to her, carrying his glass, and put an arm around her shoulders. "Come over and sit by the fire," he said. Guiding her to the fireplace, its wood laid and lighted earlier by Cavendish in preparation for Big Jim's arrival home, Delavane sat his daughter in one of the big Morris chairs and asked, "Would you like a sip of scotch before dinner?"

Francie stared incredulously at him. Dinner? "How could you bring in outsiders, Daddy?" she asked, in a tone at once incongruously pleading, accusing, challenging.

"Francie, this is a matter of simple business expediency," he explained. "I didn't go looking for these men; their superintendent got in touch with me. Their digs over in Utah tapped out and the lot of them were let go. They're family men, they need work—"

"*Our* miners are family men too," Francie declared, "and they also need work."

"The work is there for them; they won't do it. These fellows from Utah will take minimum wage and are glad to get it—"

"Daddy, this is not fair," Francie insisted. "If you bring in outsiders, it's like telling our own miners that you don't care how long they stay out on strike, that you can run the mine without them—"

"That's the general idea," Big Jim allowed.

"Oh, Daddy . . ." She shook her head, near to tears.

"Francie, honey, I know how you feel," her father said, reaching over to take one of her hands. "I know you went to school with some of those fellows who work in my stopes now; I know you've always been fond of Buck O'Crotty because your mother admired him so much, but this is business, honey."

"My God, Daddy, even business should have some ethics, shouldn't it? Some dignity, some, I don't know"—she searched for a suitable word—"some honor," she finally said, not entirely satisfied with her choice. There was equity involved here; it seemed to her that principles of integrity ought to be applied.

"I have a responsibility to my investors," Big Jim patiently explained. "They have a right to expect me to resolve these labor difficulties as efficiently and effectively as I can—"

"You're using a lot of fancy reasoning to get around the fact that this is a *human* problem, Daddy!"

"Please stop interrupting me, Francie." A dangerous edge was creeping into the mine owner's voice. "I'm merely trying to explain—"

"You mean justify."

"Goddamn it, shut up!" Delavane roared. "Let me finish a sentence, for Christ's sake!" His face flushed red with anger. "What the hell is this, some kind of inquisition? Have you joined the goddamned union on me?" Snatching up his glass again, spilling a little whiskey on the table in the process, he took a long swallow, paused to look scathingly at his daughter, then took a second, shorter drink. "You," he said meanly, pointing an accusing finger, "are getting to be just like your mother was! She never remembered which side she was on, either! And it, by God, killed her! She'd be alive today if she hadn't consorted with that rabble in town!" Overcome by emotions of resentment and loneliness, Jim

Delavane shook his head in outrage. "The bitch! The sanctimonious bitch!"

Francie stared at her father in horror. It was the first time she had ever heard him denigrate her mother's name. Though she shared her father's loss of Edith, she had never felt in her own bereavement any sense of rancor or bitterness at how or why her mother had died. As far as she was concerned, it had been a terrible accident. Francie's grief was innocent. When her father's reviling words burst from his mouth, she could only look at him with shocked repugnance.

Without a word, she rose from the chair and walked swiftly out of the room, her mind reeling with a single thought: Tony.

She had to get to Tony.

SEVENTEEN

Francie found the path that led down through the trees to the top of Gold Street rutted and uneven. Tony, she was sure, knew every stone and hollow in it, he had traversed it up and down so many times. But this was her first time, it was dark now, and she was cold and afraid. Cold because when she walked through the house to slip out the back door, she had not been able to wear a coat else she would have betrayed her intent to leave; afraid because for the first time in her life she was flagrantly and intentionally betraying her father—and the act unnerved her, frightened her. It would have been more honest and less odious, she concluded halfway down the path, to have simply walked out of the house, gotten in her car, and driven off. She was of age; her father could not have stopped her—short of using force, and he would not have done that. *Probably* would not have done that. But in her moment of turmoil and desperation, Francie had chosen the covert; now that decision plagued her conscience.

She made her way forward, downward, nevertheless, and was greatly relieved when through the trees she saw the single streetlamp at the top of Gold Street. Reaching the street, she began to trot, thankful that she had put on oxfords earlier to go over to Libby Coltrane's; she was certain she would not have had the forethought to change shoes even if she had been wearing high heels. At the corner, she turned into A Street and hurried along for several blocks, past the modest homes of store clerks, teachers, bank tellers; past Comstock Elementary with all its memories; past the Virginia City Municipal Fire Department, the public library; until finally she came to Miners Walk. Thank God it was dark, she thought. The sight of Big Jim Delavane's daughter running along the Walk at the height of a miners' strike was too ludicrous to be seen.

Francie had never been to Tony's house, the O'Crotty home; nevertheless she knew where it was because a stretch of Miners Walk could be seen from one of the favorite meeting places she and Tony had, a wooded ridge at the top of Silver Street, behind and above Sam Patch's county jail. Once when they had been lying there on the grass that edged the trees, Tony had, a little self-consciously, pointed it out to her when she innocently asked which house was his.

"Hello. You must be Kerry."

"Yes, ma'am," the girl said.

Despite the urgency of the situation, Francie was momentarily taken aback; she had never been addressed as "ma'am" before. For a fleeting moment she identified with Libby Coltrane. Her nervous smile fluctuated. "Is Tony at home, Kerry?" she asked without identifying herself.

"No, ma'am. He's on picket. No one's home but me. Denny's on picket too. And Mamma's helping with the food and coffee at the union hall. I'm not sure where Buck is."

The front door of the adjacent house opened and a woman in an apron stepped out to put an empty milk bottle with a note in it on the front stoop. She looked curiously at Francie, squinting to make her out in the light from the O'Crotty front door.

"Listen can I come in for a sec?" Francie asked, her nervousness increasing. At the moment she felt very alien.

In the modest but immaculate living room Francie was immediately aware of the meagerness of the place and had to fight the desire to be back in her own fine, elegant home on the Hill. The little O'Crotty house, while certainly not impoverished, could easily have been depressing in its comparative bleakness. Francie had a compelling urge to complete her mission and be gone.

"Kerry, could you take a note to Tony on the picket line for me?" she asked the girl.

"No, ma'am, I can't," the girl replied unequivocally. "I'm not allowed out at night alone. But Mamma will be home soon; maybe she could."

Francie bit her lower lip tentatively. She had never met Rosetta O'Crotty, although she had seen the Paiute woman in town occasionally, and naturally knew quite a lot about her from Tony. For some reason—Francie wasn't sure why; her emotions were so confused tonight—she found herself mentally resisting the idea of meeting Rosetta, at least on this occasion, under these circumstances.

"No, I'd rather not wait for your mother," Francie said. "It's important that I tell Tony something right away. I'd go myself but, well . . ."

Francie's words trailed off Kerry finished the sentence for her. "It might look funny 'cause you're Big Jim's daughter."

"Oh. You know that." Francie was surprised.

"Sure," Kerry said. "Tony told me who you were. We saw you when you and your daddy stopped at the union picnic for a little while last Fourth of July. You had on a very pretty white dress. Tony said he'd buy me one like it someday."

Francie smiled fondly. "You kind of like Tony, don't you?"

"I love Tony," Kerry said solemnly.

So do I, Francie thought, and wished fervently that she had the courage to say so as openly as this little girl did. How, why, for what reason, what purpose, toward what end, had she and Tony ever decided to keep their feelings and relationship secret anyway? Was it this class thing? Were they embarrassed by it? She because on the Hill Tony was "common"; he because on the Walk it might look like he was trying to "marry up"? No, Francie concluded immediately; those rationalizations had come much later: those were adult motives that evolved as she and Tony had matured. The secrecy had been established at the very beginning, that day in the woods when she doctored his battered face. It had been established without comment, without discussion, established *naturally*. She was from the Hill, he from the Walk: they were not supposed to fall in love. Therefore they knew not to tell anyone about it when they did. They *knew*. Had Francie's mind been in less turmoil on this hectic, unsettled night, she would have realized that she and Tony had not instituted the secrecy; it had been dictated to them by the society in which they lived.

Francie bit her lip again. The dilemma of reaching Tony was rapidly nearing the point where a solution would have to involve public exposure of the fact that she had been disloyal to her father. She had hoped to counteract Big Jim's summoning of outsiders by surreptitiously warning Buck O'Crotty of it, through Tony—but if she could not privately reach Tony, if she had to openly go up to him on the picket line, then all of Virginia City would know of her betrayal. My God, she wondered, what might such a scandal do to her father? She had already experienced deep reservations about eloping with Tony for fear of how it would affect Big Jim; how could she possibly do this, then? And why was this child, this Kerry Morrell, looking at her in such a shrewd, calculating way with those marvelous eyes of hers?

"You know a way to help me, don't you?" Francie asked. There was no conscious thought behind the question; it was something of which Francie simply became aware.

"Yes," Kerry replied. "But I don't know if I will."

"Why not? Don't you trust me, Kerry? Tony would, you know, if he were here." Francie thought she saw a tiny gleam of understanding surface in Kerry's expression: as if Kerry had realized in that instant *all* the reasons why Francie was there. Kerry's simple statement of several moments earlier—"I love Tony"—had not, it suddenly dawned on Francie, been a familial remark; it had been *a female* remark—and this half-Paiute girl with the striking eyes had meant it to be so.

"If you really do love Tony," she told Kerry, "you'll help me get to him. It is very important, Kerry."

Still the girl hesitated, studying Francie, scrutinizing her face as if looking for signs of deception, trickery, falseness. This was a nine-year-old wise beyond her years, growing up in a household not limited as most are to one culture, one religion, one language. Kerry was exposed to all manner of things white, Irish, Catholic, Paiute, Basque, union, poor, and proud. She knew of priests and medicine men, rites, dialects, prayers in English, Latin, Basque, Paiute—"No matter what language God's listening to, Kerry'll prob'ly be heard," Denny one time said with a grin. She knew of caution, cleverness, cunning, having learned them from watching and listening to Buck, Tony, Denny, and her mother. Acutely aware of her Indian blood, she felt no allegiance to any white other than the three men with whom she lived. Likewise, she harbored no animosity—but she was always wary, prudent, and patient.

Much too patient for Francie under the circumstances. "Kerry, *please*," Francie pleaded.

"Come on," Kerry said finally.

She led Francie into a small bedroom, a bedroom no larger than some closets at the mansion; plain, poor, but like the rest of Rosetta O'Crotty's house it was clean as a freshly peeled apple. A narrow cot stood against each wall; a straight wooden chair between them with a small Archer radio on it; the previous week's *Saturday Evening Post* lay partly under one cot; on the wall were pegs on which hung extra sets of miner's garb.

"Put on a pair of Tony's overalls and a coat," Kerry said. "Turn your hair up under a cap. Then keep your head down and get in the picket line. You're as big as some of the sixteen-year-olds working the mines, and it's dark out; nobody'll pay any attention to you."

With a quick surge of excitement, Francie reached for a set of clothes.

The picket line walked in a loose circle that revolved across the gated entrance to the Delavane Mine property. There were, Francie saw from the shadows, perhaps two dozen men, all with signboards: some single poster types that men held up or carried over one shoulder; others sandwich boards that hung front and back over both shoulders. All the signs were white, all the lettering black, all the messages short and to the point. "Keep it simple, keep it clear," Buck had told his volunteer sign letterers. "We aren't trying to sell anything; all we want is fair play."

Extra signs were stacked on the back of a small stake truck parked at the side of the gate. Opposite it was another vehicle, an old car. Their headlamps, illuminated, faced each other and, engines running to keep the batteries charged, threw a circle of ghostly, vaporish light into the area where the men walked.

At Buck's instruction, all men on picket were dressed in work clothes; that is, the garb they wore to and from work. Once down in the stope, where the temperature could be ninety degrees or more, depending on how close they were to a hot spring, coats and shirts came off, were folded, and laid on a shelf of rock along with a man's dinner bucket. When shift ended, no matter how hot it was in the mine, the top clothing would religiously be put back on and buttoned up tight before riding the cage back to daylight; if not, the sudden change in air temperature, especially in winter, could give a man pneumonia in minutes. The human body was not conditioned to go from ninety degrees down to ten, while a man rose from four thousand feet underground back to the surface.

Buck's theory in having the men wear tunnel garb was twofold: it gave them a uniform, military looking appearance and thus projected strength, and it also conveyed the message that they were prepared to return to work immediately once a contract was settled. The work clothes also, he knew from his experiences in the coal fields, made it more difficult to identify specific individuals when incidents of shoving and shouting occurred, as they invariably did when office employees and lower management people crossed the picket line.

Francie could have attested to the latter theory: lurking in the shadows in a set of Tony's heavy denims, oversized on her smallish frame, she tried for a quarter-hour to distinguish which of the picketers was Tony—without success. For the most part, the men walked at the edge of the pool of light, all of them well illuminated from the waist down, but from the waist up they were shadowy; even the signs they carried were indistinct. Add to that the fact that few if any people passed that way at night, and Francie decided that the night picket was completely useless. In principle, Buck would have agreed. But he had other aspects of the situation to consider besides practicality. Without night picket, there was the matter of all the men being idle at the same time—which even with the best of men was risky. Then there was the problem of non-union men knowing they could get on and off mine property at certain hours to work a scab shift without having to cross a union line—and that was altogether too tempting. Finally, of course, any possibility of Big Jim Delavane walking up at three A.M. to reopen negotiations and not finding a union representative available had to be eliminated. That would allow him to petition the U.S. Department of Labor to legally dispossess the A.M.W.N. So there had to be round-the-clock pickets, there was no option. If Buck O'Crotty learned one thing at the elbow of John L. Lewis, it was to run a strike strictly by the book at the executive level. What occurred at the subaltern level, nobody could control; angry men did angry things.

Francie finally located Tony among the moving silhouettes, but only because as he passed the truck near which she was crouched, he turned his head to look up at the starry sky and moonlight was cast upon his features. Francie hurried out of concealment, took a sign from the pile on the flatbed and, chin against her chest, cap pulled low, fell into line without incident. Tony was, she guessed, about half a dozen places in front of her by then. The picketers were shuffling along in connected yet separate clusters of three or four men. Francie was able to move up a step or two at a time, lingering at the edge of a group just long enough so as not to be obvious, then casually edging on. Twice around the circuit of the picket and she was just behind Denny Ebro, who was next to Tony. She could not move between Denny and Tony without attracting the attention of two miners very close on Tony's other side, so she took a chance and gently nudged Denny's arm. When Denny turned to see who it was, she raised her face, frowning intensely, and urgently, put a finger to her lips for silence. She shifted her wide, frightened eyes back and forth to Tony several times. Denny's lips, perpetually parted anyway, opened all the way in utter surprise. He moved them to speak, but the look on Francie's face stopped him. Because she kept walking, he kept walking; because her desperate eyes kept flicking to Tony and back, he finally composed himself enough to take Tony by the arm and change places with him. Tony looked curiously at him, and Denny used his eyes as Francie had used hers, to direct his attention to her. Tony was surprised when he saw her, but not *as* surprised; immediately grinning, he thought Francie was there for amorous reasons. Walking next to her, feeling warm and excited, he waited until they reached the turn by the truck again, then nudged her casually out of line and leaned their signs against the truck.

"Back in a minute, Lloyd," he said to Lloyd Arlen, a vice president of the local who was in charge of the picket. They walked off to the side of the road, Arlen's eyes following them curiously.

As soon as they were both in the shadows, they folded into a hungry embrace.

"Oh, God—" Francie whispered over and over again against his mouth. "Oh, God—Oh, God—"

"It's hell not seeing you," Tony told her and immediately felt foolish, as if he had stolen a line from a movie. His lips moved over her cheeks, eyes, lips, neck. "I'd like to take off your clothes and kiss every inch of your body," he whispered, and did not feel foolish about that.

"God, this is so much worse than being away at school was," Francie said, words racing. "At least at school I didn't have you so near, wasn't constantly realizing that you were close by, that I could *get* to you—I can't stand this, Tony—"

They kissed and whispered and held and touched and luxuriated in the sudden wonder of being together again, Francie as lost in the spell of the moment as Tony was. She might not have remembered her reason for being there if he had not inadvertently aborted their enchantment by asking, in curious amusement, "Where in the hell did you manage to get these clothes anyway?"

"Oh my God! They're yours. I got them from Kerry—"

"Mine? From Kerry . . .?"

"Listen. There's something I came to warn you about." She had to swallow several times to lubricate words that tried to stick in her throat. "Daddy's bringing in a trainload of out-of-work copper miners from Utah—"

"What?" Tony frowned in disbelief.

"They're getting here on the seven-thirty from Reno."

"Are you sure, Francie?"

"Yes, I'm sure."

"Jesus Christ, is he trying to start a war?"

"I don't know what he's thinking."

"What time is it now?"

"It must be past six."

"I've got to get to Buck," Tony said tensely. "Do you have your own clothes on under my things?"

"Yes."

"Take off my things and walk down the road a piece. I'll pick you up in a couple of minutes."

Tony dashed back to the picket line and found Lloyd Arlen with a curious look still on his face. "Who was that little guy with you?" the union officer asked.

"That was someone I know from town. Listen, Lloyd, there's a big problem brewing that I've got to let Buck know about. Delavane's bringing in outside workers. Don't let on to the other men yet; we don't want to start a riot. Buck will know how to handle it. I want to take the car, okay?"

"Keys are in it, Tony," Arlen said, slapping him smartly on the arm to get him going. "Good work, boy."

Tony backed the old car away, taking half the picket's light with him. He drove quickly down the road to pick up Francie.

Buck stared at Tony in astonishment.

"The fool," he murmured. "The goddamned fool." Throwing off his surprise, his rough features fixed grimly. "Who told you?" he demanded.

"I don't want to get nobody in Dutch, Buck," Tony said reluctantly.

They were in Buck's tiny office at the storefront on C Street that served as union headquarters. Tony had dropped Francie off at the foot of Sierra so that she could easily get home to safety.

Buck got up from his desk and closed the office door. "I can't act on information unless I know its source," he said. "Who was it told you?"

Oh, Christ. "Francie Delavane."

Buck became even more amazed. "In the name of God *why?*"

"We've been, uh, seeing each other—"

"You? And Frances Grace Delavane?" The older man was completely incredulous.

"What the hell's so unbelievable about that?" Tony asked with an edge. "You think she's too good for me or something?"

Buck did not answer; he merely stared at Tony for a long, unsettling moment. In his face could be seen waves of emotion ebbing and flowing. Buck exerted all the strength of his self-control to bring them to heel. Tony was riveted where he stood by Buck's stare; at the same time he was steeling himself for a battle over Francie, all the while realizing that it was unnecessary just then because Buck had to attend to the matter of the arriving outsiders first. Still, Tony knew that the subject of Francie would remain in Buck's mind, surfacing now and again at unexpected moments, until it was resolved.

"Are you convinced that she was telling you the truth? And that she knew what she was talking about?" Buck asked in a clipped tone, like a prosecuting attorney at a trial. Tony nodded emphatically.

"I'm positive, Buck."

"All right, then."

Buck opened the door and walked out into the larger part of the headquarters where volunteers, mostly women who were wives or grown daughters of miners, were typing, running the mimeograph, answering the telephone, making coffee, and wrapping sandwiches for the picketing men to eat later that night.

"Quiet, everybody, please!" Buck shouted. "Listen to me, everybody, please!"

All present immediately stopped what they were doing and looked expectantly at Buck. Several of the women could not conceal an immediate hopeful optimism: Was it over? But Buck dashed that hope at once.

"I've just received some distressing news. Management"—he did not refer to Big Jim by name during the strike—"apparently has seen fit to hire outside labor to take over our jobs. This, of course, is not acceptable to the A.M.W.N. It is legal, mind you; management has the right to do it. Our task now is to persuade the outsiders being brought in that this isn't the just and fair thing to do. They're coming in this evening, I'm told, on the seven-thirty train. Now, you've all been assigned a list of men to notify in case they're needed for an emergency vote. I want you get out your lists right now and go about notifying the men on them as quickly as you can. Tell them I want every man not on picket to meet me at the train depot at once. And tell 'em," Buck concluded ominously, "to bring ax handles. All right, hustle now!"

The volunteers in the office began scrambling about, getting lists, putting on wraps, hurrying out the door. Rosetta, who had been helping with the food, came over to Buck. "Will it be bad, do you think?"

"Could be," Buck nodded curtly. He took one of her hands and patted it affectionately. "I want you to get on the telephone and alert the people from St. Martha's Hospital who agreed to help us in case of trouble. Ask them to please stand by until notified to the contrary. Also remember where the bail funds are hidden in case the lot of us are arrested."

"Please be careful, Mr. O'Crotty," the Paiute woman said quietly. Outside their house she always addressed him formally. Buck managed a smile for her.

"Of course. Go along now."

Tony followed Buck back into the office, where the union leader put on his coat and hat. From under the desk, Buck pulled out a short, heavy club, handcarved of Irish oak. His father had brought it with him from Shillelagh, and in fact it was called a shillelagh.

"You're on picket," Buck said to Tony. "Get back to it."

"Aw, Buck!"

"Go on."

"Let me go with you, Buck," Tony pleaded. He took hold of the older man's sleeve, following him out of the office again. "Come on, Buck. Please. Jesus, I'm the one brung you the information."

Buck stopped and faced him sternly. "You sayin' I owe it to you? That you did it for me and not your union?"

"No, I'm not saying that, Buck—"

"If you're thinking there's a special reward for loyalty, you're mistaken. Loyalty is its own reward."

"I know that, Buck. I just—"

"Just what?"

"I want to be with you if—you know—"

"You just want to fight alongside old Bucko, is that it?"

They locked eyes in a moment of kinship. "Yeah, Buck," Tony said. "That's what I want."

Buck smiled broadlly. "Get yourself an ax handle. There's some in that closet there."

Together the two men, Tony now taller than Buck by an inch, strode down C Street to the corner and turned toward the railroad depot. Along the way, at every street corner, every empty lot, every alley, they were joined by other men: men in rough miners' garb, men with set, uncompromising faces, with strong, heavily veined hands curled around smooth, shiny maple ax handles. They were silent, these men, as they marched. Only while they waited for the procession to reach them did they talk angrily about the news they had just received, and only when they saw the troop of men appear, O'Crotty leading them, did they give a hearty cheer and hurry to join them. Falling in, they then fell silent; only the footfalls of their heavy shoes could be heard, like the churning of a restless sea growing with a gale.

"Back east," Buck said out of the corner of his mouth to Tony, "they call this kind of parade a 'rank and file.' " Then he bobbed his chin down the street. "There she is."

The depot was red and green, the line colors of the Virginia-and-Truckee Railroad, named after Virginia City and the Truckee River. Its long, flat-topped structure, built at the back of a raised platform, was divided into four chambers: a waiting room at the near end, marked WHITE ONLY; a baggage and freight room; a ticket office; and another waiting room at the far end for Indians, coolies, Mexicans, and the occasional Negro. The depot was the end of track for the V&T: its route snaked and twisted along thirty miles of tortuous mountain curves that wound between Virginia City and Reno, where the line connected with transcontinental trains on the Southern Pacific. Three times a day V&T trains arrived from Reno, unloaded, had their engines switched to the opposite end, and left on the return trip thirty minutes later. It took two hours and twenty minutes to make the pull uphill, fifty minutes for the run back down.

Big Jim Delavane was waiting on the platform when Buck and his men rounded a corner in sight of the depot. Dressed in tailored gray gabardine, a pinned-collar Arrow shirt, precisely knotted necktie, and highly polished black Florsheims, he stood with hands clasped behind his back, shaved chin raised slightly in defiance of something in his mind, looking as always like a figure from a play or an advertisement. Because of the silence of the union marchers, Delavane did not hear them until the swelling tide of their footsteps reached his ears. He became aware of the sound slowly, gradually, as he might have heard a humming airplane approaching from far-off skies. When he finally did recognize the sound, his head snapped around like he'd been slapped by a powerful hand. At that instant, a locomotive whistle sounded and the V&T engine came into sight half a mile downtrack.

Buck mounted the depot steps. Without a word, he strode past the mine owner and planted himself dead center on the platform: feet apart, shillelagh held horizontally in both hands. His A.M.W.N. miners fell in on both sides of him, in the same stance, forming a human line that stretched from one end of the platform to the other. Delavane's face burned with anger. The V&T engine whistled again and the smell of its burning coal preceded it. All eyes watched the colorful locomotive—painted red and black and gold—chug into the depot and grind to a halt; all eyes except those of Big Jim Delavane, which only glared hatefully at Buck O'Crotty. The passenger cars of the V&T were bright green with multicolored window awnings. When they were fully halted, a train conductor opened the door of the first car and stepped to the platform. Seeing Buck and the line of miners, he stopped uncertainly.

"Go about your job," Buck said quietly. "Get your engine switched and then stand aside. It's not the railroad's fight."

The conductor hurried along the platform, opening doors. Burly men with grip satchels in their hands or bedrolls under their arms appeared at each door to detrain. Like the conductor, they also stopped at the sight of the human wall facing them. A man Buck's age but bigger, brawnier, worked his way out one of the passenger car doors. Looking up and down the line of men, his knowing eyes fell on the only man wearing a suit, seedy and rumpled though it was; the only man wearing a necktie—over a work shirt, and tied so poorly that its bottom point hung lower than its front; the man holding a shillelagh instead of an ax handlle, with a green-and-white pin on his lapel lettered A.M.W.N. The brawny man walked over to Buck.

"Abe Bates," he said, nodding curtly. He did not offer his hand. "I'm superintendent of this crew."

"Buck O'Crotty, president of the Amalgamated Mine Workers of Nevada. The mines in this town are struck."

"We're contract miners," Bates informed him. "There's no union in Utah."

"This ain't Utah," Buck said flatly. "The only way you'll work mines in Virginia City is to cross the picket line of a legally established union."

"We'll do whatever we have to do to work," Bates said firmly. "We've all got families back home to support."

"Do y'think we haven't got families?" Buck asked indignantly. "It's partly to better their lives that we've struck."

Bates assumed an attitude of reasonableness. "Look, we

only intend to dig during the short period that you're out. Soon's you settle your differences with Delavane, we'll turn your jobs back to you and pull out. My word on it."

"Maybe we can work a deal, then," Buck replied amiably. Next to him, Tony turned in surprise and stared. Buck ignored him. "Since you wouldn't be planning to stay permanently," he said to Bates, "would you be willing to enter into a legal contract not to relocate any of your families here?"

"Well, ah, I don't know . . ." Bates had not expected conditions, just argument.

"And would you agree that none of you is to occupy company housing for the duration of your time here?"

"I couldn't agree to that," Bates said. "Where the hell would we live?"

"In the stope," Buck told him with a smile. "It's plenty warm down there, I guarantee."

"I can't have my men sleeping in a mine," Bates said.

"But it'd only be for a short time, you said so yourself," Buck reminded him.

"No, I can't go making arrangements for the future like that," Bates asserted. "Who knows how things'll work out?"

"Unless we can reach some kind of accommodation," Buck said almost blithely, "the only thing your men can do is cross our line. As their super, I presume you'll lead them?"

"That's my job."

Buck's smile turned to a cold leer. "Well, this is mine," he said.

Without warning, Buck let go of the shillelagh with his left hand and swung it with his right. Its knobby end hit Bates in the left temple with an appalling thud. The copper miner dropped like wet burlap. At once two of his men leaped out to his defense. Swinging his ax handle like a baseball bat, Tony felled the first one; a miner on the other side of Buck dealt a blow to the second. Down the line of cars in both directions, several other men leaped off the train to challenge the union line. In each instance they were stopped by a smartly swung ax handle.

When seven men lay unconscious, everything became suddenly still; the men on the train were poised to move forward, the men on the platform poised to strike—but they all froze as if in a photograph. Buck seized the moment; probably, he thought, the only one he would have.

"Listen to me, you men!" he addressed the copper miners. "You've only got two ways to go here! Stay on the train and go back where you came from—or stay here and go to the hospital!"

An angry murmur rippled through the railroad cars. Several copper miners made as if to move. The silver miners braced and stood their ground.

"We'll resist to the last man," Buck warned loudly, "whether it's one of you or one of us!"

The men on the train looked at their fallen comrades lying motionless on the platform, one of them hemorrhaging from his nose and ears. Exchanging uneasy glances, they all waited for one among them to make the next move. No one did.

"The wise man," Buck pressed his advantage, "goes his way and lives to work another day! Pick up your foolish friends here and drag 'em back on the train."

"That man," a copper miner pointed to the unconscious man who was bleeding, "needs a doctor! He's hurt!"

"We're all hurt," Buck told him. "We've hurt each other today because of the greed"—he looked down the platform at Big Jim—"of management. This is a battle nobody's won—and that's the poorest kind. Leave the man that's bleeding; we'll see he's cared for and send him home later. Get the rest aboard." Buck's sweeping glance located the conductor. "Get your train moving back downgrade as quickly as you can if you want to avoid damage to railroad property." To Terence Henny, he said, "Take over here, Mr. Henny." And to Tony, "Get yourself back to the picket."

Striding toward the platform steps, Buck passed Big Jim.

"It's not over, Buck," the mine owner warned coldly.

"I'm sure it's not," Buck replied wearily.

As Buck went down the steps, he wondered what Big Jim would do when he found out it had been his own daughter who had brought about the confrontation at the depot.

And there was no question in his mmd that Big Jim would find out.

EIGHTEEN

The heavy snow that fell on Virginia City the second week in December turned the surrounding mountain ranges and high pine forests into a glorious spectacle of unblemished white grandeur. It turned the streets of the town into an ugly morass of dirty slush.

Tony and Denny, their trouser legs stuffed into the tops of their rubber mine boots, trudged indifferently through the mess as they moved along C Street toward the union office. It was mid-morning on a weekday; a few of the merchants were still out shoveling their portion of the sidewalk clean. They looked away as Tony and Denny approached, not wanting to meet the eyes of any miners; just a few days earlier most of the merchants had posted signs in their stores that due to economic reasons all credit business was being suspended; all sales henceforth had to be on a cash-and-carry basis. Buck's union vice presidents had brought the news to him at home.

"Delavane's behind it," Terence Henny said. "I'd bet my last dollar on it."

"Him and that son of a bitch Coltrane," Lloyd Arlen agreed. Then quickly added, "Sorry, Buck. I know you don't permit swearing in your house."

"Thanks for remembering that, Lloyd. So," Buck said thoughtfully, "they're cutting off our credit. Just before Christmas too." He nodded his head. "Well, it's a good move. I should have expected it. Somehow I just didn't think Jim would—" Buck stared into space for a moment, then grimaced tightlipped. "Like I said, I should have expected it."

"Dirty low-life bastards," Arlen muttered. Catching him-

229

self again, he said in frustration, "Can we talk on the porch, Buck, so's we can speak freely?"

"Sure," Buck said. At the front door he paused to put on a worn wool sweater and his hat. The three men stepped out onto the porch. Heavy snow clouds hung low over the high little mining town, casting the day gray.

"The way me and Terry figure it," Arlen continued, his words causing spurts of vapor, "is that Harmon Coltrane, being an investor in Delavane Mines, is trying to help Big Jim put the pressure on us. The son of a bitch has probably got mortgages on half the businesses in town."

"Probably more than half," Buck allowed.

"Can the dirty prick do that, Buck?" Henny asked indignantly. "Can he tell a man how to run his business just because the man owes him money?"

"Can't tell him, no," Buck said. "But there are other ways. I imagine every business in town is behind in its payments to the bank; our strike hasn't exactly boosted the town's economy. When a business falls behind in mortgage payments, the bank usually has the right to declare the full balance due. Mr. Coltrane might have subtly suggested to certain merchants that perhaps they wouldn't have fallen behind in payments if they didn't have so much tied up in outstanding credit. He's only offering what he considers to be good business advice, and perhaps allowing the store owner to make interest-only payments for three or four months if he follows it."

"D'you think they might change their minds if you was to talk to 'em Buck?"

"Not likely," Buck shook his head. "I'll have a go at it, naturally. And I expect some of them will sympathize with us. But in the end they'll have to protect their businesses."

Later, after Arlen and Henny had left, Buck told Tony and Denny the news. "Lloyd's right, of course," he admitted to them in confidence. "The coldhearted bastard. Anything for profit—*anything*. Human beings and their struggles don't mean a thing to him. It wouldn't disturb his conscience a bit if every miner's child on the Walk went to bed hungry every night of the week, so long as he made a profit on his investment in the Delavane Mines. I don't say this about many, lads, but I honestly believe that Harmon Coltrane would order men killed for profit if he thought he could get away with it."

Buck had been right about the Virginia City merchants protecting their businesses. When he paid a personal call on each merchant, he was listened to with patience, commiserated with, and extended sympathy, and understanding—but no credit. The merchants all repeated a common excuse, as if rehearsed: they had bills to pay too, and they couldn't pay them without cash. "Putting things on the cuff is all right when there are paychecks coming in regular," the butcher shop proprietor said. "But when there's no guarantee of payment Saturday next, well . . ."

"The men are getting strike benefits," Buck tried to reason.

"Not as much as they were getting in wages," the A&P market manager argued. "They're still buying as much as if they were earning as much, but they're paying less and less on account and their balance owed keeps getting bigger."

"Besides which," the dry goods store owner added, "we don't know how long your 'benefits,' as you call them, will last."

"You're dealing with honest men here," Buck insisted.

"Good intentions don't pay bills," they countered.

So all credit along C Street was suspended; CASH ONLY signs went up in store windows. As Tony and Denny tramped through the slush toward the union hall, store owners shoveling the sidewalk offered them no greeting when they passed.

"Bastards," Tony muttered. He glared at the owner of the dry goods store, but he saw the face of Big Jim Delavane. For the first time in a long time, he thought again about physical violence. If he could catch him coming out of the mansion some night, when it was dark, bash in the back of his head with an ax handle, not enough to kill him, just enough to put him in the hospital for a month or so—

"Don't start no trouble" Denny wheezed as if reading Tony's mind " 'Member what Buck said."

The union president's advice to all his members was to maintain cordial relationships with all merchants, buy only what they could afford to pay cash for, and refrain from allowing any store owner to make individual exceptions to the new cash-and-carry policy. "Let's all stay in the same boat," Buck urged. "Exceptions will only turn us against each other. It's either credit for all—or credit for none. Let's keep the trust together."

As Tony and Denny approached the middle of C Street's second block of businesses, they saw a large flatbed truck

parked outside the hardware store, a cargo of freshly cut
pine trees about to spill into the street. A wizened old man,
red-faced and breathing heavily, was trying futilely to get a
length of rope over the top to hold them down.

"Need a hand, mister?" Tony asked, stepping off the
sidewalk. He took the rope from the old man's hand. "Denny,
grab that other end. How do you want them tied down,
mister?"

Under the puffing old man's guidance, they got the rope
crisscrossed over the top of the trees and lashed to the bed.
Leaning against the fender, still breathing heavily, his cheeks
fiery red, the old man wiped his face with a bandanna.
"Thanks, boys," he gasped. "Ain't so young as I once was."

"Know anybody who is?" Tony asked with a grin. He and
Denny started to continue on their way.

"Wait a minute, fellers," the old man called them back.
He studied Denny. "You're old Piro Ebro's boy, ain't you?"

"Used to be," Denny replied.

"You the one he disowned?"

"That's me."

"I'm Louis Axhalt. My place is down-mountain from your
daddy's lower pastures. My old woman used to be friends
with your maw afore they both died. You prob'ly don't
remember me."

Denny shook his head. "No, sir."

"No matter. You fellers looking for a little work?"

Denny shrugged but Tony said at once, "Sure. Doing
what?"

"He'ping me with these here trees. I got twenty dozen of
'em to deliver in Reno. I can take two dozen a load; that
means ten trips. I loaded this lot with a mule and a dragline,
but it 'bout wore me out. I could use some he'p. Loadin'
and unloadin'. Give you fellers two dollars a trip each and
pay for your grub. What d'you say?"

Tony and Denny asked Louis Axhalt to wait while they
ran to the union hall to get permission from Buck.

"Can't allow it," Buck said shaking his head. "If striking
workers take other employment, it diminishes the importance of the job they've struck. Gives management an in-
centive to hold out a little longer in the hope that everybody'll
find other work, then management can hire an entire new
labor force. It's self-defeating. Anyways, you've got picket
duty."

Both young men first reasoned, then argued, then erupted into dramatic litanies of pleading, appealing, beseeching, until finally Tony came dangerously close to threatening disobedience. "Goddamn it, Buck, we could have gone and done it without asking you. Maybe that's what we should have done."

"Careful, now," Buck cautioned. "Anyway, I'd've found out when you missed picket."

"Maybe, maybe not," Tony retorted. "It's not all that hard to skip picket if you've got friends to cover for you."

"Is that a fact?" Buck's eyebrows rose.

"He's right, Buck," Denny said. "We came to you 'cause we figured you'd be fair with us."

"Jesus, Buck, Christmas is just around the corner—"

"We'd like to be able to get something for Rosetta—"

"And Kerry. Christ, she's just a kid—"

Buck threw up his hands in surrender. "All right, all right, all right! On one condition," he pointed a finger at them. "You put half your wages into the strike fund. That's the only way I'll be able to justify letting you miss picket. Both agree to that?"

"Sure!" said Tony.

"Sure!" Denny echoed.

The two young men dashed out of Buck's office before he could consider changing his mind.

Francie parked her car on C Street and slid over to get out on the passenger side to avoid the slush in the street. Fur collar turned up against the early evening wind—the zephyrs were spinning like miniature tornadoes this time of year—she hurried along the sidewalk to Walker's Drugstore and pushed inside to its heavy warmth. There were two people sitting separately at the soda fountain, but none of the four booths along the back wall were occupied. Francie removed her gloves and coat, left her scarf and beret on, and took a seat in the last booth, from which she could see the entire public area of the store. The soda jerk came over to take her order.

"Cherry Coke," Francie said. "No ice, please."

"Yes, ma'am."

There it was again. Ma'am. She watched the boy walk back to the soda fountain. He couldn't have been more than three or four years younger than her.

From the boy, Francie's eyes moved to a big clock above the cigar counter with BENRUS lettered across its face. It was ten past seven. She was late. Yet Tony was not there. That disturbed her. Not since they had begun meeting at Walker's Drugstore every evening he was not on picket, had he not been there ahead of her, waiting for her. This was most unusual.

The relationship between Tony and Francie was no longer a secret in Virginia City. Since the day after the confrontation with the Utah copper miners at the V&T depot, the day after Tony's admission to Buck O'Crotty that it had been Francie who warned him about the outsiders, the day after her father had concluded that it had been his daughter who had warned the union about it, since then there had no longer been a reason for secrecy. Francie and Tony met openly, publicly, at the drugstore whenever they could. Buck O'Crotty did not approve, and constantly urged Tony to stay away from the mine owner's daughter.

"She's not for you, lad," he had told Tony after extracting from him an admission of how long the relationship had been going on—and how serious it was. "For God's sake, you haven't done anything foolish, have you?" he had to know. "I mean, you haven't—"

"No, we haven't," Tony replied indignantly. "We're not trash, Buck. We're waiting until it's right."

"For you two, it'll never be right," Buck said flatly. "Take some good advice and leave her be. There's plenty nice girls down in town and on the Walk. You keep away from Frances Grace Delavane."

Tony and Francie did not flaunt their relationship, but they no longer sneaked around either. Most nights they were there in the booth at Walker's Drugstore; whoever saw them, saw them.

The soda jerk brought her cherry Coke and she gave him a nickel. Lifting the top of a glass container on the table, she selected two straws and took a brief sip of the syrupy drink. She looked up at the clock again. Seven-fifteen.

On Francie's part, she was not forbidden from seeing Tony Donovan. She did not even know whether her father was aware of the relationship or not. Big Jim had determined, mostly out of sheer instinct, that it had been she who warned the union of the arrival of outside labor. Big Jim had known minutes after she left the house that she was

gone, but assumed she had run over to the Coltranes' looking for sympathy from Libby. He had not pursued her,
deciding to try and reason with her later, after the heat of
the moment had passed. At the depot, he had been caught
completely by surprise when Buck O'Crotty and his miners
showed up to meet the train. Only a scant few people were
supposed to have known ahead of time about the arrival of
the Utah men: Big Jim's attorney, with whom he checked
the legality of the situation; his accountant, who arranged
for the railroad tickets; Harmon Coltrane, to whom he had
mentioned it earlier that day.

Following the humiliating rout of the Utah men, Big Jim
had returned to his mansion livid. Even then it had not
occurred to him that Francie had betrayed him. Only after
he had stalked into his study, sat tensely on the edge of a
chair, and poured himself a long drink of whiskey, did he
suddenly come to that most repugnant conclusion. The whiskey did not even reach his lips; his hand holding the glass
froze as his eyes fixed on the other chair facing him, the one
in which Francie had sat earlier that evening, berating and
belittling him; the chair from which she had fled when those
careless, angry words about Edith had exploded from his
subconscious. Big Jim Delavane's eyes widened in horrible
wonder.

Francie.

It had been Francie.

The hand with the glass began to tremble and he had to
set it down to keep the whiskey from slopping out. Rising,
he walked slowly and deliberately out of the study, up the
stairs, along the hall to her bedroom door. For the first time
since she was a child of eight he entered her bedroom
without knocking, without permission. Francie was at her
dressing table, a cigarette in one hand, brushing her hair
with the other, wearing a nightgown: thin little straps holding up diaphanous material that screened but did not conceal her breasts.

They're Edith's breasts, he remembered, standing behind
her, studying them frankly and openly in the mirror. Francie,
looking at him, knew by his face what he was thinking. She
confirmed it, saying, "They remind you of Mother's, don't
they, Daddy? That's what you're thinking, isn't it?"

"Yes." It was barely a whisper, dry and hoarse.

Putting down her hairbrush, Francie used her right hand

to drop the left strap from her shoulder, her left hand to drop the right. The gown fell, gathering at her waist. Francie stared at her father staring at her breasts, eyes becoming hungry despite himself, a slight pull at the front of his trousers as an erection began.

"Now you can call me a bitch too, Daddy," she said.

Big Jim tore his eyes from her nipples and forced himself to look at her face. "You warned O'Crotty tonight, didn't you?"

"Yes." The word was defiant; her chin raised slightly, her breasts widened as her shoulders braced.

Big Jim kept his eyes fixed on her face, unblinkingly, for what seemed to Francie like a very long time. His gaze was relentless, merciless: it ate into her like acid. When she could stand it no longer, she shifted her own eyes away and pulled her gown back up.

"I won't even ask you why you warned him," her father said finally. "I don't want to know. I'm sure I've heard it before anyway, in one form or another, about one cause or another. For a lot of years I was served equity and justice and uprightness and fair play and various other combinations of morality with my dinner every night. I tolerated it from your mother in order to get certain, ah, concessions from her in return. But I'll be goddamned if I'll ever put up with it again. I want nothing further to do with you, young lady. You may continue to live in this house if you wish, but I don't want you at the table when I'm having my meals, nor do I want to engage in conversation with you at any time—"

"Daddy—"

"Kindly"—his voice rose to block the interruption—"make an effort to avoid me, and I'll do the same with you. I'll ask—no, I'll *order* you to stay out of my study; you're no longer welcome in there. That's all I have to say to you."

Ignoring the tears that welled in her eyes, Delavane turned from the dressing table and walked back across the room. Francie watched his back in the mirror. At the door, he paused and looked at her again.

"There is one other thing I have to say. You're fired. You no longer have a job at Delavane Mines."

Francie's father had not spoken to her since—more than six weeks. Several times she had made an effort to talk to him. "Daddy, we can't go on like this forever," she had said this very evening, before coming out to the drugstore to meet Tony. "We've got to talk this thing out sooner or later. Surely to God a father and daughter, two grownup people, can discuss a mutual problem."

Tonight had been like the several other times she had tried: Big Jim had listened silently to her plea, her rationale; listened patiently, almost attentively, then he had simply walked away from her without responding.

The relationship, the tension it had created, was making a nervous wreck of Francie. She was eating poorly, had lost six pounds, and was smoking nearly two packs of cigarettes a day. In the drugstore booth now, her cherry Coke untouched except for the first sip, she rummaged in her purse for the Pall Mall kings and decided she must have left them at home. Sliding out of the booth, she went to the front counter and bought a pack. By now it was half past seven and she was becoming apprehensive. Tony had *never* been late.

On her way back to the booth, Francie began to imagine all manner of terrible things that might have happened to him. Sitting down, nervously tearing cellophane and tinfoil, she managed to get a cigarette out and lit. My God, she wondered, what would she do if something *had* happened to Tony? He was all she had, the only one she could rely upon, the only person she could talk to—at least, talk to openly and honestly. Oh, God, Tony where are you . . .?

At twenty of eight, the drugstore door opened and Kerry Morrell came in. Bundled up in a mackinaw coat with a wool cap and earmuffs, the girl came directly to the booth where Francie sat.

"Hello, Kerry," said Francie, her anxiety surging. *What had happened?*

Without preliminary, Kerry pulled off one mitten to expose a folded piece of paper in her hand. "This is from Tony."

Francie grabbed it eagerly, and read it. "Oh. He's working on a truck in Reno. Thank God. I was afraid . . ." Francie expelled a sigh and some of her tension. With a wan smile she said, "Thank you, Kerry." Then she frowned. "I thought you weren't allowed out at night alone?"

"I'm supposed to be at the library. Buck dropped me off, he'll pick me up at nine when it closes."

"Would you like a soda or a sundae?" Francie asked. "My treat."

"No, thank you."

"Candy bar? Chewing gum?"

"No, thank you."

Francie reached for her coat. "Well, at least let me walk you back to the library—"

"I can get back okay alone," Kerry said. Her words were emphatic; there was no flexibility in her refusal. Francie did not argue with her.

"Why don't you like me, Kerry?" she asked instead.

"I don't like trouble," the girl replied simply. "We've got enough trouble with the strike. Now there's trouble starting between Buck and Tony because of you. Tony wants to keep seeing you and Buck's told him to quit. And I could get in trouble because I'm sneaking away from the library to give you a note from Tony. You're just more trouble. Why should I like you?"

Kerry's candor and directness, as well as the guileless logic of her conclusion, embarrassed Francie. Never in her life had she encountered such fundamental honesty as she had with this girl, Kerry Morrell. And on top of it all to have to remain fixed in the undeviating gaze of those incredible aquamarine eyes, while she listened to that frankness—it was all very distressing. But Francie had more compelling things on her mind at the moment; she could not worry about the sentiments of this—this—well, she simply could not, was all.

"I'm sorry you don't like me, Kerry," she said with a lock on her emotions. "And I'm sorry you think I'm causing trouble, because I'm not. Neither is Tony. Other people may be causing trouble for themselves, but that's something Tony and I can't do anything about. I love Tony very much and I need him very much; he's all I've got—and I do mean *all*. Thank you for bringing the note; I'm sorry you had to deceive your stepfather to do it. I'll ask Tony not to put you in this position again. You'd better go on back to the library now. Goodnight, Kerry."

"Goodnight, Miss Delavane," Kerry replied, her tone as inscrutable as her expression. It must be the Indian blood, Francie thought, that enabled Kerry at such a young age to muster such stoicism. God!

Watching Kerry leave, Francie nervously extinguished her cigarette and immediately lit another.

*   *   *

In Reno, Tony and Denny unloaded Louis Axhalt's load of pines at a large vacant lot on Second Street. Across the front of the lot, strung between two telephone poles, was a canvas banner lettered: XMAS TREES $1 AND UP. When Louis came out of the tent at the back of the lot, he handed Tony a five-dollar bill.

"Two bucks apiece for each of you, and the extra dollar's for your suppers. Down the street at Mother's Café you can get the best blue plate special in town for thirty-five cents, coffee included. I got some business to tend to, so I'll meet you boys back here in two hours and we'll head back for the next load." Louis gave them a wink and a nod, and sauntered off.

"Wonder where he's going?" Tony said.

"Probably fixin' to get his ashes hauled," Denny remarked.

"He's too old for that," Tony said. "I think he is, anyway."

Denny shrugged indifferently. "Come on, le's go tie in to them blue plate specials."

At Mother's, the two young men feasted on venison, which was in season and plentiful, mashed potatoes and venison gravy, string beans six inches long, cole slaw, hot biscuits, butter churned fresh that day, peach cobbler, and strong, rich coffee—for, as Axhalt had said, thirty-five cents each, no tax. "Mother" was a stout, yellow-bearded Norwegian who had lumberjacked to earn enough money to open the café.

"Goddamn if he don't cook pretty near good as Rosetta," Denny said as they emerged picking their teeth.

"Pretty near," Tony agreed. He looked down the night-cold street and saw a brightly lighted corner. "We've got a little while. Let's take a walk."

They walked down Second Street toward the lights, and when they got to them found that it was the corner of Virginia Street. Turning into Virginia, they entered an incredible thoroughfare of neon color. It was Reno's main street: a sparkling, flashing, pulsing valley of casinos, saloons, supper clubs, pawn shops, hotels, souvenir emporiums, Western wear haberdashers, bootmakers, and a variety of smaller, less glamorous businesses.

"Jesus," said Tony, awestruck.

"Sure beats the hell out of D Street, don't it?" Denny compared. He was talking about the single block of D Street that contained the few small gambling clubs left in Virginia

City: seedy little places with no atmosphere or ambiance, barely surviving in the town's economy; and the two brothels that were still in business: drab, uninviting houses worked by tired, used-up whores who sometimes could not pay for their required weekly medical check and had to charge it. On the whole, D Street was depressing, a place to visit in desperation or drunkenness. But *this*—Virginia Street in Reno, with a big sign across the avenue proclaiming THE BIGGEST LITTLE CITY IN THE WORLD—this was something to see!

"I never saw so many lights at once in my life," Tony marveled.

"Look at that!" Denny said excitedly, pointing to a huge sign shaped like a cowboy, who tipped his ten-gallon hat and said deeply, "Howdy, partner!"

All up and down the street were brilliantly lighted signs of invitation and enticement: Lucky Casino! Jackpot! Winner's Circle! Four Aces! Silver Dollar! Greenback Club!

At the center of it all, the grandfather of them all: Harold's Club.

Tony and Denny stopped in front of the big, glittering palace of chance and looked inside. A smiling doorman in a red uniform walked over to them. "Good evening, gents." Tony and Denny exchanged quick looks. Gents? "First time at Harold's Club, gents?" the doorman asked.

"Uh, yeah," Tony said self-consciously.

"First time in Reno," Denny added helpfully.

"Well, gents," the doorman said proudly, "you have come to the right place." Glibly he went into a practiced spiel. "Harold's Club is the preeminent gaming casino in all of Nevada. It was the first legitimate casino built after gaming was legalized eight years ago. The casino was established by Mr. Ray Smith, a well-known and highly respected gentleman gambler from California. Mr. Smith named the casino after his little boy, Harold. You will find inside Harold's Club not only the widest variety of gaming available—poker, craps, twenty-one, roulette, hi-lo, faro—but also the winningest, payingest, loosest slot machines in town, in every, denomination from a nickel to a silver dollar. So step inside, gents, and try your luck!" He pulled the door open for them. "Harold's Club welcomes you!"

"Thanks a lot!" Denny said, grinning widely. Affected by the doorman's pitch, excitement revved, he strode inside.

He was already fingering his two dollars from a shirt pocket when Tony caught up with him.

"No you don't," Tony said firmly. "Leave that money where it is."

"We might be able to win a fortune in here!" Denny said eagerly. His eyes shone with the great urge he felt.

"We can't, Den," Tony told him, taking his arm and leading him off to the side, away from the tables. " 'Member, half what we earn goes into the strike fund."

"What about the other half?"

"Let's just walk around and watch. Come on."

They wandered around for nearly an hour. Not understanding much of what they saw—the hi-lo and faro layouts were new to them; craps and twenty-one were only vaguely familiar; poker they knew how to play; roulette was not difficult to figure out—they tried to be as unobtrusive as possible, not going too close to any of it, only near enough to watch the play. People bet with chips, silver dollars, and currency. Some, apparently known to the dealers, even used markers, which they hastily scribbled out. The action was perpetual, stimulating, tantalizing, seductive.

"You know, Tony," Denny said anxiously at one point, but Tony cut him short.

"No. Forget it." Later, Tony made an observation that supported his decision. "Know what I notice, Den? Most people who stay at the tables awhile seem to have a lot of money to play with. The people who start to play with only a little money don't last very long."

The longer he watched, the more Tony became convinced that his logic was accurate. The first asset of a winning player seemed to be a bankroll. Jesus, he thought, feeling the same kind of excitement inside that Denny had manifested earlier, what a break it would be for Francie and him if he *could* win a lot of money so they could get out of Virginia City sooner. There would never be a better time: Francie was on the outs with her father; Buck was constantly needling him about seeing Francie; the strike had everybody grouchy and testy; aside from the short visits with Francie at the drugstore, and their occasional petting sessions parked somewhere in her car, neither of them was enjoying life very much. He had two hundred eighty dollars saved, hidden under a floorboard under his bed. If he brought it to Reno, to Harold's Club, maybe he could build it up to five hundred or even a thousand. A thousand dollars! With that much, he and Francie could make a good start somewhere. Denver, maybe; there were lots of mines around Denver, so finding a job shouldn't be too hard. Or even back east in the coal fields where Buck had worked. Anyplace would be all right, as long as he and Francie were together.

Almost at once, even in the exhilaration of fantasizing about winning a thousand dollars, Tony developed reservations. Suppose he didn't win; suppose he lost the money he already had? It would mean postponing their plans indefinitely because he would then have to start his secret savings all over again—something he could not even think of doing until the strike was over. Standing on the sidelines of Harold's Club, watching a twenty-one dealer rake in chips and money put on the table by losing players, Tony had a sudden feeling of nausea, as if it was *his* money, his and Francie's, the money he had saved. Seeing it slip away like that, after so many long, grueling shifts—hours, days, months in the sweltering heat of the mine—produced a bile in Tony's stomach that threatened to rise in his throat and disgorge at any second.

"Come on," he said urgently, "let's get out of here."

As they hurried out, Tony was glad the smiling doorman was looking the other way. But even as they trudged through the snowbanks toward Louis Axhalt's truck, Tony had the odd premonition that he would be coming back to Harold's Club someday.

NINETEEN

Tony and Denny made nine more trips to Reno with Louis Axhalt. On each subsequent trip except the last, they accompanied him back to his mountain timber spread and helped him load two dozen of the pine trees he had cut and contracted for. At the end of every trip, he gave each of them the agreed upon two dollars; on the last return trip, on Christmas Eve, when he dropped them off in Virginia City in front of the hardware store where he had met them, in addition to paying them, he gave each of them an extra two dollars.

"Call it a bonus, call it a Christmas present, call it anything you like," the old man said. "You're good boys, both of you, and you gave me a hand when I needed it. Wish to Christ I had a couple of sons like you." He punched Denny lightly on the muscle. "Wouldn't disown you, that's for sure."

Standing in a lightly falling snow on C Street, Tony and Denny watched him drive off, both feeling sad at the parting. "Nice old guy," Tony said.

"Yeah," Denny mused. "Maybe after you and Francie elope, I'll go up and live with him. Give him a hand with his timber."

Tony looked curiously at Denny. It had never occurred to him that his own dream of elopement would cause Denny to make any radical change in his life. "You wouldn't stay here with Buck and the family?" he asked surprised.

"Prob'ly not," Denny replied absently, watching Louis Axhalt's truck grow smaller in the snowy distance.

"Why not?" Tony wanted to know. Denny shrugged.

"I don't know." It came out, as many of Denny's sentences did, with the words run together, sounding like, "Ahohno." Since coming to Virginia City, Denny had made great strides in improving his speech: learning not to snort, not to blow the words out through his nose, most important learning to be patient and not get excited when trying to communicate. Rosetta, with her unruffled constancy, had taught him the latter. His only real remaining problem was not to make one long word out of several shorter ones.

Tony had assumed that Denny's place in the O'Crotty household was permanent. He was aware that old Louis Axhalt had reminded Denny in a way of Piro, and that Denny had felt melancholy when they were up at Axhalt's high-mountain spread, which bordered Ebro pastures. Maybe, Tony thought, that was the reason for how Denny felt at the moment. Tony decided to let the matter rest; he did not want to generate any unhappiness on Christmas Eve.

At the union hall, both young men dutifully contributed

to Paddy Herron, treasurer of the local, eleven dollars each, exactly half of their wages and bonus. "Good lads," Buck praised. "Now get on home, the two of you. I cut a small fir from out behind the house, but Kerry wouldn't hear of us trimming it until you were here to help. Tell Rosetta I'll be home in a bit; I've a couple of sacks of groceries to deliver first. Tell her we'll all go to Midnight Mass."

Before going home, Tony and Denny went to Woolworth's to Christmas shop. They went halves on a bright red apron and a bottle of Evening in Paris bath fragrance for Rosetta, and a music box with a little ballerina that did pirouettes to "The Blue Danube" for Kerry. For Buck, they went to Callahan's and bought a fifth of Canadian scotch.

When they got home, they hid the presents under the front porch before going inside. Kerry screamed with delight when she saw them; Rosetta, happy that they were home safe, gave them each a warm hug. Nothing would satisfy Kerry except immediate decorating of the little fir tree, even before the boys were allowed to take crucially needed baths. After the trimming of the tree was accomplished and Tony and Denny had cleaned up, they got some white butcher paper from the kitchen, went outside, and awkwardly wrapped everyone's present. Using the stub of a pencil, they wrote names on the gifts and put them under the tree. Kerry was beside herself to open hers at once, but Rosetta ruled that they would wait until after Mass.

When Tony felt that all his obligations at the house had been fulfilled, he put on his coat and said, "I'm going out for a while."

Rosetta gave him an apprehensive glance. Kerry became bratty and taunted, "Bet I know where you're going!"

Tony scowled at her. Rosetta followed him to the door, drying her hands on a dish towel. "Try not to do anything to upset Mr. O'Crotty tonight, Tony," she urged.

Tony felt like replying: Sure, and tell him not to do anything to upset me either.

But he was in a hurry. "Okay, Rosetta," he said instead. "I won't."

Hurrying down the Walk, Tony exchanged Christmas greetings with several people he knew. As he stepped briskly along, a flat gift-wrapped box inside his shirt rubbed against his ribs. The package contained a delicate linen handkerchief edged in silk lace. Tony had bought it in Reno, leaving

Louis Axhalt and Denny at supper one night, saying he did not feel well and was going to lie down on the seat of the truck, then running down to a store where he had seen the handkerchief in a window. For twenty-five cents extra, they had wrapped it in green paper and put a bright red ribbon and bow on it. Moving it from one hiding place to another and carrying it under his shirt had ruined the bow and Tony had thrown it away, but the ribbon was still nice.

Reaching the drugstore, Tony peered through the window and saw that Francie was not there. He walked down two doors to City Dry Cleaners, which was closed, and waited in the doorway, out of the falling snow. Maybe she would not come tonight, he suddenly thought. After all, he had not shown up for a week. But Francie knew why; Tony had surreptitiously checked with Kerry to verify that his note had been delivered. Francie would come, he decided; she would at least drive by to see if he was back.

It was, Tony reflected, going to be another depressing, dejected holiday for him, wanting to be with Francie and not being able to. It would be even worse this year for Francie, because of the silence her father was sustaining toward her. The son of a bitch. Just thinking of how Big Jim was treating her made Tony yearn to drive his fist into the mine owner's face. How could a man treat his own daughter like that? In Tony's tainted view of Delavane, there was no room for Big Jim's feelings about Francie's betrayal of her father. The only view that Tony saw was of Francie being hurt—by a man he had always found easy to hate.

As the snow began to fall more heavily, Tony saw headlights turn into C Street off Sierra. When they got nearer, he recognized that they belonged to Francie's blue Olds coupe. As soon as she was close enough, starting to look for a parking place, he stepped across the sidewalk and flagged her down. She saw him, smiled widely in surprise, and stopped. Tony opened the passenger door and slid in.

"Hi!" she said happily.

"Hi."

"God, I'm glad to see you." She shifted into neutral and turned to him.

"I'm glad to see you too—" Tony gathered her into his arms and they kissed, disregarding being in the middle of C Street, unmindful of who might see them, oblivious of everything except each other and the rapt, joyful elation of being together again. Their lips seemed to mesh and mold, and the thrill of their kiss consumed them. They felt warm, weak, alive, in love.

"I dreaded coming down here tonight, I was so afraid you wouldn't be here . . ."

Tony saw that she was about to cry. "Nothing could have kept me away tonight," he told her. He realized that the package under his shirt was being crushed, and reached between them to remove it.

"What's that?" she asked.

"Something for you that Santa Claus left at my house."

Her expression saddened. "Honey, you shouldn't have. Not being on strike allowance—"

"I've been in the lumber business all week," he bragged. "Hey, that Reno's quite a place. Den and I went to Harold's Club—"

Lights suddenly reflected in their faces from the rearview mirror as a car drew near behind them. "Guess we should get out of the middle of the street," Francie said. She shifted gears again and angled in to the curb just past the drugstore.

"Want to go in separately?" he asked.

"After the spectacle we just put on?" she asked dryly.

"I guess you're right," he admitted. As they got out of the car, Francie took a large, richly wrapped-and-tied package out of the back seat. "Jesus, Francie," he said, seeing it. "I thought we agreed to always give small gifts?"

"What makes you think this is for you?" she kidded. "Maybe it's for the soda jerk." Suddenly she was nervous; she knew the present, an expensive one, was a mistake. Goddamn it, why had she done it?

"Be serious, Francie," Tony said. "Didn't we have a deal?" They were standing on the snowy sidewalk, she with the large box, he with the small. A man and woman passed and glanced curiously at them. "Well, didn't we?" Tony insisted. He felt like a fool now with the stupid little handkerchief.

"I didn't keep my part of the bargain," Francie shrugged to cover her chagrin. "Take me to court. Are we going in the drugstore or not? I'm getting cold."

"I can't open that thing," he bobbed his chin at the large box, "whatever it is, in the drugstore. Let's get back in the car."

"Swell with me."

Francie strode back around the Olds, tossed the box into the back seat again, and slid under the wheel as Tony sat back in the passenger seat and pulled the door shut.

"This must be my Christmas to have everybody mad at me," she said self-pityingly. She rummaged in her bag for the Pall Malls. Tony stared at a chrome plate on the dashboard that read: HYDRAMATIC. Francie had been the first person in Virginia City to own a car with the new automatic transmission; Big Jim had given it to her for her eighteenth birthday. Thoughts of Harold's Club and a big win at one of the tables reverberated in Tony's mind. Francie put a cigarette between her lips and fumbled with a box of matches.

"Where's the lighter I gave you for your birthday?" Tony asked.

"It doesn't work anymore. The little spring broke."

"I might have guessed," Tony acknowledged wryly. "Where's the gold one your father gave you?"

Francie shrugged. "Lying around somewhere." In fact, it was in her purse at that moment; she never used it in front of Tony, nor had she used his inexpensive one, while it worked, in front of her father. There were easier roles in life, she imagined, than being the daughter of a mine owner and the girlfriend of a miner.

Circumstances were beginning to draw them apart, Francie thought. Circumstances that were compounding. The difference in social class; the secrecy; the availability of money on one hand, a lack of it on the other; increasing bitterness on Tony's part the longer the strike continued; her own resentment at her father for not understanding her need to warn Buck O'Crotty about the Utah miners, at Buck O'Crotty for never thanking or even acknowledging what she had done, for rewarding her by telling Tony to stay away from her; and, of course, the recent, growing pressure from the Coltranes to establish a relationship between Jack Coltrane and herself. Differences, secrecy, bitterness, resentment, pressure: all conspiring to create and widen a breach between Tony and her that neither of them could leap, a love they could not realize to culmination, to completion. Francie's troubled mind closed in on a single thought.

We can't let it happen.

Her cigarette only half smoked, she opened the side vent window and tossed it into the snowy street. Turning to Tony, she said determinedly, "Let's get married. Now. Tonight."

"What?" Tony stared at her, his chest tightening. "How?"

Francie twisted around on the seat, bringing her knees up. "Look, you've got two hundred eighty dollars saved, check? I've got the same amount. I'd have a lot more if you hadn't been so dumb and insisted that I not save any more than you were able to, so you wouldn't feel like I was putting more money into our future than you. I mean, it sounded romantic at the time, but I decided later it was silly. I never said so because you seemed so damned serious about it. Anyway, forget all that"—she waved her hands as if erasing the air—"the point is, we have nearly six hundred dollars between us, plus a car—"

"What do you mean, plus a car?" Tony interrupted. "You mean this? Your father paid for this car."

"Jesus Christ," Francie rolled her eyes. "All right, we have nearly six hundred dollars and *no* car. You don't mind just *using* the car, do you? To drive up to my house, then down to your house, then to the bus station?"

Tony continued to stare at her. This was, he realized, out of their usual realm of idle discussion, vague future plans. This was here and now and *real*. "What do you want to do?" he asked.

"Go to my house, tell my father what we're doing—if he's interested enough to listen—and pack my suitcase. Then go to your house, tell Buck O'Crotty the same thing, and pack your suitcase—"

"I haven't got a suitcase."

"Then use a pillowcase, I don't care!" she snapped. This was nervous business. "After we get our things, we'll take the ten o'clock bus to Reno and get married. The marriage license bureau is open around the clock, even on Christmas day, and there's always a justice of the peace available."

"What about my age?" Tony asked. "You're okay, you only have to be over eighteen; I have to be over twenty-one unless I have signed permission—"

"You can lie about your age. Or borrow Denny's driver's license; he's twenty-one. Anyway, they aren't that strict; as long as people *look* grownup, they don't care." Her hand worked inside his coat and shirt and she dragged her fingernails lightly down his chest. "You look grownup. Are you? Are *we?*"

Tony put a hand behind her neck and drew her face to his, opened his mouth, felt her open hers, and their tongues thrust forward, seeking, probing, mating, their mouths having the intercourse that their bodies were denied. They held their kiss of copulation for as long as they could and then released each other, the breath bursting from them in puffs of vapor.

"Well?" Francie asked, winter coat open, sweatered breasts rising and falling rapidly as she drew in snatches of air. Tony, excited, also breathing heavily, nodded briskly.

"Let's go."

Exhilarated, Francie twisted her legs back under the steering wheel and started the car. Driving to the corner, she went around the block and headed back toward Sierra Street. "Open your present on the way, Tony," she said. "Please."

"Sure." Tony reached behind the seat and pulled the big box over onto his lap. Looking at it in the dashboard light, he said, "It's wrapped so nice, I hate to open it. Did you wrap it yourself?"

"God, no. I can't cut paper straight, much less make bows. Mother was the one who could wrap packages. Every corner perfect, every ribbon just so. But I'm afraid your gift was wrapped by some lady at Pemberton's."

Tony swallowed dryly. Pemberton's was the fanciest store in Virginia City. He had never even been inside it.

As carefully as he could, Tony removed the ribbon and opened one end of the foil wrapping. Sliding it off, cringing, as it seemed to wrinkle at the slightest touch, he quickly put the paper in the back seat and opened the bright red box with PEMBERTON'S in white flocked lettering across its top. Inside, lying in great folds of soft, white tissue paper, was a rich, dark brown, leather jacket. The pungent smell of leather permeated the car in seconds. Tony rubbed his fingertips lightly over its smooth suppleness. "Jesus, Francie," he said in quiet awe.

"Do you like it?" She had to know at once. "Tell me the truth now. I can take it back—"

"You'd have to knock me out to take it back. It's the nicest thing I've ever had." But when in hell, he wondered, could he ever wear it? Then he remembered: they were leaving Virginia City. He could wear what he damned pleased.

When Francie guided the Olds into her drive and parked in front of the Delavane mansion, she said, "Now, may I please have my present?"

Tony reluctantly handed it to her: the small, plain box,

wrapped in what now seemed like hideous cheap green paper. But Francie unwrapped it as carefully as he had unwrapped his, and put the paper in the back seat as he had done. Opening the box, she unfolded the handkerchief.

"Oh, honey, it's beautiful! And it's real linen." She pressed it against her face. "You can always tell by how it smells. Oh, and Tony, the lace is exquisite!"

He shrugged self-consciously. "I saw it in a store window in Reno. I thought it looked kind of nice. Had to sneak away from Denny and the old man we were working for to buy it."

"I love it. And I love you."

They embraced and kissed again, not passionately this time but tenderly, gently, lovingly, as they had kissed the first time in the woods when they were children.

"We're going to be so happy, Tony."

"I hope so."

"I *know* so. And I want you to know so too. Now agree with me."

"I agree with you, Miss Frances Grace Delavane," he said with mock formality.

"That's better. And it'll soon be Frances Grace Donovan. I can't believe it! Do you know that I used to secretly practice writing that name to see how it looked?" They kissed again, then she asked, "Ready?"

"Let's go," he said.

Getting out of the car, they met on her side, held hands, and started across the wide drive. They had only gone a few steps when Tony noticed a car enter the drive across the snow-covered lawn, where it intersected with the top of Sierra Street. As the car entered Delavane property, its headlamps went off.

"Wait," Tony said, tensing. Stopping, he drew Francie back. As the car proceeded around the circular drive toward the mansion, Tony put an arm around Francie and guided her back to the Olds.

"What's the matter?" she asked, frowning.

"I'm not sure." Behind her car, he put a hand on her shoulder and gently pushed. "Get down."

"Tony, what's going on—"

"Just get down."

The car without its headlamps on came slowly to the front of the mansion and stopped. Four men, their faces covered with woolen neck scarves, piled out and hurried to the front of the mansion. Each man had two red bricks, and each hurled them at the stained-glass windows on the mansion's main floor. There was a loud clinking sound as brick struck glass and the windows shattered.

"Stop that!" Francie screamed. She pulled away from Tony's protective arm and stood up. "Stop that! Those are my mother's windows!"

The men whirled and stared at Francie in frozen surprise. Then they scurried back to their car. One of them took time to shake his fist at the mansion and yell, "Enjoy your fine turkey dinner tomorrow while our children eat beans, you motherless bastard, Delavane!" The car was already moving as this last man leaped inside. Gathering speed on spinning tires, it sprayed snow in Francie's face as it sped away.

Francie ran over to one of the broken windows, staring at it in revulsion. Tony hurried up and put his hands on her shoulders; she shook them off.

"My mother designed those windows!" she shouted, tears beginning to flow. "She supervised the tinting of the glass. Those were *her* windows!" Bending, she picked up a piece of yellow glass that had fallen outside and clutched it to her breast as if to protect it from further harm.

"Francie, don't," Tony said. She turned angrily on him.

"Did you know what they were going to do?" she asked accusingly.

"I didn't really know. I guessed it wasn't good when they—"

"Wasn't good?"

"—turned off their lights."

"Wasn't good! For Christ's sake, Tony, this is my *home!* Daddy was wrong to try bringing in outside labor, but *this*—this is criminal! Did you recognize who those bastards were?"

"No."

"Are you lying to me, Tony?" Francie asked. She was trembling now. Her husky voice broke when she spoke.

"I said no." Tony saw a rivulet of red run across the broken piece of yellow glass she held. "Francie, you're cut—"

The outside lights came on, the mansion door opened, and Big Jim Delavane hurried out, followed by Harmon, Libby, and Jack Coltrane, all of them in evening clothes.

Behind them came others Tony recognized: the Martin Pitts
and their son Phil, the Clinton Randalls and their son Craig,
and the Harley Kents and their son Billy, all of the younger
men accompanied by girls from other Hill families. Cavendish and two other members of the household staff came
out behind the guests.

Big Jim was the first one to reach Francie. "Are you all
right?" he asked, breaking his long silence toward her. He
saw her bloody hand. "Cavendish, quickly—"

The butler hurried up and with Big Jim guided Francie
toward the house. Several of the women followed them.

Harmon Coltrane looked at Tony, evaluating at once the
faded corduroy trousers and worn jacket. "Who are you?"
he asked coldly.

"He's Tony Donovan," said Jack Coltrane, coming forward. "One of the miners. Did you have a hand in this,
Donovan?" he demanded.

"No I didn't," Tony replied evenly.

"What the hell are you doing on the Hill then?"

"That's none of your business, Coltrane. You don't own
the Hill," Tony told him.

"Jack, dear, let him alone," purred Libby Coltrane for the
benefit of everyone there. "Maybe he was with Francie . . .?"

In his hand, Jack hefted a brick he had brought out of the
house. "Were those friends of yours who threw these?" he
demanded. Before Tony could respond, he added, "There
were women inside that house! Including my mother!"

"I don't know who threw the bricks," Tony snapped.

"I'll bet you don't," Phil Pitt sneered.

"You were probably in on the whole thing," Craig Randall accused.

"You're crazy," Tony said. *This* was crazy; it was like
they were back on the Comstock Elementary schoolyard.

When the rest of the women had gone back into the
mansion, Billy Kent said, "I think you need a good ass-
kicking, Donovan."

"There's always enough of you around to do it, isn't
there?" Tony said contemptuously.

"I can do it alone, you trash," Billy said angrily.

"Let me," Jack Coltrane said, tossing the brick down,
"since Francie's my girl."

"Francie's *your* girl?" Tony said. "That's a joke."

"Better hurry up and laugh then," Jack said, removing his

coat and handing it to Billy, "because you don't have much time." The younger Coltrane put up his fists and challenged, "All right, come on, Donovan."

Tony's eyes flicked over the men facing him: Harmon Coltrane, Martin Pitt, and the older men—all but Coltrane in the employ of Delavane Mines; their sons, led as they always had been by Jack Coltrane, one-time bully and now student of law, who in the schoolyard at Comstock Elementary or on the boxing team at Berkeley, Tony knew, could fight.

"Well, come on," Jack taunted. "Is the big, tough miner yellow?"

Tony smiled coldly, but his eyes grew fiery. For the first time he looked at Jack Coltrane and the others from the Hill without seeing the face of Big Jim Delavane. Tonight he would, for the first time, fight not a symbol of his own hate, but another person: Jack Coltrane. And he would be fighting for Francie. Unzipping his old jacket, he put it on a fender of Francie's car and raised his guard. "Okay, banker's boy, come and get it."

Jack immediately began circling slowly, his fists high in a classic boxing stance. Tony kept low: head, shoulders, fists in a protective crouch. As Jack measured him, Tony struck first, leaping forward and delivering a blow to Jack's side. Jack winced and continued circling. Tony jumped in again with an identical blow to the other side. Still Jack followed the same routine. The third time Tony attacked, Jack was ready for him: he laced Tony with two slick left jabs and a hard right cross, all to the face. Tony drew back, stung. Jack stepped in quickly, winging two more blistering jabs but missing with a right as Tony went into a crouch again. Head down, Tony ploughed forward, swinging both fists as if he had hammers in them. With satisfaction he felt two of the blows impact on Jack's face. But while he was giving, he was also taking; he felt Jack's practiced jab tagging him time after time. Tony managed to avoid the right crosses that invariably followed two or three jabs, but the damage dealt him by the jabs began to compound.

"Get him good, Jack!" Phil Pitt encouraged.

"Knock his teeth out!" Craig Randall said.

"He's bleeding, Jack! You've got him!"

Tony wasn't sure where he was bleeding from, but he began to taste blood in his mouth. Jack seemed to be moving faster, the jabs coming quicker, Tony's own punches missing more than hitting. It all seemed to culminate very quickly. One second it was a fight, the next it was all over. Jabs, jabs, jabs seemed to come out of nowhere and then Tony wasn't avoiding the right crosses anymore, and momentarily he could not see anything, and then he was on his hands and knees, head bent, watching red spots appear in the snow on the ground. When he looked up, Jack Coltrane was putting his coat back on and all the men were walking back into the Delavane mansion. Words like "showed that shanty Irishman," and "taught him a lesson he won't forget," drifted back to him. Harley Kent's voice interspersed with, ". . . starting to get serious. Clint Randall and I found roofing nails sprinkled on our driveways this week."

"And the telephone lines into the mine office were cut on Wednesday," Randall said.

"Well," said Martin Pitt, "I imagine tonight will be the last straw for Jim. Our side can play rough too. We've already been approached by a fellow named Lew Rainbolt, out of Kansas City, who's offered his services . . ."

Everyone went back inside, closing the door, leaving Tony where he had fallen. Tony looked back down at the snow. More red spots began to appear.

TWENTY

Lew Rainbolt arrived in Virginia City like a hired gunfighter riding into town on a black horse. Except that Rainbolt rode in behind the wheel of a yellow Lincoln roadster. Precisely at noon, in order to get as much public exposure as possible, he guided the long, sleek, twelve-cylinder car slowly down C Street. People stopped on the sidewalks and came out of stores to gawk. Striking miners, loitering on street corners, stopped talking and stared silently. On a sudden urge, an elderly woman made the sign of the cross.

Following a short distance behind the roadster was an ominous-looking black panel truck with white side lettering that read: RAINBOLT SECURITY CO. The panel truck was driven by a white-haired albino man. Both vehicles carried Missouri license plates.

Standing on the corner of C and Silver Streets, Buck O'Crotty watched Rainbolt pass and nodded his thick head solemnly. Tony, beside him, asked, "Is that him, Buck?"

"That's him," Buck confirmed. "That's the strikebreaker. I was afraid it would be."

In relating to Buck the incident of his beating by Jack Coltrane on Christmas Eve, Tony had recalled hearing Martin Pitt tell the other men that Big Jim Delavane had been offered the services of a man named Lew something from Kansas City.

"Rainbolt?" Buck had inquired urgently. "Was it Lew Rainbolt?"

Tony was not sure. "It might have been, Buck. I can't remember."

Buck's pug face had darkened with worry. "If Big Jim brings in Lew Rainbolt," he predicted forebodingly, "this strike will become a war. Rainbolt is one of the most notorious strikebreakers in the country. He's an absolutely ruthless man." Buck had slammed a fist into the palm of one hand. "Damn those brick-throwing idiots anyway!"

Buck O'Crotty had been incensed when he heard about the four masked men who had bombarded the windows of Big Jim Delavane's mansion.

"The fools!" he stormed. "The stupid, goddamned fools!"

Everyone in the O'Crotty household stared at him with mouths agape. It was the first time they had ever heard Buck use profanity in their home. They knew it had to be a moment of grave concern.

Buck had immediately telephoned the mansion to repudiate the act, offer to have the union pay for the damages, and assure Big Jim that if the guilty men could be identified they would be turned over to Sheriff Patch. But Big Jim refused to take his call, relaying through Cavendish that anything the union leader wished to say to him should be conveyed to his attorney, Martin Pitt. That further infuriated Buck. He telephoned his union vice presidents and summoned them to the union hall, shouting, when they protested, "I don't *care* if it's Christmas Eve! I wouldn't care if it was the *first* Christmas Eve and the Virgin Mary was in labor at this very moment! Get over there!"

At the union hall, Buck had Tony reiterate what he had witnessed and heard at the mansion. It drew puzzled frowns and prompted Lloyd Arlen to ask, "What in hell were *you* doing up there, Tony?"

"And who gave you the pasting?" Terence Henny wanted to know, scrutinizing Tony's cut, swollen lips and puffed, purplish eye.

"Never mind that," Buck snapped. "It has nothing to do with the problem at hand. I want the names of the men involved in this incident, and I want them fast! Check every man who wasn't on picket tonight. Start with the trouble-makers; you know who they are. Get your shift bosses out to help you." He pointed an intimidating finger at them. "I'm not exaggerating the seriousness of this situation. Unless we can offer Jim Delavane something to prevent him hiring a strikebreaker, we're *all* going to bleed. *Find those men!*"

The guilty men were not found. Everyone had an alibi, a witness. No one came forward. Big Jim Delavane was not placated, or dissuaded. Through Martin Pitt, he retained the services of Lew Rainbolt. For a week the rumor had spread that the strikebreaker would get to Virginia City at noon on Tuesday. He arrived on the minute.

After Rainbolt made his way slowly down C Street, he guided the yellow Lincoln to the curb in front of the Ormsby House. Getting out of the car, he walked around to the sidewalk and, to give everyone a good, close look at him, stood waiting for the panel truck to park. A tall man, well over six feet, he was telephone-pole lean and looked just as solid. The suit he wore was Western cut; his Stetson was beaver; the boots had riding heels, making him even taller. Despite the bitter cold, sunless January day, he wore no overcoat or gloves. Between the brim of his hat and the collar of his shirt lay a plane of lines, edges, and corners that were entirely devoid of curves. His features might have been hacked out with a hatchet: they were rawly angular, indelicately sharp. He was more than thirty, less than forty.

Putting a thin cheroot between his teeth, Rainbolt dug his thumbnail into a stick match and cupped his hands protectively around the flame to light it. When the panel truck was

parked, directly next to the roadster, the albino alighted and
joined Rainbolt on the sidewalk, standing to one side and
slightly, deferentially to the rear. The albino was perhaps
fifty, shorter, broader, with milky, translucent-appearing skin,
hair like tufts of raw cotton, and eyes with pink irises. As
the two men stood there, they slowly scrutinized C Street in
both directions, not warily or cautiously, not even interest-
edly, merely with the idle curiosity of men who had been in
many such towns before and had long since stopped expecting anything unique.

They stood in the cold for five or six minutes, looking and
being looked at. Just about the time observers began to
wonder what it was they were waiting for, six more cars with
Missouri plates moved in caravan down the street. Black
like the panel truck, they were all four-door sedans, each
occupied by four men.

"Right on time, Chalky," close observers heard Lew
Rainbolt say.

"Yes, sir, Mr. Rainbolt," the albino replied.

When the cars were parked, angled in to the curb at
available places as close to the roadster as possible, all of
the men got out at once. The two dozen were dressed
identically: brown-visored caps, brown leather jackets, brown
wool trousers, brown leather puttees, and brown hightop
brogans. As a group their faces were unsmiling and determined, their builds healthy and athletic; they appeared
intimidatingly formidable.

As the uniformed men were lining up on the sidewalk in a
column of twos, Sheriff Sam Patch crossed the street and
walked up to Rainbolt.

"You or your men armed, mister?" he asked without
preliminary.

"Not at the moment," Rainbolt replied. "My men arm
themselves just prior to going on duty. We're a licensed
security firm," he drew an official-looking document from
his inside coat pocket, "with a federal firearms permit valid
in all forty-eight states. We've been retained by—"

"I already know who you've been retained by," Patch
interrupted.

Rainbolt's eyes narrowed a fraction. "—by Mr. Martin
Pitt, Esquire, attorney at law," he continued, "to protect
the person and property of his client, one James Delavane."

"I said I already knew that."

"I heard you," Rainbolt said. "But I like to finish my sentences." He paused a beat, then added, "I like to finish everything I start."

"If you start anything here," Patch warned, "you'll go to jail for it."

"You mean anything illegal I presume," Rainbolt said blandly.

"You know damn well what I mean, mister," the sheriff asserted. After assuring himself that the federal firearms permit was in order, he handed it back to Rainbolt. "I ain't going to have Virginia City turned into no battleground. I give you fair warning."

"My men and I are law-abiding citizens, Sheriff," Rainbolt told him with a fixed smile. "We're here to perform a legal service that we are licensed and qualified to perform. If you uncover evidence at any time that any of us have broken a law, why, do your duty and make an arrest." The smile vanished. "But I stress the word 'evidence,' Sheriff. Unless and until you have any, kindly do not interfere with us. In any way."

Patch leaned forward an inch. "Are you threatening me, mister?"

"I never threaten. Waste of time. Plus which, it puts one's enemies on notice. Very foolish."

"Just remember what I said," Patch told him, punctuating his words with a stiff forefinger that prudently stopped short of Rainbolt's chest.

"I'll do that, Sheriff," the tall man assured him. As Patch turned and walked away, Rainbolt nodded slightly to his men. "Let's go."

The albino named Chalky and the two dozen uniformed men followed Lew Rainbolt into the Ormsby House.

The evening of his arrival in Virginia City, after an orientation tour of the area by Martin Pitt, Lew Rainbolt was taken to meet Big Jim Delavane. Over cigars and whiskey, to the crackle of a roaring fire across the study from Big Jim's desk, Rainbolt explained his operating methods.

"First and foremost, of course, Mr. Delavane, my men will protect your home. There'll be four men on duty at all times—one stationed at your front door to control entry; one on constant patrol directly around your house; one on perimeter patrol at the outer edge of your property; and a fourth on roving patrol. He might be anywhere—in the woods, on the street leading up here, on your roof. He will also be available for escort duty—I understand you have a daughter at home; escort duty for her, yourself, any members of your household staff, wherever you go.

"Secondly," Rainbolt continued, "my men will protect your mines around the clock, in six-man patrols. After seeing your property this afternoon, I will probably put one man in the mine general offices, one at the main shaft entrance, two at the gate, and have two on separate foot patrols inside the fence. With your permission, I'll also wire the fence to a generator and conductor to give it an electrical charge that will discourage anyone climbing it at night with vandalism in mind.

"Those will be the official duties of my firm," Rainbolt concluded. "Security. Protection. Peace of mind for you. My unofficial duties will be to demoralize the strikers when and where I can, in order to undermine the strike effort as quickly as possible."

"That's the part of your job we've got to get clear," Big Jim said bluntly. "I want the miners to know that I'm prepared to play as rough as they do. I don't take lightly their attack on my home on Christmas Eve. At the same time, I don't want to be responsible for escalating any violence. We don't want anything like what happened in Calumet."

Delavane and Martin Pitt were watching Lew Rainbolt closely, but he did not even wince at the mention of the infamous Michigan town. "There were several security firms employed in Calumet at the time of that tragedy, Mr. Delavane," the strikebreaker stated in a neutral tone. "No one knows for certain who was responsible for it."

The tragedy they spoke of had taken place during a long, bitter strike by members of two unions, the W.F.M., Western Federation of Miners, and the I.W.W., Industrial Workers of the World, against C&H, the Calumet and Hecla Mining Company, in the company-owned town of Calumet at the northwestern end of the upper peninsula of Michigan. With five federation locals involved, an absentee-owner parent company in faraway Boston, a divided and decentralized management, many diverse political interests, and the richest copper mines in America at stake, the dispute eventually brought in the national guard as well as at least three groups of professional strikebreakers, including the notorious Waddell-Mahon men from New York City.

With the strike in its fifth month and Christmas approaching, the women's auxiliary of the W.F.M. organized a party for children of the striking miners. The women worked day and night knitting mittens and scarves, and soliciting donations for bags of hard candy. A social hall owned by the Italian Club, upstairs over an A&P store, was secured for the event. On the afternoon of Christmas Eve, more than five hundred mostly women and children crowded into the hall. While gathered around the Christmas tree for a community sing, someone shouted, "Fire!" The crowd panicked and bolted toward the only exit: double doors at the bottom of an eight-foot-wide stairway. Those doors would not open; a steel drilling rod had been pushed through their handles on the outside.

A great tidal wave of people fell in upon itself at the bottom of the stairwell. After a quarter-hour of unremitting, screaming, writhing horror, the crush of bodies was five feet high. At the top of the pile, a dead young mother's arms protruded, holding her infant child up to save it. Seventy-four people were dead. Sixty-three of them were children. There had been no fire.

"I want nothing like that in Virginia City," Jim Delavane asserted.

"Nor do I, sir," replied Rainbolt, stiffening slightly. "My men and I are strikebreakers, not child murderers."

Big Jim revolved the cigar in his pursed lips, studying Rainbolt across the desk. The mine owner had taken an instant dislike to the strikebreaker and was trying to neutralize it. Although Delavane would have indignantly denied it, the reason was that he and Rainbolt were so much alike: both handsome in their respective ways, well-dressed, self-confident and assured, knowing they had succeeded on their own and were good at what they did. Delavane saw in Rainbolt too much of himself, too many of the traits he knew his late wife had disliked, which his daughter found objectionable: too little compassion, too much arrogance, a hard edge that rarely softened.

"Perhaps," Martin Pitt suggested, "you could give us a few examples of how you might accomplish this demoralization you mentioned. Without actually telling us what you intend to do, of course. On the record, my client is securing your services for protection purposes only."

"Of course," said Rainbolt. "At this stage, I couldn't give you any specifics anyway. Each strike presents its own possibilities. Normally we begin with tire-slashings, nuisance telephone calls, smoke bombings of the union hall, that sort of thing. Those are mild tactics that are sometimes all a particular situation calls for. The longer a walkout has continued, of course, the harsher our measures become. In this instance—"

"Never mind," Big Jim checked the strikebreaker's explanation, "I don't want to know any more. What I *do* want is to set some limits."

"That's your privilege," Rainbolt said. "You're paying the freight."

Delavane touched his desk with a stiff forefinger. "I don't want any killings. I don't want anyone badly hurt."

"Tell me what you consider 'badly hurt,' " Rainbolt requested.

"Crippled," Delavane said.

"Crippled to what extent?"

"I believe what my client means," Martin Pitt defined precisely, "is permanently injured beyond complete recuperation."

"I'll agree to that limitation," said Rainbolt. "How do you feel about property damage?"

Big Jim's lips compressed slightly. The recollection of the bricks through his windows—windows that Edith had designed and had made—caused his stomach to churn. "Sure," he said without hesitation. "As long as no one is badly hurt. So far," he pointed out, "with the exception of clubbing several outside workers I tried to bring in, the A.M.W.N. hasn't directed any real physical abuse at any of my managers or office workers. I don't want to be the one to start anything like that."

"I understand," Rainbolt assured him.

The three men talked for a while longer, finishing their cigars and whiskey, and when the attorney and Rainbolt were ready to leave, Big Jim said, "Martin, let me have a word in private with Mr. Rainbolt, will you?"

Pitt frowned briefly at being excluded, but quickly decided he was probably better off not knowing what was going to be said. "Certainly," he nodded. "I'll wait in the foyer."

When the lawyer had gone, Big Jim leaned forward on his desk. "One of the striking miners," he said quietly, "is a young man named Tony Donovan. He's been seeing my daughter Francie somewhat informally—drugstore dates, picture shows, that sort of thing. They went through elementary school together. I'm sure she feels sorry for him; maybe she's even encouraged his attentions, I don't know. At any rate, I've spoken to her about it and asked her not to see him. But I'd like you and your men to be especially alert for him, in case he tries to force a meeting with her someplace."

Delavane paused, weighing words. Lew Rainbolt said nothing, waiting, his expression inscrutable. Under the strikebreaker's steady gaze, Delavane began to feel embarrassed. Like a man negotiating with a pimp.

"Understand, I don't have anything against the young man," he attempted to rationalize. "I simply don't think he's right for my daughter; she's my only child and, ah . . ."

The mine owner's words trailed off. Drumming his fingertips soundlessly on the desktop, he thought: Go ahead. Tell this hired thug of yours to bust young Donovan up, mess up his face, put him in the hospital. . .

The hospital.

Jim's mind went back to the day when he looked in the door of a hospital room and saw Ruby Donovan nursing her newborn son.

"Congratulations on your son. May I see him?"

"I—yes, I suppose."

The black-haired infant with Ruby's swollen nipple in its mouth. "He's a handsome boy, Ruby. Do you think he looks like his father?"

For just a pulsebeat that day—

But no, he had long ago put that far-fetched notion out of his mind. Right now, he told himself firmly, he had to deal with Tony Donovan as an enemy, someone who was trying to take his daughter away from him. Delavane knew what he wanted to say to Lew Rainbolt; he wanted to tell him that Tony Donovan was an exception to the no-permanent-harm rule. Why in hell, he wondered, didn't he just say it?

"The thing of it is," he said instead, "I've been told that this young Donovan is something of a hothead. He was recently involved in a fistfight right outside my front door, as a matter of fact. Got whipped by the son of one of my neighbors, so he may be carrying a grudge." Big Jim glanced away. "I just wanted to let you know that you might have to exceed the limits we set in order to deal with him. I have no problem with it if you do." That was as close as Delavane could come to marking Tony for a beating.

"I understand," said Lew Rainbolt. "I'll make my men aware of it. Anything else?"

Delavane shook his head and walked with Rainbolt to the foyer where Martin Pitt was waiting. Francie was with the attorney. Delavane introduced his daughter to Lew Rainbolt.

"How do you do, Miss Delavane," the strikebreaker said.

"Mr. Rainbolt." Francie offered her hand and he took it. "So you're going to be our guard." Rainbolt held onto her fingers a beat longer than necessary.

"Security force, yes, Miss Delavane." His eyes sharpened. He captured her gaze with his own and would not relinquish it. "We'll do our best not to intrude on your household."

"That will be appreciated, I'm sure."

As Rainbolt put on his overcoat and hat, Big Jim and Pitt stepped aside to speak briefly, and Francie was free to study Rainbolt as closely as he was still regarding her. His eyes were frank, almost challenging, and suddenly Francie was annoyed by the way he was looking at her. Rainbolt did not even blink.

"Please feel free to call on me personally for anything you might need, Miss Delavane," he said quietly. "Anything at all."

"You're very kind, Mr. Rainbolt. However, I can take care of myself without anyone's help."

"Yes, I imagine you can," Rainbolt replied. There was just the hint of an amused smile on his lips, and it further annoyed Francie.

After all the goodnights had been said, Rainbolt left with Martin Pitt. In the lawyer's car, driving back down Sierra Street, Rainbolt decided that it might not be easy to keep Francie Delavane away from her miner boyfriend without, as Big Jim had already consented, using some extreme method. The girl had determined eyes, a determined mouth.

There was one other way, of course. As he thought of its possibilities, the amused smile returned. He could get her interested in someone else.

Himself, for instance.

*   *   *

Buck O'Crotty was in the A.M.W.N. hall, getting ready to lock up for a few hours. Denny was emptying all the wastebaskets into a burlap bag; Tony was distributing new picket assignment lists to every desk.

"Don't forget to put one of those on the bulletin board," Buck reminded through his open office door.

Tony, his back to Buck, did not reply. Glancing at a wall clock, Tony saw that it was after nine o'clock. This was the fifth consecutive night Buck had found something for him to do that prevented him from meeting Francie. Between that son of a bitch Rainbolt tagging along everywhere Francie went, and Buck keeping Tony busy from supper until bedtime, he and Francie had only seen each other twice in the ten days since Rainbolt's arrival. Both times had been in the balcony of the Strand movie house; both rendezvous initiated by Francie taking a chance telephoning the O'Crotty residence, hoping Tony would answer. Or Denny. Even Kerry. Anyone except Rosetta, of whom Francie had inexplicably developed a dread fear, or Buck, whom she was now too embarrassed and embittered over recent events to speak. During the ten-day period, Francie had actually made seven calls to the house; five times she had quietly hung up when Buck or Rosetta answered. "Nuisance calls," Buck said. "Pay them no mind. Probably Rainbolt's men; it's a common tactic."

When they arranged to meet at the movie house, Tony went in first, as soon as the box office opened; Francie was dropped off at the theater by Lew Rainbolt, who would come back for her when the picture was over. The first time Francie had unexpectedly requested an escort to the Strand, Rainbolt suspected what she was up to; the next time, he sent one of his men, wearing street clothes, in to watch her. The report he received later was of heavy petting and kissing, interrupted only occasionally by intense whispering. Rainbolt, while trying to think of the best way short of violence to stop the assignations, found himself wondering idly if Francie had slept with young Donovan. And amused at *why* he was wondering that.

The two meetings at the Strand, sweet and warm as they were, also became extremely frustrating for Tony. He knew they were going to be brief, only the length of the movie, and that he and Francie would then have to separate not knowing when they would see each other again. Tony never knew more than forty-eight hours in advance which picket shift was his; added to which Buck, by design to prevent him seeing Francie, was calling on him without notice for other assignments. And that bastard Rainbolt or one of his "cadets," as the miners referred to the security guards, was always shadowing Francie. Everybody, everything, seemed to be against them.

Francie was still very bitter about the brick throwing that had destroyed her mother's stained-glass windows. They were, Libby Coltrane had sympathized, irreplaceable; then, thinking herself thus ingratiated, had inquired, "Now *tell* me about your young miner friend, my dear. Jack is green with jealousy. Tony something, isn't it?" Francie had told her practically nothing, lying through her teeth, making up everything as she went along, depicting Tony as just a friend from town, an old grade-school chum who was hard up because of the strike, and whom she was bringing home to see if her father could move him into the office.

To her father, on the other hand, so happy was she to have the long silence at last put aside, Francie admitted that she had been "dating" Tony Donovan, that they were "interested" in each other, and that she had brought him to the mansion on Christmas Eve to have a "talk" with Big Jim. Her father had expressed an immediate disdain for Tony, insisting that he was far beneath Francie on the social ladder and, he suspected, in every other way. Francie had decided it was not an opportune time to reveal that a Christmas Eve elopement had been imminent.

Francie's main worry had been how Tony was going to react to the Christmas Eve incident. When she finally calmed down enough to think, instead of rant and rave about the windows, when she had realized, after Cavendish had bandaged her cut hand, that Jack Coltrane had beaten up Tony and left him bleeding in the snow, she had been mortified. Tony, surprisingly, had not been as humiliated by the experience as she expected.

"I've been beat up by Jack before," he told her pragmatically, at a meeting at Walker's drugstore before Rainbolt and his men arrived. "He's always been a better fighter than me. What counts is I always get in some good licks of my own—"

"You sure did!" Francie seized the moment, relieved. "You blacked his eye good."

"At least now your friends up there know about us. What did your father say about me?"

"Same thing Buck said about me. He doesn't want me seeing you." She smiled a wan smile. "I guess we're not a match made in heaven."

Tony grunted softly. "Guess not."

Both seemed to realize, without verbalizing it, that the moment, the magic, of their planned elopement, had passed. With Francie's bandaged hand, Tony's battered face, and the fact that their interest in each other was now at least superficially revealed, they tacitly agreed to wait out the beginning of the new year. Maybe it would be better than the old.

At the last meeting they were able to manage at the drugstore, a new tension had developed. Tony asked her something she did not feel was quite proper.

"Do you know anything about the strikebreakers everybody says your father's bringing in?" It was asked innocently enough, but it rankled Francie immediately.

"They're private guards, not strikebreakers," she replied, piqued. "Are you asking for yourself or for Buck O'Crotty? Or is there any difference?"

"What do you mean?" Tony did not understand her query or her irritation.

"Listen, I'm not going to get caught back in the middle of this thing a second time," she snapped. "Don't ask me any questions about what goes on in my house, and I won't ask any questions about yours."

That evening ended badly for them. Then Rainbolt and his men came to town, and their meetings were curtailed. With each passing day, Tony became more edgy, more peevish. Tonight was no exception.

"You put that picket list on the bulletin board like I said?" Buck asked as they got ready to close the union hall for the night.

"It's up," Tony grumbled.

"Denny, ready to go?" Buck called to the rear of the headquarters, where Denny had taken the trash.

"All set, Buck."

"Let's call it a night then," the union leader said wearily.

"You sure you can't find something to keep us busy for a few more hours?" Tony asked caustically.

Buck stopped in the middle of the room and looked at

him with growing impatience. "Your lip's getting a little out of hand lately."

Tony turned to face him. "I think maybe my whole life is out of hand."

"If you'd take a little good advice once in a blue moon," Buck said flatly, "maybe things would be a little easier for you."

"My problem is I'm having trouble telling the good advice from the bad" Tony retorted.

"Better button it up lad," Buck said irritably, pointing a finger at him.

"You two at it again?" Denny asked easily, ambling in from the rear. "I swear to God, you're like a couple old women."

"I'm not in the mood for any of your cracks tonight either," Buck warned.

O'Crotty held his temper in check as best he could. He knew he had been irascible of late, increasingly so since the entry of Lew Rainbolt into their volatile situation. Rainbolt and his men had been in town for ten days; Buck was laced with apprehension waiting for the strikebreaker to act. The few nuisance telephone calls, of which Buck suspected the strikebreaker, were only teasers. Rainbolt would make a major move of some kind—and soon.

"He'll have to," Buck had told Rosetta, "if he's going to earn his blood money."

"Perhaps," Rosetta reasoned, "he is only here, as he said, to protect property."

"He's here to break the strike," Buck replied unequivocally. "If all Big Jim wanted was his property protected, he could have hired Pinkerton men out of San Francisco. He didn't have to bring men all the way from Kansas City."

Buck was convinced something was coming. He cautioned all of his union officers to caution the men they were responsible for to be alert, be wary, be *ready*. Rainbolt would strike; it was only a matter of time.

As Buck let Tony and Denny precede him out of the union hall, turning to lock and double-check the door, Denny began to chastise the two of them. "I hope you guys don't carry your argument into the house again tonight, 'cause I know for a fact that all the fussing's getting on Rosetta's nerves. It's beginning to affect her cooking. Them biscuits this morning was a little heavy."

Buck muttered something unintelligible in response and Tony remained sullenly silent as the three men started down the street toward the Walk. They had gone just half a block when the union hall blew up.

The explosion was more light and sound than force; it shocked the three miners to their marrow, while not even shaking the sidewalk on which they trod. It was the sudden light of it: a blast of brightness, argent in texture, challenging the eyes and winning, gone before it could be realized; and the sound of it—a thunder-pitched boom, like a great paper bag of air being burst.

"Jesus Christ!" Denny cried out.

All three of them leaped into instinctive crouches, hands up defensively, mouths suddenly agape. The great pop of light, separating the night behind them, was too fleeting to warn them, followed too quickly by the sound itself, and then the almost melodic sharding of glass as the storefront windows disintegrated in a wave of particles.

"What the hell happened, Buck?" Denny asked urgently, still the only one to speak. "Was it the furnace?"

Buck was not there to answer. He had run into the middle of the street where, still crouched and weaving like a monkey, he was trying to see if anyone had been nearby, if anyone was hurt. He had guessed not, before he even ran to check; the union hall was invariably the only place in the block with lights and activity after dark; still he had to make sure, to know that no one needed help, before he could release his mind to other thoughts.

Tony was at his side very quickly, asking, "Was it a bomb?"

"Yes—yes, it was. It was a bomb." Buck's eyes continued to search the night.

"A bomb!" Denny cried. He ran up directly behind Tony, his nasal voice becoming incredulous. "Jesus Christ! A bomb! We coulda all been killed!"

"If they'd wanted us killed," Buck said, "we'd be dead."

"How'd they know somebody wouldn't be in there?" Tony asked.

"We were being watched, I'd guess. The bomb was prob'ly planted under the floor somewheres, and wired outside the hall to a plunger. Denny, did you see anybody out back when you took the trash? Or anything look funny to you?"

"No, Buck. It looked just like always."

"All right, come on," Buck said. Hurrying to the corner, Buck led Tony and Denny around to the alley and up to the back of the still settling, devastated union hall. "Down on all fours," he ordered. "Feel around in the dirt, dig with your fingernails; look for a wire." As they started to search, the sirens of both Virginia City fire trucks began to wail two blocks away.

Tony found the wire within a minute. "Got it, Buck!" He pulled it up from its inch-deep conduit and followed it across the dirt alley. It ran under a fifty-gallon drum used for trash. Behind the drum, the wire was connected to a small magneto plunger.

"Sure," Buck said as the scenario fell into place for him. "The garbage truck made its collection yesterday. Sometime after that, last night I'd guess, somebody shimmied under the hall and planted a satchel charge—prob'ly dynamite and a little nitro. Used a spoon or something to dig a one-inch trench over to the can, laid the wire, covered it up, and hid the plunger. Prob'ly didn't take more'n ten minutes to do it all. Tonight somebody watched us from around front. When whoever it was saw us lock up, they hurried into the alley and touched off the charge."

"The strikebreaker," Tony said, almost to himself.

"The strikebreaker," Buck verified. "Or one of his thugs." In the clear winter moonlight, Tony and Denny could see Buck's tough features turn harder. "Let's go," he said. "Over to the hotel. Right now."

As the trio hurried from the alley, Tony carrying the wire and plunger, both fire trucks skidded to a halt out front. People were running toward the scene from all directions. Sam Patch's night deputy drove up, leaped from his patrol car, and stood indecisively, not knowing what to do. As Buck passed, he slapped the young officer on the back.

"Crowd control, lad! Keep people back from all that broken glass until the sheriff gets here!" Buck knew that Sam Patch, who lived within four blocks, was probably on his way already.

Trotting past what had been their union headquarters, they paused for a better look at its remains. Between a shoe store on one side and a small furniture outlet on the other, was a gaping black hole with a cloud of dirty plaster dust churning around inside, trying to settle. The walls on each side, and the respective businesses they protected, were undamaged except for broken windows.

"A nice, clean, professional job," Buck said evenly. "It don't leave much doubt who did it. Work that neat takes practice." Buck hurried on, Tony and Denny catching up.

Reaching the Ormsby House, they found several people out on the sidewalk, straining to see what was going on with the sirens and activity far down the street. Neither Rainbolt nor any of his men were among the onlookers. Buck's jaw clenched at that. He led Tony and Denny through the glass double doors into the plush red and gold, velvet and leather lobby. Just inside the door, Buck raised a hand slightly and they halted.

Spread out all over the lobby were more than a dozen of Rainbolt's men, all in street clothes. They were variously engaged: reading newspapers, playing cards, dozing or pretending to doze, idly conversing. The albino Chalky was moving among them, serving coffee and brandy. At a small table in one corner, brandy snifters between them, Lew Rainbolt and Martin Pitt sat.

"There's too many, Buck," Denny whispered at the door.

"We need more men, Buck," Tony said quietly into the union leader's other ear.

"We're not here to fight," Buck replied in a normal voice, not caring if anyone overheard him. He took the magneto plunger from Tony's hand and stepped forward. "Watch my back," he admonished, "in case they've other ideas."

Buck walked straight toward the little corner table; Tony, swallowing, and Denny, wetting his lips, moved slightly away from him on each side and stayed several paces behind. A few of Rainbolt's trained men exchanged scoffing grins. Amateurs, their expressions said. An old man and a couple of kids.

When Buck got to the table, he smiled coldly and waved an arm around the room. "Never in my life," he said trenchantly, "have I seen more men with less curiosity. An explosion loud enough to wake the dead occurs just down the street and none of them so much as stroll out to see whether it's Armageddon or what. Remarkable."

"Maybe they're not inquisitive men," Rainbolt replied, studying Buck casually. The gladiators had met.

Buck made a complete turn where he stood, his eyes sweeping the lobby. "Fourteen incurious men. I suppose you can account for the whereabouts of ten others who would be equally uninterested in explosions?"

"If I had to," Rainbolt stated easily. "If there was legal reason for me to," he glanced significantly at Pitt. "Some of my men are on roving patrol, of course. Their whereabouts would have to be approximated."

Martin Pitt leaned forward. "For your information, Mr. O'Crotty, we are aware of what the explosion was—"

"I'm sure of that," Buck quipped coldly.

"—because several of Mr. Rainbolt's men happened to be out for a stroll when it happened. They brought us the news."

"I suppose," Buck speculated, "everyone provides an alibi for everyone else. Is that it?"

"Exactly," said Martin Pitt. "Just like when it came to identifying the vandals who smashed Jim Delavane's windows—"

"Bricks and dynamite are two different things!" Buck snapped. "Broken windows are a far cry from a blown-up building!" He slammed the magneto plunger and its attached wire onto their table, causing Martin Pitt to jump back in his chair apprehensively. Rainbolt barely blinked at the sudden, violent move. "You're a cool one, I'll say that for you," Buck grudgingly complimented.

"Calm usually prevails," Rainbolt remarked.

"*Right* prevails," Buck corrected. He braced his shoulders an inch. "The workingman will prevail. Despite all the owners and lawyers and strikebreakers, despite even dynamite, the labor union will prevail. I just came to tell you that, Mr. Rainbolt. You may make noise and cause trouble and do damage—but you won't win. Understand that. *You . . . won't . . . win.*"

"Mr. O'Crotty," the strikebreaker said quietly, "I've been involved in labor disputes since I was seventeen years old, when I went to work as a hooligan for the Atlas Guard Company to get out of the tenements of Chicago. After Atlas, I had jobs with Force Security and Logan's Private Police. Before I started my own crew, I worked as a lieutenant for Dandy Phil Donegal for three years. I've worked strikes all over America, and if I've learned one thing it's this—in a strike, *nobody* wins. It's like war—there aren't any victors, only survivors."

"If you realize that," Buck asked in some confusion, "if you feel that way about it, then why in the name of God do you stay in the vile business you're in?"

Rainbolt shrugged. "Balance, I suppose. The owners are entitled to have some muscle too. Their managers and office workers aren't going to throw bricks like your miners did. There has to be somebody around to neutralize people like you, Mr. O'Crotty. Otherwise we'd all end up being Bolsheviks."

"O'Crotty," Martin Pitt spoke again, "let's call a truce and reopen negotiations. Give up some of the concessions Delavane Mines agreed to in exchange for a wage increase. Let's get the town back to normal."

Buck shook his head. "Those concessions were for the health and safety of the men. They're entitled to decent working conditions *and* higher wages. We'll not budge an inch."

Martin Pitt looked away in frustration. Rainbolt sighed quietly in resignation. He, too, looked away.

Sam Patch strode into the lobby with two deputies carrying shotguns. They came directly to the table where Rainbolt and Pitt sat. Before Patch could say anything, Buck waved a hand preemptively. "Don't waste your time, Sheriff. Everybody here is an alibi for everybody else."

"I warned you, mister," Patch said to Rainbolt, ignoring Buck. He pulled out a pair of handcuffs. "Get up off of that chair—"

"Just a minute, Sheriff," Martin Pitt said indignantly. "Mr. Rainbolt is a client of mine. On what charge are you arresting him?"

"Suspicion of felonious property damage."

"Based on what evidence?" Pitt demanded.

"Nobody else in town would've done it," Patch declared.

Pitt rose from his chair. "That is a ludicrous statement for a law enforcement official to make. You are obviously arresting this man without any evidence whatsoever. That is malfeasance at its worst. If you do this, Patch, I intend to start recall proceedings against you the moment the courthouse opens in the morning. I won't rest until you're removed from office!"

Patch turned angrily on Martin Pitt, and Buck put a

quick, restraining hand on the sheriff's arm. "Don't make trouble for yourself Mr. Patch," he pacified. "The only evidence you'll find is that magneto plunger, and it's not likely to have any fingerprints on it except mine and Tony's. I appreciate you trying to do your honest duty; my membership is going to be told about it, you can count on that. But don't lock horns with the likes of them," he bobbed his chin in repugnance at Rainbolt and Pitt, "unless you catch 'em in the act. They're worse than diamondbacks; they don't even rattle before they strike. So be careful, Mr. Patch." Turning to Tony and Denny, he said, "Let's go," and walked away.

Before the trio was ten feet from the table, Lew Rainbolt called out, "Tony Donovan!"

The three men stopped, turning back with puzzled looks. "I'm Tony Donovan," Tony said.

Rainbolt rose and walked over to him. The strikebreaker stood several inches taller and was leagues past Tony in presence, bearing, dress. "Mr. Pitt told me who you were," Rainbolt said. "Your name was specifically mentioned by my employer as a potential trespasser. I just wanted my men to have a good look at you." To the room at large, he said, "Men, this is Tony Donovan. Be careful of him; I hear he's a hothead."

Rainbolt's men laughed loudly. Blood flowed into Tony's face. His right hand clenched into a fist; it moved six inches before Buck O'Crotty grabbed Tony's wrist. Rainbolt's men, laughter subsiding as quickly as it started, were on their feet at once, ready.

"Look around you, lad," Buck said with quiet urgency.

Tony's eyes flicked in a quick circuit of the room. Fourteen tense, unsmiling faces were waiting. Directly in front of him, Lew Rainbolt was waiting. Buck's grip on Tony's wrist tightened.

"Never fight when they pick the time and place, lad," Buck said.

Tony swallowed his fury and slowly relaxed his hand. Buck put an arm around his shoulders and guided him across the lobby, Denny following. Before they reached the door, Rainbolt spoke again, purposely loud enough for them to hear.

"All right, men. Time for rounds. I'll check the Delavane

mansion myself I want to personally make sure Miss Frances Grace Delavane is tucked safely in bed."

On his way out the door, Tony glared hatefully over his shoulder at the strikebreaker. Lew Rainbolt merely smiled.

TWENTY-ONE

In the O'Crotty kitchen, four women volunteers finished preparing the last of a shoe box full of small brown envelopes, similar in size and color to the regular pay envelopes that, prior to the strike, had been distributed at the end of shift every Saturday at Delavane Mines. Each envelope in the box showed on its face the name of a striking miner, the number of people in his household, and the amount of money he was entitled to receive weekly from the A.M.W.N. strike fund. The four women, using Rosetta O'Crotty's kitchen table since the union hall had been destroyed, wrote out the envelopes every Saturday morning, transcribing information from master lists that Buck gave them.

Buck had selected the similar envelopes and arranged for Saturday afternoon distribution of the strike funds because he felt that psychologically it was to his advantage to approximate as closely as possible the men's normal routine of compensation. Saturday was payday before the strike, Saturday would be payday during the strike. In familiarity of routine, Buck reasoned, there would be a feeling of security. He had been right—for a while.

When the strike was in its infancy, when it had vigor and spirit, when it was a cause, that was when Buck had been right. But that stage of the strike had long since passed. The A.M.W.N. walkout against Delavane Mines was now at the bottom of the shaft—in the doldrums. The men were despondent, their dispositions in a slump. Picket lines were listless: heads hung, hands were shoved into pockets, signs left leaning against truck tires. By attrition, and by attitude, the union was losing.

Still, Buck O'Crotty had confidence. Certain rules had to continue to be adhered to, a certain determination maintained, certain procedures had to continue to be followed. One of those procedures was that Saturday was payday.

"Where's Tony?" Buck asked Denny when the women had the last of the envelopes ready.

"He said he'd meet us at the bank," Denny replied. "He had something to do."

"What was it?"

Denny shrugged. "I don't know. He jus' said he'd meet us at the bank."

Buck's lips compressed. Tony knew that distribution of the strike funds had extremely high priority. The lad, Buck felt, should have kept himself available. Tony and Denny were Buck's escorts to and from the bank where they picked up enough cash each week to fill the brown envelopes. Saturday had once been the bank's busiest day; because of the strike it now only stayed open until noon. Looking at his pocket watch, Buck saw that it was already past eleven.

"Get your coat," Buck said to Denny. "Let's get going." He followed Denny to the little bedroom Denny shared with Tony, and waited as the younger man took his mackinaw off a wall peg. "If that lad's not waiting at the bank," Buck threatened, "I'll have him walking picket every night from now until we settle." As he stood there, Buck saw Denny slip something into his coat pocket. "What's that?"

"Knucks," Denny replied.

"Knucks?"

"Yeah. Brass knucks. I bought 'em from one of the railroad dicks down at the V&T yard." Denny showed him the set of brass metal finger rings attached to a transverse metal grip. When worn over the knuckles of a fist, they formed a bone-crushing weapon.

Buck snatched them from Denny's hand. "What are you, some kind of hoodlum?" he demanded scathingly. "Have you made arrangements to buy a blackjack yet, or a pistol?"

"They ain't no worse than an ax handle," Denny protested rationally.

"They are!" Buck snapped. "A hundred times worse! An ax handle is part of a workingman's tool. Sure, he uses it sometimes to defend himself or protect his job, but it always goes *back* to being part of that tool. These things"—Buck practically spat with scorn—"are carried in the pockets of gangsters and hoodlums. They were designed to be concealed by evil people, to be used for evil purposes." Buck tossed them onto Denny's cot. "What'd you give for 'em?"

"Six bits," Denny admitted sheepishly.

"Return 'em to the fellow you bought 'em from and tell him I said to give you your money back," Buck instructed. He looked at his watch again. "Come on, we'll have to shake a leg to get to the bank before it closes."

In the wooded area behind the Delavane mansion, Tony had been carefully following the progress of the sun to keep track of the time. He had fixed in his mind a point in the sky where the sun would be at approximately eleven-thirty. When it reached it, he had to hurry down the wooded path to the top of Gold Street and run from there to the bank at the corner of C and Carson, where he was to meet Buck and Denny.

Tony was not sure Francie would even try to meet him today, but he had to wait as long as he could in case she did. At their last meeting in the Strand balcony, they had, in desperation, resurrected this way of seeing each other. The place in the woods was one of their old trysting spots, used when they were in their early teens. With Buck so intent on keeping Tony occupied evenings, and Rainbolt concentrating on Francie's movements even in the afternoons—she and Tony had both been aware of the security man in the movie house—they decided that their best opportunity to get together would be in the mornings. Tony had agreed to wait in their place in the woods for as long as he could, starting at ten o'clock; if Francie could unobtrusively slip into the cellar and wait until the two perimeter sentries had passed out of sight and hearing, she would then dash back to the trees. Tony had promised not to get upset if she did not come; unless there was a perfect opportunity, she had already made it clear to him that she was not even going to try. To take a chance of exposing Tony to the rifles of Rainbolt's men, for a few minutes time together, was a risk she was not prepared to take.

For his part, Tony was not as cautious. "I'm not afraid of those bastards," he asserted, "or their guns." It was his injured manhood speaking: the Tony who had been left bleeding in the snow by Jack Coltrane; the Tony who had been made a fool of in the hotel lobby by Lew Rainbolt. He was on the verge, Francie feared, of doing something foolish, unnecessarily, to prove himself to her. The possibility of what it might be unnerved her and reinforced her determination to keep him out of harm's way to whatever extent she could. Tony had now waited in the woods on half a dozen occasions since they had made the plan; Francie had not met him there once.

Looking up at the sun beyond the needle tops of the tall pines in which he crouched, Tony calculated that it was about a quarter past eleven. Goddamn it, he thought in frustration. Once again, for perhaps the fiftieth time that morning, he carefully scrutinized the kitchen door, the cellar door, and all the back windows in the mansion. What he was looking for, he did not know. Some kind of signal, maybe; something; anything. But as before, there was nothing. Only the two uniformed sentries, one very close to the mansion, the other at the outer edge of the grounds, the two of them, with rifles slung military-like, walking their obverse posts with maddening regularity. The one on the farthest perimeter passed within thirty feet of where Tony was hidden; in the quiet of the forest, Tony could hear the man humming.

It was a puzzle to Tony how Francie and he had allowed themselves to fall back into a furtive relationship after being so close to public disclosure of the seriousness of their feelings for each other. Less than a month had passed since their exciting Christmas Eve decision to elope that very night; less than a month, and here they were—or at least, here he was—sneaking around in the woods again. What had happened, he wondered? How had everything slipped away from them; all the boldness they had built up; all the longings, the hunger, the compelling physical urges they had finally stopped keeping under rigid control by allowing themselves to meet openly at the drugstore, to be seen together in her car, to walk on the street together. There was nothing *wrong* in what they were doing even if it might be frowned upon, or disapproved socially on both class levels. Yet they were acting like criminals again.

Looking up, Tony saw that the sun had reached the point in the sky where it was time for him to leave. Frustration surged inside him like boiling water. He looked at the rear of the mansion again, tensely, desperately, as if trying to bore his vision through the walls to search Francie out. Where was she? What was preventing her from at least *trying* to get to him? This was excruciating; the torment was raw inside him. He did not know how much longer he could tolerate the situation.

But for now he had to hurry. Buck and Denny were probably already on their way to the bank to pick up the week's strike benefits money. Keeping to his crouch, Tony turned and moved deeper into the woods. Too late he realized that he had neglected to check where the sentry was—and the sentry was too close. Tony stepped on a dry pine cone and it snapped sharply. The sentry stopped and looked toward the woods.

Tony's mouth shriveled with dryness as he watched the sentry unsling his rifle.

At the bank, Buck stood patiently as a teller counted out the various denominations of currency specified on a list Buck had given her. Buck always made certain he had enough singles, fives, and tens to put the exact amount in each miner's benefit envelope, just as the mine had done with each pay envelope. The list of currency he required from the bank remained the same every week, just as if the strike benefits had remained the same—which unfortunately they had not. About every third week now Buck was forced to reduce the amount each man was allotted, not by much, but a decrease nonetheless. Instead of adjusting his Saturday withdrawal to match each lowered figure, which Buck was certain would have been reported to Big Jim Delavane by Harmon Coltrane, Buck kept the amount constant, retaining the excess for a few days, then simply redepositing it. He was not altogether certain that his ruse was fooling anyone, but felt it was worth the little effort it took, just in case.

As the money was being counted, Buck followed the tally with his eyes so he wouldn't have to recount it. Without missing a beat, he said to Denny next to him, "Check and see if Tony's coming."

Denny went to the front window of the bank and looked up and down C Street as far as he could in each direction. Like the bank itself C Street was practically deserted. Since shortly after Christmas, half the merchants in town had stopped opening at all on Saturdays; the others, following the bank's example, closed at noon. Saturday had once been the busiest trade day of the week, the miners' wives and families doing their shopping up and down the street, returning later, after shift when wages had been handed out, to settle their accounts. Now there was simply no activity; what little buying there was, mostly groceries, was done piecemeal. The Merchants Association had sent a delegation to see both Big Jim Delavane and Buck O'Crotty, imploring a settlement as quickly as possible. Nothing had come of it.

Not seeing Tony anywhere, Denny returned to Buck's side at the teller window. "No sign, Buck."

O'Crotty nodded briefly, eyes continuing to follow the teller's fingers and the count. A sudden thought from deep in his mind told him he should have summoned a replacement for Tony, he should not have depended on the lad to show up. But he had not done so because it would have been an embarrassment. To have called Lloyd Arlen or Terence Henny or anyone else, he would have had to explain why he needed them, why Tony wasn't there. There was already too much talk among the membership about Tony and his association, his *relationship*, with Francie Delavane; it was now common knowledge he and Jack Coltrane had fought, supposedly over Francie, on Christmas Eve. Buck didn't want to add any fuel to an already irritating, potentially very troublesome fire.

This thing between Tony and Francie worried Buck O'Crotty to the quick. Even with everything else he had on his mind in the now seven-month-old strike, the thought of the two of them together nagged at him like a loose tooth. God in heaven, he wondered, how could such a thing have happened? Of all the girls Tony knew—in school before he quit, on the Walk, in town—and all the young men Francie Delavane must have been exposed to—on the Hill, at college, wherever—how in the name of everything holy had they become attracted to *each other?* They were worlds apart in social class, background, upbringing; what could they have possibly found in common, what could they even talk about? Then Buck remembered the deep friendship between himself and Edith Delavane, and had to sigh resignedly. Yes, it happened. It certainly did happen.

But in this case it shouldn't, he thought, it couldn't. Tony and Francie were half brother and sister. It was unnatural and unholy. He *had* to put a stop to it.

At the bank window, when the count was finished and Buck began packing the sheafs of bills into his canvas satchel, he said, "Get the car started, Den."

Leaving the bank, Denny once more looked up and down the street for Tony without seeing him, then slid behind the wheel of Buck's old Nash and started the engine. Presently, Buck walked briskly out and got into the car on the passenger side; he held the satchel of money on his lap. Denny backed the car away from the curb and started down C Street toward the Walk. Before they reached the first corner, both he and Buck felt the cold steel muzzle of a pistol against the back of their necks.

"Keep looking straight ahead," a blunt voice ordered from the back seat. "Try anything and I'll blow your brains out."

Tensing, Buck and Denny instinctively exchanged glances. The pistol muzzle poked an immediate warning.

"Straight ahead!"

The gunman directed Denny to drive past Miners Walk and out to the edge of town. Just past the city limits, he ordered the car turned into a dirt side road.

"Stop right here," the gunman said as soon as Denny had made the turn. "Cut the motor."

The moment the engine was off, two men with handkerchiefs tied under their eyes hurried out of the trees and, at gunpoint, pulled Buck and Denny out and manhandled them up to the front of the car. The gunman in the back seat, who was also masked, got out and grabbed the bank satchel from Buck. At the same time, he slugged Buck across the cheek with the barrel of his pistol. Buck dropped to the ground.

"You son of a bitch!" Denny yelled, jerking his arm away from the man who held him. Oblivious to the threat of the guns, Denny threw a punch at the gunman who had hit Buck. Because he was off balance, the punch was awkward; it glanced off the gunman's shoulder. One of the other men struck Denny in the back of the head with a pistol handle. Denny stumbled forward and fell to his knees; as he was falling he managed to throw another punch that caught one of the holdup men squarely on the chin. The pistol clubbed him in the head again; he was on his hands and knees when one of the men kicked him in the ribs and another, on the other side, kicked him in the temple.

The gunman he had punched continued to kick him even after he was unconscious.

The sentry who heard the noise in the woods, after unslinging his rifle and scrutinizing the edge of the grounds suspiciously, took a brass whistle from somewhere inside his leather jacket and blew it loudly in three short bursts. Almost at once the sentry patrolling directly around the mansion ran out to join him. Tony, frozen in a half crouch, heard them talking.

"What's up?"

"I ain't sure. I heard something in there."

"What'd it sound like?"

"Like somebody moving."

Silence for an interminable minute. Tony's legs, held in the awkward half-bent position, felt strained. He dared only to breathe. The sentries spoke again.

"Think it coulda been a squirrel or something?"

"Sounded a lot bigger. Are there bears in these here woods?"

"I don't know. Did it sound that big, like a bear?"

"It sounded pretty big."

Tony felt perspiration surface on his forehead and nose. The calves of his legs were stiffening with the forced tension on them. He could not straighten up for fear of putting more weight on the brittle pine cone still under one foot.

"Think we ought to go in for a look-see?" one of the sentries asked.

"Why not?" the other replied.

The quiet mountain air heard the sharp, metallic sound of two rifle bolts being unlocked in unison and pulled back to jack a live cartridge into each weapon. As the sound echoed, Tony quickly straightened.

"If it's a bear," one of the sentries advised, "go for head shots. I don't think body shots will stop one."

"Right."

Footsteps crunched as the two men started into the woods. As they moved, Tony moved also, as lightfootedly as possible, watching the ground, selecting each step. He was aware that he was breathing heavily, aware that he was sweating heavily, aware that there was heavy silence around and above him. Suddenly he realized that his were the only footsteps making noise. The sentries had halted to listen again.

"Hear that? That didn't sound like no squirrel, did it?"

"It's something big, all right."

They moved forward, taking several steps before Tony realized he should be moving again also. This time he tried to match their pace, listening carefully, letting them step, then putting his own foot down while their noise still sounded. But once again they caught him; only part of a single step, but they had stopped and he had not.

"Hear that?" one of the sentries asked again.

"I heard," the other replied soberly.

This won't work, Tony's mind warned. They would keep coming until they caught up with him. He had to hide. Stopping, bracing his back against a tree, Tony frantically looked around for some place of concealment. For a brief, panicky moment, he considered climbing a tree, but realized at once the insanity of the idea; it could not be done quietly, and once up he would be trapped. Biting his lip, he listened to the steady footsteps. The sentries were no more than forty feet away.

Suddenly Tony noticed a large fallen tree lying just under a wide, sweeping fir. It had several heavy branches lying over it; branches that had snapped off the fir under the weight of a heavy snowfall the previous month. In addition, mountain winds had blown other loose forest matter onto the heap: dried mesquite, dead limbs that deer had broken off for their young to nibble.

When Tony was sure he could move again under the noise the two sentries were making, he ran in a crouch over to the downed tree and dropped to the ground beside it. As he had hoped, it was rotted on its underside from the moisture of the ground. With the toe of one shoe, Tony began to dig away the decayed, pulpy bark. As he worked, he heard the sentries moving nearer to him.

When he had six feet of the rotted tree opened up, Tony lay on his back next to it and worked his body as far under as he could. With his free arm, he dragged some of the fir branches and mesquite up close to conceal the part of him that would not fit under the tree. Then he lay very still.

When the sentries got there, Tony guessed from the sounds of their footsteps that they were walking about twelve or fifteen feet apart. One of them crunched past the fallen tree near the end under which Tony lay. The other, farther along the trunk, actually stepped up on it, causing it to sink slightly from the weight on its soft underside. The sentry quickly stepped off the shifting tree. Then both men stopped.

Tony tensed, wondering what they were doing. Sweat ran from the bridge of his nose, burning his eyes. An inch from his face, hundreds of tiny white termites scurried about in panic, disturbed by his breath, which to them was a great wave of heat. Tony began to itch all over. A dread came over him that there might be a hibernating rattler in the dead tree. He had a sudden urge to burst out and give himself up, but he was afraid the sentries would shoot him. He gritted his teeth until his jaw hurt.

The two sentries walked on a little farther, talked again, came back, walked around nearby in other directions, returned again, talked some more. Finally one of them said, "Well, whatever in hell it was sure ain't here now."

"Don't look like it. Want to grab a smoke, long as we're away from post?"

"Why not?"

It was so silent in the woods, and the mountain air so thin, that Tony could hear the match strike when the men lighted up. A moment later, pungent tobacco smoke reached his nostrils. It made him yearn desperately for a cigarette; he who was not a habitual smoker, who smoked only socially with Francie and Denny, occasionally with Buck. But at that moment he would have taken another whipping from Jack Coltrane for one of Francie's Pall Malls, or Denny's Camels, or Buck's Chesterfields.

The sentries eventually finished their smoke and left. Tony followed the sound of their footsteps until he could no longer hear them. After waiting a moment, he reached to move one of the branches to crawl out, but a sudden thought stopped him. Were they really gone? They had *said* they were returning to their posts: "Might's well get on back." He had heard them walk away. But how far had they gone? Just far enough, maybe, to make him *think* they were gone— when they were actually waiting patiently, silently, behind a nearby tree for him to make a noise so they could jump out with their rifles and drill him?

Tony eased his arm back down. Closing his eyes, he ignored the sweating, the itching, the termites, and in his mind slowly counted to one thousand. Then he listened some more, willing his sense of hearing to strain to pick up sounds. He heard nothing. Just to be on the safe side, he counted to one thousand again, a little faster this time. Finally he could wait no longer; carefully moving one of the fir branches, he raised his head.

The sentries were gone.

Quietly, but as quickly as possible, Tony moved the rest of his camouflage away, rolled out from under the old tree corpse, and hurried off.

It was past one o'clock when he got to the bank. He knew it was closed; its shades were drawn, and a round Bulova clock in one window showed the time. For some unaccountable reason, Tony tried the door anyway. Finding it locked, he stepped back onto the sidewalk and looked up and down C Street, as if by some warp of time Buck and Denny would still be in sight. But there were only a few people to be seen anywhere; the business section was practically deserted. Tony wiped his sweaty face on one sleeve.

Jesus, Buck was going to be boiling!

Hurrying down the street, Tony realized that he still had some dirt and other ground matter—leaves, twigs—on his clothes. He had tried to clean himself up once he got out of the woods, but in his haste to get to the bank he had done only a cursory job. Slowing down now, he brushed and picked away some of the forest that still clung to his coat and trousers.

He had just turned into Miners Walk when he saw Lloyd Arlen and Terence Henny running toward him.

"Where the hell were *you?*" Henny asked harshly as they came abreast.

"What's the matter?" Tony asked.

"Buck and Denny were beaten up and robbed."

"They're both in the hospital," Arlen said. "Denny's hurt pretty bad."

"Where the hell *were* you?" Henny asked again.

Tony could only stare at them as the blood drained from his face.

When Tony and the two union officers arrived at the hospital, they found Buck O'Crotty lying on an examining table. A nurse was holding an ice compress against one side of his face, while a doctor checked his blood pressure and then listened to his chest with a stethoscope. Sheriff Sam Patch was standing next to the nurse. Tony and the union officers came in and stood quietly at the foot of the table.

"What happened after that?" Patch asked.

"The one fellow kicked Denny a few more times," said Buck. "Then the three of them ran back to the highway and a car drove up and picked 'em up. That's when I stopped playing possum and dragged Denny into our car and brought him here."

"You don't think you could identify them if you saw them again?" Patch wanted to know.

"No. I told you, their faces were covered."

"What about the car?"

"I only got a glimpse of it. All's I know is that it was black—"

The doctor patted Buck's arm. "Be quiet a minute, please, Buck."

The little examining room fell silent. When the nurse removed the compress for a moment to dab Buck's face dry, Tony and the others got a look at his injury. It was an ugly, puffy bruise, deep purple along the cheekbone, swollen upward under the eye, downward nearly to the jawbone. There was a slight pinkish scratch just below the purple, but the skin had not broken. At the sight of it, Lloyd Arlen and Terence Henny exchanged angry looks. Tony's stomach tightened. *Your fault. You should have been there.*

"What are you going to do about this, Sheriff?" Arlen asked, his voice carrying a challenging edge.

"Whatever I *can* do, Mr. Arlen," the sheriff retorted, with an edge of his own. "I have to have evidence to act."

The sound of numerous voices could be heard through the hospital window. Stepping over to look out, Terence Henny saw several dozen miners gathered outside. More were arriving as word spread about the assault-robbery. "You may not have a chance to do anything, Sheriff," Henny said ominously. "The men might do it for you."

Removing the stethoscope from his ears, the doctor said, "Everything sounds okay, Buck, but I'd like to keep you here overnight for observation."

"If there's nothing wrong with me, I'm going home," Buck said.

The doctor knew better than to argue with O'Crotty. "Keep that compress on his face until I get back," he instructed the nurse. "I'm going to talk to Rosetta about keeping you overnight," he said sternly to Buck and left the room. Tony followed him out.

"Hey, Doc, where's Denny?"

"Down the hall. We took care of him first; he's not in good shape. Rosetta's with him."

Tony fell in with the doctor and walked toward Denny's room. Behind them, unseen by either, Big Jim Delavane and Lew Rainbolt went into the room where Buck lay.

Lloyd Arlen turned red with anger at the sight of the mine owner and his strikebreaker. "You two have got a lot of goddamned nerve showing your faces here!" he said hotly.

Ignoring him, Delavane stepped over to the examining table. "This wasn't my doing, Buck," he said.

"Or mine," Rainbolt added. "This isn't my style, O'Crotty."

Terence Henny, fists clenched, took a step toward them. "How in hell'd you find out about it so fast then?" he demanded.

"I called Mr. Delavane," Sam Patch said. "I felt obliged to warn him to put extra protection around his house."

"*You?*" Lloyd Arlen said incredulously. "Warned *him?*"

"I did," Patch asserted. "I didn't know how badly Buck was hurt. For all I knew, the strikers would be taking orders from hotheads like you and Henny. There's a mob already gathering out there! I felt it was my civic duty to alert Mr. Delavane."

"It might be a civic duty that costs you the next election!" Henny admonished. His meaning was obvious. An A.M.W.N. endorsement was politically important in Storey County.

"Enough of that, Mr. Henny," said Buck. Removing the nurse's hand, he said, "Thanks, miss," and held the ice pack himself as he sat up. "The sheriff's an honorable man; you know that as well as me. He does his duty as he sees it." Buck looked at Jim Delavane. "You knew nothng of this, is that what you're saying?"

"That's exactly what I'm saying," Delavane replied. "You and I go back too far for this sort of thing, Buck."

"And you, Mr. Rainbolt," Buck turned his eyes to the strikebreaker, "you didn't order it?"

"I did not," Rainbolt said evenly.

"You didn't know it was planned?"

"No."

"They weren't your men?"

Rainbolt shook his head. "Not to my knowledge."

Buck's unswollen eye narrowed. "I suppose you're going to tell me you didn't blow up my union headquarters either?"

"I'm not going to tell you anything of the kind, O'Crotty. I'm not here to discuss the destruction of your headquarters. Blowing up the center of a union's activities and destroying all its records, if it can be done without hurting any person or other property, is not a tactic of which I disapprove. Armed robbery *is*. You can believe that or not. I wasn't involved."

Buck thought about it for a moment, studying Big Jim, remembering the years gone by, remembering, for some unaccountable reason, Edith. A wave of nostalgia swept over him. He was very weary of the strike and what it was doing to his family, his men, and himself. He yearned for tranquility. Finally he nodded his head at Delavane.

"I believe you." Grimacing, he bobbed his chin slightly at the window. "Tell the men to go home, Lloyd. Tell them they'll have their strike wages by noon Monday."

Arlen and Henny again exchanged angry looks. Clearly they did not like Buck O'Crotty's decision.

In the room down the hall, Tony stood next to the hospital bed with his arm around Rosetta's shoulders. On the bed, heavily sedated, Denny Ebro lay with his head and half his face swathed in bandages, his ribcage on both sides bound with wide strips of adhesive tape, and the elbow of his right arm in a plaster cast. An intravenous needle was taped into a vein in his left arm, its tube running up to a glass jar hanging upside down from a bracket attached to the bed's headboard.

The doctor whom Tony had accompanied to the room had first listened to Denny's chest with his stethoscope, then raised each of Denny's eyelids in turn and shone a small flashlight beam into Denny's eyes. Afterward, he took a clipboard from the foot of the bed to make some notes.

"Is he going to be all right?" Rosetta asked fearfully.

"I can't tell yet," the doctor said quietly. "It was a vicious beating. Good thing it was him they gave it to and not Buck. It would have killed Buck. Speaking of whom, Rosetta, I want you to convince him to remain in the hospital overnight for observation. And to rest and keep his blood pressure under control. Will you talk to him?"

"If you think it best. I'll try. He's very stubborn. When will you be able to tell about Denny?"

The doctor shook his head. "Not before tomorrow or the next day. He has a severe concussion; there may be some brain injury. Also, that blow to the temple could have damaged his optic nerve. We'll just have to wait and see." Rosetta nodded stoically; the doctor patted her hand. "Go talk to Buck," he urged. "There's nothing you can do for Denny right now. He'll sleep for the rest of the day and all night."

Rosetta turned to Tony. "Stay with him anyway, Tony. While I go try to reason with Buck."

"Sure. Go ahead." After Rosetta left the room, Tony said to the doctor, "They worked him over good, huh?"

The doctor nodded. "It could have been worse, though," he pointed out. "They could have got him in the kidneys and testicles as well. And none of his broken ribs punctured either lung—which was *very* fortunate. But that head injury's got me worried. That could have serious long-range effects."

As the doctor was leaving, Tony asked, "No chance he'll wake up tonight?"

"No chance at all."

Tony watched from the door as the doctor walked back down the hall. As soon as the doctor was out of sight, Tony stepped over to the bed and put his hand very lightly on Denny's unbandaged cheek. "I'm going to get Rainbolt for this, Den," he whispered. "Before you wake up, that son of a bitch will be in the hospital too."

Finding Denny's clothes in the room's closet, Tony searched them for Denny's brass knuckles. They were not there and that surprised him; Denny had not gone anywhere without them since the day he bought them. The stickup men could have taken them, Tony thought. But maybe, just maybe, Denny had left them at home.

Turning to the door, Tony checked the hall again, found it clear, and hurried away. As he walked briskly through the waiting room, he saw Kerry sitting on one of the couches, her nine-year-old face strained with worry. In her fingers she fidgeted with rosary beads. When she noticed Tony, she started to cry and ran to him. Tony knelt and took her in his arms.

"Are—they—hurt bad—Tony?" she asked fearfully, as if expecting the absolute worst. She looked very Indian when she worried.

"The doctor says they're both going to be okay," Tony lied, hugging her close, patting her back, kissing the straight, shiny hair on top of her head. Holding her hand, he took her to a magazine stand across the waiting room and bought her a Baby Ruth. Back on the couch, as she ate the candy bar, he explained Buck's and Denny's injuries, omitting some of Denny's, and reassured her that in time both would be good as new. When Kerry was sufficiently calmed down, Tony said, "Listen, there's something I've got to do. You wait here for your mamma. If she asks where I am, tell her I'll be back in a little while."

By the time Tony left the hospital, the winter afternoon was waning, its shadows growing long, its thin air becoming colder. As soon as he was away from Kerry, Tony's brooding features resumed their fixed anger. An image of Rainbolt seared his mind. Obscenities flowed silently around it: words Tony had never even spoken but were the filthiest he had ever heard. So consumed was he by his hunger for revenge on Lew Rainbolt, that he did not even see Francie's car moving slowly beside him as he hurried along. She had to blow her horn to attract his attention. Stopping, blinking several times to compose himself, to return to cognizance, Tony quickly got in the car beside her.

"Drive me to my house, will you?" he said.

Francie stared at him. No kiss, no touch, not even a hello. She got a sudden chill. My God, was Buck O'Crotty dead? Or Denny Ebro? She put a tentative hand on his arm. "Tony—"

"I've got to get home quick," he insisted.

"Sure. All right," Francie said, drawing her hand back, accelerating. "Is Buck . . .?"

"Buck's okay. He just got slugged in the cheek. But Denny's busted up real bad."

"God. How bad?" Tony told her what the doctor had said. As she listened, Francie had to blink back tears. "Is there anything I can do to help?"

Tony looked at her with a frown. Glancing over, Francie caught the expression. It seemed to say: You? What could *you* do? It reminded her of the way, disdainful at best, contemptuous at worst, that he had always looked at her when they were very young, before that moment at her mother's funeral when they began to see each other differently.

"Please don't look at me like that, Tony," she asked quietly.

"Like what?"

"You know like what." She turned the corner into Miners Walk.

"When'd you see Rainbolt last?" he asked without preliminary, changing the subject. "And where?"

"A little while ago, at the house. He was there when Sheriff Patch called to tell Daddy what happened to Buck. Why?"

"Because I'm going to get him for what he did to Denny," Tony said in the cruelest tone Francie had ever heard him use. "I'm going to get a pair of brass knuckles that Denny bought, and I'm going to lay for that miserable, strikebreaking, motherless bastard and beat his face to a fucking pulp."

Francie parked the car in front of the O'Crotty house and stared incredulously at him. "Tony, he didn't have anything to do with what happened to Buck and Denny."

Tony's lips curled scornfully. "You're crazy." He got out of the car and walked briskly to the house. Francie hurried after him.

"To-ny! Listen to me," she pleaded, following him through the front door, through the living room. "I was there when both Daddy and Lew Rainbolt found out about it. They were as shocked as I was. How do you think I managed to get away from the house without an escort? They were so surprised they weren't thinking straight. I walked out to Daddy's car with them and after they drove off, I just got in my own car and left too. Believe me, Tony, neither of them knew about it until the sheriff called—"

"Look, Francie," Tony said, stopping abruptly in the hall and turning to face her, "I don't know what kind of act your old man and his hired hoodlum put on for you, but if you've got a brain in your head, you *know* Rainbolt either did it or had it done." His eyes narrowed. "Is this your way of covering for your old man?"

"No, it is not!" she seethed. "I don't have to 'cover' for anything my 'old man,' as you call him, does. *My father* didn't start the strike *or* the violence."

"He's not going to finish it either," Tony said coldly,

continuing into the bedroom. He began searching the drawers of a dilapidated bureau he and Denny shared. Francie, staying at his side, tried to hold onto his sleeve.

"Tony, you *know* I wouldn't cover up a thing like this. You know I'm just as appalled as you are about what happened to Denny. But what you're doing now is a mistake . . .!"

As Tony brushed her arm aside, he suddenly saw the brass knuckles lying in plain sight on Denny's cot. Bending over the end of the cot, he snatched them up triumphantly and shoved them into his coat pocket. As he straightened, Francie was so close to him, not giving him an inch, that his shoulder bumped her chin.

"Goddamn it, Francie—"

"Tony, *please!*" She clutched at his coat with desperate hands.

"Let go!" he snarled, and with one arm flung her roughly aside. Her hip hit the bureau, one ankle turned, and she fell heavily to a sitting position on the bare wood floor between the bureau and Tony's cot. As Tony stalked out the door, she covered her face with both hands and began to sob.

Tony stopped halfway down the hall, hands trembling, face bloodless white. Blinking rapidly several times, he put his head back and took a deep, wrenching breath. Then he rushed back to Francie.

"I'm sorry, baby—" He helped her off the floor and sat her on the end of his cot. Kneeling in front of her, he took her face in his palms and kissed her gently, lovingly, tasting tears on her lips. "I'm sorry, baby, I'm sorry," he said over and over. "Please stop crying, honey, please stop, I'm sorry . . ."

Clinging to him, face pressed to his neck, tears wetting his collar, it took Francie several minutes to bring her wracking sobs under control. Her eyes had quickly swollen, her nose turned red; she entwined the fingers of one hand in his thick hair, the better to hold him securely. Why, why, *why*, she asked herself in overwhelming despondency, were their lives so miserable?

"Tony, we've got—to get—away from here," she was finally able to say between efforts to regain normal breathing. There was, to Tony, an unnerving trepidation in the quavering statement; it was not like the grim, determined suggestion on Christmas Eve that they elope; this statement was grounded in abject fear. "We have *got* to—" She began shaking like a frightened child.

"We will," Tony soothed. "We'll make it. You'll see."

"I'm so afraid we'll never have each other—"

"We were meant to have each other, Francie."

"Tony . . ." She lay back on his cot and drew him on top of her. Fingers still in his hair, she pulled his head down and they kissed a long, hungry kiss, lips warming lips. When it was over, Francie said, "Tony, let's . . ."

Tony saw in her gray, teary eyes all the keen desire, the terrible, sweet yearning, the want that had grown in them through all the days and nights of their lives since their love began. He saw in her eyes the strain of every furtive moment they had spent together, every lie they had been required to tell in order to be together, every awful moment of parting before they were ready to part. He saw in her eyes what he knew she saw in his: what they both felt, what consumed them, nourished them, cauterized the wounds of their lives, made living at once a magnificent and terrible experience. He saw their love.

Turning, sitting up, Tony took off his coat and Francie removed hers. Together they began undressing. Tony's sweater, Francie's sweater; Tony's shirt, Francie's blouse; Tony's undershirt, Francie's brassiere. Bare from the waist up, they embraced, Francie's nipples and breasts firm and warmly defined against his chest. This was not new to them; they had stripped that far before, in the woods in summertime, in her car on lonely mountain roads. He had fondled and kissed and sucked her breasts not infrequently, especially in the past two years, and she had thrilled to it. But where before it had been the limit of their ardor, it now was to be the beginning.

"Come on," Francie said urgently.

"Okay—"

Tony's shoes came off, Francie's shoes; Tony's trousers, Francie's skirt. Tony's erection protruded from the fly of his long underwear. Francie reached down and took it in both her hands.

"Oh, God—"

Tony slipped his hand under the waistband of her knee-length winter drawers and cupped the downy soft moistness of her. Instinctively he began to gently rub, and bent his head to take a swollen nipple as far into his mouth as he could—

Then: "Stop it!" an outraged voice roared. "Jesus Christ almighty!"

Shocked, horrified, frightened, they broke apart to find Buck O'Crotty glaring red-faced at them from the door. Trembling as she had earlier, Francie reached for an article of clothing, any article, to cover herself.

Buck turned in the doorway and snapped down the hall, "Take Kerry to her room. Stay there with her."

"Goddamn you, Buck!" Tony raged. Stalking across the room, he tried to shut the door in Buck's bruised, swollen face. But Buck was far too strong; he gripped the door and held it open.

"No you don't! You," he said sharply to Francie, "get your clothes on."

Tony closed a fist and swung on Buck. The older man sidestepped the punch and, grabbing Tony by the arm, flung him into the hall.

"Mr. Arlen, Mr. Henny, take hold of this lad for me, please."

Tony was quickly restrained by Buck's two union vice presidents. He struggled against their grips with growing rage, but the combined strength of the two miners was too much for him to overcome.

"You got no right Buck!"

"I've every right," Buck retorted. "Take him into the kitchen, men."

Arlen and Henny dragged the infuriated, kicking Tony down the hall and Buck turned back to the bedroom. Francie had on her skirt, sweater, and shoes; she was holding her blouse and brassiere in one hand, reaching for her coat with the other.

"Let's go," Buck ordered. "Put on your coat on the way out." Taking the mortified young woman by one elbow, Buck walked her toward the front door. Out on the porch, he stopped and turned her to face him. "I'm going to ask you a question and I want a truthful answer, young lady. How long have you and Tony been sleeping together?"

"We haven't," Francie replied in her surliest voice.

"You mean tonight was the first time?"

"We didn't even do it tonight!" Francie snapped.

Buck stared at her for a moment, then under his breath said, "Thank you, Jesus."

Guiding Francie down the steps, he put her in the passenger seat of her car and got behind the wheel himself. Francie had left the key in the ignition and Buck started the engine. Turning on the interior lights, he took a moment to study the unfamiliar Hydramatic transmission control. Then he grunted softly, put on the headlights, shifted gears, and drove away.

Francie was silent until the car turned from poorly lighted, foreboding Miners Walk into brighter, more familiar C Street. Then she snapped angrily, "What Tony said was true! Who the hell do you think you are? You've got no right to interfere with us!"

Buck drove through town and turned off C Street into Sierra, heading up to the Delavane mansion.

"You won't keep us apart!" Francie vowed angrily. "You're not going to have your way this time!"

Buck pulled to the curb. Turning to stare at her, he said almost in a whisper, "My *way?* You little fool. Do y'think that's what this is all about—me getting my way? Do y'think I'd be doing this without a reason? A *good* reason?"

In the winter moonlight and the fuzzy dashboard lights, O'Crotty's battered swollen face was haunted. Francie stared at him with a sudden sense of dread. "What—what do you mean?"

"You can't have each other because Tony Donovan's your half-brother."

Part Five

Tony

1951

TWENTY-TWO

When the telephone rang in the count room of the Flamingo, there were several hundred thousand dollars being sorted into denominations on the count table by four men, one on each side, whose fingers were black from handling the currency. The room was heavily soundproofed because an adjoining room, which could be observed through a thick plateglass window, was the coin room; in there, thousands of coins were fed into aluminum machines that sorted them by size and funneled them to other machines that counted and rolled them. The coin room was in a constant state of clatter; the count room was completely silent except for the flutter of currency in swift, skilled fingers.

The ringing of the telephone did not distract Tony Donovan. Sitting above the table in a high chair of the type used by a baccarat pit boss, he carefully monitored the counting procedure and kept his own tally of the figures on a pad of paper as the count room manager recorded the totals on a blackboard. It was only when one of the counters reached behind himself to answer the phone, then handed it to Tony, that his concentration was broken. Frowning, because no one was supposed to disturb him in the count room, he accepted the receiver and said, "Tony Donovan."

It was Denny. "Tony, you got to come up to your office right away—"

"Goddamn it, Denny, I'm in the middle of a count."

"Rosetta's here."

"What?"

"Rosetta's here. She's got a problem with Kerry and she came down here to get us to help. She's crying, Tony. You got to come up here right away."

Tony glanced at the four counters and the count manager.

297

They had automatically suspended the count and were waiting for him to give it his full attention before resuming. Part of Tony Donovan's responsibility to Meyer Lansky was conducting random checks on the count rooms of the Strip casinos in which Lansky had a financial interest. This was to assure that the casino cash flow was being reported honestly and accurately. With new hotel-casinos continuing to be constructed in the Flamingo's wake, gambling revenues in Las Vegas had increased dramatically; already a new word had been added to casino terminology: skimming. Meyer Lansky had cautioned Tony about the comparative ease with which large amounts of unrecorded cash could be siphoned out of a casino's legitimate profit. "There's no foolproof way of preventing it," Lansky had admitted, "unless I wanted to move to Las Vegas and do the counting myself. But by hiring reliable people for the count rooms, paying them well, and imposing upon their employment the condition that you as a representative of the owners may come in anytime, unannounced, to conduct an audit, I think we will keep this skimming business down to a minimum. But you must be conscientious about your scrutiny, Tony. Very conscientious."

Tony was. Although his office was in the Flamingo, and it was there that his control was the most obvious, he was just as apt to show up at the count room of any other hotel controlled by a Lansky corporation. Only by coincidence was he in the Flamingo count room when Denny called about Rosetta.

"I'll be right up," he said. Handing the phone back, he told the count manager, "Finish without me, Ralph. Something's come up."

Riding the elevator to his office, Tony entered and found Denny on the couch with his arms around a distraught Rosetta O'Crotty. She rose and hurried to him when he entered. Tony put his arms around her.

"All right now," he comforted, patting her like a child, "what's this all about?" He guided her back to the couch. "Denny, send for some coffee."

"Already did," Denny told him. "This is Kerry's fault," he added testily. "She's not behaving like she ought to."

"No, no, it's my fault," Rosetta immediately corrected. "I've asked too much of her since Buck's death. I expected her to follow my example and go on with life, as I know

Buck would have wanted, but she hasn't been strong enough to do that—"

"She's drinking and running around with a bunch of freakos at college," Denny interjected. "Rosetta says she can't do nothing with her."

"My fault," Rosetta said again. "I haven't been there for her like Buck always was. I've been lonely, Tony"—she squeezed his hand in a plea for understanding—"I've been spending a lot of time with my people on the reservation—"

"All right, I want you to calm down now," Tony soothed as Denny went to answer a knock at the office door. A room service waiter delivered coffee. As Tony continued to console Rosetta, he was struck by the incongruity of her presence. The part of his life that included her, Kerry, Buck, Virginia City, had always remained apart from his Las Vegas life, and it was almost surreal to have a person from there suddenly appear here. In her simple, style-less dress and plain black Oxfords, hair held back with a single ribbon, she looked no more out of place than scores of other women who frequented the casinos—tourists, local matrons, housewives. Yet because Tony knew Rosetta, knew her *inside*, to him she was distinctly a foreigner here.

They got her to drink some coffee while drawing out a few more facts about the problem upsetting her. As they listened, Tony realized that it was probably not only Buck's death that was causing Kerry to act the way she was; it was also what had happened between her and Tony. Rosetta appeared to know nothing of Kerry's infatuation with and rejection by Tony. Had she known, perhaps she would not have blamed herself quite so much for Kerry's troublesome conduct. Or her own inability to temper it.

"For the first time in her life, she won't listen to me," Rosetta grieved. "Always in the past she has been reasonable and intelligent, willing to listen to advice that I gave her, or Buck gave her, even that you two gave her; now she will not listen at all. Ever since kindergarten, she has proudly shown me her school grades; this last quarter she would not. While she slept, God forgive me, I looked in her purse, a terrible thing for a mother to do, but I was worried. I found her grades: she was failing every class. I told her what I had done and she was furious. She stormed out of the house and has not been back since. I went to Reno to see her, to make peace with her. She had moved out of her dormitory and

was living in an apartment with some other girls. When I
found the apartment, she had been drinking. I asked why
she had moved. She said it was because in the apartment
there was no curfew. She said she was sick to death of
curfews and rules and always having to do what was right. I
begged her to come home with me." Rosetta's eyes lowered
in shame. "She told me to go back to the reservation where
I belonged." The distraught woman began to cry. "Tony,
Denny, what can I do? She is so young—"

"You don't have to do anything," Tony promised. "Denny
and I will go up and talk to her. This is probably just part of
her growing up, Rosetta. She's a little mixed-up right now,
Buck being taken out of her life so suddenly; he was the
only father she ever knew. All of us had other men, strong
men too, in our lives at one time. You had your first husband,
Denny had his own father, I had mine, but Kerry had no
one but Buck." Tony was talking fast to relieve Rosetta's
anguish, alleviate her tears. "Kerry's probably still in some
kind of emotional upset about Buck—"

"Like guys was shell-shocked in the war," Denny interjected
again.

"Exactly," Tony seized. "She just needs a little straightening out, is all."

The phone rang on Tony's desk and he nodded for Denny
to answer it. As Denny spoke briefly to the caller, Tony
continued to reassure Rosetta that her only daughter was
not lost and gone forever. He and Denny would see her,
reason with her, resolve the matter of her drinking and her
failing grades, and all would be well again.

"When, Tony?" Rosetta wanted to know. "When will
you see her?"

"In a couple of days."

"Not sooner? Oh, please, Tony—"

"Call coming in on the private line in five minutes,"
Denny said, hanging up the phone on the desk.

Tony nodded. Calls from Meyer Lansky were always arranged in advance over a normal telephone line so that
Tony would be at his private phone when it rang. "Get a
suite for Rosetta and assign one of the maids to her," he
told Denny. "We'll talk about this some more after I take
the call."

"Sure thing," Denny said. "Come on Rosetta"—he took
her hand and drew her off the couch—"I'm gonna show

you what the letters V.I.P. mean at the Flamingo Hotel."

After Denny left with Rosetta, Tony sat down at his desk, put a pad and pencil in front of himself and unlocked the bottom desk drawer. Almost as soon as he opened the drawer, the private phone rang.

"Tony Donovan."

"Good evening, Tony," said Meyer Lansky in the calm, confident voice that was the mainstay of his persona.

"Good evening, sir."

"How is everything going?"

"Very well, sir."

"That's fine. Tony, I'd like you to come to Havana tomorrow. There's a matter of some concern that needs to be discussed and I'd prefer not to do it over the phone, even on a private line. I'd like you to be on the ten o'clock flight to Miami in the morning from Los Angeles. I'll have a private plane bring you from Miami down here."

"All right, sir."

"You'll stay at the Hotel Nacional. I'll look forward to seeing you for dinner. Goodnight, Tony."

"Goodnight, Mr. Lansky."

What the hell was *this* all about? Tony wondered as he hung up. He had been summoned to meet Lansky before, but always in New York or Miami, never Cuba. In the back of Tony's mind was the possibility that it had something to do with the continuing investigation of Buck's murder. Agents of both the F.B.I. and the Nevada attorney general's office had questioned him several times about the case; each time he had made a full verbal report to Lansky on what had transpired. Lansky always expressed his appreciation to Tony for keeping him apprised, and invariably reassured Tony that his employers had complete confidence in him and were not disturbed by the investigations, nor should Tony himself be.

"We have our own people looking into the matter, Tony," Lansky had reassured. "We'll know soon enough where all the pieces fit."

Shortly after Buck's funeral, Tony had solicited Lansky's help in looking into the various corporations that controlled Delavane Mines, all corporations in which Harmon Coltrane had some interest. Lansky had been intrigued by the information that Harmon Coltrane was the father of Jack Coltrane, who was heading up the investigation of the so-called "organized crime" influence in Nevada's gambling industry.

"It would be very interesting," Lansky had said, "if we could prove that the senior Coltrane did have something to do with the O'Crotty murder, and that the junior Coltrane was deliberately steering the investigation away from him. Not that it would surprise me," Lansky disclaimed. "If you knew, Tony, how many duly elected and appointed public officials at all levels of government are on the take you would be shocked. I myself, in the old days, personally handed thousands of dollars to officials as high up as United States senators. Honest politicians are few and far between, I'm afraid. At any rate, we'll have a full report before long, which I'm sure will shed a lot of light on O'Crotty's death. I know it's been on your mind, Tony."

It had been on Tony's mind, relentlessly so. The unremitting guilt he felt was like a heavy yoke on his whole being. Daily as he went about his work, he endured flashes of troubled conscience. Always amounting to the same thing: would Buck now be dead if Tony had remained at his side instead of abandoning him for Las Vegas? The terrible unanswered question hung constantly in Tony's consciousness, interjecting itself at will, intruding without warning, interfering in everything from Tony's business affairs to his sex life. In the former he had to check and recheck everything he did: all figures, all reports, all decisions; in the latter, he did not even have to trouble himself, because his sex life had become nonexistent: he had not had an erection since Buck's death.

After the call from Lansky, Tony locked up the private phone, left his office, and went down to the front desk looking for Denny and Rosetta. They were nowhere in sight; the desk clerk said Mr. Ebro had not checked a Mrs. O'Crotty into a suite. Tony was about to have Denny paged when he saw him coming in the front entrance alone. Walking to meet him, Tony asked. "Where's Rosetta?"

"In a cab on her way to the bus station. She insisted, Tony," he emphasized before Tony could complain. "She had a round-trip ticket and wanted to go back tonight." Tony was astounded. The woman had ridden a bus for ten hours to talk to them for thirty minutes; now she was riding one another ten hours, without rest, to go home. As if reading Tony's mind, Denny merely shrugged. "You know how she is, Tony, once she makes up that Paiute mind of hers."

"All right, I know." Tony acceded, waiving argument; there was too much to do. "Did you get Kerry's address?"

"Yeah." Denny fished a slip of paper from his shirt pocket.

"Find somebody to fly us to Reno—tonight." Tony lowered his voice. "I have to go to Havana tomorrow, and I want this business with Kerry taken care of before I leave. I'm going to make some arrangements down here while you're getting the plane. Let's hop to it."

"Got you," Denny said, and hurried away.

Tony paused a moment and stared thoughtfully after him. Denny had shown no surprise at all at his being summoned to Havana.

It was past ten o'clock when the Reno taxi pulled to the curb in front of a small apartment building not far from the University of Nevada campus. Tony handed the driver a twenty and told him to wait. He and Denny entered the foyer of the modest building and checked the names on a row of mailboxes. They found "Morrell" printed in pencil next to two other names in number 202. Walking upstairs, they located 202 and Tony knocked. The door was opened by a young woman no more than nineteen, blonde, in a tight red sweater, a bottle of beer and a burning cigarette held in the same hand. From within the apartment came the sound of a swing band playing "Old Shanty Town" on the radio.

"Hi!" she said brightly, smiling.

"Hi. Is Kerry Morrell here?" Tony asked.

"Ker!" the blonde yelled over her shoulder. "Somebody to see you!"

"Who is it?" they heard Kerry's voice ask from another room.

"Some really dreamy guy with a scar!" the blonde shouted back, winking at Tony. But apparently she had not shouted loudly enough.

"Who?" Kerry asked again.

"Never mind," Tony said, taking the blonde's hand off the door and stepping past her. "We'll find her."

"Wait a minute now—" the blonde started to protest.

"It's okay," Denny assured her. "We're Kerry's brothers."

The blonde paled. "Why don't you just wait and I'll get her—"

Denny, eyes suddenly hard, closed a hand around her

wrist. "See that chair over there? Go sit in it. Don't get out of it until we're gone." He pointed a finger near her face. "Do like I say, hear me?"

"Sure," she said nervously. Denny's eyes frightened her. They were dark, dangerous.

When the blonde was seated, Tony and Denny followed the sound of the swing music into a small kitchen. There they found two shirtless young men, both with open bottles of beer, one of them keeping time with the music by tapping two forks drumstick-style on the table top. Dangling from his lips was a thin roll-your-own cigarette trailing peculiar smelling smoke.

"Marijuana," Denny said quietly.

In her slip, at the stove frying hamburgers, was Kerry, bouncing slightly to the music and humming as she cooked. The other bare-chested young man, also smoking a roll-your-own, was standing behind her tying a folded handkerchief around her forehead. When it was in place, he pulled several feathers out of a feather duster and stuck them in the headband. "Now you look like a real squaw," he said, laughing. Kerry laughed with him.

"Hey, comp'ny," said the one at the table when he noticed Tony and Denny. Kerry and the other youth looked around. Kerry, like the blonde, paled.

Tony crossed the room and turned off the radio. When he went over to Kerry, immediately he smelled beer on her breath. His eyes flicked angrily at the young man as he reached out and removed the headband and feathers from Kerry's head.

"Get some clothes on," he told her quietly. "And pack your things. You're leaving."

The young man's bare chest expanded. "Who the hell are you?" he asked indignantly, removing the cigarette from his lips.

"This isn't your business," Tony told him quietly. He turned back to Kerry. "Get dressed."

"Like hell I will!" Kerry snapped. "You're not my keeper, Tony!"

"You better beat it, bud," the young man said, flexing.

Tony's eyes fixed on him coldly. "What's that you're smoking?" he asked. "Marijuana? It's illegal, isn't it? How would you like to go to jail?"

The young man turned red and swallowed dryly. Again Tony turned his attention to Kerry.

"Get dressed, Ker."

"And if I won't?" she challenged, with a toss of her head. "What are you going to do, hit me?"

"No, I won't ever hit you again," Tony replied, his voice becoming very soft so that Denny would not hear.

"I warned you I was going to do this, didn't I?" Kerry said. She tried to sound spiteful and mean, but her lower lip began to tremble, moderating her words.

"Yes, you warned me," Tony admitted, "and now you've done it. So get your things and come on."

"Come on to what, Tony?" she asked, a little more forcefully. "Back to the same old thing? You going your way and me going mine?"

"I can't promise you anything different, Ker. I'd be lying if I did."

"Then I'd just as soon stay here, thank you."

Tony glanced at the two young men. "You want your friends arrested? Expelled from school?"

Kerry stared at him, becoming tight-lipped, her face flushing with anger. Presently she threw down the spatula she was holding and stalked from the room.

"Stay with these two," Tony said to Denny, and followed her.

Denny put a foot on one of the kitchen chairs and lighted a cigarette. He did not speak or smile, only stared. The two young men exchanged nervous glances and remained quiet.

In less than fifteen minutes, Tony and Denny were leaving, Kerry between them, Denny carrying Kerry's suitcase. Kerry was still angry. "You'll be sorry for this," she told them. "Wait and see."

Tony ignored her, but Denny said, "You keep your mouth shut in front of this cab driver. Don't talk about personal things in front of strangers. If you got anything to say, wait until we get on the plane."

"Plane? What plane? Aren't you taking me home?"

"No. You've caused your mother enough worry. You're coming back to Las Vegas with us."

"Oh." Kerry glanced at the silent Tony as they all got into the taxi. This was something she had not counted on: being taken to Las Vegas. Did this mean she had a second chance at winning Tony's affection—not his affection, she already had that—his *love*? Las Vegas. Suddenly she was excited at the thought of it. Of course, anything would be better than being with those idiots back in the apartment. The effort they had to put forth to force having a good time. Kerry could hardly believe she had actually taken up with them. But after Buck's death and Tony's rejection, she'd felt she had to do something; barely twenty, it seemed that life was passing her by.

Riding to the airport, Kerry was contritely silent as she mulled over this latest turn of events. She wished she hadn't drunk so much; a headache was starting and she wasn't sure she was thinking effectively. On the way, she belched loudly from the beer in her stomach; she tried to laugh it off, but Tony and Denny looked at her with unamused coolness. When they reached the airport and got into the cabin of the little six-passenger plane, Denny escorted her to a front seat by herself and buckled her in. He and Tony sat in the two rear seats. When Kerry looked back she could see them talking, but the sound of the plane's twin engines neutralized what they were saying. Of course, they were talking about her. She wondered if she would be living with Tony at the hotel. God! Surreptitiously glancing back at his somber, handsome face, she thought that maybe her little stunt had worked, after all.

The flight down was not a pleasant one for Kerry. Her headache was increased by the engine roar to a throb, and a wobbly descent nauseated her terribly. Even the sparkle of Las Vegas lights on the dark desert below failed to excite her. Everything she now wanted out of life was reduced to an Alka-Seltzer, a soft pillow, and a quiet, dark room. After they had bumped to a landing, rolled to a sudden turn-around, and the engines were shut off, Kerry thanked God for letting her get there without throwing up.

Tony and Denny hustled her off the plane and into a car. Now nearly two A.M., the lights of the Strip were ablaze as usual between the airport and the city limits. Despite her feeling of debilitation, now that she was on the ground and right in the midst of what was to her a neon wonderland—so much bigger, brighter, more dazzling than anything in Reno— Kerry began to feel stimulated. Sitting between them again, in the front seat with Denny driving, she leaned forward to look out first one side then the other, as they passed the Desert Inn, the Sands, the Thunderbird, and other palaces inspired by the Flamingo. When they went past the Flamingo without stopping, Kerry asked in surprise, "Isn't this where we're going?"

"It isn't where you're going," Tony replied. They were the first words he had spoken to her since leaving the apartment in Reno.

Kerry parted her lips to speak—a query, a protest—but quickly thought better of it. She had come this far into Tony's sphere of existence, much farther than in her wildest recent plans. There was no sense at this point in irritating Tony further by questions or complaints. Best to do it the Paiute way: patience and observation. She would get the lay of the land soon enough.

Out east of the Strip they drove, to a small housing tract surrounded by desert: an oasis of stucco, attached garages, new streetlights and rock garden front yards. On a slightly higher elevation, the houses looked down on the line of lights that was the Strip. Denny pulled into the drive of a neat corner house that had the porch light on.

"Come on," Tony said to Kerry when the car was stopped. He helped her out as Denny reached in the back seat for her suitcase.

As they walked up to the house, the front door opened and Kerry saw an attractive, fortyish woman in a bathrobe waiting to greet them.

"Hello, Madge," said Tony. He turned to Kerry. "This is Mrs. Bellamy. She works for me. You're going to be staying with her." Then to Madge again, "Sorry it's so late."

"Don't worry about it," Madge said. "Hello, Denny. Just put the suitcase anywhere. There are a couple of cold pork chops in the fridge if you're hungry." Denny headed toward the kitchen. To Kerry, Madge said with a grin, "So you're my boss's little problem, huh?"

Kerry's chin went up an inch. "Maybe."

Madge's smile widened. "Frisky, huh? I've got three just like you. We'll get along."

"Think so?" Kerry asked. It was just short of a challenge.

"Sure we will," Madge said confidently. Her expression became serious. "Want to know why?" She linked her arm in Tony's. "Because from what I've heard about you, we're both interested in staying on the good side of this fellow here. If he's happy, we'll be happy. But if he's *un*happy, everybody around him is miserable."

"That's the truth if I ever heard it," Denny commented wryly, already walking back in from the kitchen chewing on a pork chop.

Tony gave Denny an irritated look but directed his words to Kerry. "I have to leave on a short business trip in a few hours. We'll discuss your future when I get back. In the meantime, I expect you to stay here with Madge and behave yourself. If you try to run off, Denny will come after you and bring you back."

"I might strap your bottom while I'm at it too," Denny added. "I wasn't very pleased with the state I saw your mother in before we came to get you."

"You can't threaten me," Kerry said, with an effort at aloofness. "I happen to be of legal age. I can come and go as I damm well please! If either of you think—"

Kerry's voice broke and she faltered a step. Suddenly it all caught up with her: the beer, the unpressurized airplane, the noise, the lights, the lateness of the hour, the unexpectedness of everything. Her eyes rolled slightly and instinctively she put a hand over her mouth. Madge stepped in at once.

"Right this way, honey," she said, putting an arm around Kerry and guiding her quickly down the hall to a bathroom.

"I want you to keep a close watch on her," Tony cautioned Denny.

"I will," Denny said, sitting down. "I'll come get her during the day when Madge is working. Take her out to my place and let her help me run my dogs. She'll like my dogs." Denny had built a small house for himself in the desert west of town. He had half a dozen Labrador retrievers that he trained and occasionally entered in shows. A young Filipino houseboy took care of the place and the dogs when Denny was not there.

"What do you think Lansky wants you to come to Cuba for?" he asked Tony while Madge was out of the room.

Tony shook his head. "Beats me. You didn't seem very surprised that I was going."

"Nothing surprises me anymore," Denny chewed around his last bite of the chop. "Since Buck got knocked off, I promised myself I was going to be prepared for anything."

"What do *you* think Lansky wants to see me for?"

Denny shrugged. "Beats me," he said, using the same phrase Tony had. "Whatever it is, I don't think it's got anything to do with you or me." Denny leaned forward in the chair and gestured with the pork chop bone. "The way I see it, there's only one person in Vegas that Lansky can't do without—that's you. He's got a hotel manager and a casino manager at every spot on the Strip that he controls; all those guys know that you're his man, that you're watching them like *he'd* watch them if he was here. I think you're the only person in Vegas that he completely trusts." Denny smiled his crooked smile. "An' since I'm the only one around that *you* can completely trust, I think we're both home free."

Tony could not help smiling back at his longtime friend, who was as close to him as a brother might have been. "Got it all figured out, haven't you, wise guy?"

"It wasn't that hard," Denny advised him conceitedly.

Tony nodded appreciatively. He had come to the same conclusion himself. Except that Tony had carried it a bit farther. While people like Arnie Shad, Jack Coltrane, even Denny Ebro himself, were convinced that Meyer Lansky was still a racketeer, as everyone knew he had been in the old days, Tony firmly believed that Lansky's interest in Las Vegas gambling was strictly legitimate. Tony perceived Lansky to be, first and foremost, a shrewd businessman; a businessman who would always make the decision that was smartest financially. To Tony's way of thinking, the only smart way to run a casino was legitimately; it assured continued operation and guaranteed profits in perpetuity. To rig games, skim the cash flow, or take any other shortcut toward greater immediate profit, was unwise and unreasonable. Casino operators who did that were ultimately bound to be caught— and millions in long-range, down-the-line profits would be sacrificed for a few hundred thousand quick dollars. It was ludicrous to believe that Meyer Lansky would elect such an option. Shad, Coltrane, Denny, and others believed that Tony was there to see that the hotel and casino managers did not steal from Lansky. Tony's perception of his job was to see that the operations were run lawfully, that no one stole from *anyone*. That was one reason Tony had made Madge Bellamy the Flamingo's head cashier; she was as honest as they came.

As Tony was thinking of her, Madge returned to the living room with a wry expression. "She's okay," the older woman said of Kerry. "I put her to bed in Julie's room. Julie's my oldest, the one in college down in Ariozna. Here's a picture she just sent me." Madge showed Tony a framed photograph from the coffee table; Julie was an attractive young woman with glasses and a pretty smile. "She doesn't wear the glasses all the time," Madge quickly pointed out. "Just for distance."

"She's a good-looking girl," Tony complimented.

"Takes after you, Madge," said Denny, looking over Tony's shoulder.

Tony handed the picture back. "Think you can handle Kerry all right?"

"Easy as pie. Especially with Denny's help. You go ahead and make your trip and don't worry about her."

"Thanks, Madge. I owe you a big favor for this."

"Not on your life. You've still got lots of credit in my books. Now you two hit the road and let us gals get our beauty sleep."

Back in the car, Denny drove toward the hotel so that Tony could pack a bag and have the chartered plane fly him to Los Angeles in time for the flight to Miami.

"You ought to try to get a couple hours sleep, too," Denny nagged. "You need to be wide awake talking to Lansky."

Tony shook his head. "I'll just shower and change." He studied Denny's profile in the greenish glow of the dashboard lights. Finally he asked, "Den, if you knew anything you thought I ought to know, you'd tell me, wouldn't you?"

"If I knew anything about what?" Denny asked back.

"About anything. Lansky, the operation here, Buck's killing. Anything."

"What the hell kind of question is that?" Denny demanded, though not too vociferously.

"The kind you haven't answered," Tony pointed out quietly.

"Listen," Denny advised, "if you don't know by now that I'm on your side all the way, you'll never know it."

There was a heavy silence in the car as it traveled the mile back to the bright lights of the Strip. As they pulled up at the Flamingo entrance and stopped, Denny still had not answered the question.

TWENTY-THREE

Walking into the arrival terminal, Tony was met by a darkly attractive Cuban woman wearing a light raincoat over her slacks and blouse. "Welcome to Miami, Mr. Donovan," she said. "I'm Lupe Tovar. I'll be your guide and assistant while you're here and in Havana." She pronounced the name of the city Ha-*ba*-na. "If you'll come with me, we'll get your luggage and then go to the private plane. It's a very short flight, less than an hour. This way, please."

Tony followed her, impressed as usual at the efficiency of everything arranged by Meyer Lansky. Walking behind her into the baggage claim area, Tony noticed that she had on shoes with three-inch wooden wedge heels, which made her seem taller than she really was. He also noticed an enticing sway under the back of the raincoat as she walked. It brought to mind immediately his own diminished sex life. He could not help wondering, as he had scores of times already, if his impotence was permanent. The interest was still there, as now in his appreciation of Lupe Tovar's walk, but he simply could not parlay that interest into a satisfactory encounter. The several times he had tried since Buck's funeral had been exercises in frustration and futility. One woman whom he knew intimately, a lithe, firm-figured dancer at the El Rancho Vegas, had tried in an incredible variety of ways to get him erect, and failed. Tony had not made an effort since.

They landed in Havana, a boy was there to carry Tony's bag, Lupe showed a document of some kind to a Cuban immigration officer, and in minutes they were in a chauffeured limousine being driven into the city. By now it was dark and Tony could see only shadowy flashes of the area through which they passed. "It is a *barrio* anyway," Lupe advised him, "a slum. Nothing nice to see."

At the swank Hotel Nacional, which was equal to anything Tony had seen on the Strip, Lupe guided him across the elegant lobby to a private elevator that took them directly to one of four corner penthouses that shared an indoor swimming pool on the top floor.

"These suites are for very special people only," the Cuban woman told Tony as they entered a luxuriously appointed living room. "Besides Mr. Lansky, only General Batista, our former *presidente*, and a few other highly placed gentlemen can reserve these suites for someone." A pair of enormous brown eyes locked with his, and Lupe smiled a captivating smile. "So you see, you are very special, Mr. Tony Donovan."

While a valet unpacked his bag and took his two extra suits and shirts down to be pressed, Lupe showed him around the suite. It was a plush layout, obviously a high-roller suite for millionaire gamblers who patronized the Nacional's lavish casino—which, Tony knew, was also operated by a Lansky corporation. The general whom Lupe had mentioned a moment earlier was, he knew from Lansky, Fulgencio Batista, a former president of Cuba and perennially the power behind the presidency since leaving office. Lansky had once told Tony that the investors he represented paid Batista three million dollars a year for the exclusive license to operate gambling establishments on the island. It was, Tony mused, like having a monopoly on Las Vegas.

"In Cuba, we dine much later than in the States," Lupe told him when his tour was over; she pronounced the name of her country *Coo*-ba. "Mr. Lansky has arranged dinner at his home in Miramar for ten o'clock. He asks you to join him and a friend for cocktails at nine. The car will be downstairs at eight-thirty. Would you like to relax in a hot bath until your suits come back?"

"Thanks, I'll just take a shower," Tony said.

"A hot bath would make you feel good. If you want, I'll scrub your back."

"Is that part of your duties as a guide and assistant?" Tony asked.

Lupe raised one eyebrow. "Perhaps, perhaps not." She smiled again, radiantly. "Anyway, if you need me for anything I'll be available. Just call the desk." She wiggled her fingers at him and left.

I wish to Christ I *did* need you for something, Tony thought as he undressed and got into the shower. He decided that Lupe probably worked for the hotel rather than directly for Meyer Lansky. If she worked for Lansky, she would have been far more reserved and circumspect. Lansky was notorious for his propriety. Before Tony had ever met the man. Lansky's reputation for decorum had preceded him. During the construction of the Flamingo, when it was suggested at a meeting of the investors that prostitutes be allowed to operate out of the hotel, Meyer Lansky had refused to consider it. Ben Siegel, who had been at the meeting, told Tony and Arnie Shad, who both worked for him, that Lansky had been outraged by the proposal.

"Those guys were stupid even to ask," Siegel had said. "They all know, or should anyway, that Meyer is the biggest prude on earth. Christ, even in the old bootlegging days when there were showgirls, society dames, all kinds of broads practically lining up for us, Meyer never—*never*—messed around with any of them. God's truth. I've known Meyer Lansky since I was a kid, nine, ten years old. This guy, listen to this, he promised his mother he would marry a decent Jewish girl and be faithful to her—and I swear to God he kept that promise. He married this girl, Anna. Very pretty girl, dark hair, gorgeous eyes. Very religious girl. Married her in 1929 and this is 1946, so they been married for seventeen years."

Drying off after his shower, Tony reflected on what an enigma Meyer Lansky was. It never ceased to amaze him how one man could have such diverse reputations. And with most people it was either black or white: Meyer Lansky had either become as honest as Job, or was still as evil as Satan. Arnie Shad was a perfect example. Arnie had grown up in the same Lower East Side New York neighborhood that had spawned Lansky, Siegel, Lucky Luciano, and many others who had come to criminal prominence during Prohibition. Names that Tony had never heard until he went to work for Ben Siegel, Arnie Shad had known all his life. Arnie had reached the point where he now truly believed Lansky to be an evil man, capable of ordering if not personally committing the worst crimes. Yet Arnie offered no evidence, no proof. And, as Tony often reminded Arnie, the reporter's own newspaper refused to print his accusations about Meyer Lansky and so-called organized crime.

As Tony dressed for dinner, he reaffirmed his own position with respect to Meyer Lansky: he accepted him for what he knew him to be, not what others *believed*. Lansky had been good to Tony; he had given him the responsible position Tony held in Las Vegas, shown trust and confidence in him, was even helping him now look into Buck's murder. Meyer Lansky was a friend to him. That was enough for Tony Donovan.

The house in the exclusive Miramar suburb of Havana was smaller and less sumptuous than Tony expected; it was one of the smallest, simplest homes in the area. Why Tony was surprised, he did not know; he had visited Lansky's home in Miami and his apartment in Manhattan, and both had been quite unpretentious. Lansky lived well, but not luxuriously, certainly not garishly or ostentatiously.

It was Lansky himself who opened the door at Tony's ring. Smiling up at him, he shook Tony's hand with both of his.

"Tony, my boy. Good to see you again. You look marvelous, as usual, with that Vegas tan. Come in, come in."

Meyer Lansky was a compact man, well proportioned but on a smaller frame than most. His graying hair was combed straight back without nonsense, his eyes were direct, his handshake firm, and when he genuinely liked someone, as with Tony, he exuded a warmth that was unmistakable. At 49, he was in excellent physical health and of extraordinary mental capacity.

"Come into my little study, Tony, and let's have a few minutes to ourselves. A good friend of mine will be joining us for dinner but we can have a private drink first."

Lansky's study was intimate, expensively done in dark native woods and unobtrusive earth-tone fabrics. It was a cozy room, in which Tony felt, as he did with its owner, naturally comfortable. Tony sat in one of the chairs facing the desk while Lansky prepared two drinks which, Tony knew from experience, would be light on whiskey and heavy on soda. On a corner of Lansky's desk was a hinged silver frame containing one obviously very old tintype photograph of a serious-looking, long-bearded man wearing a fur cap, and a second, more modern photo of a young man in the uniform of a West Point cadet. When Lansky turned to the dcsk with the drinks and saw Tony looking at the photographs, he smiled.

"The very old and the very young," he said, handing Tony a glass. "The one is my son; the other my grandfather, Benjamin." Lansky sat in a well-worn chair behind the desk. "They never knew each other, of course, but how they would have loved one another." His eyes looked as if they might mist, but he quickly covered the possibility with a smile. "When I was a boy in Grodno—that's a little town in Poland, just next to the Russian frontier—my grandfather used to lead me by the hand to lessons at the *cheder*; he made sure I learned all the Jewish prayers, the Hebrew alphabet, everything that my parents were too busy working to worry about. My parents gave no thought to anything except accumulating enough money to leave Poland. Our little town, you see, frequently changed hands as the Polish-Russian border fluctuated. When it belonged to Russia— this was when the Czars were in power—their Cossacks regularly rode into town, stole everything of value, burned our homes, and rode off with our young women. The women were taken to Cossack camps, raped for days, then left naked in the snow so far from a village that they froze to death." Lansky, whose eyes had become fierce, put a finger to his temple. "This I remember from my own head."

Tony, who had seen the result of Japanese military atrocities during the war, shook his head incredulously. "It's hard to believe the things men do sometimes," he said.

"Not men, animals," Lansky corrected, his voice becoming quieter as he controlled his emotions. "How my Grandfather Benjamin hated them. He lived for the day when we could leave Grodno. Finally he decided there was enough money for us to emigrate to Palestine, but my father, Max, refused. My father wanted to continue saving until we had enough to go to America. He and my grandfather argued furiously over it. 'The Torah,' my grandfather would shout, pounding both fists on the table, 'teaches that good Jews go to Jerusalem!' To which my father would reply, 'America, that is the place, Papa. America, the land of opportunity!' Finally my grandfather refused to argue any longer; he took his share of the savings, he and my grandmother, Basha, packed everything they were able to carry on their backs, and they left for Palestine. My father was not worried. 'They won't get far,' he said, 'two old people like them.' It wasn't until several days passed that he realized how wrong he was. We never saw my grandparents again, but we received many letters from them—from Palestine, where they lived very happily and where they both died." Lansky gestured toward the silver frame. "Silly, I know, but I feel that keeping the photographs together somehow ties my grandfather and my son together."

"It's not silly at all," Tony said quietly. "I think it's a very nice thing to do—for both of them."

"You're very kind, Tony. But listen, enough sentimental talk. How are things with you personally? The O'Crotty murder investigation, is it bothering you emotionally?"

"A little, I suppose," Tony admitted. "Aside from hinting that you and I and others connected with Las Vegas are responsible for it, the investigators don't seem to be making any progress."

Lansky shrugged helplessly. "Blaming my associates and me is the easiest thing to do, of course. When all else fails, point the finger of guilt at 'organized crime,' as they're calling it." He held up a hand. "Listen, don't worry about it. Soon we'll have the results of our own investigation; then we should know a few facts."

"I appreciate your helping me look into it—"

Before Tony could finish expressing his gratitude, the study door opened and a somewhat swarthy, not quite handsome man about Tony's height and build, entered the room. Before he closed the door, he said, "Excuse me, am I early, Meyer?"

"Of course not. Come in. Join us." Lansky and Tony rose. "Tony, I want you to meet Charles Ross, one of my oldest, closest friends—and a major investor in our Strip hotels. Charlie, this is Tony Donovan, the young man I've had in Las Vegas since Ben's death." As Tony and the newcomer shook hands, Meyer Lansky turned to his small bar again. "Charlie, something?"

"Just a little soda water and ice, Meyer, thanks," said Ross. And to Tony, "Well, I've heard very good reports about you, Tony. Meyer tells me you do your job very capably and are completely trustworthy and loyal."

"Mr. Lansky's been a big help to me," Tony said. "I've learned a lot from him."

Ross smiled. "I don't know anyone who's ever been associated with Meyer who *hasn't* learned a lot from him—me included." He accepted the glass Lansky handed across the desk. "Thank you, Meyer. Have you talked to Tony about why he's here?"

"I was just about to, Charlie." Lansky sat down again and leaned back. "Tony, as you know, from time to time national or local politicians who want publicity get some federal or state agency to form some kind of investigating panel or committee to launch an attack on something that the press will give a lot of space to. Usually the attacks are against communism or medical malpractice, or what you and I just spoke about, this so-called 'organized crime.' You've mentioned a couple of times that this fellow you grew up with—Coltrane, is that his name?—may be doing that in Nevada to get what he calls 'gangsters' out of the legalized gambling industry. Usually these committees are here-today-and-gone-tomorrow type of things, and they don't do a great deal to change anything one way or another. But there's one gearing up in Washington at the Federal level that has us a little concerned—not because of anything we're doing, because as you know our operation in Vegas is strictly on the up and up. What we're worried about are things that might have been done in the past without our knowledge or consent." Lansky paused a beat. "Things Ben might have done before he was killed"

Tony shrugged. "Like what?"

"We're not sure," Lansky admitted.

"This committee," Charlie Ross said, "is going to be called the Special Senate Committee to Investigate Organized Crime in Interstate Commerce. It'll be made up of two Republican members of the U.S. Senate and two Democratic members; the chairman will be a third Democrat, a senator named Kefauver; insiders have already begun calling it the Kefauver Committee. We"—he gestured to include Lansky—"know all this because we have paid lobbyists in Washington to protect our interests. The five senators all come from out in the sticks: Tennessee, Wyoming, places like that. There's no time limit on how long they can keep going, and they will be allowed to travel anywhere they want to in order to hear testimony."

"Probably the biggest problem for a lot of people that they go after," Lansky spoke again, "is that Truman is going to allow them access to Federal income tax records. Which, in my opinion, amounts to an outrage. Those records have always been confidential, no matter what."

"Thanks in large part to Meyer's advice," Charlie said, "a lot of our past business associates have nothing to worry about. Meyer always cautioned us, back in the bootlegging days and back in the illegal gambling days, to operate legitimate businesses as well, and to pay taxes on those businesses. Remember, Meyer, what you used to say? 'Don't be a wise ass like Al Capone, and wind up on Alcatraz.' Meyer warned all of us about the tax thing from the very beginning."

Lansky sat forward and folded his hands together on the desktop. His expression was wry. "You see, Tony, Charlie and I, and some others, have never tried to conceal our past involvement in bootlegging and illegal gambling. Before Prohibition, I was partners with Ben Siegel in floating dice games and bookmaking all over lower Manhattan. If it hadn't been for Prohibition, I'd have remained a gambler all my life. It's my first love, gambling."

"This man," Charlie said as if bestowing a title, "developed the numbers racket, did you know that, Tony? He's the one who figured out a way for the little guy to get a shot at something by betting a nickel or a dime at odds of six hundred to one. And to know it was *honest,* that he'd get a fair shake, because the winning number was public knowledge—the last three digits of the total shares traded that day on the stock exchange. No way to rig it."

"Didn't have to rig it," Lansky said with a shrug. "The odds were nine hundred ninety-eight to one; we only paid six hundred to one. And, Tony, there's something no one ever gets around to mentioning—the numbers racket was very big business. We provided employment for literally thousands of people in that operation—even during the height of the Depression. But all that aside," he said, waving his words away with a sweep of the hand, "my point is, we never did anything that wasn't eventually made legal. We provided liquor to people who wanted it, until the government finally legalized it again. We developed a way for people to gamble without having to be rich enough to go to the racetrack or take a trip to Reno. You mark my words," he pointed a finger, "someday the government's going to realize what a bonanza bookmaking and numbers are, and you're going to see government-operated betting parlors and a government-operated numbers lottery."

"Okay Meyer enough predictions" Charlie said. "Tell Tony about the problem we've got."

"Of course. Excuse me. Tony, the main thing that's troubling us is this—when we sent Ben Siegel out to build the Flamingo, we gave him a blank check and a very long leash. He had the approval of all the investors to do pretty much what he wanted to do." Lansky shrugged again, resignedly. "Ben was headstrong, he was rash, sometimes he made hasty decisions. We frankly don't know, Tony, what Ben might have done *then* that can get us in hot water *now*. What we'd like you to do is see if you can dig up anything. Go through all books, ledgers, records, anything at all that might be subpoenaed. See if there's anything that can hurt us, anything that the government might be able to twist around to make it look like we, the investors, were involved in any way."

"I'll try," Tony said, "but I'm not sure I'd recognize anything even if I saw it.

"You would," Lansky assured him. "Things that are unusual tend to jump off a page at you. When Ben was building the Flamingo, you were with him every step of the way. You can remember things no one else could, spot things no one else could. Believe me, Tony, if you go through all the files and records thoroughly, whatever Ben might have done illegally to involve the hotel, you'll find it."

"I'll do my best," Tony promised.

Lansky smiled a pleased, almost paternal smile. "You see," he said to Ross, "I told you we could rely on this young man. He's a hundred percent okay. You agree now?"

Ross seemed to ponder for a moment, then nodded his head. "Okay."

"Should I tell him?"

Another nod. "Tell him."

"Tony," Meyer Lansky said, "everything I've told you about this gentleman is true except for his name. I'd like you to meet Lucky Luciano."

Part Six

Big Jim

1940

TWENTY-FOUR

Francie Delavane could not force herself to go home. Not yet. Not until the turmoil in her mind settled. She did not want to confront her father until she was absolutely certain that she herself was able to accept what Buck O'Crotty had finally told her.

Tony Donovan was her half-brother.

At first she had branded the statement an outrageous lie. Fresh from being caught naked in Tony's bed, from the humiliation and mortification of O'Crotty walking in on them the way he did, of his eyes turning what had been a passionate, love-filled moment into something lewd and dirty, she had lashed back at him verbally when he told her.

"You lying bastard!" she accused in the cold front seat of her car, O'Crotty hunched behind the wheel. "How dare you say that? Do you think my father will stand for you saying such a thing?"

"I don't know one way or another what your father will stand for, Frances," Buck replied levelly. "He doesn't even know it himself. But Tony's mother is the one who told me, and I believe her. I know her and your father had been sleeping together because I caught them in bed one night the same as I did you and Tony tonight. Seems like it's my lot in life to catch people doing what they oughtn't." Buck pulled the car to the curb, leaving the lights on, engine running. He had thought to drive Francie all the way home and then walk down from the Hill. Now he decided this was far enough. "Tony doesn't know either," he said. "I'll not tell him unless you force me to. What you say to your father is your own affair."

"Get out of my car, please," Francie said crisply. Even with the "please," it was an order. "If you think for

323

one second I'd believe anything as preposterous as this—"

Buck got out of the car but leaned back in. "You're a fool if you think I'd make up something of this magnitude," he said simply. "I once loved Tony's mother; I'd not sully her name with a lie. And Iron Mike Donovan was once as close a friend of mine as your father was; you can't imagine how it tears at my guts to—" He waved a hand in angry dismissal. "Never mind, that's not your worry."

Francie had slid over to get behind the wheel. Buck gripped her wrist to keep her from driving away. "Frances, I've told you this for your own good and for Tony's good. For the love of God, girl, suppose I hadn't stopped you tonight and you'd got yourself pregnant? Think what a horrible incestuous child you might have had—"

"No, I don't believe you!" Francie had shouted. "It's a lie!" She clawed at his hand. "Let go of me!"

Buck had finally backed off and she had sent the car screeching away from the curb. She raced out of town, still thinking: bastard, bastard. Up one of the nearby foothill roads she careened, her assaulted mind screaming: liar, liar, liar! When she finally ground the car to a halt and turned off lights and engine, she folded her arms across the steering wheel for a place to put her head to cry.

And admit for the first tlme that it was not a lie. It couldn't be.

Francie based her conclusion not on what she knew about her father, nor on what she knew about Buck O'Crotty, but rather what she knew and remembered about her mother. Edith Delavane had thought very highly of Buck O'Crotty; more highly than anyone else of whom Francie had ever heard her speak. Francie knew instinctively that anyone who held a position of such high esteem with her mother *had* to be a person of strict and sound standards and ethics. It was beyond the ken of such a person to even consider a lie such as this one would have to be.

Tony Donovan *was* her half-brother.

Francie put a fist to each temple. God in heaven, why had they fallen in love? What kind of diabolic fates had conspired to let such an absolutely horrible thing happen? And O'Crotty was right about a pregnancy; everyone knew what kind of mad, deformed idiots were produced by incest. Francie had been with her mother when Edith delivered a Thanksgiving basket to a family living in a shack down by the railroad tracks who had a horrible, hunchbacked, tongue-tied little boy who drooled constantly and jumped around like a monkey. Francie asked what was wrong with the boy and Edith told her his blood was tainted because his mother and father were first cousins. To think that she and Tony might have—

Angrily, Francie restarted the car, managed to turn it around on the narrow road and sped back into town. Each second that passed made her more angry at her father. By the time she got back to Sierra Street and gunned the car up its steep climb to her home, she was close to rage. Cavendish met her in the foyer, an anxious expression on his face.

"Your father had been very concerned about you, Miss Frances. He has Mr. Rainbolt out looking for you."

Just then, Big Jim came out of his study. "Francie, where in the name of God have you been? You know I don't want you running around unescorted with this strike going on—"

"May I speak to you in private, please?" she asked coolly, interrupting.

Big Jim frowned and Cavendish pursed his lips thoughtfully. "Shall I bring coffee, sir?"

"No, thank you, Cavendish," Francie answered for her father. "Please see that we aren't disturbed." She strode past them into the study. Jim Delavane exchanged glances with his butler, shrugged patiently, and followed her.

"What's this all about, Francie?" he asked as he closed the study door behind him. Her eyes, he noticed, were not even blinking.

"Did you cheat on my mother with Ruby Donovan?" she asked precisely.

"Wha—what?"

"You heard the question, Father."

"Where in the world did you, ah, hear a thing like that . . .?"

"From Buck O'Crotty. Is it true? I want to know, right now."

"Francie, honey," Big Jim spread his hands in a gesture of conciliation, "that was a long, long time ago—"

"Then it's true!"

"You weren't even born yet, honey—and she wasn't Ruby Donovan, she was still Ruby Surrett—"

"But you and mother *were* married, weren't you?" The question was scathing.

"Yes," he said abjectly, "but only just and—"

"O'Crotty says Tony Donovan is your son!" She hurled the accusation in his face like dashed water.

"What?" Bewilderment took over his expression. He stared at Francie. "Buck said that?"

"Yes, he said it. Is it true?"

Big Jim shrugged naïvely. "If it is, she never told me."

"Oh, for God's sake, Father!" Francie stormed. "Why would she have told you? Were you prepared to leave Mother for her?"

"No, of course not—" Big Jim stared into space for a moment recalling the times now and again when he'd had flashes of suspicion about Tony Donovan. Mostly they came and went, because he never allowed them to ferment. But he had wondered, since that day in the hospital when he saw Ruby with her newborn infant, he had wondered. Once, after Tony was orphaned, his suspicion had even prodded him into offering to adopt the boy; Tony had chosen Buck instead. Over the years, the suspicion had diminished and finally disappeared.

"Jesus, this can't be happening," Francie said, shaking her head, palms to her cheeks. She began to pace the big masculine room, a small frantic figure with wide, startled eyes. "My own father, a deceitful, unfaithful—"

"Francie, let's be sensible for a minute," Big Jim urged. "What the hell makes O'Crotty so sure it's true? And what was his reason for telling you about it even if it is?"

"He told me because he thought Tony Donovan and I were becoming involved," she said bluntly.

Her father's face paled, then just as quickly reddened. "Involved? What do you mean?"

"What the hell do you think I mean, Father?" she snapped. "Involved! Like you and Ruby Surrett were involved."

"You said 'becoming.' Does that mean you, ah, hadn't actually, ah . . .?"

Francie smiled tightly at his discomfort, his inability to ask if she had slept with Tony Donovan. "What's the matter, Father?" she asked cruelly. "Thinking about the prospect of an incestuous grandchild?" She shook her head in utter revulsion. "You know it's true. You know Tony is your bastard son. God, you are despicable. You have done the most awful thing to me, do you realize that? You have made me glad that my mother is dead! I hate you for that!"

Francie ran from the room, throwing the door open wide and leaving it that way. In her wake she left a man half devastated with guilt and remorse, half livid with rage at the person who had caused it. When Big Jim looked up, Cavendish had come quietly in to him.

"What may I get you, sir? How may I help you?"

Big Jim stared at his right hand, which was trembling, while his left was not; realized his right eye had begun tearing, but his left one was dry; in his right knee he felt a slight spasm, in his left none. Anguish and fury: his emotions, his mind, even his body were asunder with two responses to his daughter's assault.

"Please bring my car around front, Cavendish," he said. "I must go out for a while."

As Cavendish left Big Jim's mind reverberated with Francie's words: *You know it's true. You know Tony is your bastard son.*

He did not know. But he was going to find out.

At his desk he picked up the telephone and dialed Buck O'Crotty's number. Buck answered on the second ring.

"I want to talk to you," Big Jim said, not feeling it necessary to identify himself.

"I expected you would," Buck replied.

"I don't want to come to your home and I don't want you in mine. I suggest we meet somewhere."

"How about Callahan's back room?" Buck suggested. "We settled something important there twenty years ago; maybe we can again. Unless, of course, you'd feel uneasy going there, because of the strike—"

"Callahan's is fine. Thirty minutes."

Hanging up, Big Jim opened a desk drawer and removed a chromed .38-caliber pistol and dropped its cylinder to see if it was loaded. It was.

He put the gun in his pocket.

When Big Jim Delavane entered Callahan's, all music, all conversation, all movement stopped.

There were two dozen off-picket miners in the place, all drinking on credit. The music was being provided by Callahan's wife on an old upright piano in one corner. Callahan himself was the only one tending bar and waiting tables; during a strike it wasn't economically feasible, or necessary, to put on extra help.

Big Jim paused just inside the door to look around briefly and get his bearings. Buck O'Crotty was not being derisive when he asked whether Big Jim would feel "uneasy" about coming to Callahan's. It was definitely an enemy camp for the mine owner. In Big Jim's head were the names of several striking miners who had the potential for hotheadedness, at best, premeditated violence, at worst; they were the ones Sheriff Sam Patch suspected of stoning the Delavane mansion on Christmas Eve, and it was they whom Big Jim's eyes instinctively sought as he scanned the room, for he did not want to walk past them and give them even a slight opportunity to impress their peers with some supposedly manly but actually asinine challenge or act. Several of the troublemakers were there, but they sat at a far table out of his path. Those nearest him fell into the large majority of men who were intimidated by the mere name, not to mention the presence, of Big Jim Delavane.

In the silence generated by his appearance, Big Jim walked to the end of the bar, placed both hands on the shiny oak, and waited. Callahan, aware that the moment would be described a hundred times in the days to come, walked over to him no faster or slower than he would have for any other customer.

"Good evening, Mr. Delavane."

"Hello, Callahan. You still serve Ballymurphy Irish whiskey?"

"I do, sir. Straight, water on the side?"

"Yes." After Callahan had expertly poured the shot and served the water, Big Jim put a dollar on the bar and asked, "Is O'Crotty here yet?"

"Buck?" Callahan said, eyebrows raising. "No, sir. I don't really expect him."

"I do," Big Jim said. He bolted the shot down and took a sip of water. Glancing at the wall above the cash register, he saw that a photograph of Franklin D. Roosevelt was hanging there. "What happened to the thousand dollar bill?" he asked.

"Gone long ago, Mr. Delavane. During the Depression. No longer a need for it anyway—everybody knows my whiskey's not watered, and I don't run house games anymore. The table's there for anyone who wants to play, but I don't guarantee their honesty. Another shot?"

Big Jim shook his head. "Back room free?"

"At your disposal. Bottle and glasses?"

He shook his head again. "Just send O'Crotty back, please."

In the private room, Big Jim sat at a green felt-covered card table, in the chair that faced the door, and transferred the pistol from his pocket to a place in his waistband, just under his coat. He had barely begun to drum his fingers impatiently on the table when the door opened and Buck walked in. Pulling out the chair opposite him, the union leader sat down. He did not waver under Delavane's steady, accusing stare. Nor did he speak first. In this matter he was not going to make it one iota easier.

"Is it true?" Big Jim asked after a moment.

"It is."

"How do you know?"

"Ruby came to me when she found out. She wanted me to marry her to give the child a name. I rejected her. That's when she went to Mike."

"How long was that after she and I broke up? After the night you found us together?"

Buck shrugged. "A month, five weeks."

Big Jim's eyes narrowed a fraction. "And she wasn't sleeping with you during that time? Or with Mike?"

"You son of a bitch," Buck said very quietly. "She wasn't a slut despite spreading her legs for the likes of you. She never slept with me, not once. How soon she started sleeping with Mike, I don't know. But it was *after* she got pregnant. You're Tony's father, there's no question of it."

"Why didn't you tell me the truth? All these years—"

"Why the hell should I have? Ruby didn't want you to know; that was enough for me. Besides," Buck challenged, "what the hell would telling you the truth have accomplished?"

"I don't know," Big Jim admitted perplexedly. "I might have—I don't know—"

"Broken poor Edith's heart, that's all it would have done," Buck accused. "And maybe made the boy grow up to be like you."

"Is that so terrible, for Christ's sake?" Big Jim growled. "I'm not a goddamned monster, you know."

Buck sat back in his chair and sighed in despair. A sudden sadness came over him at the thought of people changing so much as their lives progressed. How simple life would be if you could depend on everyone to always stay the same. "I know you're not a monster, Jim," he said wearily.

"You've probably got the boy convinced that I am."

"No, I've never said a word against you to him. Except maybe on the subject of labor-management."

"What did he say when he found out I was his father?"

"He hasn't found out."

Big Jim looked astonished. "You told Francie and not him?"

"I had to tell Francie. The two of them fancied they were in love, Jim. I was afraid they might go too far. I caught them together, in Tony's room. They were on the very verge. The only way I could keep them apart was to make certain Frances would stay away from Tony. The lad has reached the point where I can't really control him that much anymore."

"Oh? What's the problem, Buck? Is the boy too strong for you? Too much like me?" Big Jim taunted.

Buck looked down at the table. "He is a lot like you in some ways, yes."

"Why the hell didn't you tell *him*?" Big Jim demanded. "Force *him* to stay away from Francie? It wouldn't have mattered what he thought of Ruby; she's dead. It does matter what Francie thinks of me. You've made my daughter hate me, Buck." Big Jim moved one hand off the table, under his coat.

What the hell? Buck forced himself not to frown or look concerned. It had not been a sudden move, not a threatening move, but it had been a *move*: not a mere shifting of weight, an adjusting of position; it had been a deliberate, purposeful move.

You're crazy, O'Crotty, he told himself. Those union payroll thieves who beat you up must have loosened a screw or two. Big Jim Delavane may be a lot of things but he isn't a madman. He doesn't shoot people, for the love of God. Settle down, O'Crotty.

"Did you hear me, goddamn it," Big Jim snarled. "Francie hates me. And it's your fault, you—"

"I did what I had to do!" Buck snapped. Big Jim's eyes grew wide and round.

"Liar! You did it to hurt me! To get back at me!"

"Get back at you?" Now Buck let himself frown. "Get back at you for what?"

"For taking Ruby *and* Edith away from you," he said,

and smiled slyly. "Oh yes, I know how you felt about *my* wife too—"

"You're crazy." Perhaps he was a madman, Buck suddenly realized. Perhaps that move . . .

"And," Big Jim persisted, "for what happened right in this room, at this very table, when I took you for everything you had in the world! When *I* became something, some*body*, and left you to go through life with dirt under your fingernails!"

Easy now, Buck warned himself. "You're mistaken, Jim, I might have resented you at one time, for Ruby *and* the game, but that was long ago. I wasn't the person then that I am now. I mean no offense by this, but I wouldn't trade places with you today for anything. And I bear you no animosity at all, outside our obvious labor-management differences. It wasn't to hurt you that I told Francie what I did; if anything, it was to help you."

"Help me?" Big Jim said scornfully. "You call it help to turn my own daughter against me?"

"No, but I call it help to prevent your son from killing you."

The mine owner squinted suspiciously. "What the hell is that supposed to mean?"

"It means," Buck said precisely, "that I was afraid if I told Tony the truth, he would try to kill you. And probably succeed. He had ten years with Ruby and Iron Mike before they died. Ten years to love his mother and worship the man he thought was his father. He's hated you since he lost his family. He blames you for what happened to them. How do you suppose he'll feel if he suddenly discovers you're his real father? Think about it for a minute, Jim. The mother he loved: first he thinks you killed her, then he finds out you slept with her. The father he loved: first he thinks you killed him, then he finds out that because of you he wasn't his father after all. Who could blame him for coming after you with murder in his heart?"

Big Jim's hand, Buck was acutely aware, had remained out of sight all the while he was talking to him. It had not moved once. Which, to Buck was ominous. Jim Delavane *could* have a gun under the table. And he could use it. He could shoot him. He could kill him.

"Would you rather be killed by your son," Buck asked quietly, "or hated by your daughter?" The instant he posed the question, Buck realized it was a mistake.

Big Jim took the gun from under the table and leveled it at him. "What you should have asked is would I rather be killed, period, than hated by my daughter. Because if a person is going to be killed, it really doesn't matter who does the job. Wouldn't you say that's true, Buck?"

Buck's mouth was too dry for him to speak. He felt sweat burst out all over his body.

"Answer me, Buck," Big Jim insisted. A leer formed on his lips. "Does it matter who kills a person?"

"Not," Buck found words, "to the one being killed. But it'll always matter to the one doing the killing."

Big Jim smiled a knowing smile. "Clever, Bucko. Very clever." He cocked the pistol's hammer. "What you're saying is that if I kill you, I'll have to face the consequences, take whatever punishment I'm given, right? Well, I don't care, Buck. Whether they hang me or send me to prison, I'll get my daughter back. She'll forget that she hates me; she'll stand by me. I know Francie. She'll overlook everything except the fact that I'm her father and I'm all alone, everybody against me. She'll be my little girl again."

Buck nodded. New words formed in his mind that caused the icy fear inside him to begin melting. "I hope you're right, Jimmy," he said. "I hope all you have to do to get your little girl back is deprive her brother of a father for the second time."

"What?" Big Jim's leer became a scowl.

"You'll be killing Tony's father a second time. I've been his father for ten years, and you're going to kill me. Iron Mike was his father for ten years, and you killed him."

"That's a goddamned lie!"

Buck shook his head. "No, it isn't. You killed Mike—"

"I didn't!"

"—and Ruby—"

"No, goddamn it, I didn't!"

"—and those two beautiful little twin girls!" Buck leaned forward, as if challenging the pistol barrel. "You did it and you know you did it! You're nothing but a dirty murderer!"

"Buck, no—please, no—"

Big Jim's hand relaxed and the pistol fell over harmlessly. The mine owner's face contorted in agony and he put his head on the table on crossed arms, sobbing.

Buck O'Crotty picked up the pistol . . .

TWENTY-FIVE

The tragedy that caused Jim Delavane to lay his head down and sob in Callahan's back room had its beginning on a sunny afternoon in May of 1929 when he parked his new Deusenberg in front of the Virginia City bank on C Street—just as Ruby Donovan pulled her new Plymouth into the space directly next to him. Jim was alone; Ruby had her four-year-old twin girls with her. The one-time lovers had not seen each other in five years. As they alighted from their respective cars, their eyes met and they stopped and stared. It was as if each had thought the other dead, as if each were seeing a ghost.

"My God," Jim finally said. "Ruby. Hello. Here, let me help you—" He hurried around to hold her car door while she got the children out.

"Hello, Jim. Thank you." A lock of hair irritatingly fell over her forehead and she pushed it back, blushing. "My goodness, how long has it been?"

"Since before these two came along," he bobbed his chin at the yellow-curled little girls. "They're beautiful, Ruby."

"Thanks. You've got quite a daughter yourself; I see her picture every year in my son's class photograph."

"Is your boy in Francie's grade?" He seemed surprised. "I should pay more attention to those things." They moved onto the sidewalk, Ruby holding each twin by the hand. "I can't believe we haven't seen each other in so long," Jim declared. "It's not like Virginia City is the size of San Francisco. It's growing, I know, but you'd think we'd run into each other more often."

"Well," Ruby said, "different circles, you know." My, God, she thought, he's still as handsome as a movie star.

333

"Come to think of it," Jim said, smiling, "I only see Mike about once a week—and he works for me."

"You've grown to be quite an important man," Ruby said, tilting her head an inch, studying him in the clear light of the sunny, day. He was a millionaire and it showed in his manner, his dress, his words. "I hear that Delavane Mines are the third richest in Nevada. And Mike tells me people call you 'Big' Jim Delavane now."

"I've tried to discourage that," he lied. "Kind of embarrassing." He put a hand on the hood ornament of her car. "I see you've got one of those new Plymouths."

"Yes. Mike read an ad in *Collier's* that said 'Look at all three,' meaning Ford, Chevy, and this one, and he did. And we bought one. I have to ask, what is that beautiful machine you're driving?".

Jim's smile widened. "It's a Deusenberg Model J. Two hundred sixty-five horsepower; she'll do a hundred and twelve on a straight highway."

"That's very fast."

"Have to go fast if you want to get anywhere, Ruby."

They looked frankly at each other for the briefest of moments, then Ruby, said, "I'm sorry, I haven't asked about Edith. How is she?"

"Oh, busy as usual," he replied, seeming to measure his words. "She's involved in a lot of civic and social work. Be honest with you, I can't keep up with half of it." He studied her now as she had studied him. "What about you, Ruby, what do you do in your spare time?"

She shrugged. "Probably the same sort of things Edith does, except, like I said before, in different circles." Ruby, forced an uneasy smile. "And speaking of things to do, I've got a million of them, including finding new shoes for these two. Would you believe they're identical twins except for shoe size? One is a half-size larger than the other. It's been nice seeing you again, Jim. Say hello to Edith for me."

She knew as she walked away that he would call her. But she did not expect it to be so soon. The telephone was ringing when she got back home and walked in the door.

"Yes, hello—"

"Guess who."

"President Hoover."

"That's close. Ruby, I just wanted to tell you how wonderful it was seeing you today. It's a great relief to me knowing that you don't have any hard feelings over the past. I've always thought you were very special—and today is an example of why." He paused a beat, and added, "You know, you're still very beautiful."

"I know I'm not beautiful at all, but thank you anyway."

"You are so," he argued good-naturedly. "I'll bet Mike tells you that all the time. If he doesn't, he's a fool. Anyway, I hope we'll run into each other again. Do you usually go uptown about the same time every day?"

"Yes. I mean, no. I mean, yes, about the same time, but no, not every day. Listen, Jim, I have to hang up," she concocted a quick lie, "one of my little girls just fell down. Thanks for calling. Bye."

She changed her trips uptown to mid-morning and began parking in the next block from where they had met. Three days later he called again.

"I haven't seen you uptown, Ruby. You're not sick, are you?"

"No. No, I'm not sick."

"That's good. I was afraid you might be sick. Didn't you say you usually came uptown about the same time every day?"

"No." Ruby replied precisely, "I did not say that at all. I do not go uptown every day." She decided to be direct. "Jim, why are you calling me?"

"I'm just trying to be friendly, Ruby. I'm so glad there are no hard feelings between us that I—well, I want us to be friends. I enjoy talking to you. Do you think you'll be going uptown tomorrow?"

"I'm not sure—"

"What about the next day?"

"I don't know—"

"I just want to talk to you, Ruby."

"Jim, there's someone at my door, I have to go—"

The next time he called, he asked jovially, "Could you use some good news? I'm giving Mike a raise in salary. Of my six mine superintendents, he's the most productive, so I decided to call him in and boost his pay. He just left my office, grinning like a kid with a new scooter. I guess the Donovan family can always use a little extra in the old pay envelope, eh, Ruby? Mike tells me you and he have a lot over on A Street and are saving to build a house."

"Yes, we are."

"Well, this should help a little."

"Yes."

Ruby did not speak of the calls to Mike. That would have required considerable explanation. However, she considered mentioning them to Buck, with whom she continued to privately correspond. Since Buck's first letter, asking her forgiveness, they had exchanged half a dozen letters a year, to and from China, then England, later New York City, and more recently Bluefield, West Virginia, where he was a coal miner and labor organizer. Because she had sent him news clippings from time to time about people he once knew in town, he had eventually ordered a mail subscription to the *Virginia City Gazette* so they could broaden their correspondence with gossip. They had, Ruby thought, established a communication frank and open enough for her to bring up a delicate subject such as the calls. But for some reason she procrastinated and never mentioned it.

The calls from Jim persisted, becoming friendlier, then more familiar, occasionally alluding vaguely to "times gone by" and how she had once "helped" him when he needed someone, how sometimes even in the best marriages a husband and wife "drifted apart" and one or the other "needed" someone or *something* else. Finally he tendered an open invitation.

"Do you ever get over to Reno, Ruby?"

"Not often." She always tried to keep her answers as concise as cordiality permitted.

"I try to get over at least once a week for the day. Have a nice rib eye for lunch at Delmonico's, sip a glass of wine with it, maybe take in a picture show. I saw *Our Dancing Daughters* with Joan Crawford last week. What a pair of legs she's got. Nothing like yours, though, if I remember right."

"Jim, please—"

"Come to Reno with me for a day, Ruby," he begged.

"For God's sake, Jim. I've got two toddlers at home—"

"Hire a Paiute woman to come in and take care of them; I'll pay for it. Ruby, I want to see you again."

"Jim, we mustn't. It isn't right—"

"Please, Ruby. Listen, just go for a ride with me then. I'll meet you somewhere and you can leave your car—"

"No. That's final. Please stop calling me."

For a while he did stop. A short time later, she understood why. At the supper table one night, Iron Mike said, "Something's come over Big Jim lately. I don't know what, but he's turning into a regular tyrant. Seems nothing I do is right anymore."

Ruby felt her spine go cold. After everyone went to sleep that night, she got out their passbook to verify how much money they had saved, then refigured her household budget so that she could put three dollars extra away each week.

At the supper table, Iron Mike's laments continued. "Big Jim says production in my shafts has fallen off. He says my figures for the month are all wrong. I don't understand it; I checked them three times. I don't see how my production could be down."

" 'Rithmetic is tricky, Pop," nine-year-old Tony commiserated. "Sometimes I check my take-aways a hundred times and still get 'em wrong."

The next time Jim Delavane called, Ruby tried to reason with him. "Jim, for God's sake, what are you doing to Mike? He's your friend; you two went through the trenches together. Please don't take out your anger toward me on him."

"My problems with Mike at the mine don't have anything to do with you, Ruby," he declared. "Mike is simply not keeping the crews up to snuff."

"But you recently gave him a raise—"

"That *was* because of you," Jim admitted. "I wanted to do something for you, make your life easier somehow; that was the only way I could think of I might as well tell you, it's caused me some problems too. The damn fool bragged about it to another superintendent and they all got up in arms and accused me of favoritism. I finally had to give every one of them raises. Your husband's not the most popular man at the mines right now—with me *or* the men."

There was no way for Ruby to challenge the veracity of what the mine owner said. For all she knew, perhaps Mike *was* falling down on the job. Although big, strong, and personable, Mike Donovan had never been the brightest employee of Delavane Mines. Ruby could only listen to his problems, minister to his needs, and encourage him to try a little harder to please Big Jim Delavane. All to no avail. While Jim continued to pester Ruby with telephone calls of ever increasing intimacy, and Ruby continued to rebuff Jim's advances, Mike Donovan continued to bemoan his apparently rapidly compounding problems at the mine.

One night Mike said angrily to his wife, "This can't go on much longer. He dressed me down today in front of an entire crew. Spoke to me like I was a kid the age of Tony there. I swear to God, Ruby, I came *that* close to hitting him."

"Why didn't you, Pop?" Tony asked encouragingly. Nightly exposure to complaints about the mine owner had already painted him an evil being in the boy's mind. "Why didn't you knock his teeth right out?" Tony asked eagerly.

"You hush," Ruby scolded. Then to Mike, "Maybe we shouldn't discuss it in front of him."

"Why not?" said the increasingly frustrated, bitter man who was caught in the middle. "He'll have to learn about bastards like Jim Delavane sooner or later."

It was the first time Tony had ever heard Iron Mike Donovan call any man a bastard; the moment sealed itself in the boy's mind. Tony did not know what a bastard was, but he knew by Mike's tone that it was bad; from then on he would forever associate Big Jim Delavane with the term in its worst application.

On an unseasonably warm day in October, Ruby reached her limit. Both twins had mumps, Tony had been sent home with a note from his third-grade teacher complaining about his conduct, the wringer handle on her washing machine had broken, and she was having the worst menstrual cramps and the heaviest flow of her entire life—when the telephone rang.

"Yes?" she answered peevishly.

"You should have gone to Reno with me yesterday, sweet Ruby," Jim teased. "Marlene Dietrich in *The Blue Angel.* She sang a torch song called 'Falling in Love Again' that must have been written for you and me—"

"You lowlife son of a bitch," Ruby interrupted.

Dead silence. Then: "What did . . . ?"

"You heard me. You are a dirty, lowlife son of a bitch!"

"Are you crazy, Ruby—"

"I must be. I must be crazy. To think that I ever considered you anything but a bastard."

"Now wait a minute—"

"You wait a minute. I have asked you time and again to stop calling me. Can't you understand that I don't want anything to do with you? If you're not getting what you want at home, why the hell don't you go to a whore and *buy* it? If you ever—*ever*—call this house again, I'm going to Edith, do you understand me? I'll tell Edith, I'll tell that brat daughter of yours, I'll walk through the streets and tell this whole goddamned town that you got down on your knees and licked my cunt!"

"You bitch, Ruby—"

"I mean it, you bastard," she swore. "Just call one more time, I dare you!"

She heard a resoumding click as he broke the connection, and her threat trailed off into a stark silence in which she stood, broken wringer handle in one hand, telephone receiver in the other, both swollen-faced twins looking at her wide-eyed, and a warm line of blood running down the inside of one thigh. All she could think of was thank God she had sent Tony to the store for a bottle of milk.

A week later, Iron Mike came home in the middle of the day, his face white as a bleached sheet.

"He's fired me, Ruby," he said incredulously. "Big Jim's fired me."

Ruby had been half expecting it, even while holding out a remote hope that it would not happen. When it finally did, she took the news as pragmatically as possible. "His isn't the only mine in Virginia City," she told her husband. There are other mines and there are other jobs."

And there were—but not for long. The next day, when Mike went to apply for a job at the Shaker Mines, the superintendent there told him, "We're holding off on hiring new men until we see what's going to happen in New York."

"New York? What do you mean?" Mike asked.

"Ain't you heard? The stock market crashed yesterday. You know—Wall Street. Everything took a nose dive. People are saying the whole country could go broke."

"Jesus," Iron Mike Donovan said, more to himself than to the superintendent.

He hurried home to tell Ruby the bad news.

Tony Donovan would remember the third grade as the blackest period in his life, this thing that people were now calling "the Depression" or "hard times." On the icy slopes of Sierra Street, where the boys from Comstock Elementary belly-flopped on their sleds and went racing all the way down to the Chinese shanties next to the railroad tracks, the talk was no longer exclusively about Gary Cooper in *The Virginian* or the new characters in the Thimble Theater comic strip who were named Popeye and Wimpy, or whether the Eskimo Pie had thicker chocolate coating than the I-Scream-Bar. Now their conversation was tinged with, "The Eclipse shut down two shafts and my pa's out of a job," and "My big brother says that over at Potosi all the haulers and hoisters is being let go and the muckers're gonna have to do their jobs," or "Overman shut down a whole shift an' now everybody in our house is laid off."

At home, Iron Mike returned each evening from unsuccessful job hunts and glumly read the *Gazette,* which they still had delivered because young Jamie Bevan was their newspaper boy and the only one in the Bevan household with an income. "There's two million people out of work," Mike would read. "Imagine that, Ruby—two *million.*"

"I know," Ruby said, "I know," as she experimented with meatless stew.

And later: "Twenty-five more banks closed, Ruby. D'you think Harmon Coltrane's bank is safe, or should we take our savings out?"

"I've already taken it out," Ruby told him. What there was left to take out, she thought.

And later: "Another hundred thousand workers were laid off in Detroit. Nobody's buying cars anymore."

"One person is," Ruby said. "Mr. Finley, the day schedule conductor on the V&T. He bought our Plymouth. You'll have to look for work on foot now." Ruby looked away. "I'm sorry."

Before taking the drastic step of selling their car, Ruby had first sought work herself going back to the Silver City hospital, her former employer, then to both the miners' hospital and the Catholic hospital there in Virginia City, and finally even spending, grudgingly, enough for gasoline to drive to Reno and inquire at the hospitals there. But nowhere was there a job for her: not as a nurse, not as an aide, not even as a janitress. So first she sold their lot on A Street, and eventually she sold the car and was thankful to get one-quarter of what they had paid for it.

And still later: "Thousands of unemployed are getting ready for a hunger march on Washington. More banks have shut down. And a woman in St. Louis threw her infant into the Mississippi River because her titties dried up and she couldn't feed it—"

"For God's sake, Mike!" Ruby slammed down a wooden spoon. "Don't we have enough troubles of our own without having to have a nightly commentary on the rest of the world's problems?" The next afternoon she caught Jamie Bevan and canceled the newspaper. Two days later she felt guilty about it and sent the Bevan family half of a fresh loaf of bread she had just baked.

At Comstock Elementary, the difference between the two strata of students—those from the Hill and those from Miners Walk—became poignant. Where once the dissimilarity in their dress had been merely between the quality and style of Pemberton's, the uptown department store, and the Sears Roebuck catalog, it now became a contrast of decent and adequate clothing versus the worn, threadbare, and frequently pitiful. Elbows and knees showed red and chapped that winter, fingers poked through mittens, cardboard was cut to fit shoes, toeless socks were folded back, mufflers fashioned from flour sacks. The children from the Hill looked all the more well-to-do as the raw edge of poverty reduced the miners' children to the condition if not the actual circumstances of vagrants. A wretched, miserable band, especially in the bitter cold of high winter, they left many a weeping mother behind of a morning. But at least at school there would be a hot meal for them at noon, which was more than their fathers had.

In Virginia City the mines closed with depressing regularity; gold and silver were no more in demand than new automobiles. News of each failure spread with the speed that only bad news seemed to generate.

"Hale and Norcross shut down today."

"Overman closed its last shaft this morning."

"The Savage digs has gone under."

"Elysian has closed . . ."

"Confidence has closed . . ."

"Fair and O'Brien has closed . . ."

Iron Mike Donovan waited like a vulture for bad news about Delavane Mines. Despite the fact that it would hurt many men who still worked there, he could not resist hoping that Jim Delavane would go broke. "It's a terrible thing to wish, I know," he confessed to Ruby, "but I can't help it. I want to see him ruined, like he's ruined me."

"He hasn't ruined you, Mike," Ruby said insistently. "Nobody can ruin you but yourself. You're still a man—and a damn good one. The Donovans will come out of this, you watch."

Delavane Mines did not go under. Big Jim Delavane made a trip to Washington to talk to some people who *did* have a continuing need for silver. He returned a week later with a two-year contract to supply processed silver to the United States mints at both San Francisco and Salt Lake City. The work would only keep half of his shafts open, but many of his employees from the shut-down tunnels were given topland jobs in the smelting plant he had to open to process his own ore. Only one in ten Delavane miners lost his job—although most had their wages reduced by at least fifty percent.

"The bastard," Iron Mike said bitterly when word spread of the new contracts. "He's got the luck of the devil."

Not luck, Ruby thought. Smarts. Though she loathed Jim Delavane the man, she could not help but admire Jim Delavane the *business*man. His success in the whirlpool of Depression failure stirred up odd awarenesses that it was Delavane blood, not Donovan, that flowed in her Tony's veins. What difference, she wondered, would that tie of blood make in her son's life? If Buck O'Crotty had been there in person, she would have discussed the matter with him, because at times she felt a great need for a confidant, but she could not bring herself to write out her doubts, fears, and cogitations, and send them off to a man she had not seen in a decade. So she kept everything to herself— more and more as things got worse, because Mike began to drink.

Ruby would have put her foot down about the drinking if Mike had been spending money on it. But he had nothing to spend, she no longer even gave him the nickel fare for the trolley that ran from the V&T depot through town and out to the mine paths. What he drank was free, paid for by those who still had jobs, when Mike would stop by Callahan's to inquire about rumors of jobs. The big ex-Marine hero had many friends who would stand him a round early in the evening on their way home if he was there, and a few backbiters later on who fed him whiskey because they perversely enjoyed seeing his hand become unsteady and hearing his words begin to slur.

The thing about the drinking that hurt Ruby was the spectacle Mike became at home when, as he invariably did, he went into long bitter harangues about Big Jim Delavane. "The bastard, the dirty bastard," Mike railed and began censuring his one-time friend for every misfortune that had come their way. Ruby watched her Tony shaggy-haired and threadbare, underfed, his young eyes becoming angry, rebellious, as he listened to Mike rant and recriminate. But there was no interfering, for Iron Mike demanded that Tony be allowed to hear each denouncement, to prepare him for the day when *he* would have to face the bastards of the world like Big Jim Delavane.

The worse their circumstances grew, the more vituperative Mike became. One morning Ruby said, "Please don't come home drunk tonight, Mike, because I need you to help me. We're moving. A smaller place on E Street. We can't afford this house any longer." Mike exploded in a rage, smashed a chair, and with one of its legs as a club, started off through the snow toward the Delavane mansion. Only a frantic telephone call to Sheriff Sam Patch, and the lawman's interception, kept Mike out of serious trouble that day.

The Donovan family's new residence was a two-room unheated frame house in the only block in Virginia City inhabited by Caucasians that was poorer than the poorest on Miners Walk. If any section of the town could be considered a slum, apart from Coolietown where the Chinese lived, it was the rundown block of E Street where Ruby was able to negotiate a two-dollar per week rent on condition that she also do laundry for the landlord, a widower, who was one of Virginia City's veterinarians. Unable to afford a stove, Ruby instead bought a secondhand corrugated washtub, put it up on bricks, and fashioned a vent for it through a window so that she could burn wood and odd pieces of coal in it for heat, and use its upturned bottom to cook. Her own Caloric gas stove was sold when they moved; there was no natural gas service past the brothels of D Street anyway.

Tony hated the new house. It was ugly inside and out, drafty, had a privy instead of an inside toilet, and was so close to the Chinese shanties that Chinese cooking and laundry odors pervaded. In addition, he no longer had a room of his own but had to sleep in the kitchen with his sisters. The twins cried a lot; it seemed they were always

either hungry or cold. Food cooked on the washtub, most of
it dough stew or gruel, was tasteless and unfilling. A constant search had to be maintained for firewood and loose
chunks of coal. The once-a-week baths that Ruby insisted
he take, in the absence of a bathroom were both freezing
and mortifying.

But the thing Tony Donovan hated most was what the
new house did to his mother's face. From the day they
moved there, all animation seemed to go out of Ruby's
expression. The confidence she had displayed to him all of
his life, the sufficiency to deal with and cope, the pride and
sometimes obstinacy, defiance, sassiness—all seemed to drain
out of her, leaving a listless imitation of the woman, the *person*,
she had been. It tore at his young heart to see her once
exuberant spirit diminish so. He tried to cheer her up: by
finding extra coal, by earning a nickel or dime shoveling
sidewalks in front of the uptown stores, by entertaining his
little sisters and making them giggle. Sometimes it worked
and Ruby would flash her old, lively smile and give him a
kiss on the cheek for his effort, but most of the time the
smile would be wan, there would be a pat instead of the
kiss, and her lethargy would continue.

Finally, Ruby could not cope any longer.

Everything bad that had happened to her family over the
many months of gradual decline, seemed to cascade into her
consciousness early one morning in a single, horrifying realization. Her once sturdy, smiling husband lay sprawled in
drunken sleep, unwashed and unshaved for a week. Her
son, in tatters, rags, hovered over the washtub of burning
wood and paper, shivering, his hands cupped around a mug
of mush made from heated water and yesterday's cornbread.
Her twins stood crying, cold, hungry, their cheeks no longer
rosy, now sallow, thick green mucus clogging their nostrils,
forbidden to go any closer to the washtub for fear they
would again burn hands already burnt. The combined effect
of Iron Mike's lax jaw—*Iron* Mike, she thought with a scorn
that shocked her; of Tony's intense, malevolent eyes—just a
boy, for God's sake, a *boy*! her mind screamed and of the
little girls, once so beautiful, now so pitiful, so wasted—
caused Ruby to stop and stare. Hovering over all other
thoughts was the most appalling realization of all: *It did not
have to be this way.*

Something new then took over Ruby's mind: new in conscience, new in purpose, and she heard herself saying to
Tony, "I want you to stay home from school today. Watch
your sisters; keep them away from the fire tub. Fix some
warm mush for your father if he wakes up." She bundled
into her now barely recognizable nurses' corps greatcoat and
tied an all but shredded muffler around her head and ears.

"Where are you going, Ma?" Tony asked, a little nervously. This was most unusual.

"To see about a job for your father," she said, thinking it
was a lie, then realizing that it was not. "Yes. To see about
a job for your father."

"Where, Ma? What kind of job?"

"I'll tell you all about it when I get back." She kissed the
girls, kissed a now apprehensive Tony, and put gentle fingertips on her husband's cheek, ashamed of the scorn she
had felt minutes earlier, thinking: I'm sorry, Mike. Sorry for
then, sorry for now. And very sorry for later.

"Watch over your sisters," she admonished Tony. Suddenly she stopped and stared at him. She put a rough palm
ever so gently on his cheek. "Always watch over your sisters, won't you, son? Sometimes women are strong and can
do all the things a strong woman has to do. But other times,
when they've used up their strength they dearly need watching over. Remember that, Tony. Always watch over your
sisters. Always be the strong one."

Ruby hurried out the door.

She made the telephone call from a grocery store on C
Street. A maid at the mansion answered. "Mr. Delavane,
please," she said. "Miss Smith calling."

"Just a minute, please. He's in the breakfast room."

Presently he came on the line. "Jim Delavane speaking—"

"Jim, it's Ruby."

A long, agonizing moment of silence.

"Did you hear me?" she asked.

"I heard you."

Ruby swallowed. "Jim, would it be possible for us to
meet somewhere today?"

Silence again, cold and reserved.

"Would it?" Ruby repeated. She had to swallow again
before she could say, "Please."

"Yes, I suppose so." His voice was reluctant, but also a
little curious. "What do you want?"

"I have something to tell you. Something important."

His voice lowered. "I haven't gotten over the last time we spoke."

"Those things were said in anger, Jim. You had pushed me to my very limit. You must realize—"

"All right," he said urgently, "let's not go into it over the phone. Do you want to drive somewhere and meet?"

"I can't. I don't have a car."

"Oh? Is Mike not working?"

"No."

"Are things not going well for you?"

"Jim, please—" Her voice broke.

"All right. Let's see. Can you walk along Baseline, near the tracks, in about an hour? I'll pick you up."

"Yes, all right. Baseline. An hour." What in the name of God, she wondered, would she do for an hour? She couldn't bear to go back home; suppose Mike was awake . . . ?

"See you then," he said.

"Yes. Good-bye."

Thanking the man at the grocery store for the use of his telephone, Ruby tied the muffler around her head again and ventured back out onto C Street. The morning was crispy cold, the sky clear blue, unthreatening. Ruby thanked God there was no fresh snow on the ground; her shoes, all but soleless, were patched on the bottom with layers of newspaper. It would take her ten minutes to walk to Baseline, that meant fifty minutes to kill. She walked along the wide main street, thin shoulders hunched against the cold, looking in windows, avoiding the glances of store clerks coming to work, eyes shifting after every few stores to the big clock in front of the bank at C and Carson, watching time go by in agonizingly slow increments: five minutes, ten . . .

By the time half an hour passed, she felt frozen to the quick. Though still early, she started for Baseline anyway. When she reached it, Ruby began to walk in the direction from which Jim Delavane would probably come. Baseline was unpaved, one of the original streets from the days when Virginia City had been a mining camp. Ruby walked along an old wooden sidewalk a few feet above the street, being careful to avoid any protruding nailheads that could snag her worn soles. As she trudged along with her head down, she wondered how Jim would react to what she was going to tell him: that Tony was his son and not Mike Donovan's.

There was a chance, she realized, that he would not believe her. In her obviously impoverished condition, he might think that it was some kind of ploy to get money from him. He had commented once, during one of his interminable telephone calls, that one of the drawbacks to being wealthy was that someone was always trying to do him out of money: by selling him something, borrowing from him, urging him to invest in this or that, and numerous other ways. "You wouldn't believe how many parasites there are in the world," he had said. Would he think that's what she was? Just another parasite?

It would have helped, of course, if there had been some resemblance between Jim and Tony, some physical characteristic—ears, nose, chin—not enough in itself to mark them father and son, yet something by which Ruby could support her claim. But there was none. The only person *Tony* looked like was *her* own father, Sean Surrett, an Irish rebel hanged by the British when she was only a baby, before her mother had emigrated to America to live with a brother in Chicago. Ruby did not remember her father, but she had several old photographs of him, and his dark, brooding countenance was an older image of her own young son.

Reaching the bottom of Sierra Street, down which she assumed Jim would be driving, Ruby turned and reversed her course. Whatever Jim Delavane's reaction to her story, she thought, at least she would have tried; she had to do that much, to keep her conscience from driving her crazy every time she knew the boy was hungry. She would ask nothing for herself, nothing for her daughters, nothing, really, for her husband—only that Jim put him back to work at the mine. Back to work as anything: mucker, hauler, hoister—Iron Mike would accept any work, Ruby knew, at any wage, just to feel like a man again: to know he was at least feeding his family.

Jim Delavane *had* to believe her, she thought desperately. He had to help her. If he didn't—

Behind her, Ruby heard a car approaching on the unpaved roadway. For a fleeting second she wished—God, how she wished!—that she was not such a pale, skinny, ragged wretch of a woman. The piercing spasm of vanity passed quickly through her and at the next set of wooden steps running down from the sidewalk, she turned to meet the car. To her surprise it was not the big, shiny Deusenberg she expected; instead it was a smaller, more conservative, dark blue LaSalle. It pulled up next to her just as she descended the steps. Only when she bent to open the passenger door did she see that the driver was not Jim Delavane.

It was Edith.

TWENTY-SIX

"Please get in, Ruby," Edith Delavane said.

Bent at the waist, one hand on the open car door, Ruby could only stare into the car at the woman who had been the maid of honor at her wedding, the woman with whose husband she had committed and recommitted the act of adultery, a woman she had not seen in nearly a decade and who looked—why in the name of God was *this* thought among the others?—who looked almost as fresh and pretty and young as she had back then.

"You might as well get in," Edith said quietly. "Jim won't be coming."

Ruby got into the car and pulled the door closed. At once she felt the warmth of thick velvet upholstery. She glanced self-consciously at Edith's sheared lamb coat with its protective calash, her fur-lined gloves, the rich cashmere muffler. Folding her arms, Ruby tried to conceal her own ragged mittens.

"There's a lap robe on the back seat" Edith suggested.

"I'm fine," Ruby replied realizing how incongruous it sounded.

"I was listening on the extension when you called Jim a little while ago," Edith said without further preliminary. "I picked up in another room just as our maid answered. Normally I would have hung up; eavesdropping isn't a habit of mine. But I was curious who 'Miss Smith' was, so I waited a moment to find out. After you two began to talk, I was frankly too surprised to hang up. I imagine you can understand that." The last statement was almost a question. Ruby half nodded.

"Yes."

"I wonder if you'd care to explain exactly what you meant by some of the things you said?" Here her question was more a request.

"Why should I?" Ruby asked curtly. "He's your husband; ask *him*."

"I did. He refuses to discuss it other than to say that you and he were—well, more than friends, before he and I were married. Is that true?"

"Yes." Precisely put, it was true.

"Do I take it that you knew each other while you were both in uniform?"

"Yes." Again, literally.

"Were you . . . ?" Edith looked away, out at the drab street, unable to form the exact words of her painful question.

"Yes," Ruby answered it anyway, "we were lovers."

"But it was a long time ago? It hasn't been a . . . recent thing?"

Ruby could feel the hurt that was inside Edith Delavane. "A very long time ago," she confirmed. "Before either of us had children." Perhaps, Ruby hoped, Edith wouldn't ask specifically whether it had been before their marriages as well. But if she did, Ruby prepared herself to lie about it. The only thing to be gained by unadulterated—there was an appropriate word—unadulterated truth, at this point, was more pain for Edith, who, like Mike, like Tony, like everyone except Jim and her, was an innocent victim.

"What did you mean," Edith asked, becoming braver, "when you said Jim had pushed you to the limit, or something like that?"

Ruby shook her head. "I don't think I want to talk about this with you, Edith. If your husband won't discuss it with you, I don't see why I should."

"Will you tell me *why* you called him, then? You said you had something important to tell him. I'd like to know what it was."

Ruby shook her head again, more emphatically this time. "I'm sorry. I, ah—no, I can't. This is . . . no, I just can't. I can't go into these things with you, Edith."

Inside, Ruby cringed at the thought of having to admit to Edith Delavane that her Tony was Jim's son and not Mike

Donovan's. The thought suddenly came rushing back to her, like some shameful long-concealed family secret, that her Tony and Edith's daughter Francie had to have been conceived around the same time. Edith would realize that, just as Ruby had long ago realized it. And although Ruby had convinced herself then that it did not matter to her that Jim Delavane had been sleeping with both of them at the same time, the prospect of admitting it, least of all to his *wife*, was something Ruby suddenly found mortifying.

"Edith, I'm sorry about this whole thing," Ruby said. "I'm really very sorry." She reached for the door handle to get out of the car, but Edith quickly put a hand on her other arm and turned to her with tears welling in her eyes.

"Ruby, please. Help me . . . cope with this . . . this—"

Ruby felt tears of her own. "Help you cope? For God's sake, Edith, look at me. Look at me. I haven't had any *underwear* for six months. Do I look like I'm capable of helping anybody cope?"

They both began to sob and instinctively fell into each other's arms. They embraced not because they were women, not because they felt pity for each other, not even because their pain was somehow mutual, somehow shared; rather they embraced because it was the human thing to do: had they been total strangers at that moment, and their individual grief secret from the other, still they would have put their arms around each other because each would have felt the depth of the other's pain.

"You *can* help me, Ruby," a crying Edith pleaded. "You're the *only* one who can help me. How could I even *talk* to anyone else about it?"

Ruby shook her head hysterically. "You don't understand. I am at the end of my rope. If I hadn't been desperate, do you think I would have—well, no, how could you? Listen, I don't want to say anymore—"

"Ruby, we *must* talk!" Edith insisted. "We *need* each other right now; you've *got* to realize that. Take your hand off the door, please. I have an idea. Let's go someplace and order some nice hot tea and rolls—"

"Oh, Edith. Look at me!" Ruby held up mittened hands with her fingers showing through worn holes. "Every piece of clothing I'm wearing is ragged. Do you think I'd go into a restaurant with you, for God's sake?"

"I'm sorry, I'm sorry. I didn't think. But we must talk"

—Edith looked around desperately—"we must work this thing out. I know you wouldn't go to my home, you probably wouldn't let me come to yours. Wait! I have another idea. Please, take your hand off the door . . ."

Ruby removed her hand and Edith, who had never stopped the engine, eased the clutch in, shifted out of neutral, and drove up to C Street. She parked at one of the smaller cafés. Making Ruby promise to wait in the car while she was gone, she went inside and a few minutes later returned with a soup bucket full of steaming coffee, two big mugs, and a paper sack of fresh, hot doughnuts. With Ruby balancing the food, Edith then drove eastward out of town and took one of the roads that wound around Mt. Davidson. "We can meet the morning sun this way," she said, making an effort to seem positive and enthusiastic. Continuing around the mountain, in a few minutes they reached a plateau where the sun shone brightly. Edith found a clearing and parked. "Let's eat first," she suggested.

"All right," Ruby agreed. "I won't pretend I'm not hungry. I haven't had coffee in two months—"

Opening the LaSalle's glove box for a makeshift table, they set out the mugs, poured their coffee, and opened the sack of doughnuts. It was a very large sack, containing more than a dozen-and-a-half homemade doughnuts. "I wasn't sure how many to get," Edith said, a little lamely.

"You bought all they had, didn't you?" asked Ruby.

"Yes," she admitted. "I thought—"

"I know what you thought. Thank you, Edith."

Ruby was not embarrassed to wolf down four doughnuts while sipping coffee continuously. It was hot enough to burn her lips and mouth a little, but it was the most delicious burn she ever felt. While Ruby ate, Edith, only nibbling, became serious again.

"I must ask this, Ruby. How do I know you're being truthful when you say you and Jim haven't—well, been together for so many years? How do I know you're not merely protecting him?"

"If all I wanted to do was protect him, I wouldn't have had to admit anything," Ruby replied. "I could have simply refused to say any more than you heard on the telephone."

"Will you tell me why you called?" Edith asked. "Please, Ruby. I've got to decide how to cope with Jim's response to you. After all, he *did* agree to see you."

Ruby's mind raced as she vigorously attacked the doughnuts. How, her survival instincts asked, could she still salvage something from her original call to Jim Delavane without admitting, even to him now, that Tony was his son? There was no way, she was certain, to do it without sacrificing *some* self-respect, some dignity, some pride. But that did not bother her; those things were retrieveable. What she had to be careful not to put in jeopardy was the Donovan name: either Iron Mike's *or* Tony's.

"Ruby—"

"Let me think about it for a minute," Ruby said. A thought was fermenting in her mind, a way out, for her, her family, for Edith—for everyone except Jim. That, she thought as it became clearer, is unfortunate—but he did, after all, start the whole thing with his persistent telephone calls, his refusal to accept *her* refusal, and ultimately his firing of Mike, which she now convinced herself conveniently, had to have been directly related to her not renewing her intimacy with the mine owner. So if Jim Delavane got his nuts squeezed a little tighter, she decided, it was because he exposed them in the first place.

"All right, Edith," she said at last. "I'm going to be honest with you. It won't be easy for either of us, and you'll probably have an even lower opinion of me after I'm through."

"Ruby, I don't feel any ill will toward you," Edith insisted. "As long as you haven't done anything to taint my marriage, I think this entire matter can be resolved."

"But I *was* going to do exactly that," Ruby admitted. She took a deep breath. The doughnuts were not settling in her stomach. "That's the reason I called Jim. What I told you about us not being together for years was true; we haven't been; but I left something out. About a year and a half ago, Jim and I ran into each other uptown. He began making overtures to revive our relationship. I'm sorry, Edith, but it's true. I resisted him, have resisted for all these months. He fired Mike and—well, you can see what the result of that has been." She began to tremble, and put a hand over her now churning stomach as if that might calm it. But the nervousness she felt, and the richness and quantity of the doughnuts, was working very quickly to make her sick. "I called Jim this morning because I'd had as much as I could stand. My children have been *hungry*, Edith, for a long time; you'll never know what that feels like unless you experience it. I asked Jim to meet me so I could tell him," she now lied, "that I would agree to start sleeping with him again, if he would give Mike a job." Bile rose in her throat. "Christ, I think I'm going to throw up—"

She managed to get the car door open in time to regurgitate on the ground, only getting a little of the foul mess on one sleeve. Edith quickly handed her some coffee and said, "Pour a little on your sleeve to clean it. Here's a handkerchief."

It was a snow-white linen handkerchief "That's all right," Ruby said, shaking her head. "It's not exactly my ball gown . . ."

Edith pressed the handkerchief into her hand. "Pour coffee on it anyway. It'll kill the odor."

"All right. Of course . . ."

When her brief episode of sickness was over, Ruby noticed that Edith's expression had tightened a little; there was severity in it for the first time. "Do you think," Edith asked, "that Jim would have done it? Would he have started sleeping with you again?"

"I don't know," Ruby replied thoughtfully. Would he, she wondered, if she *had* made him the offer? "I'm not exactly an object of desire in my present state."

"But *you* would have?" Edith asked. "You would have tainted my marriage without a second thought?"

What the hell was this "tainted" business? Ruby thought irritably. Did this woman—this woman who had everything, whose child had *never* been hungry—think her marriage was so pure and perfect as to be unaffected by the tacky little exigencies of life? For a disturbing instant, Ruby was tempted to say, "It's already tainted, Mrs. Former-Schoolteacher-and-now-Society-Leader. It was tainted night after night while your husband was winning the money and the land that made *you* what you are today. I mean, we tainted it every way you can imagine!" But that would have been foolish Ruby knew as soon as she thought it. For all of Edith Delavane's propriety and status and well-being, all of her cloying references to "tainting," Ruby had no desire, indeed no legitimate reason, to hurt her any more than she had already been hurt. Besides which, Ruby still had something to accomplish in the matter—and to do so she had to have Edith Delavane's understanding. At the moment she felt dangerously close to losing it.

"I said this wasn't going to be easy for either of us," Ruby reminded her. "I've told you the whole story, which is what you wanted. I've been honest with you, which is also what you wanted. If you change what you said earlier, if you now want to let yourself feel ill will toward me for doing what you wanted me to do, I'll just have to accept that."

Edith bit her lower lip and looked away. Having been decent, understanding, charitable, and forgiving all of one's life, she found now, was an insurmountable burden when she tried to be accusing and vindictive. Her eyes misted again and for some reason she thought of Francie. At whatever cost, she must not let this business become known to Francie.

"Edith, please remember," Ruby said, "that even though I was willing, today, because of my circumstances, to give in to Jim, my telephone call this morning was not what started this whole thing. Jim put constant pressure on me to begin seeing him again; that's what I meant when I said he pushed me to the limit. It was Jim who started it, not me. Please remember that when you're judging me."

"I'm going to try hard *not* to judge you," Edith said, facing her again. "And I'm not going to allow myself to feel ill will toward you. We've both been taken advantage of, both been treated unfairly. My problem is going to be how to resume my life with Jim. I don't know whether he would have started a relationship with you again; naturally I'd like to think that he would *not* have, that he would have given Mike a job without requiring that you compromise yourself that he would have been compassionate and benevolent—"

There, Ruby thought. *Now.*

"Then make him be those things, Edith," she suggested quietly, as neutrally as she could make her voice. "Let him have the benefit of the doubt. Have him give Mike a job, any job, without even being asked by me. *You* do it, Edith. You help him." She paused just enough for effect. "Help *all* of us."

Edith's eyes lost their worry and immediately glowed with enthusiasm for Ruby's suggestion. Yes. Of course. Help *everyone.* She squeezed Ruby's hand.

"I'll do it," she said.

Ruby was elated. Not in her most optimistic imagination had she dared hope that things would possibly turn out as well as they had.

Edith had given her personal assurance that there would be a job for Mike at Delavane Mines beginning the following morning. She had guaranteed it. Ruby had sought to counteract any resistance from Jim Delavane by asking Edith how she could be so certain her husband would agree.

"How could he not?" Edith had replied. "To refuse to give Mike a job would be the same as admitting to me that he *is* still interested in you, that he wants to keep that advantage in reserve to influence you in the future. Don't you see that?"

"Yes, I do now," Ruby encouraged. The way it worked out, Ruby concluded happily, was perfect.

When she got home, Ruby found turmoil. Mike was sick and throwing up, running a slight fever, and Tony was trying to help him at the same time he had to contend with the crying twins who could not understand where their mother was and why their brother was at home and in charge of them. Ruby solved their problems and Tony's with the rest of the bag of doughnuts, and turned to attend her ailing husband. While she was helping him clean up and settle down, giving him free aspirin from the Virginia City clinic for his fever, along with the heated-up remains of the soup bucket of coffee Edith had bought, she told him about the job. The big man's eyebrows raised and held in interest until she finished talking. Then he said, "Edith Delavane? Offered to do that for me?"

"Yes. I'm sure it won't be the mine superintendent's job, but it will be a job. You wouldn't mind being a hoister again, would you? Something like that?"

"Mind?" Iron Mike's eyes misted. "I'd get down on my knees and beg for a hoister's job."

"Well, you won't have to. Not now."

"You mean not now that you've done the begging for me?"

"I don't mean that at all. And it's not true anyway," she insisted. "You know as well as I do that no one has to beg Edith Delavane for anything. I think her feelings would be hurt if she heard you say such a thing."

"I guess you're right," Mike said after reflection, sipping the coffee she gave him. "I'll have to find some way of thanking her, won't I? Wonder what Jim'll have to say when she asks him?"

"I wouldn't worry about it," Ruby said. "I imagine Edith

Delavane can handle her husband"—she leaned over and kissed Mike briefly on the lips—"as easily as I can handle mine."

"Is that so?" he scoffed and pulled her onto his lap. "Maybe later tonight we'll see who does the handling in this family."

"Maybe we will," Ruby agreed. "But first you've got to break the fever you're running, and I've got to get a decent meal into you tonight so you'll be fit for work tomorrow."

"Work," Iron Mike said softly. "The word sounds good, don't it?"

"Yes, darling, it does." Ruby kissed her husband again, then set about getting her household in order. Wood was added to the embers in their makeshift washtub stove and water was heated in buckets to pour into a big wooden tub in which she threw the twins, their clothes after them, for a serious scrubbing. Tony, sensing what was coming, was almost out the door when his mother stopped him.

"No you don't, young man. You're next." To his vociferous complaints and indignant reminders that it was not Saturday, she ruled, "From now on the Donovans are going to be clean every day. When your father gets his first pay envelope, we'll see about buying you some new school clothes; meanwhile what you have will at least be washed. Now strip."

While Iron Mike laughed and kidded him, Tony was given the same kind of scrubbing as the twins, then all of them huddled under blankets on the bed while their clothes were dried before the open fire. Afterward it was Mike's turn to be washed, the children's to giggle, as he got the full treatment including a shave and hair trim. "You're going to be the best-looking man reporting to work tomorrow," Ruby promised, heating her flatiron to press his old moleskin pants and a corduroy shirt, the closest he had to underground wear. "We'll have to get you some proper work duds as quick as we can," Ruby said. "Maybe Anson's Clothing Store will let us open an account now that you'll have steady wages."

While everyone was waiting for their clothes to dry, Ruby got out the Mason jar in which she kept her meager household money. There was less than four dollars in it. Biting her lip as if it caused her physical pain to do so, she took half of it. Throwing her tattered coat back on, she hurried

off to the market and returned an hour later with a small
bag of groceries. "We're going to have a proper meal tonight," she told her family. Looking around the dingy little
house, she added, "And we're to have it in a clean house. I
want the four of you to sit over there in the corner and stay
out of my way."

For two hours she dusted, swept, scrubbed, aired, and
rearranged. When she finished, the impoverished little place
still looked poor, but it no longer looked dirty poor; it
looked, as Ruby wanted *them* to look, proud poor. By the
end of the long afternoon, there was nothing left to clean
except herself. She had Mike hang a blanket across the
corner of the kitchen and behind it she actually languished
in the wooden tub of hot water for a few minutes, smoking
one of five cigarettes she had bought for a penny each. The
day, she thought, had been incredibly long; it seemed like
an eternity since she had made up her mind to call Jim
Delavane—yet it had only been eight hours. Such a short
time in which to have brought about such drastic changes:
everything clean again, attitude positive again, outlook cheerful again—and all because of a job. Or rather, the promise
of a job. Suddenly Ruby realized that nothing in their lives
had actually changed yet except what *she* had made change.
She could have done exactly the same thing without the
prospect of Mike going back to work. True, there would
have been less enthusiasm for it, but it still would have
boosted everyone's morale a bit. Ruby blamed herself for
allowing the Donovan family to sink into such a pit of
despair. She should have been stronger, given them more;
she should have kept their pride polished—especially her
husband's and her son's. Men, she had learned, wore pride
well, but were often deficient in its maintenance, sometimes
sacrificing it too easily. She made a promise to herself to
always help *her* men keep their pride, from that day forward.

It felt glorious to be clean and fresh, dressed in whatever
odds and ends she could scavenge, with the house actually
smelling good and her scrubbed family waiting patiently for
the "proper" meal she had promised. Ruby fried a skillet of
thinly cut pork chops, cooking them to a crispy dark brown
so she could drain off all the fat and grease to mix into a
thick gravy for a pan of hot biscuits she managed to bake by
putting the dough under a bucket inside her washtub stove.
She prepared half a dozen unskinned yams the same way,

and served it all with glasses of milk from a bottle she had put on the outside window sill to get cold.

"My God," Mike said, "I'd forgotten what it was like to have a family meal together." He reached over to touch his wife's hand. "Let's not forget again, however little we might have to eat."

"We won't," Ruby promised.

By the time supper was over, Ruby was exhausted. Mike insisted she lie down while he and Tony cleaned up the table. In minutes she was fast asleep. Mike kept the house quiet for her, put the twins to bed when they got sleepy, and later, after a couple of games of Old Maid with Tony, their first good time together in months, sent the boy off to his own cot in the corner.

Tony was dozing, in and out of light sleep, eyes opening, then closing again, when he saw Iron Mike first check to make sure Ruby was still asleep, then retrieve from under a floorboard of the room a pint bottle of whiskey. Tony knew that Callahan had given Mike the bottle in payment for chopping firewood. Tony had been there at the time, helping Mike stack the wood, and had been admonished not to "mention this to your mother, hear me?"

With his feet propped up near the washtub fire to keep warm, the big ex-Marine now pulled the cork and took a long swallow from the bottle. Tony tried to stay awake; if Mike got drunk, he would have to be put to bed. But the bath, the supper, the relaxation of the Old Maid games, all conspired against him. Finally his eyes closed tightly and he slept soundly until the pungent smell of smoke brought him awake coughing.

Bolting upright on the cot, Tony stared in horror at live, dancing flames. He could see clearly how and where they had started: a single burning ember of wood had popped out of the tub, fallen to the floor, and spread out from there along the line of floorboards where there was cool, thin air on which it could rapidly feed. It spread in a dark circle, like spilled oil, singeing, then it combusted and began burning the floor and the chair on which Iron Mike dozed.

"Pa!" Tony yelled, leaping across the room to shake him awake. The bottle on his lap was still nearly full and Tony realized with relief that Mike was not drunk, had probably only taken the one drink. "Pa!" he yelled again, and Mike came awake instantly. "The house is on fire, Pa!"

"Jesus Christ!" Mike kicked the burning chair away. At the same time they both saw in horror that the ceiling was on fire too, from a single trail of flame that had climbed like a burning vine up one corner of the room. "My God—"

As they were watching, part of it sagged and caved in above where the twins were sleeping on a pallet, and they heard agonizing little voices scream in terror from within the flames.

"Jesus Christ, Jim Delavane has destroyed us all!" Mike yelled incongruously. Then he seized Tony with powerful arms and, like a man shifting a sack of grain, swung him through the nearest window.

Tony felt himself propelled through the window as if in a nightmare. The breaking pane sliced open his left cheek in a thin, almost surgical line. He landed in a bank of frozen snow, now dirty and crusty, left from the last snowfall. Sitting up dazed, he heard his mother scream. He saw the outside wall of the little shanty collapse and brilliant fiery embers gush up like a burning mushroom.

Tony struggled to his feet, intending to rush back into the inferno to help his mother, but before he could take the first step a blackness dropped over him and he fainted.

TWENTY-SEVEN

In the back room at Callahan's, Buck O'Crotty unloaded Big Jim Delavane's pistol and put the bullets in one coat pocket, the gun in another.

Big Jim's head was down again, as it had been periodically during the telling of that part of Ruby's story which he knew. Though his voice was hoarse, he kept raising his head to add a fact, an afterthought, a conjecture.

"Edith had her breakdown that same night," he said now. "Almost as soon as she heard about the fire. We had al-

ready been through a very strained evening anyway, discussing her meeting with Ruby, my intentions in agreeing to
meet her, that sort of thing. Edith was being very understanding, very reasonable. I admitted that in trying to entice
Ruby back into a relationship I had been weak and stupid; I
promised her I'd never do such a thing again—and I meant
it, Buck, as God is my witness. At that moment, with her
being so forgiving about everything, I loved Edith more than
I ever had. She asked me to show good faith by putting Iron
Mike back to work, and I agreed immediately." He looked
at Buck with haunted eyes. "When the doctor told me what
young Tony said Mike's last words were—'Jim Delavane has
destroyed us all'—it made me sick. I won't lie about why I
fired him: yes, it was to hurt Ruby. But to hold me responsible for everything that happened after that? To blame me
because they became poverty stricken? Good God, Buck, it
was the Depression! Then to carry it further and say they
died because of me, because they were *there* because of
me—why, that's ridiculous, Buck. That's unfair." Delavane
looked pleadingly at Buck. "You don't see it that way, do
you? Those things you said earlier, that was just to get the
gun away from me, wasn't it? You don't believe—"

"You want the truth, Jim?" Buck challenged. "Are you
ready to face the truth after all these years?"

Delavane did not answer. He could only stare at Buck as
dread seeped into his mind and his expression.

"Of course you're responsible, Jim," the union leader
said, as gently as possible. "If you'd let Mike go because of
the economic conditions of the time, then I could accept
that it was the Depression that put them in that shanty
where they burned up. But you fired him because his wife
wouldn't sleep with you. It was your own rejected lust that
started them downhill to that tragedy. Accept it, Jim."

Still staring, his eyes starkly wide, Delavane nodded a
barely perceptible nod. "My God . . ." he whispered.

Buck rose, patted the mine owner briefly on the shoulder,
and said, "Stay here." Leaving the little room, he went out
to the bar. The miners in the saloon fell silent and watched
him as he asked Callahan for a bottle and two glasses. No
one, Callahan included, presumed to ask him what was going
on, and Buck volunteered nothing. Buck knew everyone would
assume that he and Big Jim were having an impromptu labor
negotiations meeting. He would let them think that.

Back in the little room, he poured two shots of whiskey and put one in front of Delavane. The mine owner bolted it down and Buck poured him another.

"Why don't you take that gun and shoot me, Buck?" he asked. "I've got it coming."

"Odd you should ask me to," Buck replied quietly. "The day I took Tony to live with me, I promised I'd help him kill you if I ever believed you were responsible for what happened to his family. Now, well—" Buck downed his own drink. "It's not up to me to punish you, Jimmy. I'm not God."

"It doesn't really matter" Delavane said solemnly. "I'll punish myself I'm sure" He drank his second shot and pulled the bottle over to pour a third. "Or maybe you should tell young Tony and let him do the job for both of us."

"Adding a new tragedy to an old one wouldn't solve anything," Buck reasoned.

Jim stared at his whiskey for a moment. "It's odd, but one of the last things Edith said that night, before we heard about the fire and she collapsed, was that she had the most overwhelming feeling that there was something else Ruby had to tell, something she had not discussed that day. I realize now that it was probably the fact that Tony was mine." He looked curiously at Buck. "In all the time Edith worked with you in your various causes, didn't she ever suspect?"

"Never," Buck said absolutely. "I'd have known if she had."

"And the boy himself?"

"Good God, no," Buck affirmed. "Such things would never occur to him."

Jim smiled wryly. "For a lot of years I bemoaned the fact that I didn't have a son to carry on my name. Half the time when I had suspicions about the Donovan boy being mine, I think it was because I *wanted* him to be mine. It took me years to finally put that out of my head. Now I've found out for a fact that he *is,* and it doesn't matter to me. All I can think of is that I might lose my daughter. And if I do, I'll have lost my last link to Edith . . ."

"Time will help with Francie," Buck assured him. "It's been a terrible shock to her; a necessary shock, to keep her from going to bed with her own half-brother, but terrible all the same. She's a smart girl, though, and she's got enough of Edith in her to eventually realize that it was for the best, and that the charitable thing to do is to forgive her father. Have patience, you'll see." Buck's mind was racing to find a way to protect Tony from all of this. "The important thing, as I see it," he rationalized to Delavane, "is to try and keep the situation contained where we've got it now. Keep it from spreading any further; especially keep it from Tony. He's a hothead; there's no doubt in my mind he'd do something rash if he found out.".

Jim nodded slowly. "Whatever you think is best, Buck. All I really want is to get my daughter back; I've lived all my life without a son—I can continue to do so."

"Wise choice," Buck told him. "Come on, wash up a bit now before you go back through the saloon. I'll walk to your car with you, in case there are any off-picket trouble-makers out there having a drink."

"Yes," Jim said, rising, walking toward the bathroom, "I want to get back home as soon as I can and see if Francie will let me talk to her."

A few minutes later, as the two men left the back room and walked the length of the bar, the saloon falling silent in front of them as it had when Big Jim first entered, their course was followed by several flat, angry stares from a table behind them.

"Look at the son of a bitch," one striker said quietly of the mine owner after he passed. "Dressed to the teeth while our kids ain't even getting enough to eat."

"He can keep the mine closed as long as he wants and never go hungry," said another.

"D'you think they was trying to work out a settlement back there, him and Buck?"

"It didn't sound like it," one said. "When I went out back to take a leak, I listened at the window for a few seconds. Sounded to me like they was talking about Iron Mike Donovan."

"Iron Mike? I remember him. Fine figure of a man. Arms like tree trunks."

"Jesus, what a tragic thing that was, that fire. Did y'ever see those yellow-haired little twin girls of his? More beautiful children never drew breath."

"Y'know, the only reason the family was living in that firetrap of a shack was because Big Jim and Mike had a falling out and Big Jim fired him. There's some say he even blackballed Mike with the other mine owners so's Mike couldn't get work."

One of the men turned to look out the window where Big Jim was getting into his car. "And there he goes with no problems of conscience at all. Getting into his big car—"

"A Deusenberg, no less. He don't even drive an American car."

"—and driving back up to his mansion on the Hill. Ever get a close look at that place?"

"Not since Christmas Eve," one of them replied with a smirk.

"It's a palace. My Jennie worked there in the old days when Mrs. Delavane was still alive. They sleep on silk sheets."

"A fine house, all right. Got everything it needs, I guess. Except a firebreak." The smirking man leaned forward, his forearms on the table. "If it was my house, I'd have a firebreak dug. What with all the dried mesquite and such in the forest this time of year."

"No firebreak at all, you say?"

"Not a sign. Forest comes almost down to his back door."

"Wouldn't that be one for the books now, if Big Jim went the same way as Iron Mike did?"

"No firebreak at all? You're sure?"

"I'm as sure as I'm sure the devil always gets his due. Undersand my meaning?"

For the next few minutes, the striking miners drank in silence, each with his own thoughts.

When Big Jim Delavane arrived home, Lew Rainbolt was at the front door with one of his sentries. "Has my daughter come back yet?" Big Jim asked.

"Not yet," Rainbolt said. "I have my men scouting the town for her. I'm sure she's all right, Mr. Delavane."

"I hope so. Please let me know as soon as you locate her."

"Certainly."

After Big Jim went inside, Rainbolt winked at his sentry in the light of the illuminated front entry, and walked over to his big yellow roadster parked at the edge of the drive. Opening the door, he said, "It's okay now. He went inside."

As Rainbolt got in behind the wheel, Francie Delavane sat up in the passenger seat where she had been crouched down out of sight. "Thanks," she said. "I wasn't sure I could trust you."

"Now you know," Rainbolt said.

"God, this has been a rotten night." Francie rummaged in her purse. "Do you have a cigarette? I'm out."

"No. I don't smoke cigarettes. Just these," he said, taking from a leather case a thin cheroot cut square at both ends. Lighting it, he took a long drag and said, "Want to try a puff?'"

Francie shook her head. "No."

"What's been so rotten about the day?" he asked, rolling down the car window. "You mean your boyfriend's foster father getting beaten up and losing the strike funds?"

"I'd practically forgotten that," Francie admitted. Throughout her earlier encounter with Buck O'Crotty, his shocking disclosure had so numbed her mind to everything else that O'Crotty's bruised, swollen face had not really registered in her thoughts. "No," she said to Rainbolt, "I was talking about other things. Things you don't know anything about; things too involved to go into, so please don't ask me about them."

"All right."

"You can stop referring to Tony Donovan as my boyfriend, too," Francie said.

Rainbolt's eyebrows raised in interest. "That so?"

"Yes. You can tell your men they won't have to worry anymore about me slipping off to meet him. I won't"—her voice broke but she quickly controlled it—"I won't be seeing Tony anymore."

"He wasn't really man enough for you anyway," Rainbolt commented.

"Just what is that supposed to mean?" Francie challenged irritably.

"Someday you'll understand."

"I'm not in the mood for games," she said archly. She reached for the door to leave.

"It isn't a game." Rainbolt closed strong fingers around her wrist and drew her very close to him.

"Let go of my wrist," she said.

He continued to hold her.

"Let go!"

She tried to pull away but his grip tightened and held.

"Goddamn you, let go of me!" Her eyes widened in anger

and her nostrils flared. Still Rainbolt held on, the vise of his fingers holding her like a lock. Their faces were very close. She could feel his breath, smell him. There was a muskiness about him: like the leathery, tobacco smell of her father, but without the body tonic fragrance added; and like the brown soap smell of Tony. Wonderful, she thought. A combination of my two biggest problems.

While she was thinking that, Lew Rainbolt kissed her.

"Why did you do that?" Francie asked.

"Because I wanted to. I've wanted to since the night we met." A slight smile played at his lips. "The night you assured me you could take care of yourself."

"I could," she reasserted. "I mean, I can. I can still take care of myself."

"You don't need to depend on your father?"

"No." Emphatically.

"Or Tony Donovan?"

"No." Less emphatic but determined.

"Prove it," Rainbolt challenged.

Francie stared at him in the murky night light, then leaned forward and kissed him. It was a short, rebellious kiss. When it was over, Rainbolt drew her back and they kissed together, kissed each other, for the first time mutually. During this third kiss he let go of her wrist and she was free to pull away, to go. But she did not.

They sat in silence for several minutes. Rainbolt finished the cheroot he had held throughout and tossed it out the window. Taking her hand, he held it to his lips without speaking.

"You're very gentle when you want to be," Francie said. Why in the name of God did he smell like *both* of them? She let him kiss each of her fingertips and the palm of her hand, not resisting, not *wanting* to resist. His lips felt so damned good, no matter where he put them. "I've got some real problems," she suddenly blurted out—for what reason she did not know; she certainly had no intention of talking about them.

"Not with me you don't," Rainbolt quietly pointed out.

Francie found herself feeling very warm, *too* warm—and too comfortable. "Listen, I have to go in now."

"All right." He gave her hand a final kiss. "Anytime you need someone . . ."

"Thanks." The word was not casual; it was as real as the gratitude she felt.

Francie got out of the car and hurried away. Rainbolt waited until she was past his sentry, safely in the house, before he started the car and headed downtown to the Ormsby House to find Chalky. He had a very important errand for his albino valet.

Tony Donovan had come back to the place where the devastating evening had begun: Denny's hospital room. His friend lay on his back, in the deep, unremitting sleep that the doctor had promised would last until the following morning. It was now near midnight and this was the only absolutely quiet place Tony could think of to get away from everyone.

After Buck had walked in on Francie and him in bed, Tony had been subjected to the most humiliating experience of his life: being dragged into the kitchen of the O'Crotty home and forcibly restrained there by Terence Henny and Lloyd Arlen. It had not been the reality of their combined strength overpowering his that mortified him so; it was the fact that he had been helpless to defend Francie against Buck's accusing manner, protect her from Buck's immediate assumption of authority over both of them. Buck had dealt with them as if they were still children, as if they were too immature to love, to desire, to *need*. Just as he did with everything else in his life, Buck O'Crotty had applied his own morals, his own standards and ethics, to a situation and summarily declared it wrong.

The son of a bitch, Tony thought, pacing the dimly lighted room, grinding one fist into the other palm. The son of a bitch! He was *not* going to get away with it—not this time!

In Tony's seething mind there was already expanding an angry desperate plan. It was actually the same plan he and Francie had talked about sporadically for years: running away together. Except now it had a headlong urgency attached to it, even more so than their aborted elopement on Christmas Eve. This time, Tony thought, overwrought, it was now or never. With Buck's interference no longer merely superficial, he and Francie had to make the break with their lives in Virginia City at once—or, he was certain, never have the chance again.

The first thing he needed was a car. He was still determined not to leave town in Francie's—a car bought and paid for by Big Jim Delavane. There was a car for sale down at

Callahan's: a '36 Chevy left on consignment with the saloon-keeper by a miner from the McKeith digs who had joined the navy. Callahan was to sell it for him and send the money to him, less ten percent commission. The previous week, Tony and Denny had inquired about the vehicle and been told its price was sixty-five dollars.

If he could get that car, Tony thought, and somehow get word to Francie that he had it, maybe Francie could get away from Lew Rainbolt's goons long enough for Tony to pick her up someplace and they could make a run for it. He shook his head in irony; it sounded as if they were criminals. Bonnie and Clyde all over again. But he realized he had to think that way, because there *would* be people after them: Buck, Big Jim, Rainbolt and his men, maybe even Sam Patch if Buck swore out a warrant for Tony as a runaway because he was still under twenty-one.

The only thing that disturbed Tony about running away was not being able to say good-bye to Denny. Standing at the side of the hospital bed, he put his hand very lightly on his friend's arm. Denny would understand, Tony was sure of that; with his crooked grin and nagging, sarcastic manner, he would probably never admit it—but he would under-stand. And Tony would write him after a time, when he and Francie were safely settled somewhere, legally married, so that no one could interfere with them.

"So long, Den," he whispered. "I'll be in touch soon."

As he slipped out of the hospital room, Tony realized that it had not occurred to him that Denny might not recover; he was simply assuming that he would. And with good reason. Denny was tough, all the way to the core; he had been ever since he learned to make a fist.

Hurrying through the night back to the town end of Miners Walk, Tony stayed in the shadows, and when he got to Callahan's crept to a side window and peered in to see if Buck was there. He wanted to avoid any further contact with his foster father if at all possible, wanted, in fact, to get out of Virginia City without even seeing him again. He was not surprised to find that Buck was not there; it was now well past midnight. Easing his way inside, Tony went to the end of the bar and bobbed his chin at Callahan. The saloonkeeper came over and Tony said, "I've decided to buy that Chevy you're holding. Can you give me the key tonight and I'll pay you the money after the bank opens Monday morning?"

"Sure, I'll do that for you, Tony," Callahan said, "if you'll give me your word you're not going to back out on me. Have we got us a done deal?"

"A done deal," Tony said, offering his hand. The two shook and Callahan cranked open the drawer of his old ornate cash register and handed Tony a key. "Thanks, Callahan," Tony said, and left the saloon.

Tony walked briskly around to the rear where the Chevy was parked. Getting into the car, he tried to start it. The engine ground and churned, but would not turn over. "Son of a bitch," Tony muttered, getting out and opening the hood. Unable to see anything, he returned to the front seat and found a flashlight in the glove box. Shining the beam around on the engine, he saw nothing obviously wrong. As he was searching, he heard a voice say, "Mr. Donovan, suh?"

Startled, Tony extinguished the flashlight and stepped quickly away from the car. He held his arms ready apprehensively.

"Who's there?" he asked sharply.

"It's Chalky, suh. Mr. Rainbolt's man. I has a message fur you from Mr. Rainbolt."

"What is it?"

"I'd like to come a little closer, suh, so I doesn't have to talk too loud. This here's personal."

"All right," said Tony, straightening a little, "come on."

Chalky stepped out of the shadows into a circle of fuzzy illumination thrown by a streetlight at the corner of the alley. His milky skin and white hair looked ghostly and unreal in the gray cast. When he was close enough, Tony saw that his pink irises looked like a rabbit's eyes. "That's close enough," Tony said. "What's the message?"

"Suh, Mr. Rainbolt say to tell you that Miss Francie Delavane done tol' him she don't want no more to do with you. He say he ain't been enforcing Mr. Delavane's order to keep you away from her 'cause she wanted to see you. But now that she say she *don't* want to see you no more, he say to let you know that he gonna be carrying out that order from now on. He say if you smart, suh, you stay away from Miss Delavane."

It was a lie, Tony thought. Francie was tricking them in some way. He nodded curtly. "Anything else?"

"No, suh. That's it."

"Okay, you told me." Tony waited a moment but the albino made no move to leave. "Well?" he said bluntly.

"You having some car trouble, suh?" Chalky asked with a smile.

"Maybe," Tony replied.

"I'm a first-class auto mechanic," Chalky told him. "I takes care of Mr. Rainbolt's car personal. Why, shoot, he won't let nobody 'cept me *touch* that roadster of his."

"That so?"

"God's truf'. I be glad to take a look at yours."

"Why?" Tony asked curiously.

"Why not?" Chalky countered with a shrug. "We ain't got nothin', agin' each other, you and me. Has we?"

Now Tony shrugged. "No, I guess not."

"Well then," Chalky said, walking up. "Turn your flashlight back on and le's see what the problem be."

After checking the cables, coils, and connections, and finding nothing wrong, Chalky had Tony get in the car and try to start it. He listened to the grinding and churning only a moment before waving for Tony to stop.

"Batt'ry's just low," he ruled. "Wait here; I'll give you a push to get it started."

A couple of minutes later, Tony was surprised to see the albino, smiling a smile as white as the rest of him, drive up in Lew Rainbolt's yellow roadster.

"Hey," Tony said, "you won't get in any Dutch for doing this, will you?"

"Naw," Chalky scoffed. "But I 'preciate you asking." He tilted his head an inch. "You know, you seems like a nice young man, Mr. Donovan. Mind a little free advice?"

"No, go ahead."

"You don't wants to mess with my Mr. Rainbolt, you know what I mean? Once he gets set on something, like he is on keeping you and Miss Delavane apart, why, he can be pretty mean if he gets any interference. *Real* mean, hear me? Broken-knee mean. Fractured-skull mean. That kind of thing. You be doing yourself a big favor to take that into consideration."

"Okay," Tony said, "I will. Thanks for the warning."

"Right. Now listen, after I push you and your engine gets to going, you drive it around for 'bout a quarter-hour to get that batt'ry charged up."

"I will. Thanks a lot, Chalky."

The albino grinned and winked, and a minute later Tony's old Chevy was being pushed down the alley by Lew Rainbolt's fancy yellow roadster.

Tony slept in the back seat of the car, huddled under an old lap robe he found in the trunk. He woke at dawn, stiff with cold, and drove to the edge of town to an all-night café where he got hot coffee and toast. Buck, he knew, would be up and out of the house as usual by seven o'clock, despite his beating the day before. Or perhaps because of it; he might, Tony decided, feel he had to make a show of still being in charge—of the men, the union, the strike—in spite of the setback caused by the robbery of their strike funds. It was Sunday, so he definitely would put in an appearance at Mass with Rosetta and Kerry at ten. Tony hung around the café until six-thirty, then drove back to Miners Walk and parked a few doors down from the O'Crotty house.

Buck left at ten of seven. As soon as his car turned the corner, Tony pulled up to the house and hurried inside. Kerry was at the kitchen table, still in her nightgown, eating oatmeal. When Tony came in, her ten-year-old face animated with excitement.

"Tony! Where have you been all night!" Blustering, her mouth full, oatmeal ran down her chin. "Mamma's been worried sick!"

"Wipe your chin," Tony said, walking past her. As he hurried down the hall to his and Denny's room, he heard Kerry yell, "Mamma, Tony's back!"

In the bedroom, Tony had begun piling his few extra clothes on his cot when Rosetta hurried in. Her fierce black eyes shone with worry. "Where have you been all night?" she said. "Mr. O'Crotty has been very concerned. What are you doing?"

"I'm leaving, Rosetta," he said. "I'm sorry, but I just can't live with Buck anymore. I bought a car and I'm going away." He almost added that he was taking Francie with him, but some instinct told him that would not be wise.

"Tony, you can't do this," Rosetta pleaded. "I know you and Buck have your differences, but this isn't the time. He's just been beaten and robbed; Denny's lying in the hospital in serious condition; there's no end in sight for the strike. Please, Tony, don't give him any more burden than he already has—"

"I'll bet he's running off with Francie Delavane!" Kerry said from the doorway.

Rosetta gave her a scathing look. "Get back to the table and finish your breakfast! Tony, please, listen to me—"

"My mind's made up, Rosetta." He made a bindle-pack out of two shirts and stuffed all his clothes into it, and got his savings passbook from a cigar box on the shelf. As Rosetta was pleading with him, they heard a siren begin to whine at the Virginia City firehouse several blocks away. Ignoring it, Rosetta said, "Tony, at least have some breakfast before you go." If she could get him to stay a few minutes, maybe she could change his mind.

In the kitchen she persuaded Tony to put down his pack and sit at the table with Kerry, who promptly stuck her tongue out at him.

"I'm gonna smack you," Tony warned.

"I'm going to do worse than that," Rosetta seconded, emphasizing with a threatening finger. She began to crack eggs at the stove. The firehouse siren was still sounding.

"I hope it's the schoolhouse," Kerry said spitefully. Rosetta reached over and with her fingertips slapped the girl's mouth. Just then the telephone rang in the living room.

"Get up here and watch these eggs, young lady," Rosetta told Kerry, and hurried to answer it.

As Kerry tended the stove, her brattiness dissolved and the anxiety she was trying to conceal came to the surface. Her eyes became teary. "Are you really going away, Tony?" she asked, sniffing.

"Yeah, I am," he said gruffly. Then he saw her eyes and suddenly felt very tender toward her. Going to the stove, he put his hands on her shoulders and kissed the top of her head. "But I'm going to write you," he assured her. She began to whimper anyway. "And, listen," he added quickly, "when you're older you can come visit me, wherever I am. How would you like that?"

"Can't I go with you now?" she asked urgently.

"No, honey—"

"You *are* taking Francie Delavane, aren't you? I knew it!"

"Kerry, listen—"

"Why do you have to take her?" Kerry wanted to know. "Why can't you take me instead? I could take care of you better than *she* could. Look, I can cook, I know how to make beds and do laundry—"

Rosetta hurried in to interrupt them. "That was Buck. There's a brush fire. It's burning down toward the Delavane mansion." As she spoke, the siren stopped. The worry in Rosetta's eyes increased. "Buck says that for some reason the fire engines haven't left the firehouse."

Tony's eyes widened in fear. *Francie!*

He bolted to the door, snatching his bundle of clothes as he went, Rosetta and Kerry rushing after him automatically with no real purpose in mind except an anxious desire to keep him in sight for as long as possible. As they watched him drive away, the four eggs Rosetta had been cooking for him scorched and began to burn.

Tony tried to drive up to the Hill, but his way was blocked. Sierra Street was congested with people spread all the way to the front of the Delavane property, watching the fire that raged behind it. They ignored the honking of Tony's horn. Finally, in frustration, he parked just off C Street and started making his way uphill on foot, trotting. Many of the men milling about were off-picket miners, some of them with wives and children.

As Tony neared the top, he saw with relief that the fire had not reached the mansion. The fire chief's red car, its emergency light flashing, was at the entrance to the Delavane driveway. The fire chief and Big Jim Delavane were arguing heatedly as the gathering crowd listened. Tony moved closer.

"—expect me to do what, Mr. Delavane?" the chief was pleading. "My trucks won't *start*. The carburetors is all clogged. Something's been poured in the gas tanks. Sugar, most likely."

"I'll have your goddamned job for this!" Big Jim roared. "And if my house burns, I'll see that you go to jail for criminal negligence!"

Two firemen, their faces and uniforms partially blackened from smoke, came hurrying from the woods off to one side of the mansion and rushed up to the chief. "Coal oil," one of them panted, out of breath. "Smell it clear as day back there."

"The fire was *set*?" Big Jim asked incredulously.

"How fast is it moving?" the chief asked his men, ignoring Delavane. How the fire started was the last thing that concerned him at the moment.

"Slow but steady," the fireman replied. "The piñon and

juniper still got some sap in them, but there's lots of mesquite that's blowed down from up high and it's dry as dust."

"Winds are whipping it pretty smart too," the other fireman said. "It's gonna horseshoe on all three sides."

Big Jim grabbed the chief's arm. "Was this fire deliberately set?" he demanded to know.

"It appears that way, Mr. Delavane," the chief replied
impatiently, "but if I was you I wouldn't worry about that
right now—"

"The bastards," Big Jim muttered, eyes locking coldly on
some miners gathered nearby.

"—I'd be worried about how to stop it," the chief
continued.

Francie, who was standing nearby with Lew Rainbolt,
pushed her way up to them. "What should we do, Chief?"
she asked, without looking at her father. "I don't want my
mother's house to burn."

"Only one thing to do—dig a firebreak." The chief's eyes
scanned the extensive perimeter of the Delavane property.
"Gonna take a lot of help, though. My firemen can't do it
alone."

"All of my men are at your disposal, Chief," Lew Rainbolt
said. He whistled at a nearby sentry. "Get down to the hotel
and send the entire force up here," he ordered. "Have them
bring every shovel and pick they can find!"

"Still gonna need more help," the chief said. "We'll have
to dig a break two-fifty or three hundred yards long."

Big Jim Delavane turned to face the gathered crowd.
"You men from town, listen to me! I'll pay ten dollars to
every man who gets a shovel and helps dig a firebreak! You
all know me; I'm good for my word! Ten dollars!"

It was, in the strike-poor town, an enticing sum. A number of merchants and clerks rushed off to get shovels. Not a
miner moved. Francie saw Tony, stared at him momentarily, then turned to hurry back toward the house with her
father and Rainbolt.

Tony watched her go, the words she had spoken a moment earlier reverberating in his head. *"I don't want my
mother's house to burn."*

He remembered Christmas Eve when she had seen the
bricks crashing through the mansion windows. *"Those are
my mother's windows . . ."*

Staring at the retreating figure of Jim Delavane, Tony

knew that if it was just the mine owner, just Delavane's house, it could burn to ashes and he would not lift a finger to help. But this was Francie's house too, and Francie's mother's house. He had to help Francie, for himself. And Edith Delavane, for Buck.

Pushing forward, Tony started toward the mansion, but Lloyd Arlen and several miners blocked his way.

"You wouldn't be thinking of giving them a hand, would you, Donovan?" the union vice president asked. "We're still on strike, remember?"

"Get out of my way, Arlen." Tony tried to push through but felt his arms being grabbed. The miners tightened around him, capturing him with their bodies. "You bastard, Arlen!" he cursed.

"Keep a hold on him, men," Arlen said. His lips curled in a sneer at the struggling Tony. "We don't want him embarrassing the union by running to help his rich girlfriend."

The fire chief and his men went to work. When the rest of Rainbolt's force arrived, they also began digging. Cavendish and the other members of the Delavane domestic staff did likewise. Big Jim rolled up his sleeves and picked up a shovel for the first time in two decades. Even Francie fell into line, beside Lew Rainbolt, and used a hatchet to break ground. Tony, seeing Rainbolt working shoulder to shoulder with Francie, struggled with all his strength but was unable to extricate himself from the press of the circle of miners that held him.

"What d' you think?" one of the miners asked Lloyd Arlen. The union officer surveyed the extensive property line; only about one-third was being dug. He glanced at the slowly approaching smoke in the woods beyond. Finally he shook his head.

"They'll never make it without more help." Arlen's eyes flicked to the incline of Sierra Street, up which a number of townsmen were now returning, tools in hand. "You know what to do, men," he said to the assembled miners at large.

As the townsmen hurried up to the Delavane driveway, miners fanned out in a human wall to bar their way. The townsmen slowed, tentatively stopped, muttered and grumbled, but having no leader did not proceed. Lloyd Arlen moved to the center of the line and addressed several of those nearest him.

"You men don't want no part of this," he rationalized.

"You want to stay neutral, not take sides against the miners' union. Think of the business we give you when we ain't on strike."

"The man's paying ten dollars!" one of the townsmen argued.

"Ten dollars won't pay for a busted skull," Arlen said pointedly.

The townsmen milled about like edgy cattle, griping malcontentedly as their ten dollars slipped away, but none of them moving to challenge the tough, scowling miners.

"Don't listen to Arlen, men!" Tony suddenly shouted. "This has got nothing to do with the union or the strike! That was Edith Delavane's home! She was always there to help anybody who needed help! Don't let her home burn because of this bastard!"

The townsmen continued to mill about and mutter—but none of them tried to get past the miners. Lloyd Arlen grinned maliciously at Tony.

Behind all of them—the townsmen, the line of miners, the mixed group frantically digging the firebreak—relentlessly came the fire. Interspersed in the roiling gray smoke now could be seen spurts and darts of live flame as a tall tree burned in its high branches. And there could be felt by all the gentle brush of a breeze that told them the creeping fire was being breathed along by the wind. In minutes the rolls of smoke had reached the edge of the large clearing on three sides of the mansion, and yellow flames began licking at the dry grass that the fire found there.

"Shouldn't we use water?" Big Jim, face sheeted with sweat, paused to gasp to the fire chief.

"Be like spitting in a hot skillet," the chief panted in reply. "Nothing's going to do it but a firebreak!"

"I don't think we'll make it in time!" Big Jim yelled.

"I don't either!" the chief agreed. "But we've got to try! Listen up, everybody! Keep it shallow! Six inches! Try to cover more ground!"

But even as they dug, all of them could see that it was no use. The fire moved in a steady, wiggling line like a long, writhing snake crawling sideways. It inched closer and closer to the people digging.

As the miners, and the townsmen behind them, watched the threatening inferno in morbid fascination, they all heard at once a rough, authoritative voice command, "One side!

Out of my way!" Heads turned in unison to see Buck
O'Crotty muscling his way through the crowd, battered and
bruised face fixed in a glowering scowl. "Move aside!" he
ordered, and everybody did.

When Buck got to the center of the crowd, to the point
where the wall of miners still loosely held back the unorga-
nized townsmen, not a word was spoken. The union leader,
seeing the desperate digging being done on the Delavane
property, looked at the townsmen with disdain, at his miners with disgust, and snatched a shovel from the hand of the
nearest man. Pushing angrily through the line, he started
across the expansive lawn.

"Buck!" Tony yelled.

Buck paused and looked back. He saw Tony's plight at
once. "Turn him loose!" he ordered.

The men around Tony relaxed and gave way. Tony roughly
pushed his way through them and, as Buck had done,
snatched a shovel from a townsman. Hurrying over, he
joined Buck. Together they stalked forward. They fell in to
work beside Big Jim Delavane. The mine owner missed two
beats, staring at them in surprise, then quickly resumed
digging.

Back at the entry to the drive, another miner followed
Tony's example, and another after him. Then a townsman
stepped forward to join in. Presently, like the flow through
an ever-widening hole in a dam, a gush of men with shovels,
picks, axes, and hoes surged across the driveway and spread
out like locusts along the three endangered property lines.
There was a man and a tool for every three feet of ground.
Beginning to dig, they quickly gouged a formidable trench
in the face of the fire, a furrow two feet deep and equally as
wide, the displaced dirt from it thrown forward onto and
into the encroaching flames.

When the cut was finished, the workers backed away
from it toward the big mansion, waiting to see if it would do
its job. For the most part, it did—halting the creeping blaze
on the outer edge of the break. In the few places where the
fire jumped the gap, men hurried forward to beat it out with
the backs of shovel scoops. The ground still smoldered, the
burned woods still smoked, but as a fire, as a threat, it was
over.

As the last sputter of it was snuffed out, as Cavendish
helped Francie Delavane back to the house, a great sponta-

neous cheer arose from the melange of men: miner, strike-breaker, townsman, servant; their voices melded as one, the hail praising them all. The laughter that followed quickly subdued as Big Jim Delavane walked over to Lew Rainbolt.

"I'm terminating your employment, Mr. Rainbolt," Big Jim said. "I appreciate the help you and your men gave me today, and I'll see that you're paid for the full contract, including bonuses."

"Fair enough," Rainbolt said. A slight smile came to his lips; this was not the first time an employer had gone soft on him for one reason or another.

Big Jim turned to Buck. "You and your negotiators come to my office at two this afternoon, Buck. I'll sign your new union contract giving you everything you asked for. This strike is over."

Another cheer filled the air. Rainbolt, walking toward the mansion for his car, said to one of his lieutenants, "Let's get the entire force out of town while everyone's still so happy. Pack up and head for San Francisco. Take a week off, then contact me at the Fairmont Hotel."

When Rainbolt walked around to the side of the mansion where his roadster was parked, Francie came out onto the terrace, her hands around a glass of iced tea Cavendish had prepared for her. "Did Daddy fire you?" she asked.

"You know your father very well," he said by way of confirmation.

"Where do you go now?"

"Who knows? The grape pickers in the Imperial Valley have been a little restless lately; maybe we'll head down there." He turned on a garden faucet and washed his hands and face, drying them on a handkerchief. "Ever been to the Imperial Valley?"

Francie shook her head. "No."

"Terrible place. Hot as hell. Windy. Sandy. Nothing to do at night but eat, drink, and sit around an air-cooled hotel room in your underwear. It's a good place," he pointed out, "to go when you want to leave all your troubles behind."

"Is it really possible to leave your troubles behind?" Francie asked. There was an almost weary plea in her voice.

"Absolutely," Lew Rainbolt assured her confidently. "I do it every time I leave a town."

He reached into the roadster's glove box for a cheroot and lighted it. Francie thought of the previous night when she and Lew Rainbolt had sat in his car and kissed. She thought of her father and how much at that moment she still wanted to hurt him. She thought of Tony Donovan and the temptation of a love, now forbidden, that she knew would nevertheless not go away. The Imperial Valley, where all one had to think about was eating, drinking, and keeping cool in one's underwear, sounded like paradise.

Rainbolt came up to the edge of the terrace. "Want to try it?" he asked quietly.

Francie stared at him for a long thoughtful moment. Then she said, "Why not?"

Rainbolt took the glass from her hands, set it aside, and helped her down. She got into the roadster on the driver's side and slid across the leather seat, her skirt raising high on one thigh as she did. When Rainbolt got in, he put his hand on her knee.

"We'll go to San Francisco for a week first," he said.

"Whatever you want," Francie replied.

"I like that."

Rainbolt started the roadster and drove away.

Tony Donovan came around the corner of the mansion just in time to see them leave.

TWENTY-EIGHT

Denny Ebro was sitting up in his hospital bed a month after the beating when the telephone rang next to his bed. It was Tony.

"Where the hell are you?" Denny asked irritably. "I nearly died and you wasn't even here."

"You didn't nearly die, you phony," Tony chided. "I've been calling the hospital every three days to check. You weren't even close to dying."

"Where the hell are you?" Denny asked again, ignoring the fact that he had been caught in a lie.

"Just outside Reno," Tony told him. "I've got a rented shack."

"Oh, yeah? Where you working at?"

"I'm in business for myself. Want to go in with me?"

"What kind of business?" Denny asked skeptically.

"I'll show you when you get here."

Denny grunted more skepticism. "I've got a feeling it's something Buck wouldn't like."

"Buck's not running my life anymore," Tony said sternly.

"Yeah well, Rosetta's been worried sick about you," Denny charged. "You ought to have more concern for her feelings."

"I know, I know. I'm sorry. I just couldn't tell Rosetta where I was without Buck finding out too. Tell her I'm okay, will you?"

"Sure. But if I come up there with you, I'm gonna tell her where I'm going. I'm not gonna worry her like you did."

Denny left the hospital a day earlier than scheduled, leaving a letter for Rosetta and Buck explaining that he was joining Tony in Reno so that he could "look after him and keep him out of trouble." He promised to call or write to them very soon.

Tony picked him up in the old Chevy he had bought to run away with Francie. On the way to Reno, Denny brought him up to date on what had happened since Tony left. "Strike's over, I'm sure you know. Delavane Mines is open again; two shifts going. Big Jim gave Buck everything the union wanted—wage increases, new ventilation system, new drainage system—the whole deal. There's a rumor that Big Jim is personally paying for all the improvements, that it was the only way he could get the new contract approved by the investors. There's also a rumor that he's hitting the bottle pretty hard since Francie ran away with that bastard Rainbolt." He looked curiously at Tony. "How'd you take that?" he wanted to know.

Tony put a tight check on himself. "It hasn't bothered me that much." He had never told a bigger lie. From the moment he saw Rainbolt and Francie driving away, he felt like a fire had been lighted inside him. Whenever he thought of her, he wanted to lash out with his fists. Not at Francie, but at others: at Big Jim for hiring Rainbolt, at Rainbolt for taking her away, at Buck for driving her to it. Mixed in with his seething anger, he ached for her persistently every day, constantly at night when he tried to sleep.

But he could not admit any of that to Denny; it was too painful to admit. He could only say, "It hasn't bothered me that much."

"Well, I'm glad of that," Denny remarked. "She's never been nothing but a problem for us."

The shack that Tony rented, for five dollars a month, was just that: a shack. It was much like the one Tony remembered living in the last year his parents and sisters had been alive: two rooms of frame board with a corrugated tin roof that had long since turned to rust. There was a potbellied wood-burning stove for both heating and cooking, a sink with a hand pump, and an outhouse in back. Tony had bought two cots, a wooden table, two straight chairs, a large iron skillet, two tin plates, two tin cups, and some utensils. That was it.

"I'm used to a little better than this," Denny sniffed when he saw the place. Then he noticed a wooden tub half filled with a watery paste, and two sluice pans lying next to it. "So you're high-grading," he said.

High-grading was the practice of underground miners picking up and pocketing chunks of ore that looked to be rich in gold or silver. It was done by men who over the years had become poignantly aware of the great imbalance that existed between their wages and their contributed effort and assumed risk. It was an imbalance that even unionizing could not correct, an imbalance that bred steadily growing resentment. If a man could smuggle a potato-size piece of ore out of the mine and sell it to an assayer for fifty cents, it somehow seemed to alleviate the inequity of the miner's lot.

When Denny saw the homemade ore-processing apparatus, he at once assumed that Tony was not only high-grading but processing the ore himself.

"You're close," Tony said. "I couldn't be high-grading because I don't have a job. But I *am* processing filched ore. I'm getting it at night from Delavane's spoil-rock pit."

"Jesus," Denny said. "You could be taking a hell of a lot of risk for nothing. And doing a hell of a lot of work."

"I knew that when I started," Tony said. "It's a chance I'm willing to take."

The spoil-rock pit was a ground-level hole into which was dumped the spoil rock, or waste: diggings considered too barren of silver to be commercially profitable. When the pit was full, the diggings were sold to the operator of a non-precious metal smelter that extracted the lead, copper, and zinc from the ore, letting what little silver there was, usually only traces, wash away. The trace silver might be high or low in purity; even if it was high, however, its value would never cover the overhead of processing it commercially.

"I've been driving up every night," Tony said, "sneaking into the pit after the second shift closes down, and hauling away as much as I can carry. I'm doing all the processing myself; I buy the little bit of mercury I need from a guy who works at Washoe Smelter." Tony's eyes become intense. "It'll take a long time to collect enough to sell and when I do get enough it might be so impure that I won't get much for it. But—it *could* be very pure too, in which case I'll get a good price. If I do, if I get a good stake, I'm going to take a shot at Harold's Club. I'm going to see if I can win a big bankroll."

"To do what?" Denny wanted to know.

"I'm not sure," Tony shrugged. "Maybe go up in the mountains and buy into old man Axhalt's place, become a timber baron. Maybe open a bar like Callahan's got. I don't know. All I do know is I want something better than the mines—and I intend to get it."

"What do you plan to live on while you're stockpiling this fortune in silver?" Denny asked.

"Money I had saved to elope with Francie. I figure there's enough to carry us through the winter. If you don't eat too much, that is."

"I ain't said I was in yet," Denny pointed out. "I just come from six weeks in the hospital. I ain't anxious to go back in with my ass full of buckshot from Delavane's night watchman."

"I've got the watchman's routine down solid," Tony assured. "I've been in the pit six times already. Look." He knelt, pulled up a floorboard, and drew out a suede pouch. Hefting it, he said, "Nearly four ounces already. By myself The two of us can do twice that, maybe more. Come on, Den, what d'you say?"

Denny pursed his twisted lips in thought for a moment, and finally said, "Okay, but I have to do all the cooking. You're not worth shit in the kitchen."

That night, Tony took Denny on their first trip to pilfer ore together. They left the shack outside Reno at midnight and drove to Virginia City. By two A.M. they were lying on their bellies outside the mesh fence that enclosed the Delavane Mine main digs. Just inside the fence was the spoil-rock pit.

"I've got a hole dug under the fence right next to that post," Tony whispered. "When I leave, I fill it with loose dirt and leaves. All we have to do to get in is scoop it out."

The hole was just long enough and deep enough for them to lie on their backs and snake under the fence. Each had a burlap bag tied around his waist. Once under, they crept to the pit, slid quietly into it, and began to feel around in the dark for the larger chunks of ore. Tony was acutely aware of the night watchman's schedule; they had thirty-five minutes to get in, get ore, and get out. They filled the burlap bags only until the bags were as thick as their own bodies, to facilitate dragging them back under the fence. Even so, they were almost too heavy to carry, the unprocessed diggings being solid—clay and rock—filled dead weight. To avoid suspicion, they had to park the car at least half a mile away. The trek back to it, in the dark, carrying the ponderous bags, was usually the worst part of the night. That and the always present fear of being shot with the night watchman's scatter gun.

In the shack, during the day, they processed the pilfered ore. By hand, because they had no tools, they crushed and pressed the fist-size chunks of ore in the wooden washtub partly filled with water. When they had the ore mashed into a watery paste, they added small quantities of the mercury that Tony purchased from the Washoe Smelter workman. With sluice pans—ordinary pie tins with the bottoms cut out and replaced by small-mesh wire—they agitated the mixture until bits of silver paste attached itself to the mercury globules. The watery paste was then strained through broadcloth of some kind—in their case an old shirt—causing the globules to adhere to the fabric. The broadcloth was subsequently folded and gently pressed with the palm, squeezing the mercury into liquid and filtering it, too, through the cloth. There was then left only a thick, pasty residue: silver that could be heated and cast into bars or other shapes.

"Pretty, isn't it?" Tony asked as he carefully scraped the amalgam off the shirt into a collection pan.

"I'll think it's pretty when I find out how much it's worth," Denny said.

"Look at it this way," Tony rationalized, "we're going to

be taking the spoil rock over a long period of time, right? Even if we get some impure silver part of the time, we're bound to also get some pure stuff too. I figure the worst that can happen is we end up with fifty-fifty."

"I hope you're right," Denny said. "I'd hate to work all goddamned winter for nothing."

"We won't. Anyway, winter will go by before we know it."

That was wishful thinking. The only thing winter did differently that year was come early. The two young men woke up one morning to find that the temperature had plummeted. The shack was freezing cold. They found out within hours that the potbellied stove only heated a radius of about three feet. Many cracks in the frame walls readily accommodated the thin, chilling wind. And there was ice on the boards of the outhouse.

"I think I should have stayed with Buck," Denny grumbled.

The winter was long, bitter, and miserable. Trips to the spoil-rock pit became tests of endurance. The ground froze; a new crawl hole had to be dug every time they breached the fence. The ore itself froze; pieces had to be pried from the pile. The frozen digs were heavier; they were able to carry back less each trip. The first stage of the processing was torture; it took three times as long to mash the ore into paste, and doing it turned their hands raw and stripped their knuckles of top skin. During the short, gray sunless days they had to work by lantern light because the shack had no electricity. The water pump froze at least once a week and had to be primed with heated rocks.

The two young men themselves soon became as stark and haggard as their environment. To save money they cut each other's hair with a pocketknife, with disastrous results. A steady diet of greasy fried foods, unsupplemented by green vegetables or fruit, kept them intermittently constipated and diarrhetic. Their eyes became hollow from lack of comfortable sleep, their joints chronically ached from the cold, their lips were constantly chapped and split. Sometimes an entire day would go by without them speaking: they passed like zombies, grimly going from the tub where they agonizingly crushed the ore to paste, to the stove to thaw out their throbbing, bluish hands. The one thing that kept them going, and on which they refused to skimp, was coffee: they drank quarts of it, black, strong, and steaming, every day. It kept them awake, kept them warm, kept them lucid.

For Tony, there was the additional stimulation of his thoughts of Francie. Beyond what he had told Denny of his scheme to use their bankroll to buy timber interests or a bar, Tony had private plans. Nightly in his dreadful existence he plotted the finding of Lew Rainbolt and the taking of Francie. He had convinced himself that she had gone with Rainbolt out of desperation, been driven to it by the conclusion that he and she would never be permitted—by her father, by Buck, by their class difference—to ever have the kind of life together that they desired. She had, Tony was certain, grabbed at the easiest way out of her dilemma and the environment that had produced it. Rainbolt was an escape, nothing more.

Before he went after Francie, however, Tony was determined to become something in life. He would never again offer himself to her with a shovel over his shoulder. The next time they met, he would *be* somebody. To that end, through everything, he watched their stockpile of silver increase: four ounces, eight ounces, ten, twenty . . .

But he could not look at it without wondering tensely: How much was it going to be worth?

The day before Christmas, they had a visitor. There was a knock on the door and when Tony answered it he found Buck O'Crotty standing there.

"I've been sent by Rosetta," Buck said, "and Kerry, to invite the two of you to turkey dinner tomorrow. It's not my idea, mind; it's theirs. Both of them have been whining around for a month about you two being all alone on Christmas. How about it?"

"Hiya, Buck!" said Denny, coming up behind Tony. "Sounds good to me."

"How'd you know where to find us?" Tony asked curiously. Buck bobbed his chin at the old Chevy, parked outside.

"Callahan recognized the car on his way to Reno one day. He mentioned it to me and I didn't have the presence of mind to keep it to myself. I've not had a peaceful evening since I told Rosetta and Kerry I knew where you were. But it's Christmas"—he waved a hand peremptorily—"so let's let bygones be. You'll come down, then?"

"You bet!" Denny said eagerly. "Hope it's a big turkey."

"Big enough." Buck squinted curiously at them. "I have to tell you the two of you look like hell. Are you working?"

Denny glanced away; Tony said, "We're working, sure. Kind of."

"Kind of?" Buck's eyebrows went up. "I've heard of lots of jobs, but never a 'kind of' job." Denny's discomfort was too obvious not to notice. "Mind if I come in?"

"I don't think you'd better," Tony said.

"*I* think I'd better," Buck declared. With the palm of one hand, he pushed the door back. Tony did not try to stop him. The first thing Buck saw when he stepped inside was the processing apparatus. "I'll be damned," he whispered.

"It ain't what you think, Buck," Denny defended at once. "We ain't high-grading. It's spoil rock."

Buck turned on him. "Spoil rock? From where?" Denny looked down and did not answer. Buck's eyes flicked to Tony. "From Delavane's? Answer me!"

"Yeah," Tony admitted.

"So," Buck said, hands going to hips, "it's a thief I've raised. Not a decent workingman, not a respectable citizen, but a thief who steals in the night from a man who once employed him. And," he pointed to Denny, "makes a thief out of his best friend, as well."

"For Christ's sake, it's only spoil rock," Tony argued.

"It ain't *your* spoil rock, it's Delavane's!" Buck roared. "That makes it theft when you take it!" The bandy-legged union leader paced the little room in overwhelming frustration. "A town that was full of bad and bitter memories," he accused, "I came back to—for you. A woman I barely knew, I married—for you. A little girl that isn't mine, I'm raising—for you. A career at the side of this county's greatest labor leader, John L. Lewis, I gave up—for you. I've done it all for you—and this is how you choose to repay me?"

"Wait a minute, Buck," Tony challenged. "Has it really been all for me? Just me? Or was there some other reason too? I'm not a kid anymore, Buck. I don't believe you came back out of the goodness of your heart just to save a poor orphan. I've always thought it went deeper than that, always thought there was part of it I didn't know, part of it you didn't tell me. What's the big secret, Buck? What have you been keeping from me all these years?"

Buck O'Crotty stared at him as if thunderstruck. It's a

bluff, he told himself at once. He couldn't know. But he was getting close.

"Believe what you like," Buck retorted cautiously. Seeking to change the subject, he bobbed his chin at their makeshift processing works and the two burlap bags next to the tub. "The two of you will probably be wealthy men in forty or fifty years," he said scornfully. Tony came right back at him.

"We don't expect to get rich off the silver, Buck," he said, coldly and deliberately. "We're only going to use that as a stake. To try and hit it big in the casinos."

"So that's it!" Buck stormed with new rage. "Doing it like the sharpies and slickers do! Trying to make it at the gambling tables! Going for the quick silver!"

"That's right!" Tony snapped. "Why shouldn't we? Do you think we'd ever make it in the mines?" Cruelly, he added, "You didn't."

"You're a young fool," Buck said, shaking his head reprehensively. "You're both young fools. I ought to turn you over to the law and see you go to jail. But I won't. Going to jail would be too easy on you. I'm going to let you go right ahead with what you're doing; you'll both see what it gets you."

Buck started to leave. At the door he paused and turned back to Denny.

"You don't have to stay with him, you know. You can come back home with me."

Denny shifted his eyes, looking down at the floor. "I guess I'll stay," he mumbled, barely audibly.

"Suit yourself."

Buck walked out, slamming the door.

TWENTY-NINE

When spring arrived, Tony decided they might have enough silver to provide a stake that would give them a reasonable chance at the Harold's Club tables. It would depend on that one unknown factor over which they had no control: how pure was the silver? Cleaning up and making themselves as presentable as possible, they drove into town and took their pouch of silver to an assayer who was also a silver broker. A glance at their hands told the assayer that the young miners had processed the silver themselves. It could, the man knew, be high-graded ore, pilfering from a spoil-rock pit, quick silver stripped from a surface dig, or an entire winter of scraping skim ore from one of the mines that closed down when a rich ore vein played out. The assayer, although not legally obligated to determine the source of any precious metal he purchased, decided that it was probably the latter: skim ore.

"Looks like you gentlemen might have good skimmings here," he commented as he carefully scooped an ounce from the bag. Standing in front of his assay table, Tony and Denny exchanged glances but made no comment. Both knew what he thought; they let him go on thinking it. Their eyes followed every move as he spread the silver on a glass plate and with a flat wooden stick pulverized it enough to pass it through a one-hundred-mesh sieve. Over a Bunsen burner he then heated the sample until the ore was decomposed, after which he added lead oxide. In a clay crucible he added soda ash and increased the heat until fluid was produced. The fluid was poured into a conical iron mold where it immediately began to set. As soon as the mass had solidified, the cubical shaped button of lead and silver that resulted was tapped out and its slag scraped off; the button

387

was put into a small porous vessel called a cupel. Over low heat the lead monoxide was melted off leaving a bead of silver. The assayer put the bead onto a finely calibrated, very delicate scale and weighed it. Tony and Denny knew at once by the surprised expression on the man's face that the news was favorable.

"Very good," he said. "Very good indeed. On a fineness scale of one thousand, what you've got here, gentlemen, is about nine hundred fifty. Do you want to sell it outright or leave it on consignment at a fee for me to take bids?"

"Outright," Tony said, "if the price is right."

"Oh, it will be," the assayer assured them. "I wouldn't risk losing stuff this good over a few dollars. Let me just weigh the rest of it in bulk—"

Tony put his hands in his pockets to keep them from shaking. Denny, he noticed, looked as calm as could be, thumbs hooked in his suspenders, watching the assayer like a hawk lest he spill a grain. Finally the involved procedure was over and the assayer made a few figures on a pad, punched some keys on an adding machine, pulled the handle several times, and smiled.

"Twelve hundred thirty dollars," he said.

Tony and Denny were astounded. For two young men who had last earned forty-five cents an hour in the mines, it was an enormous sum. Even with the new Fair Labor Standards Act in force, requiring employers to pay time and a half for all work over forty hours, Tony and Denny earned only twenty-three dollars in wages for a grueling forty-eight hours underground. In more than four years of conscientious and dedicated saving for his and Francie's future, Tony had been able to save less than three hundred dollars. Now, with little more than a single winter's work, his share was twice that. It would have been a wonderful moment, except that his astonishment was tainted by the memory of Buck O'Crotty's words: *It's not your spoil rock, it's Delavane's!*

We're thieves, just like Buck said, Tony allowed himself to realize for the first time. This is stolen money.

After looking at the disturbed expression on Tony's face, Denny found the presence of mind to say, "We'll take it," to the assayer's offer. "Make it cash."

Five minutes later, they left the office with six hundred fifteen dollars each in their pockets. The sight and feel of the money worked to somewhat assuage Tony's conscience. Despite Buck's words and his own guilt, Tony realized that the deed was done; they couldn't put the silver back. After they ran their bankroll into some *real* money, maybe he could figure out a way, perhaps through Buck, to pay Delavane Mines the fair amount it would have received for the spoil rock they took if it had gone to the non-precious metals smelter. That would be about ten percent of what the silver brought them. Jesus, Tony thought, if spoil rock produced that much good silver all the time, it would be worth a man's while to *buy* it and process it himself. But Tony knew it did not; usually, the lead, copper, and zinc, which were easier to smelt, exceeded in combined value the worth of the silver. He and Denny had been very lucky to chance consistently on ore as rich as they did.

"What now?" Denny asked when they got outside.

"A hotel room," Tony decided. "A hot bath. A haircut. New clothes. And the two biggest steaks we can find in Reno!"

Denny grinned. "Now you're talking!"

That evening, as the two young miners finished their steaks—Denny having ordered, and eaten, two of them—they were also finishing their second glass of wine, which had made them lightheaded and decidedly cheerful. They were in Delmonico's, the best restaurant in Reno. Each was wearing a new double-breasted suit, Arrow shirt, ready-made bow tie, wingtip shoes, and new underwear and socks. They had been barbered, shampooed, and half manicured—the manicurist having given up in defeat after only managing to get their abused hands and chewed nails clean; there was no way she could file them.

"What time do you have?" Tony asked with a grin as he drank the last of his wine. Denny pulled back a cuff to look at the watch on his wrist.

"Half past six." He finished his own wine. "What time do *you* have?" he asked back, with the same sly grin, which on him looked idiotic.

"I have half past six too," Tony said.

The wristwatches were new: Helbros brand, they had cost twenty-five dollars each. They were the first watches either of them had ever owned; both felt markedly mature wearing them. They asked each other the time every few minutes.

At a table across from them sat an older man in the company of a bosomy younger woman with chestnut hair falling past her shoulders. She and Tony were facing each other across the space between the tables. Every so often their eyes met and she smiled slightly. Tony smiled back, wondering if the man with her was her father. They made him think of Big Jim Delavane and Francie.

Denny glanced over his shoulder to see what was occupying Tony's attention. When he saw the young woman, he said, "Don't you think we ought to get going?"

"Sure," said Tony.

They paid the check, exchanging surprised glances at the amount of it, then walked over to Harold's Club, complaining along the way about the high price of eating out in Reno. Reaching the dazzling casino, they loitered on the sidelines, as they had done the Christmas they helped Lew Axhalt deliver trees, watching the play at the various games.

"Don't look all that easy, does it?" Denny said skeptically.

"Can't be all that hard either," Tony reasoned, "with so many people playing."

They watched a craps table for a while, without being able to figure out how the game worked. Sometimes a player won when he rolled a seven, sometimes he lost. It seemed very complicated. They moved to a Twenty-one table.

"I think they add up the cards to see how close they can get to twenty-one points," Tony said. "Face cards are worth ten, looks like."

"That can't be right," Denny said. "A guy just won with a face card and an ace; that only makes eleven."

Finally they discovered the roulette wheel. It looked remarkably simple: select a color, red or black; a number; or both. The interesting thing they noticed at once was that players, when they won, seemed to win more than at other games.

"Looks pretty easy," Tony said. "What d'you think?"

"Sure," said Denny. "I got a few lucky numbers to try."

Nervously, wetting their lips, they sat down at the table and pulled out a hundred dollars each. The money was gone in an instant, replaced by a stack of ten-dollar chips in front of each of them. Smiling tentatively at each other, they began to play.

They placed their bets in the worst possible fashion: selecting single numbers where the odds were thirty-seven to one against them. The numbers were chosen out of their heads, at random; their birthdays and ages, shoe sizes, the number of letters in their names, what time it was when they glanced at their new wristwatches: seven forty-five called for bets on seven, four, and five. Neither of them knew enough to increase their chances of winning by decreasing the odds with bets on six numbers at five to one, four numbers at eight to one, three at eleven to one, or even two at seventeen to one. Neither knew to reduce their losses each spin with even-money bets on red or black, high or low, even or odd. As an example of their foolish play, Tony locked onto number twenty on each spin; twenty was the number of letters in Frances Grace Delavane's name, and because he knew deep down that she was the inspiration behind his ambition to succeed, to be somebody, he did not see how the number could lose. It did, consistently. The single-number bets chewed into their bankroll like a voracious shark.

After an hour, Tony began to see what they were doing wrong. Watching others place bets on blocks of numbers from a dozen down to two, he began to decrease his single-number bets and follow suit. His losses started to lessen. From time to time he won, fifty dollars or eighty, but because it was a zero and double-zero wheel, and because the house collected all bets when one of those numbers was hit, the house advantage of five and one-quarter percent relentlessly worked at taking his money. It did not help that Denny refused his advice and insisted on continuing to play the single numbers.

"Just leave me alone, okay," Denny said, shunning Tony's coaching, "I'm gonna hit any minute now. Just one win will be three hundred and fifty bucks."

They had begun play at seven-thirty with a little more than a thousand dollars. By nine o'clock that amount had been reduced by half. Tony began to worry seriously. At a craps table across the casino he saw the chestnut-haired woman from the restaurant, with one arm around the man who, Tony decided, was obviously not her father. The man was drinking and shooting dice. The woman's glance and Tony's met briefly and she held up her glass to him. He nodded, wondering if their luck was any better than his and Denny's.

Tenaciously, the two young men kept playing. Denny finally came around, after losing thirty consecutive single-number ten-dollar bets, and began playing as Tony played, in combinations of numbers. Even so, by ten o'clock Tony had the ill feeling that it was too late, that there was no way they were going to beat this capricious, colorful wheel with its contra-rotating little ivory ball. He had a desperate desire to back away from the table with whatever money they still had and at least salvage that much. He was about to suggest it to Denny when, as if reading his thoughts, the wheel paid Denny one hundred seventy dollars on a seven-eight double-number bet.

" 'Bout time," Denny muttered. He tossed a crooked grin at Tony. "I think our luck might've just changed."

It had not, but another hour passed before they were convinced. Shortly after eleven o'clock, they were down to less than a hundred dollars between them. That was when Denny became visibly nervous for the first time. "Jesus, what should we do, Tony?" he asked in a quick whisper. Seeing Denny losing his composure somehow helped Tony regain his own. He put a calming hand on Denny's arm.

"Relax." Tony gave him four ten-dollar chips. "Pick four single numbers," he said. Maybe after all the betting Denny had done on single numbers, it was time for him to win. Tony himself played the last five of their chips, spreading them out on red and on predominantly red four-number bets at the upper and lower ends of the table.

The wheels were spun. Chips continued to be placed until the ivory ball slowed and the croupier said, "No more bets."

Tony and Denny waited tensely for the ball to fall into a compartment. When it did, Tony stood at once and walked away from the table. After several seconds, Denny followed him. All of their bets had lost.

At midnight they were sitting on the curb of a side street a block from the casino, too physically and emotionally wasted to even walk back to the hotel room they had already paid for. Between them they now had seven dollars and some change.

"I can't believe it," Denny said incredulously. "I can't believe we lost that much."

Tony did not respond, merely stared down at the dark street. He could not believe it either, but his concept of their loss was in terms of time and effort; he could not believe all those miserable months and all the agonizing work had gone down the drain in just four hours.

"It's my fault," Denny lamented. "I shoulda listened the first time you tol' me to lay off the one-number bets."

"It wouldn't have mattered," Tony consoled. "We might have lasted a little longer, but in the long run it probably would have turned out the same. This is exactly the reason Buck didn't turn us in to the law back in December, exactly the reason he let us keep breaking our balls the way we were. He knew what would happen."

"Jesus," Denny whined, "why didn't he tell us?"

"He did," Tony said. "He told us we were fools. We are."

From the corner nearby, Tony and Denny heard a raucous male voice say, "Hey, come on now, honey!" Looking toward the sound, they again saw the chestnut-haired young woman with her older male companion. The man was obviously drunk and the woman was struggling to keep him upright. Two cowboys in Levis and western hats were pestering her. "What do you want with an old coot like that for, honey?" one of them asked.

"You look like you could handle a lot younger stud, Red," the other said. He laughingly tried to separate her from the shaky gentleman she was maneuvering; the older man almost fell but the woman managed to keep him up.

"Have a heart, fellows," the woman pleaded in a slow Southern drawl. But the cowboys persisted in harassing her.

Tony got up from the curb. "Come on," he said. He and Denny walked over to the conflict and Tony took the swaying man's opposite arm to steady him. "Looks like you've got your hands full," he said quietly to the woman.

"What are you butting in for?" one of the cowboys asked indignantly.

"You son of a bitch!" Denny growled nasally. He shoved one of the men into the street. "How'd you like to try picking up your teeth with a broken arm?" Denny aimed a vicious kick at the second cowboy, who jumped back just in time to miss getting a toe in the testicles. "Get out of here before I kick your asses black and blue!"

In the face of such confident threats, the two cowboys immediately retreated, Denny harassing them a dozen yards down the street.

"Where are you trying to take him?" Tony asked the woman. "We'll give you a hand."

"Gosh, thanks. The Hollister," she brushed her hair back and pointed to a tall hotel sign two blocks away.

Tony and Denny helped the unsteady older man to the Hollister, through the lobby, and up to his suite on the fourth floor. They stretched him out on the bed where he promptly went to sleep. The woman covered him with a blanket.

"Thanks, fellows," she drawled. "I don't know what I'd have done without you. I asked him not to drink so much. Speaking of which, can I offer you one? In appreciation?"

"Take a bottle of beer if you got one," Denny said.

"Coming right up." In the parlor she opened a refrigerated section on the bar and took out three bottles of Carling's Black Label. "My name's Virginia Hill," she said. "What's yours?"

"Tony Donovan. He's Denny Ebro."

"Well," she said, opening the bottles, handing them theirs, and raising her own in a toast, "thanks again, fellows." After her first swallow, she said, "Say, you fellows hungry? How about I get room service to send us up a late supper?"

Tony and Denny shrugged. "Sure, okay."

After she ordered the food, Virginia kicked off her high heels and sat down with them. "So how'd you fellows do at roulette?" she asked.

"Lost everything," Denny replied guilelessly. "Everything we worked for all winter long. More'n a thousand dollars."

"Honest to God?" Virginia asked, surprised. "You wouldn't kid a girl, would you?" She looked at Tony. "Is he on the level?"

" 'Fraid so," Tony admitted, embarrassed. "Let's don't tell the whole world about it," he said irritably to Denny.

"Listen, don't be self-conscious around me," Virginia said, her Southern drawl taking on a tone of camaraderie. "You wouldn't believe"—she waved a hand in dismissal—"some of the mistakes *I've* made. That drunk in there on the bed is just the latest one. Can you imagine, he's a bigshot producer for Columbia Pictures?" She named the last two movies he had produced. "A friend of mine got me into Columbia's acting school. I'm what you call a starlet. My friend told me to be nice to producers. That's what I'm doing on this trip to Reno."

At her urging, Tony told Virginia how he and Denny had worked all winter to get a bankroll; he modified the story to the extent that they were strip mining a closed shaft, which was legal, instead of pilfering spoil rock, which was not.

Both Tony and Denny found Virginia Hill extremely easy to talk to and be around. She was unpretentious, candid, understanding, and possessed of a sense of humor that at once put them at ease and let them laugh at themselves. While she could put on a pout for them as she sympathized with their atrocious luck at the roulette table, she also chided them enough to make them realize it was not the end of the world.

Later, after their food arrived and they were eating, Virginia told them about herself.

"I came from a little wide place in the road down in Coffee County, Alabama. My daddy was what they called a jack of all trades and master of none. Two things he knew how to do *real* well were drink bootleg hooch and make babies. I was the first one he made and there were nine more after me. By the time I was fifteen I was taking care of all the younger ones 'cause Mamma always had to work. I got tired of that *real* quick and when I was sixteen I ran away. Hitchhiked over to Birmingham and got a job waiting tables in a café. I always looked older than I was until I got to be twenty and started looking younger than I was. Reason I looked older, of course, was because of these." She jerked a thumb at her abundant bosom.

"Anyway, while I was in Birmingham I read in a movie magazine that some guy named Mike Todd was looking for well-built girls to dance in his 'Streets of Paris' exhibition at the World's Fair in Chicago. By then I had a few simoleons saved, so I decided, what the hell, you never know unless you try, right? I was seventeen, I had *really* blossomed, and had visions of becoming the belle of the World's Fair." She pulled a sad face. "Didn't quite make it, gents. Gal named Sally Rand took that honor with a couple of ostrich plumes. I did get a job at the fair, though. I worked at one of the

Libby, McNeill and Libby stands where pineapple juice was first sold." She waved a hand again. "People either loved it or hated it; nobody was ever neutral about pineapple juice.

"I worked for Libby until the fair closed and then I got a job as a soda fountain waitress at the big Drexel drugstore at State and Lake streets, right across from the Chicago Theatre. That's where they had all the big stage shows. Jane Froman, Ray Bolger, Marilyn Miller, Jack Oakie—they all played there. And all the big bands—Benny Goodman, Harry James, Glenn Miller. Between shows a lot of them would come over for Cokes and sandwiches. They'd sit around and talk and laugh and kid, you know? They all seemed like very happy people, really enjoying life. It was a real kick just being around them.

"It was while I was working at Drexel's that I met my friend Joe Epstein. I didn't pay much attention to him at first; he used to come in and drink malted milks and watch the show people. He was a real fan, crazy about movie stars, vaudeville teams, singers—anything and everything to do with show business. We started talking, you know, and found out we had a lot in common, me wanting to get into dancing and all; finally we started dating and eventually I moved in with him. He was older than me by fifteen years— hell, I was only eighteen at the time—and he wasn't much in the looks department; he was short and wore real thick glasses, but he was a really nice guy. And we had great times together. We went out every night, saw every act that played Chicago—all the stage shows, the supper club performers, the dance bands—we never missed any of them. All the time I thought Joe was just an ordinary accountant," she claimed blandly, "but later I found out he was a *mob* accountant. He worked for Jake Guzik, who worked directly for Al Capone. Joe's job was to see that none of Capone's bookies ever got hit too hard; he laid off big bets to other bookmakers in the west and east. After I found out what he was, he used to take me to all the mob parties. I met Guzik, Frank Nitti, lots of big shots, never got to meet Al Capone himself though."

"So how'd you end up in Hollywood?" Denny asked around a mouthful of food.

"Joe fixed it for me to get into Columbia's acting school. We both figured that if Evelyn Keyes and Rosemary Lane and gals like that could make it in the movies, I could too. So here I am—being nice to producers."

"Have you been in any movies yet?" Tony asked. He immediately regretted the tactless question.

Virginia shook her head. Both young men caught a flash of sadness in her emerald eyes as she said simply, "No. Not yet."

By the time they finished eating, drinking, talking, it was nearly two A.M. Tony and Denny prepared to leave. "Thanks for the supper," Tony said. "I hope you make it in the movies."

"Listen, thank *you*," Virginia said, "both of you, for helping me with those two cowboys. Wait a sec, I want to give you something." She hurried into the bedroom and returned a moment later with her purse. Opening it, she took out a roll of fifty-dollar bills and peeled off one for each of them. "To help you get started on a new bankroll," she explained. When Tony started to protest, she disclaimed, "Call it a loan. Pay me back someday when you see me making a personal appearance somewhere. Go on, take it. I've got plenty. Joe sends me a shoe box full of bookie money every month so I can keep up appearances. I think it's his insurance policy so when I hit the big time, he can say it was all his doing."

They took the money and did not even have time to thank her as Virginia hustled them out the door of the suite, planted a warm kiss on the cheek of each, and admonished them not to gamble anymore.

"That's for the suckers," she asserted. "You can't beat the people who run the game—ever." She winked. "Better to join them," she said as she closed the door.

Tony and Denny returned to their own hotel, to the room they had paid for twelve hours earlier—it seemed like an eternity ago—when they still had all their money. Now they had only a few dollars plus what Virginia had given them, but oddly they did not feel deflated or defeated; the few hours spent with Virginia, the exposure to her effervescent personality and positive philosophy had somehow smoothed the jagged edge of losing. Virginia Hill had made an extraordinary impression, especially on Tony; he had the odd feeling that they would meet again some day.

Going to bed that night, Tony and Denny did not even

talk about their disastrous experience at Harold's Club. Instead, they gratefully fell into immediate, deep sleep. It was nearly noon when they awoke the next day, and two hours later by the time they returned to their dilapidated shack at the edge of town.

Lloyd Arlen was there waiting for them.

"There's been a cave-in," he told them tensely, as soon as they drove up. "The number eleven stope gave way. Buck and a dozen others are trapped."

THIRTY

Tony and Denny rode with Lloyd Arlen back to Virginia City because his pickup truck was faster than Tony's old Chevy.

"Buck was down making a routine inspection," the union vice president said. His knuckles were white on the steering wheel as he raced the truck over the twisting road back. "I was up topland checking on some spalled bits that was supposed to be finished. All of a sudden, I feel the floor of the toolshed shake under my feet. First thing I knew, the top hoisters are yelling, 'Cave-in! Cave-in!' I ran to the cage and got down there as quick as I could."

"How bad is it?" Tony asked. His face, like Denny's, was as white as Arlen's knuckles.

"Bad as it can be," Arlen confirmed. "We only got as far down as the number six stope when we hit dust."

Tony and Denny exchanged ominous glances. 'Dust' was the wave of hazy, dirt-filled air that gushed through a tunnel following a cave-in. The farther the wave got through the stope behind it, the greater the air disturbance had been; the greater the air disturbance, the more serious the cave-in.

"When we got to number eleven and managed to blow

enough dust out so's we could see, we found the ceiling down and the whole of the tunnel blocked."

"What about the power lines and the ventilation hoses?" Tony asked.

"All buried. The power lines might be intact; they ain't broke on our side, so the men might have light in there. But the ventilation hoses is smashed flat; no good air's going in, no tainted air's coming out."

"What kind of rescue work have you started?"

"Terry Henny and a couple of crews have put extra shoring in the front of eleven and started digging. But the stuff fell hard, Tony, dropped like lead; it's jammed tight as hell. Digging ain't going to do it."

Arlen's expression became self-conscious. "There's an adjacent stope that runs parallel to the one that's blocked. A sealed tunnel, about twenty feet away. It's the one that was closed back in '37."

"I remember it," Denny said. "The vein ran out in the fourteenth or fifteenth stope."

"That's the one. We could get to them quicker by knocking a hole between the two, only—" Arlen's self-consciousness turned to embarrassment.

"Only what?" Tony asked.

"We can't get no volunteers to go in there," Arlen admitted. "The contract says nobody has to enter a tunnel closed for more than three years—"

"Those lousy bastards," Denny snarled. "They won't go in? To help Buck?"

"It's the firedamp, Denny." Lloyd Arlen shrugged, as if no further explanation was required. "The men are afraid of it."

Tony stared at the union officer. Firedamp was carbureted hydrogen, produced in closed tunnels by decaying pine timbers used in shoring. Dangerous to breath, it was also highly volatile and could be touched off by candle or lantern fire into a brilliant flash of combustion that would singe a man hairless, eyebrows and all, and in some cases blind him as well.

"That's why I come for you and Denny," Arlen told Tony. "I knew you two would go in for Buck. Henny and I will too. The four of us can handle two jackhammers and one sinker drill. I figure we can do it. What d'you think?"

Tony nodded tensely. They would *have* to do it.

Or leave Buck O'Crotty and the others in there to suffocate.

When they reached the mine, Arlen drove right up to the cage. Terence Henny was waiting there with overalls and coats, ventilating masks, and battery lanterns. As they got dressed, Denny looked scornfully at the miners assembled around the shaft.

"You lousy bastards," he said. "After all Buck's done for you!"

"Cut it out, Denny," Tony said. "Buck wrote the contract, remember?"

"That don't make no difference!" Denny had tears of anger in his eyes. The four men got into the cage. "Bastards!" Denny cursed them one last time as the cage started its descent. It went down slowly, noisily, to bottom of shaft: thirteen hundred feet.

"The sealed tunnel's at great depth," Terence Henny said, meaning four thousand feet.

The men entered the main tunnel and began a further descent, hurrying along by foot on an incline graded so that it was hardly noticeable. The main tunnel was well-lighted, dry, unobstructed. They could have moved faster, could even have trotted, but they did not. At the depths to which they were descending, breathable air was more important than speed. They wanted their lungs as untaxed as possible when they unsealed and entered the old stope.

At great depth, where the main tunnel was cut open in many different directions like the tributaries of a river, the men paused long enough to connect two jackhammers and a sinker drill to air hoses and electrical current. Then they each took a crowbar and pried off the thick, crisscrossed planks that had been used to seal the old tunnel.

"This ain't gonna be pretty," Terence Henny said ominously as they attacked the last layer of planks.

When the tunnel was open, the men lashed picks and shovels to their utility belts, put on the ventilating masks, switched on their powerful battery lanterns, and stepped cautiously into the old tunnel. It was like entering another world. Ahead of them, everywhere they looked, was fungi of monstrous, incredible growth, assuming uncouth and frightening forms. Long, twisting, serpent-like lengths of it clung to the walls; broad, slimy curtains of it hung from the ceiling. In some places it was mucousy, like the inside of a worm; in others it reminded of bread that had molded green, gray, and black. The stench, without their masks, would have been unbearable.

"Jesus," said Lloyd Arlen.

"This must be what it's like in a grave," Denny said fearfully.

"Come on," Tony said, moving forward with a jackhammer.

They made their way through the first stope, staying close to the outside rail of the narrow gauge track on which the ore car had run. At the end of the stope, where the track curved down to the next level, they lowered their drills and stepped around onto a ladder to climb down. The same procedure was repeated at the end of that stope, and the next, and each one after that, as the four men went deeper and deeper into the body of the earth. At the beginning of stope number nine, they came across an empty ore car standing forlornly on the track.

"Will you look at that!" Terence Henny said amazed. "A perfectly good dumper just left standing."

"Must've been your crew that was down here last," Lloyd Arlen said. "Mine wouldn't have been so careless."

"Like hell."

"Don't talk unless it's necessary," Tony reminded them. "Save the air."

When they reached stope number eleven, the men used their picks and shovels to clear away the repulsive layers and sheets of fungi to expose one wall of the tunnel. "They should be right through there," Lloyd Arlen said. It seemed odd to realize that the trapped men were only twenty feet away.

"We should be able to put a hole in to them in about four hours," Terence Henny calculated.

Tony set his jackhammer in place. "Let's dig," he said, and turned it on. The other three men tensed. Sparks flew as the pneumatic bit jacked into the earth of the wall. After a moment, the men breathed a sigh of relief; no firedamp ignited. The tunnel apparently was safe. Denny picked up the other jackhammer and joined Tony in drilling. Arlen and Henny started swinging their picks.

For two hours the digging went well. The men took turns using the jackhammers to break the wall, and picking and shoveling away the muck. The sinker drill they had dragged in from the main tunnel lay idly on the ground, unneeded.

For two hours the spirits of the four men rose steadily as it began to appear that they would get to the trapped men with plenty of time to spare.

Then their luck ran out. At twelve feet, they hit solid rock. Thinking it might be a boulder, they first tried to dig around the barrier. It quickly became apparent that it was not a boulder; it was a wall.

"Looks like we didn't waste our time bringing this down, after all," Terence Henny said, bringing over the sinker drill.

Lloyd Arlen and Denny, the two strongest, set the drill in place and turned it on. Its bit ground against the rock face for a full minute without cracking the surface, then broke off. A fresh bit was put on. It did the same. A third bit. It also broke.

"Son of a bitch. We're gonna have to have a drifter," Arlen said, referring to the next larger underground drill.

"Tony and I will get one," Henny said. "You two rest."

Tony and Terence Henny returned to the main tunnel, climbing back stope-by-stope, and found a heavy-duty drifter drill. Lugging it between them, they laboriously made their way back down to number eleven. The sinker drill was disconnected from its power, the drifter connected in its place, and once again Denny and Lloyd Arlen braced themselves to drill.

The drifter lasted three minutes before its bit snapped like a dry twig. Four new bits were tried; all of them broke.

Lloyd Arlen and Denny came out of the hole with sweat sheeted on their faces. "We'll have to get a stoper," Arlen panted.

"There's none down below," Henny said. "We'll have to go all the way topland."

Once again Henny and Tony went back up the ascending stopes. They hurried a little more now, despite the extra oxygen it cost them, because both were acutely aware of the valuable time being expended. From great depth to bottom of shaft they went, and into the cage for the ride back to the surface. The mine crews were still assembled when they reached the top; they had been joined by some Delavane Mines management.

"You men," Henny shouted to the nearest miners, "get a stoper drill from the tool shed! Look alive!"

As the men hurried away, Harley Kent, the mine general manager, asked, "How is it going, Henny?"

"Fair." His eyes swept the little management group. Lawyer Martin Pitt was there, accountant Clinton Randall, and several others of lesser capacity. But there was no sign of the mine owner. "Where's Big Jim?" Henny asked pointedly.

"Mr. Delavane is ill," Martin Pitt said blandly, answering for Kent.

"Is he now?" said Henny, eyes knowing.

When the big stoper drill was brought forward, Henny said loudly, "We could use some help with this thing! There's no firedamp in the tunnel."

"You mean it ain't combusted yet," one of the miners said skeptically.

"Wait until *that* monster starts throwing sparks," predicted another, bobbing his chin at the stoper drill, "the whole tunnel will torch up."

One of the younger miners stepped forward. "I'll give you a hand. I ain't a family man anyway."

"Me too," said another. "What the hell."

"Fools!" someone said from the crowd.

"Fuck you!" Tony shouted at the unknown voice, his eyes flashing anger. "Why don't you step up here and say it?"

"Never mind," Terence Henny calmed, "we've got two good men, that's all we need. Let's go."

When they were in the cage being lowered, Terence Henny smirked, "So Big Jim's ill, is he? Ill from the bottle, I'll bet."

The trip back down seemed interminable; they could not hurry because of the awkward, ponderous stoper drill, a brute of a boring instrument that was used only to penetrate the most difficult obstacles. At the end of each stope in the old tunnel, one pair of men had to lower it to another pair; it would have been impossible to bring it down without help, or without summoning Denny and Lloyd Arlen.

Finally they got it there, got it connected, got its great steel rotary bit in place, and turned it on. All four of them held the bit in place, keeping it hard against the rock wall they had to breach. It heated and smoked, ground and whined, screeched until their skin crawled, but it did not break the wall. Instead, to the amazement of the men, the big rotating drills failed completely as their steel bits disintegrated against the solid mass as fast as they could take one off and put a new one on.

"I don't believe it," Lloyd Arlen said, gasping for breath, "I never seen nothing like it."

Terence Henny stared at the eight-by-eight-foot breast of rock. "Bedrock," he said, barely whispering the word.

Arlen's eyes widened. "Do you reckon?"

Denny nodded solenmly. "Bedrock," he said again.

Tony, Denny and the two young miners who had helped with the stoper drill were also staring at the wall. They had all heard of the dreaded bedrock, but none of them had ever actually seen it. Some miners, if they were lucky, went all their lives without seeing it. Sometimes called the "Devil's Wall," it was an igneous formation of molten magma that had solidified harder than the hardest granite. Impenetrable to drills, impervious to dynamite, it usually represented only one thing: a dead end.

Lloyd Arlen, his underground gear soaked through from the heat generated in the twelve-foot-long escape hole, slumped against a wall of the larger tunnel and let himself slide wearily to the floor. "If only Buck was out *here* instead of in *there*," he wished. "He could show us how to crack this bastard."

"What do you mean?" Tony asked.

"He done it once before. Years ago. He was working some copper digs in Tonopah, must've been 1910 or thereabouts, and they hit bedrock. Buck told me about it once. They broke it with fire somehow; I don't recollect exactly what it was they did. Jesus, if only we could talk to Buck—"

"We don't have to," Tony said quietly. "There's somebody else who knows."

Thirty minutes later, Tony and Denny drove up to the front of the Delavane mansion in Lloyd Arlen's pickup truck.

"Remember," Tony said, as they parked and got out, "nobody stops us. *Nobody*."

Denny nodded brusquely. They went to the big front door, both still in their sweaty, grimy underground gear, and Tony tapped with the knocker. Cavendish opened the door.

"We have to see Jim Delavane," Tony said. "It's an emergency."

"I'm sorry, but Mr. Delavane has retired for the evening," Cavendish said. His eyes swept over the two young men.

"There's been a cave-in at the mine," Tony said. "We *have* to see him."

"Mr. Kent is the mine general manager," Cavendish said. "His house is just down Sierra Street. Perhaps he could—"

"Harley Kent is already there," Tony said. "We need Delavane." He pushed past Cavendish, Denny following him. "Where is he?"

"Now see here—"

"Watch him," Tony said to Denny. "Keep him away from the telephone."

Tony began to run in and out of rooms, looking for the mine owner. So urgent was his mission, so intense his concentration on why he was there, that he experienced no waves of nostalgia at all from the fact that this was Francie's house—or had been. Snatching open one door after another, Tony looked in a solarium, breakfast room, dining room, parlor, library, and finally the big private study; there he found the mine owner slumped in a chair, chin on chest, empty whiskey glass in one limp hand.

Tony stared at Jim Delavane. How many times, he thought, had he imagined a moment such as this? Just Delavane and himself, alone. The man who had destroyed his family: fired Iron Mike and turned him into a ranting drunk; turned Ruby into an impoverished wretch; sent them all, little Megan and Maureen included, to live in that clapboard shanty, that tinderbox—

Kill him, a voice said from deep in Tony's mind. Lock your fingers around his throat and choke the breath out of him. Put your lips by his ear while you're strangling him and whisper their names for him to hear: Mike Donovan . . . Ruby Donovan . . . Megan and Maureen Donovan . . . *Buck.*

Tony shook his head, jarring the voice to silence. Buck needed him. He crossed the study to Delavane.

Looking up, Big Jim watched Tony approach. "What do *you* want?" he asked thickly.

Tony stopped in front of him. "You worked some digs in Tonopah with Buck O'Crotty" he said flatly. "You hit bedrock and broke it. Buck's trapped in a cave-in with some others. We've got bedrock to go through to get to them. You're going to show us how."

Big Jim's expression went from slack to concerned to helpless. Grunting absently, he said, "At the moment, I couldn't show you how to use a shovel. I am very—very—drunk."

"You won't be for long," Tony said grimly.

Tony returned to the foyer. "Take the butler into the kitchen," he instructed Denny. "Have him make a pot of strong coffee."

Back in the study, Tony dragged Jim Delavane roughly out of the chair and stood him upright. Big Jim dropped the glass he was holding and threw an awkward punch that Tony easily stepped inside of. Then Tony bent and threw the mine owner over his shoulder. Faltering slightly under Delavane's weight, he staggered out to the wide main stairway with him. Pulling himself along the banister with one hand, he managed to get to the second floor, where he went through a bedroom and found a bathroom. Lowering Delavane into the tub fully clothed, Tony turned on the cold water through a gooseneck shower apparatus that extended from the main faucet. He directed the spray onto Delavane's head.

Fifteen minutes later, Denny and Cavendish came into the bedroom with the coffee. Cavendish helped Tony get Big Jim out of the tub and strip off his wet clothes. The butler briskly rubbed him down with a Turkish towel and wrapped a blanket around him, while Tony started giving Delavane short swallows of the hot coffee. Presently Big Jim pushed the cup away and looked intently at Tony.

"How long have they been in there?" he asked soberly.

"Going on seven hours."

Turning to Cavendish, the mine owner said, "Show these gentlemen to the foyer, please, then get my car. I'll be down shortly."

They only had to wait ten minutes before Big Jim came downstairs. Dressed in duckcloth hunting clothes and high, lace-up boots, he moved with a vitality and alertness that belied his earlier alcoholic consumption. Although there was a slightly pasty tone to his complexion, the perfectly combed hair, handsome line of chin, and steady, penetrating eyes were ready to dominate immediately any scene into which he stepped.

"Let's go," he said, striding through the foyer without pause. Following him out, Tony and Denny started for the pickup. "You come with me," Big Jim said to Tony.

Exchanging uncertain glances with Denny, Tony handed him the keys to Lloyd Arlen's pickup, and followed Big Jim. When they got to the Deusenberg, Big Jim went around to the passenger side, saying, "You drive." Tony's lips parted incredulously, but there was no opportunity to protest because the mine owner was already getting in. As Tony slid behind the wheel, soft leather seat molding to him at once, he saw Big Jim point. "Starter's there. Let's go."

Tony started the big engine and put the car in gear. The quiet power of the car was obvious to him at once; he felt like a pilot instead of a driver. For the briefest of moments, the urgency of his reason for being there was infiltrated by a sudden feeling of power.

"You're Tony Donovan, that right?" Big Jim asked rhetorically as the car turned down Sierra. "The hothead."

Tony glanced coldly at the mine owner but did not reply.

"I was told you'd left Virginia City. Right after the strike was settled. That true?"

"It's true," Tony said.

"You wouldn't by any chance know where my daughter Frances is, would you?"

"No." Another glance. "Don't you know?"

Delavane did not answer, but in Tony's peripheral vision he saw him shake his head sadly. Serves you right, you son of a bitch, Tony thought. Instantly, he hated the big luxury car and was disgusted with himself for driving it. He stepped down on the accelerator, disregarding caution.

As the car arrived at the mine and pulled up at the cage, Big Jim was alighting before it even stopped. At once, he assumed total command. "Henny, Arlen, let's go," he said to the two foremen, who had returned to the top to rest. "You too, Donovan." As they got aboard the cage, Denny crowded on with them. "Who're you?" Big Jim asked.

"He's with me," Tony said, expecting a challenge. Instead, Big Jim merely nodded.

"Let her down!" the mine owner ordered. The cage began to lower.

Minutes later, at great depth in the main tunnel, Henny found Big Jim a ventilation mask and the group went into the unsealed tunnel. Big Jim led the way, his stride that of a younger, stronger man, his demeanor that of the man in charge: forceful, direct, unmindful of the awful fungi, the putrid air, the darkness, the dampness, the unknown. This was *his* tunnel; he moved through it with authority.

At the escape hole in stope number eleven, Big Jim examined the broken drill bits from the sinker and drifter drills, and the partly disintegrated rotary bit from the big stoper drill. Then he went into the escape passage to look at the breast itself Aside from several barely discernible scratches where the various drills had scraped the surface, the wall was unmarked. The mine owner brushed away some dirt with one sleeve and put his fingertips lightly, almost reverently, on the surface. "Well, well," he said quietly to himself.

"Is it bedrock, sir?" Lloyd Arlen asked.

"Nothing but," Big Jim affirmed, coming back out. "Let's go," he said, striding past them.

Back in the main tunnel, Big Jim went over to a double cord of shoring timbers stacked against one wall. He turned to Lloyd Arlen. "Get back topland. I want an auxiliary ventilator brought down here, and I want enough drawing pipe to reach from the vents here all the way to stope eleven. Get some men to take the pipe out of these open drifts. I also want two high-pressure water hoses the same length. I want all of it ready in twenty minutes. And send two dozen men down here to move this timber to the escape hole. Get moving!" As Arlen hurried off, Delavane jerked a thumb at Denny and Terence Henny. "You two start moving the timber down the stopes." Picking up two axes and handing one to Tony, he said, "You come with me, boy."

"I'm not a boy," Tony said coldly.

Big Jim smiled a spare smile. "We'll see," he said. "Let's go."

Big Jim led Tony back down to stope eleven, then on into stope twelve. There he took his axe and shaved a sliver of wood from one of the timber shores supporting the ceiling.

"I want one sliver of wood from each beam," he said, cautioning, *"only* one. We don't want this tunnel caving in too. Pile the strips of wood over there."

In twenty minutes, when the auxiliary ventilator pipe had been expanded all the way to stope eleven, and the high-pressure hoses coupled one onto another until they, too, reached all the way in, Big Jim and Tony had sliced off and carried six armfuls of pine slivers into the escape passage. The wood was arranged along the base of the bedrock wall like kindling in a fireplace. The men Lloyd Arlen had sent down were formed into a long relay line through the first ten stopes and were sending in the planks of shoring timber. These were some of the same men who earlier had refused to enter the unsealed tunnel. With Big Jim himself now overseeing the rescue operation, they had reconsidered their previous position.

Within an hour after Big Jim's arrival, the eight-by-eight-foot wall of bedrock was covered with a layer of stacked wood. More planks were piled at the entry to the escape passage. "Put a keg of powder, a box of dynamite, and half a dozen fuses in stope number eight," Big Jim instructed Lloyd Arlen. "When you get back topland, pressurize the hoses." Looking around, he waved an arm, saying, "You all did a good job! Everybody clear out now!" Again he looked at Tony. "Except you. You stay."

When the tunnel was cleared except for himself and Tony, the mine owner extracted a leather cigar case from somewhere under his coat, put an expensive panatela between his teeth, and said with a smile, "Live flame is the ultimate test for firedamp. If you'd like, I'll give you time to get a few stopes away."

Tony grunted derisively. Delavane's smile widened. He brought out a lighter and looked at it wistfully. "Francie gave me this for my last birthday. Now it could be what I kill us with."

He snapped the lighter to flame and, along with Tony, stared at it for several seconds. There was no explosion. Smiling again, Big Jim lighted his cigar. Then he knelt and held the flame to the kindling at the bottom of the wood. It ignited quickly and fire began to spread across the base of the bedrock wall. Big Jim walked out of the passage, into the tunnel, and sat on some of the extra timber. He noticed that Tony looked perplexed and uncertain.

"Relax," he said in the kindest tone Tony had ever heard him speak. "We'll get old Bucko out."

Nodding briefly, self-consciously, Tony sat down on the timbers also, not exactly with Big Jim but not removed from him either.

"What'd you think of my Deusenberg?" Big Jim asked conversationally, puffing almost nonchalantly on the cigar.

Shrugging, Tony replied, "It's okay, I guess." Twelve feet into the escape passage, he could see the timbers begin to burn against the bedrock.

"Buck taught you to drive, I'll bet. In that old Nash of his."

"Yeah."

"I always wanted a son," Big Jim admitted. "Somebody I could teach to do things. Francie always seemed to learn everything without me. Hell, my butler Cavendish taught her to drive." He peered in and saw that the bedrock wall was ablaze with burning timber. Smoke was moving in rolls along the ceiling. Clamping the cigar in his teeth, Big Jim rose and said, "Give me a hand."

Together they lifted a fresh timber, carried it into the passage and threw it onto the blaze. Soon the entire hole was thick with smoke. Big Jim dragged the auxiliary ventilator over to the entry and throttled it on. Immediately it began to draw smoke into its long, tubelike pipe that extended up the stopes to the main shaft ventilating system. As soon as the hole was clear, Big Jim pointed to another timber. "Let's go."

For an hour, they kept the fire going against the bedrock wall, throwing on fresh timber every time the blaze seemed to lessen. During the process they became even grimier and sweatier than they had been, and their faces were soon soot blackened, their lips and throats parched from the heat. All the while, Big Jim continued to puff on his cigar until it was down to a butt, then threw it, too, into the blaze.

"I don't understand what the hell we're doing!" Tony finally complained in frustration.

"You will," Big Jim promised.

When Big Jim felt the fire had been kept burning long enough, he gestured for Tony to follow him and went over to the pair of high-pressure hoses that, like the ventilator shaft, stretched all the way back to the piped water supply in the main tinnel. Because the hoses had been pressurized from that water supply they were already fully bloated, straining with the water being held back by their closed nozzles.

"Okay, kid!" Big Jim shouted. "Let's put out that fire!"

Each grabbed a hose and aimed it into the twelve-foot passage, pulling back on the nozzle release handle to deliver two great streams of water onto the fiery timbers. The flames were quickly extinguished, sizzling steam being created in their wake. The jets of water then drove into the burned timber, breaking it up, spewing wet, sooty ash over the walls and floor of the passage. When it appeared that their job was done, Tony started to lower his hose.

"Keep that water going!" Big Jim yelled. "Blast that wall!"

The two men aimed their hoses at the bedrock, blasting the hot wall with cold water as it, like the burned timbers, sizzled and steamed.

"Hold it steady!" Big Jim shouted..

The big hoses vibrated in their arms, shuddering, jerking, straining their muscles as they struggled to keep them from jumping away and going out of control. After several excruciating minutes of it, both men heard a sharp lightninglike sound as the great wall of bedrock cracked and split before their eyes.

Shutting off the water, both men dropped to their knees, panting in exhaustion, arms and legs quivering, hearts pulsating, stomachs convulsing, bowels quaking. They stared almost dumbly at the long, slanted, still steaming crack.

"Jesus—" Tony gasped.

Big Jim lumbered to his feet. "Let's . . . go."

Tony followed him to stope number eight where they got the dynamite, black powder, and fuses. Back at the bedrock, they began to carefully work sticks of dynamite into the crack. In and around the sticks, they poured black powder. They tamped it with handfuls of thick mud created on the ground by the same water that had cracked the wall.

"We'll fire it in four places," Big Jim said, unwrapping the fuses and quickly twisting them into place. "We'll each light two and run for it. We'll have to be quick." He slapped Tony on the shoulder. "You with me?"

Tony stared for a split instant at this man whom he had hated for almost as long as he could remember but for some peculiar reason did not hate at that moment. He slapped Big Jim on the shoulder and said curtly, "Let's go!"

Big Jim got out his silver lighter, ignited a spare fuse for himself and handed the lighter to Tony. "Use this, kid."

Each man moved into place. Their eyes held for a blink of time, then Delavane nodded. He touched his burning fuse to two others as Tony snapped the lighter to fire and lit his own two.

With the fuses burning, they began their run through the stoped tunnel. From eleven, they quickly climbed the ladder to ten and ran as fast as they could across that level. At the end of ten, Tony leaped onto the ladder and climbed to nine, turning to offer a hand to Big Jim, right behind him. Both men dashed across nine to the ladder leading up to eight. Once again Tony jumped halfway up the ladder, vaulted to the top, and turned to help Big Jim. Just as his hand was extended, and Delavane reached for it, the rung which the mine owner gripped with his other hand broke off. Tony's and Big Jim's fingers touched for a microsecond before Delavane pitched backward and fell into the abandoned ore car the men had seen earlier. The car began rolling back down the stopes.

"Get out!" Tony screamed. He leaped down to nine and tried to catch the car, but it quickly went over the hump and picked up speed.

At the ladder leading down to ten, Tony could only watch helplessly as the little car, Big Jim stuck in it backwards and upside down, rolled along its narrow gauge track and took the mine owner directly into the face of the explosion.

Part Seven

Tony

1951

THIRTY-ONE

After his first trip to Havana, Tony was summoned back to the Cuban city once a month for meetings with Meyer Lansky about the Kefauver Committee. Sometimes Lucky Luciano was at the meetings, sometimes not; Lansky explained that since Luciano had been deported by the United States to Italy four years earlier, he had difficulty moving freely in the Western Hemisphere. Although not specifically prohibited from entering any country except the United States, that government's State Department had exerted pressure on neighboring countries to exclude him also. Luciano used the name Charles Ross when he traveled, but was careful always to carry his authentic Italian passport, in his real name of Salvatore Lucania, to avoid arrest for illegal entry.

"It's just another example of how the U.S. Government plays dirty," Lansky said with rancor. "During the war, when Charlie was still in prison, I made a deal with certain officials that Charlie would use his connections on the New York docks to eliminate pilferage and cargo theft for the duration of the war, in order to combat black marketeering. Also, through contacts he still had in Italy, he provided up to date, detailed maps of various coastlines for the invasion landings that were being planned. In exchange for that and some other things, when the war ended, Charlie was to be released from prison on the condition that he leave the U.S. and go live in Italy. Nothing was said about him having to *stay* in Italy exclusively. Far as the arrangement was concerned, he was free to go wherever he wanted, except back to the U.S. But the government doesn't see it that way; it resents the fact that it had to keep its part of the bargain. See, some of the officials involved wanted to back out after

415

the war and not let Charlie out of prison; I threatened through our lawyers to go public with the deal, tell the press, everything—anyway, make a long story short, to get back at Charlie because they had to release him, now they hound him every time he wants to travel outside Italy. Dirty pool, is all it is."

At their meetings, with or without Luciano's presence, Lansky briefed Tony on the progress of the Kefauver group; the actual members who had been named, the attorneys and investigators they had appointed, who had been subpoenaed so far to testify before the panel, and what, in Lansky's opinion, the committee might hope to prove by each witness. The purpose of the monthly briefings, per Lansky, was to try to determine as accurately as possible whether any witness or potential chain of evidence would lead back to Ben Siegel and the Flamingo Hotel. In four lengthy meetings on the subject, no such link had been established.

Each time Tony returned to Havana, Lupe Tovar came to meet him in Miami with the private plane, and each time she accompanied him to one of the four penthouse suites at the Nacional. Tony began to look forward to seeing her, and she him.

"I like you, Tony Donovan," she told him on his third trip. Tony smiled at her engaging directness.

"Tell me why," he said.

"Well, in Cuba," she explained, "is not always so easy for a woman to get along, you know? Especially if she is from a poor family, like me. It's either marry, have babies, and stay poor all your life, or go out on your own and try for something better. For something better there is always the price to pay." Lupe's voice softened. "Mos' visitors, especially the men who stay in these suites, they walk in here and expect me to right away pay the price for keeping my job. They expect me to put out, you know? But you din't. Tha's why I like you."

"Maybe," Tony said, "there's a reason why I haven't. Maybe there's something wrong with me."

For a moment she studied him gravely, uncertain whether he was serious. Then she smiled her brilliant smile and shook her head. "It makes no difference. I *know* you are not the kind of man who would take from a woman jus', because he *could*. You would only take if she wanted to give. Can you tell me honestly that I am wrong?" Tony shrugged an admission that she was right. "See?" Lupe said triumphantly.

Before Tony's fourth trip to Havana, Meyer Lansky had called him on the private line and asked, "Tony, do you still have any contact with Virginia Hill?"

The question came as a complete surprise. Tony rarely even thought of Virginia anymore. He told Lansky as much.

"There is some indication from Washington that the Kefauver investigators may be negotiating with her to come back from Europe and testify before their committee. Ask around there in Vegas, will you; people who knew her, anyone she might still be in touch with. See if there are any rumors to that effect."

"Sure."

After he hung up, Tony sat back and thought about Virginia Hill, recalled her as the young Columbia Pictures starlet "being nice" to the movie producer in Reno, and how he and Denny had helped her out of the situation with the two rowdy cowboys. Tony had suspected then, so long ago, that he and Denny had not seen the last of Virginia— and he had been right. After the war, they had run into her in Las Vegas and Tony had talked her into asking Ben Siegel, whose mistress she had become, to give them jobs during the construction of the Flamingo. Since Ben's death, she had lived in self-imposed exile in Austria.

After the request from Lansky, Tony made a few discreet inquiries, and had Denny do the same, but no one on the Strip had heard from, or anything about, Virginia Hill in years. Tony reported that back to Lansky.

"I'll check into it further in Washington," Lansky said.

When Tony made his next trip to Cuba, Luciano showed up for the meeting in Lansky's study. Charming, soft-spoken as usual, he greeted Tony cordially. Lansky, who looked worried for the first time, said "Tony, I'm afraid it looks like we might have a problem with Virginia."

"Has she agreed to come back?" Tony asked. Lansky shook his head.

"Not yet. All we know is that one of the committee's investigators made a trip to see her; when he came back, one of the lawyers went over. We're waiting to see if they issue a subpoena for her; they wouldn't bother to do that, with her residing in Europe, unless she's made a deal to come back. I'm keeping my fingers crossed that she'll turn them down, but—" Lansky shrugged with uncertainty. Folding his hands on the desk, he pursed his lips in thought for a moment. "Tony, we're going to level with you, Charlie and me. We had wanted to keep you completely removed from knowledge of anything illegal, but it doesn't look like we'll be able to. So here it is. Ben was never completely legit. We wanted him to be, and despite a golden opportunity to go straight once and for all, he just couldn't keep his fingers out of other things. We know, for instance, that he was part of a protection racket being worked on bookmakers who used a West Coast wire service for race results. We suspect he was enticed into the operation, allowing his name to be used. Ben had a very heavy reputation in the old days, and a lot of people were still afraid of him; just the possibility of him being an enforcer for this protection scam would have been enough to convince a lot of bookmakers to fall in line."

"There were one or two other things too," Luciano added. "Mostly deals involving the same people. A Chicago group. We think," he spoke very quietly, "they may have been the ones responsible for Ben's death."

"What we need to determine," Lansky said, "is whether Ben did anything that might even remotely involve Charlie and me, or any other Flamingo investor, in these sideline activities of his. Could there have been any transfers of money, any fixes to allow big winnings to his other partners, any payoffs under the table . . . ?"

Tony shook his head. "I've been through every ledger, every file folder, every scrap of paper that's been kept as a record," he declared, "and I couldn't find anything the least bit suspicious. Ben was a fanatic about the Flamingo's books from the very beginning. Even the petty cash account always balanced to the penny."

"The fact that the books balanced wouldn't have eliminated skimming," Luciano pointed out. "Skimming takes place in the count room, with the cash, before the bookkeepers even get to it."

Tony shook his head. "I don't think Ben was skimming. He wanted the hotel to succeed too badly."

"You liked Ben, didn't you, Tony?" Luciano asked.

"Yes, I did," Tony replied. "Ben Siegel gave me a break and a job after the war. I was indebted to him, just as I am to Mr. Lansky. If it weren't for them, I might be back working in the mines." That was not true, Tony would never have gone back into the mines, but it made a point.

Meyer Lansky shook his head emphatically. "Never. Cream rises to the top, Tony. If I hadn't hired you, someone else with an eye for smarts would have. You'd have gone places one way or another."

"Meyer tells me that Virginia Hill was responsible for Ben giving you a job," Luciano said.

"Yes, she was. I'd done her a favor once—that is my friend Denny Ebro and I had—and a few years later she paid us back by getting Ben to give us jobs."

"I see." Luciano nodded. Then, "Excuse me for asking, Tony, but is it possible that you might still feel enough of your old friendship for Ben that you'd consider covering up anything incriminating that you found?"

Tony locked eyes with the soft-spoken Sicilian. "Anything's possible."

"Suppose I asked you to assure me of your loyalty?"

"I couldn't do it," Tony replied.

Claustrophobic silence filled the little room. Tony and Luciano matched unblinking stares; animosity surfaced between them. Behind the desk, Meyer Lansky remained silent. Presently a flicker of a smile came to Luciano's lips.

"Suppose," he said, "I asked you to assure me of your loyalty to Meyer?"

"That I can do," Tony said unequivocally.

The tension in the office evaporated.

When that visit to Havana was over, Meyer Lansky personally rode with Tony back to the airport instead of having Lupe Tovar accompany him.

"I'd like to ask you a favor, Tony," he said in the back seat of the limousine. "Try not to take too personally anything Charlie might say. Like that loyalty business. Charlie's a naturally suspicious man; all Sicilians are. But in addition to his natural inclination, he's also very gun-shy because he's had so many people turn on him over the years. People he trusted, people he thought were reliable and dependable, people he considered friends. Also, I suspect that the reason he wants to be absolutely sure of you is for my sake, not his. When you get right down to it, there's not much the Kefauver Committee can do to him. When he tries to test you, I'm sure it's in my interest. You'd be doing me a big favor if you'd keep that in mind."

"Sure," Tony said. "I'll try."

At the airport, Lansky gave him a list of thirty names, neatly typed on a single sheet of paper. "I want you to go through the Flamingo books again; it's a nuisance, I know. I wouldn't ask if I didn't think it was necessary. See if you run across any of these names. If you do, put the books aside to bring down on your next trip. Oh, and Tony, I meant to mention it earlier: next time you're here, I should have the report of our investigation into Buck O'Crotty's death." Lansky smiled warmly and put out his hand. "Have a good trip back, Tony. Thanks very much for coming."

After shaking hands and boarding the private plane that would fly him to Miami, Tony for the first time failed to experience the confident feeling of well-being that Meyer Lansky usually gave him. Acutely aware of its absence, he wondered why. Only after the plane was airborne and his thoughts were among the high, dark clouds, did he decide why.

It was because of Luciano.

There were no feelings of security when Lucky Luciano was around.

THIRTY-ONE

Tony had not been back in Las Vegas ten days before he was summoned again to Havana.

"It's confirmed about Virginia," Lansky told him on the private line. "She's agreed to come back to the States and testify when the Kefauver hearings move to New York. You'd better come on down, Tony. We need to talk about this."

Luciano was there again and the three of them dined on the open terrace of a private club which sat on a bluff only fifty feet above the Caribbean. Surf rushing against the rocks was their dinner music. Tiki torches cast dancing light and deep shadows. At a respectful distance, a sommelier and two waiters stood silently and watched for any sign that service was needed. They dined on wild boar and wild dove, both dead less than six hours, and drank Chateau Margaux bottled between the two world wars.

"I kept hoping," Lansky said, "that we wouldn't have to deal with Virginia, that she'd use her head and stay in Europe. But apparently that isn't going to be the case. Our informants in Washington have confirmed exactly what we were afraid of—the government wants Virginia to testify because they know how close she was to Ben. Whatever he was doing, chances are she knew all about it. We"—Lansky pointed at himself and Luciano—"have got to find out whether Ben in any way involved us in anything crooked or under the table. It's the only way we can take steps to protect ourselves and our interests."

"Things would be a lot simpler," Luciano said, "if she could be persuaded *not* to testify."

"Persuaded how?" Tony asked bluntly.

"However," Luciano replied. "Whatever it takes."

"Isn't there some kind of law against interfering with witnesses subpoenaed to a government hearing?"

"I'm sure there is," Luciano said archly. "There's laws against just about everything."

"I don't think, Charlie, that it's necessary to try and persuade her not to testify," Lansky said. "And, Tony, it is certainly not our intent to interfere with a witness. We wouldn't ask Virginia to change a word of what she's willing to testify to. All we're concerned with is knowing ahead of time whether any of it involves us. We just want to protect ourselves. Isn't that fair?"

"Sure it is," Tony agreed.

"The best protection," Luciano insisted, "is for her not to testify at all."

"Nobody would argue about that," Lansky agreed, "but would it be the smartest move? It's entirely possible that there's nothing at all in her testimony to hurt us."

"Do we know *why* she decided to come back?" Tony asked.

Lansky shook his head. "We haven't been able to find that out. The government must be promising her *something* —we just don't know what it is."

"Revenge, maybe?" Tony asked pointedly. He looked

from Lansky to Luciano and back again. "Maybe she knows something that will hurt whoever she thinks killed Ben."

"That's possible," Luciano admitted. He spread his hands apart. "Look, this Kefauver thing is going to open a lot of closets. Everybody who ever peddled hooch in the old days will be a target, everybody who ever ran a betting parlor or a numbers route; it isn't going to make any difference whether they're legit now or still breaking the law. Hell, some of the biggest distillery presidents in the country today once ran liquor with Meyer, Ben, and me. Some of the biggest casino owners and investors in Nevada once operated bookie joints and worked the numbers racket. But as far as the government is concerned, a man don't go straight. Once a lawbreaker, always a lawbreaker—and they'll get you when and where they can, any way they can." Luciano put a finger on Tony's arm for emphasis. "Tom Dewey once sent me to Dannemora on perjured testimony that he and I and the judge and everybody else *knew* was perjured testimony. As a reward he got to be governor of New York state—and later he got to run for President of the United States. I'm not complaining, understand; I was crooked at the time and deserved to go to jail. I just didn't deserve to go for what I got sent for, which was prostitution, which I was never involved in. My point, Tony, is that we can never count on fair play from *anybody*—not even from the federal government."

"Especially in the federal government," Meyer Lansky added wryly. He put his napkin on the table and rose. "Excuse me, gentlemen. Nature calls."

The waiters cleared the table, removed the top tablecloth, and served coffee on fresh linen while Lansky was gone. Luciano waited until it was all done, and he and Tony were alone at the table, before he spoke again. Then he said. "I didn't get a chance to tell you the last time you were here, Tony, but I was very glad to hear you say you were loyal to Meyer. He needs that loyalty, and he needs your help."

Tony sipped his coffee and said nothing. Pursing his lips, Luciano looked away for a moment, staring out in the direction of the unseen sea, appearing to ponder something weighty. He silently drummed the fingertips of one hand on the crisp white tablecloth. When he continued speaking, he did so without looking at Tony, speaking toward the blackness.

"I've been friends with Meyer Lansky since 1912. Nearly forty years." An almost imperceptible smile settled on Luciano's lips. "When I was fifteen years old, back in New York, I had a gang of very tough guys, all Sicilians like myself. We controlled everybody on Hester Street who was fourteen and under. They all had to pay us a nickel or a dime protection money every week; either that or never leave their homes. We got payoffs from all of them—the Irish, the Jews, Italian kids who weren't in with us; it didn't matter—a coin was a coin. One day a guy in my gang, Frankie Castiglia—later changed his name to Costello—he points out this little Jew kid coming down the street with a big pan in his hands. In it was what they called 'cholent,' which was a dish that the women prepared ahead of time to be eaten on Saturday, the Jewish Sabbath, when no cooking was allowed. Meyer's mother, Yetta, used to make her cholent out of brown eggs, potatoes, green beans, and all different kinds of other vegetables—plus a little meat when they could afford it. The families ate it cold on Saturday; it was delicious, I found out later.

"Anyway, in the tenements, you know, all the women had to share a building's oven, and they weren't very big ovens to begin with. So the neighborhood bakers, for a nickel, used to bake the cholent for a lot of families. Now, normally my gang never bothered a kid taking cholent to the baker. We knew he had a nickel, but we also knew what it was for. And most of the kids was paying us at other times anyway. But on this particular day, Frankie points out this little Jew kid and says, 'Sal, that's a kid there who don't pay us.' I was called 'Sal' in those days because my real name was Salvatore Lucania. I changed it, like Meyer did, so as not to embarrass my family. Anyway, we spread out on the sidewalk and blocked this kid's path, see. He stops, holding this cholent pan in both hands, and I explain the facts of life to him. Then I tell him to hand over his nickel." Luciano turned to face Tony now. His eyes, Tony saw in the tiki-torch light, had a gleam of amusement in them. "This little runt of a Jew kid, who was not even eleven years old yet, stuck his chin out and said to me, 'Go fuck yourself, guinea.' " Luciano chuckled and shook his head. "I won't forget that if I live to be a thousand. 'Go fuck yourself, guinea.' Jesus, what balls."

"Did you take his nickel?" Tony asked.

Luciano shook his head. "Course not. How could I? My guys wanted to plaster him *and* his cholent all over the sidewalk, but I wouldn't let them. Balls like that, you just didn't kick." Luciano leaned forward on his elbows. "I have a brother that I'm very close to, Tony. And Meyer has a brother that he's very close to. But between Meyer and me, for nearly forty years, has been a closeness that is closer than brothers become. I can honestly say that in forty years we have never had an argument. Disagreements, discussions, sure, but we never argued like people do when they become angry. We never fought. Never has a cross word passed between us. We became friends shortly after the day I just told you about, and we have remained friends. Most of the people we've been associated with over the years, we've never been able to trust very much. Nobody ever felt they owed anybody for anything; everybody was always out strictly for themselves. That's why I'm glad you said what you did about owing Meyer your gratitude."

Luciano's voice now became feathery soft. "Meyer needs your help on this Virginia Hill thing, Tony. Personally, I don't give a damn for myself what she says; I was deported to Italy after I got out of prison, so the American authorities can't touch me anymore. As for my holdings over here, if I lost them all it wouldn't change my life for a minute; I've got more than enough in European banks to live well for the rest of my days. But with Meyer it's a different story. He still lives in the United States. He's got a family in the United States. You saw the picture on his desk of his son in West Point? Well he has another son too, a son that has had cerebral palsy all his life. Meyer doesn't talk much about him, but the young man is in and out of hospitals a lot, and his father constantly worries about him. Now this Virginia Hill thing is on his mind too. You and I, Tony, have got to do whatever we can to relieve some of the pressure on him."

"What do you have in mind?" Tony asked.

"I'm for going back to my original suggestion—persuade the broad not to testify."

"How?"

Luciano's eyes narrowed a fraction. "Any way we can." He leaned forward. "Look, Tony, I think you probably realize that I'm not as completely on the up and up as Meyer. There are some things I'll still do—or have done for me—if I think they're necessary."

Listening to Luciano, Tony suddenly knew: he'll have Virginia killed. It was not a guess; Tony did not wonder about it. Without qualification it was there as a known fact. Luciano was ready to kill Virginia—just like that.

I can't let this happen he thought. I can't let this man drag Meyer Lansky and me and our legitimate Las Vegas operation back into the gangster gutter where he still operates. I can't let him prove that everything Arnie Shad has said is true, prove that Lansky is as bad as Luciano. Lansky's done too much for me, brought me too far; at times, Lansky had been like a—

Tony shook the thought out of his head.

"Let me go see her," he said to Luciano. "Let me try to find out why she's coming back and what she intends to say."

"What makes you think she'll tell you?"

"We used to be friends. I've done her some favors. I think she'll level with me."

Luciano tapped a knuckle against his lips, considering it.

"Be a lot easier to get Mr. Lansky to go along with it this way than the other," Tony pointed out. "This way is the careful way."

Luciano continued to ponder.

"If it works," Tony pressed, "it could save a lot of trouble all the way around."

Finally Luciano nodded. "Okay, why not? There'll still be time if your way doesn't work."

When Lansky returned to the table, Luciano told him what Tony had offered to do. Lansky seemed moved, some of the worry left his eyes.

"That's very good of you, Tony," he said. "I didn't want to ask, even though I realized that you would be the perfect one to contact her for us. You have no police record, no past involvement in anything illegal; you can approach her as a friend." He put a hand on Tony's arm. "I want you to know that I appreciate this, Tony. Very much."

"Yeah, me too," Luciano said. "And, Meyer, like I told Tony, if it doesn't work, there's always time for persuasion."

Tony felt a wave of relief. He had pulled it off, suckered Luciano. And if my way doesn't work, he thought, Luciano wouldn't get a chance at his. Tony made up his mind to warn Virginia that Lucky Luciano would be out to get her.

*   *   *

It was one o'clock in the morning when Tony got back to his suite at the Nacional. Lupe Tovar was curled up on the couch, asleep, her raincoat covering her, shoes on the floor. A layer of lustrous black hair had fallen over part of her face. Tony closed the door quietly so as not to disturb her and went into the bedroom.

On the bed table he found a thick file that Lansky had told him to expect. It was the report of Lansky's private investigation into the murder of Buck O'Crotty. With his shoes removed, and his coat and tie off, Tony propped himself up on the bed and began to read.

It was a lengthy file, covering a period of several months of investigation which began some six months after the actual incident. An introductory section, titled "Purpose of Inquiry," stated that the investigation was being conducted in order to ascertain through a careful scrutiny of the facts whether an impartial effort was being made by the law enforcement agencies involved to determine the actual murderer of Buck O'Crotty, or whether the thrust of the official investigation was rather to connect with the crime certain businessmen whom the agencies believed to be part of a so-called "organized crime network."

Meyer Lansky, Tony suddenly realized as he perused the long report, had not ordered the investigation for Tony's sake alone: he wanted a hole card—an independent study of the facts—in case the threats made by Jack Coltrane, the brash public statements of Arnie Shad, and the impending Senate hearings, somehow resulted in a charge against him.

Tony was impressed by the obvious scope of the private investigation. Not only had undercover agents lived in Virginia City for up to eight weeks, posing as itinerant workers, but the detective firm had somehow obtained access to many federal, state, and union records in order to develop background information. The list of people they had talked to in Virginia City and other places, both informally while undercover and in subsequent formal interviews, created waves of nostalgia for Tony. His eyes flicked down once and still familiar names like Terence Henny, Lloyd Arlen, Callahan, Harmon and Libby Coltrane, Jack Coltrane, Martin Pitt, Clinton Randall, Harley Kent, Sam Patch, Father Juan Gomesa, even, Tony was surprised to see, the Delavane butler Cavendish, and Chalky, the albino, who were found living in the Delavane mansion.

Tony turned at once to the pages listed for the two latter interviews, hoping there might be some word of Francie in them. Upon quick reading, he found there was, but it was sketchy and told him nothing new. Cavendish had claimed he was retained by Miss Frances Grace Delavane to reside in and keep in livable condition the interior of the mansion. He was allowed a budget for one person to assist him—that was Chalky. Miss Delavane was not concerned with the exterior of the property, which would have required at least two other full-time employees to keep up, therefore did not budget for it, hence the shabby appearance of the outside. Miss Delavane sometimes stayed at the mansion and sometimes did not; the two employees professed no knowledge of where she was during her absences.

Disappointed, Tony went on to read some of the other interviews. Terence Henny, the new president of the A.M.W.N., had said he felt the murder was part of a long-range plan by gangsters to take over Nevada unions; he pledged to fight the gangsters with all his resources. Lloyd Arlen, who had moved to Washington to work for the United Mine Workers, disclaimed Henny's theory and said it would probably turn out that some disgruntled lower management person, whom Buck had been influential in getting fired, had harbored a grudge for years and finally returned for revenge. It was likely, Arlen opined, that the killer would never be apprehended. Callahan, the saloon owner, like Henny believed the murder had something to do with gangsters. Harmon Coltrane, now in his seventies but still president of the bank and active in financial dealings, had no doubt whatever that the murder was somehow involved with union politics. His wife, Libby, had no real opinion on the killing, gave the impression that it was of no import at all to her, and would not discuss it further. An aside to the report on Libby mentioned the fact that she spent most of her time at the Coltranes' second home in Palm Springs where, at the age of 47, she was a stunning woman, known to be having an affair with her thirty-year-old tennis instructor. Her son, Jack Coltrane, at his office in the Nevada Department of Justice building, had refused to discuss the handling of the O'Crotty case, was incensed that a private inquiry had been commissioned, and demanded to know who was paying for it. When told that was confidential information, he had angrily promised to take legal steps to find out. Martin Pitt, whose muscular son Phil had been killed in the war, was still attorney for Delavane Mines, which, as Tony knew, was now operated by Consolidated Minerals and Manufacturing. Pitt declined comment on the basis of possible legal repercussions. Clinton Randall, former accountant for Delavane Mines, had his own Certified Public Accounting firm with his son Craig as a junior partner; the firm was retained by Consolidated Minerals and Manufacturing to audit the books of Delavane Mines. Both Randall and his son attributed the murder of O'Crotty to the close ties between organized labor and organized crime. Harley Kent, still the mine general manager but now employed by CM&M, felt that Buck had been killed by some miner he had been obliged to fire, or some union member who had dipped into A.M.W.N. funds, or some similar revenge-motivated individual. Longtime sheriff Sam Patch declined to comment on the investigations being conducted by other law enforcement agencies, but did not hesitate to admit that as far as his small department was concerned, the case was at a complete standstill. Patch had not a suspicion as to who killed Buck O'Crotty, not a clue to go on, and was leaving further inquiry to state and federal authorities. Father Juan Gomesa, pastor of Saints Peter and Paul Church, depicted Buck as a crusader for right and good, involved in many worthy causes, and pointed out that such a person invariably aroused enmity in others who opposed him. Buck, he believed, could have been killed by any number of persons, for any number of reasons. The important thing was not who killed him, but that he had been a decent man, supported his church, and was now in heaven.

So it went. There were other interviews, some with persons Tony had never heard of; most of the results were speculative, inconclusive, vague, vindictive, or self-serving. F.B.I. and other Department of Justice records, U.M.W. and A.M.W.N. records, employment records from the coal mines in West Virginia, military records, and other files, some of which Tony suspected had been illegally obtained, likewise contained no categorical evidence pointing to any individual or group as having both motive and opportunity to kill Buck. Nowhere had there been found any facts or data upon which to base the belief that Buck's killing had been caused or committed by "gangsters" or members of an "organized crime" cartel or by "criminal elements" alleged to have interests in or control of gambling in Las Vegas and elsewhere in Nevada. Similarly, nothing was uncovered to advance the theory that the murder was union related. And despite the fact that Harmon Coltrane was involved in all three corporations that now controlled Delavane Mines, and the fact that all of Big Jim Delavane's original management cadre were still running the operation, there was no indication that any of them, Coltrane included, would have had serious reason to want Buck killed. That the silica dust problem could have been their motive was considered but dismissed; the mine owners claimed they had already given O'Crotty verbal agreement to correct the problem by developing new underground breathing masks.

The underlying conclusion of the report seemed to be that the person who shot Buck O'Crotty had not been connected with him in any way, but had simply come into his life for that brief violent moment of tragedy, and then passed on. As difficult as that was for anyone to accept, there was simply no evidence to the contrary. As much as Tony wanted to know who had killed Buck, he could not help feeling a great wave of relief at the thought that the act was apparently not related to anything that directly or indirectly involved him. Not the gambling industry, not the union, not his failure to remain at Buck's side, not the silica dust problem—nothing causally connected to him. As that realization came over him, Tony paused in his reading, leaned his head back, and closed his eyes.

Okay, Buck, he thought, I didn't contribute to it. Now I'll be trying to find out who did it because I promised you I would. Not because I feel guilty myself.

Feeling better, Tony resumed reading and was intrigued by the light the report shed on Buck O'Crotty's decade-long absence from Nevada, beginning with his sudden and unexplained departure from Silver City in 1920, until his return to Virginia City to adopt Tony in 1930. Buck had never talked much about that period of his life, other than to say he had "knocked around a bit" and "seen me a little of the world" before settling down as a coal miner in West Virginia. In truth, Tony learned from the investigation report's synopsis of the murdered man's life, Buck had gone from Silver City to San Francisco where he had reenlisted in the Marine Corps. Tony knew that Buck had served in the Marines during World War I, with Big Jim Delavane and

Tony's father, Iron Mike Donovan, but he had not been
aware that Buck had served a subsequent enlistment. The
photostatic copy of Buck's military record showed that he
had reentered the Marines at the rank of corporal, and upon
reporting to his assigned duty station, with the Fourth Marine Regiment in China, had been promoted to his former
rank of sergeant. For the next four years, Buck served in
the guard at the United States Legation at Tientsin. Several
retired Marines who had known him had been located during the investigation and through them it was learned that
O'Crotty had joined a "study group" formed by a Protes-
tant missionary in the city to learn about and possibly alleviate the terrible class system that had made virtual slaves of
the Chinese coolies. It was at this point in time, according to
one confidential interview, that Buck began to equate the
oppression of the Chinese coolies with the miners and their
problems with the mine owners in Nevada.

Part of the investigation document included a report made
internally by the Marine Corps regarding Buck O'Crotty's
friendship with one Harry Morse, a young English lance
corporal attached to the British Legation. Morse, once a
miner himself, had been involved in the General Strike of
1922 in Great Britain, in which three million workers be-
longing to the Trade Union Congress had struck the entire
country for nine days. Fascinated by the concept of broad
organized labor, Buck joined with Harry Morse in forming
their own study group devoted to discussion of ways to
improve the workingman's lot in various countries. The
Marine Corps had investigated the group due to suspicion
that it might be advocating Bolshevism or other political
philosophies to which the Corps objected. It found nothing
on which to base a specific court martial against Sergeant
O'Crotty, however, and had to be content to call him up for
an office hours hearing at which he was given two week's
extra duty and fined ten dollars pay for having membership
in an unapproved organization. The study group had subsequently disbanded.

When Buck's enlistment was up, he returned to the United
States and joined a fledgling group that called itself the
Congress of Industrial Organizations, and therein came un-
der the influence of the bushy-browed Welsh coal miner's
son who was behind it: John L. Lewis. The C.I.O. took
Buck to the West Virginia coal mines, and there he stayed

for several years, as a miner and a union organizer, until learning of the tragedy that had left young Tony Donovan an orphan.

Tony was amazed, not only at the amount of information gathered about Buck, but at how Buck's devout belief in labor unions had begun and how it had grown. Through all Tony's years as boy and man he had known that Buck was dedicated almost fanatically to the principle and philosophy of unions; it simply had never occurred to Tony that Buck had ever been any other way. To read all this background was enlightening; sighing, Tony wished he had known the details years earlier. Perhaps he would have respected Buck more and been more tolerant of his sometimes constricted attitudes. Perhaps, Tony thought, he would have had a better understanding of mining, the sacredness Buck felt for the life of each miner who went underground. Maybe it would have helped him rationalize his own love-hate feelings that had finally caused him to turn his back on both the mines and on Buck. The things we don't know, Tony thought with a soft grunt, aren't supposed to hurt us.

While he read, Tony had stretched out and turned sideways on the bed. Now he felt movement behind him and turned to find Lupe sitting down and leaning on his thigh.

"Why didn't you wake me when you returned?" she asked indignantly.

"You looked too peaceful," Tony said. He reached over to touch her raven hair. "Like a little girl who was very tired."

"If we want to talk about looks," she said, "you look a little sad right now. Are you?"

"A little," Tony admitted.

"Because of what you are reading?" Lupe asked, bobbing her oval chin at the sheaf of papers.

"In a way." Tony put the report aside. "How about a drink?"

"You bet," Lupe replied with a delighted smile.

She fixed martinis for both of them and they sat on the terrace of the suite overlooking Havana.

"The thing you are reading that makes you sad, it is about the past, yes?" Lupe asked.

Tony nodded. "How did you know?"

The dark young woman shrugged. "A guess. Thinking about the past always makes one very sad or very happy. One is never indifferent about the past."

Tony's eyebrows went up pensively. "You're right. I never thought of it quite that way before." He smiled. "You're smart, Lupe."

She shrugged again."Not so smart. I jus' try to get along, you know. The bes' I can."

"By paying the price?" he asked gently. She shrugged. "When I have to."

Tony pursed his lips. "Next time you go to Miami," he said, "get on a plane and come to Las Vegas. Come and see me at the Flamingo Hotel. I'll give you a job where you won't have to put out."

Lupe set down her glass and came over to sit next to his chair, crossing her arms on his knee.

"You are very nice, Tony Donovan," she said. "But I think that someday in Cuba things will change. I have a brother who is in Mexico City studying with a man named Dr. Castro. In his letters he says that Dr. Castro—Fidel, he calls him; he is a lawyer—believes that the more corrupt a government becomes, the weaker it grows. He thinks that the Cuban government will soon reach a state where it has no moral fiber or strength at all, and that if challenged it will collapse. He sees a future Cuba in which all people work for a common good, and no one mus' pay the price to work. I think I will stay and be a part of that Cuba."

Tony raised his glass to her. "I hope you make it."

"In the meantime," Lupe said, one hand moving casually to the inside of his thigh, "I do not like you to be sad thinking about the past. Can I not do something to make you be happy?"

Tony was surprised to feel warm stirrings near her hand. He thought about the report he had just read, and the conclusions that alleviated the guilt he felt about Buck's death. Had that been the cause of his impotence, he wondered, thinking he was somehow to blame for what happened to Buck? It must have been. The problem began as soon as Buck was killed, when Tony began weighing his own culpability. It had continued all this time. Until now.

As he felt an erection begin, Tony set his own drink aside. Bending forward, he put a hand on Lupe's neck and kissed her warmly, softly on the lips. She kissed him back, hungrily, tasting him wetly, her hand sliding upward toward his expanding heat, feeling his hand slip down to cup one of her hanging breasts.

When their kiss was over, she said, "I want to make love with you, Tony Donovan. Not put out. Make love."

"I want to make love with you too, Lupe," he answered. "Come on—"

She rose and went into the suite, pausing every few steps to disrobe and discard her clothing—shoes here, blouse there, slacks dropped where she stepped out of them, bra draped over a chair—until at last he was following a tall, slim, brown body with only a pair of delicately lace-trimmed panties over buttocks that swayed enticingly with every step.

Their lovemaking was spectacular: they enjoyed each other's body in long uninhibited solo ministrations interspersed with passionate couplings that were almost machinelike in their precision.

"Jesus—it's like—we've been doing this together—for years," Lupe panted.

They rolled smoothly from position to position, mouths, breasts, legs, genitalia always rotating to the perfect place without awkwardness. Whatever they did, however they moved, singly or together, it felt good, looked good, tasted good. They had ninety minutes of raw ecstasy.

When it was over, Tony tried to sleep but could not. After an hour he eased out of bed, put on his travel robe and slippers, and returned to the terrace. With a fresh drink, smoking a rare cigarette, Tony stood at the edge of the terrace. The lights of Havana twinkled below but instead of seeing them he stared across them to the dark sea and sky beyond. He thought of the incredibly skilled young brown woman sleeping inside between rose-colored satin sheets, thought of what she had done to him and for him, thought of how good it felt to be able to get hard again, to make love, to come.

It made him remember the war, and how it had felt when he found Francie again.

Part Eight

Francis

1943

THIRTY-THREE

Tony woke up in the middle of the night with the light of a full moon in his eyes. His feet and crotch, both fungus-infected, were itching relentlessly. Sitting up in the half-darkness, he lowered his dungaree trousers and skivvy shorts, and poured calamine lotion over his testicles and inner thighs. He did the same with his feet. Then he lay back gritting his teeth as the pink liquid burned furiously for a full three minutes, bringing tears to his eyes. When the burning eventually stopped, Tony sat up to dress; one of his socks disintegrated as he pulled it on. He crawled over to a nearby tree where Denny was sitting, smoking a cigarette held inside a canteen cup for concealment.

"You got an extra sock?" Tony asked.

Denny stuck his cigarette in a puddle of water next to him and rummaged around in his field pack. He handed Tony a stiff, mud-caked sock. "Hate to break up my last clean pair," he said.

"I'll pay you back," Tony promised. "I expect the navy to deliver my laundry any day now." That was a running joke; the navy had abandoned the Marines almost as soon as it landed them on Guadalcanal.

Tony and Denny continued to talk until a voice hissed from the darkness, "Will you guys shut the fuck up? I'm trying to have a wet dream about Betty Grable."

"Think about sheep," Denny advised. "That'll work faster."

Tony sat up against the tree, shoulder to shoulder with Denny. "What day is it?" he asked idly.

"I don't know. Tuesday, I think. Maybe Thursday." Denny fished out a box of Japanese cigarettes rolled in rice paper. Captured smokes were all they had. "Want one?"

"Sure."

Together they worked a rubberized poncho over themselves tent-fashion and lighted up. At that moment it began to rain so they stayed under the shelter, exhaling through the opening in the center.

"Quiet tonight," Tony said. "For a change."

"Ain't over yet," Denny replied pessimistically.

"The scuttlebutt is that scouts found some more caves up the Tenaru today. We're supposed to move on them tomorrow."

"Life's just a bowl of cherries," Denny said.

There was a sudden rustling at the edge of the poncho and a young Marine named Grubb crawled in with them. He was grimy, unshaven, extremely pungent. His odor quickly filled the little space.

"Jesus, when's the last time you washed, Grubb?" asked Denny.

"July. Gimme a smoke."

Denny passed the Japanese cigarettes over. "What do you want anyway?"

"Company. You guys are keeping me awake with your grab-assing." He lighted up and looked at Tony. "Our squad moving on the caves tomorrow, Sarge?"

Tony, a buck sergeant, shrugged. "I haven't gotten the word if we are." He had a sudden inspiration. "Why don't you ask Timmons? He'll know." Timmons was a staff sergeant and platoon leader.

"Where's he at?" Grubb asked.

"Somewhere close to the shit pit, I think. He's got dysentery."

"I'll go find out," Grubb said, dousing the cigarette after only one drag. It did not matter; their outfit had captured thousands of boxes of Jap supplies.

"Nice work," Denny said with a crooked grin after Grubb left. "He's prob'ly the only one on the island who stinks worse than we do. Only enlisted man, that is."

When they finished their cigarettes, they stretched out and spread the poncho over their middle, leaving heads and feet out, oblivious to the continuing tropical rain. "What's the date?" Tony asked.

"Hell, I don't know," Denny replied irritably. "What's with you anyway? What day is it, what's the date—shit, what's the *difference?* You ain't going anywhere, are you?"

"I was just thinking about how long we'd been away from home," Tony said, overlooking Denny's irascibility. Denny had been ill-tempered, as had many others, for several weeks, as the campaign to capture the 'Canal continued with no end in sight. "Been nearly a year since Pearl Harbor, hasn't it?"

"Pretty close," Denny confirmed.

"It's a good thing ol' Buck forgave us and let us move back home after the cave-in," he reflected. "If he hadn't, we'd prob'ly be back stealing from Delavane's spoil-rock pit."

"If we were," Tony asserted, "at least we wouldn't be giving our profits to Harold's Club. We're a lot smarter now."

"Yeah," Denny said wryly, wiping rain from his face and turning onto his side in the mud, "we've come a long way."

A few minutes later, they had almost managed to drift off when Grubb scurried back between them.

"Timmons says we're on for tomorrow," he whispered excitedly. "The caves up the Tenaru." Tony and Denny could see him smile in the moonlight. "I'm gonna get me some gold tomorrow!"

Grubb was one of the battlefield ghouls who carried a pair of pliers to extract gold teeth from the enemy dead.

At daybreak the company moved out, platoon by platoon, squad by squad, in a column of twos along the sandy bank of the Tenaru. These were the Marines who called themselves "raggedy-assed," who had been subsisting for weeks on rice, canned seaweed and crabmeat, and rice beer—all captured from the Japanese; their own supply lines, from the sea, had been nonexistent since three days after they landed. Plodding up the river, they resembled traveling tinkers: their web belts strung with first-aid kits, canteens, bayonets, mess kits, hand shovels or picks, and hand grenades laced together with shoestrings. Bandoliers of extra ammunition crisscrossed their chests. The weight of it all caused them to sink an extra inch into the marshy ground and their boondockers to make sucking sounds with each step. Under mixing-bowl helmets, their young faces were yellow-casted from daily doses of the malaria-suppressant, quinacrine.

A two-hour forced march, first along the river through the jungle, then out across a wide plain of tall yellow kunai grass that led down to a valley of sorts, brought the Marines to a series of steep hills into which the Japanese caves had been dug. The approaches to the caves were guarded by machine gun emplacements on bulldozed dirt patios in front of each cave. Marine officers leading the march halted the column three hundred yards away and deployed the men into nine zones. Tony was in charge of zone one, at the left flank of the caves. After a meeting of company commanders, it was decided to attack the caves straight on with fire teams from zones two through eight, while sending zones one and nine up each side to set up a crossfire on the machine gun nests. As soon as the machine guns were neutralized, demolition teams would throw shape charges of explosives into the caves, after which flamethrowers would be used to make certain all enemy were dead.

"You people remember," the lieutenant colonel in charge said, "that these are Bushido troops. These are the same savages that beheaded the members of Carlson's Raiders captured on Makin Island, and cut up Marines and fed them to the fish at Tassafaronga. Don't fuck with these animals in any way. Take no prisoners."

The assault shoved off at ten hundred hours. Tony led three fire teams up the east flank; Denny, who was a corporal, and three riflemen made up one team; a Browning automatic rifle team made up the second; four more riflemen, including Grubb, formed the third. On their initial assault, the thirteen men advanced ninety yards before being pinned down. When Tony reported their position, he was surprised to learn that the seven middle squads had only made it forty yards. "What the hell happened?" he asked Staff Sergeant Timmons on his field radio.

"Heavy machine gun fire, what the fuck do you think?" Timmons told him. "Make a second advance at ten-forty hours. Got that?"

"Aye, aye," Tony replied.

On the second push, although still under heavy fire, Tony's squad moved sixty additional yards to an imaginary line halfway to the caves. On the radio again, he was told that the middle troops had gone a scant thirty additional yards. A subsequent third assault, at eleven-twenty hours, took them only twenty yards farther, while Tony's men gained fifty yards and were within one hundred yards of the elevation on which the caves sat.

"Donovan," Timmons radioed, "pull your men back."

"What? Repeat, over—"

"We can't hold under this concentrated fire. We're pulling back to re-form. Bring your squad back down."

Tony, lying behind a rock, said, "Bullshit. I can practically spit to those caves!"

"Goddamn it, we are ordered to fall back and re-form." Tony twisted around where he was lying and looked down the hill: two hundred yards from where they started. If he pulled his squad back, he knew those two hundred yards would have to be taken all over again. Clicking on the field radio, he said to Timmons, "We're staying here."

"You are, like hell! Get your asses back down here with the rest of us!"

"Fuck you, Timmons. Out."

Tony did not acknowledge any further calls from the platoon leader. A few minutes later, a new, more precise voice, that of the company commander, came over the radio.

"Sergeant Donovan, this is Lieutenant Eggars. Bring your men the fuck back down here at once! Do you read?"

Tony looked at the grimy, sweat-streaked faces of his men; he saw fatigue, frustration, fear.

"Re-form, Donovan! That's an order!" Eggars barked.

"No, sir!"

"What? *What?*"

"I said, No, sir! My men aren't fighting for the same goddamned ground twice! We'll hold here until the rest of you catch up."

"Donovan, I'll court martial your ass!" the lieutenant threatened. "I'll have you put under arrest!"

Tony cut him off. "Dig in," he told his squad.

After half an hour another voice came through. "This is Colonel Edson, Sergeant. What the fuck do you think you're doing?"

"Holding, sir."

"What?"

"Holding, sir. My squad has taken two hundred uphill yards, sir. We're holding it."

The radio was silent for a long moment. Then: "What are your casualties, Sergeant?"

"None, sir."

Silence again. Then: "Can you advance any farther, Donovan?"

"We can try, Colonel."

"Try," Colonel Edson said, "then report back."

"Aye, aye, sir!"

There was no radio traffic for an hour. The rest of the outfit pulled back and re-formed. At half past noon, Tony called Edson's command post. "Sergeant Donovan reporting as ordered, sir. We're forty yards closer."

"You mean to say," Edson asked incredulously, "that you're only fifty or sixty yards from the cave elevation?"

"Aye, sir."

"What's your situation? I don't hear any firing."

"We're not *under* any fire, Colonel," Tony told him. "I don't think the Japs know we're here."

"Jesus Christ," Edson said to himself.

Tony was on his knees, carefully studying the terrain remaining between his squad and the caves, as well as an interesting strip of thickly overgrown brush that extended up the side of the hill to a point above the caves. As his eyes measured the distance to the overgrowth, Tony felt a wave of excitement.

"Colonel, I think we can get above and behind the caves," he said,

"Charging or infiltrating?" Edson asked tensely.

"Infiltrating."

"How long will it take you?"

Tony quickly scanned the strip of brush again. "Two hours. Want us to try?"

"By all means, son," Edson replied without hesitation. "Go to it. Keep me informed. Out."

By fourteen hundred hours, Tony and his twelve men had crept, crawled, and climbed the additional sixty yards of hilly terrain up to the cave level, then slipped beyond that point to a terrace of ground approximately fifty feet above that. Snaking to the edge of that plateau, Tony could look directly down on a three-man machine gun crew in front of the cave on the top of which he was lying; he could also see, along that same level, eight other emplacements in front of caves roughly one hundred feet apart. His body churned and vibrated with fear at being that close to Bushido troops. If he and his men were seen, he was certain that squads of enemy would rush out of the caves and overwhelm and butcher them. Rolling back from the precipice, Tony made his way to the overgrowth of brush where his squad waited.

With a stick, he drew a diagram in the dirt to show the men how he planned to assault the caves. When he was certain they all understood, he removed his dungaree jacket and collected all of their hand grenades. Fashioning a makeshift bag, he slung the grenades from one shoulder and radioed the command post.

"Colonel Edson," he reported as loudly as he dared, "attack in ten minutes, sir. Repeat, attack in ten minutes."

"Where are—" the colonel started to ask, but Tony shut off the radio. "Deploy," he told his men.

Denny put an arm around him. "Watch your ass."

"You watch yours," Tony replied, patting Denny's unshaven cheek. Denny, a deadly shot, patted his rifle and winked.

As the dozen men moved out, Tony made his way stealthily down a narrow ravine alongside the first cave. Crouching at the foot of it, he watched in frozen silence as Denny and the others spread out along the upper ridge. Because he expected enemy soldiers to flood out of the caves as soon as the machine gunners were killed, it was necessary to have two men above each cave to cover him. With twelve men, only the first six of the nine caves would initially be under fire; the last three might or might not turn on him: it would depend on how fast—hell, or *whether*—the rest of the outfit attacked. At best, it was a risky action, but it was necessary if they were to clean out the caves.

The squad began to fire on the machine gunners as soon as they were all in place. The fusillade was sudden and shocking; one moment Tony was reflecting on his plan, the next he was seeing Japanese soldiers being shot down from above, and his frightened mind was screaming *Go*! Go, go!

Leaping from the concealment of the ravine, he ran past the falling enemy to the mouth of the first cave where, crouching with his back to the wall, he lobbed four grenades into the cave as fast as he could pull their pins and let fly their spoons. As he was doing so, the insane thought flashed in his mind that there were not enemy soldiers in the cave, but silver miners. The cave suddenly became a mine tunnel.

As the grenades were exploding, Tony dashed to the next cave and repeated his bombardment. Before he got to the third cave, soldiers came rushing out. Tony threw three grenades directly into them.

At the fourth cave, there were no soldiers and Tony

fleetingly suspected that it was probably a supply cave of some kind. He was already pulling a pin, letting a spoon fly, and releasing a grenade in an underhanded toss when the thought sped through his mind that if it *was* a supply cave, he should not be blowing it up. But by then it was too late, the momentum of his assault was carrying him irreversibly forward, and he had put a second grenade into the opening before he could accelerate movement and get past it.

At the fifth cave, a Japanese officer shot him with a pistol. The bullet cut a hole through the top of his left shoulder and knocked him off his feet. A spurt of automatic rifle fire from above cut the officer down and Tony, more stunned than hurt, scrambled to his feet and bombarded the cave entrance just in time to stop a dozen half-naked enemy from charging out. In front of him now, soldiers were swarming around the last four caves, trying to simultaneously defend the high ground behind them and the slope in front of them. Tony felt a surge of exhilaration at seeing them fire downhill; it had to mean that Colonel Edson had launched a frontal assault. Crouching next to the opening of cave five, his shoulder searing with pain, Tony began lobbing grenades overhanded into the wildly confused enemy ranks. One of the Japanese machine guns turned around and made a sweeping strafe of the upper ridge. A body plummeted from above and landed like a sack of grain just feet from Tony. He scurried out to it but saw at once there was nothing he could do; it was Grubb and the top of his head was gone, only pulp left. As Tony started to rush back to his cover, he was shot again, in the right side this time, much more directly: the bullet, from a rifle, ricocheted into him from the front as he was running. He had the sensation of being kicked by a powerful foot and, as he hurtled back, he was acutely aware that his ribs were breaking, giving in. He landed very close to Grubb and drew in his breath, biting down hard on the insides of his cheeks to keep from yelling, forcing himself to remain very still all the while certain in his mind that some slimy-faced Nip with a Bushido scarf around his head was going to rush over with a samurai sword and cut off his head—

That was his last thought as he blacked out.

THIRTY-FOUR

Darlene, a big-boned nurse, entered the solarium of the naval hospital to tell him, "Donovan, you're wanted over at Fleet Marine Headquarters to get your medal. Come on and I'll help you dress."

Tony, who had been lying in the Hawaiian sun in robe and pajamas, one arm in a sling, rose and left the glass-walled room and a chorus of whistles and lewd comments from the other patients.

"Don't pay any attention to them, Lieutenant," Tony said as he accompanied Darlene down the hall.

"I *never* pay any attention to Marines," she replied acidly.

It was two days before Christmas and the hospital corridor was decorated with red crepe-paper bows and strings of silvery tinsel. Soft holiday music played through a speaker somewhere. Tony and the nurse turned into a two-bed room and Tony removed a summer service uniform from a locker while Darlene got him fresh underwear and socks from a drawer. As she helped him out of his robe and pajama top, which had been buttoned over his slung arm, he asked, "Do you think I'll get the Navy Cross, Lieutenant?"

"Could," she said. "If not, the D.S.M. for sure." The D.S.M. was the Distinguished Service Medal, which was a lesser decoration than the Navy Cross. Tony had already received the Purple Heart.

"If I get the Navy Cross, will you go out with me, Lieutenant?" Tony asked. Every patient in the wing was trying to get Darlene into bed.

"I only go out with officers, Donovan," she said. Crouched in front of him to help him out of his bottoms and into his shorts, Darlene looked with interest at his ample penis, then quickly buttoned his shorts and stood up. She had a pert,

445

baby face that belied both her size and experience. "Why don't you stop down on Kuhio Street if you want to get laid?" Kuhio was the tenderloin section of Honolulu where young girls were getting rich servicing servicemen.

"I'm a wounded man," Tony said. "I need the attention of someone with medical experience. I can't even undress myself."

"You don't have to," she said, working an undershirt over his arm and head. "All you have to do is unzip. There are girls down on Kuhio who do it with their mouths. Some of them are supposed to be very good at it. There's a rumor they practice by sucking marbles through a garden hose." When she had him dressed, Darlene walked with him to the military bus stop. "Get laid before you come back, will you, Donovan?" she requested. "You've got a beautiful cock and it's becoming more tempting every day."

With half an erection, Tony got in the brown army bus that stopped, taking a seat next to a window. As the bus pulled away, he watched Darlene walking back to the hospital, her rounded buttocks swaying enticingly under her starched white uniform. If I get the Navy Cross, he promised himself, I'm going to get Darlene too. With the Navy Cross and a beautiful cock, he could not miss.

As the bus made its circuitous way through wartime Honolulu, Tony did what he could to get comfortable. With wounds on both sides of his body, it was not easy. The first bullet that had hit him back on the 'Canal had smashed his clavicula, and torn apart his vena subclavia, arteria subclavia, and musculus trapezius, rendering his left arm virtually useless. The second round had pierced his oblique external abdomen muscle, broken five os costale bones, collapsed his right pulmo, punctured his colon ascendens and his duodenum, and grazed his pancreas, before exiting his transverse abdomen muscle. He had been stabilized and stitched at an aid station, opened and patched at a field hospital, opened again and temporarily repaired on a hospital ship, and finally evacuated by air to Hawaii where he was opened for the third time and extensively operated on to correct all his internal damage. He had been recuperating for two months and his prognosis called for complete recovery in two more. As evidenced by his preoccupation with Darlene's body, he was, except for minor discomfort, feeling fine already.

As the bus wove its way past Kapiolani Park, Tony no-

ticed an oddly familiar figure leave the curb and hurry
across the street behind it. Twisting his head around for a
better look, he suddenly remembered the white-washed complexion and cotton-tuft hair.

Chalky!

Jesus Christ . . . ! Tony leaped from his seat and ran to
the front of the bus. "Stop!" he yelled at the army corporal
who was driving. "Stop the bus! Stop it!"

"What the hell's a'matter, Mac?" The corporal pulled to
the curb and ground to a halt. "You having a fit or what?"

Tony grabbed the pneumatic hand control and pulled the
door open. Hurrying off the bus, he rushed back down the
block to where he had seen Chalky cross. Dodging traffic,
he ran into the park and scanned the area. There were
people everywhere—uniformed servicemen, civilians, children—but no sign of Chalky.

"Hey, buddy," Tony stopped a sailor and a girl coming
out of the park, "did you see an albino guy anywhere in
there?"

"A what?" the sailor asked suspiciously.

"Never mind." Tony hurried deeper into the park, his
eyes darting frantically.

He searched for an hour without any luck. Reluctantly,
despondently, he walked back to the bus route.

At Fleet Marine Headquarters, Tony stood at rigid attention before the desk of a full colonel.

"Sergeant Donovan," the colonel said, "you are here to
be presented with the Navy Cross for heroism. Normally a
formal ceremony is held for such an occasion, but due to the
exigencies of our wartime emergency situation, we have had
to dispense with that. This in no way diminishes either the
award or the act of gallantry which resulted in your being
cited for it."

As the colonel rose and removed from its envelope a
parchment scroll, Tony tried to keep his attention directed
on what was transpiring at that moment. But all he could
think of was Chalky, and the possibility that Lew Rainbolt
was in Honolulu—and that Francie might still be with him.
The colonel began to read from the scroll.

" 'On ten October, Nineteen Hundred and Forty-two,
during a continuing offensive campaign against troops of the
Imperial Japanese Army on the island of Guadalcanal, in

the Solomon Islands, Sergeant Tony Donovan, 1172307, United States Marine Corps, did, at risk to himself above and beyond the call of duty, lead a twelve-man squad in an assault upon heavily and strategically entrenched enemy, did bravely expose himself to enemy fire, and although subsequently seriously wounded did inspire and prolong that assault to the end that a support assault did successfully overwhelm and defeat the enemy. Because the foregoing act of gallantry was in keeping with the highest traditions of the United States Naval Service, Sergeant Donovan is hereby awarded the Navy Cross for heroism. Signed, Merrit Edson, Lieutenant Colonel, Commander, First Raider Battalion, United States Marine Corps. Endorsed, Alexander A. Vandegrift, Major General, Commander, First Marine Division, United States Marine Corps. Approved, Thomas Holcomb, General, Commandant, United States Marine Corps.' "

The colonel stepped around the desk and from a leather box removed and pinned on Tony's arm sling the blue-and-white-ribboned, gold cross. Tony's throat went dry as he felt the medal being attached—the same award given to Iron Mike Donovan by the Marine Corps in World War I.

"Congratulations, Donovan," said the colonel, shaking hands. "I have one other thing to give you, also on the recommendation of Lieutenant Colonel Edson." He handed Tony a small box containing two gold bars. "You're being given a battlefield commission to the rank of second lieutenant. And Colonel Edson wants you back in his unit as soon as you're certified fit for duty."

When Tony left Fleet Marine Headquarters, his mind was in a frenzy. The pride of receiving the Marine Corps' second highest medal, the surprise of summarily being commissioned an officer, a sudden end to the suspense of wondering where he would be assigned when he left the hospital, all competed for attention in his thoughts—and all were overcome and subdued by the nagging presence of Chalky—and, by association, Francie.

He went immediately back to Kapiolani Park and looked around again. When he saw no sign of Chalky, he crossed to several stores and began making inquiries. At a poultry market run by a Portuguese woman, he found his first lead.

"Sure, I know who you mean," the woman said. "Got skin like milk, yeah? Sure, he's here two, three times a week. Lives somewhere above the park, I think, up there on one of the highland streets."

Assuring the woman that Chalky was not a wanted fugitive, Tony proceeded to the highland streets that bordered and looked down on the park. In the first block he stopped a boy delivering the *Honolulu Courier*.

"Yeah, I know of a guy like that," the Hawaiian boy said. "He takes care of a house down the street. The one with the green shutters, third from the corner."

"Thanks." Tony gave him a dollar.

Walking briskly down the block, Tony reached the house. The front door was open, the screen door latched. There was a green Christmas wreath on it. All the front windows across the porch were open. Tony peered inside; no one was in the living room. Leaving the porch, he walked along the side driveway to the back of the house, where he found another, smaller porch, this one enclosed by screens. From inside he heard the sound of a radio playing a popular song by the Kay Kyser band, with Trudy Erwin singing the lyrics. A throaty feminine voice in the kitchen was vocalizing along with the radio:

Who wouldn't love you,
Who wouldn't care—
You're so enchanting
People must stare—

Tony quietly climbed the back stairs. There was no doubt in his mind who it was. The naturally hoarse voice was ummistakable.

You're the dream that dreamers want to dream about
You're the breath of spring that lovers gad about, are
mad about—

Looking in the back door, he saw her standing at the kitchen table, chopping vegetables with a butcher knife. Her back was to him, she was dressed in white shorts and a halter, and as she kept beat with the music she bounced slightly from foot to foot. She was, Tony saw, still a few pounds overweight for the fashion, and brown as a nut. Her auburn hair was as short as a boy's.

Who wouldn't love you,
Who wouldn't buy—
The west side of heaven
If you winked your eye—

In the alcove off the kitchen, Tony noticed a small writing desk. On it was a framed photograph of Lew Rainbolt and Francie standing next to the yellow Lincoln roadster, parked beside a roadsign which read: Welcome to Texas. Their arms were around each other and Francie's head was on Rainbolt's shoulder.

Tony swallowed and turned away. As quietly as he had climbed them, he descended the steps. She made her choice, he told himself. She went with Rainbolt, and she stayed with Rainbolt. What right did he have to come wading into her life now, stirring up muddy waters of the past? She had run away to rid herself of Big Jim, of Buck, maybe even of himself. She had chosen not to tell anyone where she was: Martin Pitt had not even been able to find her when Big Jim was killed; her father had been in his grave more than a month when the lawyer finally tracked down Lew Rainbolt, at an oilfield strike in Texas, and gotten a message to her. Even then, Francie had not come back to Virginia City; she had signed papers giving Pitt permission to sell the stock she had inherited in Delavane Mines and put the proceeds into a bank account in her name. She gave Cavendish an authorization to draw on the account to keep up the Delavane mansion, her mother's house, in her absence—and that was the last that had been heard of her.

She obviously was content to keep all ties severed with Virginia City and everybody there—including himself. Tony concluded. It was her way, he imagined, of avoiding all the heartbreak and grief that the two of them endured the last few years before she ran away. If he suddenly stepped back into her life now, Tony thought, it would only subject her to more of the same. Tony loved her too much to do that.

Walking back around the side of the house, he was almost to the sidewalk when he heard a voice say, "Hey! Is that you? I'll be damned!"

Turning, Tony saw Chalky grinning at him from a small square of planted ground off to the side of the house. He had just dug up some carrots and was standing with them in his hand. Glancing anxiously at the house, Tony walked over to him.

"Hello, Chalky."

"Well, Mr. Donovan! I'll be double-damned!" He turned worried eyes to Tony's arm. "You been hurt bad, son?"

"Not too bad, Chalky. I'll be all right. How are you?"

"Why, I'm fine, Mr. Donovan. Got me a nice little Victory garden here—peas, carrots, and such. You been in to see Miss Francie?"

"Ah, no. I started to, Chalky, but I changed my mind. I'd appreciate it if you wouldn't tell her you saw me." Because Chalky was looking at him so curiously, Tony shrugged and smiled tentatively. "I decided it might be better if I didn't drag the past back into her life. If she's happy here with Rainbolt, it's probably best just to let things be—"

Chalky was shaking his head so that Tony stopped in mid-sentence, confused. "I guess you don't know," the albino said. "Mr. Rainbolt's dead. He was killed in the pineapple plantation riots the month before the war started. Miss Francie, she's all alone now."

Tony stared incredulously at Chalky. Before he could recover from the surprise and speak, he heard Francie's voice behind him. "My God—"

Turning, he found her standing on the drive, fingertips of one hand to her lips, as astonished by the moment as he was.

"Hello, Francie." His whole being seethed with feelings of love that had lain dormant but never died.

"Tony. Oh, Tony—"

Tears ran down her cheeks as she walked slowly to him and gently put her arms around him.

THIRTY-FIVE

They sat in a swing on the screened back porch in the cool of the evening, drinking beer. Chalky, who had a room over the garage, had gone to bed. Francie's radio was still on; Dick Jergens and his band were playing "One Dozen Roses."

"We came to the islands in September of last year," Francie told Tony. "Lew and his force were hired to patrol the pineapple fields on Lanai. There were riots the following month by Hawaiian field workers. During one of them, while Lew and his men were trying to protect the home of the plantation owner, Lew was stabbed to death. One of the servants in the house did it; a maid who saw him shoot her son, who was participating in the riot. She just walked up and plunged a kitchen knife into his heart. He was dead in minutes."

"Tough," Tony said, trying to sound sincere.

"We were living here at the time. Lew had a Gloster two-seater that he flew back and forth to Lanai. After his death, most of his men returned to the States. Chalky and I didn't know what to do, where to go; we had both been so dependent on Lew. After Pearl Harbor, travel became so restrictive that we just ended up staying here. I manage to keep pretty busy." She ticked off activities on her fingers. "Mondays and Wednesdays I roll bandages and pack medical kits for the Red Cross. Tuesdays I drive a pickup truck and collect tin cans from all the restaurants. Thursdays I run a movie projector at the enlisted men's movie house at Hickam Field. Friday and Saturday nights I'm a hostess at the U.S.O. canteen downtown. In between times, I help Chalky with his Victory garden."

"Quite a schedule," Tony said. He was impressed. "Sounds

452

like the kind of stuff your mother would be doing if she was
. . . here."

Francie smiled. "I often think of Mother, and how I used
to go all over Storey County with her on those 'missions of
mercy,' as my father used to call them." Her eyes settled on
him. "I understand from Martin Pitt that you were with my
father when he was killed."

"Yeah." Tony sighed quietly. "Matter of fact, I have
something of his you might want." Fumbling in his trouser
pocket, he drew out the cigarette lighter Big Jim had tossed
to him when they were lighting the fuses to blow open the
cracked bedrock. "I didn't know what to do with it, so I've
just been carrying it."

Francie turned the silver Ronson over in her hand a few
times, looking at it thoughtfully; then she handed it back to
him. "You keep it, Tony." He tried to object but she
insisted, pressing it back into his hand. "Please. I want you
to." *He was your father too.*

Francie was not surprised that Tony obviously did not
know the truth. After all, who would have told him? Not
Big Jim; if he had, Martin Pitt would have said something
when he finally located her in Texas. And not Buck O'Crotty;
he would have wanted, as he had *always* wanted, to protect
Tony from the possible influence of the upper class, the
management class, that he was always so fearful would
corrupt his beloved workingman. No, when she summarily
left Virginia City with Lew Rainbolt, she effectively closed
the valve on that bit of information, and insulated Tony,
insulated her *brother*, against the news that had so numbed
her.

"I hoped you would come back home when you found out
about your father," Tony said now.

Francie's smile was part self-conscious. "There was no
reason to come back," she said. "My father was already
buried. Martin was taking care of everything else. There
wasn't as much of an estate as most people imagined; my
father had taken a very heavy financial loss when he personally funded the new union contract. Not only did he not
make any money at all for himself after that, but he also had
to put up quite a lot of his own cash to subsidize the new
wages he agreed to."

"I didn't know that," Tony said. He wondered if Buck
had known?

"I did get an inheritance," Francie said, "don't get me wrong. I have enough to get by on and to keep up my mother's house, but I'm not independently wealthy by any means."

The radio began to play a new song called "Don't Get Around Much Anymore." Tony reached over and took Francie's hand. "What happened with us, honey?" he asked quietly, almost a plea. "How'd we lose each other?"

"People—just change," Francie said, trying to hold back tears. God, she wondered, why *do* things like this happen in life? She loved this man just as strongly and demandingly as she always had—*and in the same way*. The homogeneity of the blood in his veins and in hers had not changed that one iota. She loved and desired Tony Donovan just as she had since she had been a girl. God*damn* her father!

"I've asked myself a thousand times what went wrong," Tony said. "On the 'Canal I'd lie awake at night thinking about you, wondering where you were, wanting you—"

"Tony, don't," she said, as if in sudden panic. She drew her hand away from his. It did not dissuade him; he moved closer and put an arm around her.

"I keep thinking it was my fault," he admitted. "That there was more I could have done—"

"It wasn't your fault *or* mine, Tony," she insisted. "It was circumstances—our backgrounds, the interference of others, the strike and all its bad feelings . . ."

"And those are all things that are behind us now," Tony said. "There's no one to interfere in our lives anymore; nothing to cause bad feelings; no class difference to keep us apart. I still love you, Francie, just like I always have. Can't we try again?"

"I don't know, Tony," she said, an obvious strain in her already taut voice. Slipping out from under his arm, she rose and put her empty beer bottle and his into a trash can. Stepping partway through the kitchen door, she opened a refrigerator and fetched two more bottles, removing their tops at a bottle opener affixed to the porch railing. Handing Tony one, hoping that holding it, drinking it, would occupy his hands, she sat down again, wondering why—*why?*—this burden had fallen on her. "Tony, so much has happened," she said, and realized at once how lame it sounded.

"Have you stopped loving me, Francie?" he asked suddenly.

"No, Tony, no. I'll always love you—"

"Did you love Rainbolt?" He had to know.

"I needed Lew," she said. "And I might have thought I loved him. There were times," she admitted, "when I told him that I loved him. But I don't think I ever did, not really." She noticed Tony adjust his position and wince slightly. "Are you in pain?" she asked. "Would you like to lie down?"

"I'm okay. Just not used to being up so long."

"You never did tell me about your wounds," she said, in an effort to redirect the conversation.

Tony shrugged. "They're just wounds. One in the shoulder, one in the side. They're mending."

"You won't have to go back into combat, will you?"

"Sure I will. I'll go back to my outfit as soon as I'm able. That's not the reason you're being so distant, is it? What might happen to me in the war?"

"Well, it's something we have to think about," Francie said, seizing on the suggestion. Tony laughed and took her hand again.

"You don't have to worry about that," he assured her. "Do you have any idea what the odds are against me getting hit again? People don't get wounded twice, Francie. Hell, I'll be so safe when I get back, guys will be fighting to stand next to me."

He's going to die in combat, Francie thought.

She did not know why she thought it, or why it was suddenly such a given in her mind. Perhaps it was his laughter, his conviction that he would *not*. But whatever the perverse reason, she had absolutely no doubt at that moment that Tony Donovan, her half brother, would not survive the war. Now it was she who instinctively clasped his hand.

"Couldn't you get out of a combat assignment if you wanted to?" she asked.

"I don't know." Tony replied quietly. A slight reservation crept into his tone. "I never thought about it."

Could she ask him to do that? she wondered. Without offering him anything in return. "It just seems that you've done your part already," she said, and again her words sounded lame. "I'm sorry," she quickly apologized. "Just forget I said that. It was stupid."

A few minutes later, after she had gathered her thoughts

and had her feelings under control, she said earnestly, "Tony, listen to me for a minute. Try to understand what I'm going to say, even if I say it in my usual haphazard way. When I left Virginia City with Lew, I was very—I don't know, mixed-up, I guess, is the best way to put it. I felt that I had to get away from everything and everybody that was putting pressure on me, boxing me in, making demands. I kind of felt like I might lose my mind if I didn't. I felt like I had to find some way to breathe. Do you understand that?"

"Yeah, I guess so," he said.

Good, Francie thought, because it's the best lie I can think of, the best excuse I can make up to cover the fact that I ran away to hurt my father because I found out he was *your* father too.

"I kind of feel the same way now," she continued, "first with Lew being killed so violently, now with you wounded like you are. I feel like circumstances might be closing in on me again, making me want to bolt. Making me want to run away."

Francie put a palm on his cheek and let it slowly move down to rest on his neck. *Was she actually going to do this?*

"I love you very much, Tony. I want you very badly. But I don't want to make any plans. I don't want to count on any tomorrows. I don't want to look ahead and try to decide what the future should be—for either of us."

"You just want right now, is that it?"

"Yes." She leaned forward and put her lips on his. It was the kind of soft, gentle kiss that they had first shared in the forest when she had tasted the blood of his beating. Not knowing she was tasting her own blood. "Let's make a pact," she said. "Let's not talk about who we are, or what we are, or where we came from, or anything about the past. And, for God's sake, let's not worry about the future. Let's just love each other—now and until you leave. Can we do that, Tony?"

"We can do anything you want us to, Francie." Her kiss was still warm on his lips. "Anything you want us to."

She took the bottle of beer out of his hand and set it down with her own. Gently she pulled him to his feet. *Are you going to do this?* her mind screamed again. Yes, yes, yes! Her arm slipped around Tony's waist and she felt his good arm come around hers. They walked inside, through the kitchen, past the photograph of the dead Rainbolt, into the bedroom.

Are you . . . ? Yes!

"How badly are you still hurt, my darling?" she asked softly as she unknotted his tie.

"My stitches are all out," he said. "I can't do anything real fancy—"

"You don't have to. Leave the fancy stuff to me."

She got his shirt off, and his undershirt, and put his bare arm back in the sling. There was a metal clip visible in his collarbone. Sitting him on the side of the bed, she removed his shoes and socks, then stood him up again. Undoing his trousers, she got her first look at the ugly scar coming around his side and down his abdomen.

"My poor baby—" Then his erection came out of his shorts and she smiled. "Well, what have we here?"

"I've been told as recently as this morning that it's beautiful."

"Oh? Who by?"

"A nurse named Darlene."

"Well, mister, you just got a second vote. Darlene's right; this is gorgeous." She closed one hand around him and squeezed.

"Jesus, be careful—it's been a long time—"

Getting his shorts off Francie sat him back down, naked, and quickly removed her own clothes, dropping them on both sides of her as they came off. When she was naked too, she pushed him gently back onto the bed and put a pillow under his head. Straddling him, she locked her legs and lowered herself toward him.

"This isn't—going to take much—" he cautioned.

"You mean the first time won't," she amended. "I know it. But that's only the beginning . . ."

Francie let her torso down until the hair between her widely spread legs was barely touching the head of his rigid shaft. Bracing back on outstretched arms, she moved against him with the lightest of contact. Tony raised his head an inch and took in the incredible sight of her: bent toes, raised heels, widely separated knees, large flexed thighs, marvelous hair-surrounded cunt, and back beyond it her smooth belly, quaking breasts, raised chin, open mouth, dancing eyes, flowing hair . . .

"Francie—"

"Yes, my darling—"

"I can't wait—"

"Then don't, darling—"

Reaching forward with one hand, Francie seized him and held him steady as she thrust herself over him. A second later she felt him gush in the warm, wet darkness of her.

Right or wrong, it was done.

She did not regret it.

THIRTY-SIX

Their time together in Hawaii was idyllic. For days on end, they somehow managed to do the incredible if not the impossible: they forgot the past and ignored the future. So finely did they tune their minds to *now*, that they did not, until the last minute, plan even one day ahead. Everything was today for them—and only today.

They found that they loved to dance together, something they had missed during their adolescence because of their social separation.

"We do so well!" Francie marveled on the dance floor. "Even with your arm in that sling."

"Wish I could jitterbug with you," Tony said. "Bet you're good at that."

"Not really," she told him. "I like to watch, though."

There were half a dozen dances to choose from every night on Oahu: U.S.O. dances, ladies' auxiliary dances, nurses' corps dances, war bond dances—always some affair, always held in a hall or Quonset hut with the windows heavily draped due to the blackout. Popular music was played by military bands, high school marching bands, U.S.O. entertainment troupes, temporary groups using borrowed instruments, or phonograph records hooked up to loud-speakers. Someone was assigned to handle the lights, turning them up for "Perdido" and "Jingle Jangle Jingle," down low for "I Don't Want to Walk Without You" and "I've Heard That Song Before." When the music was slow and they swayed around dim little floors, Francie kept one hand at the back of Tony's neck and often whispered the lyrics in his ear. Tony loved it when she did; he had spent so many sleepless hours thinking of her throaty voice, that it now seemed like a miracle to be hearing it. When she whispered the words to "Don't Get Around Much Anymore," Tony had said happily, "That's not us. We're getting around plenty."

"Making up for lost time," Francie agreed.

When the musicians stepped up the tempo to "Jersey Bounce" or "Beat Me, Daddy, Eight to the Bar," Tony and Francie would stand on the sidelines under posters that said "Keep 'em Flying" and "Loose Lips Sink Ships," drinking three-point-two beer, always sure to stand close enough so that some part of them touched. It was so important to them, the physical contact that said *I'm yours,* that told the world *We belong to each other.*

Their days, when Francie was free of her volunteer work, were spent down on Waikiki lying on towels in the sun, listening to the surf lick at the shore. Francie rubbed lotion on him and regimented his positions so that he would tan evenly. "We've got to get some color on you," she said administratively. "That solarium at the hospital is okay for your face and hands, but the rest of you looks like a ghost. I want you tan all over—like me."

Soon he was. They had a favorite spot under a palm tree, "their" spot, just as Sierra Street had been "their" street, although they never mentioned that because it was part of the past. Francie always brought a blanket and a basket of food; they had shade when they wanted it, sun when it was time for Tony to sunbathe. Afternoons were balmy and peaceful; rarely when he was lying there with her fingers playing lightly in his hair, did he not fall asleep for an hour. From Francie's portable radio he might drift off to Kitty Kallen singing "Star Eyes," and wake up listening to Dinah Shore's sensuous "You'd Be So Nice To Come Home To."

Some nights they stayed at home eating ribs that Chalky would barbecue for them, playing cassino, listening to records of the Andrews Sisters, Helen Forrest, the Ames

Brothers, Jo Stafford. Always Francie played new records that she had just bought or borrowed; she had dozens she had brought from the States, but they were older songs, had memories attached, so were never played. Sometimes late at night, Francie would make an omelette, which Tony loved, from cheese purchased with valuable red ration stamps that were used primarily for meat and butter. After their midnight supper, they might go to one of the movies which were run around the clock at the movie houses on Kalakakua; they cried at the end of *Casablanca* when Ingrid Bergman flew away, cheered Brian Donlevy and Robert Preston in *Wake Island*, and talked excitedly about a new young actor named Alan Ladd they saw in *This Gun for Hire*.

But always there were the dances, never did two nights go by without finding a dance. The music of their "now" time was part of everything they did, and they felt drawn to embrace and dance to it. The songs of their war told lovers to kiss once, kiss twice, kiss once again, and they did; to stroll the lanes and laugh at the rains together, and they did. They clung to each other and listened to the music as if no one else on earth could hear the melody and whisper the words.

And when the dancing was over, there was their love. When the musicians called it a night, Tony and Francie had the little radio. When the dance floor darkened for a few hours, they had their candles in her bedroom. They made love every night, in every way. Francie watched her days carefully, and exercised subtle but preemptive control on what they did, and when. Buck O'Crotty's comment about the horror of an incestuous child haunted her memory, and she took all necessary precautions. She would not make Tony use a rubber; she wanted nothing between them when he was inside her, but on days when there was danger, even slightly, she took over the scenario, became the aggressor, and got it out of him with her mouth, or her hand, or awkwardly with her squeezed breasts.

"I wish I was as big as Darlene," she said once after doing it the latter way. She had met Tony's nurse at a hospital dance.

"You're plenty big enough," Tony said.

"I'll bet she can put lotion on hers, hold them together, and make a regular tunnel for it. Has she admired your cock any more?"

"No, I mostly dress myself now," Tony half lied. Darlene *had* indicated her receptiveness in light of his commission. She had come into his room one morning when he was alone, her uniform unbuttoned on top to show some enticing cleavage.

"Well, *Lieutenant* Donovan, congratulations," she said. "Are you still interested in getting together?"

"Sorry, no, Lieutenant," he had replied with a wide smile. "Now that I'm an officer and a gentleman, I only go out with civilians."

"Suit yourself," she had said good-naturedly. "You don't know what you're missing."

"But you do," Tony reminded her.

From then on one of the married nurses seemed to draw Tony for a patient; Darlene never helped him dress again.

There were other things Tony kept from Francie too, but they all involved Virginia City: letters he received from Buck, Rosetta, and Kerry. Buck wrote of the mines being converted to metals like copper and lead, with the precious metals, silver and gold, although more valuable, now much less essential to the war effort and therefore not mined as primary products any longer. He praised the government for putting a freeze on food prices but complained that it had allowed "profit-mongering businessmen" to raise the cost of food more than sixty percent before finally stopping them. And always Buck spoke of the day when Tony would return and go back into the mines and the union. In his letters to Buck, Tony never responded to those comments. He had made up his mind not to return to the life of a miner. The caves on the 'Canal, with the eerie association to mining he experienced during the grenade attack, had started him thinking about it. Finding Francie had inspired further thoughts. Now he no longer believed he could make it as a miner; thoughts of the darkness and the depths depressed him. He did not want to remain a manual laborer. Since his exposure to the privileges of being an officer, he had decided that there had to be many cleaner, quicker ways of earning a living. Buck, he knew, would oppose his decision, and Tony knew he would have to cope with that in the future.

Rosetta's letters to Tony were about her Victory garden, about milk deliveries being reduced to every other day, and about her volunteer work with the Red Cross and V.F.W. auxiliary. Kerry, approaching her teens and about to graduate from the eighth grade, wrote about a young actress named Margaret O'Brien whom she had seen in *Journey for Margaret*, and a book she had read called *The Song of Bernadette*, and how she was looking forward to high school where she hoped to be treated more like a grown-up.

Most of Kerry's letters were adolescent in tone, but an occasional one, Tony noticed, sounded more grown up. In those, she told Tony how much she loved—really *loved*— him, not as a sister, but as a girlfriend. She went to sleep every night thinking about him, she said, feeling warm and cozy, pretending he was lying beside her. Tony did not let himself become too disturbed by the girl's love letters, they were not that frequent, but they did remind him every so often that there was no blood between Kerry and him. His own sisters, the little twins, were still very much in his memory.

Tony felt guilty about not answering the letters from home as punctually and enthusiastically as he knew he should, but he could not bring himself to take time away from Francie. While she was doing her volunteer work his time was usually taken up by physical therapy to restore the use of his arm. He did write brief notes to each one in the O'Crotty household assuring them that he was recuperating nicely and always promising to write more when he could. And he sent off several short letters to Denny, addressing them to the Fleet Post Office, First Marine Division, but did not know whether Denny got them or not; he never received a reply. The only way he knew that Denny was still alive was that Buck had not been notified to the contrary.

For the most part, Tony's life was all Francie: making love with her, walking and talking with her, dancing and lying on Waikiki with her, thinking of her, looking at her, waiting for her, laughing with her, sharing the incredible feeling of love that each knew the other felt so equally compelling. For Tony, there was nothing, no one, except Francie. And for Francie, nothing, no one, but Tony—and her own relentless conscience.

Francie knew what she was doing was very wrong, as wrong as anything she *could* do. This man she was making love with was her half brother, whose being, whose beginning, came from the same place from which her being, her beginning, had come: from the manhood, the excitement, the lust, the seed of Jim Delavane. At night sometimes, with Tony sleeping naked beside her, she would lie awake and see the faces of her father and Buck O'Crotty, the only people who knew the awful secret, floating over the bed in the darkness. They looked at her with scorn and contempt, their lips mouthing silent vilifications at her: tramp, slut, whore, incestuous bitch. How grateful she was that her mother's face did not join them; she would not, she feared, have been able to stand that.

Recriminate as she might, Francie had no intention of reversing the course of action she had chosen. There was still her utter conviction that Tony was doomed, that he would not survive the war, that he would die in combat. It never occurred to her that she might have subconsciously fabricated that conception to justify her illicit conduct with him. Such a possibility was beyond her consideration; she truly believed that the gift of love she was sharing with Tony was the last he would ever receive. She could not, would not, deprive him of it; could not, would not, send him back to the hell of combat rejected by her, without knowing why. And she could not tell him—that was totally, completely, irrevocably unthinkable. Not simply because she lacked the capacity to tell him; she was glad no one else had either. She did not want him to know . . . ever.

So their time together passed, happy days flowing into wonderful weeks, glorious nights melding into scores of precious memories, their love expanding, enveloping, encompassing all that they allowed: today, the moment, *now*. All the while Tony's wounds were healing and his war was waiting.

Early in February, Tony's doctor gave him a thorough physical examination and said, "You ready to get back in it, Donovan?"

"Yes, sir," Tony replied. The duty he felt to the Marine Corps—for his citation, his commission, his country—was the only thing he could even remotely imagine that he would allow to take him away from Francie. He had to go back; that was inflexible.

That night, after he had been certified fit for active duty, she did what she had promised herself she would not: she challenged his return to combat.

"You've been seriously wounded and you've been decorated for heroism. There's no *reason* for you to go back! Let them send somebody else! They could give you a training assignment somewhere—"

She began to cry and Tony put his arms around her. He held her, comforted her, without speaking. It was not necessary to say anything; they both knew he would go back to combat, and they both knew why. Combat was where the Marine Corps needed him.

As they had agreed in the beginning, they did not talk about the future, even on their last night together. They spent that last night, as they had spent so many others, embracing on a crowded floor, dancing to the music of their time, their love, their war. They talked little, except to whisper "I love you" over and over again. And Francie softly sang love lyrics in his ear.

When the dancing was over, they went to their place under the palm tree on Waikiki and sat in each other's arms listening to the moonlit surf just yards away. At three A.M., when the beach was deserted, they rose and silently took off their clothes. Standing up against the palm tree, they made slow, smooth, warm, wet love: multi-orgasmic for Francie; prolongingly explosive for Tony.

At dawn they walked through the park and up to her house, and she cooked breakfast for him. Then he got his seabag out of the bedroom and Chalky drove them in Lew Rainbolt's yellow roadster out to Hickam Field. In a staging area, Tony shook an almost tearful Chalky's hand and told him good-bye; then Tony and Francie walked to the embarkation gate together.

"This is my address," Tony said, pressing a piece of paper into her hand.

"Tony—"

"I know. No tomorrows. But just in case, okay?"

"Okay." She took the piece of paper.

"Take care of yourself honey," he said softly.

She put a palm on his cheek and her face contorted as the sobs burst from her. "Oh, Tony—"

From a loudspeaker: *All transfer personnel please board the aircraft!*

With one arm around her waist, Tony kissed her. "I love you, Francie."

"I—love you—too, Tony—"

In the clear Hawaiian morning, Tony fell in with the line of men crossing the tarmac to a waiting C-54. Francie walked sobbing back to the yellow roadster, dropping the slip of paper behind her as she went. She did not want to know when he died.

Part Nine

Tony

1951

THIRTY-SEVEN

Tony could not help feeling that Rosetta was lying to him about Buck's murder.

As much as he wanted to believe her, as much as he had been conditioned over twenty years to depend upon her honesty, her inability to equivocate, something deep in his gut told him that now, in this most important subject they had ever discussed, she was, if not lying, at least withholding something from him. Feeling that way, he asked her the same question he had sometime earlier asked Denny.

"Rosetta, if you knew anything that I wanted to know, you'd tell me, wouldn't you?"

"You asked me a similar question right after Buck's funeral," she reminded him. "I'll give you the same answer I did then—if I knew anything that would help you, Tony, and not hurt you, yes, I would tell you."

And you, Tony thought, are the one who decides whether it will help me or not, hurt me or not. Which gives you a lot of flexibility in your decision.

Pursing his lips, Tony rose from Rosetta's kitchen table to pour himself some more coffee. He had not remembered asking her the question previously, only that he had asked Denny. This is not good, he thought. I am asking the people closest to me to reaffirm their loyalty to me—and then forgetting that I asked them. I've got to stop trying to make people promise to tell me the truth and assume that they are. If they aren't, I should be able to tell.

Tony had flown up to Virginia City the previous day and given Rosetta the private investigation report on Buck's murder. He had done so after obtaining permission from Meyer Lansky.

"Of course, Tony," Lansky had said on the phone from

his Manhattan apartment. "Listen, we're playing all our cards above the table in this. That report is the end result of a legitimate inquiry conducted for a justifiable reason by a reputable private investigation firm. Share it with whomever you wish, please."

"Would you mind," Tony had requested further, "if I make direct contact myself with the detective agency and ask for some follow-up work? At my own expense, of course."

"Have them do any additional work you wish, Tony," he was told by Lansky, "and at *our* expense. Consider it an extra bonus for the good job you're doing for us. You won't be taking a lot of time away from the hotels, will you?"

"No, sir, not at all," Tony assured him. "Just a day now and then."

"Let me know any way I can help you, Tony."

After leaving the report with Rosetta to read overnight, Tony had come back to discuss it. "What did you think of it?" he asked.

"It seems to be very thorough," Rosetta commented. "But it answers none of your questions, does it, Tony?"

Tony frowned. *My* questions? Didn't she also want to know who killed Buck?

"I thought maybe your reading the interviews with the various people contacted might generate some thought about some of them. About their relationships with Buck, maybe some old grudges you might have forgotten. Anything."

"I'm sorry, Tony. The report gave me no new thoughts. I'm glad you have it, though; it seems to be pretty definite that none of the people you work for were involved. Of course, I never really thought they were."

"Why not?" Tony asked curiously.

Rosetta shrugged. "Unlike Buck," she said, "I was never really convinced that you had turned into some kind of gangster. Naturally, with others, I never contradicted his position. But I did in private, with him."

"I wasn't aware of that."

"There was no way for me to tell you. I was never able to change his mind, even a little bit. He was convinced you had turned bad."

"Yet just before his death he was going to contact me," Tony reminded her. "He was going to try and resolve the trouble between us. Why, Rosetta?"

"Tony, dear," she took his hand in both of hers, "all I

can tell you is that Buck, like the rest of us, got wiser as he grew older; he began to relax some of his rigid ways, change a few of his longtime values. He began to see some things in new light. Even though he was convinced you had turned your back on everything he held high in his mind, perhaps he also felt that if he gave a little and you gave a little, the two of you could at least meet again on common ground. There were things he wanted to tell you, Tony, that he felt only he was qualified to tell; only he had the *right* to tell. That burden weighed very heavily on him in what turned out to be the last week of his life."

A sudden thought occurred to Tony. "You don't suppose he might have left some written record of what he wanted to tell me, do you? A diary or journal or something?"

"If he did, I know nothing of it. There was no such thing among his personal effects. I don't know about his union papers; Terence Henny took charge of all those. I think Mr. Henny would have told me if he found anything personal."

"Probably," Tony agreed. "I might ask him anyway."

Later that day, Tony went uptown to the union office and spent a few minutes with Terence Henny. He asked him first about the interview with the private investigator, in which Henny had connected Buck's murder with an attempt by "organized crime" to take over Nevada unions. The new union president brushed it aside good-naturedly.

"Hell, that's political talk, Tony," he scoffed. "That's stockpiling votes for the next union election. Makes the men down below think their president is concerned with important, even dangerous, matters. Gives them something to think about besides the next dime-an-hour wage hike." He winked at Tony. "If I only get 'em a nickel an hour, well at least I'll have kept the gangsters out of our union too, so they'll vote for me one more time. Union politics, Tony, that's all."

It seemed Henny had no more idea who killed Buck O'Crotty than anyone else did. The silica dust problem, he admitted, might have produced enough enmity at one time to constitute a motive, but that had been resolved amicably before the murder. There was nothing else, Henny claimed, of any consequence that might involve the union.

Tony then asked whether anything personal of Buck's had been found in the union office. "Any kind of diary or log, maybe?"

"Nothing like that," Henny told him. "There was this, though," he said, taking from his safe an old Cavalier Supreme cigar box and handing it to Tony. "I didn't give it to Rosetta because there's a picture of some woman in there and—well, I didn't know—"

"My mother," Tony said, staring at the copy of the photograph that Buck had once given him; that he in turn had given back to Buck in his casket. Now it was almost as if Buck was returning it to him from the grave.

"I didn't know who she was," Henny said self-consciously. "I just thought—"

"It's all right," Tony said. He looked through the other items: some old union pins from the coal mines, a few postcards, Marine Corps sergeant chevrons, a photograph of Buck, John L. Lewis, and another man, and a Purple Heart and three campaign medals from World War I. "This is all?" Tony asked.

"That's the lot," Henny assured him.

Tony sighed resignedly. "If you should run across anything else, let me know, will you, Terry?"

"You can count on it, Tony, my boy," Henny said, patting him on the back. "After all, us hardrockers have to stick together."

Tony left the union office with the distinct feeling that he had been handled.

He had promised Rosetta he would come back for supper, but before he did, Tony stopped in to see Sheriff Sam Patch. "I'm curious, Sheriff," he said. "I've been in town since yesterday and you haven't bothered me. No warnings, no one following me. Why's that?"

"Maybe I've decided you're not a troublemaker, after all," the longtime sheriff said. He sat far back in a swivel chair and with a bone-handled jackknife sliced off a plug of Red Man and put it in one cheek.

"I thought maybe," Tony said, "whoever told you to do it last time, told you not to this time."

"Don't nobody really *tell* me to do or not to do things." he replied easily. "I'll take advice, and I appreciate tips, but I usually call the shots myself. I hope you're not implying to the contrary."

Standing before Patch's desk, Tony recalled the night that his father, with a wooden chair leg for a weapon, had started in a drunken rage for the Delavane mansion to settle with Big Jim Delavane for the Donovan family's slide to poverty. Ruby had telephoned Patch and the sheriff had stopped Iron Mike from making a bad mistake. Another time, Tony recalled, when Buck had returned to Virginia City to adopt him, and Big Jim Delavane had also tried to get him, it had been Sheriff Patch who suggested that Tony himself be allowed to decide with whom he wanted to live.

"Sam," Tony asked now, "how did you and I get on different sides?"

"Don't know," Patch said. "Want to talk about it?"

"Let's."

The old sheriff smiled a grizzled smile and said, "Sit down, Tony. I'll get the coffee."

They talked for an hour, explaining their positions, resolving their real and imagined differences, and concluding that they both really wanted the same thing: to find out who killed Buck.

"I can't believe," Tony said, "that he was killed by some shadowy person who moved in and out of his life just long enough to end it. That wouldn't have happened to Buck."

"I agree," Patch said. "But right now that's sure as hell how it looks. The state police, the state's attorney general, the F.B.I., and my own little department have all conducted investigations. There was some private investigation too—"

"That was mine," Tony told him.

"Well, then you know. Not a single clue points toward anyone. It's a dead end, Tony."

"Does that mean you're giving up on it?"

"I'll never give up on it," Patch said. "It'll always be an open case. But it'll get older every day too."

"I intend to keep looking," Tony said.

"Wouldn't expect you to do no different," the sheriff allowed. "You'll get no trouble from me so long as you don't get nobody in town upset. Keep things quiet, know what I mean?"

"Sure," said Tony.

He left the sheriff's office feeling a little better at having resolved things with Patch, and went back to Rosetta's for supper. When he got there he found Kerry helping her prepare the meal. Mother and daughter both laughed at his surprise.

"I called her and told her to come down," Rosetta admitted.

"And I," Kerry said in mock horror, "cut classes for the afternoon."

"But it's all right," Rosetta excused, "because her grades are back up where they should be. She's getting an A in everything except—what is it, honey? Agents?"

"Agency," said Kerry. "And I'm getting a B in that, so it's okay." She put her arms around Tony's neck. "Are you glad to see me?"

"If you're behaving yourself I am," Tony replied, kissing her lightly on the cheek.

"None of that," she said roughly and gave him an unsisterly kiss on the lips. Rosetta looked at them curiously and Tony felt himself blush. To cover his embarrassment, he gave Rosetta the cigar box he had acquired from Henny, minus the photograph of Ruby, which he kept for himself. For several minutes she and Kerry had a good cry going through Buck's mementos.

Kerry had been back in school nearly an entire semester since her rebellious conduct had brought Tony and Denny to Reno to take her in hand. They had kept her out of school for four weeks, making her stay with Madge Bellamy. Madge tried to be her friend. "Seems to me, honey, the simple answer to the whole problem is for you to settle down, go back to college, and be the person everybody wants you to be. Tell you one thing—you'll stand a lot better chance getting Tony that way."

"Is it that plain?" Kerry had asked.

"It is to me, honey."

Kerry had ended up crying like a child in Madge Bellamy's lap—then telling Tony and Denny she was ready to beg her mother's forgiveness, go back to school, and straighten up and fly right. Which is ultimately what she did. Surprising Tony at her mother's house was the first time she had seen him since returning to school.

"Sounds," Tony said at supper, "like you've got all your courses under control again if you're getting such good grades."

"I have," Kerry said. "Even with two law courses, agency and contracts, I'll still make the dean's list." Although technically in prelaw, through a newly instituted advanced courses examination, Kerry was being allowed to do first-year law school work along with her undergraduate studies. This, after having made up for the month of studies she missed during what she now referred to as her "problem stage."

"I am so proud of her again," Rosetta praised. "Imagine, the dean's list. How Buck would have boasted. Not to mention Mr. Morrell, her blood father." Rosetta quickly crossed herself. "God rest both their souls."

"Not Buck's, I don't think, Rosetta," Tony said quietly.

"What do you mean?" Rosetta asked, staring.

"Let's don't pray for Buck's soul to be at rest. He wouldn't want that. Not until his murderer is found."

Rosetta looked at him unblinkingly for a long moment, her steady Indian eyes probing for some deeper meaning than was obvious in his words. "I'm not sure," she said after a moment, "that I agree with you, Tony. Suppose the person is never found?"

"The person will be found," he assured her. "Too many people want it to happen for it not to. And," he added quietly, "I made Buck a promise at his grave, that *I* would find out who did it."

Rosetta put a hand to her lips. "I didn't know that."

"It was just between Buck and me. I didn't want to put any extra burden on you and Kerry then. But it's a year now and it's still unsolved. So I want your help, both of you. Will you give it to me?"

"Of course, Tony," said Rosetta.

"Sure," Kerry replied, "you know we will. What do you want us to do?"

"For now," Tony said, "I want you to be observant with everyone you come into contact with who was associated in any way with Buck. Watch people, listen to them, remember what they say. Be alert not only to what they say but *how* they say it. If anything—anything at all, however slight—impresses you as suspicious, I want to know about it. Call me. I'll pass the information on to the detective agency; they're going to continue to keep their investigation active for the time being, so they'll be ready to act on anything we give them."

"Will they be coming back to Virginia City?" Rosetta wanted to know. "Asking questions around town again?"

"That's possible," said Tony. He sensed that she was bothered by that. "Why?"

"I was just curious," the Paiute woman said.

But Tony got the distinct impression that it was more than that. And the expression on Kerry's face told him that Rosetta's daughter had the same feeling.

Later that night, after Rosetta had gone to bed, Tony and Kerry sat in the front porch swing to talk. Kerry lighted a Kool, saying, "It's the one bad habit I still have, other than being in love with you."

"That'll pass when Mr. Right comes along," Tony told her easily.

"To quote you," she replied, " 'Sure, sure.' " She had a portable radio on the porch and reached over to turn it on. After it warmed up, it began playing Hank Williams, singing "Cold, Cold Heart." Kerry laughed quietly. "How appropriate. I dedicate this song to you, Mr. Donovan."

Tony reach past her and turned it off "I have something to ask you."

"The answer is yes and I'd like a simple wedding."

"Is it possible for you to be serious for a minute?" he asked, a little harshly.

"Okay," she said contritely. "Sorry." She swallowed, embarrassed. "What do you want to ask me?"

"Has it ever crossed your mind," he lowered his voice, "that your mother might not have been completely honest with us in what she knows about Buck's death?"

In the moonlight Tony saw her look away, toward the dark silence of G Street. In profile, he could see that she was biting her lower lip. He knew her answer before she spoke it.

"Yes," she admitted, "it has."

Tony's stomach churned a little as he heard what might be, he thought, the first completely honest answer he had gotten from anyone regarding Buck's killing. Knowing how Kerry must feel about having to make the admission, he took one of her hands in the dark. "Listen to me, Kerry. If Rosetta is lying to us, she has a damn good reason for it. And she's hurting inside for having to do it. If we find out why, we can help her. Understand?"

"Yes."

"What is it that you think she hasn't told us?"

"Tony, I don't know," Kerry declared. "I'm not even sure *why* I feel the way I do. I thought it was just me, that I was upset over losing Buck, upset because I'd made a fool of myself with you—"

"You didn't, Kerry."

"Oh, like hell. I threw myself at you like a high school sophomore. I did everything wrong. Then I went and pulled that Miss Disgraceful act and made a fool out of myself again. I know how I've messed everything up. My point is, that's why I wasn't sure about Mother, why I thought it was just poor, mixed-up me. I had no idea you suspected the same thing."

"Do you have any gut feeling about what she's holding back, or why?"

"Not a clue," Kerry said. "You?"

"No, nothing. I'm like you—I wasn't sure it was anything except my imagination." He slipped an arm around her shoulders. "Earlier tonight I asked you and Rosetta to listen to people and observe them. I want you to do that for us with Rosetta."

"I don't know, Tony," she said skeptically. "I don't know about spying on my own mother—"

"Not spying," he asserted. "Trying to help. If she's not being honest with us, two of the three people in this world that she cares the most about, then she *needs* our help. And you may be the only one who can figure her out, Kerry."

"Because I'm her daughter?"

"Partly. And partly because you're an Indian like she is."

Kerry turned to stare at the dark street again. As she did so, Tony had the strange sensation that they were not alone on the porch. His eyes searched the shadows around them. They stopped at a window near the swing. It was open a few inches at the bottom, just enough for part of a curtain hem to blow through. As Tony raised his eyes midway up the window, he was certain he saw a figure in white inside, backing away. Rosetta, he thought. In her nightgown. How long had she been there? he wondered. What had she heard? He was reaching up to put a cautioning finger to Kerry's lips when Kerry gave him her answer.

"All right, I'll watch Mother as closely as I can when I'm home. But I'm not sure how I'm going to feel about doing it. I might back out on you."

"If you have to, okay." He lowered his own voice even more, hoping she would do the same, although he was sure Rosetta had now backed too far away from the window to hear them any longer. Just to be on the safe side, he took Kerry's hand. "Let's go for a walk."

He could see her moonlit smile as she suddenly reverted to her less serious self. "Hmm. Things may be looking up."

Tony forced himself to laugh softly with her, even though his mind was on the woman back in the house.

THIRTY-EIGHT

Before he drove to the airport in Reno the next morning, Tony left the Ormsby House on foot and walked to the top of Gold Street. A row of fairly new tract homes ran along part of one side where the street dead-ended at the foot hills, but adjacent to the yard of the last house there was still some slight sign of where his old footpath had once begun. Hoping no one in the little end house was observing, he left the sidewalk and began to make his way into the forest.

Memories charged his mind as he proceeded along the pine-needled floor. He knew exactly which tree he sat under, bleeding and crying, after his beating in the schoolyard by Jack Coltrane and the other Hill boys; knew exactly which side of the tree he had sat on, which direction he had been facing, when Francie had so quietly come up next to him. Stopping by that tree now, he touched it almost reverently as bittersweet images of her young face reeled in his mind. God, he thought, how he had loved her and how indescribably sweet had been the sensations of that first love; how compelling and consuming that love had been; how it had mastered every emotion in his being, been able to summon in an instant the keenest ecstasy, the deepest agony. That young love, that first love, had generated in him a sensation so near to sexual climax that he had never forgotten it. How he *had* loved her? No—how he *still* loved her. And was convinced that he always would.

Deeper into the forest his old footpath was even more intact, and he saw individual rocks he actually remembered, individual stepping places he had used to climb where the terrain rose abruptly, even a hollow under one rock where he used to leave his pocket change so it would not rattle when he sneaked into the cellar of the Delavane mansion. Memories were like a drug-induced euphoria, like the intensity of the morphine during the hours between the time he was wounded on Guadalcanal and when he finally reached the naval hospital in Hawaii: a feeling of softness, warmth, suspension.

Finally Tony reached the stand of pines at the back edge of the Delavane property. The rear of the mansion was in even worse disrepair than he remembered the front being when he had seen it a year earlier. Shutters had paint peeling from them, weeds had grown unchecked all along the foundation, a once lovely patio extending around from the west side, where it got the afternoon sun, was unswept, its wicker furniture strewn with blown leaves, strung with spider webs. Once again Tony thought, how Edith Delavane would hate this, how it would hurt her to see it. He could not understand, given the deep love Francie had always had for her mother, how she could let the house decay this way.

As Tony stood looking out of the shadows of the trees, the mansion's back door suddenly opened. Startled, Tony tensed, instinctively crouched, and remained absolutely still. Francie, he thought. Francie, he begged. Francie—God, let it be Francie.

It was Cavendish.

The Delavane butler, whom Tony had not seen in more than a decade, came out of the house wvith a grocery sack in his hands and went down the porch steps to a pair of metal trash cans standing next to the outside cellar door. As he lifted the lid on one of the cans to put the sack inside, a few things spilled on the ground and Cavendish stooped to pick them up. Tony quickly estimated the distance between himself and the porch steps, and between Cavendish and the porch steps—and without hesitation moved from the concealment of the trees and hurried across the backyard. He had plenty of time; Cavendish was slow in picking up what he had dropped, did not hear as well as he once had, and was not aware of Tony's presence until he put the lid back on the trash can and turned to find Tony walking past the porch steps toward him. The butler's face drained of color.

"Why . . . Mr. Donovan . . ."

"Hello, Cavendish." Tony kept his tone conversational. "How've you been?"

"Ah, I've been quite well, thank you." His eyes flicked to the rear door and back. "And you, sir?"

"Pretty good, Cavendish. It's been a long time."

"Yes, sir, it has." Although English, the butler had only an occasional trace of British left in his speech.

The two men could not resist studying each other, and remembering. What Tony saw was a man once tall and erect who had been the epitome of fastidiousness: precisely trimmed hair, so closely shaved his cheeks were pink, attired in three suits every day—one for mornings, afternoons, and evenings—who now had a stubble of white beard, who wore a plaid woolen shirt under a worn cardigan sweater, who had been reduced to taking out the garbage. What Cavendish saw was an intense, brooding boy with dark eyes, his cheek scarred from a terrible tragedy, who had become a confident, controlled, perhaps less intense, but still scarred—on the surface and no doubt inside—perhaps dangerous man, who at the moment, the butler felt nervously, had him at a distinct disadvantage. Cavendish ran his tongue over suddenly dry lips.

Tony realized that the older man was afraid of him. He did not want that. "When was the last time we saw each other, Cavendish?" he asked easily. "The spring of 1941, wasn't it? The day of the cave-in?"

"I . . . yes, sir, I believe it was . . ."

The back door closed and both men heard a quiet but unmistakable click as it was locked.

"Someone has locked you out, Cavendish," Tony said. Spoken as a simple statement, both men knew it was a query.

"Chalky, sir," the butler told him. "Do you remember Chalky? He came to town with Mr. Rainbolt?"

"Yes, I remember him."

"He works for me now. Two of us make up the entire household staff." Cavendish looked helplessly around at the disreputable condition of the mansion exterior and the grounds. "As you can see," he said apologetically, "we can't possibly keep up with everything that, well . . ." The older man sighed an abjectly weary sigh that made Tony suddenly feel sorry for him. But Tony could not allow himself to lose control of the conversation.

"Why would Chalky lock you out, Cavendish?" he pressed.

"Perhaps he doesn't realize I'm out here," the butler said lamely.

"Should we knock on the door and tell him?"

"There's no hurry, sir. I've some things to do out here for a while." Cavendish straightened his shoulders slightly, as if reconciling his unexpected situation, and realizing that all he knew about Tony Donovan made him conclude that he was in no real danger here.

"Cavendish," Tony decided to be direct, "I'd like to go into the house and see Miss Delavane."

"I'm sorry, sir, but Miss Delavane is away."

"Away where?"

"I really can't say, sir."

Tony let his expression harden. "Can't say or won't say?"

"Can't say, sir. I do not know where Miss Delavane goes when she leaves here."

"Cavendish," Tony said ominously, "suppose I insisted on going inside to see for myself whether Miss Delavane is there or not. Do you think you and Chalky could stop me?"

"I think we would probably telephone Sheriff Patch, sir. You see, we have strict instructions from Miss Delavane that no intruders are to be permitted on the grounds."

Tony's expression and voice became nonthreatening again. "Do you really consider me an intruder?" he asked in quiet reproach.

The butler's weary face became sad. "I don't, Mr. Donovan. I think you know that, sir. But I'm not at liberty to exercise my own feelings and judgment. Miss Delavane is my employer and I—" He held out his hands in a gesture of helplessness. "Please understand, sir."

Tony found himself incapable of backing the poor old man any further into a corner over something that was not his doing. "I do understand, Cavendish. I'm sorry." He suddenly felt very sad himself "You know I still love Francie very much, don't you?" It was the first time he had ever used her given name in conversation with Cavendish. To the butler it was like a handshake.

"I do know that, yes. I have wished many times that—" His voice broke and he sighed again, shaking his head in defeat. "I am only a servant," he said finally, his excuse and explanation for all in the world that he could not control and of which he did not approve.

Tony patted the butler on the shoulder. He bobbed his chin at the back door. "Tell Chalky I don't hold it against him."

"He'll be glad to know that, sir. He's always held you in very high regard. Let me belatedly say too, Mr. Donovan, how sorry I was about Mr. O'Crotty's death. I've never had the chance to tell you, but I always greatly admired him. He was an exemplary man who always treated everyone like an equal, no matter what their station. His kind are few and far between."

"Thank you, Cavendish. Buck would be pleased to know you felt that way." Tony glanced at the back door again and decided there was nothing further to be gained there unless he actually did force his way into the mansion, which would serve to put him in bad stead with Sam Patch again, whether Francie was inside or not. It was essential in continuing to look for Buck's killer, that he stay on the sheriff's good side. Smiling, he shook hands with the elderly butler. "Good-bye, Cavendish. Take care of Francie."

"Always, sir."

Tony left the yard and walked back to the forest.

At the Reno airport several hours later, Tony was drinking coffee out of a paper cup in the terminal when he saw Arnie Shad standing nearby, doing the same. The two men nodded reservedly and, after hesitating, Shad walked over.

"You on the two-thirty flight?" he asked.

"Yeah. You too?"

"Yeah." Arnie took a sip of coffee. "You think they'll ever have decent coffee in airports?"

"Someday, maybe," Tony replied noncommittally. He started to mention a new product being developed by a dietetic laboratory in Ohio; called Pream, it was a powdered instant cream for use in coffee. Tony had been advised to invest in it. But the man who gave him the advice was Meyer Lansky, and Tony knew better than to mention Lansky to the maverick reporter.

The two men fell awkwardly silent. They had not seen

each other since the evening of Buck's funeral. Arnie had called him once since then to say he had completed the series of articles on Buck and wondered if Tony cared to read them before publication, as Rosetta was doing, to check for accuracy. Tony said he would and Arnie sent the galleys over by messenger. Tony read the entire series that night and called Arnie first thing the next morning.

"It's a fine piece of writing, Arnie," he told the reporter. "I was very moved by a lot of it. I'm sure Rosetta will be too."

"I'm glad you like it, Tony," Arnie replied. "I know you and I don't see a lot of things the same way anymore, but it was important to me that you approve of this. I hope Buck would have liked it too."

"He would," Tony assured him. "I guarantee it."

The series, in six parts, entitled "Hardrock: The Story of Buck O'Crotty," began in a Sunday edition of the *Las Vegas Star* and ran in the next five daily editions. It was widely praised throughout Nevada and subsequently syndicated to a number of newspapers, especially in mining communities, all over the western states. Arnie was presented a plaque by the Nevada Newspaper Association at their annual awards dinner in Carson City and also received a scroll for outstanding journalism from the United Mine Workers. Tony had been proud of him and thought several times about calling and telling him so. But he never did. Standing in the airport, Tony tried to think of a way of telling Arnie now but the reporter started talking first.

"So, how are things going?"

"Okay," Tony replied.

"Been up visiting Rosetta or what?"

"Yeah. I had a report from a private investigation firm regarding Buck's killing that I wanted to go over with her."

Arnie's eyebrows went up. "Private investigation firm, huh? They come up with anything?"

Tony shook his head. "They found a lot of evidence to show who didn't do it, but nothing to indicate who did. My theory about the mine operators and the silica dust problem was all wet. Buck apparently had resolved that with them before he was killed."

"I know," Arnie said. "I checked into that possibility myself" Tony looked surprised. "I'm a good newspaperman," Arnie shrugged. "I check all angles."

"That's the first time I've known you to look into any possibility that didn't support your 'organized crime' stand."

"Speaking of which, did your investigation explore the possibility of a Lansky-Luciano involvement?"

"Yes, it did. The conclusion was that the murder was not connected in any way to a national crime syndicate or to anybody believed to be part of such a thing. Sorry to disappoint you."

"Into each life a little rain must fall," Arnie said philosophically. "It'll all come out in the open some day and then I'll say I told you so." Arnie glanced around the terminal and lowered his voice. "Are you up to date on what's happening in Washington? The Senate crime commission?"

"More or less."

Arnie pursed his lips in thought, then said, "They've got a secret witness that you'll probably find very interesting."

"You mean Virginia?"

The reporter's mouth dropped open. "I'll be damned. That's supposed to be a well-guarded secret."

"How'd you know, then?"

"I've got connections."

Tony nodded curtly. "So have I."

Their flight was announced and the two men discarded their unfinished coffee and walked onto the field to board. Once they were airborne, their discussion continued.

"You know I'm covering the state crime beat now," Arnie said, "which means I pick up a lot of inside stuff that the state attorney general's office is involved in. There's a state investigation committee also being formed; its goal is going to be to clean out crime syndicate members who have investments in Nevada casinos."

"That's nothing new," Tony pointed out. "Jack Coltrane threatened me with that when I went up for Buck's funeral. It's never materialized."

"It will. It'll go to work as soon as the Kefauver hearings are over. The state attorney general doesn't want anything to impede that investigation because he hopes that the federal boys will do part of his work for him. He hopes that by the time the Senate gets through, half the racketeers who are involved in Las Vegas casinos will either be out of business, in jail, or both. And that includes your friend Lansky."

Tony grunted softly. "All they do is make insinuations that nobody ever backs up."

"They'll be backed up someday," Arnie asserted.

"Sure, sure," Tony scoffed. "That kind of bullshit has been spread about Lansky for years. You know, Arnie, after Ben was killed, I went over all the things you'd told me about Lansky since you quit working for the Flamingo. You had me scared that maybe Lansky *was* this cold-blooded gangster you say he is. So I started doing a little checking on my own, through some contacts I've made myself over the past few years. You want to know the sum total of Meyer Lansky's crimes—his *real* crimes?"

"I can hardly wait," Arnie said.

"Sure, be a wise guy. But it's pretty hard to argue with the facts. And the facts, Arnie, are that Meyer Lansky has only been convicted of one crime in his entire life—in 1918 when he was sixteen years old, he was found guilty of fighting on a public street, served four days in jail, and was fined two dollars for it! And this is the man you want me to believe is Public Enemy Number One?"

Arnie was shaking his head furiously. "You're missing the point, Tony. It's not just Lansky you have to look at; it's Luciano too. They've been like Siamese twins ever since they were kids. What Luciano has been guilty of, Lansky has too."

"Bullshit. That's not the way it works, Arnie. You *wish* it worked that way. If Lansky was guilty of everything Luciano was guilty of, why wasn't Lansky sent to prison like Luciano was? Why wasn't Lansky deported like Luciano was?"

"Because he's smarter than Luciano," Arnie excused.

"Sure, sure," Tony scoffed again. "Know what your problem is, Arnie? You can't stand to be wrong. You think because you're a hotshot newspaper reporter that your opinions ought to be chiseled in granite. I hope somebody sues your ass for libel someday and wins. It'd serve you right."

"Won't be Meyer Lansky," Arnie replied confidently. "To sue me, he'd have to appear in a court of law. He'd rather cut off his toes."

"Incredible," Tony marveled. "I can't believe you."

"You'll see," Arnie Shad predicted. "Someday you'll see."

When the plane landed in Las Vegas, the two men were not speaking. They deplaned together because they had been sitting together, crossed the tarmac toward the terminal together, walked inside together. In the baggage claim area they stood together but apart, hands in pockets, each trying to avoid looking at the other. Presently a caterpillar pulled up with a wagon of luggage behind it and two baggage handlers began setting suitcases on a low counter. Arnie's garment bag and portable typewriter were put up before Tony's two-suiter; the reporter took one in each hand and peremptorily turned to go. But he stopped without taking a step.

"The fact that you know about Virginia coming back to testify tells me that Lansky knows too. And Luciano. I want to warn you right now that if anything happens to her, if she has any kind of 'accident' while she's back to testify, I'm going to give your name to the Kefauver investigators; I'm going to tell them that you *knew* in advance that she was coming back."

Tony's eyes went cold. "Don't threaten me, Arnie. I don't like it."

Arnie walked away and Tony watched him carry his luggage out to the curb where a *Las Vegas Star* car was waiting for him. It was the first time in their up-and-down relationship that Arnie Shad had issued such an explicit warning. As Shad got in the car and it pulled away, Tony wondered what the reporter would do if he knew that arrangements had already been made for Tony to see Virginia Hill before she went before the Kefauver Committee?

He was meeting her in New York the following week.

Part Ten

Virginia

1946

THIRTY-NINE

Tony and Denny stood in the doorway of the Oasis Café, on Fremont Street in Las Vegas, with their jacket collars turned up against a chill midday wind blowing in from the winter desert. Fremont was all but deserted: a few prewar automobiles moved up and down; a *Review-Journal* carrier trotted the sidewalk, delivering newspapers from a canvas sack slung over one shoulder; across the street, two women in tight Western pants hurried from the Recreation Bowling Lanes into the Boulder Club next door; a Blue Cab taxi cruised the main drag looking for a fare.

"What d'you want to do now?" Denny asked, his stomach contentedly full of chili. Tony looked up and down the street.

"I don't know," he replied absently. It was January 1946. They had been home from the war several months; for the past three weeks they had been in Las Vegas, looking for work, prospects, business opportunities, anything of interest. They had found nothing. The town was dormant.

"We've seen the picture at the El Portal, and the Palace don't have a matinee," Denny said, effectively eliminating a movie. "We could go back to the hotel and sit in the lobby." They were staying at the National on South 3rd; it was cheaper than the Fremont Street hotels.

Tony shook his head. "Let's walk up to the Horseshoe," he said. "Watch the play for a while." Tony was becoming edgier each day; he had expected something to turn up for them before now.

They left the protective doorway, hurrying along as the wind flattened their trousers against their legs. By the time they reached the Horseshoe Club, their foreheads felt frozen and it hurt their chests to breathe the thin, cold air.

"Jesus, I thought—the desert—was hot," Denny panted when they were safely inside.

"Must be—all that time—we spent in the Pacific," Tony reasoned. "Maybe—our blood's thinned out."

"If we'd tried to spend the winter in Virginia City," Denny said when his breath became even, "it would've killed us."

Turning their collars down and unzipping their jackets, they idled through the moderately busy casino, relishing the warmth and listening to the easy tempo of chips, dice, silver dollars, cards, wheels, and muted voices. Now and again they paused to watch the action at one table or another, then moved on. Once Denny stopped to drop a nickel in a slot machine shaped like an Indian. He lost the nickel and Tony said wryly, "When are you going to learn?"

They strolled over to watch a craps table. While they were standing there, each felt an arm around his waist as a generously proportioned woman with long chestnut hair squeezed between them. "I thought I told you guys to stay away from the gambling joints," she chided with a smile.

Tony and Denny looked at her, at each other, and at her again as memory activated and recognition dawned.

"Virginia Hill!" Tony said.

"Hey, yeah!" Denny grinned widely.

Each of them hugged her as if she were a lost friend for whom they had conducted a long search. Many times during the Pacific campaign they had talked about Virginia Hill and wondered what had happened to her. They told her so now as they all kept smiling widely and repeating the hugs.

"Every time we saw an American movie in Wellington, we always used to look for you in it," Tony told her. "Whether it was a Columbia picture or not."

"I thought I saw you in a cowboy picture once," Denny said. "Me and Tony argued about it all the way to Okinawa."

"Wasn't me," Virginia said. "My dazzling smile and gorgeous figure never graced the silver screen." She made a sour face. "I ditched that place, but fast. You never saw so many phony-baloneys in your life as there are in the movie racket. I don't mean the actors—most of them are okay; I mean the producers—talk about overworked zippers!"

She asked what they were doing in Las Vegas and they told her. While they were talking a boyishly handsome man in his late thirties, with glossy black hair, nattily dressed in a pinstriped suit and wide silk necktie, came over and said unsmilingly to Virginia, "Is there a problem here, Flamingo?"

"No, honey," Virginia quickly replied, "these two fellows helped me out of a pickle one time up in Reno. Remember, I told you about the night the cowboys bothered me when I was there with that jerk from Columbia."

"Yeah, I remember." The handsome man smiled slightly. Quick blue eyes scrutinized Tony and Denny in a split second. Virginia told him their names and said in her lazy drawl, "Fellows, this is my guy, Ben Siegel. He calls me 'Flamingo' on account of my hair."

As they were shaking hands, another man approached, shorter, with ears too large for his head and a dead nerve in his cheek that pulled up the left side of his mouth slightly. "What's the trouble?" he asked, eyeing Tony and Denny.

"No trouble," Ben Siegel said easily. His eyelids drooped very slightly, giving him a sleepy look that was totally deceptive, for he was keenly aware of everything around him, and had a hair-trigger alertness. "This is Moe Sedway," he introduced the little man to Tony and Denny. Then he asked Sedway, "Where's Arnie?"

"Bringing the car around. You wanted to go out to the place where you're gonna build the hotel, remember?"

Ben Siegel nodded. He had not forgotten; he never forgot anything. But pretending to forget gave him a few extra seconds to think. A few extra seconds, he had learned long ago, could sometimes make a difference. "Tell me when the car gets here," he told Sedway, and walked to a nearby craps table.

Still standing with Virginia, Tony asked with interest, "He's going to build a hotel?"

"Yeah," she smiled. "More like a resort, actually. A group of investors sent him out from New York. He was handling some other business for them in Hollywood; we met at the racetrack one day."

"Listen," Tony said eagerly, "is he looking for anybody to work for him?"

"You mean you two?" she bobbed her chin at Denny and him. "No, I don't think so, kids."

"We're not kids, Virginia," Tony said with an edge of impatience. "We've both been through the war—"

"Tony was an officer," Denny interjected.

"Even so," Virginia demurred, "I think this might be a

little out of your line. Ben and the men he works for are—well, not your average businessmen."

"I don't care whether they're average or not," Tony said. His eagerness increased to urgency. "Look, if he's new to Nevada, he's going to need somebody who knows the area, the people. I think Denny and I would be a definite asset to him, Virginia."

"I don't know," she said, still hesitant.

"We could save him a lot of running around to get things done. He'd have more time to spend with you." Tony put a hand on her arm. "Talk to him for us will you?"

With a bemused smile, Virginia said, "I don't remember you being such a fast talker."

"I told you, he was an officer," Denny reminded.

"Come on, Virginia," Tony urged. "Be a pal. You won't be sorry."

"Such moxie," she said, removing his hand. Then she patted his cheek. "Okay, I'll try."

Tony and Denny watched her go over to Ben Siegel, whisper in his ear, then take his arm and lead him away from the table. Standing alone with him, she put one palm against his chest as she talked. Listening, Ben kept his head inclined toward her, but his eyes were all over the place. Nobody came near him, not even a cigarette girl, without swift scrutiny, mindful appraisal. He reminded Tony of a watchdog. While they were talking, Moe Sedway walked up and told Ben the car was ready. Ben came over to Tony and Denny.

"Virginia tells me you two guys are looking for work," he said. "Come on and take a ride with me; we'll talk about it."

Out front, they all dashed across the windy sidewalk and piled into a brand new DeSoto station wagon with genuine pecan wood panels in the doors. A wiry young man Tony's age, pleasant looking except for sad eyes, was behind the wheel, an unlit cigarette in one corner of his mouth. As Tony and Denny got into the front seat with him, Ben introduced them. "This is Arnie Shad. He's just back from the war too; he was a *Stars and Stripes* reporter."

With Ben, Virginia, and Moe Sedway in the back seat, Arnie Shad guided the car down Fremont and turned south out of town. After only several blocks they were on Highway 91, moving through mostly undeveloped, windswept desert. There were only two hotels outside the city limits, and they drove past both of them: El Rancho Vegas and the Frontier. Both were rustic, Western-style establishments.

"Sawdust joints," Ben Siegel said derisively. "Cowboy corrals. No style, no class, just like the joints downtown. Know what the problem is?" he asked no one in particular. "People around here got no imagination, that's what the problem is." Six miles outside town, Ben said, "Pull over, Arnie."

Shad parked on the shoulder of the highway and all six occupants of the DeSoto got out. The wind had calmed down some and in the openness there was warmth from the sun.

"This is it," Ben Siegel said, pointing across the highway to a rundown eight-cabin motor court. "This dump is now owned by the Nevada Projects Corporation, of which my partner, Meyer Lansky, is an officer. And right here, on thirty acres, I'm going to build the biggest and most luxurious goddamned resort hotel and casino the world ever saw." As he stared out at the desert, his youthful face glowed. "It's going to have half a dozen restaurants and bars, the biggest swimming pool in the state, a nightclub with a revolving stage, and the best entertainment money can buy; plush carpet so thick you'll sink in it; urns and statues, and paintings on the walls; outside landscaping with palm trees, green grass, bubbling fountains. Everything's going to be pink and white, like my girl here," he put an arm around Virginia and pulled her close. "As a matter of fact, I'm going to name the place after her. I'm going to call it Ben Siegel's Flamingo."

Turning to Tony and Denny, he said, "Moe here is my right-hand man. Arnie is going to be in charge of publicity, promotion, advertising, that kind of stuff. Virginia is going to take care of all the decorating and furnishing. But I guess I can use a couple of extra guys. You two want to work for me?"

"Sure," Tony said at once.

"Yeah, you bet," Denny chimed in.

Ben bobbed his chin at Sedway. "Put 'em on the payroll, Moe. Fifty a week." He gave them an ingenuous smile. "From now on," he said simply, "you do only what I tell you to. Understand?"

"Right," Tony quickly replied.

Inside, he felt a new and different kind of excitement from any he had known before.

That night, after Ben had Tony and Denny move into the Fremont Hotel where the rest of them were staying, Arnie Shad brought some beer to their room and filled them in on some background.

"Ben Siegel is a very tough individual," he cautioned. "He's legit now, but there was a time when he was considered one of the most dangerous guys in New York. He and Meyer Lansky and Lucky Luciano all grew up together. They were involved in illegal gambling, hot cars, bootlegging during Prohibition, loan sharking. Ben was an enforcer—he'd go out and break a guy's arms if the guy didn't pay back a loan. They used to call him Bugsy because half the people who knew him thought he was crazy. But," Arnie cautioned solemnly, "don't *ever* use that name around him; he hates it. And has he got a hot temper! I might as well tell you too—he's probably killed half a dozen people, guys from other gangs back in the old days. Anyway, I'm told that's all in the past. I wouldn't be here if I didn't believe it. I got my job through my father; he used to work alongside Meyer Lansky in a tool-and-die works."

"Who's Meyer Lansky?" Tony asked.

"The brains behind this plan. A financial genius, got a photographic memory. Got in the rackets in the old days by hiring out to change the serial numbers on hot cars, something that's duck soup for a tool-and-die maker. My father used to cover for him while he went out back of the shop to a car someone would bring over; he paid my father back by giving me this job. Ben got this deal because he saved Meyer's life one time. A rival mobster named Waxey Gordon put a bomb in Meyer's office on Grand Street in Brooklyn; Ben spotted it and tossed it out the window just as it went off. Meyer didn't get a scratch, but Ben was cut up pretty badly by flying glass. Meyer's been like an older brother to him ever since."

"This hotel project and everything," Tony asked, "is all legal, isn't it?"

"Has to be," Arnie assured him. "All the shareholders of the corporation have to be approved by the state for a casino license. If Ben and Lansky and the rest weren't legit now, there'd be no license issued. Hell, the other stockholders are people like Billy Wilkerson—he publishes the *Holly-wood Reporter* and owns Ciro's nightclub in Hollywood—and Samuel Rothberg, who's a big shot at American Distillers, and Charles Straus, a big banker down in Phoenix, Arizona. I don't think men like that would be involved with Lansky if he hadn't gone straight."

"Makes sense," Denny said solemnly.

"Yeah, I guess," Tony agreed. After a moment, he asked, "What do you think he'll have Denny and me doing?"

Arnie shrugged. "Who knows? Whatever it is, I'll guarantee you one thing: working for Ben Siegel won't be boring."

Tony felt the new excitement again.

FORTY

For the first few weeks after ground was broken for the new hotel, Tony and Denny were given mostly errand work to do: going to the post office, chauffeuring Ben around, taking Virginia to and from the airport for her frequent trips to Beverly Hills, going for coffee, getting the newspapers, keeping Ben company at dinner when Virginia was gone, picking up the cleaning, answering the telephone. Ben had rented a small suite of offices on Carson Street, and it was from there they operated. So that they could all get around, two additional cars were purchased, both of them the new model Frazers that Henry J. Kaiser was manufacturing. Arnie had his own office, with a new Royal typewriter on which he continuously composed teaser press releases about the new hotel being built. While the grading and surveying of the land was being completed, Ben constantly had the hotel's architects in to make changes. Their original designs had called for the casino to be in a room off to one side, almost unobtrusive.

"No, no, no!" Ben growled irritably. "I want the casino

right in the middle of everything. I don't want anybody to be able to get to their room, to a restaurant, to any bar, to the swimming pool, barber shop, beauty shop, even to the john to take a piss, without passing through my casino. All traffic has got to go through the casino!"

When Virginia came back with design sketches of the interior, Ben went through them room by room and put a red crayon mark through every place where a clock had been included in the decor. "No clocks," he told her. "We're not building a goddamned bank. I don't want a clock anyplace to remind the gamblers what time it is."

When the architects returned with a new design, it had windows in the casino. For the first time, Tony and Denny saw Ben fly into a rage. "Windows! You dumb *fucks!* Don't you have any brains at all? Didn't you learn to do anything in college except jack off? You know what that fucking window would do? Every time a truck passed, my players would be distracted. Every time a car horn blew. Every time a broad with big tits walked by." Crumbling the blueprints into a large ball, he threw it at them. "Take out the windows, you assholes!"

Del Webb, the Phoenix contractor hired to do the building, had expressed concern from the outset about the availability of certain materials. Plumbing fixtures, cement, plaster, pipes, tubing, lumber, and many other items were still under wartime priority. A construction purchasing agent reported daily to Siegel by telephone to advise him of the needed items which they were unable to secure through normal channels. When the list got long enough, Tony Donovan was given his first important assignment.

"Go up to the state capitol at Carson City," Ben instructed. "Go to the office of Senator McCarran, that's Pat McCarran, he's a U.S. Senator. Ask for this guy here" —Ben wrote a name on a slip of paper—"sit down with him and work out where and when we can get the stuff on this list. I don't expect them to get it all, but don't let them know that; make sure they guarantee at least half of it."

"I'll take care of it," Tony said.

As soon as he left Ben's office, he hurried into Arnie's office and quietly closed the door.

"How'd you like to give a friend some advice?" he asked tensely. He told Arnie about his assignment. "I've never done anything like this in my life," he admitted anxiously.

"I wouldn't know even how to act in the office of a senator. Help me out, will you, Arnie?"

"Calm down," Arnie said. "Don't get so nervous." He looked Tony up and down, rubbing his chin thoughtfully as he studied Tony's corduroy sports coat and flannel shirt. Putting the cover on his typewriter, he said, "Come with me."

Arnie took Tony over to Fremont Street to Beckley's Men's Furnishings.

"A suit for my friend here," he told the haberdasher. "Something in a banker's gray. Double-breasted."

Two hours later, Tony was completely outfitted down to mid-calf socks with garters. His suit trousers had even been cuffed while he waited, a new snap-brim hat blocked to fit, and two Wings shirts unfolded, pressed, and put on hangers.

That evening in Arnie's room, Tony was given a crash course in how to conduct himself. "First of all," Arnie pointed out, "remember that nobody knows you didn't finish high school, nobody knows you worked in a mine; all anybody will know is what they *see.* I want you to think back to how you felt when you were a Marine Corps officer. Think back to Honolulu, wearing a dress uniform, walking down the street, being saluted by enlisted men. Some of those enlisted men were probably better educated than you, but *they* didn't know it. All they knew was what they saw—an officer with bars on his shoulders. For all they knew, you could have been a graduate of Harvard. You know what I'm saying?"

"I think so, yeah."

Arnie put a cigarette between his lips, as usual without lighting it. He began to pace. "Okay, now picture yourself in the new clothes you just bought. You walk in the door of Senator McCarran's office. There'll be a receptionist or a secretary there. She'll look up without smiling; civil servants are never pleasant. She probably won't speak first, so you'll have to. What's the name of the guy Ben wants you to see?" Suddenly Arnie raised a hand. "Wait, never mind. I don't want to know his name; this is probably an under-the-table deal and I don't want to know any of the details. Let's say his name is Smith, John Smith. You step up to the desk and say, 'Mr. Donovan to see Mr. Smith.' Say it."

Tony repeated the phrase. "Mr. Donovan to see Mr. Smith."

"Say it with authority," Arnie insisted. "This is a secretary you're talking to, not the senator. Say it like this—'Mr. *Donovan* . . . to see Mr. Smith.' Then immediately look at your watch as if you're in a hurry. If she asks if you have an appointment, you say, 'No. Just tell him I'm here.' Then you turn away from her and sit down. That will prevent her from arguing; civil servants love to argue. But you ignore her; sit down, cross your legs, put your briefcase on the floor next to the chair—"

"I don't have a briefcase."

"You can use mine. It's well worn, make a nice contrast to your new clothes. Now, when you're shown into this guy's office, you call him by his first name, John. Under no circumstances call him 'Mister' like you did with the secretary; that was just to keep her in her place. But with him, you put out your hand and say, 'John, I'm Tony Donovan.' Let's practice it," Arnie said, sitting down. "I'll be Smith and you pretend you've just walked into my office . . ."

They worked in Arnie Shad's room for four hours that night. It was the first of many lessons the young New York journalism graduate would give the young Nevada silver miner. From the very beginning, the lessons were successful.

On his first trip to the state capital, his first meeting with Senator McCarran's aide, Tony found that he was able to assert himself with confidence and assurance that he had not even been aware he had. The aide's name was Lester Phelps, and while he addressed Tony as "Mr. Donovan," Tony adhered strictly to Arnie's instruction and called him "Lester." Tony realized in minutes that it gave him a definite advantage of some kind over Phelps, like the edge an adult has over an adolescent. As soon as he became aware of the advantage, Tony locked onto it tenaciously.

"Were you in the war, Lester?" he asked, noting the absence of a discharge button in the aide's lapel.

"Uh, no. The senator felt he needed me on the home front."

"A lot of Marines in my command were from Nevada, thought you might have been one of them." Tony smiled and opened his—Arnie's—briefcase. "Nice of the senator to help us with the supplies on this list. Our hotel will do a lot for the future of southern Nevada—"

"We haven't really made a commitment regarding these materials yet," Phelps hedged. "The senator only agreed to take a look at your requirements. There may be some commodities he isn't in a position to help with—"

"Yes, we know," Tony countered. "We've already eliminated the items that might be a problem for him. I think you'll find the ones that are left pretty easy to deal with."

There were fourteen items on Ben Siegel's list, none of them easy to procure: cement, copper tubing, piping, plumbing fixtures, and ten other of the scarcest postwar tangibles of the day. Lester blanched when he read the list. "My God. I'm afraid there are only a couple here that we can do anything about."

"Which three can you help us get?" Tony asked, uncapping his—Arnie's—fountain pen and posing it to write.

The aide selected three, returned the list, and gave Tony the names of suppliers who would, at the senator's request, provide the materials. After Tony wrote everything down, he leaned forward confidentially.

"What can *you* help me with, Lester?"

"Me? Nothing, I'm afraid. I—"

"Lester," Tony chided, "you can level with me. Look, you and I are in the same boat. We both work for important men who probably couldn't get anything done without us. We help them a lot more than they realize, but we have to help each other too. I'm building up my own list of helpful people—friends, actually—who will be welcome guests of mine anytime after the Flamingo opens. I'd like to include you among those friends, Lester. And your family too, naturally. You married, Lester?"

"Uh, yes, I am—"

"Be nice to be able to bring your wife down to Las Vegas for a weekend at the Flamingo. Have dinner in the show room. Watch Vivian Blaine or Phil Silvers perform. Have breakfast by the pool the next morning—"

"Mr. Donovan—"

"Call me Tony."

"Tony, okay. Look, Tony, ah—" Lester mulled it over for a moment, grimaced a little, then said, "Let's see the list again."

Lester personally committed for three items, then Tony steered him back to more items to be obtained under the senator's approval. When he had nine of the fourteen, two more than Ben had specified, he could have quit. But he felt that he was on a roll with Lester, so kept at it.

"Jesus, I'm going overboard here," Lester said at one point. "Tony, if this ever gets out, I mean, Christ, there's veteran housing being delayed down there because they can't get some of these materials—"

"Veteran housing is important" Tony conceded. "But so are *jobs* for vets, Lester. The Flamingo has several hundred men working on its construction crews. And when it opens, it will provide six hundred permanent jobs."

Tony got Lester to commit to two more items. When he left the senator's office, he had purchase permits or contacts through which to obtain eleven of the fourteen items on Ben Siegel's list. When Tony returned to Las Vegas, Ben was astounded.

"What the hell did you do, kid, put a gun to his head? You're terrific! What am I paying you, fifty a week? From now on it's a hundred!"

For the first time in his life, Tony felt he was going somewhere.

While in Carson City, Tony had taken some time to go over to Virginia City to see Rosetta and Kerry. He showed up at their door with candy and flowers for Rosetta and half a dozen records for Kerry. They were both delighted by the surprise visit; Kerry almost swooned over his new clothes. "You look like Tyrone Power in *Nightmare Alley!*" Tony was surprised at how much her appearance had changed in just a few months; a high-school senior now, she had adopted the "new look" of long, peg-topped skirt, tight V-neck sweater, and saddle shoes. Under the sweater, she had noticeably filled out.

Rosetta, as usual, insisted on feeding Tony even though it was too early for supper. While he ate, he told them all about his new job, the fabulous luxury hotel he was helping build, and the fact that he had just come from the office of United States Senator Pat McCarran. "Of course, I didn't see *him*," he admitted, "he's in Washington. I just saw one of his aides."

"Imagine that, a *senator's* office!" Rosetta exclaimed, impressed. "How well you're doing! And look at you: dressed like a banker!"

"Actually that's what the suit color is called," Tony told them, "banker's gray." He glanced at his watch. "I should probably leave before Buck gets home."

"Nonsense," Rosetta said firmly. "You stay right here. You two have got to end this quarrel between you sooner or later; today is as good a time as any."

The quarrel had been a bad one.

It happened a short time after Tony and Denny returned from the war. They had all been sitting at the table with Buck, who was telling them about a new breathing problem that miners were experiencing.

"It's caused by something called 'silica dust,' " Buck said. "What it is, is finely pulverized bits of quartz, porphyry, and granite. It's produced by the new high-speed rotary drills. This dust has needle-sharp edges. The lungs are incapable of dissolving the particles, and once they get in there two things happen—first, those sharp edges cut the delicate tissues of the lungs; second, the particles eventually release something called 'silicic' acid that slowly petrifies, or hardens, the lung tissue. The result is that the lungs gradually deteriorate and lose their ability to provide the blood with oxygen." Buck paused for effect, a moment of ominous quiet. Then he concluded solemnly, "The afflicted person then suffocates, very slowly, until he's dead."

"Jesus," said Denny. Then at once, "Sorry, Buck. Didn't mean to swear."

"This stuff is bad enough to make anybody swear," Buck excused. "I'm glad you're both back home, lads. We're going to need as many union men as we can get when it comes down to fighting the owners over this issue. Here"—he pulled an envelope from his pocket—"I've got your new membership cards—"

"I'm not coming back to the mines, Buck," Tony told him quietly.

Buck looked at him, mouth agape. "Not coming back to the mines? What do you mean? Why not?"

"I don't want to be a miner now, that's all."

"What *do* you want?"

"I'm not sure. I just know I don't ever want to see the inside of another mine." Tony sat forward restlessly, leaning on the table. "It's kind of mixed up in my mind, Buck. When I was a little kid, I used to love the mines. I loved being a miner's son, part of a miner's family. After the fire, well—for a long time I hated the mines, mostly I guess because I hated Delavane so bad. Then, when I had lived with you for a while, I stopped hating them; I even wanted to *be* a miner. But after the cave-in, after Delavane was killed, I started feeling the other way again. The war came along and took me out of the mines. I think that was some kind of fate. I don't think I'm *meant* to go back underground."

Buck's eyes shifted to Denny. "You too? Are you in on this?" he demanded, as if it were an evil conspiracy. Denny shrugged.

"I'm doing whatever Tony does, Buck."

Across the table, Kerry was looking at Tony in stunned disbelief. She had so many adolescent plans, the main one being that Tony, in his dress blues, wearing his decorations, would take her to the junior-senior dance.

Sitting next to her daughter, Rosetta was not so surprised she could not try to prevent an altercation.

"Maybe the boys aim to go to school, Mr. O'Crotty, on that G.I. Bill they passed."

"Not me," Denny declared peremptorily. "I ain't going to school."

"We're not sure what we want to do," Tony tried to explain. "The G.I. Bill also helps vets go into business; we've talked about that . . ." It was hard to put into words that he thought Buck would understand. Aside from the negative things that were cemented in his mind—the memory of the dreariness and darkness down below, the pervasive heat, the threat of cave-in, faulty blasting, water scald, now this silica dust business, and the occasionally recurring nightmare of the caves on Guadalcanal—there was the positive aspect of his desire to make a lot of money. He was determined to find Francie—find her and *have* her—and for that he needed money. Not merely workingman's wages —*money*.

"Is it because the Marines made you an officer," Buck asked reproachfully, "that you think you're too good now to be a workingman?"

"That's got nothing to do with it, Buck—"

"I'd counted on you. Counted on your help. Counted on you coming back into the union. I'd planned a place for you. Planned to put your name up for the next election—"

"I'm sorry, Buck—"

"Look," the union leader said, his voice shifting into its reasoning tone, its negotiating mode, "maybe it's just that I haven't explained it well enough to you. Maybe I haven't given you the whole picture so's you could see the importance of it—"

"It's not that," Tony said.

"No, no, listen to me," Buck insisted. "There's a great opportunity—*right here*. Look, Nevada is one of the few great undeveloped regions left in the country. There are hundreds of thousands of acres that aren't any good for mining, aren't any good for ranching or farming, have no potential at all as far as big American business is concerned. But it's land that can be *industrialized*. Here," he leaned eagerly over the table, "supposing I could get a shoemaker's union in Massachusetts to put up a sum of money, and a garment worker's union in New York to put up a sum of money, and a furniture maker's union in North Carolina, and a teamster's union, an electrical worker's union, and so on. Use the funds to start a vast industrial complex right here in Nevada—a *union-owned* complex. With its own trucking terminal. Its own labor force. Its own housing tracts. Homes built by union men *for* union men, with no profit for a middle man because there wouldn't *be* a middle man. It would be a grand experiment, don't y'see? A union *city*. With all the different organizations melded into one great body, one great union, the strongest ever. I've even got a name for it: Amalgamated Workers of America. A.W.A. How does that sound to you? What do you . . .?"

Buck stopped speaking, stopped as suddenly as he had started. He knew by the way Tony and Denny were looking at him that he could be speaking in tongues for all the impact his words were having on them. He had their attention; their eyes were on him; they did not interrupt. But their expressions were blank, unconcerned. They were not moved.

"You don't care, do you?" Buck asked in quiet accusation. "You're not interested in making things better."

"We just finished fighting a long, dirty war to make things better," Tony reminded him.

"Well, then!" Buck exclaimed, as if just gaining an advantage. "Why stop now? There's still a big job to be done, still a long ways to go. Keep up the battle—but now do it for the union!"

Tony and Denny exchanged unimpressed glances. "We'd rather do it for something *we* pick," Tony said quietly. "Instead of something that's picked for us."

"All right, look then," Buck said. "There's something else I've been giving thought to. Politics. Management has its men in the state legislature, why shouldn't we? You'd make a crackerjack state senator, Tony. And getting you elected would be duck soup. Why, with your war record—"

"Buck, I don't want my life planned out for me!" Tony snapped. "I want to go my own way."

Buck sat back and studied them, eyes flicking back and forth, expression gradually becoming knowing. "You're going for the quick silver again, aren't you, boys?" he asked slyly. "You're going for a spoilrock pit and Harold's Club all over again."

"That's not it at all, Buck."

"You haven't learned your lesson yet, neither of you."

"You're wrong," Tony insisted.

"No," Buck snapped, "not anymore I'm not. I've been wrong all along about you two. But not now. I see you for what you are now—and you know something? I'm glad. I wouldn't *want* you in my union." He picked up the two new union membership cards lying on the table. Putting them together, he tore them in half.

Tony nodded curtly. "Thanks, Buck. You made it easy."

Rising, Tony walked out of the room. Denny quickly followed.

Back in that same room now, at the same table, Tony tried to convince Rosetta that he should leave before Buck got home. But Rosetta would not hear of it. They were still debating it when they heard the thud of a rubber-tipped cane on the wooden back porch and Buck came in. Stopping in the doorway, he tilted his head slightly and scrutinized Tony's appearance with obvious disparagement. "My, my," he said handing his hat to Kerry; he sat down opposite Tony at the kitchen table. "You're looking prosperous, Mr. Donovan." The tone of his voice was the same one he used when discussing management profits.

"He's got a very good job, Mr. O'Crotty," said Rosetta. "In the hotel business. Tell him about it, Tony." There was forced cheerfulness in her voice; her hands were already wringing nervously. Kerry retreated to a corner of the kitchen.

"By all means," Buck encouraged. "Tell me about your newfound success."

Buck folded his hands and sat like a schoolboy giving his

undivided attention to a teacher. Somewhat self-consciously, Tony described how he and Denny had managed to get jobs working for the man who was in charge of building a lavish hotel complex in Las Vegas.

"Ah, yes," said Buck, "I recall reading about that in the Reno paper. There was an editorial that pointed out that at least four of the shareholders behind that hotel have criminal records. Did you know about that?"

"I know that some of them used to be bootleggers and run illegal gambling joints—"

"Which makes them criminals," Buck said firmly.

"No more so than your friend Callahan," Tony defended. "He operated a speakeasy all during Prohibition, and ran a card game in his back room for years without a gaming license."

Buck's lips became a tight line and he drummed his fingers irritably on the table. "Callahan's an honest man. He did what he had to during the hard times."

Tony refused to back down. "The men I work for probably did the same thing. I don't think any of them are involved any longer in illegal activities. If they were, the Nevada Casino Commission wouldn't have granted them a license."

"For the right amount of money in the right place," Buck retorted, "Satan himself could get a gaming license in Nevada."

"There's just no talking to you, is there?" Tony said in frustration. "You think you know everything."

"I know right from wrong," Buck declared, "and what you're into is wrong!"

"Have it your own way, Buck," Tony said, shaking his head wearily. Without finishing his meal, he rose from the table. "I'm sorry, Rosetta, but I have to go." He hugged and kissed her, then Kerry, who was trembling and on the verge of tears.

Buck did not rise or offer to shake hands, but he did turn in his chair and point a warning finger at Tony.

"You're riding for a hard fall, young man. You mark my words. A very hard fall."

As Tony walked out the door, he replied, "If it happens, I hope you're there to see it, Buck. I know it'll make you very happy."

* * *

Before Tony left Virginia City, he drove up Sierra Street to the Delavane mansion, on the off-chance that he could get an answer at the door. Parking in front on the circular drive, he rapped loudly with the door knocker and waited. As usual, there was no response; there was never any response. He had looked for Francie at the mansion a number of times before moving to Las Vegas, and never had he found anyone there.

Walking back to the car, dejected over the altercation with Buck and their continuing estrangement, frustrated at his failure to find any trace of Francie, Tony leaned for a moment against the fender and massaged his temple. He began thinking again about hiring a private detective agency to look for Francie.

When he returned from the war, one of the first things Tony had done was go up to the mansion, on foot. He had walked across the broad expanse of lawn to the front door and, as he had today, rapped with the door knocker. When no one answered, he knocked again, louder. And again, very loudly. There had been no response. Tony had stepped back to the circular drive and scrutinized all the windows. Then he walked around to the back of the house and knocked loudly at the rear door. He tried it, wondering why he had not done the same in the front, but found it locked. Suddenly inspired, he went over to the cellar door that he had used so often in the wintertime to sneak in and meet Francie in the warmth next to the mansion's furnace room. But the cellar door was also locked. Dejectedly, Tony had walked back around front. Without optimism, he had tried the front door and, as expected, found it locked too.

Walking back downhill to C Street that day, Tony had gone to the office of Martin Pitt. After a few minutes wait, he was shown into the lawyer's private office.

"What can I do for you, Donovan?" Pitt had asked without preliminary.

Tony tried to be cordial. "I appreciate you seeing me, sir. I was very sorry to hear about Phil." The lawyer's son had been killed in action in Europe.

Pitt's eyebrows raised. "I was under the impression that you and my son were not friends."

"We weren't, exactly. We did go to school together—"

"Actually, you didn't even like each other, did you?" Pitt challenged.

Nothing's changed, Tony thought. "No, we didn't like each other," he admitted. "I'm sorry he got killed anyway."

"What can I do for you?" the lawyer asked again.

"I'd like to get in touch with Francie Delavane. I was hoping you could tell me how."

Pitt shook his head. "I'm not at liberty to do that. Miss Delavane wants her whereabouts to remain private."

"Will you pass on a message to her?"

"This is a law office, not a message service, young man. Unless it pertains to some legal matter regarding Miss Delavane—"

"You know it isn't a legal matter, Mr. Pitt," Tony interrupted, as calmly as he could. He was talking to the Hill again, and an old familiar anger was waking. "Suppose I write Miss Delavane a letter. Suppose I mark it 'personal.' And send it here registered mail. As her lawyer, you'd be obligated to forward it to her, wouldn't you?"

"If I knew where she was, yes," Pitt admitted. "However, that isn't always the case."

The two men locked eyes across the desk; Tony knew the conversation was over. He rose.

"Thank you for your time, Mr. Pitt." At the door, he said, "I'm still sorry about Phil."

"Yes, so am I," replied Martin Pitt. "Pity it couldn't have been someone else instead of him."

Hearing the lawyer's words, Tony became aware that the anger inside himself had suddenly neutralized. Another emotion overcame it that day, one that was totally alien to any feeling Tony had ever had for any of the men from the Hill. The new feeling both surprised him and, oddly, relieved him. He felt *pity* for Martin Pitt.

After that, Tony had checked periodically at the mansion and asked a few people around town who might have known, but he could uncover no knowledge of Francie.

A private detective agency might be the answer, he thought now. At least it was something to look forward to; as soon as he had enough money saved, he would ask Arnie how to go about it. It felt good knowing he had a friend like Arnie Shad to count on. Arnie was a different kind of friend, a kind like Tony had never had; a friend he could learn from, *had* learned from. Tony was glad too that Virginia was his friend, and through her, Ben.

He was getting somewhere for the first time in his life.

Going someplace. Accomplishing something. When the time
came to find Francie, he would be ready. He would have
money, position, a future.

Looking at the big, silent, foreboding mansion, Tony
thought: Someday, Francie. Someday.

He got back in the car and drove away.

FORTY-ONE

When actual construction of the hotel began, it was a
nightmare.

Nothing went right, from the very beginning. On the day
the concrete foundation was due to be completed, Ben and
his entourage drove out to see it and found the job less than
half done. Furious, Ben found the construction foreman,
seized him by his collar, and demanded an explanation.

"Manpower, Mr. Siegel," the frightened man explained.
"The contractor didn't hire enough cement finishers to meet
the deadline."

An enraged Siegel telephoned the contractor's office in
Phoenix and was told, "We couldn't get enough local labor,
Mr. Siegel, and the project accountants wouldn't authorize
the extra money to bring them in from out of town."

Ben called the accountants. "You fucking idiots!" he
screamed. "If you ever fuck up my construction schedule
again, you'll be keeping books with your toes because your
fingers will be broken!" Trembling so with anger, it took
Virginia, Tony, Denny, and Moe Sedway, all four, to restrain him from physical violence.

"Let Tony see what he can do about it," Virginia pleaded
and Ben finally said okay.

Tony went back to the job foreman, apologized for Ben's
earlier conduct, slipped him a fifty-dollar bill, and asked his
advice on solving their problem. The foreman accompanied

Tony back to his office, they got on the telephone, and by that afternoon there were a dozen cement finishers en route from Salt Lake City at top pay plus twenty dollars per day bonus.

The first inside room to be completed in the new structure was to house the hotel's boiler. When it arrived, a giant crane was unable to lower it into place because the room was too small; someone had misread the specifications on the plans: an area that should have been thirty-two feet wide was only twenty-three. "It'll take a week to tear out, another week to rebuild," the foreman estimated.

"Blow it up," Siegel told him. "That'll save a week."

The foreman refused to take responsibility for blowing up the room; he feared it would damage the rest of the structure. Siegel made a telephone call, two men arrived the next morning, and the room was blown up. The rest of the structure was unharmed.

The company that was supposed to supply the tile for the guest bathrooms went into bankruptcy and its inventory was frozen by the federal court. The Flamingo's priority permit to buy the scarce commodity was tied up in red tape. Ben sent Virginia on a frantic trip all over Mexico to locate a quantity of the same tile. Then Ben made another phone call and arranged for it to be smuggled across the border.

When the inside walls were being done on the main floor, Ben discovered he could hear through them. "Why aren't they thicker?" he demanded of the already terrified architects' assistants. "What the hell am I building here, a god-damned shanty in old shantytown? This is a *class* hotel. If a guest is fucking his wife in one-ten, I don't want the guest in one-twelve to hear the goddamn bedsprings creak! Fix the fucking walls!" The thickness of the walls was doubled.

A rumor reached them one day that the electricians doing the foundation wiring were grumbling about working conditions; there was talk of a walkout. "That does it!" Ben stormed. Throwing off his coat and rolling up his sleeves, he strode from the office, vowing, "I'm going to make an example of somebody! The first electrician I find, I'm going to put the son of a bitch in the hospital!" Again the group around Ben managed to restrain him and Tony went to deal with the unrest. It turned out to be a simple matter of inferior sandwiches and coffee being catered to the job site. Tony changed caterers and the problem was solved.

But the more things went wrong, the more volatile Ben Siegel became. His temper was hair-trigger and no one was exempt from it. If Virginia put his coffee in the wrong place on his desk, he berated her for it. If Tony failed to answer the telephone quickly enough, he was screamed at. When Arnie Shad used his typewriter without closing the door, Ben hurled an ashtray into his office. Moe Sedway was developing serious stomach ulcers from the constant harassment he endured. Even Denny, who as a rule took no lip from anyone, walked on eggs around the scowling, muttering man they worked for.

Yet he needed them, and they all knew it. In rare moments of tranquility, he would drape an arm around the shoulders of one of them and say, "How's it going, champ?" Or throw a confidential wink and his winsome smile at someone and it would renew his loyalty and dedication instantly. Virginia, who was closest to him, took more than the others. If her blouse or dress was cut too low, he would snarl, "Get your ass back to the hotel and change clothes! I don't want you showing your tits to every hick in town!" Or if she was too long at the beauty parlor or manicurist, it would be, suspiciously, "Where the hell you been? Who you been with?" A threatening finger would jab her shoulder. "I ever catch you with anybody, you cunt, and you know what'll happen. To *both* of you." But always she was there for him, at the end of the hectic, tedious, nerve-wracking days, there to help him into one of the loud sport coats he had taken to wearing, to hook her arm in his and say, "Come on, baby. Let's go home." Like a punch-drunk fighter at the end of a tough ten-rounder, he would shuffle off with her to the hotel.

And always—*always*—Ben would come back the next morning fresh, fit, alert, and smiling. "What a woman," he would say. "What a goddamned *woman!*"

Ben came to depend more and more on Tony. After Tony's success on the first trip to Carson City, he was sent back several more times to deal with Lester Phelps, always with similar results. And he was sent on other trips, to Hollywood as a liaison with Billy Wilkerson, the publisher and nightclub owner, who was helping obtain from some movie studios other scarce material needed by the Flamingo contractors. The studios, exempt from rationing during the recent war as an essential industry, had stockpiles of lumber, upholstery material, and plaster used for movie sets. When Wilkerson did not have the necessary influence, Tony would be referred to Los Angeles, to an unsmiling little man named Mickey Cohen, who would check a list of debts owed by various studio executives to an illegal gambling house in the Hollywood hills called the Clover Club. Tony was amazed at the number of famous names he saw on the list: Clark Gable, Cary Grant, Gary Cooper, Ronald Colman, and numerous others. But it was always a name that Tony did not recognize, a studio executive, that Cohen would call. Usually the conversation was very brief, a line would be drawn through the mogul's debt, and whatever material the Flamingo needed would shortly be delivered.

"Nice going, buddy," Arnie Shad would compliment when Tony had solved a sticky problem or handled a troublesome situation. "You're learning."

And Tony was. Not only in his continuing instruction from Arnie—how to dress, sign a check, give an order, write a letter; how to listen, remember, evaluate—but also from people he observed wherever Ben sent him, from reputable respected businessmen to smalltime hoods, executive secretaries to airline stewardesses, anybody and everybody. Tony found that he could learn something from just about everyone—and he did.

But the problems never let up. When summer came and the desert temperatures rose, the teamsters' union decided that its truckers did not have to drive in areas where the heat was one hundred degrees or more, which effectively eliminated all deliveries to Las Vegas. Fuming, Ben had to make a trip to New York, then to Chicago. When he returned, the trucks began making deliveries again, but every time Ben Siegel looked at a driver it was with murder in his eyes.

"He had to bribe the teamster officials," Arnie whispered to Tony in confidence. "Moe said it cost him a hundred grand."

Tony was astounded. His only experience with a union having been at the side of Buck O'Crotty, it had never occurred to him that such an organization could be dishonest. Tony was learning.

Labor problems never ended. Las Vegas had such an inferior labor force that it was a constant battle to get workers. Carpenters had to be imported from Denver, plumbers from Phoenix, plasterers from Portland. Sometimes they stayed, sometimes the heat drove them off, sometimes they quit because they were unable to endure the swearing, shouting, threatening man in the loud sport coat who made so many sudden, unannounced appearances at the job site.

Errors were constant. An inferior grade of carpet was shipped by mistake and began to wear thin in the halls from the shoes of the workmen moving furniture into the rooms. It had to be removed and replaced. Hundreds of pairs of drapes were found to be flammable and had to be returned to the manufacturer for fireproofing. A large crate containing two thousand coffee cups was dropped during unloading; only one cup remained unbroken. Instead of going into a rage, as everyone expected him to, Ben Siegel took the accident as an omen, lovingly rescued the lone cup, and had it bronzed. Convinced it would bring him good luck, he used it as a paperweight on his desk.

Siegel's genial attitude in the cup incident was an exception; his anger was the rule. Wherever he went, he stalked, always scowling, accusing, warning against any waste of time. He never spoke in a normal voice anymore, always a yell. Cigarette butts on the floor infuriated him, smudge marks on the wall turned him red in the face; one day he kicked—literally, with his foot—a carpenter off the job for spitting on a newly tiled area. When the spring rains came, halting all exterior work, Ben stood out in the downpour and shook his fist at the sky.

There was another matter that for a while puzzled all of them. Ben would prowl around the partially constructed premises with a perplexed frown on his face, stopping here and there to study a wall or a pillar or a section of floor. Sometimes, rubbing his chin and muttering to himself, he would borrow a carpenter's tape and measure whatever area interested him. If Virginia or anyone else asked what he was doing, he would say, "Nothing, nothing," and walk away. This went on for two weeks, and then one day after the construction crews went home, an unmarked panel truck with California plates pulled up and two men in coveralls unloaded a large, heavy box, tools, and an acetylene torch. Ben personally kept everyone away while the men were inside, five hours. The next day, Virginia told Tony and Arnie what it was all about.

"He's had a secret safe put in," she said.

"Do you know where?" Tony asked.

"No," she winked and pursed her luscious lips, "but I will."

If she did, she never told either of them.

One day, Gus Berman showed up. A big muscular man with an oversized lower lip, he represented another Lansky corporation that planned to open a legal house of prostitution for the exclusive use of the Flamingo's high rollers. "Since Lansky won't let my girls work out of the hotel," he told Ben and his staff at their first meeting, "I thought you and I could work out some kind of limo service or something to take them back and forth. Be a nice piece of side money for us. Maybe your doll here," he nodded to Virginia, "could even be in charge at this end. Kind of give the johns a preview of what's waiting for them at the other end."

Ben Siegel's blue eyes had turned to ice while Berman spoke and the little finger of his right hand began to twitch, a signal that physical violence was not far from erupting. Virginia noticed the sign and immediately stood behind Ben's chair and massaged his neck. When Berman finished talking, Ben leaned forward away from her soothing hands and pointed a silver letter opener at the burly man.

"First of all," he said in a tightly constrained voice, "Miss Hill is not a 'doll.' She is an executive of this hotel. Second thing, we are setting up a respectable hotel and casino operation here and we don't want anything to do with you and your whores. If guests or players want to leave here and go down to Block 16, that's their business. They can arrange their own transportation. None of my people are going to be involved in a limo service or anything else. None of my employees are going to refer guests to your whorehouse or any other whorehouse. That's all I've got to say. Now get out of my office, you fucking pimp."

"You cocksucker," Gus Berman snarled, leaping to his feet, right hand going under his coat. Little Moe Sedway was instantly at his side, a cocked revolver against Berman's ear. Berman froze, but his angry expression became a sneer. "I can remember when you used to handle your own muscle," he said, paused, then added, "Bugsy."

Virginia's eyes rolled upward in horror and Moe Sedway swallowed dryly. Tony and Denny only sat and stared incredulously. Siegel rose and went around the desk. He stood very close to Berman and, to everyone's amazement, smiled. It was a tight smile, cold and humorless, but it was a smile, and it brought relief to the others in the office who expected the worst.

"Stay away from me and stay away from my hotel when it's finished," Ben said quietly. "My people and I don't want anything to do with lowlife scum like you. Show him out, Moe."

After Moe had taken Berman away, Virginia threw her arms around Ben's neck and exclaimed, "I can't believe it! You were wonderful! You didn't threaten to kill him or anything, even when he called you Bugsy."

Ben removed her arms and adjusted the knot of his tie. "I'm a businessman," he said archly. "I don't threaten people."

The very next day he chased a delivery man across the parking lot for not wiping his feet before walking into the newly carpeted lobby.

Miraculously, it somehow came together. The paving, landscaping and fountains, the carpeting and draperies, the fixtures and furnishings, the kitchen, the showroom, the casino floor. Key personnel were hired and massive interviewing began for the small army of service people they would command. A date was selected for the grand opening: December 26th. Ben hoped that the celebration would last all the way through New Year's Eve. Extravagant plans were finalized.

"I got him!" Arnie Shad said gleefully one day, bursting into Ben's office. "I got Jimmy Durante for opening week!"

"Beautiful!" Ben exclaimed. "What about a band?"

"I'm waiting for final confirmation on Xavier Cugat and his orchestra right now. But I'm sure it's in the bag."

"Okay." Ben put a finger to his temple as a thought struck him. "Listen, you know that list of newspaper columnists that you've been sending all the press releases to? I want you to send each one of them a case of whiskey as an opening night present."

Arnie pursed his lips, glancing tentatively at Tony and Virginia. "I'm not sure we want to do that, Ben."

"No? Why not?"

"Well, it's kind of like—you know, a bribe. You have to be careful with newspapermen."

"You can make sure they understand it's not a bribe," Ben said. "It's like a thank you, only in advance. Like insurance. I can't take any chances that they won't play the Flamingo up big in their columns for opening night."

"I still think it's a bad idea—"

"Just send the whiskey, Arnie," Ben Siegel ordered. Arnie shrugged and did as he was told.

A week before opening night, tough-guy actor George Raft arrived for an advance tour. He and Ben had been boyhood pals on the lower east side of New York, and had renewed their friendship when Ben moved to Hollywood to handle Meyer Lansky's West Coast business affairs.

"Jeez," Denny said when he saw the actor crossing the lobby, "I didn't realize he was so short."

"He wears a corset too," Virginia whispered to Tony and Denny. They were both aghast. "It's the truth," she swore. "Ben and I have spent the night at his house a couple times. He never goes out in public without being laced into his corset. That's why he walks so straight. You'll never see him bend over, either."

Ben personally escorted Raft all over the new complex. "I'm going to have a couple of Lockheed Constellations in Los Angeles to fly you and all the stars you can get directly here on opening night," he told his old friend. "Who do you think you can get?"

"I'll get 'em all, Ben," Raft boasted. "Jim Cagney, Joan Crawford, Spence Tracy. I'll fill the planes for you, pal."

Ben hugged the movie star. "I knew I could count on you, Georgie."

Ben had a tailor flown in from Beverly Hills to measure Tony, Denny, and Moe and all his pit bosses and managers for tuxedoes. Virginia had a flowing rosy-white gown made for the occasion by designer Howard Greer at a cost of thirty-six hundred dollars. Arnie Shad announced another coup.

"George Jessel has agreed to a one-night stand as our official greeter and master of ceremonies."

"Wonderful, kid!" Ben slapped him fondly on the back. Then he asked, "Did you arrange for that whiskey?"

"Just like you said, Ben. But I still think it's a mistake."

"You worry too much, kid," Ben told him jovially. For the first time in a year, things were running smoothly. "Flamingo," he said walking through the fabulous new hotel with an arm around Virginia's waist, the rest of the entourage following them, "I think we're home free, baby." Pausing, he looked at them almost teary eyed. "I want to thank all of you. You helped me crawl up out of the sewer, and I appreciate it."

The day after Christmas, ten hours before the official opening of the new hotel, Ben Siegel had his first inkling that something was wrong. George Raft telephoned him, sounding upset.

"Ben, something fishy is going on. I've been getting calls all last night and again this morning from people who are canceling out on us. Ty Power called, Hank Fonda, Linda Darnell—"

"What's going on?" Ben asked, surprised. "They know it's not costing them anything, don't they?"

"Sure. They've all got half-assed excuses. Rita Hayworth says she's worn out from Christmas. Judy Garland claims she has to rehearse. Ronnie Colman says he won't travel in this kind of weather—"

"What's wrong with the weather?"

"There's a report of a big ice storm in the mountains between here and there. Lots of people are scared to fly. I'm thinking of driving down myself."

"Jesus, make some calls for me, will you, Georgie?" Ben pleaded nervously. "Invite anybody—starlets, bit players, cowboy actors—I don't care. Just get me some movie stars, George."

"Do my best, pal."

When Ben hung up and told Virginia and the others, a general feeling of apprehension settled over them. A sense of disaster began to ferment. Virginia tried to generate optimism. "Come on, you guys! A few cancellations don't call off a party! This joint will be crawling with movie stars tonight, wait and see!"

Later that morning, the other shoe fell: Raft called again. Tony was able to intercept the call.

"I think I know what the problem is," Raft said. "William Randolph Hearst, the big newspaper publisher, found out you guys sent cases of booze to some of his columnists. He blew his stack over it. Then he did some checking and found out that some of the guys behind the hotel have criminal records. Now he's got Louella Parsons spreading the word that the Flamingo is operated by gangsters. She's calling everybody she knows—which *is* everybody—and advising them to skip the opening night, telling them it could hurt their careers."

Tony's stomach churned. "Can you get *anybody* to come?" he asked.

"A few maybe. But the storm over the mountains is still getting worse. A lot of people won't fly in weather like that—"

"Listen," Tony said with sudden inspiration, "there's a train that leaves Los Angeles at noon and gets in here around four. How about if I get a private club car put on it—would that help?"

"Jesus, yeah, that's a great idea," said Raft.

"Okay, I'll work on that and you start lining up people to come by train. We've got to get some movie stars here for Ben."

Tony told Virginia what had happened; they agreed to tell Ben about the train, but not about the stars that William Randolph Hearst was influencing not to come. In private, Virginia seethed in anger at Hearst. "That cocksucker! What did we ever do to him? It's okay for him to keep that whore Marion Davies in his castle in California, but everybody else is supposed to be Snow White, is that it? The two-faced bastard!"

Tony was successful in making last-minute arrangements for the private club car. When Raft telephoned to confirm it, they could not keep the call from Ben.

"Who were you able to get, Georgie?" he wanted to know.

"George Sanders is coming," Raft said enthusiastically. "Sonny Tufts. Charles Coburn—you know him, wears a monocle, great character actor. Georgie Jessel—"

"I'm paying him," Ben said glumly.

While Raft was still on the line, Tony talked to him again. "Were you able to get anybody on those planes?"

"Sure. They'll both be filled. Nobody really big—Bill Elliott and Don Barry, they're cowboy stars; Yak Canutt and some other stunt men; Andy Devine; some starlets. Real cute babes—"

Despite the news, the rest of the afternoon was like a wake. Ben went up to the apartment and sat staring gloomily out a window. As evening approached, he refused even to change into his dinner jacket. "It's a bust," he muttered over and over again. "The whole fucking thing is a bust."

"It is not!" Virginia shrieked when she found him. "Now come *on*," she tugged at him. "Get showered and put on that tux! I am *not* going to handle this night by myself!"

Tony finally had to be summoned to help her get him dressed. The spirit had gone out of him entirely. He felt like he had fought for the title and lost—by a split decision. It took them an hour to get him ready. Virginia even had to comb his hair.

When they finally got Ben dressed and downstairs, he and Virginia made a spectacular couple: the leggy, bosomy, chesnut-haired, drawling beauty from Alabama, and the boyishly handsome, blue-eyed, Dead-End-Kid-in-a-tuxedo from Hell's Kitchen. Ben cut the ribbon across the front entrance, flashbulbs popped, the doors were opened to a modest local crowd, the celebrities already inside moved onto the casino floor, and the first house dice were officially rolled. They came up seven and the shooter won. The Flamingo had lost the first bet it covered. It might have been an omen.

An hour later, Tony had to bring Ben more bad news. "The planes from Los Angeles won't be here. They're grounded because of that storm in the mountains."

Ben shrugged, almost as if he had expected as much.

Later in the evening, Ben walked up to Arnie Shad, who was with a group of publicists, and said, "You're fired, Arnie. Be out of the hotel in an hour or I'll have my security men throw you out." A dumbstruck Arnie could only stare mutely as Ben Siegel blithely walked away.

When Tony happened on Arnie cleaning out his desk and learned what happened, he stormed into Ben's office where Ben and Virginia had taken a break from the festivities. "What the hell did you fire Arnie for?" Tony demanded.

"He fucked up the opening night with that whiskey he sent," Ben replied. George Raft had told him what happened.

"That was *your* idea, Ben!"

"He was supposed to make sure nobody thought it was a bribe. He didn't do that. William Randolph Hearst got his nose out of joint over it and because of him I don't have any decent movie stars downstairs—"

"For Christ's sake, Ben, you can't blame Arnie for something William Randolph Hearst did!'' Tony was livid. For a fleeting second he had an image of himself acting as Ben had been acting those past months: like a raging maniac.

"I can do anything I want to do," Ben told him evenly. "This is *my* hotel. Shad is fired." He pointed a warning finger at Tony. "You may be too if you don't button your lip."

"Fuck you, Ben!" Tony shouted. "And fuck your hotel! I quit!"

Tony stormed out of the office with the same anger with which he had stormed into it. When he got back to the office they shared, Arnie was already gone. Tony started cleaning out his own desk. He was halfway throuh it when Virginia hurried in. She came around the desk, made him stop what he was doing, and put her arms around his waist.

"Listen to me, Tony," she said, her drawl very quiet, "you can't walk out on Ben right now."

"Like hell I can't." Tony tried to pull away, but she held him with surprising strength.

"Listen to me," she said again. "That man in there needs you. I know he's a first-class prick sometimes; I know he's one of the most aggravating son of a bitches that ever drew breath; I know he's unreasonable, hot-tempered, self-centered, and completely unbearable at times. But I also know something else—he's your friend. He gave you a break and you're learning this business because of him. You owe him, Tony. And he's in trouble."

Virginia's eyes were teary, the first time Tony had ever seen them that way. "What kind of trouble?"

"He had to borrow several million dollars from some people back east to get this place finished. Now he's got to make it successful or else. The casino is losing money like crazy right now; I think half the dealers we hired are cheating us. Ben *needs* us, Tony. All of us."

"He doesn't seem to think he needs Arnie," Tony said bitterly.

"Yes, he does. He knows he made a mistake. You can tell Arnie he's still got a job."

"Ben said that?"

"Ben said that," Virginia assured him. Her arms went up around his neck. "Come on, say you'll stay," she urged. "Please, Tony."

Virginia laid her head against his chest. Tony was sure she

did it to keep him from seeing her cry. He could do nothing but put his arms around her and pat her shoulder comfortingly.

"Okay," he finally told her, "I'll stay."

He had the feeling he had just made a terrible mistake.

FORTY-TWO

Late one afternoon in April, Tony was called into Ben Siegel's office. Ben looked haggard, depressed, run-down, as he had for weeks. The face that once had been boyish was growing old fast.

"Tony, I want you to do something for me," he said. Even his voice had changed; no longer spirited and enthusiastic, he often barely whispered. "That guy Gus Berman has got his whorehouse open out on Sahara Road. He calls it the Ranch. Take a run out there and look the joint over for me, will you? See if it looks like it's making any money." Before Tony left the office Ben added, "Listen, ask around and see if Berman is bad-mouthing me around town. I've got a feeling he's knocking me to the people back east."

"Sure, Ben."

The assignment did not surprise Tony. More and more, Ben was turning to Tony for things that he once would have done himself. It was, Tony suspected, because Ben was so disheartened by the Flamingo's failure to make a profit. He was very tired, listless. Had it not been for Virginia and Tony, the hotel would have had to close. Together they kept it going, on sheer determination.

When Tony told Virginia about his latest assignment, she rolled her eyes toward the ceiling. "Christ! The people back east are leaning on him because the casino has lost more than half a million dollars since we opened. But he thinks everybody back there is still his friend, like in the old days; he's got himself convinced all he has to do to stay in their good graces is keep Gus Berman from back-stabbing him. Honest to God, he's like a little kid sometimes; he absolutely refuses to face reality." Virginia rose and paced her little office. Her face, like Ben's, showed signs of strain and worry. "It's easy to understand how the boys back east feel," she reasoned. "Hell, we can't explain the losses even to ourselves. We've replaced every crooked dealer we found; you and Ben oversee the count room yourselves; we've been getting as much play as the other casinos—yet we keep losing money. What the hell's wrong?" she asked.

"You really want to know?" Tony asked.

"Of course I do," she said, throwing him a curious look. She sat back down and tilted her head back to use a nasal spray for her spring allergies.

"All right, I'll tell you," Tony said. He spoke with complete self-assurance. "Our overhead is killing us, Virginia. We've had bad weather off and on since we opened, and it's kept our vacancy rate around seventy percent—yet we continue to try and operate like we've got a maximum occupancy. We keep a full staff of maids, a full staff of waiters. We spread guests all over the hotel, so we have to use full electricity, full gas heat. We keep our show room open every night; do you know, Virginia, that Lena Horne only drew *fourteen* people to one of her dinner shows. Fourteen dinners won't pay Lena Horne's salary."

Virginia was studying him closely, with keen interest. Her knowing eyes measured not only what he said, but how he said it. She was aware that, unlike Ben, who asked no one for advice, Tony was constantly seeking to learn from people around him who knew more than he did. He was not reluctant to ask waiters for advice about food service, bellmen for advice about guest logistics, bartenders about liquor purchases. Over the months she had seen Tony's knowledge of hotel and casino operations increase by volumes, until he had become a knowledgeable, efficient manager—with nothing to manage because Ben personally ran everything himself. Maybe now, she decided, was the time to make use of what he knew.

"What can we do?" she asked. Tony, encouraged, leaned forward eagerly.

"I've done a check on every separate area of our operation to see where we're making money and where we're losing it. I think I've come up with a good plan to help us start making a profit, but it'll mean cutting down a lot of our operation. I'm not sure Ben will go for it—"

"Never mind Ben, what would you cut?" Virginia asked.

"The show room, for one thing. Close it down completely except on weekends. Book acts only for weekends. Cut back on all hotel personnel to conform with our occupancy rate. Reduce all food purchases drastically to decrease spoilage. Put guests on the lower floors only and close off the upper floors; that'll cut our electric bill by a third, our heating bill by—"

"Is all this written down on paper?" Virginia interrupted to ask.

"It's mostly just notes, but I can write it all out."

"Do it," Virginia ordered. She gave Tony a wink. "Maybe you and I can keep the good ship Flamingo from sinking in the desert." As an afterthought, she added, "If the guys back east will give us enough time."

Tony took Denny with him to make the visit to Gus Berman's 'Ranch.' As they drove out Sahara Road in the cool early evening, Tony contemplated asking Arnie Shad to help him put his plan for the hotel into the proper words. Denny advised against it.

"I don't think it's smart to trust Shad," he said. "He ain't one of us anymore."

"Oh, bullshit. He's still a friend."

"I wouldn't be too sure of that," Denny replied doggedly.

Arnie Shad had not come back to work for the Flamingo after Ben Siegel fired him, despite Tony's pleading that he do so. "I'm out," Arnie had said stubbornly the next day. "Ben fired me and I'm staying fired."

"He was upset," Tony tried to explain. "The opening day bust pulled the rug out from under him, Arn. Give him a chance to make up for it."

"Look, Tony," his friend replied quietly, "I'm not so sure I would have stayed around much longer even if he hadn't fired me. There are things going on that—well, I just don't want to be a part of."

"If you're talking about the cases of whiskey sent to those columnists, Ben knows he was wrong about that—"

Arnie had shaken his head emphatically. "It's not that. It's not any one thing that I can put my finger on. It's more like, I don't know, an *attitude*. That probably sounds pretty crazy to you, I guess," Arnie admitted resignedly. "You grew up in a little mining town where if a kid turned out to be a thief or a killer, it was a big shock to everybody. Where I grew up, there was a fifty-fifty chance of it happening. It didn't matter if a kid was Irish like you, or Jewish like me, or Italian like Lucky Luciano; everybody was vulnerable, because everybody was exposed to the same temptations. But the ones who took the wrong path always seemed to have the same *attitude*. It was the attitude that they were going to do what they *wanted* to do—whether it was right or wrong." Arnie shrugged, almost apologetically. "That's the attitude Ben has. And Virginia." His voice grew quieter. "It's an attitude I don't want to take a chance of developing myself."

Arnie had urged Tony to leave the Flamingo too. "You've got a good reputation in town," he said. "Some of the smaller casino owners really like you, and they know you're a hard worker. You could find another job easily. You'd be smart to get away from Ben and Virginia and Denny Ebro—"

Tony had drawn inward at once. "Denny's been my friend for fifteen years," he said, in a tone that carried a hint of warning.

"That doesn't mean you know him," Arnie pointed out. "Sometimes you can be so close to a person that you don't know him at all."

"I know Denny," Tony had insisted.

In the end, Arnie had gone his own way, obtaining a job as reporter for a fledgling newspaper, the *Star*. But he and Tony had remained friends; they met for lunch a couple of times a week, on neutral ground, and avoided talking about Ben Siegel or the Flamingo operation.

"Arnie's interested in Las Vegas as a community," Tony told Denny as they drove toward the Ranch. "He wouldn't be interested in saving Ben's ass, but he knows if the Flamingo folds, it's going to hurt the town. For that reason I think he might help me."

"Have it your way," Denny conceded. He shook his head. "You get more like Buck every day."

When they got to the Ranch they found it to be an

expensive single-story, U-shaped building with a large
barroom-reception area from which walkways led in opposite directions to separate wings of motel-like rooms. A
stout but very shapely woman of perhaps fifty, dressed in
expensive Western riding clothes and heavy silver-and-
turquoise jewelry, greeted them in a small but plush foyer
off the barroom.

"Good evening, gentlemen. Welcome to the Ranch." Her
eyes swept over Denny and stopped on Tony. "Mr. Donovan, I believe, of the Flamingo."

"Have we met?" Tony asked with a smile that covered his
surprise at being known.

"Actually, no. I'm Lily Baker, the assistant manager. Mr.
Berman, our manager, showed me pictures of Mr. Siegel
and his staff from your grand opening. He was sure someone from the Flamingo would come around sooner or later.
He wanted to be sure he got to show you around personally.
If you'll make yourselves at home, I'll let Mr. Berman know
you're here."

"Thanks very much," Tony said. He and Denny entered
the larger room and walked to the bar.

"Guess Berman's smarter than Ben gave him credit for,"
Denny said.

"Could be," Tony admitted.

The room they were in was rustic but cozy: an open-beam
ceiling and cream-colored adobe walls culminated in a floor-
to-ceiling natural stone fireplace with deep plush couches
and loveseats positioned around it on bright Indian rugs.
There was a small bar on each side of the room; white
bartenders and black waitresses wore Western shirts and
lariat ties. At a red grand piano in the center of the room,
an older, silver-haired man in a fringed buckskin shirt was
playing a slow rendition of "Ragtime Cowboy Joe." At
various locations throughout the big room, sitting among
themselves or with customers, were two dozen girls and
women, ages sixteen to thirty, all in some form, mostly
abbreviated, of cowgirl dress. Each costume had its own
enticing feature: leather skirts slit high on the thigh, transparent blouses, red bandanna halters, spike-heel boots with
black net stockings, riding chaps with bare buttocks exposed.

"Sluts," Denny sneered. "And look at that piano—looks
like it was painted with nail polish—"

Denny stopped talking when he noticed that Tony had stopped walking. Turning, he saw that Tony was standing stock still, staring at a trio of girls on a nearby couch. One of them was Francie Delavane.

"Jesus Christ . . ." Denny muttered, moving back to where Tony stood. He followed as Tony walked slowly over to the girls and stood in front of the couch.

"Hi, handsome!" one of them said. "Would you like to buy me a drink?"

Francie looked up, started to put a similar line to Denny, but suddenly seemed to realize who he was, and frowned deeply. In the next instant she shook her head briefly in self-chagrin and smiled lazily. "Hi, there," she said in her throaty voice.

Tony knelt in front of her. She was wearing one of the transparent blouses that tightly covered but did not conceal her breasts; under it, Francie's nipples were darkly rouged.

"Hi, there," she said again, voice and eyes very sleepy. She seemed to be swaying slightly.

"Francie, look at me," Tony said. He took her hands. "Don't you know me?"

Denny bent down and studied Francie's eyes. "She's on something," he said quietly. Tony frowned.

"What's the matter with her?" he asked the girl next to Francie.

"You a friend of hers, mister?" the girl wanted to know.

"Yes, I'm a friend of hers. Tell me what's the matter with her."

Glancing fearfully around, the girl whispered, "She's a smoker. Opium."

Tony looked down at the floor. "Jesus."

Glancing around, Denny saw that others were watching them, including a husky man sitting alone in a corner, whom Denny suspected was a bouncer. "What do you want to do?" he asked Tony, wetting his lips.

"Get her out of here," Tony said. He rose, still holding Francie's hands. "Francie, honey, come with us." He tried to draw her to her feet, but Francie resisted; Tony had to pull her up forcibly. Denny saw the bouncer rise and start toward them. He also saw Gus Berman come in, looking ludicrous but formidable in Western garb.

"Shit," Denny muttered to himself.

"Come on, Francie," Tony said, one arm around Francie's shoulders, urging her away from the couch.

Berman, who had been smiling as he walked in, began to scowl as he neared them. He met Tony and Francie halfway to the door, blocking their way.

"What gives, Donovan?" he bobbed his chin at Francie. "What's going on?"

"This is an old friend of mine—"

"Where do you think you're going?" Berman held up a beefy hand. "My girls don't leave the premises. House rule." Still guiding Francie, Tony tried to brush past him. Berman grabbed him by the arm. "Just a fucking minute!"

Letting go of Francie, Tony whirled and drove his fist into Berman's groin, not once but twice. The big pimp doubled up, clutching himself with one hand but instinctively swinging on Tony with the other. Tony leaned out of the way of the punch, grabbed Berman by the hair and one ear, forced him to his knees, and jerked his face down hard against a coffee table. Berman let out a scream like a wounded elephant and fell across the table.

The bouncer broke into a run and from both sides of the room bartenders rushed toward the fracas. Denny's hand shot under his coat and, as little Moe Sedway had once done, he put the muzzle of a pistol against Berman's head.

"Freeze, everybody, or I'll kill him!" he warned loudly.

The running men came to abrupt stops. Tony stared at Denny in astonishment.

"A gun? What the hell . . .?"

"Never mind!" Denny snapped, eyes darting nervously. "Let's get out of here, goddamn it!"

Grabbing Berman by the collar, Denny dragged the groggy, bleeding man to his feet and held him steady. Tony lifted Francie in his arms and hurried to the door with her. Denny backed to the door, holding the staggering Berman with one hand, the gun with the other. His eyes were fierce, his moustache-covered harelip drawn tightly over his teeth. Lily Baker was in his path to the door; he drew the gun back threateningly as if to pistol whip her. "Get out of the way, you filthy, fat whore!" he snarled viciously.

Outside, Tony was behind the wheel of their car, the engine running, Francie propped up beside him in the middle of the front seat. As employees and customers of the Ranch watched from the entrance, Denny flung Gus Berman over the hood of a convenient Cadillac, quickly got into the idling car, and yelled, "Let's get the fuck out of here!"

Tony sprayed gravel for thirty feet as he gunned the car off the lot.

"When the hell did you start carrying a gun?" Tony asked as they sped along Sahara Road.

"A while ago," Denny replied vaguely. "What difference does it make? Goddamn good thing I *was* carrying one tonight."

Tony wet his lips and twisted to look behind them. No headlights were following. Between them, Francie swayed lazily back and forth with the motion of the car. She stared straight ahead, eyelids heavy, lips slack.

"We're up shit creek now," Denny said. "Might as well drive right out of town and not come back."

"I don't think so," Tony disagreed. "That other girl said Francie was on opium. What's Berman going to do? Call the law and say we kidnapped a dope addict from him? For damn sure he's not going to want Ben to know about it, because Berman won't want the people he works for back east to know about it. He might keep the whole thing quiet."

"Sounds like a long shot to me," Denny said skeptically.

"All we can do is wait and see," Tony decided. When they got to the Flamingo, he pulled around to a side entrance. "In case I'm wrong about Berman, I want you to stick close to the hotel. Keep Ben in sight, or at least know where he is. Warn security to be extra alert. But don't mention to anybody what happened."

"What are you gonna do with her?" Denny asked, bobbing his chin disgustedly at the doped-up Francie.

"I'm not sure. I'll call you later and have you paged."

Tony reached over, pulled the door closed, and sped away.

There were only two people he could go to for help: Virginia Hill or Arnie Shad. Virginia, he knew, would have done what was best for *him*; Arnie would do what was best for Francie.

He went to Arnie.

Parked behind the apartment building where Arnie lived,

after telephoning him, Tony felt tremendous relief when the restless young reporter, ever present unlighted cigarette between his lips, hurried out and got into the car. Arnie turned on the interior light so he could look at Francie's eyes. She smiled wistfully at him. Tony was acutely aware of her breasts being visible under the transparent blouse, but Arnie seemed to pay no attention.

"Opium, the girl said?"

"Yeah. That she was a smoker."

Arnie turned the light off.

"Jesus, I don't know, Tony. There's a doctor named Mildren that has a sanitarium out on the Salt Lake Highway for drunks who want to dry out. But I don't know if he takes in dopers or not."

"How can we find out?"

"Let's go out there. If he won't take her, he can probably recommend someplace in California or Arizona. Wait here a minute—" Arnie hurried back into his apartment building and several minutes later returned with a lady's cardigan sweater. "I borrowed it from my landlady."

"Thanks, Arnie."

They got Francie into the sweater and buttoned her up, then Tony drove out the Salt Lake Highway until, a few miles out of town, Arnie spotted the place they were looking for. Set back from the highway amidst desert landscaping in an oasis of palm trees, it looked more like a country home than a sanitarium. Dr. Mildren was a stooped man in a long white coat. With the assistance of a powerfully built but pleasant nurse, he gave Francie a quick preliminary physical examination.

"She seems fairly healthy," he told Tony and Arnie when he finished. "There shouldn't be any medical problem in withdrawing her from the drug. You must understand, however, that this is a facility for alcoholics. I have no opium or access to it, so I can't withdraw her gradually. I can keep her sedated enough to make shock withdrawal easier, and see that she has enough intravenous nourishment to maintain her health, but it will still be a very trying ordeal for her. And"—he looked at Tony, who was holding Francie's hand—"for whoever goes through it with her. Are you the young lady's husband?"

"Yes," Tony lied.

"If you'd rather take her out of state—"

"No, we'll do it here, where I can be with her every day."

"As you wish. One thing about our method," the doctor said, "it will certainly be quicker. You understand, of course, that the responsibility of staying off the narcotic will rest with the patient. She'll have to *want* to remain unaddicted."

"She will," Tony said. "I'll see to it."

This time, Tony promised himself he was not going to lose her again. To anything.

FORTY-THREE

Tony was correct in his appraisal of Gus Berman: there was no public word on what had happened at the Ranch, and no repercussions from any source in the week that followed. Tony reported back to Ben Siegel as if the visit had been without incident.

"It's kind of a tacky place," Tony said. "Like a set for a low-budget movie. A lot of fake Western decorations. Red piano. But it looked busy. I think it's the kind of place that'll draw business."

"What'd the girls look like? Good-looking or beasts?"

"Good-looking. Lot of them look pretty young."

"That fucking Berman is probably white-slaving underage cunt," Ben said contemptuously.

"I didn't think Mr. Lansky would be involved in anything like that," Tony said.

"He wouldn't," Ben assured him. "Thing is, Meyer's just one guy in the different groups that form these corporations. He can advise and suggest, but in the end he can only vote his shares just like everybody else. He probably didn't like the idea of opening a cathouse even if it is legal, but if the others decide to do it anyway, he either has to go along or pull out. That can be touchy sometimes, depending who the other guys are. The corporation that owns the Ranch isn't the same bunch that owns the Flamingo. I don't know who Meyer's in with on the Ranch deal."

Ben had counted on increased business in April and May as more tourists made the five-hour drive from Los Angeles. Business did increase—but profits did not. Ben Siegel's Fabulous Flamingo seeméd to be laboring under some terrible jinx, some incredible hex or spell. It simply could not seem to make any money.

Virginia was becoming more and more nervous. "They're not going to give him much longer," she said to Tony. "This place has *got* to make a profit."

"Did you show him my plan for closing the show room and making the other cutbacks?" Tony asked.

"Yeah. He wouldn't go for it." Her expression softened. "He appreciated the effort, Tony. And the thought."

Tony felt badly about the plan—not because Ben had rejected it, but because he himself had not put as much thought into it as he could have. Unexpectedly having Francie thrust back into his life, with all the attendant problems, had caused him to give everything else a lesser priority. Tony had not asked Arnie Shad for help in outlining the plan for the Flamingo, as he had considered doing, because he felt he had imposed on Arnie enough in getting help for Francie. And he had not redone the plan himself as he intended to, had not reworked the figures, not put into it any more of the time and effort that would have been required to polish it and make it palatable to Ben Siegel. Tony was not surprised that Ben turned it down; it had become a plan without enthusiasm.

Tony had no enthusiasm for anything—except keeping Francie.

Francie's withdrawal from opium addiction was, as Dr. Mildren had predicted, an ordeal. The doctor sedated her as much as was medically prudent; the rest of the time she had to battle her demons the hard way—in a straitjacket, in a small room that had heavy pads on the walls and floor. Tony stayed with her much of the time; when he was not there, the burly but gentle nurse, Miss Moon, took his place.

The most excruciating period was naturally the first week: during that period Francie was a snarling, biting, spitting, cursing lunatic. Bereft of any emotion or desire except for the opiate upon which her nervous system had grown to depend and expect, she became a raving, demanding monomaniac, then a panic-stricken, pleading, crying childlike figure, and finally a delirious, incoherent mass of pale, shivering humanity that Tony was certain would die.

"Oh, no," Miss Moon reassured him, "we're not going to lose our girl, don't you worry about that. We just have to see that she doesn't go into shock. She's going to be fine; it'll just take time."

It tore at Tony's guts to see Francie reduced to such a pathetic, groveling thing one minute, a wild, abandoned thing the next. He tried to hold and comfort her despite the awkwardness of the restraining jacket she wore, then had to defend himself against her kicks and head butts when she went wild.

"Tony, oh Tony, my Tony, help me, please," she would beg. "Sweet Tony, darling Tony, please help Francie. Francie loves you so . . ."

When it did not work, when he failed to provide her with the relief she needed: "You son of a bitch! Fuck you, Tony! Get out of my sight, you bastard, I hate you!"

Once, when she was trying to be cunning, she was lucid enough to remember the thing that she knew and that he did not. "Tony, darling, if you'll help me, I'll tell you a deep, dark secret. All you have to do is get me just one teensy-weensy pipeful. Gus will give it to you; just tell him it's for me. Do that for me and I'll tell you the biggest secret you'll ever hear."

"I can't, honey," Tony told her, as gently as he could.

She flew into a rage, yelling and kicking for fifteen minutes, and forgot what the secret was.

After ten days, she awoke one afternoon serene and in repose. "Tony," she said quietly. "Is it really you?"

"It's me." He sat on the side of the bed and took her hand.

"I thought you were part of my nightmare," she said. "I guess I've probably been part of yours. Was I terrible?"

"You've got a couple of spankings coming, but you can take them later."

"Where are we?" she wanted to know.

Tony told her everything she could not remember, beginning with him recognizing her at the Ranch. When he finished, she covered her face to hide the shame she felt.

"Tony, I'm so sorry. To have you find me like that, in a place like that . . ."

Tony gently pulled her hands away and stroked her hair. "How I found you, where I found you, doesn't matter, honey. The only thing that matters is that I did find you." He leaned close to her. "Do you still love me, Francie?"

"Yes, Tony. God, yes—" She began to cry. "I've never stopped loving you, not for a second. Wherever I've been, whoever I've been with, whatever—" She bit her lip. She had been about to say, "whatever I've learned about us," but caught herself in time. She had no recollection of how closely she had come to telling him the secret during her withdrawal; all she knew was that she must not tell him now. "Whatever I've been through," she amended, "I've never stopped loving you."

"When you didn't write after Hawaii," he said, wringing the words out of himself "all those months, when you didn't answer any of my letters, I—I didn't know what to think—"

There was a light knock on the open door and Miss Moon came in. "Mr. Donovan, you just had a call from a Mr. Ebro at the hotel. He said there was a serious emergency and asked if you could come to your office right away." She came over and felt Francie's forehead. "Feeling better, sugar?"

"Yes, thanks," Francie said.

Frowning, Tony wondered what was wrong at the hotel. Ben and Virginia had been at their house in Beverly Hills for the weekend, Virginia insisting that Ben get away from the Flamingo for a few days. Maybe they were back and Ben was in one of his rages about something. It crossed Tony's mind that the call might have something to do with Gus Berman, but Tony doubted it. Ten days had passed since the incident at the Ranch; Tony was convinced Berman was not going to stir up further trouble. Given the Flamingo's ongoing luck, the emergency was probably some high roller who was about to win the hotel. Which might be a blessing for everyone.

"Go ahead," Francie said, squeezing his hand. "You can come back later and we'll talk."

"We want to try and get some soup into her anyway," said Miss Moon. She patted Francie's shoulder. "Maybe we'll even fix your hair a little, if you're up to it."

Tony kissed Francie good-bye and left. Miss Moon sighed when he was gone.

"That man's been with you practically day and night since

he brought you here. You're a lucky girl to have a husband like him."

Francie stared at her for a moment, then nodded thoughtfully.

When Tony walked into the Flamingo, the front desk manager hung up the phone and hurried over to meet him.

"That was a call from the airport. Mr. Lansky's on his way here. He wants someone to meet his limo at the back door so he doesn't have to use the lobby."

For a moment, Tony was incredulous. Meyer Lansky. Ben's boss. The man behind the Flamingo. Tony had been hearing about him for three years but had never met him. This would be his first visit to the hotel.

"Mr. Siegel's not back?" Tony asked. The manager shook his head. "All right, I'll take care of it. Where's Denny Ebro?"

"Your office, I think."

Tony ignored the elevators and climbed the stairs two at a time to the second floor. When he walked into his office he caught a glimpse of Denny sitting on the couch, a bloody towel wrapped around one hand. Then a pistol butt came down hard across Tony's right shoulder and he was knocked to the floor. As he tried to regain his balance, he was kicked solidly in the ribs. The room started to spin.

"All right," a voice said, "get him on his feet."

Tony was dragged upright and held. Pain seared from his shoulder up into his neck and down into his arm. His ribs hurt from the kick, but not enough to keep him from being fleetingly thankful he had not been kicked on the side where he had been shot, where his ribs were weaker. Squinting against the pain he saw Gus Berman smiling coldly at him. Berman had three men with him, two holding Tony's arms, one standing at the office door. I should have listened to Denny, Tony thought. Denny had told him a dozen times that Berman would not let the conflict between them rest.

Suddenly Tony remembered Meyer Lansky. What the hell did he have to do with all this? Shaking his head, he saw Gus Berman's face move close to his.

"Hello, tough guy," Berman said.

Tony looked over at Denny. His face was white and he had been crying. He was holding the bloody-towel-wrapped hand up close to his chest protectively.

"Your pal's got lots of guts," Berman said, bobbing his chin at Denny. "We stuck a handkerchief in his mouth and pulled out three of his fingernails with a pair of pliers before he'd tell us where you were."

"You son of a bitch," Tony muttered.

Berman's hand shot up and gripped Tony's throat. He put his face closer to Tony's, his oversized lower lip wet with saliva. "You fucking mick bastard. An hour from now you'll be kissing my shoes, begging for your fucking life." Letting go of Tony's neck, Berman jerked a thumb at his man at the door. "Let's go."

Berman and one thug flanked Denny, the other two stayed on Tony, and they assembled at the door. Denny's bloody hand was pushed under his coat where it could not be seen.

"I'm sorry, Tony," Denny sniffed. "But they been working me over for an hour—"

"Shut up, splitlip," Berman ordered. To Tony he said, "We're taking the elevator to the lobby, then right out to the side parking lot. Either of you tries anything cute," Berman pulled an automatic from a shoulder holster, "we'll not only let you have it right there, we'll give it to everybody else in sight. We'll shoot up the whole fucking lobby. Got that?"

"Got it," Tony said tightly. As he glanced back at Denny, he was suddenly struck by a surprising realization. *They did not know Meyer Lansky was on his way.*

Denny said they had been working him over for an hour. But the manager had just received the call from the airport as Tony walked in downstairs.

"Berman, wait a minute," Tony said quickly. "Don't take us through the lobby—"

"Why the fuck not?" Berman demanded.

"I don't want the place shot up. There are security guards in the lobby; they might realize what you're doing. Use the service elevator and take us out through the kitchen. You can get to the side parking lot just as easy that way."

Berman glared suspiciously at him. "You trying to pull something on me, you cocksucker?"

Tony shook his head. "I just don't want the lobby shot up, Berman." Pausing a beat, he decided to take a chance and added, "Neither would Mr. Lansky."

Tony saw uncertainty flash in Berman's eyes. But nothing else; he made no retort about Meyer Lansky. Tony was sure then that he was right: Berman was unaware that Lansky was on his way to the Flamingo.

"Okay," Berman decided, "we'll go the back way. Same rules. Either one of you or anybody else tries anything, we start blasting." He smiled sadistically at Tony. "When I get you out on the desert, you're gonna wish your mother had flushed you down the toilet when you were a handful of blood," he promised. "And when I'm finished with you, I'm gonna get that cunt Francie out of the hospital and put her back where she belongs, peddling her pussy. Now move!"

The second-floor hallway was deserted. The two trios of men walked quickly to the service foyer and Berman pressed the elevator call button. In the unmuted light of the foyer, Denny looked even paler, a sick bloodless white. Tony wondered if he might be on the verge of shock.

The elevator arrived, empty. They got aboard. Berman pressed the button marked KITCHEN. "Remember," he warned again, "no funny business."

Tony's mind raced. If Lansky's limousine had not arrived yet, Tony would have to make some kind of alternative move: trip one of the thugs holding his arms, shove the other one into Denny and his two captors, jump Berman and try to get his gun—

Risky. Dangerous. A gut feeling warned Tony that it would not work. But the thought of Berman going after Francie tore at his insides.

The elevator door opened onto a busy kitchen. The six men made their way through the beehive of activity almost without being noticed. Cooks and waiters who did notice their presence were too preoccupied to give them more than a cursory glance. They filed out the back door of the hotel. Berman's thugs guided them toward the side parking lot. As they were walking, Tony noticed a limousine pull onto the parking lot, heading directly toward them. Whether it was Lansky or not, he decided, when it got close enough he was going to jump Berman—

The limo did not get close enough. It stopped twenty feet in front of them and its rear doors opened. Three men in dark business suits got out, two of them husky, unsmiling, younger men, the third a compact older man. The older man's eyes evaluated the scene in front of him with a single glance. His expression darkened.

Gus Berman's mouth opened incredulously.

"Mr. Lansky—" he said, almost choking on the name.

Ten minutes later, all nine of them were in Ben Siegel's office. Meyer Lansky sat at Ben's desk while his bodyguards searched everyone and disarmed Berman and his men. Berman, as pale as Denny now, said, "I was just throwing a scare into them, Mr. Lansky—"

"Excuse me," Lansky said evenly, interrupting him, "but when I want you to speak, I will ask you to speak."

"I felt it was necessary to keep them in line," Berman persisted. One of Lansky's men stepped over and put a warning finger on Berman's chest.

"Shut up," he said. Berman swallowed dryly and shut up.

"Where is Ben?" Lansky asked. "Anyone know?"

"Los Angeles," Tony answered. "Probably on his way back right now."

"You are . . .?"

"Tony Donovan. I work—"

"For Ben, yes, I know about you."

"Mr. Lansky," Tony said quickly, "this is Denny Ebro, who also works here. He needs medical treatment; Berman pulled out some of his fingernails."

Lansky put a palm on his forehead and sighed quietly. "Is there a hotel doctor on retainer?"

"Yes, sir."

"Call him."

Tony picked up the phone on Ben's desk and dialed the hotel chief operator. "This is Tony Donovan. Will you get in touch with Dr. Lattimer and ask him to come to my office as quickly as he can, please." Tony was aware that Meyer Lansky was watching him closely. "Denny Ebro's had an accident," Tony told the operator. "He closed a car door on his fingers." Lansky's eyebrows raised slightly. He was obviously impressed.

As Tony hung up the phone, the office door opened and Ben Siegel strode in, Virginia just behind him. "What the hell's going on—" He saw Lansky and stopped, surprised. Quickly he smiled a wide smile. "Meyer! Hey!"

Lansky rose as Ben hurried toward him. The two men embraced and Ben kissed Lansky on his cheek. Lansky patted Ben fondly on the side of the head as an adult would do a child. "Benny," he said. *"Shalom."* Stepping past Ben, he briefly hugged Virginia also. "Hello, my dear."

"What's going on here?" Ben asked. His eyes locked on Berman. "I thought I told you to stay out of my hotel," he said in an ominously quiet voice.

"Gus was just leaving," said Meyer Lansky. He turned to Berman. "Take your boys and go back to the Ranch. Stay there. I'll talk to you at your office in the morning, at ten o'clock. Goodnight."

One of Lansky's bodyguards held the door for Berman and his three men to file out.

"My God, Denny! What happened to your hand?" Virginia asked in alarm as the men were leaving. She went over and put her arm around him.

"You have a very alert girlfriend, Ben," said Meyer Lansky. "She notices one of your men is hurt before you do." Ben turned red and Lansky turned to Virginia. "My dear, would you take Denny into Tony's office and wait with him there until the doctor comes? I'd appreciate it."

Virginia left with Denny. Lansky nodded to his two bodyguards and they also left the office. Now there were just the three of them left, and Lansky returned to the chair behind the desk and gestured for Ben and Tony to take chairs facing him. Folding his hands on the desk, Lansky looked disapprovingly at Ben Siegel.

"I'm not going to ask you what happened here tonight, because obviously you wouldn't know, Ben. You weren't here taking care of business as you should have been. So *I'll* have to tell *you*—at least as much as I know. I arrived at this hotel less than one hour ago; I found that a man who works for you had just had some of his fingernails pulled out; I found that he and another man who works for you were being taken from this hotel out into the desert, ostensibly to be taught a lesson about something, but I suspect for a far more serious purpose. Gus Berman and the three men you saw with him were doing the taking. Can you explain any of this to me, Ben?"

"I don't know anything about it, Meyer," Ben said, flabbergasted.

"You are supposed to be running this operation," Lansky said evenly. "You are supposed to be in charge." He turned to Tony. "I'd like you to tell me everything you know about this unfortunate situation, please."

"Yes, sir," Tony said, wetting his lips. "It's really all my fault, Mr. Lansky. Ben's not involved in it at all."

"Please," said Lansky, raising a hand, "no judgments, just facts."

"Yes, sir." Tony took a deep breath. "The whole thing started about ten days ago—"

He told Lansky everything that had happened, beginning with his and Denny's visit, at Ben's request, to look over the Ranch. Omitting nothing, he emphasized that Ben Siegel had not been aware of either the initial incident at the Ranch or anything that had transpired since. He also pointed out that Denny had urged him to tell Ben and took full responsibility for not doing so. As Lansky listened, his penetrating gaze never left Tony's face. His expression remained inscrutable; he neither nodded nor shook his head at any time. When Tony finished speaking, Lansky pursed his lips in thought, unfolded his hands, and drummed his fingertips silently on the desktop.

"This young lady, this Francie," he asked presently, "you've known her how long?"

"All my life, nearly," said Tony. "Since first grade."

"She's your childhood sweetheart?"

"Yes, sir."

"If you'd come to me," Ben interjected, "I could have helped you."

"I realize that, Ben. I'm sorry."

"She's going to be all right now?" Lansky inquired. "From the addiction?"

"I think so."

"That's good," he nodded. "Nasty business, narcotics." Turning to Ben, he said, "Benny, do me a favor. Have one of the cooks fix me a small New York cut and a nice salad, would you? I'd like to eat it upstairs in the apartment with you and Virginia. In about thirty minutes. Tony will keep me company here while you do that for me, all right?"

Ben shrugged. "Sure, Meyer." He hesitated and Lansky smiled.

"Thank you, Ben. I'll see you upstairs in thirty minutes."

"Sure, okay." Ben rose and self-consciously left the office.

Meyer Lansky looked at his watch, then wound it a few turns. "So, Tony, what do you think of Ben Siegel?"

"How do you mean?"

Lansky shrugged. "As a man. An employer. A manager. Just in general."

"I think a lot of Ben," Tony said. "He gave me a job in

an area where I had no experience, gave me a chance. I was just back from the service—"

"I understand you were given a battlefield commission," said Lansky. "And decorated for heroism."

"I was," Tony confirmed, "but aside from fighting in the war, and working in a silver mine prior to that, I was a very inexperienced person, especially as far as business is concerned. Ben Siegel gave me an opportunity to see what kind of savvy I had. That kind of confidence goes a long way with me." Tony stiffened in the chair slightly, as if bracing himself. "I really don't have anything negative to say about Ben Siegel, if that's the purpose of this conversation."

Meyer Lansky pursed his lips and drummed his fingertips again. Then he said, "The purpose of the conversation, Tony, is me getting to know you a little better. I've followed your employment under Ben with a good deal of interest. You've come a long way in a relatively short time. I must admit that I'm very impressed by your ambition to get ahead and your ability to learn new things so quickly. And I particularly appreciate your loyalty to Ben; I hope you'll feel the same way about me someday. Right now I'd like to ask you to help me help Ben. He's tired, overworked, physically and mentally drained; he needs a rest. Can you look after the hotel while he takes one?"

"Sure, if he wants me to."

"He'll want you to," Lansky assured. "If he has time, he'll talk to you about it before he leaves. And also about some new management, which is what I came out to discuss with him. The investors have decided to hire experienced hotel and casino managers to be responsible for the separate operations here. We're looking at candidates now. After we find the right people, I'd like to talk to you about a new position I intend to create in our operational structure: a very special, liaison-type position, much like an aide-de-camp in the military. In the meantime, it would greatly relieve my mind if I knew that I could count on you fully during this interim period. You're getting a salary of one-fifty a week right now; let's increase that to six hundred. And to show you how much I appreciate your relieving *my* mind, I want to relieve yours. We're closing the Ranch. Gus Berman will be leaving Las Vegas tomorrow, permanently. I'll see to it that he doesn't harass your young lady any further." Lansky abruptly rose, smiling. "Do we have a deal, Tony?" he asked, extending his hand.

Tony got quickly to his feet and shook hands. "Yes, sir."

"Wonderful. Now if you'll excuse me, I want to change before I go have my steak and talk with Ben. I'll see you sometime tomorrow and we'll visit further. Goodnight, Tony."

Lansky left the office. It had all happened so quickly that when Tony was alone, he had to recap it for himself. He had gone into the conversation determined not to betray or undermine Ben Siegel in any way, but somehow had come out of it as Ben's replacement, at least temporarily, at the Flamingo. It disturbed him slightly that there had been talk of *his* future, not Ben's; but Tony remembered Arnie Shad's insistence that Lansky and Ben were like brothers.

The main thing in Tony's mind at the moment was the tremendous relief he felt knowing that Francie was safe from Gus Berman. He realized in retrospect that during the entire confrontation with Berman and his thugs, his uppermost priority had not been his own safety or Denny's, but the protection of Francie. He knew there was no one, including himself that he would not sacrifice for her.

After making certain that Denny had gone with Dr. Lattimer to get proper medical treatment for his fingers, Tony left the hotel and hurried back to the sanitarium. He felt a compelling urge to resolve with Francie once and for all that they were now going to remain together. He found her sitting up in bed, hair brushed and a dab of makeup on, leafing through a movie magazine Miss Moon had given her.

"Hi," she said brightly.

"Hi." He stood by the bed, looking down at her.

"Dr. Mildren was in while you were gone. He's a dear, isn't he? He was very pleased with my progress. He said in another week or so I could go"—she looked down—"could leave."

"That's good."

"Are you okay?" she asked curiously.

"I'm fine." His side was throbbing from Gus Berman's kick, but he was not going to tell her that.

"I seem to remember" she said, "your wanting to know why I didn't answer your letters after Hawaii—"

"Francie, that isn't important," Tony said, with a new urgency in his voice. Sitting on the bed, he leaned close to her as he had earlier that day, and took her hands again. "Francie, we've got to get our lives in order, you and I. We can't go on coming together and then being pulled apart like—like—I don't know, like we're living our lives in a pinball machine."

She started to speak but he put his fingers on her lips.

"No, let me finish," he said firmly. "I love you, Francie. I want you. But more than that, I've got to know that you're going to be mine—*permanently*. I want to plan my life, get somewhere, accomplish something, but I can't do it wondering if we'll be together today and apart tomorrow. I can't keep going through that for the rest of my life . . ." His words trailed off.

"Oh, Tony," she said, suddenly hugging him to her with an urgency of her own. "Tony, my darling, my dearest, please forgive me for hurting you so often in the past—"

"Forget the past!" he said insistently. "The past only hurts us!"

"Yes, yes, you're right. It does, doesn't it? It does hurt us!" Francie said it as if realizing it for the first time.

Their embrace tightened; Tony held her as if against the whole world. "Promise me there won't be any more yesterdays," he pressed. "Promise me we'll only have tomorrows."

"If I do, Tony, will you promise me something?"

"Anything."

"Promise me that we'll never have to go back to Virginia City, ever. And that we won't let Virginia City, or anybody there, come into our life together. Promise you'll keep me free of Virginia City completely."

"I promise. Virginia City is dead and buried."

"Then, Tony," she said, pulling her lips toward his, "we *will* have only tomorrows. And we *will* be together."

They kissed a kiss that was so long and sweet that, for each of them, it was like their first kiss all over again. For a splendid moment in time, they returned to innocence.

FORTY-FOUR

Tony found a house for them, one of a dozen new prefabricated models just built southwest of the downtown area. It was a cheerful little two-bedroom stucco with an attached garage. At Brown's Furniture on Fremont Street, he picked out a bedroom set and had it delivered. He moved out of the room in which he had been living at the Flamingo and neatly arranged all his clothes in closets and drawers at the house. At the J.C. Penney store he bought bed linens and an assortment of towels. There were a hundred other things he knew they needed, from a can opener to a refrigerator, but he decided to let Francie do the shopping for those items. It would help her keep busy, which Tony had been told was essential to her therapy.

Dr. Mildren had said Francie could leave the sanitarium after three weeks if she would promise to adhere for a month to a high-calorie diet he designed to help her gain some weight. Tony gave her money and Francie had Miss Moon buy her some Western slacks, a couple of pullover sweaters, underwear, and a pair of sandals. Early one afternoon, she said good-bye to the doctor and his nurse, and Tony drove her to the house.

"You mean this is *ours*?" she asked in delight when they arrived. "Honest? We *own* it?"

"Us and the First State Bank," Tony said. "I bought it on the G.I. Bill. Do you like it?"

"I *love* it!" She went from room to room like a child in toyland, her hospital-pale face glowing as she opened and closed doors, drawers, cabinets. "Aha," she said when she got to the large bedroom, "I see someone has already moved in."

"This is the only room with any furniture in it," Tony told

542

her. "I thought I'd let you pick out the rest of what we need."

"Oh let's do it together, Tony," she said excitedly. "It'll be such fun."

When they were outside talking about shutters, they met another young couple, David and Julie Webb, who had moved in next door. Francie introduced herself as "Francie Donovan." David Webb was assistant to the trainmaster at the Union Pacific depot. Tony said that he was in hotel administration at the Flamingo. Tony and David agreed to go halves on a common fence along their property line, while Francie and Julie discussed the relative merits of the Electrolux versus the Stewart-Warner refrigerator. They promised to invite each other over to barbecue in the backyard.

"They seem like nice neighbors," Tony said.

"Yes. Julie said they were planning a family right away." After a moment, Francie added, "I'm not sure I even want any children. How do you feel about it?"

"All I want is you," Tony declared, taking her in his arms. "I don't care if we never have a kid, a dog, a cat, a goldfish; I don't even care if we have a radio. Just you—and I'll be completely happy."

"Good," she said adamantly. "Let's keep it that way. Just you and me. Who needs a lot of brats running around the house? Right?"

"Absolutely."

"Just the two of us, deal?" she asked.

"Deal," Tony agreed.

Ceremoniously they shook hands. Francie had intentionally kept it as light as possible; inside, she was tremendously relieved that Tony had gone along with her.

That evening Tony took her out for dinner. They went to the Grotto dinner club on the highway north of town. During dinner, Francie felt she had to put something to rest.

"I know we've agreed to keep the past out of our lives, but I've got to clear my conscience about not answering your letters, and explain how I ended up at the Ranch. Okay?"

"Just this once," Tony allowed. "Then we forget it, right?"

"Right." She took a deep breath, as if fortifying herself "After you left Hawaii—actually, even before you left—I had convinced myself that you weren't going to make it through the war. I had a premonition that you were going to be killed—and I did not want to know about it. I didn't want to know when or where; the only memory I wanted of you was our time together on Oahu." Francie lowered her gaze to the table. "I was on a long waiting list for a travel permit for Chalky and me to go back to the mainland. I tried to keep busy, but—I started seeing someone—an army officer—"

"Francie, this isn't necessary," Tony interjected.

"Yes, it is, Tony, please." After a moment, she continued. "He was a major. I went with him for about a year. When he received a transfer to the Presidio in San Francisco, he arranged travel for Chalky and me also. I took Chalky to live in Virginia City with Cavendish; I went back to San Francisco and moved in with the major. A year or so later, he left me and returned to his family in South Carolina. I hadn't even known he was married." Francie began to fidget with a fingernail. "After the war there was a lot of high times and fast living going on in San Francisco. I kind of fell into it; I was a natural, I guess—an unattached young woman with a small trust income. One of the fellows I was seeing was a little on the shady side; he took me to Chinatown a few times and eventually introduced me to opium. I didn't put up much resistance, especially after being told that I'd forget all my troubles. I still loved you very much, Tony, but by then I had convinced myself that you were probably dead. I hadn't left a forwarding address in Hawaii, so none of your letters reached me after I left there; I wasn't in close contact with Cavendish and Chalky, so I didn't learn you had actually returned from the war. Then after . . . after I got hooked on smoking opium, it didn't really matter; all I wanted was my water pipe.

"Eventually, of course, my habit far exceeded my trust allowance. My friend offered to introduce me to someone who could help me both make money and get my dope. That kind of person, to an addict, is like God. It turned out to be Gus Berman. He was starting a whorehouse in a newly developing place called Las Vegas, and he wanted some fresh faces, not just the same old bags. From San Francisco he got me and a sixteen-year-old Chinese girl that he leased for a year from her family. We were taken by car to Los Angeles, where we picked up a young Negro woman and a white beauty contest winner who had flunked her screen test. The four of us were driven across the state line to

Nevada in the middle of the night like bootleg liquor. You know the rest of it. I had been at the Ranch about two weeks when you found me."

After she told the story, Francie felt as if she had been hosed down inside and out. She felt clean—almost. The one terrible secret remaining she would keep forever.

When they finished dinner, Tony drove them back to their almost empty little house. Since they had no furniture except in the bedroom, they sat for a while on the steps of their slab front porch, in the dark, enjoying the balmy air of the desert spring.

"Somehow it doesn't seem real, does it?" Tony said. "Our being together at last."

"No, it doesn't," Francie agreed. To her it seemed surreal, but she did not say so.

"I must have imagined moments like this a million times," he mused.

"Me too." No matter how hard she tried not to.

"Sometimes I think all I've lived for is to find you . . ." Swallowing heavily, he looked up at the starry sky, as if giving thanks.

"Tony—"

She took his hand and they got up together and went into their bedroom. They began undressing each other.

"We can't turn on any lights because we don't have drapes or blinds yet," Francie whispered, as if there were someone there to hear her.

"The bathroom window is up high," Tony reminded. "We could have the light on in there."

"Oh, good," Francie said. Naked, she led him into the bathroom. "I need light to see what you're going to put into me. That cock the nurse in Hawaii thought was so beautiful."

"You did too," he reminded her.

Closing the door, turning on the light, she looked at his erection and smiled. "Still do," she said happily. She sat up on the built-in vanity counter, braced her feet widely apart on the shower stall, and said, "Get me wet, honey . . ."

As Tony knelt and his head came up between her thighs, Francie found that she could look into the angled mirrors of the bathroom and see herself and Tony reflected many, many times, into infinity. Tony saw it too.

"That's us," he whispered. "Together like this forever."

"Yes," she said, and closed her eyes as he bent to her.

But she could not keep her eyes closed. At some point she opened them and stared at her reflection in revulsion.

Early in June, Denny came into Tony's office one afternoon and said, "Virginia's getting out of a cab out front."

Tony went to the elevator to meet her. She came off dressed in beige and gold, with brown alligator accessories. Her long chestnut hair was rolled in a French twist in back. She looked gorgeous and she gave Tony a radiant smile.

"Hiya, kid," she greeted him, throwing her arms around him. She gave Denny a peck on the cheek and said hello to Tony's secretary and a couple of waiters who were passing.

"No bags?" Tony asked.

"Still at the airport," she said. "I'm just passing through on my way to Chicago. Have you got a few minutes, Tony?"

"Sure. Come on in," he gestured toward his office.

"Not using Ben's office?" Virginia asked, eyebrows raising.

Tony did not respond until they were inside with the door closed. Then he said, "As far as I'm concerned, I still work for Ben. The office is there for him, just like the apartment is still there for both of you."

"I should have figured," she said. "You always have been a different cut." She took a chair and the smiling, cheerful exterior she had shown outside the office now faded. "Tony," she said somberly, "I stopped by to ask you if you've heard anything, anything at all, about what Meyer has planned for Ben?"

"No, I haven't. Why?" He tilted his head slightly, frowning. "You look worried."

"I'm more than worried. There's a rumor around that a contract has been set on Ben."

"A contract?"

"A murder contract."

"Come on, Virginia," Tony said lightly. "Ben's out of that kind of stuff now. Anyway, why would anyone want him killed?"

"I don't know, Tony. All I know is what I hear. Very strong rumors—from people in positions to know. I'm going to Chicago and see if any of my old friends there can shed any light on it. If not, I'm heading for New York to make some inquiries. And if I strike out there . . ." She paused deliberately, studying Tony.

"Yeah?" he asked. "If you strike out there?"

"Then," she said very quietly, "I'm going to fly to Rome and ask Lucky Luciano himself. No mob hit gets approval without Luciano knowing about it."

"Virginia, if you're serious," Tony said, "shouldn't you contact the police?"

"God, I wish it was that simple," she said wearily.

"Does Ben know about this?"

She nodded. "He doesn't believe it. And if you talk to him," she implored, "for God's sake, don't say I was here, or that I said anything about it. Ben thinks I'm on a trip just to visit friends."

"Do you have any idea who could be behind it?" Tony asked. "Assuming it is true."

Virginia shook her head. "None. I thought if Meyer had indicated what he's going to have Ben doing, it might give me a clue. That maybe somebody was being eased out somewhere and was sore. Hell, I don't know," she said wearily.

"What can I do to help you?" Tony asked.

Virginia shrugged. "Just keep your ears open. If you should hear anything, even idle gossip, call Ben direct. He's at the Beverly Hills number. Maybe if he hears it from somebody besides me, he'll take it seriously." Virginia took a monogrammed cigarette from a silver case in her purse, and Tony came around the desk to light it for her. "How's business?" she asked.

"Picking up, I'm happy to say." Tony did not elaborate. He could justifiably have added, "Now that Ben's not around to poke his nose into everything." But he did not.

Under Meyer Lansky's long-distance guidance, and by observation of the casino, hotel, restaurant, and beverage managers put in by the corporation, Tony had now undergone a crash course in just how bad a manager Ben Siegel was. No one man, Tony now knew, could *personally* run a huge complex like the Flamingo. A man could not supervise the front desk *and* the kitchen, the blackjack tables *and* the show room, the pit bosses *and* the cocktail waitresses. Responsibilities had to be delegated and shared. One person could only oversee, double check, function as a safety valve against inefficiency, as Tony was now doing for Meyer Lansky at the Flamingo, and would begin doing at two other casino-hotels that Lansky corporations planned to build. If a man spread himself too thin, as Ben had done, nothing could be

accomplished with any degree of reasonable cost effective-
ness. The Flamingo was a very expensive monument to the
veracity of that business maxim.

But none of that would Tony ever say, to Ben *or* Virginia.
They were his friends. At the urging of one, the other had
given him a chance to become something, some*one*. He
would never hurt either of them.

When Virginia was preparing to leave, she put a finger on
Tony's cheek and said, "How's that girl you're shacked up
with? She doing okay?"

Tony blushed, and hated it. "She's doing fine, Virginia.
Thanks."

"Well, I hope she's good enough for you, kid. You love
her? She love you?"

He nodded. "Yes to both."

"Wonderful. When it's both ways like that, there's nothing like it. I've only had it one time in my life—with Ben.
But I'll tell you something, kid, I wouldn't trade it for
anything." She kissed him on the lips, lingering just a fraction. "Take care of yourself Tony."

"I will. You too."

"Always have," she said, throwing him a wink.

From the office window, Tony watched her get into a taxi
for the ride back to the airport. In a single, meshed pair of
thoughts, he was very glad that Ben had Virginia and that
he had Francie.

Ten days later, Tony no longer had Francie.

When he got home from work, she was not there. He
looked around for a note, but there was none. Looking in
the garage, he saw the little Willys Jeep they had bought for
Francie to shop and run around in. If the Jeep was there,
Tony thought, Francie had to be close by. Probably gossip-
ing with Julie next door. Leaving his coat and tie in the
kitchen, he went to the Webbs' back door.

"No, I don't know where she is, Tony," said the young
housewife. "I saw her leave early this afternoon, but I don't
know where she went. She was with a short man who had a
limp. He used one of those rubber-tipped canes."

Tony could only stare incredulously at Julie. It was as if
his mind could not accept and process Julie's words, as if
they were either foreign or simply too horrible for Tony's

consciousness to permit. The stunned expression on his face frightened the neighbor.

"Tony, what's wrong?" she asked apprehensively. A nervous hand went to one cheek. "Who was that man? Do you know . . .?"

"Sure," Tony replied quickly, forcing a half smile. "I just forgot he was coming. It's someone from our hometown." He parted Julie's arm. "Sorry I scared you."

Back in his own kitchen, Tony leaned heavily against the refrigerator and stared into space. Was this a nightmare? Had he died and gone to hell: a place where he and Francie found each other over and over, and Buck O'Crotty always separated them? This couldn't be happening . . .

Shaking his head violently to purge the monstrous, near-nauseating astonishment from his mind, Tony began to stalk through the house. *There has got to be a note.* Bedroom, bathroom, living room, tables, counters, dresser: there was nothing. None of her clothes appeared to be missing. The little cash they kept in the house was still there. Even the purse Francie had used last was still there; in it was her new driver's license: a driver's license listing her name as "Frances Grace Donovan."

Nothing was gone except Francie. As if she had simply been lifted out of their life by the hand of some god. Or devil.

Tony stood like a zombie in the middle of their bedroom. The bed was three feet away; he could easily have sat, or lain. But he stood, a mortal being held fast by the gravity of a world spinning too rapidly for him. His mouth did not gape, his shoulders did not sag; he was not defeated, as such, but for the moment he was neutralized. In defense against a shock too traumatic with which to cope, his mind had made him embryonic.

He remained that way for an hour. Outside the sun slipped down in the sky; inside, the shadows of their furniture lengthened. Tony's eyes continued blinking, his chest rose and fell slightly with normal breathing, his arms and hands hung relaxed. When he finally stepped away from the trance, it was to him as if only a moment had passed. Walking into the bathroom, he rinsed his face with cold water. As he dried, he went into the living room, where their telephone was.

There was a scheduled Bonanza flight to Reno at nine-thirty, but he did not want to wait. He called the charter desk at the airport. There were two private planes available; one would be fueled-up and its pilot ready when Tony got there.

It was midnight when Tony arrived at the Delavane mansion.

"Don't look like there's nobody, home," the Reno taxi driver said. "Place is all dark." His voice was uneven, indicating his nervousness. He found Virginia City spooky as hell at night, and the silent, moody man with the scar on his face wasn't helping matters. When the man had first come out of the Reno airport and offered him double fare to be driven to the mining town, it seemed like a windfall. Now the cabbie wasn't too sure. Dark mansions high on a hill at midnight weren't among his favorite destinations.

"Wait here," Tony said.

The driver watched as his customer loudly sounded the door knocker, rapped heavily on first-floor windows with his knuckles, and finally stood well back on the drive and yelled demandingly, "Francie!" It was like a plea he was wrenching from within himself "Francie!"

There was no response, no light went on. But the shouting man was not dissuaded.

"Francie!"

He yelled at intervals of perhaps twenty seconds, for several minutes. A light went on in a house back down Sierra Street. The driver got out and went over to Tony.

"Look, mister, I'm afraid somebody's gonna call the cops on us. I don't want to get in no trouble."

Tony stared at him for a moment, then nodded understandingly. "Okay, let's go," he said.

Tony gave him directions. The driver thought they were leaving town; he almost balked when he was told to turn into Miner's Walk. Deserted like everything else at that hour, the narrow, foreboding little street looked like it led to eternal darkness.

"Park here," Tony, said in front of the O'Crotty house. "Wait." The driver now had no choice; there was thirty-one dollars on his meter, at regular fare.

Tony saw light coming from the rear of the house. He walked around to the back door and through a porch window saw Buck in the kitchen. At the table, chin on chest,

Buck stared wearily at a cup of coffee. His rubber-tipped cane hung from the tabletop next to him. Tony opened the back door and stepped into the kitchen.

Buck looked up.

"I've been half expecting you," he said.

Tony leaned back on the closed door. His eyes riveted on the older man. Buck studied him for a moment, then nodded toward the stove.

"There's coffee."

"How do you do it, Buck?" Tony asked, ignoring the inane offer. "How do you make Francie turn her back on me so easily?"

"I only talk to her," Buck said simply. He raised both hands slightly from the tabletop, as if explaining the most obvious thing in the world. "I point out to her what I believe to be wrong in what she's doing, what you both are doing—"

"Wrong *how*?" Tony demanded. "Wrong *why*?"

"There are some people, some men and women, who are not meant to be . . . together," Buck said lamely. "Your mother and I, for instance—"

"*No!*" Tony snapped. "Don't go back to 1920 again! You can't justify everything with examples from the past! This is 1947! Tell me why Francie and I can't have each other *now!*"

Buck shook his head, expressing amazement. "You can't separate now from then, lad. Now *is* then. Then *is* now. You see—"

His words broke off and Buck stared at nothing for a moment, frowning. Then he looked up at Tony with heart-felt empathy. Jesus, Mary, and Joseph, he thought, *why* can't I tell him—here and now? Why, must I go on hurting him to keep the wish of a woman dead nearly two decades?

Buck sighed heavily and picked up his cup of coffee. He held the cup close to his lips but did not drink. It's not only for Ruby, he reminded himself. He had a promise to keep to Frances Grace too: a promise not to tell Tony the truth if she would leave him. Not to tell Tony that he had committed incest—and that she had let him.

So, Buck thought, putting the cup down without ever tasting the coffee, what he was doing was not only for the dead, but the living as well. But if it was the right thing to do, he wondered, why it was tearing his guts out?

From the door, Tony scrutinized the older man thoughtfully, tongue wetting his lower lip. Tony's throat had suddenly become sore from the yelling he had done at the mansion. Stepping to the table he sat opposite Buck.

"I think you're crazy, Buck," he said without rancor. "I think you've lost your mind."

Buck grunted in quiet derision and shook his head briefly. "No, I haven't."

"Yes," Tony said. "You're either crazy or you're a fool. To convince yourself that you've been so right for so long, you have to be one or the other. Not that I care which it is; I don't. It no longer makes any difference to me *why* you interfere in my life. But I want you to tell me *how* you do it. What kind of control are you able to exert over Francie?"

"Common sense, that's all," Buck declared.

"There has to be more to it than that," Tony said. "She was happy with me in Las Vegas. We were making a life for ourselves." Tony suddenly frowned. "How did you even know she was there?"

"How I knew she was there isn't important—"

"Did *she* call you?"

"—what's important is that you and she be prevented from doing something that could ruin the lives of you both—"

"*How?*" Tony demanded, pounding a fist on the table.

"You keep your voice down," Buck ordered, pointing a threatening finger.

"I won't!" Tony shouted. "You're going to tell me what I want to know!"

"I won't sit here and be bellowed at," Buck announced, reaching for his cane. Tony knocked the cane away, sending it flying across the room with a sweep of his arm. "How dare you?" Buck asked, incensed.

Tony reached across the table and jerked Buck forward by the front of his shirt. "Tell me!" he demanded, face livid with anger at the same time his eyes were moist with hurt. "Tell me why she turns on me every time you want her to! Tell me, you son of a bitch!"

Buck's right hand lashed out in a stinging slap across Tony's cheek. "No man calls me that," he growled in an odd guttural voice. Tony drew back a fist.

"Tony, no! Don't hurt him!"

The shrieking voice startled both of them, causing their heads to snap toward the sound. It was Kerry, in her nightgown, gripping the doorjamb leading from the hallway as if terrified.

"Please, Tony, don't hurt him," she begged. "Please . . ."

Buck's chin went up and his chest puffed out in righteous indignation. "Take your hands off me," he demanded. "Can't you see you're frightening the girl?"

Tony let him go. He slumped back in the chair; now he was defeated.

"My cane," Buck said to Kerry. Retrieving it, she hurried to him. He stood, cane in one hand, the other arm around Kerry's shoulders. For a moment he stared down at Tony, eyes, expression, his very being laced with sadness, hurt, and a gnawing, oppressing feeling that what he was doing— had *done*—might possibly *not* be right.

We can't go on like this, Buck thought. If we do, it'll come to murder someday.

"Leave this house, Tony," he said, with the last ounce of emotional strength he had left. "Never come back."

Guiding a weeping Kerry alongside himself, Buck walked out of the kitchen.

It was three in the morning when Tony got back to the Reno airport. The meter on the cab was fifty-eight dollars. Tony gave the driver six twenty-dollar bills. "Sorry I made you so nervous," he apologized.

While he waited for the pilot to file a flight plan back to Las Vegas, Tony washed his face and hands in the men's room. Looking in the mirror to comb his hair, he stopped suddenly with the comb poised. All the way back to Reno, he had played the scene with Buck over and over in his mind: the angry words, the raised voices, the physical violence. He had reviewed everything said and done on his part, everything said and done by Buck, and the extreme upset caused to Kerry. But at no time until that very moment, staring at himself in the washroom mirror, had it occurred to him that a key figure in the scenario had been missing.

Not Francie. She was not expected to be there.

But Rosetta was.

And had not been.

"Ready to go when you are, Mr. Donovan," the pilot said, sticking his head in the door.

"Right with you," Tony replied.

He finished combing his hair and, frowning tightly, walked

out into the terminal. *Where the hell had Rosetta been?* The thought would have nagged him all the way home, but as he walked past the closed newsstand, a man hurried in from a truck and dropped a bundle of morning newspapers on the floor. Tony caught a glimpse of the headline. He stopped and stared at it in horror.

GANGSTER BUGSY SIEGEL SLAIN

Part
Eleven

Tony

1951–1952

FORTY-FIVE

"Hello, Tony. Come on up."

The voice, as always, was a shade suggestive.

When Ben Siegel had been alive, when Tony, Arnie Shad, and Virginia Hill had all been together in Las Vegas helping him oversee the building of the Flamingo, Ben had often chastised Virginia for her invitational tone. "No matter what you say," he complained, "it sounds like you're asking somebody to go to bed with you. You can say, 'Eggs over easy,' and it sounds like you're asking to get laid."

Tony still remembered Virginia's wry reply: "So I'll stop eating eggs, Ben, all right?"

Hers was a voice that matched the rest of her: it was straight like her shoulders, tapered like her long legs, robust like her bosom, alive like her eyes, and its tone matched her stride when she walked, the slight Southern accent in step with her natural strut. Suggestive, inviting: that and more, but also natural and healthy, uninhibited and unashamed. She had what she had, was what she was, and anyone who didn't like it could go fuck themselves. That was Virginia Hill. Always. She never changed.

In the elevator of the Plaza, after he had called Virginia's suite, Tony felt a nervous thrill at the realization that he was actually on his way to see her after three years. It was the weekend before she was scheduled to testify for the Kefauver Committee; it was the trip he had volunteered to make for Lansky and Luciano. Why he felt so nervous, he did not know. Virginia was, had always been, strictly a friend. But Tony, like nearly every other man, and even some of the women, who had known her, could not help thinking of her in a personal, physical way. There was something so sensual, so earthy about her—the resplendent chestnut hair,

557

round red cheeks, pursed lips, sculpted shoulders, grandiose breasts, floating hips, and those long, elegant legs—that lent even the most platonic relationship an aura of physicality, an emanation of sex that pervaded every contact, however brief, with everybody. She was a rough-cut goddess, and no one who ever met her ever forgot her.

When the elevator stopped, Tony got off, paused at a foyer mirror to remove his overcoat and check his tie, and walked down the hall to her suite. Tapping with the knocker, he swallowed, wet his lips, and waited. Then the door opened and she was there, hair upswept, gorgeous in a green cocktail dress, neck draped with diamonds, smile as dazzling as a Klieg light, the same ageless twenty-five she had always been although now a decade past that. Only her eyes were older. Tony could do nothing but stare until she who had cast the spell broke it.

"Hello, Tony."

"Hello, Virginia."

They stepped into each other's arms as if it was the most natural thing in the world for them to do, and their lips came together in a kiss so delicious that Tony felt it to his ankles.

It was the first time he had ever kissed a woman and not thought of someone else: Francie. But he knew by Virginia's tears that it was she who was thinking of someone else.

The memory of Ben Siegel hung heavily over them.

After Virginia had a good healthy cry, purging her emotions of the moment, she left Tony's embrace and retreated to the powder room where she remained for fifteen minutes.

When she emerged, she was radiant again. And raunchy. "Jesus, I haven't been kissed like that since I was with Ben. You didn't take lessons from him, did you?" She winked. "Because if he taught you anything else, I'll take you back to Salzburg with me."

Tony laughed. "I think some of Ben rubbed off on everybody who knew him."

Virginia sighed. "Ain't that the truth. How about a drink? Then we'll have dinner sent up."

Without asking what he wanted, Virginia mixed him a dry martini with three olives, exactly the way he liked it. After he took his first sip, he said, "Perfect. How'd you remember?"

She winked again. "A smart girl never forgets what a man

drinks." Sitting on the couch with him, her own drink held in a cloth napkin, she said candidly, "So. I take it my coming back to testify is a cause for concern in certain quarters."

Tony took another sip of his drink, remembering Buck O'Crotty's long-ago advice: In a sticky situation, never comment unless you have to. He said nothing.

"Who am I making nervous, Tony?" she asked directly. "Meyer and Charlie?"

"Mr. Lansky," Tony said, not wanting to bring Luciano's name into the conversation, "is worried that he might not know everything Ben did while the Flamingo was going up. Since Ben technically and legally worked for Mr. Lansky directly at the time, he's afraid that if Ben was involved in anything shady, he himself might end up being held responsible for it today. With Ben dead, Mr. Lansky might have trouble proving he wasn't involved in anything Ben might have done on his own."

"Has he sent you here with some kind of offer for me, Tony?" she asked.

"Not at all," Tony said quickly. "It's not his intent to interfere with your testimony; in fact, he told me that he *wants* you to tell the truth about everything you know. He said if there was any past wrongdoing connected with any of his current holdings, he would rather get it out in the open and do whatever's necessary to resolve it instead of having it forever hanging over his head. Now that Mr. Lansky is completely legitimate, he's trying very hard to disassociate himself from his past."

"Do you believe he is completely legitimate, Tony?" Virginia asked evenly. There was no shading in her tone to indicate her own opinion.

"Yes, I do," Tony asserted. "I've worked for him directly for more than three years now. During that time I haven't known him to be involved in anything—any business, any activity at all—that wasn't completely on the square." Virginia noticed that Tony was gesturing with one hand as he talked, much as Ben used to do. "Lansky's involved in gambling in Nevada," Tony continued, "which is legal. He's involved in gambling in Cuba and the Bahamas, which is legal. Would you like to know where his other interests lie?" He began to enumerate them on his fingers. "Something called a transistor, which he believes will replace radio and television tubes. Something he refers to as a 'conglomerate,' which is a single group of managers running a lot of different companies that are involved in seasonal products; he says it's an entirely new concept of management. Something called hexachlorophene, which can be put in soap to help prevent body odor. He's got investments in a search for bauxite ore in Jamaica; that's what aluminum comes from. He's invested in powdered cream for coffee, in elevator doors that open automatically and don't need an operator, in complete dinners that are frozen and can simply be heated up and served, in a chain of pizzerias that would extend from coast to coast. He's backing the construction of a hotel and some other businesses in Israel, where he hopes to retire some day . . ." Tony paused, trying to think of other things to add, then finally gave up and concluded with a shrug, "He is a legitimate businessman with interests in a wide range of businesses, new products, research and development, speculations, just about anything you can name—all legal."

Virginia's eyes were fixed on Tony in quiet study. "Sounds like you kind of like the man," she commented when he stopped talking.

"Sure. He's been good to me. If it wasn't for him and Ben—"

"Let's talk about Ben for a minute," she cut in. "There are some people who think it was Meyer who had Ben killed."

"I don't believe that," Tony shook his head adamantly. "I've been in Meyer Lansky's company when he spoke about Ben's killing and tears came to his eyes."

"Has he ever said who *he* thinks did it?"

"In a way," Tony temporized. It had actually been Lucky Luciano who expressed the opinion. "Some people from Chicago were mentioned. No specific names. I think they were involved in some kind of wire service to bookmakers." Tony decided to see whether Virginia was going to be frank with him. "Was Ben involved in anything like that?"

"Yes," she replied without hesitation. She leaned forward to get a cigarette from the coffee table; down the front of her dress, Tony could not help seeing her exquisite breasts shift and reform in a half-cup bra. Sitting back, Virginia held the cigarette and waited. It took Tony a moment to realize what she was waiting for.

"Oh, sorry." He picked up a lighter and snapped it for her.

"I warned Ben not to get mixed up in the wire service thing," she elaborated, exhaling. "I *begged* him not to. But he'd already made up his mind. He wanted something on the side to put money away for his two little girls to go to college. The deal was a cream puff, he said. Remember that's what he used to call easy pickings? Cream puff deals. Maybe in this one," she concluded bitterly, "the cream went sour."

"The Flamingo wasn't involved in any way, was it?" Tony asked. "He didn't put casino money into it or anything like that?"

"No. Hell, no," she assured him, "he didn't put any money at all into it. The men operating it just wanted the Ben Siegel name; it still carried a lot of muscle." Virginia stared at her drink and sighed. "But in the end, I guess not enough." Looking up, she forced a smile. "Hungry yet?"

"Sure."

Just as with the drink, Virginia did not consult him about dinner, merely went into the bedroom, called room service herself, and ordered what she knew he would like. When it was served an hour later, he was not surprised to find well-done tournedos with a brochette of extra bacon on the side, richly creamed spinach, and potatoes au gratin with sesame seeds mixed liberally into the baked bread crumbs. The wine was a Chateau Lafite-Rothschild, vintage 1937, which the room service captain handled as if it were a newborn babe. After the waiters left, Virginia lighted two tall candles in silver holders and turned the room lights low. Tony poured the wine and they toasted.

"To old times."

"Yes, old times." Virginia's eyes started to mist again but she suppressed more tears by forcing herself to reminisce about happy things. "Ben and I used to eat by candlelight," she said dreamily. "At first he wouldn't do it; he claimed candlelight was for faggots. After I finally nagged him into it, he said he hated it, tried to get me to believe he couldn't see his food. Then for a long time he didn't say anything at all. One night I neglected to put candles on the table and I thought he was going to have a fit. You would have thought he caught me in bed with another man. He said if that was the best I could set his table, he might as well eat his meals in the coffee shop from then on. Anybody listening to him would've sworn he'd been eating by candlelight since birth. God, he was something."

"He was indeed," Tony said, and at once realized how much that phrase made him sound like Buck O'Crotty. For an instant he thought it strange that Buck should come to mind at such an odd moment: in the company of a woman like Virginia Hill, conversing about a man like Ben Siegel. Then Tony realized something that had not occurred to him before. Ben and Buck had something very much in common: both had been close to him, at different times and in different ways, and both had been murdered by a person or persons unknown. Carrying that thought to a further parallel, it occurred to him, also for the first time, that Arnie Shad, although he had never said so in a single, specific accusation, believed Meyer Lansky to be indirectly responsible for *both* murders. Three men who had most influenced his life, Tony thought, all linked together by unproved charges of unsolved crimes.

"A penny," Virginia said quietly.

Tony came out of his reverie and instinctively camouflaged his true thoughts. "Just thinking about Ben," he half lied.

"He's easy to think about," she said. After a beat, she added quietly, "Sometimes."

When they finished dinner, Virginia closed the curtained French doors of the little dining alcove and led Tony back to the living room where she poured him a brandy.

"Take your coat and shoes off if you want to," she said. "I'm going to get out of this garter belt so I can relax."

Tony took off his coat and loosened his tie. Sniffing his brandy by one of the windows, he looked down on a night-lighted, snow-covered Central Park and tried not to think about Virginia taking off her clothes in the next room. Trying not to think about it gave him a partial erection and he quickly took a swallow of brandy and walked around the room.

When Virginia returned, she was in a soft green peignoir that should have concealed her figure with its yards of flowing silk, but which actually only served to accentuate individual parts of her depending on how she moved: an arm bent to pour her brandy molded the silk onto a breast; reaching under the bar for a fresh napkin clearly outlined her buttocks; joining him on the couch again, drawing her legs up under her, accentuated her marvelous thighs. Gone was all the makeup now, the jewelry, the image she showed the world. Left was the woman: freshly scrubbed, freckled, a few lines showing, a pound or two not constricted by latex, chestnut hair disappearing past her shoulders. Tony could not take his eyes off her.

"Why are you staring at me, sir?" she asked coyly.

At the moment, Tony lacked the capacity for anything except simple truth. "I can't decide whether you were more beautiful before you went into the bedroom or after you came out."

"Oh, Tony." Touched, she took his hand. "That's sweet." Tilting her head an inch, she said, "I have to hand it to Meyer: he knew just who to send tonight. Anybody else from the old days would have shown up at my door, I probably would have kicked him in the grapes and told him to tell Meyer that if he wanted to know what I was going to say to the Kefauver Committee on Thursday, he could watch it on television. You knew they were televising it, didn't you?"

"Yes."

"What a kick," she made a wry face and took a long swallow from her glass, which Tony noticed had twice as much brandy in it as she had poured for him. For a moment she kept the glass in front of her face, looking at him over its crystal rim, her greenish-gray eyes emotionless, penetrating. Under her gaze Tony felt like a specimen being scrutinized prior to dissection. He was glad he had told her only the one inconsequential lie that night; if he had been lying all evening he suspected he might now expect to be verbally castigated, castrated, and crucified. Instead, Virginia said without further preliminaries, "Okay. So you want to know two things. One, why I came back to testify. Two, what I'm going to tell them. Am I right?"

"Right." The word almost stuck in his throat. For a brief moment he felt almost like a hypocrite for being there. But he reminded himself that if it had not been him here, it would have been someone else: somebody selected by Luciano. And he admitted to himself that *he* wanted the information she had, just as Lansky and Luciano did, to protect his position as well as theirs. And as the evening wore on, he was becoming more and more attracted to her as a woman, the friendship going on reserve. So he could no more tear himself away from the moment at hand than he could touch her lips without also touching her neck, her nipples, all of her. She held him there, captive, by what she knew and by what she was.

"My reason for being here isn't all that involved," she finally told him. "I don't know whether you knew it or not, but my house in Beverly Hills, where Ben was shot, well, everything in it was seized by the Feds, supposedly because of back taxes I never paid. The real reason, of course, was to try and get me to come back to the States so they could question me about Ben's murder. I told them to go to hell and take me to court for the back taxes. They never have, but they've never let me claim my things either. A lot of what they seized, Ben and I bought together, like our bedroom furniture, some paintings, Oriental carpets, quite a few rare books, some antiques we had throughout the house. They took a set of sterling silver service for twenty-four, all my beautiful Limoges china, my Waterford crystal glassware. Other things of mine had been gifts from Ben—a lot of jewelry, my furs . . . in that house I left two mink, one ermine, one sable, and two Persian lamb coats. There were some gold and silver picture frames that he also gave me. And some very personal items—photographs, letters, even some love poems—did you know that Ben wrote poetry?"

"No, I didn't."

"I know a few literary people in Europe; they've read Ben's poetry and thought it was very good. Irwin Shaw was particularly moved by it."

Tony nodded. He did not know who Irwin Shaw was.

"Anyway," Virginia continued, "you get the general idea. Uncle Sam has custody of a lot of my belongings, some of which are very dear to me. The government offered me a deal—if I would come back and testify before the Kefauver Committee, all my property would be returned."

As she talked, she had not put the brandy down, had never let the glass get too far from her pale, scrubbed lips, and soon it was all gone. Virginia rose to pour herself some more. Tony watched her long stride-strut across the room, remembering how she had turned heads when she walked through the Flamingo. Ben had finally banned her from the casino, where she all but stopped play. "Stay the hell away from the tables," he had ordered. "Every time you sashay through there, you probably cost the house a thousand dollars."

As Tony watched her go to the bar and back, tides of green silk flowing with each step, each move she made, he experienced the same surge of desire that he had felt when she was in the bedroom changing clothes. Shifting his position on the couch to check the start of another annoying erection, he became irritated with himself for not being able to control his thoughts and emotions. This woman still loved someone else, just as he himself loved someone else. Ben was dead and Francie was remote and unattainable, but those circumstances did not alter the love that their memories generated. Ben had been Tony's friend, his mentor, the person who gave him his first chance to make of himself something besides a hardrock miner. As much as Tony's physical desire for Virginia was asserting itself he could not avoid feeling that it was somehow disloyal of him to want her. Allegiance did not stop at the grave.

Virginia returned to the couch with her fresh brandy. This time when she sat down facing him, feet up on the cushions, she hiked the gown above her knees for comfort. The front of one exquisitely turned calf lay against his thigh as she resumed talking.

"As for what I'm going to tell the committee," she said, "the answer is easy—not a goddamn thing. There's nothing in my deal with Uncle Sam about *how* I'll testify; just that I will." She smiled knowingly. "With five United States senators and half a dozen high-powered federal attorneys and investigators, I guess they didn't think it was necessary to guarantee ahead of time what a hick from Alabama like me was going to say. They're pretty sure that as smart as they all are, it'll be easy enough to wrap me around their little fingers." Her smile hardened like granite. "Thursday should be a very interesting day." Her eyes again locked on Tony. "Satisfied?"

"Yes." Tony wanted to end the deception and the doubt.

"Think Meyer and Charlie will be too?"

"Yes."

She nodded slowly, with finality. "Good. Because after this stop, I'm leaving the bus. I'm through, finished. I want to get my property back and say good-bye to the past forever. I never want to see this country again, I want to forget everything and everybody I knew here." She raised the glass and drank all the remaining brandy in three quick swallows. When she put the glass down, a drop of brandy clung to the corner of her bottom lip.

"Even Ben?" Tony asked quietly. "Do you want to forget Ben?"

She looked away blinking back tears. "I don't know, Tony. Sometimes I feel very mixed up about Ben." Turning back, she locked eyes with him. "Like right now. The thing I want most in the world right this minute is for you to fuck me. But it's the thing I want *least* too—because of Ben. Does that make sense?"

"Yes, it does." Tony took her hands. "I feel exactly the same way. I want you very badly. But I know I'd hate myself for it." With one finger he lifted the drop of brandy from her lip and put it on his tongue.

"So we won't do it, will we?" It was a statement as much as a question.

"No," Tony said, "we won't."

She nodded a sad, resigned smile. But after a moment the smile became teasing and one eyebrow arched tantalizingly. With a fingernail she made soft circles in the palm of his hand. "We're going to regret this night, Donovan."

"I know."

Tony put an arm around her and she laid her cheek against his chest. They sat embraced for a long time, neither speaking. "I'm glad you came, Tony."

"So am I," he said.

Because now, he thought, Lucky Luciano would be satisfied. No one would have to die.

FORTY-SIX

Tony Donovan and Denny Ebro, both deeply tanned, lay stretched on chaise longues in the warm Jamaican sun at Ocho Rios. Next to them, in a comfortable beach chair under an umbrella, Meyer Lansky was extolling latent evils of big government.

"A disgrace," the older man said in his usual calm but considered manner. "Millions upon millions of tax dollars were spent to fund this folly known as the Special Senate Committee to Investigate Organized Crime in Interstate Commerce. And to what end? Accomplishing what? I'll tell you what—absolutely nothing."

"Scared hell out of a lot of people, though," Denny commented. Tony glanced at him, wishing he would shut up. Unlike Tony, who mostly listened, Denny persisted in conversing with Lansky, even to the point of guilelessly disagreeing with him sometimes. To Tony's amazement, Lansky seemed to enjoy the exchanges; he was fond of Denny and had lately developed the habit of having Tony bring him along to their meetings.

"Oh, yes," Meyer Lansky quickly agreed, "it certainly did scare hell out of quite a few, myself included once or twice. But I ask you: is it a proper function of government to frighten, to mentally and emotionally intimidate? This is not czarist Russia, you know. Or Nazi Germany. If there is evidence against a man for committing a crime, then arrest him. Charge him. Try him. But this so-called investigating committee that pries, insinuates, uses its congressional privilege to accuse *without* formally charging—this, I tell you, boys, is wrong."

"Maybe we should write our congressman," Denny cracked.

"That's very funny, Denny," said Tony without a smile, thinking Lansky, might be offended. But Lansky defended Denny.

"Actually, that's not a bad idea," he pointed out. "If the committee had continued much longer, we were going to do just that—use *our* congressmen and senators to combat the proceedings. We hesitated having to ask our men in Washington to take a public stand, but it almost came to that. Fortunately, the national elections are coming up and this fellow from Tennessee, Kefauver, wants to run for president, so he had to start campaigning."

"Wonder what the future holds for the other committee members?" Tony asked. Lansky shrugged.

"Depends on whether Kefauver gets the Democratic nomination and is elected. If he is, those four I'm sure will receive very lofty appointments; after all, they've given most of the limelight to Kefauver for a year and a half; they've grabbed onto his coattails; now they'll have to see where he takes them."

Meyer Lansky took a sip of iced tea and shook his head wryly.

"I was not against that committee, you know," he said rhetorically. "No, I was all for it—*but,* I wanted it to be done properly. Efficiently and effectively. And I could see from the outset that it was not. First of all, instead of putting senators on the committee who were familiar with big city life, big city crime, senators who had risen in politics in cities like New York, Chicago, Miami, they pick men from Maryland, New Hampshire, Wisconsin, Wyoming. I ask you," Lansky emphasized, spreading his hands helplessly, "what kind of crime do they have in Wyoming? Cattle rustling? And Wisconsin? The dairy capital of America? From places like that we choose our representatives to investigate so-called organized vice, illegal gambling, narcotics smuggling?" He shook his head. "Incredible." Picking up a pitcher, he asked, "More iced tea boys?"

Tony and Denny both wanted something stronger, a nice Planter's Punch maybe, but Lansky disapproved of alcoholic beverages before sundown.

"From start to finish," Lansky condemned as he filled their glasses, "it was a disgraceful waste of taxpayer dollars. For a year and a half those five hick senators had a long, all-expense-paid vacation. They traveled to thirteen cities to take testimony; thirteen"—he ticked them off on his fingers— "Tampa, Miami, New York, Cleveland, St. Louis, Kansas City, New Orleans, Chicago, Detroit, Philadelphia, Los An-

geles, San Francisco, and Las Vegas. All their secretaries
had to go along, naturally all their clerks and aides and
investigators, everybody. A regular traveling road show.
Staying in suites at the best hotels, naturally, riding in
limousines, dining in the best restaurants—all on the taxpay-
ers. And what did it accomplish? Nothing."

Lansky sat forward, elbows on his bare knees, holding the
glass of tea in both hands. His expression became melancholy, almost sad.

"Look at the men they, forced into court and put on
display for the television cameras. Joe Costello, Albert An-
astasia, Paul Ricca, Joe Adonis, Moe Dalitz, Louis Rothkopf
Charley Fischetti. Some, like me, used to be crooks; maybe
some still are; some never were. All lumped together by the
committee; all guilty by association. Oh, it wasn't a complete failure, not at all. Poor Charley Fischetti, an old-time
rum runner, was put under such a strain that he had a heart
attack and died. Vito Genovese got so scared that he skipped
the country and hid out down here in the Caribbean. The
best witness they had was Willie Moretti, who was so sick in
his mind with advanced paresis caused by the syph—same
thing Al Capone had toward the end—Willie was so out of
control in his mind, knew he was dying, that he actually
paid for his own killing. Bought a contract on himself to end
all the misery. Everybody knew he did it; nobody ever talks
about it, and naturally the federal government claims it was
an 'organized crime' murder.

"And look," he continued, as close to vehemence as
Tony had ever seen him, "what they did to Virginia Hill.
They made promises"—he punctuated the air with an accusing finger—"there were understandings. Agreements were
reached. Her part of the bargain was to testify, to appear.
No arrangements were made as to what she would say, oh
no; the committee was so sure that it could outsmart her on
the witness stand, all she was asked to do was show up and
be sworn in. So she makes an appearance—and what an
appearance! You boys saw her on television the same as me.
In she struts, dressed to the teeth, that wide-brimmed hat,
tailored suit, gloves, a full-length mink—the works. Now,
I'll be the first to admit that Virginia has never been my
favorite person. When she and Ben started living together,
and it reached the point where Ben's wife wanted to divorce
him—you boys never met his wife, I know; a wonderful

Jewish girl named Esther he had been married to for years; they had two lovely daughters together—well, I broke a longstanding rule never to interfere in other people's personal matters. I went to Esther and asked her to hold off on divorce proceedings; I went to Ben and tried to talk some sense into him. He wouldn't listen, of course, always had to be a hardhead. I take part of the blame; I had sent him to the West Coast to manage our gambling enterprises out there and he turned Hollywood on us. Had Esther and the girls living in a palatial Beverly Hills mansion that he rented from Lawrence Tibbett, the opera singer. Going to Santa Anita racetrack every day with George Raft. Things like that. I think, looking back, that maybe I put Ben in over his head. Anyway, I did try to get him to stop seeing Virginia after he took up with her, but it didn't work. He had fallen for the girl and that was that; it broke up his marriage. So I wasn't exactly partial to Virginia at any time. But"—again the punctuating finger—"what the federal government did to her was dirty pool."

"I'm with you a hunnerd percent on that, Mr. Lansky," Denny said indignantly. "Those dirty bastards broke her heart."

"Exactly right, Denny. She handlled those senators like they were schoolboys, did not give the committee a shred of damaging evidence against anybody—and they made her pay for it. Sold at auction everything of hers that had been confiscated—jewelry, furs, furniture, personal items—all of it. Then sent news photographers to tell her about it so they could get pictures of her breaking down and crying. Nice men, our public officials." He shrugged resignedly. "Ah, well, at least they can't hurt her any further. She's back in Austria, she has a nice income, and she'll never return to America." He made the latter statement, Tony observed, as if there was no question about it.

Lansky sat back in his chair and fell quiet for several minutes, sighing as if a heavy burden had just been removed from his shoulders, as if he had managed to purge himself of something inherently distasteful. Tony and Denny remained silent also, respecting the older man's need for a moment in which to regroup his emotions after addressing what to him was obviously a trying subject. Denny got up once during the suspension of talk and moved the umbrella to keep Lansky out of the encroaching sun; Lansky enjoyed the outdoors but had recently developed an allergy to direct sunlight. In a little while he sighed a final sigh and shrugged as if in final resignation that the world would never be an ideal place.

"Excuse my tirade, please, boys," he apologized almost shyly. "As I grow older, I unfortunately become less tolerant. By the time I am very old, probably nobody will be able to stand having me around. I suppose I should be grateful that so-called gangsters like myself are being left alone, now that the government has its House Un-American Activities Committee getting the headlines. They are now attacking some of America's really dangerous enemies . . . like Lillian Hellman. But"—he smiled—"we are not sitting on this lovely Caribbean beach to discuss things like that; we are here to talk about the future. How would you boys like to move down here and work closely with me?"

Tony and Denny exchanged surprised looks. "You mean leave Las Vegas?" Tony said. "Leave the Flamingo?"

"Exactly. As you boys know, my friend General Batista is once again back in office in Cuba. This means that we are not only in a position to expand our Cuban enterprise but will also have a firm base of operations to branch out all over the Caribbean. Preliminary negotiations are already under way with the governments of Bermuda, the Bahamas, Haiti, and the Dominican Republic to establish broadscale tourist facilities in each of those countries—with, of course, large casino operations at each. If these negotiations conclude satisfactorily, which I expect them to, our corporations will be able to establish a vast legal gambling empire more profitable than Las Vegas, Reno, Monte Carlo, or anyplace else you can name. And, once the casinos are operating on land, my intent is to also set them up at sea, on deluxe cruise ships that will sail from New York and Miami to all the island countries, providing gambling not only there but to and from as well. Gambling has always been my first love," Lansky said with satisfaction, "so for me this will be a dream come true. But I will need help, lots of help. Reliable help. You two boys are the first ones I thought of; I can't think of anyone more dependable than you. What do you think of the idea?"

Denny, who knew that he should defer to Tony when the situation called for it, kept quiet and waited for his friend to answer for them. Tony was a little overwhelmed by the prospect. "We've never really considered leaving Nevada before," he told Lansky. "Except for the war, we've spent our whole lives there."

"I know it's hard to leave one's roots," Lansky sympathized. "It didn't bother me to leave Poland; I was still so young. But let me tell you, when I left New York City for Miami, you'd have thought I was leaving a leg behind. How I mourned! But, believe me, a person adjusts. A person *has* to adjust."

"Will you give us a little time to talk it over?" Tony asked.

"Certainly." Lansky rose to go into the hotel. "One important thing" he said. "When we get the Caribbean operation going, I've decided to liquidate the holdings in Las Vegas. There's another grand jury probe gearing up at the state level in Nevada, and I don't want to be bothered with it. I'll be selling the Flamingo and the other Vegas properties. The new owners may or may not retain your particular function in their operation, Tony, which means you may or may not have a job. You might want to take that into consideration."

Lansky gave them a paternal nod and walked off the beach, leaving Tony and Denny staring after him. He had, Tony realized, just told them that he was changing their entire lives. Whether they chose to move to Cuba or not, everything would soon be different. Lansky's words reverberated in Tony's mind:

I've decided to liquidate . . .
I don't want to be bothered . . .
I'll be selling the Flamingo . . .

It had not been investors nor a corporation speaking. It had been one man. Meyer Lansky. Speaking as an individual.

Only at that moment did Tony understand how powerful Lansky was. And how much control Lansky had over his life.

For the first time, Tony felt the tiniest flicker of fear about Meyer Lansky.

FORTY-SEVEN

Tony had called his secretary from Los Angeles to have his car taken out to the Las Vegas airport, and it was waiting there when he and Denny returned from Jamaica. As they put their suitcases in the trunk, Tony asked, "You coming to the hotel with me or you want me to drop you at home?"

"Home," Denny said. "I want to see my dogs. Unless you got something for me to do?"

"Nothing that can't wait until tomorrow."

Tony drove off the airport lot onto Highway 91 and turned north. Just past the Hacienda, which was the hotel-casino farthest out the Strip, he turned west and headed into the desert. Tony had traded his 1949 Porsche for a 1950 BMC, traded that for a 1951 Gran Torque from Argentina, and now had gone back to Porsche for its 1952 model. On the open stretch of desert blacktop he slowly accelerated the sports car to ninety-five.

"I'm not in no hurry," Denny said acidly. Denny was conservative about speed.

"Relax," Tony said. But he raised his foot and let the car gradually slow down.

Denny's house was a flat-roofed white stucco affair set back off the secondary road all alone in its own little oasis of desert landscaping and a few shade trees. While the house itself was compact and ordinary, a kennel out back was large, elaborate, and completely equipped—to the extent that it was heated in winter, cooled in summer. When Denny told Tony he had bought the property and was planning to build the place, Tony had asked how he could afford it. Denny had merely shrugged. "I'm thrifty," he said. "I've got money saved. I make a little off the investment tips Lansky gives us, just like you do. I pick up a little bit gambling, now that I know what I'm doing. Anyway, I won't be spending any more on my house than you do on those fucking sports cars."

Tony supposed he was right; the sports cars were an expensive hobby. And the new house, when it was finished, did get Denny out of Tony's daily personal routine, which was something of a relief; Denny could be an awful nag. But he seemed happy out here on the desert, Tony reflected, as they neared the house. Denny had taken a young Filipino busboy, Lee, out of the Flamingo kitchen, made him a houseboy, and was teaching him how to train and show the Labradors, something Denny learned from a Dunes pit boss who had done it professionally for years. The Filipino had sent for his teenaged brother, Kim, and Denny had sponsored the younger boy's immigration from the Philippines. Now he, too, was learning to train Labs.

"What will you do about Lee and Kim and your dogs when we move to Cuba?" Tony asked.

They had accepted Meyer Lansky's offer. It would have been difficult to turn down; Lansky had told them unequivocally that acceptance would guarantee that they would become wealthy.

"Take 'em with me," Denny said.

"Two Filipino kids?" Tony glanced at him. "And six dogs?"

"What else can I do?" Denny asked. "They all depend on me. I'm their sole support."

"I'm not sure you'll be able to," Tony said. "Lee and Kim are resident aliens. And I don't know if you're allowed to take dogs to Cuba."

"Lansky'll fix it for me" Denny said confidently. "He likes me."

Tony shook his head in wonder. The guy, he thought, never worried about anything. Tony knew that if he himself were responsible for two young Filipino boys and six Labrador retrievers, he would be chewing his nails over it. The thought of not being close enough to Kerry to keep an eye on her for Rosetta was already beginning to trouble him. He was very glad that Lansky had assured them of six months to wind things up in Nevada. At least he could work out some orderly transition in his life.

As Tony pulled up in front of Denny's house, both Filipino boys and all six Labs came running out to welcome

Denny home. The boys were shiny clean, smiling as they got Denny's bag out of the trunk; the dogs were barking and jumping about exuberantly. Tony did not get out of the car; Denny's dogs were overly friendly and he could not take all of them at once.

"If you want to stay awhile, I'll barbecue some steaks for supper," Denny offered.

"No, I'm too tired," Tony declined. "I'll see you in the morning."

Driving back to the Strip, on the long, straight, desert road, his headlights two demanding probes in the darkness, the black horizon ahead sprinkled with the tall lights of the Sahara, Thunderbird, Stardust, Tropicana, Dunes, Hacienda, and in the middle of them all the one that had started it all, the Fabulous Flamingo, Tony felt a sudden exhilaration and in seconds pushed the car up to one hundred ten miles an hour. I'm going to make it, Francie, he thought. I'm going to be as wealthy as Big Jim Delavane ever was. Other things, whatever they may be, might continue to keep them apart, but it would never again be money. In Cuba he would have as fine a home as the Delavane mansion, with servants like the Delavane mansion had, and a big private study for himself, like the one he had glimpsed briefly the night of the cave-in, the night Big Jim Delavane died . . .

Tony refused to give up on Francie. Somehow, someday, he would penetrate the barrier she had put around herself; he would get past Cavendish and Chalky, get into that now run-down house on the hill where she remained so reclusively . . .

As he drove up to the Flamingo, Tony saw the doorman notice him and pick up the telephone in the kiosk next to the entrance. By the time a valet had opened his car door and Tony got out, the doorman had hung up and was walking over to him.

"Good evening, Mr. Donovan. I just let Mrs. Bellamy know you'd arrived, sir. She said she'd meet you at the elevator."

"Thanks, Fred." Tony frowned as he walked inside to the muted sea of sound generated in and by the casino. It was nearly nine o'clock; if Madge Bellamy was there that late, it meant a problem. Only when he reached the lobby did he realize he had forgotten his suitcase; he asked the bell captain to have it sent up to his apartment.

Madge was waiting for him when he stepped off the elevator on the fifth floor, where his apartment was, the same apartment that Ben Siegel had designed into the hotel for Virginia Hill and himself.

"Kerry's here," Madge said.

"What's wrong?" he asked.

"She should tell you, Tony." She put a hand on his arm. "I'll be down in the cage if you need me."

"Sure," Tony said, frowning. "Thanks."

Kerry was on the couch in the living room, legs drawn up under her, clearly overwrought, teary, her fingers worrying a badly wrinkled handkerchief. The teariness turned to sobbing as Tony sat down and put his arms around her.

"What is it, honey?" he asked.

"Mamma"—Kerry choked on the word—"Mamma's got . . . cancer."

An hour later, Tony and Kerry were at Tony's private table in a corner of the Flamingo's gourmet restaurant. Tony had a double martini and Kerry was sipping tentatively at a glass of wine, as they waited for their dinner. Kerry had contained her grief enough to talk.

"Mamma didn't tell me," she said. "I found out by accident. A girl I went to high school with, Dottie Sayers, is an X-ray technician at the Virginia City hospital. I drove down from school this morning to spend the weekend with Mamma and I stopped in town to pick up a few things. I ran into Dottie at the drugstore. She took my hand and told me how sorry she was about Mamma. She must have seen at once that I didn't know what she was talking about because she turned beet red. First thing she said was, 'Oh my God, I'll lose my job.' They're not supposed to talk about anybody's X-ray results. Dottie said she just assumed I knew by now because Mamma was told two months ago." Kerry looked down at the table and had to bite her lower lip for control. "It's in—in her kidneys. She only has a—a few months left—"

Tony felt sick, much worse even than he had felt when he learned of Buck's death. Denny, he knew, would be devastated by the news. Taking Kerry's hand on the table, he probed for hope of some kind.

"Is there any kind of treatment?" he asked. "Maybe at someplace like the Mayo Clinic?" Meyer Lansky, he knew, would help him financially or in any other way he could.

Kerry shook her head. "I don't think so. I made Dottie come sit in the car and tell me everything she knew. Mamma was told she could go to Reno twice a week for some kind of treatments, but because the disease is so far along, the doctors didn't think the treatments would do much good. Plus which they told her that there would be side effects—severe nausea, skin lesions, hair loss. Dottie said Mamma decided not to take them." Now Kerry gripped Tony's hand. "We've got to talk to her, Tony. You, me, and Denny. We've got to persuade her to take the treatments. If there's any chance at all that they might help her—"

"We'll see," Tony said, less than enthusiastically. He saw a frown pinch the top of Kerry's nose.

"You don't sound like you want to." It was less than an accusation, but not by much.

"I don't want to try persuading Rosetta to do anything she's made up her mind not to do," Tony said. "Especially when it concerns something like this."

"Not even if it might save her life?" Now it was an accusation.

"Apparently she doesn't believe it will save her life," Tony reasoned. "Have you talked to her at all about this? Or have you just talked to your friend Dottie?"

"Just Dottie," Kerry admitted. "I was too upset to confront Mamma. Tony, how could she not *tell* me? I'm her daughter, for God's sake—"

"You're half Paiute, Kerry. You shouldn't have to ask that question. You know Rosetta's philosophy about life and death; you saw it at work when Buck was killed. Rosetta believes in living life as free of complications as possible. She knows you will be hurt by this; she doesn't want you to be hurt for any longer than necessary. I think she'll tell you when she has to—not before."

"And what am I supposed to do in the meantime?" Kerry demanded. "How am I supposed to act?"

"Like Rosetta's daughter," Tony said with quiet firmness. "Treating your mother with the respect she deserves. Letting her accept death, if that's her choice, just as she has lived life—with dignity."

"I'm not sure I can do that, Tony," she said flatly.

"You may not be able to," he allowed. "What's important, for you as well as Rosetta, is that you try."

She looked penetratingly at him across the table. "You

make it sound so—I don't know, predetermined. Like there's no other way. I'm really not so sure of that, Tony." She nervously fingered the stem of her wine glass. "Where's Denny anyway? Shouldn't he be here?" She knew instinctively that Denny, who was as emotional as she was, would support her. Denny would want to rush to Rosetta *now,* if for no other reason than to put his arms around her and cry.

"We can talk to Denny tomorrow," Tony told her. "He and I just got back from Jamaica; it was a long trip. We can tell Denny about it in the morning, after he's had some rest."

"Jamaica," Kerry said. "I thought your tan looked renewed. Down there to see your Mr. Lansky?"

"On business, yes," Tony replied. Something about the way she said "your Mr. Lansky" irked him slightly. It sounded almost like Buck talking.

"All right," she conceded, "we'll wait and see what Denny has to say. Where's the ladies' room?"

Tony gave her directions and held her chair when she rose. As he sat back down, he saw Arnie Shad leave a table across the restaurant and make his way toward him. At the table Shad left, Tony recognized the publisher of the *Las Vegas Star* and several other newspaper employees.

"Have you got a minute?" Arnie asked.

"Sure," Tony said. He bobbed his chin at one of the extra chairs. Arnie and he had not spoken since their plane ride together from Reno, when Arnie had warned him not to bother Virginia Hill. "What's on your mind?" he asked the reporter.

"What's the chance of coming by your office in the morning?" Arnie inquired. "I want to talk to you about something very serious."

"Talk about it right now," Tony said. Arnie shook his head.

"It has to be private. Uninterrupted. Like I said, it's *very* serious."

Tony shook his head. He did not care to be drawn into another of Arnie's speculative intrigues about organized crime. "Arnie, I've got a lot on my mind at the moment—"

"You're going to have a lot more very shortly," Arnie cut in bluntly. He lowered his voice almost to a whisper. "I have it on very good authority that you're about to be indicted by a secret grand jury that has been examining evidence of organized crime interests in Nevada gambling."

"I've heard that before."

"Well, this time it's going to happen," the reporter assured him. "Your old friend Jack Coltrane is behind it. You're being indicted, and so is Denny Ebro."

"Denny?" Tony grunted softly. This was more preposterous than usual. "What the hell could a grand jury indict Denny for?" he asked disdainfully.

"Meet with me in the morning and I'll tell you everything I know," Arnie promised. "It isn't a hell of a lot, but it might keep you from going to jail."

Tony's first inclination was to tell Shad he was simply too busy to devote any time or thought to another idle threat of indictment. Rumors had been rampant for months about a secret grand jury, secret witnesses, secret testimony, and deals of immunity; Lansky had even mentioned it in Jamaica. Tony had reached the point where he paid no attention to it anymore. Someone, it seemed, in Carson City, was always threatening to indict half the population of Las Vegas.

But, he thought, this was the first time there had ever been any mention of Denny being indicted. Why, he wondered, was this time different?

"I go for a swim about seven, then have breakfast at the pool," he told the reporter. "Come by if you like."

"See you then," Arnie said, nodding brusquely. Rising, he noticed Kerry coming back to the table. "Is that who I think it is?"

"Kerry Morrell. Buck O'Crotty's stepdaughter."

"She looks all grown up," Arnie said admiringly.

"She is," Tony said, adding, "sometimes." He was not thrilled by the interest with which Arnie watched Kerry cross the restaurant. "See you in the morning," he said by way of dismissal.

"Right." Arnie left the table and walked directly toward Kerry. He intercepted her several tables away and, to Tony's annoyance, she stopped to talk to him. Tony was further irritated by the fact that when Arnie held his hand out, Kerry took it and they stood like that for longer than he considered necessary. Jesus Christ, he thought, I'm becoming as big a prude as Lansky.

When Kerry got back to the table, Tony asked, "What was that all about?"

"What was what all about?"

"Shad. What was he talking to you about?"

"Oh. He's the one that did the newspaper series on Buck—"

"I know who he is. What did he say?"

Kerry shrugged. "Just that he was on assignment a lot up north. He asked if I was still in school in Reno. I told him I was, and he asked if we could have lunch sometime. I said sure. He's going to call me." Kerry studied Tony thoughtfully. If she didn't know better, she would have sworn she detected jealousy in his query.

"I'm not sure I like the idea of you seeing him," Tony said.

Kerry raised one eyebrow. "Oh? Well, let me know when you decide, won't you?"

"Remember that he's a newspaper reporter. Whatever you say to him could end up in print."

"I'll keep that in mind." He *was* jealous. My God.

Under her curious stare, Tony drank the rest of his martini and for several moments seemed to concentrate on stirring the ice cubes around in his glass. He sorely wished that he had not objected to her seeing Arnie. The reporter was, after all, a decent man despite his vivid imagination and outrageous conjectures. Arnie would, Tony thought, probably be very good for Kerry right now. If Rosetta truly was dying of cancer, and if Kerry was going to be able to control her youthful emotions through the ordeal, she would need something or someone to help take her mind off what was happening. Arnie Shad might be just the person to do that.

"Forget what I said about seeing Arnie," he told her. "He's a nice guy. See him all you want."

"I probably won't," Kerry said. "I don't know what I'm thinking; how can I talk about lunch dates when Mamma's dying? Jesus—"

She started to become teary again and Tony reached for her hand once more. He wished to hell their dinner would come so she could occupy herself eating. In the morning, he thought irritably, he was going to call in the head chef and find out why it took so goddamned long to get two simple steak dinners—

All right, he thought, all right. Calm the hell down. Too much was happening too quickly and it was drawing an edge on him. Lansky, moving to Cuba, the Caribbean operation, Rosetta having cancer, Kerry finding out about it before

Rosetta wanted her to know: it was all coming down like a waterfall. And in the midst of it, something else now, something he was finding more troubling with each thought.

On what possible grounds could a grand jury be planning to indict Denny?

FORTY-EIGHT

Tony came out of the shallow end of the pool after swimming ten laps. Arnie had arrived when Tony was in the middle of his morning regimen; he had sat at the table which had been set for Tony's breakfast, drinking coffee and fingering the inevitable cigarette that he rarely lighted. As Tony walked over and picked up a terrycloth robe, Arnie noticed that Tony's deep tan almost eradicated the ugly scar around his right side.

"I told you the sun would cover that scar," he reminded Tony. "I told you that back in the summer of '46. Remember?"

"Sure, I remember," Tony said. "It was the last time you were right about anything."

"Very funny." Arnie poured coffee for both of them as Tony toweled his hair and sat down. "You know, despite everything that eventually came of it," he reminisced, "I still think back on 1946 as probably the best year of my life. The war was over, I had survived, I had an exciting job helping build the first great hotel-casino in Las Vegas, I had a good friend—nice young guy named Donovan—wonder what ever happened to him?"

"He got old," Tony said, sipping his coffee. "Did you get up this early just to kick around old times?"

"Not really. But we did have some times, didn't we?" Arnie grinned, unable to let go of the subject. "Remember how you, me, and Virginia used to go for midnight swims in this very pool, before the hotel opened? Used to drive Ben crazy; he'd always come out and check to make sure we weren't skinny dipping. You know, at one time I really liked Ben Siegel—even if he was a psycho."

"Lay off Ben, will you, Arnie," Tony said without rancor. "He did a lot for both of us."

"You're right. I forget that sometimes."

"You forget a lot of things sometimes."

"You're right about that too," Arnie conceded. "I try to make up for it when I can. For instance, I never forget for a minute that without my help you wouldn't be where you are today. And I don't say that to get credit, believe me; I *regret* ever having helped you. You'd be better off if you'd stayed in the mines and never seen Las Vegas—"

"That's your opinion," Tony said.

The reporter's expression became as somber as Tony remembered it the morning Arnie had told him about Buck's killing. "I want you to listen to me, Tony," he urged. "You may never have the opportunity again. All the information I've got right now is off the record and unofficial. That's why I feel free to share it with you. Once it becomes official, once I'm given certain facts for publication, it'll be too late to do you any good. This may be the only time I'm in a position to help you."

"The last time we talked," Tony reminded him, "you were half convinced that I might be involved in some plan to cause Virginia to have an 'accident' before she testified. Now you want to do me a favor. Why?"

Arnie shrugged. "Guilty conscience, I guess. For helping make you what you are today. You're my Frankenstein monster." Arnie tilted his head an inch. "As long as we're on the subject of motives, what about you? Usually you won't even listen when I talk about a Nevada grand jury. But this time you're interested. Why?"

"I don't mind answering that," Tony said. "I'm not concerned about me being indicted; I know exactly how vulnerable I am at all times. It's what you said about Denny that worries me. I'm always very careful to keep him from becoming personally involved in anything that could hurt him. If Jack Coltrane is seriously planning to indict Denny, it must be for something I don't know anything about. If you can tell me what that is, I'd appreciate it."

Arnie shook his head. "I can't do that, not yet; I don't know what the specific charges against him are going to be.

Maybe you can figure it out when I tell you who the attorney general's secret witness is."

"Okay. Who?"

"Gus Berman."

Tony frowned deeply. "Berman? What the hell does Berman have to do with all this? He's a pimp."

"Not anymore. He's come up in the world. Six months ago," Arnie explained, "Gus Berman and two other hoods landed a light airplane out on the desert near Jackass Flats. They were a little too close to the restricted area where the government has its nuclear testing facility, and they were detained by Atomic Energy Commission security guards. The A.E.C. searched the plane, found it was carrying a cargo of marijuana, and turned the men over to the Nevada Highway Patrol, which in turn called in the state attorney general's office. Jack Coltrane apparently remembered Berman from when he was first trying to put together a case against mob-infiltrated gaming and prostitution in Nevada; that was when the state put its investigation on hold to let the Kefauver Committee proceed without any duplication of investigative effort. Now that Kefauver is finished, and nothing was done about the Nevada problem, the state geared up to proceed again. Then Berman fell into Jack Coltrane's lap. Coltrane made arrangements for Berman to be given immunity from the narcotics smuggling charge—which could have put him away for fifteen years because of the quantity involved—and to beome part of what Coltrane is calling a 'secret witness program' to enable punks like Gus Berman to rat on their associates." Arnie began to fidget with the unlit cigarette. "The information I get from my source at the attorney general's office is that Berman has given Coltrane and the grand jury enough to indict you, Denny, Meyer Lansky, and half a dozen others who are involved in either the ownership or operation of several strip hotels."

"What are they going to charge me with?" Tony wanted to know.

"So far, skimming. Or as they refer to it, 'Illegal Retention of Profits to Avoid Payment of State Gaming Taxes.' Now here's the curious part—Denny isn't being charged with skimming. The charge against him, whatever it is, hasn't been formally made yet. But the rumor is that it's a more serious charge than skimming, and involves interstate commerce in some way." Arnie pursed his lips slightly. "Got any idea what it could be?"

"Not a clue," Tony said, shaking his head. "Berman's probably making up stuff so he'll look good, Arnie. He's never been close enough to a casino operation to know anything about skimming or how we control it or anything else."

"Is there skimming going on?" Arnie asked bluntly.

Tony had never admitted it before. "Sure, some," he now said frankly. "We keep a lid on it as much as possible, but it's like enforcing an ordinance not to spit on the sidewalk—some people are going to do it, and some who do it are going to get away with it."

"Berman has Jack Coltrane convinced that it's much more serious than that," Arnie said. "Berman says that hundreds of thousands of dollars are skimmed every week—"

"Bullshit."

"—from every casino that Meyer Lansky and his corporations have an interest in. He claims that he knows it because he was Lansky's bag man for a while. He says he collected the money from the skimmers and delivered it wherever he was told—Los Angeles, Chicago, St. Louis." Arnie fixed Tony with a flat stare. "Carrying illegally obtained money across state lines is a violation of the interstate commerce laws. Do you think that's what Denny might be doing?"

Tony stared back at the reporter, suddenly realizing how possible it seemed. And how much it would explain. Denny's financial ability to build his house, for instance. His casual confidence about Meyer Lansky "fixing" it for him to take his Filipino houseboys and all of his dogs to Cuba. And the dogs, Tony realized, gave Denny the excuse he needed to travel: now that Tony thought about it, Denny frequently made overnight or long weekend trips, ostensibly to dog shows around the country. What better cover could a bag man want?

"You don't have to answer me," Arnie said after a moment. "I can tell by your expression that there's a good chance that it's true. Didn't it ever occur to you before?"

Tony shook his head. "How could it? I never believed that any serious skimming was going on. And I'm not sure I believe it now. Berman's got it in for me, because of what happened with Francie—"

"I realize that," Arnie said.

"His whole story could be one big lie, giving Coltrane what he wants to hear, and getting even with me at the same time."

"On the other hand," Arnie argued, "it could be true."

Tony rose and walked to the edge of the pool, coffee cup in hand. He had once asked Denny whether he would keep anything from him, if he knew it was something Tony would want to know. Denny had never answered specifically, only saying that if Tony didn't trust him completely by then, he probably never would. The question had seemed to irritate Denny at the time; Tony had made up with him by assuring Denny that he trusted him completely. Now Tony was not so sure he had been right in the decision.

As Tony was pondering the problem, Denny came out of the hotel and started around the pool toward them. Arnie immediately rose, saying, "I've told you all I can, Tony. I hope it'll be of some help. To Denny too, if he deserves it. See you."

"Yeah, sure. See you." Tony turned to shake hands but Shad was already walking away. "Thanks, Arnie," he said, and the reporter waved over his shoulder without looking back.

"What the hell did *he* want?" Denny asked sullenly when he walked up.

"To talk." Tony pursed his lips slightly in thought, then asked, "Want some breakfast?"

"I ordered inside; they'll bring it out." Denny glanced after Arnie Shad. "What'd he want to talk about?"

"A state grand jury that might be getting ready to indict me."

"Ho hum. Same ol' record." Denny's splayed lip curled into a sneer. "That asshole."

"He says Coltrane's got Gus Berman for a witness." Tony watched closely but Denny's expression did not change.

"So? What does that pimp know?"

"He must know something. Apparently he's been testifying before this grand jury on and off for quite a while, helping Jack Coltrane build a case of some kind—"

"Coltrane's an asshole too."

"—against me." Tony paused for effect. "And against you." Denny's eyebrows raised. "Against me? For what?"

Tony shrugged. "I don't know. There aren't any specific charges yet."

"Those bastards," Denny said resentfully. "One of the reasons they can't solve Buck's murder is 'cause they're too fucking busy trying to send innocent people to jail."

"Are we innocent?" Tony asked.

"I am. I ain't so sure about you." Denny grinned.

"Be serious. I don't think it's a joke this time."

"Okay," Denny said. His grin faded. "Sure we're innocent. Name one thing we've done to make us not innocent."

"I can't."

"Well then?"

"Look, Den, Jack Coltrane is no fool. He's a damn smart prosecutor. What could Gus Berman be telling him—and the grand jury—that they'd all believe?"

"Just about anything, as long as it was bad," Denny declared. "And as long as it had something to do with 'organized crime' or the 'syndicate' or that kind of stuff. Since the Kefauver hearings on television, it ain't hard to convince people that the whole country is being run by gangsters."

"Arnie thinks some of the indictments are going to be for large-scale skimming."

"That's bullshit," Denny said. "Aside from petty stuff there ain't no skimming and you and I both know it. Not in Lansky hotels anyway."

"Berman claims he was a bag man for Lansky. That he picked up and delivered skimmed money."

"He's lying, Tony. He's just trying to save his own ass."

Tony stared at Denny as he had stared earlier at Arnie Shad. A stare of realization. Denny already knew about Berman.

"Save his own ass from what, Den?" he asked quietly.

Denny stared back at him for a moment, then looked away. "Shit," he said, almost to himself.

The hotel door opened at that moment as Kerry came out to join them. Denny turned to Tony in surprise.

"What's she doing here?"

Tony had been worrying all night exactly how to break the news to Denny about Rosetta. Now, in a moment of exposure, of betrayal, it seemed like an insignificant concern.

"She's brought some bad news," he said simply. "Rosetta's dying."

Part
Twelve

Denny

1952–1953

FORTY-NINE

The three of them were in Tony's office; Kerry and Denny were crying.

"I don't care what you say, Tony." Denny sniffed back tears. "If Rosetta's dying, we owe it to her to spend as much time as possible with her."

Tony looked at him across the desk, trying to formulate an argument about Rosetta. It was extremely difficult; the thought that kept dominating was: *He knew about Gus Berman—and didn't tell me.*

"I agree with Denny," Kerry said tearfully. "Mamma's only keeping this from us so *we* won't be hurt as much or as soon. It's not right of us to let her protect us like that. It's selfish."

"What do you suggest we do?" Tony asked. "All barge in on her unannounced and say 'Rosetta, we've found out that you're dying and we want to get in on it?' Then we all have a good cry together and when that's over we sit around and take turns asking her how she feels?"

Denny was unmoved. "I don't care what you say," he told Tony again. "I'm moving back home until it's over."

"Wonderful," Tony scorned. "Don't give her any privacy or freedom at all. Make sure she has to concern herself every day with how *you* feel. Let her spend the last days of her life making your goddamned breakfast every morning!"

"Fuck you, Tony!" Denny snapped. "I ain't listening to you this time!"

Tony's jaw tightened. *He knew about Gus Berman and didn't tell me.*

"Tony, we can't let her spend her last weeks and months by herself." Kerry pleaded in sobs. "Me up in Reno in school, you and Denny down here, her all alone—"

"She's not all alone," Tony reminded. "You said yourself that she's been going out to the reservation a lot, like she did after Buck was killed."

"Sure!" Denny yelled. " 'Cause her family ain't with her! She's gotta do something!"

"That's not it at all." Tony shook his head adamantly. "Rosetta is doing what she believes she must do to get ready for the next lifetime that she believes is waiting for her. She is dealing in her own way with the disease that she knows is killing her. Part of the plans she is making include telling us about her illness; she's probably already chosen the time and method to do that." Tony sat forward and put a rigid forefinger on his desk. "Remember, she is going to have to deal with *our* emotions too. To make her do that before she's ready would be wrong."

Disconsolately, Denny sat down on the couch and put his face in his hands. Kerry came around the desk and Tony stood up to let her put her arms around him and weep against his chest. Looking over her head at Denny in his abject misery, Tony could not help, despite the Gus Berman thing, feeling pity for him. Denny, he knew, could not have loved Rosetta more had he actually been born of her. Tony guided Kerry over to where Denny was so they could all sit together.

"Look," he said quietly, "we three are the closest people in the world to Rosetta. We simply cannot intrude on whatever plans she has made or is making for the rest of her life. She has a right to die with dignity in her own way—and that includes the right to tell us about her illness when she is ready to tell us. If we interfere in any way, we'll never stop regretting it."

Neither of them, finally, argued any further.

Tony waited until they got Kerry on a plane home. On the way back from the airport, he pulled off on the shoulder of the highway and parked. He knew that Denny was still feeling some of the shock of learning about Rosetta, but that couldn't be helped. Gus Berman had to be talked about.

"How long have you known about it?" he asked. He did not have to elaborate; Denny knew exactly what he meant.

"Since the Jamaica trip," Denny admitted. "Lansky told me."

Tony stared incredulously at him. "Three goddamn months? A man you know hates my guts is helping another man you know hates my guts get a criminal indictment against me, and you keep it from me for *three goddamn months*?"

"It's nothing to get hot about," Denny declared. "Look, Lansky happened to mention it when you weren't around for a few minutes one day. He asked me not to mention it to you because he didn't think anything would ever come of it. He said you were going to have enough on your mind helping him wrap things up here in Vegas before our move down to Cuba; there was no reason to burden you with this—that's the exact word he used—'burden.' All I done," Denny stressed, "was what Lansky asked me to do."

Tony turned in his seat and riveted Denny with his eyes. "Have you been bagging skim money for Lansky?" he asked flatly.

"Absolutely not!" Denny swore indignantly. His own eyes narrowed suspiciously. "Did that fucking Shad accuse me of that?"

" 'That fucking Shad' hasn't accused you of anything," Tony snapped. "All he's done is offer some help—to both of us."

"Then why ask me about bagging skim money?" Denny demanded to know.

"Arnie says the indictment against you is some way involved in violation of interstate commerce. Crossing state lines to commit a crime." He kept his eyes fixed on his longtime friend. "What could that be?"

"Beats the hell out of me," Denny assured him. "Maybe Berman is making something up to get me framed. The son of a bitch prob'ly figures if he helps send you to prison, that I'll come after him for it." Denny held out his right hand for Tony to see the three pinkish, misshapen fingernails that had grown back. "He's got reason to think I'm pretty loyal to you, remember?"

Tony turned to look out the window. He suddenly felt very ashamed. This *was* the friend who had stuck with him through everything, all the way, when it seemed that everyone else, even Francie, had quit on him. Denny's excuse for not telling him about Gus Berman was perfectly logical; it was exactly the kind of thing Meyer Lansky would do. Maybe Denny sincerely believed he was merely insulating

Tony from the "burden" of an unnecessary worry. Tony sighed quietly.

Hearing his friend sigh, Denny put a hand on his shoulder. "Come on, Tony, what difference does all this make anyway?" he asked. "We'll be long gone to Cuba before Coltrane can indict either one of us. If what I done was wrong, I'm sorry. But this ain't no time for us to be on the outs, with Rosetta sick like she is."

Tony found himself nodding and saying, "Sure. You're right. Let's forget it."

But he knew even as he spoke that he would *not* forget it.

Kerry returned to school and continued to go home for weekends as if nothing had changed. If Rosetta suspected that her daughter knew the truth, she never let on. Tony and Denny talked to Rosetta on the telephone, as usual, and made separate trips to spend an occasional evening with her, on the pretext that they were north on business. In private they marveled at the composure of the woman: she presented herself to them exactly as they had known her all of their lives.

"It's how she wants us to remember her," Tony said, when they discussed it. Kerry and Denny finally understood the position he had taken.

After two months, when Rosetta's gradual weight loss began to show and it became necessary for her to begin taking medication for her pain, she told them. Kerry first, when mother and daughter were alone in the house one evening. Tony and Denny the following weekend when they were invited up at her request. All of them were appropriately shocked and solicitous, but whether they fooled Rosetta or not, they would never know.

"I'm so grateful to you, Tony," Kerry told him one day when she called him from school. "When I see the dignity we've left Mamma, I shudder to think of the mess Denny and I might have made of it. What you did for her, what you made us do, makes me love you all the more. Do you realize that, have you felt it?"

"Yes," he admitted. "I have." He had experienced an unfamiliar feeling of late toward Kerry, an emotion that was somehow different from the past. He had been giving thought to Kerry's future after Rosetta was gone. He and Denny would be in Cuba; the prospect of Kerry remaining behind, with no family, deeply disturbed him.

"I'm going to need somebody when Mamma's gone," she said nervously over the phone. "I'm not sure I can cope all alone—"

"You won't have to," Tony promised.

"Can we talk about it when you come up this weekend? After Mamma's asleep?"

"Sure."

"Will Denny be coming with you?"

"I don't know." Since their discussion of the Gus Berman matter, there had been a definite strain between them. Denny had pretty much gone his own way.

"What's happened between you and Denny?" Kerry asked now. "I know something's wrong."

"It's nothing you need to be bothered about," Tony told her.

"I hope you're not being too hard on him about whatever it is," Kerry said sympathetically. "He depends on you, just like I do. And you know he's under a lot of stress over Mamma's illness."

"Don't wyorry about it," Tony advised.

"Well, I know how you get sometimes," Kerry asserted, trying to be a conciliator. "And you know that Denny always means well. Even when it looks like he doesn't. Even when it causes lots of trouble. He *meant* well when he called Buck and told him Francie was in Las Vegas living with you. I know that it caused terrible consequences, but—"

"Wait a minute," said Tony. He was not sure he had heard her right. "Called Buck when?"

Kerry hesitated a beat, perhaps sensing her mistake. "The time Buck went down there and got Francie. I asked Denny at Buck's funeral if you knew he had called; he said you did. He asked me not to mention it back then because he said you and he had put everything to do with Francie behind you."

Inside, Tony's stomach had started churning and a fist-size knot tightened in his chest. He could tell by a quake in Kerry's voice that she was afraid she had made a bad mistake. Quickly, he covered his surprise. "Don't worry about Denny and me; we always work things out. Listen, Kerry, I have another call," he cut the conversation short. "I'll talk to you tomorrow, okay?"

After he hung up, Tony stared at the telephone for several long, silent minutes. The blood drained from his face, leaving him pale; his hands trembled slightly. Was nothing ever the way it seemed anymore? he wondered. Was there no one in his life who did not wear a mask of some kind to cover his real face, no one who did not casually lie to him or conceal things from him? Didn't he have one person upon whom he could depend for complete honesty? Denny had always been the rock for Tony to fall back on: always there, always supportive—even when he disagreed, always reliable. From the schoolyard to the mines to the Marines to the Flamingo, Denny had been his back-up.

Now Denny, too, had failed him.

Eyes flat, mouth an angry line, Tony picked the receiver up and dialed the chief operator.

"Locate Mr. Ebro for me, please. Have him come to my office."

As he waited for Denny, he felt sick inside, miserable to the core; the unthinkable was gnawing at his emotions like a chainsaw. He had not felt this bad since the terrible day that Buck had come to get Francie, taking her away from him for the last time—and now to learn that it had been Denny who caused that terrible hurt: it was almost too much. Tony frowned. That had been the same night he learned of Ben's murder. He remembered that Denny had been waiting for him when he got back to Las Vegas.

Tony had never remotely suspected what he had done that day.

It was a little four-seater plane that had flown him to Las Vegas. Tony had kept the newspaper spread open on his lap, its ugly headline telling him: GANGSTER BUGSY SIEGEL SLAIN. Using a map light above the seat, Tony had read the story. It was the initial report; there were only the barest of details. Benjamin Siegel, age forty, well-known alleged underworld figure and part owner of the luxurious Flamingo Hotel and Casino in Las Vegas, had been slain the previous night in the living room of a mansion at 810 N. Linden Drive in Beverly Hills, California. While Siegel had been sitting on the living room couch, reading a newspaper, an unknown assassin, firing through a window from outside, had shot him with a .30-caliber rifle. Two high-powered slugs had killed the victim instantly: one had struck him in the right eye, one in the skull. Preliminary statements by police indicated that there was no immediate clue as to who the killer had been.

Tony returned to the Flamingo in a state of stunned disbelief. Denny was waiting in his office, drinking coffee, looking haggard. "Where the hell you been?" he asked irritably. "Lansky's been calling. You heard what happened?"

Tony nodded despondently. "Francie left me again. I made a trip north to try and talk to her. I got this at the airport when I started back," he handed the newspaper to Denny.

"You better call Lansky right away," Denny said, sitting down to read the paper.

Tony took out the private telephone and got Meyer Lansky on the line. The older man's voice, for the first time in Tony's experience, was something other than calm and reassuring; it was tinged with sadness.

"Benny was headstrong and hasty," Lansky said; "something like this was bound to happen, I suppose. But the shame of it, Tony, the shame of it, the waste."

"I'm very sorry, Mr. Lansky. I know you and Ben were close—"

"Twenty-eight years I knew him, since he was a little boy." Lansky grunted softly. "What am I saying, 'since he was a little boy'? Benny has always been a little boy. I blame myself for this, Tony. I should have kept him with me—"

"It's not your fault, sir," Tony interjected.

"—right by my side, where I could have guided him. He needed to be with his own, not out in Hollywood with *ganefs* like that George Raft and baggage like Virginia Hill—"

"Virginia loved him, Mr. Lansky," Tony defended. "She'll be as hurt by this as you are."

There was a silence on the line that seemed somehow icy. Tony realized at once that it had not been the most tactful comment to make, but he did not retract it. Virginia would be devastated by Ben's killing. Meyer Lansky had been his friend, his "brother," but would his grief be greater than that of the woman who had shared Ben's bed and, more important, his dreams these past years? Perhaps, perhaps not. Tony only knew that someone had to defend Virginia's place in Ben's life, and at that moment he felt it was himself.

"I trust, Tony, that I may continue to count on you there

in Las Vegas during this difficult period," Meyer Lansky said at last.

"Yes, sir."

"I appreciate that. I'll talk to you again soon. Good-bye, Tony."

"Good-bye, Mr. Lansky."

It had been several hours later that the overseas call from Virginia came in. She had been having dinner in Paris when a rumor of Ben's killing reached her. Breaking into sobs after Tony verified it for her, Virginia said her life was over and swore never to come back to the United States. Tony would not hear from or see her again until the evening they would spend together in her Plaza suite just prior to her Kefauver Committee testimony.

Terrible memories of that double-trauma night—Francie leaving him the final time, Ben being killed—tormented Tony relentlessly in the months that followed. Only with the increasing responsibility that Meyer Lansky continued to give him, with the gin that he began to consume on a regular basis, with the powerful sports cars that he bought with a constantly increasing income, with the pills to make him sleep at night—only with all that was he able to move forward in life with any degree of stability. He put a moratorium on all of his relationships, past and present: on the dead, like Ben; the removed, like Virginia; the unobtainable, like Francie; the intruders like Buck and Arnie Shad, who both tried to influence how he lived his life; even the innocent, like Rosetta and Kerry, whom he stopped seeing altogether. Of everyone in his life, only Denny remained. Denny the faithful, Denny the rock that was always there.

Then Buck had died and some of the relationships had begun again: Rosetta, Kerry; to a slight degree, even Arnie. And new torments of Francie: was she back in the mansion, was she ill, was she . . .?

Now Rosetta was dying.

And again the long-ago night of the double trauma came out of the grave of memory to plague him.

To deprive him of the person he had trusted the longest and the most.

Denny walked into Tony's office without knocking. "You want to see me?"

"Sit down," Tony said, controlling his voice.

Denny sat and lighted a cigarette. Tony leaned back, clasping his hands behind his neck in case the anger he felt made them tremble.

"Remember the night Ben was killed?" Tony asked. It was a rhetorical question, but Denny answered it anyway.

"Yeah, I remember."

"Remember earlier that day was when Francie left and went back up north with Buck?"

"Yeah?" Denny shrugged—but he also glanced away.

"I've always wondered how Buck found out she and I were together again."

Denny nodded resignedly to himself; then grunted quietly. He took a drag on his cigarette, exhaled, and stared thoughtfully at the smoke as it dispersed.

Tony drummed his fingertips on the desk, a habit he had picked up from Meyer Lansky. "You have anything to say to me?" he asked.

Denny shook his head. "I ain't gonna play your games, Tony."

"You called Buck, didn't you?"

"Yeah, I did."

"Told him Francie and I were living together. Told him where we were living."

"Yeah, I told him everything."

"Why?"

"Couple of reasons," Denny replied calmly. "First off, it was for your own good—"

"Oh, Jesus—" It was like Buck's voice screaming from the grave.

"It's the truth. You *never* had good sense when it came to Francie," Denny accused. "Admit it. Every time you had anything to do with her, it went wrong. She got you beat up by them Hill punks and then dumped you to run off with Lew Rainbolt. She dumped you again after Hawaii, when you got sent back to our outfit in the Pacific. For two fucking years I had to listen to you whine 'cause she didn't answer your letters. Then we find her in a fucking *whorehouse,* a fucking *dopehead,* and have to risk our asses getting her out. Which ended up costing me three fingernails and almost getting us buried out on the goddamned desert! Jesus Christ, anybody in their right mind would have figured out a long time ago that this fucking broad is bad fucking

news—but not you! Oh, no! You keep going back for more—
and you keep dragging me with you. I was sick of it, Tony!"

Denny reached over and crushed his cigarette in Tony's
ashtray as if he were trying to annihilate it rather than
merely put it out. His face had turned an angry red and his
mouth hung open slightly as it did when he got excited and
found it difficult to breathe. Tony's own face was white, his
anger bloodless around a clenched jaw and grim lips.

"You said a couple of reasons," Tony reminded him.
"What's the other one?"

"What difference does it make?" Denny asked, suddenly
listless. Rising, he stood behind the chair, placing both
hands on its back, eyes downcast. "Look, Tony—"

"I want to know the other reason," Tony insisted.

Denny sighed wearily. Then he shrugged and faced Tony
directly. "You weren't taking care of business the way you
should've been. I took a call from Lansky one day when you
weren't in your office. He talked to me about you, said he
was a little disappointed in your performance since he sent
Ben away. His exact words were that you 'seemed distracted.' He asked what was going on with Francie, and I
told him. We had a long talk, Lansky and me—and it wasn't
the last one we had either. Anyways, he asked me to help
you in any way I could. I figured the best thing I could do
for you was to get that goddamned broad out of your life
before she fucked it up again. I called Buck and asked him
if he had any advice or ideas. He said he had a way to
convince Francie to leave. He wouldn't tell me what it was,
just said leave it to him. I did."

Tony's eyes were like bullet holes. He had to exert extreme effort to keep from diving across the desk to get at
Denny's throat. In his lifetime he had hated with a murderous passion only two men: Big Jim Delavane and Buck
O'Crotty. Now there was a third.

"You son of a bitch," he said. "You double-crossing son
of a bitch. I loved you like a brother."

"Well, I loved you *more* than a brother," Denny said.
Blinking rapidly several times, he looked away.

Tony saw a deep hurt in Denny's eyes and frowned tightly.
Facets of realization bombarded his mind: the scorn Denny
had for most women, the isolated house in the desert, the
two young Filipino boys . . .

Denny looked yearningly at him. "Didn't you never feel

nothing for me, Tony? All these years? Didn't you never feel how *I* felt?"

Tony could only stare at him, stare without understanding, without compassion, without even the need to communicate further. Ultimately he felt that the revelation was but one more betrayal by Denny Ebro. Tony shook his head in anger instead of sadness.

"Get out, Denny. Stay away from me and stay away from my hotels. We're quits. For good."

Denny wet his impaired upper lip and swallowed heavily. His expression tightened. "Sure, Tony. I'll get out." A slight cynical smile surfaced. "But only 'cause I want to," he added.

At the door, Denny turned back. He studied Tony's uncompromising expression and merciless eyes. After a moment, he sighed a deep weary sigh and then shrugged again, resignedly.

"Just so's you'll know, Tony, it was me that called Sheriff Sam Patch, too. 'Member that morning after Buck's funeral, when you was gonna go confront Harmon Coltrane?" Denny shook his head hopelessly. "Like I said, you didn't always use good sense. You're lucky you had me around all those years. I don't know how you'll get along now." He winked and grinned. "So long, Tony. I'll always love you."

FIFTY

The body of *Pav-ot-zo*, who was also called Rosetta Morrell O'Crotty, wrapped in a cloak of white rabbit fur, was lying on a travois on the bank of the Truckee River. The travois, which had just been lowered from a platform on stilts ten feet high, was made of cedar and ash and pine that had been freshly cut when the travois was made, so that the fragrance of each would surround the dead woman. The travois had lain on the platform for a day and a night while women of the Paiute tribe sat under it, rocking back and forth, singing death prayers. Now it was time to send the dead woman to her place of rest.

At Rosetta's request, only three white people attended her funeral: Kerry, Tony, Denny. Kerry fingered rosary beads without really praying. On one side of her, Denny sniffed back tears; on the other, Tony stared solemnly at Rosetta.

During the chanting, a canoe of white birch had been brought to the riverbank and the young girls of the tribe had come with baskets of wild flowers and knelt beside it. A bed of flowers—yellow primroses, white wild lilies, red coralroot, and blue lobelias—was made in the canoe. When it was ready, the prayer chants stopped.

"It's time to tell her good-bye," Kerry said in a quiet, broken voice. "Please don't forget to tell her that you love her . . ."

Six women of the tribe, wearing skins smeared with ashes, lifted the travois and brought it forward. They stopped in front of the white mourners and Kerry stepped forward. Putting her arms around her dead mother, Kerry laid her face on Rosetta's still bosom and wept. After several moments, she said, "Good-bye, Mamma. I love you."

Tony was next. Bending, he kissed Rosetta on the cheek. "Good-bye, Rosetta. I love you."

Then Denny, who was now sobbing. He covered her folded hands with his and kissed her forehead. " 'Bye, Rosetta. I love you. You're the on'y one in this world ever really gave a damn about me. I know you're going to heaven for that. 'Bye . . ."

The body was put on the bed of wildflowers in the canoe, and the women in ash-smeared skins walked along the bank pulling it behind them by a rope.

"They'll float the canoe down to the tribe's sacred burial ground," Kerry said. "A grave has already been prepared for her. After she's buried, all the flowers from the canoe will be spread over her grave. When the flowers die, their seed will take root and new blossoms will grow every spring." She glanced from Tony to Denny. "We can walk along the bank as far as the boundary of the burial ground," she told them, "but we can't go onto the sacred ground."

Denny shook his head. "I'm gonna leave now, Kerry," he

said. "I can't take no more. You know I loved your mamma, don't you? And she loved me too—"

"I know, Denny."

As they embraced, Tony stepped off to the side and watched the canoe. Rosetta's funeral was the first time he and Denny had seen each other since their confrontation in Tony's office. Stubbornly, they had not spoken. Kerry, in her grief, had not been able to generate enough anger to rebuke them for it; all she had said was, "Mamma would be very disappointed in both of you."

But they could not overcome their feelings. Denny walked away, alone, weeping, while Kerry joined Tony in walking along the riverbank, following the canoe.

Driving her car back toward Virginia City, Kerry reached over and opened the glove compartment. Tony saw a white envelope inside.

"That's yours, Tony," she said. "A letter from Mamma."

His brow pinching, Tony took the envelope out and closed the glove compartment. He stared apprehensively at the envelope without opening it. Inside, he felt like a man able to see the date of his own death, but afraid to look. Kerry glanced understandingly at him.

"I won't mind if you want to wait and read it in private," she told him quietly.

"Do you know what it says?" he asked.

"Yes."

Wetting his lips, Tony looked out at the barren Nevada landscape, all rock and sagebrush and stillness. He tapped the envelope against one knee. "Is it bad, Kerry?" he wanted to know.

She bit her lip to hold back tears. "Yes."

Tony tore open the end of the envelope and shook the letter out. In Rosetta's neat, parochial-school cursive, it read:

My dear Tony

I will now tell you in death what I was sworn not to tell you in life.

Mr. O'Crotty's efforts to keep you and Francie Delavane apart were made always in good faith and with good reason. What he would never tell you was that Francie is your half-sister.

"I don't believe this," Tony said. He looked at Kerry almost angrily.

"Please, Tony, read it all," she implored. "Don't judge yet."

He resumed reading:

> Your blood father was Jim Delavane. There is no documentary proof of this other than the enclosed note which Mr. Delavane sent to Mr. O'Crotty.

Tony quickly looked at the sheet of paper behind the letter. On Jim Delavane's personal stationery was written in bold longhand: "Bucky: I hope you'll be alive to read this tomorrow. For whatever good it might do now or in the future, I hereby acknowledge Tony Donovan as my natural blood son. I leave it to you whether he ever sees this. Your old friend, Jimmy." Below the name was Delavane's full signature. The note was dated April 11, 1941.

"The day of the cave-in," Tony said, half to himself. Turning to Kerry again, he added, "He must have written it while Denny and I were waiting to take him to the mine."

"Buck was the only one to know for years," Kerry said. "Mamma was finally told after Buck went to Las Vegas and brought Francie back with him. He knew you'd come after her, so he had Mamma take her out to the reservation to hide."

"Then Francie knew," he said, more a statement than a question.

"Yes, Tony. For a long time. Buck told her after he caught you and her in bed. It horrified him to think you and she might unknowingly commit incest." Kerry shook her head in empathy. "God knows what it must have done to Francie to find out. I'm sure it was the reason she ran away with Lew Rainbolt."

And the reason she did a lot of other things too, Tony thought. Realizations cascaded through his thoughts: in Hawaii she had resisted loving him again, resisted going to bed with him, until his presence, his own love, had worn him down, until she had conquered her conscience and her morals, convinced herself that she could not send him back to war, to combat, without giving back the love he needed so badly; then not answering his letters, escaping the stigma again, turning to drugs for sanctuary; and in Las Vegas, wanting him again, loving him even more because he had brought her out of the nightmare of the Ranch, but fearing the stigma still, making him promise to keep Virginia City out of their lives, hoping against hope that they could find the forbidden happiness after all.

Incest, Tony thought. What a mean, hateful little word. How many times had that word punctured Francie's heart like a knife, sliced her mind like a razor? It wasn't incest for him, not at the time, because he didn't know; for him it was the pure, consuming love it had always been. Only for Francie had it been incest, and therefore torture. Maybe worse . . .

She's not the same as she used to be . . . a recluse up in the mansion . . . they say she's lost her mind . . .

"She's been in the mansion all along, hasn't she?" he asked. Kerry nodded.

"Yes. After you had that last fight with Buck and went back to Las Vegas, Mamma brought Francie in from the reservation and left her with Cavendish and Chalky. They've been looking after her ever since. A month ago, when Mamma knew the end was near, she told me everything." Kerry paused a beat, then said, "I—I've been up to see her a couple of times . . ."

"Take me to her," Tony said. "Right now."

"All right," Kerry agreed without argument. "But please finish Mamma's letter first."

Again Tony resumed reading.

> It has hurt my heart terribly that I could not tell you these things while I lived, Tony, and could not help soothe the hurt I know you must feel. But I made a sacred vow not to tell you. Kerry will explain it to you.

"A vow?" Tony said. "To who?"

"To Buck," Kerry told him. "When he brought Francie back from Las Vegas and told Mamma the whole story, she wanted to tell you the truth at once. Buck wouldn't hear of it; he made her swear she would not tell you as long as she lived. She was still bound by that vow when Buck was killed. She felt that it was fate for her to keep the secret until after she died."

Tony read the last of the letter.

> I hope you will not hate me for the hurt that my
> vow to Buck caused you to suffer. I have loved you
> like my own son. You must believe that even if you
> had been of my blood, as Kerry is, I would have
> done no differently. Please forgive Ruby Donovan
> and forgive me. As your mothers, we did the best
> we could for you. As I die, my undying love stays
> with you.
>
> Rosetta

Tony wept softly as he put the letter back into its envelope.

At the Delavane mansion Kerry tapped with the knocker
and the big front door was opened for them almost at once.
They were met in the foyer by Cavendish and Chalky. The
longtime Delavane butler, wearing one of his day coats
which now had worn cuffs and threadbare lapels, looked
very old, slightly stooped, but still alert. Chalky, whose
albino hair had always been white, at first looked no older
than usual; then as he approached, Tony saw that his milky
skin was becoming shiny and wrinkled, like old parchment.

"Good afternoon, Mr. Donovan," Cavendish said.

"Hello, Mr. Tony," said Chalky with a tentative smile.
Tony shook hands with both men. Chalky's smile widened
confidently. "I sure am glad you're here, Mr. Tony." He
nudged Cavendish. "Things gonna be all right now."

Kerry looked inquiringly at Cavendish. "In the study," he
told her quietly.

Kerry took Tony's arm tightly, and her eyes began to
mist. She led him to the study door. As Cavendish and
Chalky started to follow, Cavendish drew Big Jim Delavane's
silver-plated revolver from a pocket of his day coat and
removed its safety catch. Chalky reached to take the weapon
from his hand, but Cavendish jerked away, looking at him
threateningly. The butler returned the gun to his pocket and
hurried after Kerry and Tony; the albino hurried fearfully
after the butler. The four of them filed into the study
together.

In Big Jim Delavane's easy chair in front of the fireplace,
Francie sat. In her arms she cradled the Shirley Temple doll

Tony had given her when they were adolescents. She hummed as she rocked the doll.

Frowning, Tony knelt by the chair. "Francie . . ."

"Hello," she said, smiling slightly. In her eyes Tony saw no recognition. She held the doll up. "Francie's too little to talk."

"Francie, don't you know me?"

A frown replaced the slight smile. "You're not Francie's daddy are you? This is her daddy's chair. We're waiting for him here."

Tony felt Kerry's hand on his shoulder. "She thinks she's her mother. She calls herself Edith and the doll Francie."

Tony stared at her, studying her eyes. Gone now was the self-confidence of the Francie he knew in elementary school, gone the determination of the Francie he loved in adolescence, gone the wordliness of the Francie of Hawaii, the desperation of the Francie of Las Vegas. In her eyes now was only a void. Swallowing hard, Tony stood up. Kerry took his arm again.

"She hasn't been right for a long time. After I came up and found her this way, and talked to Cavendish and Chalky about her, I asked one of the psych professors at school about her condition. He said it sounded like 'reactive regression.' Because of some terrible guilt or fear, Francie was going back to a time of innocence. The psych professor said she would block out any period of time that caused her to remember the thing she felt guilty about, or feared. He said it was possible that she could regress all the way to her early childhood." Kerry bit her lower lip. "I think that's what she's done."

Still staring, Tony slowly nodded understanding. "She became her own mother," he said quietly, almost to himself, "because Edith Delavane was the most innocent person she had ever known." Shaking his head, Tony turned toward the door. "I don't want to look at her like this—"

"Just a moment, please." It was Cavendish speaking. He sat in Big Jim's chair behind the desk. From his pocket, he removed the gun and placed it on the desk in plain sight, keeping his hand close to it. "Please sit down, Mr. Donovan, Miss Kerry," he said.

Tensing at the sight of the gun, Tony cautiously guided Kerry to the chairs Cavendish had indicated in front of the desk. They both sat down. Off to the side, Chalky stood quietly. Francie remained by the fireplace, rocking the doll; she resumed humming, as if she were again alone in the room.

"I suppose, Mr. Donovan, that you're wondering about the gun?" Cavendish asked. Tony met his eyes but did not respond. "This is the revolver that killed Mr. O'Crotty," Cavendish said.

Tony took care not to register surprise. His wariness was increasing. These were not stable people.

"He came up to the house one day," Cavendish said, "and asked to see Miss Frances. This was while she was still lucid part of the time. At first she refused to see him, but he insisted, saying he had to talk to her about you. Finally she allowed me to let him in; they came in here to the study. I could hear them arguing very loudly. Mr. O'Crotty was saying he had made up his mind to tell you something, that it was the only way he could reconcile with you and bring you back into his family where you belonged. Miss Frances became very angry; she said that Mr. O'Crotty had sworn not to tell you whatever it was they were talking about. She shouted at him that she had kept her part of the bargain and warned him that he had better continue to keep his. He told her he was sorry but he could not. He said he had to tell you the truth; there was no other way. He pleaded with Miss Frances to talk to you with him; he said it might help you to understand why they had both deceived you for so many years. Miss Frances said 'Never.' Mr. O'Crotty asked her to think it over; he said he'd wait until the next day to contact you. He told Miss Frances that if she changed her mind, to come to the union office at ten the following morning and they could call you together. Then Mr. O'Crotty left. Miss Frances was beside herself with anger."

Cavendish paused, glancing instinctively over at Francie, as if to reassure himself that she was all right. Still he kept a hand close to the gun.

"The next morning, which was Sunday, Miss Frances said she was going for a walk in the woods. I found that peculiar, because she almost never went out. I followed her. She seemed to know a path that led through the forest down to the top of Gold Street. From there it was only two short, undeveloped blocks to the rear door of the union hall. I was very surprised when I saw that was where she was going, even more surprised to see her draw this gun from her pocket as she entered. I hurried to the door as quickly as I could, but just as I got there the shots were fired . . ."

Tony now looked back at Francie for a moment. She was still rocking the doll, humming, seemingly unaware of anyone around her. My God, he thought. What we drove you to—

"I saw at once that nothing could be done for Mr. O'Crotty," Cavendish assured Tony. "He had been killed instantly. The only thing left was to get Miss Frances out of there. That wasn't difficult; I simply took her back the way we had come. That part of town is deserted on Sundays; no one heard the shots or saw us." Cavendish sighed quietly. "It was only after I got Miss Frances safely back here that I learned what it was she feared Mr. O'Crotty would tell you."

"After it was over," Chalky suddenly put in, "me and Cavendish made a pact to protect Miss Francie—from the law, from you, from everybody. We had done seen signs that Miss Francie was . . . well, not quite right."

"It wasn't long," Cavendish resumed, "before her mind started to go altogether. We felt we could continue to take care of her indefinitely, but," he shrugged, "her inheritance is almost gone. We both have a little money of our own, but it won't last long."

"When Miss Kerry came the first time," Chalky said, "we decided it was time to tell someone the whole story."

Cavendish's eyes riveted their gaze to Tony. "May I ask, Mr. Donovan, how you feel about the situation, sir?"

"You've got a gun practically pointed at me, Cavendish," Tony replied bluntly. "Are you afraid I won't give the right answer?"

Cavendish pursed his lips in thought for a moment. "Nothing personal is intended, sir. It's just that Chalky and I don't, ah, want to take any chance of Miss Frances being . . . punished . . . in any way."

"Are you prepared to shoot me if I disagree?" Tony challenged.

Again Cavendish paused in thought, studying Tony across the desk. "I suppose not, Mr. Donovan," he finally admitted. Looking very tired, Cavendish released the pistol's cylinder and ejected its bullets onto the desktop.

Relieved of having to consider the gun, Tony rose and

went over to where Francie sat. He stood beside her chair and she smiled briefly up at him.

"You want to know how I feel about it, Cavendish?" he asked. His eyes were harsh judgers. "I feel as if we've all committed some terrible crime. Buck, Big Jim, you, Chalky, even me—although, God knows"—he shook his head in frustration—"all I ever did was love her. If I had known any of it, I would have let her alone; I would have stopped trying to force her to stay with me. I never would have—" His eyes flicked to Francie and his statement abruptly stopped. He shook his head in great remorse. Francie was staring at him now, almost as if she knew what he was thinking. *I did this to her.* And it drove her mad. If he let it, he sensed, it might do the same to him. So he knew he must not. *Her love was incest; his incest was love.* There was a difference. That difference had to be his salvation, because now more than ever, Francie needed him. He looked into her wide, gray eyes, once so knowing, now so innocent with the void in her mind. "I hope you or God or somebody forgives us for what we've done, Francie," he said quietly.

"All any of us ever tried to do was help her," Cavendish pleaded. "Surely you can see that?"

"What I see," Tony said, "is that *everyone,* beginning with her own father, left it to be her burden alone. She was the one involved in something dirty, something forbidden, she was the one who had to run away, who had to carry all the guilt, the shame, who finally had to hide up here in this decaying house." He looked sadly down at Francie. "It's no wonder she's the way she is."

"Tony, it isn't hopeless," Kerry interjected urgently. "She *can* be helped—"

"She's been 'helped' enough!" Tony snapped. Taking Francie's hand, he drew her to her feet. "Come with me, Francie—"

But Francie held back. Clutching her doll close, she looked fearfully at him. "Francie can't go with you," she said. It was clear that she was talking about the doll.

"Then you come with me, Edith," Tony said. "And you bring Francie."

"No," she shook her head, "we have to wait for Francie's father to come home." She pulled her hand away from Tony's; he reached to take it again. "No," she said firmly.

"Francie—I mean, Edith—"

"No!"

Dashing away from him, she ran over to Chalky, who put a protective arm around her shoulders. Tony stared at her, hurt and confused. He took a step toward her and she cringed.

"Leave me alone!" she spat. "I don't want to go with you! I don't like you!"

"She don't mean nothin' by it, Mr. Tony," Chalky placated. "She jus' don't remember you."

"Sure," Tony said. The word was spoken listlessly. He felt wasted and empty. Francie, he was certain, was lost to him forever, even as a sister. To Kerry, he said, "Let me know how much money they need to keep taking care of her. I'll see that they get it."

Before she could protest, Tony left the room and walked out of the mansion. On foot, he started down Sierra Street.

You won, Buck, he thought. You did it from the grave, but you won.

FIFTY-ONE

J ust before noon, there was a light tap at Tony's office door and Madge Bellamy entered. She was carrying a cupcake with a lighted candle on it. Behind her came Tony's secretary, carrying another one. They began singing. "Happy birthday to you, happy birthday to you—"

Tony looked at them with mouth agape, then checked the calendar on his desk. It *was* his birthday; he had not even remembered it. He was thirty-three years old.

"—happy birthday, dear bo-sssssss . . ."

Smiling, he shook his head in surprise and let them finish their harmony. Then he said, "See the entertainment manager. I think we can use you in the lounge."

"We're not that bad," cracked Madge. She blew out the

candle on her cupcake and set it on his desk. "Come on, we're taking you to lunch for your birthday."

"And we are *not* eating in the hotel," his secretary pledged. "I swear, you haven't seen sunlight in two months."

It was true. Since returning from Rosetta's funeral and his visit to the Delavane mansion, he had thrown himself entirely into preparing the Flamingo and the other Lansky hotels for transfer to their respective new owners, and for his own imminent move to Cuba. He seldom left the premises of the Flamingo, except to check the other hotels, and that he did at night.

"I appreciate the luncheon invitation, ladies," Tony demurred, "but I'm having a sandwich sent up. I've got to work on some figures—"

"We're not taking no for an answer," Madge declared, and the two women proceeded to come around the desk and coax him bodily from the chair and into his coat.

"You can't handle us both at once, Mr. Donovan, so you might as well give in," his secretary insisted.

"Okay, okay," he capitulated. "But after lunch, you're both fired."

One on each side of him, they escorted him to the elevator and down to the lobby. As they walked toward the front entrance, Tony heard his name called: "Tony, wait up!" Turning, he saw Arnie Shad hurrying across the casino from the side door. When the reporter reached them, he said nervously, "I've got to talk to you, Tony—"

"You want to join us?" Madge asked. "It's his birthday and—"

"Tony, I've *got* to talk to you," Arnie insisted. "Right now." He started pulling Tony aside.

"Wait for me at the desk," Tony told the women. "I'll be right with you." He let Arnie guide him over to a deserted slot machine alcove. Then he said irritably, "If this is about Francie—"

"It's not about Francie," he was assured. Arnie had been seeing Kerry up north; several times she had enlisted his help to try to reason with Tony about Francie's situation. Tony refused to do anything except provide money to support the Delavane mansion and would not discuss the matter with Arnie. He rarely even talked to Kerry anymore, usually having his secretary tell Kerry he was out when she called. He no longer even tried to cope with the problem.

"What is it, then?" Tony asked impatiently.

"The state grand jury handed down its indictments this morning. You, Lansky, and twelve others are charged with skimming. But it's the indictment against Denny that packs the wallop. Remember the interstate commerce violation we couldn't figure out? We thought Denny might be bagging?" Arnie shook his head emphatically. "Nothing so simple. It's for conspiracy to commit murder. Denny and Meyer Lansky."

"Murder? Denny? I don't under—"

"Tony," the reporter said, putting his hands on Tony's shoulders, "Denny killed Ben. Meyer Lansky ordered it."

Tony drew his head back, as if in revulsion. "What? That's crazy—"

But even as he voiced the protest, pieces fell into place. Denny, the Marine Corps expert rifleman. A high-powered rifle used to shoot Ben. Denny's confidence in his place in Meyer Lansky's esteem. The fact that even after Tony fired him, Denny was still assured a position with Meyer Lansky's operation in Cuba. "I hope you don't mind, Tony," Lansky had said to him over the telephone. "Your differences with Denny appear to be personal. That's no reason he can't continue to be an asset to our organization. You won't be required to work directly with him, of course . . ."

Staring at Arnie Shad, Tony's initial, instinctive disbelief quickly dissolved. "Are they positive?" he asked. Arnie nodded.

"Gus Berman made a full confession under the new immunity law. He was Denny's driver. Meyer Lansky had them work together on it in order to neutralize the bad blood between them. Berman's reward was the narcotics operation that eventually got him arrested out in the desert. He said Denny wouldn't take any reward for doing the actual shooting, said Denny enjoyed it. Berman claims Denny is homosexual and was very jealous of your close relationship with Ben—" As Arnie spoke, Tony turned and walked quickly away. Arnie caught up with him. "Where are you going?"

"To find Denny."

"What the hell for?"

"To warn him."

"Wait a goddamned minute, Tony!" Arnie grabbed Tony's arm and spun him around. "This is confidential information!"

"Then you shouldn't have told me!" Tony retorted, jerking his arm free.

"I didn't tell you so you could go warn a killer!"

"I'm not!" Tony immediately lowered his voice. "I'm not warning a killer. I'm warning a kid I grew up with and taught to make a fist. A kid I never should have brought to Las Vegas in the first place. Don't try to stop me, Arnie." Then he added, less forcefully, "Please."

The reporter put a hand to the back of his neck and bent his head forward, as if he had a migraine. "Jesus," he said. Taking an unlit cigarette from between his lips, he broke it in half and tossed it down. He slapped Tony smartly on the arm.

"Come on. My car's at the side entrance."

At Denny's house in the desert, Lee, the oldest of the two Filipino brothers who were Denny's houseboys, opened the door with a wide smile.

"Ah, Mi'ter Tony. Mi'ter Denny not here."

"Where is he, Lee?" Tony asked.

"Go out of town. Be'ness. Back tonight or tomorrow." Lee glanced warily at Arnie, whom he did not know.

"Where did he go?"

"Not say." The houseboy averted his eyes.

"He's lying," Arnie said.

"Lee, I have to talk to Denny right away," Tony said sternly. "Is he here?"

"Not here," Lee insisted. Behind him, Kim, the younger brother, stretched to look out the door.

Tony removed Lee's hand from the door and pushed his way into the house, Arnie following behind him.

"Mi'ter Denny say let no one in," Lee protested. Kim cowered back fearfully.

In the living room there were a dozen large boxes in various stages of being packed. Tony strode through the house, looking for Denny. There were more boxes in every room. In Denny's bedroom, a closet door was open, its light on. On a wall of the closet was a rifle rack with braces for three rifles. There were only two rifles on the rack. Swallowing dryly, Tony hurried back to the living room.

"He's gone," Tony told Arnie. Taking each houseboy by the arm, Tony sat them side by side on the couch. He knelt in front of them.

"Lee, Kim, you both know that I'm Denny's friend—"

"I don't 'sink so, anymore," Lee contradicted.

"Mi'ter Denny say you, him, fall out," Kim accused.

"That's right, we did fall out," Tony admitted, "but I came here today to ask him to be friends with me again—"

"Make up?" Kim asked brightly.

"Yes, make up," Tony seized. "I want to make up. But I have to know where he is."

"Come back tomorrow" Lee advised. "Mebbe here to-morrow. Make up then."

"Lee, listen to me. Denny is in trouble. Someone wants to hurt him. I want to warn him before he gets hurt—"

"Mi'ter Denny get hurt?" Kim asked in alarm.

"You shut up!" Lee snapped. Irritably he lambasted his younger brother in Filipino.

Tony took Kim's arm and drew him off the couch. Bobbing his chin at Lee, he told Arnie, "Keep him here." Tony guided Kim into the kitchen. Putting his hands on a half-packed carton of dishes, he said, "Kim, if Denny has already left for Cuba, he's in no danger. But—"

"Mi'ter Denny not go Coo-ba," Kim said. Glancing anxiously back toward the living room, he whispered, "Go 'Ginia City."

"Virginia City? Do you know why?"

"Mi'ter Ransky say go."

"Mr. Lansky?"

"That right. He call 'urry this morning, still dark. Mi'ter Denny listen on tel'phone, say okay, then get dress and go. I make four san'wich for him eat in car."

"Thanks, Kim," Tony said, patting him on the back. He strode back through the living room, jerking his head at Arnie. "Let's go!"

As they hurried out to Arnie's car, they heard Lee screaming at his younger brother and the sound of blows landing. Kim ran out of the house sobbing and stumbled toward the kennels; Lee chased him, waving a shoe.

As Arnie tooled the car back toward the paved road, Tony asked, "Where is Berman being held?"

"In a safe house."

"A safe house in Virginia City?"

Arnie glanced at him in surprise. "How the hell did you know?"

"That's where Denny's headed. With a rifle."

"Jesus. Are we too late to stop him?"

"I don't know. He's driving, with maybe a seven-hour headstart."

"We can use the paper's plane and be in Reno in an hour," Arnie said. "We keep a car at the Reno airport too. While we're on our way, I can have someone down here try to find out exactly where the safe house is—"

"You won't have to," Tony said. "Jack Coltrane's parents have a house up on the Hill, near the Delavane mansion. It stays closed most of the time because his father retired last year and both parents live in Palm Springs. If Jack's got Berman in Virginia City, he's probably keeping him at the Coltrane house."

"Sounds logical."

Reaching the paved road, Arnie eased the accelerator to the floor and sped toward the airport. Halfway there, Tony decided to tell him the rest of what he had learned from Kim.

"Lansky called Denny this morning, before Denny left."

Arnie shrugged. "Figures. Either to tell him where Berman's being kept, if he managed to find out, or to tell Denny to follow Jack Coltrane until he led him to Berman. Lansky knows all of you grew up together; he probably figured Denny was perfect for the job—he knows Coltrane, knows the area—"

"And he's a crack shot," Tony said darkly, thinking of Ben. "He's already proved that." Turning to the reporter, he said, "Arnie, when this is over, I'm getting out. I'm quitting Lansky."

"I hate to be the one to tell you this, pal," Arnie said somberly, "but Lansky might have other ideas about that."

"He can't stop me," Tony asserted.

Arnie glanced over at him.

"Sure he can. The same way he stopped Ben."

The two men drove into Virginia City at three o'clock, with Tony behind the wheel. Tony guided the car along C Street to Silver Street, then detoured to the sheriff's office.

"You get out here, Arnie, and get to Sheriff Patch. Have him put out a call for his patrol cars to look for Denny. I'll head on up the Hill and cruise around the area of the Coltrane house. Maybe I can spot Denny before the law does."

As Arnie got out, he turned and said, "Don't take any foolish chances, Tony. You don't know what's in Denny's head right now."

"Denny wouldn't hurt me."

"Just be careful," Arnie warned as he slammed the door.

Making a U-turn, Tony drove back to C Street and cut over to Sierra. There were now several other streets that extended all the way up the Hill, but like others who had grown up in Virginia City, Tony without thinking, always used Sierra, the original and once the only street to the top.

The Coltrane house was set one block down from the summit, on what had been the highest plateau below the huge top lot on which Big Jim Delavane built his mansion. As Tony drove past, the house appeared to be unoccupied: the drapes were drawn and there were no cars in the driveway. Tony continued on, up to the circular road that let to and from the Delavane mansion. As he turned the car around, he saw the front of the mansion, still unkempt and forlorn in its austerity. Momentarily, he wondered if the money he was sending was enough; he had asked Kerry for a figure, and she had obtained one from Cavendish. If it was not enough, he presumed someone would have advised him by now. Briefly he wondered how much his income would be affected when he left the Flamingo. He had been offered other jobs on the Strip, at independent hotels not operated by a Lansky corporation, but he was not certain how much money he could expect if he accepted one. Certainly nowhere near the fifteen hundred a week Meyer Lansky was paying him. At this point, facing an indictment and probable trial, Tony was not even sure the job offers would still be valid. Fortunately, except for his sports cars, he had been fairly thrifty; he had a sizeable savings account.

Leaving the Delavane mansion behind, Tony cruised back in front of the Coltrane house again. This time, as he was almost past it, he thought he saw one of the drapes move slightly. Stopping, he scrutinized the house for a long moment but saw nothing further. Off behind the house, where there had once been nothing but forest, Tony now saw a small apartment complex: A-frame architecture in distressed wood, with covered outside walkways leading to units on two floors. The complex faced the back of the Coltrane house across a wide meadow.

Driving back a couple of blocks, Tony took one of the

cross streets and cut over to a new incline street that seemed to run roughly behind the Coltrane house and adjacent to the apartment complex. When he reached the top, where the street dead-ended at the woods, he saw that the apartment complex was on ground slightly raised on one side of the street, while the rear and one side of the Coltrane house lay at a slightly lower elevation on the other side.

Tony parked and looked down on the Coltrane patio, recalling how Francie had once shared with him the conversations she often had with Libby Coltrane while the latter painted her landscapes. Francie had taken delight in never feeding Libby's insatiable appetite for scandalous gossip, no matter how cleverly Libby tried to manipulate her into telling all. It seemed like so long ago.

As Tony was sitting there, two sedans came up the street behind him and parked one block back. The driver of each got out and looked down toward the Coltrane house. Tony followed their gaze and saw the patio doors suddenly slide open and an entourage of men hurry out of the house. There were six of them; four formed an uneven box around one, while the sixth man led the way. Gus Berman was the man in the box; Jack Coltrane the one leading them.

Glancing at the two drivers on the street where he sat, Tony saw that they were scrutinizing everything around them: meadow, trees, apartment complex, pedestrians. In front of the apartments, a gardener was trimming hedges, a young couple held the hands of a toddler walking laboriously between them, a tall woman in a green dress was bent over the open trunk of a car.

Tony's eyes flicked back to the meadow. The hurrying group of men were halfway to the waiting cars now. The drivers were still flicking their eyes in perpetual scrutiny. Tony looked back toward the apartments: the gardener, the young couple and their child, the woman in the green dress; she was standing up now, looking toward the meadow. She was very tall—

Suddenly Tony froze. His mind polarized in a single thought: the memory of Kim's words several hours earlier about Denny's call from Meyer Lansky. "Mi'ter Denny listen on tel'phone, say okay, then get dress and go." Tony had thought the last phrase was simple pidgin English for "get dressed and go." Now he realized in a horrible instant that Kim had spoken literally.

The tall figure in the green dress was Denny, wearing a wig, moustache shaved, lipstick on his twisted lips. As Tony watched in revulsion, Denny took a scoped rifle from the trunk, expertly adjusted its sling around his left elbow and knelt.

Sliding across the seat, Tony threw open the door and leaped out the passenger side. As he broke into a run across the meadow, the two men near the cars saw him and rushed after him, drawing guns from under their coats.

"Jack!" Tony yelled, waving his arms. "Go back!"

The entourage of men stopped in confusion, the four around Berman also drawing guns. Coltrane looked angrily at Tony and threw up a hand in warning.

"Keep away from this witness, Donovan!"

"Goddamnit, go back!" Tony shouted.

But it was too late. A single sharp crack of rifle fire split the air and Tony saw the top of Gus Berman's head—hair, skull, brain matter—rise from his face and fly away in a burst of blood.

Jack Coltrane and the four men around the prisoner whirled toward the sound. Tony hesitated only a step, then charged toward the group.

"Jack!"

Coltrane's eyes locked on Tony in confusion as Tony bore down on him like a fullback.

"What the hell . . .?" Coltrane started to say.

Then Tony's hands were on him, throwing him roughly to the ground as a second rifle shot sounded.

The bullet slammed into Tony's upper body, its impact knocking both men to the ground. Coltrane regained his balance and scurried into a crouch. Groaning in pain, Tony rolled onto his back, his head flopping to one side.

Tony's eyes were open. He watched helplessly as the figure in the green dress stood up, painted lips agape.

"Tony . . .?" Denny said. Then Denny saw the two drivers rushing him with guns drawn, and he screamed. "Tony!"

The two men stopped and poured pistol fire into him.

Part
Thirteen

Tony

1953

FIFTY-TWO

At times, Tony thought he was back on Guadalcanal. In his delirium he never lost awareness that he had been shot, but his mind rejected at every channel the realization that he had been shot by Denny. Whenever the moment of the shooting manifested in his thoughts, he would immediately reject the images of Jack Coltrane, Gus Berman, and the others at the scene, and quickly substitute for them a swarm of faceless Japanese soldiers in whose midst he fell again. Some rebellious part of his mind kept relentlessly foisting reality on him, and just as relentlessly he stubbornly blocked it. He felt exhausted and feverish, but he would not surrender. At one point he heard a female voice say, "He just won't settle down, doctor; he's tossing and turning like he's having a nightmare."

"Must be trauma of some kind associated with being shot," a male voice replied. "He needs to quiet down to let his surgical repair start healing. We'd better give him a shot of chloral hydrate."

Presently Tony felt a hypodermic needle in his arm and a short time later he went into a deep sleep free of disturbing mental conflict.

From time to time Tony came awake, briefly, to find concerned faces peering down at him. Kerry was sometimes there, looking pale and distressed; Arnie was sometimes there, more serious than usual, worried; Jack Coltrane was there, Sheriff Sam Patch, unfamiliar doctors, nurses, orderlies. Tony wove in and out of consciousness randomly, wondering whose image would come into focus each time he opened his eyes. It became a game with him. Just as silence became a game: to their inquiries of how he felt, could he hear them, was he in pain, he did not reply. It was not contrariness; he did not want to talk to anyone because he did not want to ask about Denny. And he knew he would have to.

Finally he woke up one time to find only Arnie in the room. Wetting dry, puffy lips, he said "Now you show up."

Arnie hovered over him. "I told you to be careful. But no, not you."

"Where are you when I need you?" Tony asked.

"*Shlemiel*," Arnie chided. "You never listen."

Tony was aware of thick bandaging under his right arm and on his upper back. "How bad did I get hit?"

"How 'badly,' " Arnie corrected. "Not too," he then answered. "You took the slug on an angle—went in your right shoulder blade and came out just under the armpit. You'll live."

"But will I be able to play the piano?" Tony asked weakly.

"I've heard that one." Arnie squelched the wisecrack. "Listen, I'm supposed to call them if you wake up."

Tony shook his head. "Later."

Arnie started to argue, then shrugged. "Okay, later." He drew a chair up next to the bed. "Kerry's been here a lot."

Tony nodded. "Coltrane too."

"Yeah. He wants to talk to you when you're up to it."

"I won't have anything to tell him," Tony said.

"I told him that."

"How'd you know?"

"I know you. Anyway, I think he understands."

Tony sighed quietly and looked up at the ceiling for a few moments. Next to his bed on the other side, clear glucose dripped from a hanging bottle into an infusion tube attached to a needle taped to the back of his left hand. Where the needle entered his vein, there was a persistent itch that he could not scratch because his right arm was bound close to his body. As he stared at the ceiling, Tony tried to concentrate on the itch. It was impossible. The figure in the green dress would not let him. Turning his face to Arnie, Tony finally, sadly said, "Okay. Tell me."

"They got him right after he got you," Arnie began.

"He wasn't aiming at me, you know," Tony stressed.

"I know that. So does Jack Coltrane. Gus Berman is dead, of course; Denny's first shot was perfect—"

"He could drill an apple at a thousand yards," Tony boasted. He swallowed tightly.

"Naturally, they had to take a lot of pictures," Arnie said, "at the scene and later at the morgue. The two local papers and both wire services agreed to kill the photos; everybody felt they would be too sordid for publication. Jack agreed to let the news stories just say that Denny had been wearing a disguise, without going into details. I kept Kerry out of it until all the formalities were over with; Denny was all cleaned up by the time she claimed his body."

Tony sighed a deep, hollow sigh that caused him to momentarily shudder all over. He had to blink back tears. Because there was no place else accessible, Arnie put a comforting hand lightly on Tony's chest.

"His funeral was yesterday. He's buried in Miners Cemetery next to Buck—"

He'd rather be next to Rosetta, Tony thought. But that was impossible.

"There was quite a crowd at the service," Arnie said. "Kerry was really surprised—"

Tony wasn't surprised. Through good times and bad, Denny had always been well liked. Hardly anyone ever got angry at Denny except Buck, and that was usually an afterthought to ire directed at Tony.

"The Marine Corps had a color guard there," Arnie continued. "They gave Kerry the flag . . ."

Tony finally had to turn his face away and close his eyes. The hurt he felt inside was exceeded only by his deep sense of regret. As with Buck, Tony's last meeting with Denny—at least at which they spoke—had been a hostile and antagonistic one.

It's got to be me, Tony thought. These people love me and somehow I seem to let them down terribly just before they die.

He wondered if the reason was that he did not really care for them at all? Or for anyone? Was he what he had always thought Jim Delavane to be: cold and unfeeling? Did the Delavane blood in him sometimes control how he acted?

Was he turning into a Jim Delavane after all?

The thought plagued him long after Arnie left that day.

When he felt well enough to sit up and talk, Jack Coltrane came to see him. Kerry and Arnie, who were already there, offered to excuse themselves, but Jack shook his head.

"Nothing I've got to say is confidential," the assistant state attorney general told them. "I just want to set the record straight on a few things. I'm dropping the indictments against you, Lansky, and the others," he told Tony. "Without Berman's testimony, most of the charges, the way they're structured, won't wash. That was my mistake; I never should have built the case around evidence from one source. The conspiracy charge relating to Ben Siegel's murder goes down the drain, too, so Lansky is off the hook on that score also. My only consolation there is that both men who participated in the actual murder are now dead—even if the man who ordered it isn't. On that note, it's only fair to warn you that I intend to start at once building a new skimming case against all of you. If you'd be willing to cooperate with me, Donovan, I could work out an immunity arrangement for you—"

"I don't know anything that could help you," Tony said by way of refusal. "I haven't been involved in anything illegal and I don't have any firsthand knowledge of anyone who has."

"Not even Meyer Lansky?" Jack Coltrane asked. Tony grunted softly, glancing at Arnie.

"Especially Meyer Lansky," he replied unequivocally.

Coltrane put one finger vertically across his lips and studied Tony indecisively. "Donovan, I know you probably saved my life last week—"

"No probably about it," Tony interjected. "If I hadn't knocked you down, your head would have gone the same way Berman's head went. But I didn't do it for you; I did it to keep Denny from getting in worse trouble than he was already in. I was trying to help him, not you."

"Even so," Coltrane said, "I nevertheless feel personally indebted to you. And because I do, I'd like to give you as much benefit of the doubt as I ethically can. But it's a real test of my credulity to accept that you've been employed by Meyer Lansky all these years, yet are not criminally involved in any of his activities."

"If you need somebody to vouch for his naïveté and bullheadedness in that regard," Arnie Shad said wryly, "I'll be happy to accommodate."

"You keep out of this, Arnie," said Tony. Then to Coltrane, "I don't care whether you believe me or not. I'm not Gus Berman: I won't say something just because I think it's what you want to hear. And I don't need your immunity; I haven't done anything."

"You don't still believe that Lansky is nothing more than a reformed bootlegger now operating legitimately, do you?" Coltrane challenged.

"Maybe I do, maybe I don't," Tony hedged. "It seems funny to me that not you or anybody else can get anything solid to prosecute him with, except by the testimony of some scum like Berman—and you have to *buy* that with immunity."

"If that's how you feel," Coltrane retorted, "then why are you getting out?"

Tony gave Arnie Shad a withering look. The reporter shrugged. "You didn't say not to repeat it," he excused.

Kerry came over and stood next to the bed, putting an arm around Tony's neck. "Maybe he's getting out because of what happened to Denny," she said quietly.

Tony turned to look into her eyes, surprised that she could see him so clearly. That was exactly why he was quitting: because—everything else aside—he was convinced that Meyer Lansky was responsible for what Denny became: a cold-blooded murderer.

In the end, Jack Coltrane committed himself to a fair and impartial evaluation of Tony's entire career in the legalized gambling industry. "If you are clean" he said "I'll personally see to it that the rest of the industry—the *honest* gambling community—is made aware of it."

"That's big of you" Tony said. "You people from the Hill always did have a lot of heart."

"Lot of tolerance too," Coltrane replied curtly. "We have to have, to put up with people like you from Miners Walk." He looked at Kerry. "Nothing personal, Miss Morrell. That was for him." His eyes appraised Kerry with interest. "When you finish law school, why don't you come around and talk to me. My office is always looking for new talent. Legal talent, that is."

"Thank you," said Kerry, suppressing a smile. "I'll remember that."

"Hey, hands off," Arnie said to Coltrane. "She's coming to Las Vegas to work in my paper's legal department. Aren't you, Ker?" he asked familiarly.

"We'll see," Kerry replied. Smiling a soft, pleased smile,

she nevertheless kept her arm around Tony's neck—and both men noticed it.

When he was ready to leave, Coltrane said good-bye to Arnie and Kerry, shaking hands with both, but merely bobbed his chin at Tony and said, "See you around, Donovan."

"I hope not," Tony answered.

Later, after Kerry and Arnie also departed, Tony was left to himself and to his own thoughts and doubts. As much as he wanted to believe in the truth of what he had told Jack Coltrane, as much as he wanted to feel in his heart that he had saved Coltrane's life to help Denny, there was a gnawing lack of conviction in that belief. Tony kept remembering the forest fire that threatened the Delavane mansion, and how Buck O'Crotty had led the way in getting miners and townsmen to cross the class line and help dig a firebreak. Had Buck done that to help Jim Delavane? Would it have mattered whether that mansion belonged to Buck's worst enemy, best friend, or a total stranger? Tony thought not. He now realized why Buck did what he did. And he had to wonder if indeed it was the same reason he himself had saved Jack Coltrane's life.

Simply because it was the right thing to do.

It was well past visiting hours the next night, after the intravenous needle had been removed and he was able to get comfortable, that Tony was dozing and suddenly sensed the presence of someone in the room. He opened his eyes and found Meyer Lansky standing next to his bed. Tony's lips parted in surprise and he felt his mouth suddenly go dry.

"Good evening, Tony," said Lansky in a quiet, conversational tone. "I'm sorry to visit so late, but in light of recent events I'd prefer not to be seen. How are you feeling?"

"All right," Tony replied. Sitting up slightly, he saw the ubiquitous two bodyguards next to the door. "What are you doing here?" he asked.

"I came to consult with you, Tony. To discuss this very unfortunate situation. Just as Mr. Coltrane came to see you, I'm certain for the same reason. And of course, to offer my sympathy for what happened to Denny. Very untimely, very tragic."

"Why did you do it?" Tony asked in a voice as quiet as

Lansky's. The room, the corridor, the hospital was silent around them. "Why did you make a killer out of Denny?"

"Nobody *makes* anything of anyone," Lansky replied, shaking his head sagely. "We are all many things inside of ourselves. There's a killer in you, Tony, there's a killer in me, just as there was one in Denny. You and I, we're smart enough and strong enough to keep it under control. Denny was not. It was always right there on the surface for anyone who could recognize it. Ben saw it; he was the one who told me about it."

"And you used it, you used Denny, to kill Ben." Tony's words were a clear accusation. The compact little man shrugged slightly.

"I was against killing Ben, I hope you believe that. But when it became an inevitable thing, I was obligated to step in and see that it was done in a way that would be the least harmful to us. Those animals in Chicago, Tony, they would have shot him down right in the Flamingo casino. How would that have looked, after all our efforts there?" Lansky shook his head. "I couldn't have bullets and blood dirtying a major investment like that, so I had to supervise Ben's departure myself. I got him away from us, away from our property and our holdings, and I let him die in Beverly Hills with that *shmir* out there; they're really the ones who killed him—the movie stars, the high living, the *shlock* glamour—"

"But you *used* Denny," Tony accused again.

"In business one matches the person to the task. One uses to best advantage the resources one has."

Tony stared intently at Lansky. "Isn't there any difference in your mind between resources and people?"

The older man smiled—barely. "Difference? Of course not."

Tony's eyes narrowed. "And me? You used me like you used Denny?"

"I made incredible use of you, Tony," he said proudly. "You have been the most perfect front man ever. You know why? Because you *believed*. Most front men have one glaring weakness—they are playing a part and they know it. But you *lived* the part; you were honest and sincere." Now Lansky smiled warmly. "Tony, my boy, our scam in Las Vegas has been so good that there are still people who believe that casino profits are honestly accounted for and accurately reported."

There it was. The final admission. "How much is skimmed?" Tony asked. Lansky leaned close enough for Tony to feel the little man's breath in his face. It was sour, smelling of decay.

"Millions," Lansky whispered. He straightened up, squaring his shoulders and pushing out his chest expansively. His chin jutted out in the same way Tony remembered Big Jim Delavane's chin doing. "Now then," Lansky said, resuming his businesslike tone, "this is the time to put behind us all of the unpleasant experiences associated with Las Vegas, and move on to bigger and better things. Cuba awaits us, Tony. The Bahamas. The Dominican Republic. All of the Caribbean. And don't think," he emphasized, holding up a rigid forefinger, "that I'm talking about ordinary employment anymore; I'm not. I'm talking partnership, my boy; I'm talking percentage." He smiled. "Before we get into that, however, I'd like to know a little about your visit from Mr. Coltrane. I hope you haven't made any, ah, arrangements with him."

Tony shook his head. "No."

"Wonderful," Lansky nodded approvingly.

"I'm not going to make any arrangements with you either," Tony said bluntly. "I've quit. I don't work for you anymore."

Lansky's eyebrows went up. "Since when, may I ask?"

"Since I found out that Denny killed Ben. I've been out."

Lansky shook his head very slowly. "I'm afraid not, Tony. I wouldn't be comfortable with you out. You've been given too much confidential information about the Caribbean operation. I'd feel much better if you were close to me, Tony, so I could be assured that you weren't going wrong."

Tony now shook his head as Lansky had, slowly but emphatically. "I'm through."

Lansky's expression darkened and his lips pursed in dissatisfaction. "I think you should give your decision further consideration," he said very evenly. "You have responsibilities, you know. It will be expensive, caring for a woman who's going insane—"

Tony stared at him in astonishment. "How do you know about her?"

"I told him, Tony," said a new voice from the door.

Tony and Lansky both looked around in surprise. It was Arnie. As the reporter started to enter the room, one of

Lansky's bodyguards stepped out to stop him. Lansky shook his head and the bodyguard moved back. Arnie came over to the bed.

"*You* told him?" Tony asked in disbelief.

"The paper got in touch with me this morning to tell me that Meyer Lansky was at the Flamingo," Arnie said. "I thought I saw an opportunity to settle this matter quickly and without further trouble for you. I thought I could reason with him. So I called him. I explained the extent of your personal problems and asked him, one human being to another, to let you quit. He told me very politely that your employment was none of my business. I figured he'd show up here; I had one of our stringers watching the Reno airport. From what I heard a moment ago, he doesn't plan to let you walk away."

"You haven't told Tony the whole story, Arnold," chided Lansky. He looked at Tony. "To show you that everyone has his price, Tony, Arnold tried to bribe me. In exchange for letting you leave my organization, he offered to stop writing entirely all stories about organized crime."

"*Schmuk,*" Tony said quietly to Arnie. Lansky's eyebrows rose again.

"So, Arnold, it's not just proper English you've been teaching our Tony."

"I try to impart knowledge anywhere there's a need, Mr. Lansky," Arnie replied, directly addressing the older man for the first time.

"I declined his offer, of course," Lansky told Tony. "Since the Kefauver hearings, Arnold and other news media people have had much greater success in getting their stories before the public, but my associates and I aren't bothered much about it. People are funny in America. Half of them don't believe the stories; of the half that does, there is always a percentage that looks upon us—the so-called 'gangsters' or 'racketeers'—as heroes. Did you know that Lucky Luciano has several fan clubs right here in this country, just like Clark Gable? Anyway, my point is, the press doesn't concern us. *You* don't concern us, Arnold. We are only concerned," he looked at Tony, "by people who can hurt us."

"Maybe I *can* hurt you, Mr. Lansky," Arnie Shad told him flatly.

"Please, Arnold, no more," Lansky said, holding up a

hand impatiently. "Tony, I'm going to arrange for a private ambulance plane to move you out of here—"

"Maybe I can hurt you," Arnie continued, "by telling where Ben Siegel's secret safe is located."

Lansky's eyes fixed on the reporter at once. The older man made a supreme effort to keep his expression inscrutable, but an undeniable wave of concern seeped through—and both Tony and Arnie saw it. "By telling where what is?" he asked blandly.

"Ben Siegel's secret safe," Arnie repeated.

A hint of a smile played at Lansky's lips. "You wouldn't try to bluff an old card player, would you, Arnold?"

"I wouldn't be that foolish," Arnie disclaimed.

"I suppose you are going to tell me that there is something highly incriminating in the safe?" Lansky's expression became smug.

Arnie shook his head. "I have no idea what's in it," he replied candidly.

The smugness disappeared and a tiny pinch formed at the top of Meyer Lansky's nose. "If Ben did have a safe, why would he tell you where it was?"

"He didn't. After it was installed, I accidentally overheard him tell Virginia Hill where it was."

Lansky clasped his hands behind his back and walked to the foot of the bed. Arnie's eyes flicked from him to the silent but watchful bodyguards at the door.

"I've already written a story about the safe," Arnie said. "It's in a sealed envelope; my publisher has it. If anything happened to me, it would be opened."

Lansky studied the young reporter for several long moments. There was an uncertainty in his bearing now, a definite hesitancy. "With you, Arnold, it's always been difficult to tell where truth stops and imagination begins."

"Maybe I can help you," Arnie said. "Do you remember my father?"

"Of course."

"I love my father very much. I would never show disrespect for his name. And I swear to you now, on the life of my father, that what I have just said about Ben Siegel's safe is the truth."

Meyer Lansky raised both hands, palms inward, and shrugged dramatically. "Against that I cannot argue." His eyes flicked from Arnie to Tony and back again. "What do you want?"

"Just what I asked for when I called you. Let Tony walk away. Forget you ever knew him. Let him forget he ever knew you."

"But will he?" Lansky asked, looking pointedly at Tony. Arnie looked at him too.

Tony nodded. "I will."

Meyer Lansky studied them long and hard, his eyes cold and emotionless, expression completely devoid of compassion, sympathy, charity of any kind. He was like an executioner with his hand on the lever. Except in this case the choice of whether to trip the lever was his. As Tony looked at him, in a terrible moment of silence, he felt in his heart for the first time that Meyer Lansky was evil.

"All right," Lansky said at last, looking steadily at Tony but speaking to Arnie, "I never knew him."

Meyer Lansky left the room, his bodyguards following.

FIFTY-THREE

Tony felt strangely free.

He felt as if the last in a series of shackles had been unlocked and removed—not from his ankles but from his mind, his conscience. He knew it was not solely because the tie with Meyer Lansky had been broken, although just now that was his main relief. There had been a moment while Lansky was in the room when Tony had felt cold fear of the man—and he sensed that Arnie had too.

"Do you think that's the last we'll hear from him?" Tony asked after Lansky departed. Arnie nodded nervously.

"I think so. He plays the odds. In this case, the odds are more in his favor if he leaves us alone."

"Did you really find out where Ben's safe is?"

Arnie shook his head. "For me to have overheard Ben tell Virginia where that safe is, I'd've had to be in bed with them."

Tony smiled. "I guess you're right." His smile became fond. "Ben and Virginia. They were something, weren't they?"

"I'll say," Arnie agreed.

The two men fell silent, each with his own thoughts, memories, realizations. After a while, Arnie asked, "Where do you go from here?"

Tony shook his head. "I don't know." There was concern in his eyes.

"When you get out of the hospital, why don't you come on down and bunk with me for a while? You can ask around and see if any of the other hotels need a good man."

"Maybe I'll do that," Tony said. Arnie detected no enthusiasm, or even interest, in his tone.

"Maybe," Arnie said, "you should do what Buck wanted you to do right after the war—go into politics. With what you know now, you could probably do a lot for Nevada. The state could use a senator who knew the dangers posed by both Meyer Lansky *and* Jack Coltrane."

"Interesting thought," Tony allowed.

"Kerry thinks you're going to take off," Arnie told him candidly. "She thinks you're going to do exactly what Buck did when he wanted to get away from your mother—run away."

Tony grunted softly. "It's tempting."

Arnie looked down for a moment, as if pondering, then said, "Kerry hasn't told you this, but she's taken Francie to live with her. She's found a doctor in Reno who thinks he may be able to help her. Cavendish and Chalky have been given the mansion to live out their days in, but Kerry's determined that Francie isn't going to waste away up there. She says that Francie is as much her sister as you are her brother," Arnie winked at him. "Lots of guts, that girl."

Before they could do any more talking, a night nurse came in and chastised Arnie for being there so long after visiting hours. "You'll have to leave at once, sir," she ordered.

"Give some thought to that political thing," Arnie urged as he was being guided out.

"I will, Arnie. Thanks for everything," Tony said. "So long."

As he said it, Tony was aware that it sounded like a final farewell. He put his head back. The future, in his mind, was as empty, he realized, as the past was full. For the first time in his memory, he had no goals, no desires, no plans. He did not, surprisingly, even feel any compelling loves or hates. It was as if with a single rifle shot he had been rendered a neutral being. He felt no debits, expected no credits. The book of life, in his case, was even.

Maybe, he thought, it's time to die.

Tony waited until the wing was quiet and still again, then got out of bed. He had been going to the bathroom for several days, so he knew how steady he could expect himself to be. The bandage he now had on was taped from his collarbone, across his armpit, and around his shoulder blade, leaving his right arm free with about fifty-percent movement. His left arm was unimpaired.

All of his clothes, except for his shirt and undershirt, were in the closet; the shirts had probably been too bloodsoaked to keep, he thought. His suit coat, he saw when he took the garments out, had a small patch of dried blood around the entry bullethole, but no blood at all under the sleeve where the slug exited.

Laying his clothes on the bed, he slowly and methodically managed to dress: socks, shorts, trousers, shoes. He kept on the hospital gown for a shirt, tucking it into his trousers. The suit coat he put only his left arm into, pulling the other side over his shoulder and putting the sleeve in the pocket. His personal effects, from the drawer of the nightstand— watch, keys, handkerchief, wallet—he put in the other coat pocket.

When he was ready, Tony stepped over to the partly open door and looked up and down the corridor. Except for a lighted nurses' station midway along the hall, there was no sound and no one in sight. Near his room, Tony saw a door with an illuminated sign over it: EXIT. He walked to the door, opened it, and found a flight of stairs. Several moments later, on the ground floor, he opened another door and left by way of the hospital parking lot.

Turning up the collar of his coat against the cool night air, Tony walked along deserted D Street, past the elementary school playground and the fire station. When he got to

Sierra, he turned away from the Hill and cut down to C Street. At that hour, he saw not a person nor a car moving in any direction, all the way down to Miners Walk. Just into the Walk was the first sign of life: Callahan's.

As Tony stepped inside, the saloonkeeper, past seventy, not so wiry now, was saying, "Well, this Marciano may be Eye-talian and all, but at least, by God, he's white. We've not had a white heavyweight champion since Jimmy Braddock wore the crown, and I say it's high time—" Callahan's words broke in mid-sentence when he saw Tony. After staring for a moment, he muttered, "I'll be damned."

The miners to whom Callahan was talking looked over, but they did not know Tony and he did not know them. Tony stepped to the end of the bar and Callahan hurried down to him.

"How are you, lad?" he asked warmly.

"Not bad, thanks, Callahan. How are you?"

"I've arthritis and gallstones," Callahan replied, treating the question literally, "plus one or two other troubles, but I manage to endure the pain." Callahan reached for a decanter with "Private Stock" etched in its crystal face and poured a shot for each of them. For a long moment they studied one another, each oddly a little self-conscious, as if knowing more than they should about the other. Then Callahan raised his glass in a toast. "Here's to them that ain't here to drink with us anymore. God bless 'em all."

"All," said Tony, and the two drank in unison.

As Callahan wiped his mouth on the back of his hand, he asked, "What brings you to the Walk, lad?"

"I don't know," Tony replied. There was a vacant look to his face. "I don't know."

"Heading anywheres in particular?"

"No. I don't know where I'm heading, Callahan."

The saloonkeeper scrutinized him for a moment before nodding sagely. "At loose ends, eh, lad? Well, that's what life generally comes down to—a lot of loose ends. When it happens, no one living on earth can help you tie 'em together. You got to do it yourself. Not that you can't get help, if you really want it."

"Where?" Tony asked, with an odd urgency. "From who?"

Callahan nodded at the door. "All the way down to the end of the Walk, lad. There's plenty down there who'll talk to you—if you'll listen."

Callahan moved back along the bar to serve someone else.

The Miners Cemetery was silver gray under a three-quarter moon, its paths and lanes and markers clearly defined in eerie light. Tony moved slowly among the gravestones, his eyes flicking from one chiseled name to another.

> MICHAEL ANTHONY DONOVAN
> RUBY SURRETT DONOVAN
> MEGAN MARY DONOVAN
> MAUREEN MARIE DONOVAN

Farther along, he came to:

> GERALD ARTHUR O'CROTTY

And next to him, in a fresh grave with a new stone:

> DENNIS ALBERT EBRO

There were three unused gravesites in Buck's plot: one for Rosetta if she had chosen to be buried there, one for Kerry, the third for Tony. On the site that was his, Tony sat down and leaned against the side of Buck's gravestone.

"You can't take the quick silver from the earth and expect it to last you," Buck had told him once. *"If something's good, it don't come fast and it don't come easy. The long haul is the thing. Trade part of your life for the quick silver, and you're a fool. Take it from deep in the earth, the hard way over the long haul, and you're a man. Be a man, Tony, not a fool."*

When had Buck said that to him? Tony tried to remember. Was it sometime very long ago? Sometime later on? Or—

Right then?

Tony shook his head, puzzled. With some difficulty, he got back to his feet. Being on the ground, even for such a short time, had made him cold; he held the lapels of his coat close to his neck. Staring at Buck's grave, he continued to wonder. He was sure Buck had spoken the words to him at some time; he just could not recollect exactly when. But he knew he couldn't have remembered them if Buck had not said them. The words were very clear, very precise in his mind; it was odd, he felt, that he had never remembered them before.

But at least he had remembered them now. When he needed them.

Stepping over to his mother's grave, Tony could not contain a wry smile. Ruby, Ruby, he thought. You must have been something, Ma: the woman inside you that I never knew. Iron Mike loved you, Buck loved you, even Delavane must have loved you. Why you went to him, I'll never know—but it doesn't matter. What I am, I got from you, not him. You must have given me strength long ago, without me even knowing it, just like Buck did, just like Rosetta did. The blood in your veins doesn't make you what you are; the people who love you make you what you are.

Glancing at the graves of his little twin sisters, Tony remembered a morning long ago when Ruby had said to him, "Sometimes women are strong and can do all the things a strong woman has to do. But other times, when they've used up their strength, they dearly need watching over. Remember that, Tony. Always watch over your sisters. Always be the strong one."

Always be the strong one. Who were his sisters now, and who was the strong one?

Tony walked out of the cemetery. Instead of going back down Miners Walk to C Street, as he had come, he cut along the street that paralleled the cemetery until he came to G Street. From one corner of that intersection, he could look up at the Hill and see the Delavane mansion silhouetted against the moonlit sky. Staring at it, a rush of memories flooded him. Inside, he was still warm from Callahan's whiskey, but outside the night had begun to make him shiver. Reaching under his coat, he felt fresh blood seeping through the bandage on his armpit, wetting his side.

Hurrying along G Street to one of the darkened little houses, Tony climbed to the porch and rang the doorbell. He had to ring several times before a light came on and Kerry, in her nightgown, peered out at him. She quickly opened the door.

"My God, Tony," she said, helping him in. "You shouldn't—"

"Help me, Kerry," he interrupted, putting an arm around her shoulders.

She got him inside and closed the door. Cowering across the room, also in a nightgown, Francie stared apprehensively at them. The suitcoat slipped off Tony's shoulder revealing the blood. He held out his bandaged arm.

"Help me, Francie—"

She frowned deeply, but a flicker of recognition shone in her eyes. Her lips parted slightly.

"Help me, Francie," Tony said again.

Francie came over and took Tony's injured arm. The two women guided him toward the couch.

"No," he said. "Put me there."

They helped him where he directed, into Buck's old chair.

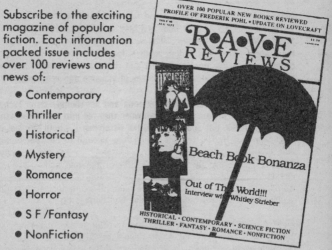